Левъ Толстой

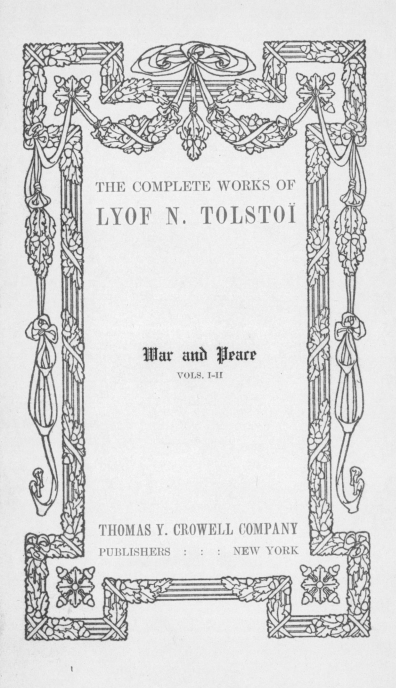

THE COMPLETE WORKS OF
LYOF N. TOLSTOÏ

War and Peace

VOLS. I-II

THOMAS Y. CROWELL COMPANY
PUBLISHERS : : : NEW YORK

WAR AND PEACE

VOL. I

EDITOR'S PREFACE

MEN occasionally appear who by the force of their personality challenge the attention of mankind. Their message may not be altogether welcome, but we listen to it perforce. We may not accept it, but we become conscious that it is affecting the thought of our time, and unconsciously, perhaps, is changing our own lives.

Such a man is Count Lyof Nikolayevitch Tolstoï. Few have seen more widely contrasting phases of life, have experienced a more inclusive experience of the whole gamut of human life and passion. Born into the higher circle of the Russian aristocracy, serving in the army of the Caucasus and during the Crimean war, received into the intimacy of the best writers of his day, he has gradually worked his way up to the loftiest plane of ethical Christianity, and now, repudiating the form of his former literary activity, he preaches a doctrine of equal labor for all men, of non-resistance no matter what the provocation may be, and of a literal acceptation of the words of Christ regarding most of the points of Christian profession and practice.

Striking out from the highway of Fame and Success, he seems to be the personification of Russia's traditional peasant-hermit who lives in the forest and turns the leaves of the golden book, and with infallible instinct answers even the most difficult questions that are propounded to him.

Count Tolstoï himself in "What is Art" very distinctly states his own judgment of his works. Those that he has written for his peasant readers he regards as his best. Those that he wrote for Art's sake he places in a lower category. But a man cannot put his life-work out of sight, and the world has with wonderful unanimity accepted his earlier stories as masterpieces, which no one doubts will retain their place among the masterpieces of universal literature. It is an interesting and instructive task to trace the development of Count Tolstoï's "Doctrine" from its first germs in his earliest sketches through "War and Peace" even to his purely religious works. It will be found that the fundamental tendencies of his writings have ever been the same. The dazzling and multifarious episodes of his romances, drawn from every phase of life, have been like the débris piled on the bottom granite of the religious theory.

From either point of view it is remarkable; in the books written for Art's sake, simply as novels, the ethical background is noticeable; in the later stories, written for the sake of the doctrine, the supreme art of the story-teller is no less manifest. He can rid himself of neither. In either case he holds his unique place as one of the greatest writers of all time.

A new and uniform edition of Count Tolstoï's works has been long a desideratum, and the present series of volumes aims to present practically everything that has proceeded from his pen. Not only have they been translated from the original with the approval of the author, but especial pains have been taken to give them full and complete revision. Thus "My Religion," which has hitherto existed only in a version made from the

French, is now here translated directly from the original. The editor has seized the opportunity of making a new translation of "Anna Karénina." Miss Hapgood has also carefully revised her versions of "Childhood, Boyhood, and Youth," "Sevastopol," and "Life."

A number of Count Tolstoï's later works, stories, and critical articles have been added, and it is believed that these volumes in which this remarkable body of literature appears will find a warm welcome from the thousands of Count Tolstoï's admirers in this country.

NATHAN HASKELL DOLE.

NOVEMBER 1, 1898.

INTRODUCTION

COUNT TOLSTOÏ in the early sixties began to write a novel, the characters of which were intended to portray some of the surviving members of the famous December conspiracy of 1825, returning to the emancipated Russia of 1856. He wrote one chapter of this novel, which was entitled the "Dekabrists," but his mind was irresistibly drawn back to the conspiracy itself, and finally to the first causes of the conspiracy, which lay in the fateful epoch of the first quarter of this century. Thus originated "War and Peace."

This panoramic novel was published between 1864 and 1869. In the original it has upwards of 2000 pages, and contains not far from 650,000 words. Yet in spite of its multiplicity of characters there is no confusion in the delineation of types. Count Tolstoï's brother-in-law, Professor C. A. Behrs, says : "There is no doubt that in 'War and Peace' Prince Nikolaï Andreyevitch Bolkonsky and Count Ilya Andreyevitch Rostof are intended to represent the Count's grandfathers, Prince Volkonsky and Count Tolstoï." He also thinks that his mother, the Princess Mariya Volkonskaya is the prototype of Prince Andreï's saintly sister ; his father, Count Nikolaï Ilyitch, that of young Lieutenant Rostof, though the story of his capture by the French is transferred to Pierre's experiences. G. H. Perris says : "One feels that the writer must have split his own soul in twain to make those two chief figures of Prince Andreï Bolkonsky and Count Pierre Bezukhoï — the proud and elegant gentleman, cold, skeptical, even as to the power of reason, yet visited with spasms of spiritual anxiety especially after the death of his wife, whom he has despised; and then the more typical Slav — gentle, emotional, weak of will, but full of humane desires." And he adds, "Every character is, indeed, in a sense which can hardly be used of any other modern artist, the overflowing of some side of his own opulent and varied character."

In this novel, which is an implicit protest against war, we have a kaleidoscopic succession of life-views. One follows the other without confusion, naturally, with entrancing interest. "The court and camp, town and country, nobles and peasants, — all are sketched in with the same broad and sure outline. We pass at a leap from a *soirée* to a battle-field, from a mud hovel to a palace, from an idyl to a saturnalia. As we summon our recollections of the prodigal outpouring of a careless genius, a troop of characters as lifelike as any in Scott or in Shakespeare defile before our mental eye. Tolstoï finds endless opportunities of inculcating his favorite themes: the mastery of circumstance over will and desire, the weakness of man in the front of things, and the necessity for resignation."

But, not alone as a novel is "War and Peace" remarkable. It is the basis and illustration of a theory of Fate. Count Tolstoï shows that the great man is as much a puppet as the merest soldier; Napoleon or Kutuzof or Bagration, seeming to direct great movements, were, in reality, no more the efficient cause of them than the striking of the clock is the cause of a sunset.

In support of this theory, Count Tolstoï introduces the great men of those famous Napoleonic days, and shows how they, as well as men unknown, were led, often with eyes wide open, into courses where destruction infallibly awaited them. His arguments on this subject, scattered here and there through the book, were extracted without change and published in France in a separate volume entitled "Napoleon and the Russian Campaign." The epilogue has also been published by itself under the title "Power and Liberty."

CONTENTS

PART I (1805)

xi

CONTENTS

CONTENTS

CONTENTS

CHAPTER I. PAGE 155

The Russian army and Kutuzof near Braunau. Preparation for inspection. Condition of the regiments. The regimental commander. A
change of orders. Dolokhof cashiered. The blue capote. Captain
Timokhin of Company Three.

CHAPTER II. P. 161

Arrival of Kutuzof. The review. Prince Andreï and Nesvitsky.
Zherkof. The hussar mimic. Prince Andreï reminds Kutuzof of Dolokhof. Timokhin's account of Dolokhof. Regimental comments on Kutuzof. "Singers to the front!" Zherkhof tries to make friends with
Dolokhof.

CHAPTER III. P. 170

Kutuzof and the member of the Hofskriegsrath. Kutuzof's excuses
for not taking an active part in offensive operations. Change in Prince
Andreï. Kutuzof's report of him to his father. How regarded by the
staff. Arrival of the defeated General Mack. *Le malheureux Mack.*
Preparations for the campaign. Zherkhof insults General Strauch. Prince
Andreï's resentment.

CHAPTER IV. P. 178

Nikolaï Rostof as yunker. Nikolaï and his horse. His conversation
with his German host. Description of Denisof. Lieutenant Telyanin.
Disappearance of the purse. Nikolaï forces Telyanin to refund.

CHAPTER V. P. 188

Nikolaï refuses to apologize to the regimental commander. Discussion
of the matter. Nikolaï's pride. End of inaction.

CHAPTER VI. P. 192

Kutuzof in retreat. The army crossing the Enns. The scene. View
from the hill. Firing from the battery.

CONTENTS

PRINCIPAL CHARACTERS IN "WAR AND PEACE"

Count Kirill Vladimirovitch BEZUKHOÏ [*Graf Kir*-íl *Vlah*-dee-*meer-o-vitch Be*-zoo-*ho-ee*]. A wealthy old grandee of the Empress Catherine's time. At his death his illegitimate son Pierre inherits his title and estates.

Monsieur Pierre, afterwards Count Piotr Kirillovitch BEZUKHOÏ [*Pee-6-tr Ki*-ríl-*o-vitch*, shortened into *Kiríltch*]. The old count's illegitimate son, educated abroad, and easily led both into dissipation and into idealistic theories of life, "gentle, emotional, weak of will, but full of human desires." He marries first the Princess Ellen, and afterwards the Countess Natasha Rostova.

Prince Nikolaï Andreyevitch BOLKONSKY [*Kniaz* (K-nee-áz) *Nee-ko*-láh-*ee An*-dré-*ye-vitch* (or *An*-dré-*yitch*) *Bol*-kon-*skee*]. A harsh martinet, full of old-time prejudices, living a bitter, lonely life at his estate of Luisiya Gorui (Lwee-*see-ya* Gór-*ee*), or Bald Hills: father of Prince Andreï and the Princess Mariya.

Prince Andreï Nikolayèvitch (Nikolaïtch) BOLKONSKY [*Kniaz An*-dré-*ee Nee-ko*-láh-*ye-vitch; (Ni-ko*-láh-*itch*). Also called André and Andre-yusha (*An-dre*-yoo-*sha*)]. Adjutant or aide to General Kutuzof; wounded at Austerlitz; proprietor of Bogucharovo [*Bo-goo*-tcháh-*ra-va*]; engaged to Countess Natasha Rostova.

Prince Nikolaï Andreyevitch (Andreyitch) Bolkonsky [*Kniaz Nee-ko*-láh-*ee An*-dré-*ye-vitch* (or *An*-dré-*itch*)]. Called by the pet names Niko-lusha, Nikolenka [*Nee-ko*-loó-sha, *Nee-kó-len-ka*], Prince Andreï's baby son.

Princess Yelizavieta Karlovna BOLKONSKAYA (*née* Meinen) [*K-nee-a*-ghee-*nya Yel-ee-zahv*-yét-a Kárl-*ov-na Bol*-kón-*ska-ya*]. Known as Liza or Lise; Prince Andreï Nikolayevitch's wife, who dies in giving birth to the little Nikolusha.

Princess Mariya Nikolayevna Bolkonskaya [*K-nee-azh*-ná *Mah*-ree-ya *Nee-ko*-láh-*yev-na*]. Known as Marie, Masha, Mashenka [Má-*shen-ka*]; afterwards the Countess Rostova [*Gra*-feen-*ya* Rós-*to-va*].

Prince Vasili Sergeyevitch (or Sergeyitch) Kuragin [*Kniaz Va*-see-*lee Sier-ge*-é-*ye-vitch* (or *Sier-gee*-é-*itch*) *Koo*-ráh-*gheen*]. Vasili is Basil.

Prince Ippolit Vasilyevitch Kuragin [*Kniaz Ip-o*-leet *Va*-seel-*ye-vitch*]. In the diplomatic service, but dissipated and foolish. "Le Charmant Hippolyte."

Prince Anatol Vasilyevitch Kuragin [*Kniaz An-a*-tól *Va*-seel-*ye-vitch*]. A spendthrift who aspires to the Princess Mariya Nikolayevna's hand, but proves himself unworthy.

Princess Yelena Vasilyevna Kuragina [*Kniazhna Yel*-é-na *Va*-seel-*yev-na Koo*-ráh-*gee-na*]. Also known as Ellen, Hélène, Elena, Lyolya [*L*-yó-*l-ya*], afterwards the unfaithful wife of Pierre Bezukhoï.

Count Ilya Andreyevitch (or Andreyitch) Rostof [*Graf Il*-yá *An*-dré-*ye-vitch* Rós-*tof*]. A wealthy but extravagant proprietor or pomyeshchik [*pom*-yés *tchik*], whose affairs go from bad to worse.

Count Nikolaï Ilyitch Rostof [*Graf Nee-ko*-láh-*ee Il*-yítch]. Known as Nikolenka [*Nik-ó-len-ka*], Nikolúshka, Kólya, Kokó. Open-hearted, gallant, generous; serving in the cavalry; at first engaged to his cousin Sonya, afterwards married to the Princess Mariya Bolkonskaya.

Count Piotr Ilyitch Rostof [*Graf Pee-ó-tr Il*-yítch]. Known as Petya [Pét-*ya*], Petrúshka, Pétenka.

Countess Natalya Rostova (*née* Shinshina) [*Grafinya Na*-tál-*ya* Rós-*tov-a; Shin-shin*-á].

Countess Viera Ilyitchna Rostova [*Grafinya Vee*-é-*ra Il*-yitch-*na* Rós-*to-va*]. Known also as Vierushka [*Vee*-é-*roosh-ka*], Vierotchka [*Vee*-é-*rotch-ka*]. Afterwards married to Alphonse Karlitch Berg.

Countess Natalya Ilyitchna Rostova [*Grafinya Na*-tál-*ya Il*-yítch-*na* Rós-*to-va*]. Also known as Natalí, Natasha [*Na*-tá-*sha*]. Engaged to Prince Andreï Bolkonsky, but after his death married to Count Pierre Bezukhoï.

Sofya Aleksandrovna Shinshina (?) [Sŏf-*ya Al-ex*-án-*drov-na*]. Known as Sophie, Sonya [Sŏ-n-ya], Sonyushka [Sŏ-*n-yoosh-ka*]. The niece of the Rostofs; engaged at first to Count Nikolaï Rostof; "a sterile flower."

Alphonse Karlovitch (or Karluitch) Berg. A conceited young officer, who "gets on," and marries the Countess Viera Rostova.

Prince Boris Drubetskoï [*Kniaz Ba*-rís *Droo-bet*-skŏ-*ee*]. A relation of the Rostofs; he is cold, calculating, and selfish, and through influence is rapidly advanced. Known also as Borenka [Bŏ-*ren-ka*].

Princess Anna Mikhaïlovna Drubetskaya [*Kniagina* Anna *Mi*-háh-*ee-lov-na Droo-bet*-ská-*ya*]. Poor but intriguing; the mother of Boris.

Julie Karagina [*Ka*-rá-*ghee-na*]. Afterwards marries Boris.

Princess Yekaterina Semyonovna Mamontova
[*Kniazhna Ye-kat-er*-ee-*na Sem*-yón-*ov-na* Máh-*mon-to-va*]. Known as Catherine, Katish [*Ka*-teesh], Catiche.
Princess Sófya Semyónovna Mámontova.
Princess Olga Semyónovna Mámontova. } Pierre's three cousins.

Vasili Feodorovitch Denisof [*Va*-see-*lee Fee*-ŏ-*do-ro-vitch De*-nee-*sof*]. Gallant soldier and poet, in love with Natasha. Known as Váska.

Feodor Ivanovitch Dolokhof [*Fee*-ŏd-*or Ee*-ván-*o-vitch* Dól-*o-hof*]. A gambler and *roué*, who offers himself to Sónya, but is rejected; brave but bad.

Marya Ivanovna Dolokhova [Már-*ya Ee*-ván-*ov-na* Dól-*o-ho-va*]. The fond mother of Feodor.

Marya Dmitrievna Akhrasimova [Már-*ya* Dmee-*tree-ev-na Ah-khra*-sím-*o-va*].

Piotr Nikolayevitch Shinshín [*Shin*-sheen].

Prokhor Ignatyevitch Timokhin [Pro-hór *Ig*-nát-*ye-vitch Tim*-ŏ-*hin*].

Osip (or Iosiph) Alekseyevitch Bazdeyef [Ó-*sip A-lex*-é-ye-*vitch Baz*-dé-*yef*]. The Freemason, Pierre's "Benefactor."

Marya Ignatyevna Peronskaya [Már-*ya Ig*-nát-*yev-na* Pe-rón-*ska-ya*].

Platon Karatayef [Pla-tón *Ka-ra*-táh-*yef*]. The philosophical peasant; also known as Platósha and Platoche.

Pelageya Danilovna Milyukova [*Pel-a*-gé-*ya Dan*-ee-*lov-na Mil-yoo*-kó-*va*].

Anna Pavlovna Scherer [Páv-*lov-na*]. Lady-in-waiting to the empress.

Mikhaïl Nikanorovitch [*Mee*-há-*il Nee-ka*-nór-*o-vitch*]. The little uncle.

Mlle. Amélie Bourienne, sometimes called Burienka.

Semyón Chekmár, Danílo (Daníla) Teréntyitch, Éduard Karluitch
    Dimmler, Zakhár, Luíza Ivánovna Schoss, Tíkhon, Máksimka, Márya
    Bogdánovna the midwife, Feoktíst the cook, Praskóvya Sávishna the
    old nurse, Ivánushka the old pilgrim, Fedósyushka, Father Amfilókhi
    [*Am-fee*-ló-*hi*], Mavrúshka the maid, Gerásim the servant, Ilyúshka
    the gipsy, Yákof Alpátuitch, Lavrúshka, etc.
The Emperor Alexander Pávlovitch (Románof).
The Emperor Napoleon Bonaparte.
Mikháíl Iliáronovitch Kutúzof [*Mee*-há-*il Il-ya*-rón-*o-vitch Koo*-too-*zof*].
Pável Ivánovitch Kutúzof.
Feódor Vasílyevitch Rostopchín [*Ras-tap*-tcheen].
Prince Adam Czartoruísky [*Char-to*-rís-*ky*].
Count Ostermann-Tolstóï [*Tol*-stó-*ee*].
General Prschebiszewsky [*Presh-ebi*-shev-*sky*].
Mikháíl Mikháílovitch Speránsky.
Alekséï Andréyevitch Arakchéyef.
General Milorádovitch.
Yúri Vladimírovitch Dolgorúkof or Dolgorúki.
Count Viázemsky.
Prince Aleksandr Naruíshkin [*Nar-ý*sh-*keen*].
Feódor Petróvitch Uvárof [*Oo*-vá-*rof*].
General Benigsen (or Benningsen).
Countess Potocka [*Po*-tót-*ska*].
Count Máïkof.
Prince Soltuikóf [*Sal-ty*-kóf].
Generals Winzengeróde, Karl Bogdánovitch Schubert, Barclay de Tolly,
    Yermólof, Count Orlóf-Denísof, Poniatówski [*Pon-ya*-tóv-*skee*],
    Novosíltsof, Weirother, Balashóf, Murat, Davoust, Pfuhl (Pfühl),
    Rumyántsof, Stoluípin, Grand Duke Kónstantin Pávlovitch, Potémkin
    [*Pat*-yóm-*kin*], Suvórof [*Soo*-vór-*of*, known in history as Suvarof,
    Suwarrow], etc.

In the foregoing list of names an attempt is made to represent the
pronunciation. The stress comes on the syllable left unitalicized. The
transliteration and pronunciation of Russian names offer some difficulty.
The accent is even more capricious than in English. Only an approxima-
tion to accuracy is possible. An unaccented *o* sounds like *a*; an accented
e sometimes sounds like the *e* in yelk, that is, like *yo*. Thus, Potemkin is
Pat-yóm-keen, Orel like Ar-yól. Masculine proper names are made feminine by a change in the ending, generally by the addition of the syllable *a* or
aya, but though the word may be lengthened the accent remains on the
same syllable. Thus, Mámontof's wife is Mámontova, but Shinshín's wife
is Shinshiná. The accent on the town Rostof is on the ultimate, but the
family name is Róstof, Róstova. The patronymic endings *evitch*, *evna*,
(*vitch*, *itch*, *vna*) are used with the Christian name of the father, somewhat
as *O'*, *Mac*, and *Ap* show the family origin of Celtic names. Russian has
an abundance of diminutives and augmentatives used in familiar discourse.
These are for the most part noted in the list of characters.

Count L. N. Tolstoï, 1868.

WAR AND PEACE

PART FIRST

CHAPTER I

" WELL, prince, Genoa and Lucca are now nothing
more than the apanages of the Bonaparte fam-
ily. I warn you that if you do not tell me we are going to
have war, if you still allow yourself to condone all the
infamies, all the atrocities, of this Antichrist, — on my
word I believe he is Antichrist, — I will not recognize
you; that is the end of our friendship; you shall no
longer be my faithful slave, as you call yourself. There
now, cheer up, cheer up, I see I frighten you. Come,
sit down and tell me all about it."

Thus on a July evening in 1805 the well-known Anna
Pavlovna Scherer, maid of honor and confidential friend
of the Empress Maria Feodorovna, greeted the influential statesman, Prince Vasíli, who was the first to
arrive at her reception.

Anna Pavlovna had been coughing for several days;
she had the *grippe*, as she called it — *grippe* being then
a new word used only by a few.

Her notes of invitation, distributed that morning by
a footman in red, had been written alike to all : —

"Count (or Prince), if you have nothing better to do, and
if the prospect of an evening with a poor invalid is not too
frightful, I shall be very glad to see you to-night at my house
between seven and ten.

"ANNA SCHERER."

"Oh! what a cruel attack!" exclaimed the prince, as he came forward in his embroidered court uniform, stockings, and diamond-buckled shoes, and with an expression of serenity on his fleshy face: he was not in the least disturbed by this reception.

He spoke that elegant French in which Russians formerly not only talked but also thought, and his voice was low and patronizing, as becomes a distinguished man who has spent a long life in society and at court.

He went up to Anna Pavlovna, kissed her hand, bending down to it his perfumed and polished bald head, and then he seated himself comfortably on the divan.

"First tell me how you are feeling; calm your friend's anxiety," said he, not altering the tone of his voice, which, in spite of the gallant and sympathetic nature of his remark, still betrayed indifference and even raillery.

"How can one be well — when one's moral sensibilities are so tormented? How in these days can any one with feelings remain calm?" exclaimed Anna Pavlovna. "You will spend the evening with me, I hope?"

"But the English ambassador's reception? To-day is Wednesday. I must show myself there," said the prince. "My daughter is coming for me, to take me there."

"I thought that reception had been postponed. I confess all these *fêtes* and fireworks are beginning to grow tiresome!"

"If they had known that you had wished it, they would have postponed the reception," said the prince, from habit, like a watch wound up, saying things which he did not expect to be believed.

"Don't tease me! Well, what has been decided in regard to Novosiltsof's despatch? You know everything."

"How can I tell you," said the prince, in a cold tone of annoyance, "what has been decided? It has been decided that Bonaparte has burnt his ships, and I believe that we are ready to burn ours."

Prince Vasíli always spoke indolently, like an actor rehearsing an old part. Anna Pavlovna, on the contrary, in spite of her forty years, was full of vivacity and impulses.

Her character of an enthusiast had given her a peculiar position, and sometimes, even when it was contrary to her inclinations, she worked herself up to enthusiasm, so as not to disappoint the expectations of her acquaintances. The suppressed smile constantly playing over her face, although incongruous with her faded features, expressed, just as in the case of spoiled children, the ever present consciousness of her amiable weakness, which she could not and would not correct, and which she did not think it necessary to correct.

In the midst of their conversation about political matters Anna Pavlovna grew heated, —

" Oh! don't speak to me about Austria. Perhaps I do not know anything about it, but Austria has never wished for war, and she does not now. She is betraying us. Russia alone must be the savior of Europe. Our benefactor realizes his lofty mission, and will be faithful to it. That is one thing in which I have a firm belief. The grandest part in the world lies before our kind and splendid sovereign, and he is so benevolent and good that God will not abandon him, and he will fulfil his mission of crushing the hydra of revolution, which is now more monstrous than ever, in the face of this murderer and scoundrel. We alone must redeem the blood of the just. .... On whom can we rely, I ask you? .... England with her commercial spirit does not understand and cannot at all conceive the Emperor Alexander's loftiness of soul. She has refused to evacuate Malta. She is anxious to find, she is seeking for, some secret motive in our actions. What did they say to Novosiltsof? Nothing! They do not and they cannot understand the self-denial of our emperor, who wishes nothing for his own gain, but everything for the good of the world. And what have they promised? Nothing! Even what they have promised will not be performed. Prussia has already declared that Bonaparte is invincible, and that all Europe is powerless before him. ..... And I have not the slightest faith in Hardenberg or in Haugwitz. This famous Prussian neutrality is only a snare. I believe in God alone, and in the high destiny of our beloved emperor. He will save Europe!".....

She suddenly paused, with a smile of amusement at her own impetuosity.

"I think," said the prince, smiling, "that if you had been sent instead of our dear Wintzengerode, you would have taken the king of Prussia's consent by storm. You are so eloquent! Will you give me some tea?"

"Directly. *À propos*," she added, becoming calm once more, "this evening two very interesting men will be here: the Vicomte de Montemart, connected with the Montmorencys through the Rohars, one of the best names in France. He is one of the decent emigrants of the genuine sort. And then the Abbé Morio; do you know that profound mind? He has been received by the sovereign. Do you know him?"

"Ah! I shall be most happy," said the prince. "But tell me," he went on to say, as if something just at that moment for the first time occurred to him, whereas in reality the matter regarding which he was asking this question was the chief object of his visit, "is it true that the empress dowager wishes Baron Funke to be named as first secretary at Vienna? It seems to me that this baron is a wretched creature."

Prince Vasíli was anxious for his son to get the appointment to this place, which a party was trying to secure for the baron through the influence of the Empress Maria Feodorovna.

Anna Pavlovna almost closed her eyes, to signify that neither she nor any one else could tell what would satisfy or please the empress.

"Baron Funke was recommended to the empress dowager by her sister," said she in a dry, melancholy tone. Whenever Anna Pavlovna spoke of the empress, her face suddenly assumed a deep and genuine expression of devotion and deference tinged with melancholy, and this was characteristic of her at all times when she was reminded of her august patroness. She said that her majesty had been pleased to show Baron Funke her good-will, and again her face became melancholy.

The prince said nothing and looked indifferent. Anna Pavlovna, with feminine quickness and a courtly dexterity characteristic of her, was desirous of giving the prince a rap because he had dared to speak in dispraise of a person recommended to the empress, and at the same time she wished to console him. " But speaking of your family," she added, " do you know that your daughter, since she came out, has roused the enthusiasm of our best society. She is considered to be as lovely as the day."

The prince bowed in token of his respect and gratitude.

" I often think," pursued Anna Pavlovna, after a moment's silence, drawing a little closer to the prince and giving him a flattering smile, as if to imply that nothing more was to be said about politics and society, but that now they might have a confidential chat: " I often think how unfairly good things of life are distributed. Why should fate have given you two such splendid children (I don't count Anatol, your youngest, I don't like him," she said decisively, in way of parenthesis, and raising her brows), two such lovely children? And really you do not prize them as much as others do, and therefore you do not deserve them."

And she smiled her enthusiastic smile.

" *Que voulez-vous ?* Lavater would have said that I lack the bump of philoprogenitiveness," said the prince.

" Now stop joking. I wanted to have a serious talk with you. You must know, I am out of patience with your youngest son. Between you and me (here her face assumed its melancholy expression), they have been talking about him at her majesty's, and they feel sorry for you."

The prince made no reply, but she paused and looked at him significantly while waiting for his answer. Prince Vasíli frowned.

"What do you wish me to do!" he exclaimed at last. "You know I have done everything for their education that a father can do, and both have turned out imbeciles. Ippolit is at least only an inoffensive idiot, but Anatol is a nuisance. There is that difference between them," said he, with a smile more natural and animated than usual, and at the same time very distinctly displaying an unexpectedly coarse and disagreeable expression in the wrinkles around his mouth.

"And why is it that such men as you have children? If you were not a father, I should not be able to find fault with you about anything," said Anna Pavlovna, lifting her eyes pensively.

"I am your faithful slave, and I can confess it to you alone. My children are the stumbling-blocks of my existence. This is my cross. That is the way that I explain it to myself. *Que voulez-vous?*" —

He paused, expressing with a gesture his submission to his cruel fate. Anna Pavlovna was lost in thought.

"Has it never occurred to you to find a wife for your prodigal son? They say old maids have a mania for match-making; I am not as yet conscious of this weakness, but I know a young girl who is very unhappy with her father: she is a relative of ours, Princess Bolkonskaya."

Prince Vasíli made no reply, but the motion of his head showed that, with the swiftness of calculation and memory characteristic of men of the world, he was taking her suggestion into consideration.

"Did you know that this Anatol costs me forty thousand a year?" said he, evidently unable to restrain the painful current of his thoughts. He hesitated: "What will it be five years hence, if it goes at this rate? That is the advantage of being a father. Is she rich, this princess of yours?"

"Her father is very rich and stingy. He lives in the country. You know, he is that famous Prince Bolkonsky, who retired during the lifetime of the late emperor. He was nicknamed 'The King of Prussia.' He is a man of genius, but full of whims, and a trial.

The poor little girl is as unhappy as she can be. She has a brother who recently married Lise Meinen. He is on Kutuzof's staff. He will be here this evening."

"Listen, my dear Annette," said the prince, suddenly taking his companion's hand and bending it down for some reason. "Arrange this business for me, and I will be your faithfullest slave forever and ever. She is of good family and rich — that is all I require."

And with that easy and natural grace for which he was distinguished, he raised her hand, kissed it, and having kissed it, still retained it in his, while he settled back in his arm-chair and looked to one side.

"Just wait!" said Anna Pavlovna, after a moment of consideration. "I will speak about it this evening to Lise (young Bolkonsky's wife), and perhaps it can be arranged. I shall begin my old maid's apprenticeship in your family."

CHAPTER II

Anna Pavlovna's drawing-room gradually began to be filled. The highest aristocracy of Petersburg came; people most widely differing in age and in character, but alike in that they all belonged to the same class of society. Prince Vasíli's daughter, the beautiful Ellen, came, in order to go with her father to the ambassador's reception. She was in ball toilet and wore the imperial decoration. There came also the little, young Princess Bolkonskaya, known as the most fascinating woman in Petersburg. She had been married during the winter before, and now, owing to her expectations, had ceased to appear at large entertainments, but still went to small receptions. Prince Ippolit, Prince Vasíli's son, came with Montemart, whom he was introducing to society. The Abbé Morio and many others also came.

"Have you seen my aunt yet?" or "Do you know my aunt?" asked Anna Pavlovna of her guests, as they came in, and with perfect seriousness she would lead them up to a little old lady wearing tremendous bows,

who had sailed out from the next room the moment
the guests began to arrive, and she presented them by
name, deliberately looking from guest to aunt, and then
going back to her place again.

All the guests had to go through the formality of an
introduction to this superfluous and uninteresting aunt,
whom no one knew or cared to know. Anna Pavlovna,
with a melancholy, solemn expression of sympathetic
approval, silently listened to their exchange of for-
malities.

"*Ma tante*" spoke to all newcomers in precisely the
same terms about their health, her own health, and the
health of her majesty, "which was better to-day, thank
God." All those who fell into her clutches, though
from politeness they showed no undue haste, made their
escape with the consciousness of relief at having accomplished a disagreeable duty, and took pains not to stay
near the old lady or to come into her vicinity again
during the evening.

The young Princess Bolkonskaya came, bringing
some work in a gold-embroidered velvet bag. Her
pretty little upper lip, just shaded by an almost imperceptible down, was rather short, but all the more fascinating when it displayed her teeth, and more fascinating
still when she drew it down a little and closed it against
the under lip. As is always the case with perfectly
charming women, her defect of a short lip and a half-
open mouth seemed like a distinction, her peculiar
beauty.

It was a delight for all to look at this beautiful young
woman so full of health and life, and so gracious with
the promise of coming motherhood. Old men and
surly young men, soured before their time, as they
looked at her seemed to become like her, after being in
her presence and talking with her for a little time.
Whoever spoke with her and saw her bright smile, and
her shining white teeth displayed at every word, was
sure to go away with the impression that he had been
unusually agreeable that day. And every one felt the
same.

The young princess, with her workbag in her hand, waddling along with short quick steps, passed around the table, and joyously disposing her dress, sat down on the divan near the silver samovár, as if all that she did was a delight for herself and all around her.

"I have brought my work," she said, opening her reticule, and addressing the whole company. "Now see here, Annette, don't play a naughty trick on me," she went on to say, turning to the hostess. "You wrote me that it was to be a little informal *soirée;* see how unsuitably I am dressed!"

And she spread out her arms so as to display her elegant gray gown trimmed with lace and belted high with a wide ribbon.

"Do not be disturbed, Lise," replied Anna Pavlovna, "you will always be the most beautiful of all."

"You know my husband is deserting me," continued the young princess, still in French, and addressing a general, "He is going to meet his death. — Tell me, why this wretched war?" she added, this time speaking to Prince Vasíli; and without waiting for his rejoinder, she had some remark to make to Prince Vasíli's daughter, the handsome Ellen.

"What a charming creature that little princess is!" whispered Prince Vasíli to Anna Pavlovna.

Shortly after the young princess's arrival, a huge, stout young man came in. His head was close cropped, he had on eyeglasses, and wore stylish light trousers, an immense frill, and a cinnamon-colored coat. This stout young man was the illegitimate son of Count Bezukhoï, a famous grandee of Catherine's time, and now lying at the point of death in Moscow. He had not as yet entered any branch of the service, having just returned from abroad, where he had been educated, and this was his first appearance in society.

Anna Pavlovna welcomed him with a nod reserved for men of the very least importance in the hierarchy of her salon. But notwithstanding this greeting, almost contemptuous in its way, Anna Pavlovna's face, as Pierre came toward her, expressed anxiety and dismay such as one experiences at the sight of anything too huge and out of place.

Pierre was indeed rather taller than any one else in the room, but the princess's dismay may have been caused only by the young man's intelligent, and at the same time diffident, glance, so honest and keen that it distinguished him from every one else in the room.

"It is very kind of you, Monsieur Pierre, to come and see a poor invalid," said Anna Pavlovna, looking up in alarm from her aunt, to whom she was conducting him.

Pierre blurted out some incoherent reply, and continued to let his eyes wander around the assembly. He smiled with pleasure as he bowed to the little princess as if she were an intimate friend, and went on toward the aunt.

Anna Pavlovna's alarm was justified, for Pierre, without waiting for the old lady to finish her discourse about her majesty's health, left her abruptly. Anna Pavlovna in dismay detained him with the words, —

"Don't you know the Abbé Morio?" she asked, "he is a very interesting man."

"Yes, I have heard of his plan for a perpetual peace, and it is very interesting, but hardly feasible."

"Do you think so?" said Anna Pavlovna, for the sake of saying something, and once more returning to her duties as hostess; but Pierre was now guilty of an incivility of an opposite nature. Before, he had left a lady without allowing her to finish speaking; now he insisted on detaining his companion to hear what he had to say, though she wished to leave him.

Bending his head down, and standing with his long legs spread apart, he began to show Anna Pavlovna why he conceived that the abbé's plan was chimerical.

"We will talk about that by and by," said Anna Pavlovna, with a smile.

And having turned away from this young man who had such bad manners, she once more devoted herself to her duties as hostess, and continued to listen and look on, ready to lend her aid wherever conversation was beginning to flag. Just as the proprietor of a cotton mill, who has stationed his workmen at their places, walks up and down on his tour of inspection, and when he notices any spindle that has stopped, or that makes an unusually loud or creaking noise, hastens to it, and checks it or sets it going in its proper rote, even so Anna Pavlovna, as she walked up and down her drawing-room, came to some group that was silent, or that was talking too excitedly, and by a single word or a slight transposition, set the talking machine in regular decorous running order again.

But while she was occupied with these labors, it could be seen that she was in especial dread of Pierre. She watched him anxiously while he went to listen to what was said in the circle around Montemart, and then joined another group, where the abbé was discoursing.

Pierre had been educated abroad, and this reception at Anna Pavlovna's was his first introduction to society in Russia. He knew that all the intellect of Petersburg was gathered here, and like a child in a toy-show, he kept his eyes open. He was all the time afraid of missing some clever conversation that might interest him. As he saw the assured and refined expressions on the faces of those gathered here, he was ever on the lookout for something especially intellectual.

He had finally come to where Morio was. The conversation seemed to him interesting, and he stood there waiting a chance to air his opinions, as young men are fond of doing.

CHAPTER III

Anna Pavlovna's reception was in full swing. The spindles on all sides were buzzing smoothly and without halt. Not counting *Ma Tante*, near whom sat only one elderly lady with a thin tear-worn face, a poor soul rather out of place in this brilliant society, the guests were divided into three circles. The Abbé Morio formed the center of one, for the most part composed of men; in the second, mainly young folks, were that beauty, the

Princess Ellen, Prince Vasíli's daughter, and the pretty little Princess Bolkonskaya, fair and rosy, but too stout for her age.

In the third were Montemart and Anna Pavlovna.

The viscount was an attractive-looking young man, with delicate features and refined manners. He evidently regarded himself as a celebrity, but through his good breeding modestly allowed the company with which he mingled to profit by his presence. Anna Pavlovna was evidently serving him up as a treat for her guests, just as a good *maître d'hôtel* offers as a supernaturally delicious dish some piece of meat which no one would feel like eating were it seen in the unsavory kitchen; so this evening Anna Pavlovna served up to her guests first the viscount, then the abbé, as some sort of supernatural delicacy.

In Montemart's circle they had immediately begun to discuss the murder of the Duc d'Enghien. The viscount maintained that the duke had fallen a victim to his own magnanimity, and that there had been personal reasons for Bonaparte's ill-will.

"Ah! there now, tell us about it, viscount," said Anna Pavlovna, eagerly, with a consciousness that this phrase —"*tell us about it, viscount*," sounded *à la* Louis XV.

The viscount bowed in token of submission, and smiled urbanely. Anna Pavlovna made her circle close in around the viscount, and invited all to hear his account.

"The viscount knew the duke personally," whispered Anna Pavlovna to one of her guests. "The viscount is a wonderfully clever story-teller," she said to another; "How easy it is to tell a man used to good society," she exclaimed to a third; and the viscount was offered to the company in a halo most exquisite and flattering to himself, like roast beef garnished with parsley on a hot platter.

The viscount was anxious to begin his narration, and smiled faintly.

"Come over here, *chère Hélène*," said Anna Pavlovna,

to the lovely young princess, who was seated at some little distance, the centre of the second group.

The Princess Ellen smiled; she stood up with that unchanging smile with which she first came into the room — the smile of a perfectly beautiful woman. With the rustle of her white ball dress, ornamented with smilax and moss, with shoulders gleaming white, with glossy hair and flashing gems, she made her way through the ranks of men who stood aside to let her pass, and not looking at any one in particular, but smiling on all, and as it were, amiably granting each one the privilege of admiring the beauty of her form, of her plump shoulders, of her beautiful bosom and back, exposed by the low cut of dresses then in vogue, seeming to personify the radiance of festivity, she crossed straight over to Anna Pavlovna.

Ellen was so lovely that not only there was not a shade of coquetry to be perceived in her, but on the contrary, she was, as it were, conscience-stricken at her indubitable and all-conquering maidenly beauty. She seemed to have the will but not the power to diminish the effect of her loveliness.

"What a beautiful girl!" was remarked by all who saw her.

The viscount, as if overwhelmed by something extraordinary, shrugged his shoulders and dropped his eyes as she took her seat in front of him and turned upon him the radiance of that perpetual smile.

"Madame, I fear that my ability is not on a par with such an audience," said he, inclining his head with a smile.

The young princess rested her bare round arm on the table, and did not think she needed to say anything in reply. She smiled and waited. All the time that he was telling his story she sat upright, glancing occasionally now at her beautiful plump arm, which by its pressure on the table altered its shape, now at her still more beautiful bosom, on which she adjusted her diamond necklace; once or twice she smoothed out the folds of her dress; and when the story was particularly impressive, she would look at Anna Pavlovna and for an instant assume the very same expression of face as her hostess, and then again resume her calm, radiant smile.

The little Princess Bolkonskaya had also left the tea-table and followed Ellen.

"Wait a moment, I am going to bring my work!" she had exclaimed. "Why are you in a brown study?" she added, addressing Prince Ippolit — "bring me my workbag!"

The princess, smiling, and having a word for every one, had quickly effected her transmigration, and as she took her seat, merrily arranged herself.

"Now I am comfortable," she had exclaimed, and begging the viscount to begin, had devoted herself to her work again. Prince Ippolit had brought her the bag and, placing his chair near her, sat down.

The charming Hippolyte struck one by his extraordinary likeness to his sister, the beautiful Ellen, and still more by the fact that in spite of this likeness he was astonishingly ugly. His features were the same as his sister's, but in her case all was illumined by her radiantly joyous, self-contented, unfailing smile of life and youth, and the remarkable classic beauty of her form. In the case of the brother, on the contrary, the same face was befogged with an idiotic look, and invariably gave the impression of a self-conceited and peevish disposition, and his body was lean and feeble. Eyes, nose, mouth, all were fixed, as it were, in a vague and querulous grimace, while his arms and legs always assumed some unnatural attitude.

"It is not a ghost story, is it?" he had asked, as he sat down near the princess and hastily put on his eye-glass, as if without this instrument it were impossible for him to say a word.

"Why no, my dear," replied the astonished narrator, shrugging his shoulders.

"Because I detest ghost stories," he added, and it was plain from his tone that only after he had spoken these words he realized what they meant.

The self-assurance with which he spoke made it difficult for any one to tell whether his remark was very witty or very stupid. He wore a dark green coat, pantaloons of a shade which he called *cuisse de nymphe effrayée*, and stockings and pumps.

The viscount gave a very clever rendering of an anecdote at that time going the rounds, to the effect that the Duc d'Enghien had gone secretly to Paris to see Mlle. George, and there met Bonaparte, who also enjoyed the favors of the famous actress; and that Napoleon on meeting the duke there happened to fall into one of the epileptic fits to which he was subject, and thus came into the duke's power, but the duke refrained from taking advantage of it, while Bonaparte revenged himself for such magnanimity by compassing the duke's death.

The story was very nice and interesting, especially at the place where the rivals suddenly recognize each other, and the ladies, it appeared, were moved.

"Charming!" exclaimed Anna Pavlovna, looking interrogatively at the little princess.

"Charming," whispered the little princess, looking for her needle in her work, as if to signify that the interest and fascination of the story had prevented her from going on with her sewing.

The viscount was flattered by this mute tribute of praise, and with a gratified smile was about to continue; but at this instant Anna Pavlovna, who had kept her eye constantly on the young man who seemed to her so dangerous, noticed that he and the abbé were talking altogether too loud and energetically, and she hastened to carry aid to the imperilled place.

In reality Pierre had succeeded in leading the abbé into a conversation on political equipoise; and the abbé, evidently interested by the young man's frank impetuosity, was giving him the full benefit of his pet idea. Both were talking and listening with too much natural ardor, and this was displeasing to Anna Pavlovna.

"How can it be done?—the balance of Europe and the right of nations," the abbé was saying. "It is possible for one powerful empire like Russia, having the

repute of being barbarous, to take her stand disinter-
estedly at the head of an alliance which should have
for its aim the balance of Europe — and she would save
the world!"

"How would you bring about such a balance of
power?" Pierre was beginning to ask; but just at this
instant Anna Pavlovna joined them, and, giving Pierre
a stern glance, asked the Italian how he bore the climate of Petersburg.

The Italian's face instantly changed and took on an
offensively, affectedly soft expression, which was evidently habitual with him when he engaged in conversation with women.

"I am so enchanted by the charms of the wit and
culture, especially among the women of the society into
which I have the honor of being received, that I have
not as yet had time to think of the climate," said he.

Anna Pavlovna, not allowing Pierre and the abbé to
escape from her, brought them into the general circle,
so that she might keep them under her observation.

At this moment, a new personage appeared in the
drawing-room. This new personage was the young
Prince Andreï Bolkonsky, the husband of the little
princess. Prince Bolkonsky was a very handsome
young man of medium height, with strongly marked
and stern features. Everything about him, from the
dull and weary expression of his eyes to the measured
deliberation of his step, presented a striking contrast
with his little lively wife. He was not only acquainted,
it seemed, with every one in the room, but found them
so tedious that even to look at them and hear their
voices was a great bore to him. Of all the faces there
which he found so tiresome, the face of his lovely little
wife was apparently the one that bored him the most.
With a grimace which disfigured his handsome face,
he turned away from her. He kissed Anna Pavlovna's
hand, and with half-closed eyes looked round at the
assembly.

"So you are getting ready for war, prince?" asked
Anna Pavlovna.

"General Kutuzóf has been kind enough to desire me as his aide-de-camp."

He spoke in French and like a Frenchman accented the last syllable of Kutúzof's name.

"And Liza, your wife?"

"She will go into the country."

"Isn't it a sin for you to deprive us of your charming wife?"

"André," exclaimed the little princess, addressing her husband in the same coquettish tone that she employed toward strangers, "such a fascinating story the viscount has been telling us about Mlle. George and Bonaparte!"

Prince Andreï frowned and turned away. Pierre, who from the moment when Prince Andreï entered the room had not taken his merry kindly eyes from him, now came up and took him by the arm. Prince Andreï, without looking round, again contracted his face into a grimace expressing his annoyance that any one should touch his arm, but when he saw Pierre's smiling face, he smiled with an unexpectedly kind and pleasant smile.

"What is this! — you also in gay society?" said he to Pierre.

"I knew that you would be here," replied Pierre. "I will go home to supper with you," he added in a whisper, so as not to disturb the viscount, who was proceeding with his story; "may I?"

"No, it's impossible!" said Prince Andreï, laughing, and by a pressure of the hand giving Pierre to understand that he had no need of asking such a question.

He had something more on his tongue's end, but at this moment, Prince Vasíli and his daughter arose and the two young men stood aside to give them room to pass.

"You will excuse me, my dear viscount," said Prince Vasíli to the Frenchman, courteously pulling him down by the sleeve to make him keep his seat; "this unfortunate reception at the embassy deprives me of a pleasure, and compels us to interrupt you — I am very sorry to leave your delightful reception," said he to Anna Pavlovna.

His daughter, the Princess Ellen, gracefully holding the folds of her dress, made her way among the chairs, and the smile on her lovely face was more radiant than ever. Pierre looked with almost startled, enthusiastic eyes at the beauty as she passed by him.

"Very handsome," said Prince Andreï.

"Very," said Pierre.

As he went by, Prince Vasíli seized Pierre by the hand and turned to Anna Pavlovna.

"Train this bear for me," said he. "Here he has been living a month at my house, and this is the first time that I have seen him in society. Nothing is so advantageous for a young man as the society of clever women."

CHAPTER IV

ANNA PAVLOVNA smiled and promised to look out for Pierre, who was, as she knew, on his father's side related to Prince Vasíli.

The elderly lady who had been sitting near *Ma Tante* jumped up hastily and followed Prince Vasíli into the entry. Her face lost all its former pretence of interest. Her kind, tear-worn face expressed only anxiety and alarm.

"What can you tell me, prince, about my Bóris," she said, as she followed him (she pronounced the name Borís with the accent on the first syllable); "I cannot stay any longer in Petersburg. Tell me what tidings I can take to my poor boy."

Although Prince Vasíli's manner in listening to the old lady was reluctant and almost uncivil, and even showed impatience, still she gave him a flattering and affectionate smile and took his arm to keep him from going.

"What would it cost you to say a word to the emperor and then he would be at once admitted to the Guards!" she added.

"Be assured that I will do all I can, princess," replied Prince Vasíli; "but it is hard for me to ask his majesty; I should advise you to appeal to Rumyantsof through Prince Galitsuin. That would be wiser."

The elderly lady was the Princess Drubetskaya, and belonged to one of the best families in Russia, but she was poor, had long been out of society, and had lost her former connections. She had now come to town in order to secure the admittance of her only son into the Imperial Guards. Merely for the sake of meeting Prince Vasíli, she had accepted Anna Pavlovna's invitation and come to the reception; merely for this she had listened to the viscount's story. She was dismayed at Prince Vasíli's words; her once handsome face expressed vexation, but this lasted only an instant. She smiled once more and clasped Prince Vasíli's arm more firmly.

"Listen, prince," said she, "I have never asked anything of you, and I never shall ask anything of you again and I have never reminded you of the friendship that my father had for you. But now I beg of you, in God's name, do this for my son and I will look upon you as our benefactor," she added hastily. "No, don't be angry, but promise me this. I have asked Galitsuin, he refused. Be kind as you used to be!" she said, trying to smile, though the tears were in her eyes.

"Papa, we shall be late," said the Princess Ellen, turning her lovely head on her classic shoulders as she stood waiting at the door.

Now influence in society is a capital which has to be economized lest it be exhausted. Prince Vasíli understood this, and having once come to the conclusion that if he asked favors for everybody that applied to him, it would soon be idle to ask anything for himself, he rarely exerted his influence. The Princess Drubetskaya's last appeal, however, caused him to feel something like a pang of conscience. She reminded him of the fact that he owed to her father his first advancement in his career. Moreover he saw by her manner that she was one of those women, notably mothers, who having once got a notion into their heads do not desist until their desires are gratified, and in case they fail are ready every day, every moment, with fresh urgencies, and even scenes. This last consideration turned the scale with him.

"*Chère* Anna Mikhaïlovna," said he, with his usual familiarity and with ill humor in his voice; "it is almost impossible for me to do what you wish; but in order to show you how fond I am of you, and how much I honor your father's memory, I will do the impossible; your son shall be admitted to the Guards, here is my hand on it. Are you satisfied?"

"My dear, you are our benefactor. I expected nothing less from you — I knew how kind you were." — He started to go. — "Wait, two words more — when once he is admitted," — she hesitated. "You and Mikhaïl Ilarionovitch Kutuzof are good friends, do recommend Bóris to him as aide-de-camp. Then I should be content, and then — "

Prince Vasíli smiled.

"That I will not promise. You have no idea how Kutuzof has been besieged since he was appointed commander-in-chief. He himself told me that all the ladies of Moscow had offered him all their sons as adjutants."

"No, promise me; I will not let you go, my dear friend, my benefactor, — "

"Papa," again insisted the beautiful Ellen, in the same tone, "we shall be late."

"Well, *au revoir*, good-by. Do you see?"

"Then to-morrow you will speak to the Emperor?"

"Without fail, but I cannot promise about Kutuzof."

"No, but promise, promise, Basile," insisted Anna Mikhaïlovna, with a coquettish smile, which perhaps in days long gone by might have been becoming to her, but now ill suited her haggard face. She evidently forgot her age, and through habit put her confidence in her former feminine resources. But as soon as he was gone, her face again assumed the same expression as before, of pretended cool complacency. She returned to the group where the viscount was still telling stories, and again she made believe listen, though she was anxiously waiting for the time to go, now that her purpose was accomplished.

"But what do you think of all this last comedy *du sacre de Milan?*" asked Anna Pavlovna, "and the new comedy of the people of Genoa and Lucca coming to offer their homage to Monsieur Bonaparte sitting on a throne and accepting the homage of nations. Oh, this is delicious! No, it is enough to make one beside one's self. You would think the whole world had gone mad."

Prince Andreï looked straight into her face and smiled.

"'God has given me this crown; beware of touching it,'" he said, quoting Bonaparte's words at his coronation. "They say he was very handsome as he pronounced these words," he added, and he repeated them in Italian: "*Dio mi la dona, guai a chi la tocca.*"

"I hope," pursued Anna Pavlovna, "that this will at last be the drop too much. The sovereigns cannot longer endure this man who imperils everything."

"The sovereigns? I do not mean Russia," said the viscount, politely, but in a tone of despair: "The sovereigns, madame? What have they done for Louis XVIII., for the Queen, for Madame Elizabeth? Nothing!" he added, becoming animated. "And, believe me, they are suffering their punishment for having betrayed the cause of the Bourbons. The sovereigns? They are sending ambassadors to compliment the usurper!"

And with an exclamation of contempt, he again changed his position.

Prince Ippolit, who had been long contemplating the viscount through his lorgnette, suddenly at these words turned completely round to the little princess, and asking her for a needle proceeded to show her what the escutcheon of Condé was, scratching it with the needle on the table. He explained this coat-of-arms for her benefit, with a consequential air, as if the princess had asked him to do it for her.

"*Bâton de gueules engrêlé de gueules d'azur* — the house of Condé," he said.

The princess listened with a smile.

"If Bonaparte remains a year longer on the throne of France, things will have gone quite too far," said the viscount, still pursuing the same line of conversation, like a man who, without listening to others, and considering himself the best informed on any subject, insists on following the lead of his own thoughts. By intrigue, violence, proscriptions and capital punishment, society, I mean good society, French society, will be utterly destroyed, and then — "

He shrugged his shoulders and spread open his hands. Pierre was about to put in a word, the conversation interested him, but Anna Pavlovna, who was watching him, broke in : —

"The Emperor Alexander," said she, with the melancholy which always accompanied any reference of hers to the imperial family, "has declared that he will leave it to the French themselves to choose their own form of government. And I think that there is no doubt that the whole nation, when once freed from the usurper, will throw itself into the arms of its rightful king," said Anna Pavlovna, striving to be gracious to the *émigré* and Royalist.

"That is doubtful," said Prince Andreï. "The viscount is perfectly right when he remarks that things have already gone too far. I think it will be difficult to return to the old."

"I have recently heard," remarked Pierre, with a flushed face, again venturing to take part in the conversation, "that almost all the nobility have gone over to Bonaparte."

"That is what the Bonapartists say," replied the viscount, not looking at Pierre. "It is hard nowadays to know what the public opinion of France really is."

"Bonaparte said so," said Prince Andreï, with a sneer.

It was evident that the viscount did not please him, and also that the viscount, without especially addressing him, directed all his remarks at him.

" ' I have showed them the path of glory,' " he went on, after a moment's silence, again quoting Napoleon's words, " ' and they would not enter it; I opened my antechambers to them, and they rushed in in throngs,' I know not how far he was justified in saying that."

" Not at all," said the viscount; " after the murder of the duke, even the most partial ceased to look on him as a hero. Even if he was a hero for certain people," continued the viscount, addressing Anna Pavlovna, " since the assassination of the duke there is one martyr more in heaven, one hero less on earth."

Anna Pavlovna and the others had not time to reward the viscount with a smile of approval for his words, before Pierre again rushed into the conversation, and Anna Pavlovna, though she had a presentiment that he would say something indecorous, was unable this time to restrain him.

" The punishment of the Duc d'Enghien," said Monsieur Pierre, " was an imperial necessity, and I for one regard it as magnanimous of Napoleon not to hesitate to assume the sole responsibility of this act."

" *Dieu! mon Dieu!* " exclaimed Anna Pavlovna, in a whisper of dismay.

" What, Monsieur Pierre! you see magnanimity in assassination? " exclaimed the little princess, smiling and moving her work nearer to her.

" Ah!.... Oh! " said different voices.

" Capital," said Prince Ippolit, in English, and he began to slap his knee with his hand.

The viscount merely shrugged his shoulders.

Pierre looked triumphantly at the company over his spectacles.

" I say this," he went on to explain, in a sort of desperation, " because the Bourbons fled from the Revolution, leaving their people a prey to anarchy. And Napoleon was the only man able to understand the Revolution, to conquer it, and consequently, for the sake of the general good he could not hesitate, before the life of an individual."

"Don't you want to come over to this table?" suggested Anna Pavlovna.

But Pierre, without heeding her, went on with his discourse.

"No," said he, growing more and more excited, "Napoleon is great because he stands superior to the Revolution, because he has crushed out its abuses, preserving all that was good — the equality of citizens, and freedom of speech and of the press, and only thus he gained power."

"Yes, if, when he gained the power, instead of using it for assassination, he had restored it to the legitimate king," said the viscount, "then I should have called him a great man."

"But he could not do that. The power was granted him by the people, solely that he might deliver them from the Bourbons, and because they saw that he was a great man. The Revolution was a mighty fact," continued Monseiur Pierre, betraying by this desperate and forced proposition, his extreme youth, and his propensity to speak out whatever was in his mind.

"Revolution and regicide mighty facts!.... After this .... but will you not come over to this table?" insisted Anna Pavlovna.

"*Contrat social*," suggested the viscount, with a benignant smile.

"I am not talking about regicide, I am talking about ideas."

"Yes, ideas of pillage, murder, and regicide," suggested an ironical voice.

"Those are the extremes, of course, and the real significance is not in such things, but in the rights of man, in emancipation from prejudices, in equality of the citizens, and all these principles Napoleon has preserved in all their integrity."

"Liberty and equality!" exclaimed the viscount, scornfully, as if he had at last made up his mind seriously to prove to this young man all the foolishness of his arguments. "All high-sounding words, which long ago were shown to be dangerous. Who does not love liberty and equality? Our Saviour himself preached liberty and equality. But after the Revolution were men any happier? On the contrary! We wanted freedom, and Bonaparte has destroyed it."

Prince Andreï with a smile looked now at Pierre, now at the viscount, and now at the hostess. During the first instant of Pierre's outbreak, Anna Pavlovna was appalled, notwithstanding her experience in society; but when she saw that Pierre's sacrilegious utterances did not make the viscount lose his temper, and when she became convinced that it was impossible to check them, she collected her forces, and taking the viscount's side, she attacked the young orator.

"*Mais, mon cher* Monsieur Pierre," said Anna Pavlovna, "how can you call a man great who can put to death a duke, simply a man, when you come to analyze it, without trial and without cause?"

"I should like to ask," said the viscount, "how monsieur explains the Eighteenth Brumaire. Was it not a fraud? It was a piece of trickery wholly unlike what a great man could have done."

"And the prisoners in Africa, whom he killed?" suggested the little princess. "That was horrible!" and she shrugged her shoulders.

"He is a low fellow, whatever you may say."

Monsieur Pierre did not know which one to answer; he looked at them all and smiled. His smile was unlike other men's, falsely compounded of seriousness. Whenever a smile came on his face, then suddenly, like a flash, all the serious and even stern expression vanished, and in its place came another, genial, frank, and like that of a child asking forgiveness.

The viscount, who had never seen this young Jacobin before, recognized clearly that he was not nearly as terrible as his words.

All were silent.

"How can you expect him to answer all of you at once?" said Prince Andreï. "Besides, in the actions of a statesman, one must distinguish those of a private individual, a general, or an emperor. So it seems to me."

"Yes, yes, of course," put in Pierre, delighted at this ratification of his ideas.

"It is impossible not to acknowledge," pursued Prince Andreï, "that Napoleon was great as a man on the bridge at Arcola, or in the hospital at Jaffa, when he shook hands with the plague-stricken soldiers, but — but there are other actions of his which are hard to justify."

Prince Andreï, who had evidently been desirous of smoothing over the clumsiness of Pierre's remark, got up, with the intention of leaving, and giving his wife the hint.

Suddenly, Prince Ippolit arose, and with a gesture of his hand detaining the company, and begging them to be seated, he went on to say: —

"Oh, I was told to-day such a charming Russian story. I must give you the benefit of it. You will excuse me, viscount, I must tell it in Russian. Otherwise, the flavor of the story will be lost."

And Prince Ippolit began to speak in Russian, with much the same fluency as Frenchmen who have spent a year in Russia usually attain. All stopped to listen, because Prince Ippolit had been so strenuously urgent in attracting their attention to his story.

"In Moscow there is a lady, *une dame*, and she is very miserly. She has to have two footmen behind her carriage. And very tall ones. That was her hobby. And she had a chambermaid, who was also very tall. She said — "

Here Prince Ippolit paused to think, evidently at a loss to collect his wits.

"She said, — yes, she said, 'Girl (*à la femme de chambre*), put on a livery and go with me, behind the carriage, and make some calls.' "

Here Prince Ippolit snickered and laughed long before his hearers and their silence produced a very disheartening effect upon the narrator. However, a few, including the elderly lady and Anna Pavlovna, smiled.

" She drove off. Suddenly a strong wind blew up.
The girl lost her hat and her long hair came down."

Here he could not hold in any longer, but through
his bursts of broken laughter he managed to say these
words, —

" And every one knew about it."

That was the end of the anecdote. Although it was
incomprehensible why he told it, and why he felt called
on to tell it in Russian rather than French, still Anna
Pavlovna and the others appreciated Prince Ippolit's
cleverness in so agreeably putting an end to Monsieur
Pierre's disagreeable and stupid freak.

The company, after the anecdote, broke up into little
groups, busily engaged in insignificant small talk about
some ball that had been or some ball that was to be, or
the theatre, or when and where they should meet
again.

CHAPTER V

CONGRATULATING Anna Pavlovna on what they called
her charming *soirée*, the guests began to take their
departure.

Pierre, as we have already said, was awkward. Stout,
of more than the average height, broad-shouldered,
with huge red hands, he had no idea of the proper way
to enter a drawing-room, and still less the proper way
of making his exit; in other words he did not know
how to make some especially agreeable remark to his
hostess before taking his leave. Moreover, he was
absent-minded. He got up, and instead of taking his
own hat he seized the plumed three-cornered hat of some
general, and held it, pulling at the feathers until the
general came and asked him to surrender it. But all
his absent-mindedness and clumsiness about entering a
drawing-room, and about suitable subjects of conversation, were redeemed by his expression of genuine goodness, simplicity, and modesty.

Anna Pavlovna turned to him, and with Christian

sweetness expressing her forgiveness for his behavior, nodded to him, and said, —

"I hope I shall see you again, but I hope also that you will change your opinions, my dear Monsieur Pierre," said she.

He could find no words to answer her; he only bowed, and let every one again see his smile, which really said nothing, except this : "Opinions are opinions, and you can see what a good and noble young man I am." And all, Anna Pavlovna included, could not help feeling this.

Prince Andreï went into the anteroom, allowed the lackey to throw his mantle over his shoulders, and with cool indifference listened to the chatter of his wife and Prince Ippolit, who had also come into the anteroom.

Prince Ippolit stood near the pretty little princess, and stared straight at her through his lorgnette.

"Go back, Annette, you will take cold," said the little princess, by way of farewell to Anna Pavlovna. "It is all understood," she added, in an undertone.

Anna Pavlovna had already had a chance to speak a word with Liza in regard to the suggested match between Anatol and the little princess's sister-in-law.

"I shall depend upon you, my dear," said Anna Pavlovna, also in an undertone. "You write to her and tell me how her father will look at it. *Au revoir.*" And she went back from the anteroom.

Prince Ippolit came to the little princess, and bending his face down close to her began to talk to her in a half-whisper.

Two lackeys, one the princess's, holding her shawl, the other Prince Ippolit's, with his overcoat, stood waiting until they should finish talking, and listened to their chatter, which being in French was incomprehensible; but their faces seemed to say, "We understand, but we do not care to show it."

The princess, as always, smiled as she spoke, and listened, laughing gayly.

"I am very glad that I did not go to the ambassador's," said Prince Ippolit, "a bore — we've had a lovely evening, haven't we, lovely."

"They say it will be a very fine ball," replied the princess, curling her downy lip. "All the pretty women in society will be there."

"Not all, because you are not there, certainly not all," said Prince Ippolit, gayly laughing; and taking the shawl from the servant he even pushed him away and began to wrap it round the princess. Either through awkwardness or intentionally (no one could tell which), it was a long time before he took his arms away from her even after the shawl was well wrapped round her, and he seemed to be embracing the young woman.

Gracefully, and still smiling, she drew back a little, turned around and glanced at her husband. Prince Andreï's eyes were closed; he seemed so tired and sleepy!

"Are you ready?" he asked, glancing at his wife.

Prince Ippolit hastily put on his overcoat, which being in the latest style came below his heels, and stumbling along in it rushed to the steps after the princess, whom the lackey was assisting into the carriage.

"Princess, *au revoir*," he cried, his tongue as badly entangled as his feet.

The princess, gathering up her dress, took her seat in the darkness of the carriage; her husband was arranging his sword; Prince Ippolit, in his efforts to be of assistance, was in everybody's way.

"Excuse me, sir," said Prince Andreï in Russian, in a cold, disagreeable tone, addressing Prince Ippolit, who stood in his way.

"I shall expect you, Pierre," said the same voice, but warmly and affectionately.

The postilion whipped up the horses and the carriage rolled noisily away.

Prince Ippolit laughed nervously, as he stood on the steps, waiting for the viscount, whom he had promised to take home.

"Well, my dear fellow, your little princess is charming, very charming," said the viscount, as he took his seat in the carriage with Ippolit, "yes indeed, she's charming." He kissed the tips of his fingers.

"And really quite Frenchy."

Ippolit roared with laughter.

"And do you know, you are terrible with your little innocent ways," continued the viscount. "I pity the poor husband, — that little officer who puts on the airs of a reigning prince."

Ippolit again went off into a burst of laughter, through which he managed to articulate : —

"And yet you said that the Russian ladies were not anywhere equal to the French ladies! One must know how to manage them."

Pierre, being the first to reach the house, went into Prince Andreï's own room, like one thoroughly at home, and immediately stretching himself out on the divan, as his habit was, took up the first book that he found on the shelf — it was Cæsar's Commentaries — and leaning on his elbow began to read in the middle of the volume.

"What have you been doing to Mlle. Scherer? She will be quite laid up now," said Prince Andreï, coming into the room and rubbing his small white hands together.

Pierre turned over with his whole body, making the divan creak, looked up at Prince Andreï with an eager face, smiled and waved his hand.

"No," said he, "that abbé is very interesting, only he does not understand the matter aright. .... In my opinion, permanent peace is possible, but I cannot tell how .... certainly not through political equilibrium."

Prince Andreï was evidently not interested in these abstract questions.

"It is not good form, my dear fellow, always and everywhere to say what you think. But have you come to any final decision yet as to your career? Will you be a horse-guardsman or a diplomat ?" asked Prince Andreï, after a moment's silence.

Pierre sat up on the divan, doubling his legs under him.

"You can imagine, I have not as yet the slightest idea. Neither the one nor the other pleases me."

"But see here, you must come to some decision. Your father is waiting."

Pierre at the age of ten had been sent abroad, with an abbé for a tutor, and had remained there till he was twenty. On his return to Moscow, his father dismissed the abbé and said to the young man: —

"Now go to Petersburg, look about, and take your choice. I give my consent to anything. Here is a letter to Prince Vasíli, and here is money for you. Write me about everything, and I will help you in any way."

Pierre had been trying for three months to choose a career, and had not succeeded. It was in regard to this choice that Prince Andreï spoke. Pierre rubbed his forehead.

"But he must be a Freemason," said he, referring to the abbé whom he had met that evening.

"That is all nonsense," said Prince Andreï, again stopping him short; "let us talk about your affairs. Have you been to the Horse Guards?"

"No, not yet, but here is an idea that occurred to me and I wanted to tell you; now there is war against Napoleon. If it had been a war for freedom, I should have taken part, I should have been the first to enter the military service; but to help England and Austria against the greatest man in the world, that is not good."

Prince Andreï merely shrugged his shoulders at Pierre's childish talk. He pretended that it was impossible to reply to such stupidities, but in reality it was difficult to settle this naïve question in any other way than as Prince Andreï did answer it.

"If all men made war only for their convictions, there would be no war," said he.

"That would be splendid," said Pierre.

Prince Andreï laughed.

"Very likely it would be splendid, but it will never be."

"Now, why are you going to war?" asked Pierre.

"Why? I don't know. It must be so. Besides, I'm going" — He paused. "I am going because the life which I lead here, my life, is not to my mind."

CHAPTER VI

THE rustle of a woman's gown was heard in the adjoining room. As if caught napping, Prince Andreï shook himself, and his face assumed the same expression which it had worn in Anna Pavlovna's drawing-room.

Pierre set his feet down from the sofa.

The princess came in. She had already changed her gown for another, a house dress, but equally fresh and elegant.

Prince Andreï got up and courteously pushed forward an easy-chair.

"Why is it, I often wonder," she remarked, speaking as always in French, and at the same time briskly and spryly sitting down in the easy-chair, "why Annette never married. How stupid you all are, messieurs, that you never married her. You will excuse me for saying so, but you have not the slightest notion how to talk with women. What an arguer you are, Monsieur Pierre."

"Your husband and I were just this moment arguing. I cannot understand why he wants to go to war," said Pierre, addressing the princess without any of the embarrassment so commonly shown in the relations of a young man toward a young woman.

The princess gave a start. Evidently Pierre's words touched her to the quick.

"Ah, that is exactly what I say!" said she. "I do not understand, really I do not understand why men cannot live without war. Why is it that we women do not want it and do not need it at all? Now you be the judge. I will put the matter just as it is: here he is adjutant to uncle, a most brilliant position. Everybody knows him. Everybody esteems him. The other day at the Apraksins' I heard a lady asking: 'Is that the famous Prince Andreï?' On my word of honor!"

She laughed.

"He is received so everywhere. He might **very**

easily be even one of his majesty's aides. You know the
Emperor spoke very cordially with him. Annette and
I have talked it all over; it might be very easily ar-
ranged. What do you think?"

Pierre glanced at Prince Andreï, and seeing that this
conversation did not please his friend, made no reply
to her.

"When are you going?" he asked.

"Ah! don't speak of going, don't speak of it. I do
not wish to hear a word of it!" exclaimed the princess,
in the same capriciously vivacious tone in which she had
spoken to Ippolit. It was obviously out of place in the
family circle, in which Pierre was an adopted member.

"To-day when it came over me that I had to break
off from all these pleasant relations — and then, you
know, André"— She blinked her eyes significantly at
her husband. "I dread it, I dread it," she whispered,
making a shiver run down her back.

Her husband looked at her with a surprised expression, as if for the first time he had noticed that any one
besides himself and Pierre had come into the room.
Then with a cool politeness he addressed his wife, inquiringly : —

"What is it that you dread, Liza. I cannot understand," said he.

"Now how selfish all you men are, all, all selfish.
Simply from his own whim, God knows why, he deserts
me, shuts me up in the country alone."

"With my father and sister, don't forget that," said
Prince Andreï, gently.

"All alone, just the same, away from *my* friends —
and he expects me not to be afraid."

Her tone grew querulous; her lip was lifted, so that
her face looked not mirthful, but repulsive and like a
squirrel's. She paused, as if she regarded it as indecorous to speak of her condition before Pierre, though
this was the real secret of her fear.

"And still I do not understand what you dread," said
Prince Andreï, deliberately, not taking his eyes from his
wife.

The princess blushed and spread open her hands with a gesture of despair.

"No, André, I insist upon it, you have changed so!"

"Your doctor bids you go to bed earlier," said Prince Andreï. "You had better retire."

The princess made no answer, and suddenly her short downy lip trembled; Prince Andreï, shrugging his shoulders, began to walk up and down the room.

Pierre gazed through his glasses with naïve curiosity, first at him, then at the princess, and made a motion as if he also would get up, but then changed his mind.

"What difference does it make to me if Monsieur Pierre is here!" suddenly exclaimed the little princess, and her pretty face at the same time was contracted into a tearful grimace. "I have been wanting for a long time to ask you, André, why you have changed toward me so? What have I done to you? You are going to the army, you do not pity me at all. Why is it?"

"Lise!" exclaimed Prince Andreï, but this one word carried an entreaty, a threat, and above all a conviction that she herself would regret what she had said; but she went on hurriedly:—

"You treat me as if I were ill or a child. I see it all. You were not so six months ago."

"Lise, I beg of you to stop," said Prince Andreï, still more earnestly.

Pierre, growing more and more agitated as this conversation proceeded, arose and went to the princess. He evidently could not endure the sight of tears, and he himself was ready to weep.

"Calm yourself, princess. This is only your fancy, because, I assure you, I myself have experienced.... and so.... because.... No, excuse me, a stranger is in the way.... No, calm yourself.... good-by."

Prince Andreï detained him, taking him by the arm:—

"No, stay, Pierre. The princess is so kind that she will not have the heart to deprive me of the pleasure of spending the rest of the evening with you."

"Yes, he only thinks about his own pleasure!" exclaimed the princess, not restraining her angry tears.

"Lise," said Prince Andreï, dryly, raising his voice sufficiently to show that his patience was exhausted.

Suddenly the angry, squirrel-like expression on the princess's pretty little face changed to one of alarm, both fascinating and provocative of sympathy; her beautiful eyes looked from under her long lashes at her husband, and there came into her face that timid look of subjection such as a dog has when it wags its drooping tail quickly but doubtfully.

"*Mon Dieu! Mon Dieu!*" muttered the princess, and gathering up the skirt of her dress with one hand, she went to her husband and kissed him on the forehead.

"Good-night, Lise," said Prince Andreï, getting up and courteously kissing her hand, as if she were a stranger.

CHAPTER VII

THE friends were silent. Neither the one nor the other felt like being the first to speak. Pierre looked at Prince Andreï; Prince Andreï rubbed his forehead with his slender hand.

"Let us have some supper," said he, with a sigh, getting up and going to the door.

They went into the dining-room, elegantly, newly, and richly furnished in the latest style. Everything, from the napkins to the silver, the china, and the glassware, had that peculiar imprint of newness which is characteristic of the establishment of a young couple.

In the midst of supper, Prince Andreï leaned forward on his elbows, and, like a man who has for a long time had something on his heart and suddenly determines to confess it, he began to talk with an expression of nervous exasperation such as Pierre had never before beheld in his friend: —

"Never, never get married, my friend! This is my advice to you. Do not marry until you have come to the conclusion that you have done all that is in your power to do and until you have ceased to love the woman whom you have chosen, until you have seen clearly what she is; otherwise you will make a sad and irreparable mistake. When you are old and good for nothing, then get married. .... Otherwise, all that is good and noble in you will be thrown away. All will be wasted in trifles. Yes, yes, yes! Don't look at me in such amazement. If ever you have any hope of anything ahead of you, you will be made to feel at every step that, as far as you are concerned, all is at an end, all closed to you, except the drawing-room, where you will rank with court lackeys and idiots. — That's a fact!"

He waved his hand energetically.

Pierre took off his spectacles, and this made his face, as he gazed in amazement at his friend, even more expressive than usual of his goodness of heart.

"My wife," continued Prince Andreï, "is a lovely woman. She is one of those few women to whom a man can feel that his honor is safely intrusted; but, my God! what would I not give at this moment if I were not married! You are the first and only person to whom I have said this, and it is because I love you."

Prince Andreï, in saying this, was still less like the Bolkonsky who, that same evening, had been sitting in Anna Pávlovna's easy-chairs, murmuring French phrases as he blinked his eyes. Every muscle in his spare face was quivering with nervous animation; his eyes, in which before the fire of life seemed to be extinguished, now gleamed with a fierce and intense brilliancy. It was evident that, however lacking in life he might appear in ordinary circumstances, he more than made up for it by his energy at moments of almost morbid excitability.

"You cannot understand why I say this to you," he went on. "Why, it is the whole history of a life. You talk about Bonaparte and his career," said he, although Pierre had not said a word about Bonaparte. "You talk about Bonaparte, but Bonaparte, when he was toiling, went step by step straight for his goal; he was free;

he let nothing stand between him and his goal, and he reached it. But tie yourself to a woman and, like a prisoner in chains, your whole freedom is destroyed. And in proportion as you feel that you have hope and powers, the more you will be weighed down and tormented with regrets. Drawing-rooms, tittle-tattle, balls, vulgar show, meanness, — such is the charmed circle from which I cannot escape. I am now getting ready for the war, the greatest war that ever was, and yet I know nothing and am fit for nothing. I am very, very likable and very keen," continued Prince Andreï, "and at Anna Pavlovna's they like to hear me talk. And this stupid society, without which my wife cannot live, and these women .... If you could only know what all these distinguished women and women in general amount to! My father is right. Egotism, ostentation, stupidity, meanness in every respect — such are women when they show themselves as they are. You see them in society and think that they amount to something, but they are naught, naught, naught! No, don't marry, my dear heart, don't marry," said Prince Andreï in conclusion.

"It seems ridiculous to me," said Pierre, "that you should regard yourself as incapable and your life as spoiled. Everything is before you — everything. And you ...."

He did not finish his sentence, but his very tone made it evident how highly he prized his friend and how much he expected from him in the future.

"How can he speak so!" thought Pierre, who considered Prince Andreï the model of all accomplishments, for the very reason that Prince Andreï united in himself, to the highest degree, all those qualities that were lacking in Pierre, and that more nearly than anything else expresses the concept, — *will-power.*

Pierre always admired Prince Andreï's ability to meet with perfect ease all sorts of people, his extraordinary memory, his breadth of knowledge, — he had read everything, he knew about everything, he had ideas on every subject, — and, above all, his powers of work and study. And if Pierre was often struck by Andreï's lack of aptitude for speculative philosophy — which was his own specialty — he at least regarded it not as a fault but as a sign of strength.

In all the best relations, however friendly and simple, flattery or praise is indispensable, just as grease is indispensable for making wheels move easily.

"I have reached the end of things," said Prince Andreï. "What is there to say about me! Let us talk about yourself," said he, after a short silence, and smiling at his consoling thoughts. This smile was instantly reflected on Pierre's face.

"But what is there to say about me," asked Pierre, his lips parting in a gay, careless smile. "What am I, anyway? I am a bastard!"

And suddenly his face grew red. It was evident that he had exerted great effort to say that. "Without name, without fortune!.... And yet it is true....."

He did not say what was true.

"I am free for the present, and I like it. Only I don't know what to take up. I should like to have a serious talk with you on the subject."

Prince Andreï looked at him with kindly eyes. But his glance, friendly and affectionate as it was, betrayed the consciousness of his superiority.

"I am fond of you for the special reason that you are the only live man in all our circle. It is well with you. Choose whatever you like, it is all the same. It will be well with you anywhere; but there's one thing. Stop going to those Kuragins' and leading their kind of life. That sort of thing does not become you: all those revels, that wild life, and all — "

"What do you care, my dear fellow," exclaimed Pierre, shrugging his shoulders, "women, my dear, women!"

"I don't understand it," replied Andreï. "Respectable women, that is another thing, but Kuragin's women, women and wine, I don't understand it."

Pierre had been living at Prince Vasíli Kuragin's, and had been taking part in the dissipated life of his son Anatol, the very same young man to whom it had been proposed to marry Prince Andreï's sister in order to reform him.

"Do you know," said Pierre, as if a happy thought had come unexpectedly into his mind, — "seriously, I have been thinking about it for some time. Since I have been leading this sort of life, I have not been able to think or to come to any decision. My head aches; I have no money. This evening he invited me, but I am not going."

"Give me your word of honor that you will not go again."

"Here's my word on it!"

CHAPTER VIII

It was already two o'clock when Pierre left his friend. It was a luminous June night, characteristic of Petersburg. Pierre took his seat in the hired carriage, with the intention of going home, but the farther he rode the more impossible he found it to think of sleeping on such a night, which was more like twilight or early morning. He could see far down through the empty streets. On the way it occurred to him that the gambling club were to meet as usual that evening at Anatol Kuragin's, after which they were accustomed to have a drinking bout, topping off with one of Pierre's favorite entertainments.

"It would be good fun to go to Kuragin's," said he to himself, but instantly he remembered that he had given Prince Andreï his word of honor not to go there again.

But, as happens to men of no strength of character, he immediately felt such a violent desire to have one more last taste of this dissipated life, so well known to him, that he determined to go. And, in excuse for it, the thought entered his mind that his promise was not binding, because, before he had given it to Prince Andreï, he had also promised Anatol to be present at his house; moreover, he reasoned that all such pledges were merely conditional and had no definite meaning, especially if it were taken into consideration that perhaps by the next day he might be dead, or something might happen to him so extraordinary that the distinctions of honorable and dishonorable would entirely vanish. Arguments of this nature often occurred to Pierre, entirely nullifying his plans and purposes.

He went to Kuragin's.

Driving up to the great house at the Horse-Guard barracks, where Anatol lived, he sprang upon the lighted porch, ran up the steps, and entered the open door. There was no one in the anteroom; empty bottles, cloaks, and overshoes were scattered about; there was an odor of wine; farther on he heard loud talking and shouts.

Play and supper were over, but the guests had not yet dispersed. Pierre threw off his cloak and went into the first room, where were the remains of the supper: a single waiter, thinking that no one could see him, was stealthily drinking up the wine in the half-empty glasses. In a third room were heard the sounds of scuffling, laughter, the shouts of well-known voices, and the growl of a bear. Eight young men were eagerly crowding around an open window. Three were having sport with the young bear which one of their number was dragging by a chain and trying to frighten the others with.

"I bet a hundred on Stevens," cried one.

"See, he can't hold him," cried a second.

"I bet on Dolokhof," cried a third. "Get those fellows away, Kuragin."

"There, let Mishka go! This is the wager."

"Without stopping to breathe, or he loses," cried a fourth.

"Yakof, bring the bottle, Yakof!" cried the host of the evening, a tall, handsome fellow, standing in the midst of the crowd, in a single thin shirt, thrown open at the chest. — "Hold on, gentlemen! Here he is, here is our dear friend, Petrushka," he cried, addressing Pierre.

A short man, with clear blue eyes, whose voice,

among all those drunken voices, was noticeable for its tone of sobriety, shouted from the window : —

"Come here and hear about the wagers."

This was Dolokhof, an officer of the Semyonovsky regiment, a well-known gambler and duelist, whose home was with Anatol. Pierre smiled, as he gayly looked around him.

"I don't understand at all. What's up?"

"Hold on! He's not drunk. Bring a bottle," cried Anatol, and taking a glass from the table, went up to Pierre, —

"First of all, drink."

Pierre proceeded to drain glass after glass, at the same time closely observing and listening to the drunken guests, who had again crowded around the window. Anatol kept his glass filled with wine, and told him how Dolokhof had laid a wager with Stevens, an English naval man who happened to be there, that he, Dolokhof, was to drink a bottle of rum, sitting in the third story window with his legs hanging out.

"There, now, drink it all," said Anatol, handing the last glass to Pierre, "I shan't let you off."

"No, I don't wish any more," replied Pierre, and pushing Anatol aside, he went to the window. Dolokhof was holding the Englishman by the arm, and was clearly and explicitly laying down the conditions of the wager, turning more particularly to Anatol and Pierre, as they approached.

Dolokhof was a man of medium height, with curly hair and bright blue eyes. He was twenty-five years old. Like all infantry officers, he wore no mustache, so that his mouth, which was the most striking feature of his face, was wholly revealed. The lines of the mouth were drawn with remarkable delicacy. The upper lip closed firmly over the strong lower one in a sharp curve at the center, and in the corners hovered constantly something in the nature of two smiles — one in each corner! and all taken together and especially in conjunction with a straightforward, bold, intelligent look, made it impossible not to take notice of his face.

Dolokhof was not a rich man, and he had no influential connections. But although Anatol spent ten thousand rubles a year and it was known that Dolokhof lived with him, nevertheless, he had succeeded in winning such a position that Anatol and all who were acquainted with the two men had a higher regard for him than for Anatol. Dolokhof played nearly every kind of a game and almost always won. However much he drank, he never was known to lose his head. Both Kurágin and Dolokhof were at this time notorious among the rakes and spendthrifts of Petersburg.

The bottle of rum was brought. Two lackeys, evidently made timid and nervous by the orders and shouts of the boon companions, tried to pull away the sash that hindered any one from sitting on the outer slope of the window-seat.

Anatol, with his swaggering way, came up to the window. He wanted to smash something. He pushed the lackeys away and tugged at the sash, but the sash would not yield. He broke the window-panes.

"Now you try it, you man of muscle," said he, calling Pierre.

Pierre seized hold of the cross-bar, gave a pull, and the oaken framework gave way with a crash.

"Take it all out, or they'll think I clung to it," said Dolokhof.

"The Englishman accepts it, does he? — All right?" asked Anatol.

"All right," said Pierre, glancing at Dolokhof, who took the bottle of rum and went to the window, through which could be seen the sky where the evening and morning light were beginning to mingle.

He leaped on the window-sill with the bottle in his hand.

"Listen!" he cried, as he stood there and looked back into the room.

All were silent.

"I wager," — he spoke French so that the Englishman might understand him, and spoke it none too well either, — "I wager fifty sovereigns; or perhaps you prefer a hundred?" he added, addressing the Englishman.

"No, fifty," replied the Englishman.

"Very well, then, fifty it is, — that I will drink this whole bottle of rum without taking it once from my mouth; drink it sitting in this window, in that place there" — he bent over and pointed to the sloping projection of the wall outside the window, — "and not holding on to anything. Is that understood?"

"Very good," said the Englishman.

Anatol turned to the Englishman, and, holding him by the button of his coat and looking down on him, — for the Englishman was short, — began to repeat the terms of the wager in English.

"Hold!" cried Dolokhof, thumping on the window with the bottle, in order to attract attention, — hold, Kuragin, listen! If any one else does the same thing, then I will pay down a hundred sovereigns. Do you understand?"

The Englishman nodded his head, though he did not make it apparent whether or no he were prepared to accept this new wager. Anatol still held him by the button, and, in spite of the nods that he made to signify that he understood all that was said, Anatol insisted on translating Dolokhof's words for him into English.

A lean young Lifeguardsman, who had been playing a losing game all the evening, climbed on the window, leaned over, and gazed down, —

"Oo! Oo! Oo!" he exclaimed, as he looked down from the window to the flagstones below.

"Hush!" cried Dolokhof, and he pulled the officer back from the window, who, getting his feet entangled in his spurs, awkwardly leaped down into the room.

Placing the bottle on the window-sill so as to be within reach, Dolokhof warily and coolly climbed into the window. Letting down his legs and spreading out both hands, he measured the width of the window, sat down, let go his hands, moved to the right, then to the left, and took up the bottle. Anatol brought two candles and set them on the window-seat. although it was now quite light. Dolokhof's back, in the white shirt, and his curly head were illuminated on both sides. All gathered around the window. The Englishman stood in the front row. Pierre smiled and said nothing. One of the older men present suddenly stepped forward, with a stern and frightened face, and attempted to seize Dolokhof by the shirt.

"Gentlemen, this is folly; he will kill himself," said this man, who was less foolhardy than the rest.

Anatol restrained him, —

"Don't touch him; you will startle him, and then he might fall. What if he should? Hey?"

Dolokhof turned around, straightening himself up, and again stretching out his hands.

"If any one touches me again," said he, hissing the words through his thin compressed lips, "I will send him flying down there! So now!"

Thus having spoken, he resumed his former position, dropped his hands, and seizing the bottle he put it to his lips, bent his head back, and raised his free arm as a balance. One of the lackeys, who had begun to clear away the broken glass, paused in his work, and, still bending down, fixed his eyes on the window and Dolokhof's back. Anatol stood straight with staring eyes. The Englishman, thrusting out his lips, looked askance. The man who had tried to stop the proceeding repaired to one corner of the room and threw himself on the divan, with his face to the wall. Pierre covered his eyes, and though the feeble smile still hovered over his lips, his face now expressed horror and apprehension.

All were silent. Pierre took his hand from his eyes. Dolokhof was still sitting in the same position, only his head was thrown farther back, so that the curly hair in the nape of his neck touched his shirt-collar, and the hand holding the bottle was lifted higher and higher, trembling under the effort. The bottle was evidently nearly empty and consequently had to be held almost perpendicularly over his head.

"Why should it take so long?" thought Pierre. It seemed to him as if more than a half-hour had elapsed.

Suddenly Dolokhof's body made a backward motion and his hand trembled nervously; this tremor was sufficient to make him slip as he sat on the sloping ledge. In fact, he slipped, and his arm and head wavered more violently as he struggled to regain his balance. He stretched out one hand to clutch the window-seat, but refrained from touching it.

Pierre again covered his eyes, and declared to himself that he would not open them again. Suddenly he was conscious that there was a commotion around him. He looked up. Dolokhof was standing on the window-seat; his face was pale but radiant.

"Empty!"

He flung the bottle at the Englishman, who cleverly caught it. Dolokhof sprang down from the window. He exhaled a powerful odor of rum.

"Capital!" — "Bravo!" — "That's a wager worth while!" — "The devil take you all," were the shouts that rang from all sides.

The Englishman, taking out his purse, was counting out his money. Dolokhof was scowling, and had nothing to say. Pierre started for the window.

"Gentlemen! Who wants to make the bet with me; I will do the same thing," he cried. "But there's no need of any wager. Give me a bottle. I will do it anyway. Bring a bottle."

"Let him! Let him!" said Dolokhof, smiling.

"What is the matter with you?"—"Are you beside yourself?" — "We won't let you!" — "It makes you dizzy even on a staircase," were shouted from various sides.

"I will drink it; give me a bottle of rum," cried Pierre, pounding on the table with a drunken and resolute gesture, and climbing into the window. He was seized by the arm, but his strength was so great that whoever approached him was sent flying across the room.

"No, you will never dissuade him that way," said Anatol. "Hold on; I will deceive him. Listen, I will make the wager with you, but to-morrow; but now we are all going to ——'s."

"Come on," cried Pierre, "come on! And we will take Mishka with us." And seizing the bear, he began to gallop round the room with him.

CHAPTER IX

PRINCE VASÍLI fulfilled the promise which he had made to the Princess Drubetskaya, when she asked him on the evening of Anna Pavlovna's reception, to help her only son, Borís. The request had been preferred to the emperor, and contrary to the experience of many others, he was allowed to enter the Semyonovsky regiment of the Guard as ensign. But in spite of all Anna Mikhaïlovna's efforts and intrigues, Borís failed of his employment as aide or attaché to Kutuzof.

Shortly after Anna Pavlovna's reception, the princess returned to Moscow and went straight to her rich relatives, the Rostofs, at whose house she always stayed when visiting in Moscow, and where her idolized Borenka had been educated from early childhood and had lived some years, waiting to be transferred from the Line to his position as ensign of the Guard. The Guard had already left Petersburg on the twenty-second of August, and the young man, delayed in Moscow by his uniform and outfit, was to join his regiment at Radzivílof.

The Rostofs were celebrating the name-day of the mother and the youngest daughter, both of whom were named Natalia. Since morning there had been an unceasing stream of carriages coming and going with guests, who brought their congratulations to the countess's great mansion on the Povarskaya, so well known to all Moscow. The countess herself and her eldest daughter, a beautiful girl, were in the drawing-room receiving the guests, whose places were constantly filled by newcomers.

The Countess Rostova was a woman of forty-five, of a thin Oriental type of countenance, and evidently worn out by her cares as mother of a family of a dozen children. Her deliberateness of motion and speech, arising from her lack of strength, gave her a certain appearance of dignity which commanded respect.

The Princess Anna Mikhaïlovna Drubetskaya, in her capacity of friend of the family, was also in the drawing-room, helping to receive the company and join in the conversation. The young people were in the rear rooms, not considering it incumbent upon them to take part in receiving the visitors. The count met the guests, and escorted them to the door again, urging them all to dine with him.

"Very, very much obliged to you, *ma chère* or *mon cher*" (*ma chère* or *mon cher* he said to all without exception, without the slightest shadow of difference whether his guests stood high or low in the social scale), "much obliged to you for myself and for my dear ones whose name-day we are celebrating. See here, come in to dinner. You will affront me, if you do not, *mon cher*. Cordially I invite you, and my whole family join with me, *ma chère*."

These words he repeated to all, without exception or variation, with an unchanging expression on his round, jolly, and clean-shaven countenance, and with a monotonously firm grip of the hand, and with repeated short bows. Having escorted a guest to his carriage, the count would return to this, that, or the other visitor still remaining in the drawing-room; dropping down on a chair, with the aspect of a man who understands and enjoys the secret of life, he would cross his legs in boyish fashion, lay his hands on his knees, and shaking his head significantly, would set forth his conjectures concerning the weather, or exchange confidences about health, sometimes speaking in Russian, sometimes in very execrable but self-confident French, and then again with the air of a weary man, who is nevertheless bound to fulfil all obligations, he would go to the door with still another departing guest, straightening the thin·gray hairs on his bald head, and dutifully proffering the invitations to dinner.

Sometimes returning through the entry to the draw·

ing-room, he would pass through the conservatory and butler's room to the great marble hall where covers were laid for eighty guests, and, glancing at the butlers who were bringing the silver and china, setting the tables and unfolding the damask table-linen, he would call to him Dimítri Vasilyevitch, a man of noble family, who had charge of all his affairs, and would say : —

"Well, well, Mítenka, see that everything is all right. That's good, that's good," he would say, glancing with satisfaction on the huge extension table. "The principal thing is the service. Very good, very good."

And with a deep sigh of satisfaction, he would go back to the drawing-room once more.

"Marya Lvovna Karagina and her daughter," announced the countess's footman, in a thundering bass voice, coming to the door. The countess was thoughtful for a moment, and took a pinch of snuff from a gold snuff-box ornamented with a portrait of her husband.

"These callers have tired me out," said she. "Well, she is the last one I shall receive. She is very affected. — Ask her to come in," said she to the footman, in a mournful voice, as if her words had been : "Kill me and have done with it."

A tall, portly, haughty-looking lady, in a rustling gown, came into the drawing-room, followed by her round-faced, smiling young daughter.

"Dear Countess, it has been such a long time...." she has been ill in bed, poor girl.".... "At the Razumovsky ball ...." " *Et la Comtesse Apraksine* ...." "I have had such an enjoyable time...." Such were the phrases, spoken by lively feminine voices interrupting one another, and mingling with the rustle of silks and the moving of chairs.

That sort of conversation had begun which is expressly contrived so that at the first pause the visitor is ready to get up and, with a rustling of garments, to murmur : "I am charmed .... mamma's health .... and the Countess Apraksina" —and again with rustling garments to beat a retreat into the anteroom, to throw on the shuba or the cloak, and to depart.

The conversation was turning on the chief item of city news at that time, namely, the illness of the well-known old Count Bezukhoï, one of the richest and handsomest men of Catherine's time, and also about his illegitimate son, Pierre, the same young man who had conducted himself in such an unseemly manner at Anna Pavlovna's reception.

"I am very sorry for the old count," said one of the ladies, "his health is so wretched, and now the mortification his son causes him—it will be the death of him."

"What is that?" asked the countess, as if she were not aware of what the visitor was talking about, although she had heard fifty times already the cause of Count Bezukhoï's mortification.

"It all comes from the present system of education. Sending them abroad!" pursued the lady. "This young man has been left to himself, and now they say that he has been carrying on so horribly in Petersburg that the police had to send him out of the city."

"Pray, tell us about it," urged the countess.

"He made a bad choice of friends," remarked the Princess Anna Mikhaïlovna. "Prince Vasíli's son, this Pierre, and a Dolokhof, they say, have been doing—heaven only knows what. But all of them have had to suffer for it. Dolokhof has been reduced to the ranks, and Bezukhoï's son has been sent to Moscow, and Anatol Kuragin has been taken in charge by his father. At all events, he has been sent away from Petersburg."

"Yes, but, pray, what have they been doing?" asked the countess.

"They acted like perfect cutthroats, especially Dolokhof," said the visitor. "He is a son of Marya Ivanovna Dolokhova,—such an excellent woman, just think of it! Can you imagine it? the three of them, somehow, got hold of a bear, took it with them into a carriage, and carried it to the house of some actresses. The police hastened to apprehend them. They seized the officer and tied him back to back to the bear, and then threw the bear into the Moïka; the bear floated off with the police officer on his back!"

"Capital, *ma chère*, what a figure the officer must have cut!" cried the count, bursting with laughter.

"Oh, how terrible! how can you laugh, count?" But the ladies had to laugh in spite of themselves.

"It was with difficulty that they rescued the unfortunate man," pursued the visitor. "And to think that a son of Count Kírill Vladímirovitch Bezukhoï should find amusement in such intellectual pursuits," she added. "But they say he is so well educated and clever! That shows what educating young men abroad makes of them! I hope that no one will bring him here, though he is so rich. They wanted to introduce him to me. I decidedly refused; I have daughters."

"Why did you say that this young man was so rich?" asked the countess, bending away from the younger ladies, who immediately pretended not to hear what she was saying. "You see, he has only illegitimate children. It appears — and Pierre is also illegitimate."

The guest waved her hand: "I imagine he has a score of them."

The Princess Anna Mikhaïlovna took part in the conversation, with the evident desire of showing off her powerful connections and her acquaintance with all the details of high life.

"This is the truth of the matter," said she, significantly, and also in a half-whisper, "Count Kírill Vladímirovitch's reputation is notorious; as for his children, he has lost count of them, but this Pierre has been his favorite."

"How handsome the old man," said the countess, "and only last year too! I never saw a handsomer man!"

"Now he is very much changed," said Anna Mikhaïlovna. "As I was going to say, on his wife's side, Prince Vasíli is the direct heir to all his property, but the old man is very fond of Pierre, has taken great pains with his education, and has written to the emperor about him; so that no one knows, if he should die, — he is so weak, that it may happen any moment, and Dr. Lorrain has come up from Petersburg, — no one knows, I say, which will get his colossal fortune, Pierre or Prince Vasíli. He has forty thousand serfs, and millions! I know all about this, because Prince Vasíli himself told me. Yes, and besides, Kírill Vladímirovitch is my great-uncle on my mother's side. And he is also Borís's god-father," she added, pretending that she attributed no significance to this circumstance.

"Prince Vasíli came to Moscow, yesterday. He is on some official business, I was told," said the guest.

"Yes, but *entre nous*," said the princess, "that's a pretext; he has come principally on account of Count Kírill Vladímirovitch, because he knew that he was so sick."

"At all events, *ma chère*, that was a splendid joke," said the count; and perceiving that the elderly visitor did not hear him, he turned his attention to the young ladies. "Charming figure, that cut by the police officer, — I can imagine it!"

And imitating the way the unfortunate police officer would have waved his arms, he again burst out into a ringing bass laugh, which made his portly form fairly shake, as men laugh who always live well, and indulge in generous wines.

"So glad to have you dine with us," said he.

CHAPTER X

A SILENCE ensued. The countess looked at the caller, smiling pleasantly, but nevertheless making no pretense to hide that she would not be sorry if she got up and took her departure. The daughter was already arranging her dress and looking inquiringly at her mother, when suddenly there was heard in the next room the noise of several persons running toward the door, then the catching and upsetting of a chair, and instantly into the drawing-room darted a maiden of thirteen, folding something in her short muslin skirt. She halted in the middle of the room, and it was evident that her wild frolic had carried her farther than she had intended. At the same instant there appeared in the door a student with a crimson collar, a young officer of the Guard, a maiden of fifteen, and a plump rosy-faced little boy in a frock.

The count jumped up, and opening out his arms, threw them around the little girl who had come running in.

"Ah! here she is," he cried, with a jolly laugh. "Her name-day, *ma chère*, her name-day!"

"My dear girl, there is a time for all things," said the countess, feigning severity. "You are always spoiling her, *Élie*," she added, addressing her husband.

"How do you do, my dear; I congratulate you," said the visitor. "What a fascinating girl!" she added, turning to the mother.

The little maiden was at that charming age when she is no longer a child nor yet a young lady. . She was full of life, but not pretty. Her eyes were black and her mouth was large; her bare childish shoulders were rising and falling in her bodice from the excitement of her race; her dark locks were tossed back; her thin arms were bare; she wore lace-trimmed pantalets and her low shoes displayed her slender little ankles.

Tearing herself away from her father, she ran to her mother, and giving no heed to her stern reproof, hid her blushing face in the lace folds of her mother's mantilla, and went into a fit of laughter. The cause of her laughter was the doll which she took out from under her skirt, trying to tell some fragmentary story about it.

"Do you see? .... my doll.... Mimi.... You see...."

And Natasha was unable to say any more, it all seemed to her so ludicrous. She leaned on her mother and laughed so merrily and infectiously, that all, even the conceited visitor, in spite of herself, joined in her amusement.

"Now, run away, run away with your monster," admonished the mother, pushing away her daughter with pretended sternness. "She is my youngest," she added, turning to the visitor.

Natasha, for a moment raising her face from her mother's lace mantle, glanced up at the stranger through her tears of laughter and again hid her face.

The visitor, compelled to admire this family scene, felt it incumbent upon her to take some part in it. "Tell me, my dear," said she, addressing Natasha, "what relation is this Mimi to you? She is your daughter, I suppose."

Natasha was displeased by the condescending tone in which the lady addressed her. She made no reply and looked solemnly at her.

Meantime, all the young people — the officer, Borís, the son of the Princess Anna Mikhaïlovna, Nikolaï the student, the count's oldest son, Sonya, the count's fifteen-year-old niece, and the little Petrusha, his youngest boy — crowded into the drawing-room, evidently doing their utmost to restrain within the bounds of propriety the excitement and merriment that convulsed their faces. It could be seen that there in the rear rooms, from which they had rushed so impetuously, they had been engaged in much more entertaining conversation than town gossip, the weather, and the Countess Apraksina.

Occasionally they would glance at one another and find it hard to refrain from bursting out laughing again.

The two young men, the student and the officer, who had been friends from childhood, were of the same age and were both good-looking, but totally unlike each other. Borís was tall and fair, with regular, delicate features and a placid expression. Nikolaï was a short, curly-haired young man, with a frank, open countenance. On his upper lip the first dark down had already begun to appear, and his whole face was expressive of impetuosity and enthusiasm. Nikolaï's face had flushed crimson the moment he entered the drawing-room. It was plain to see that he strove in vain to find something to say; Borís, on the contrary, immediately regained his self-possession, and began to

relate, calmly and humorously, how he had been acquainted with this Mimi-kulka when she was a fine
young lady, before her nose had lost its beauty; how
since their acquaintance, begun five years before, she
had grown aged and cracked as to the whole surface
of her cranium!

As he said this he looked at Natasha, but she turned
away from him and looked at her little brother, who was
squeezing his eyes together and shaking with suppressed
laughter, and finding that she could no longer control
herself, snickered out loud and darted from the room as
fast as her nimble little feet would carry her. Borís
managed to preserve his composure.

"*Maman*, do you not want to go for a drive? Shall
I order the carriage?" he asked, turning to his mother
with a smile.

"Yes, yes, go and order it, please," said she, returning his smile.

Borís quietly left the room and went in pursuit of
Natasha; the plump little boy trotted sturdily after
them, as if he was vexed at heart at the disarrangement
made in his plans.

CHAPTER XI

OF the young people, not reckoning the young lady
caller and the count's oldest daughter, who was four
years older than her sister and regarded herself as already grown up, only Nikolaï and the niece Sonya
remained in the drawing-room.

Sonya was a slender miniature little brunette, with a
tawny-tinted complexion especially noticeable on her
neck and bare arms, which were slender, but graceful
and muscular. She had soft eyes shaded by long
lashes, and she wore her thick black hair in a braid
twined twice about her head. By the easy grace of her
movements, by the suppleness and softness of her
slender limbs, and by a certain cunning and coyness of
manner, she reminded one of a beautiful kitten which

promises soon to grow into a lovely cat. She evidently considered it the right thing to manifest her interest in the general conversation by a smile; but her eyes involuntarily shot glances of such passionate girlish adoration from under their long, thick lashes at her cousin who was soon to join the army, that her smile could not for an instant deceive any one, and it was plain to see that the kitten had only crouched down in order to jump and play all the more merrily with her cousin, as soon as the two followed the example of Borís and Natasha, and left the drawing-room.

"Yes, *ma chère*," said the old count, turning to their caller and pointing to Nikolaï, "his friend Borís, here, has been appointed an officer in the Guard, and they are such good friends that they cannot be separated; so he throws up the University and his old father, and is going into the military service, *ma chère*. And yet there was a place all ready for him in the department of the Archives, and all. That's what friendship is," concluded the count, with a dubious shake of the head.

"Yes, there's going to be war, they say," said the visitor.

"They have been saying so for a long time," replied the count, "and they will say so again, and keep saying so, and that will be the end of it. *Ma chère*, that's what friendship is," he repeated, "he is going to join the hussars."

The visitor, not knowing what reply to make, shook her head.

"It is not out of friendship at all," declared Nikolaï, flushing and spurning the accusation as if it were a shameful aspersion on his character. "It is not from friendship at all, but simply because I feel drawn to a military life."

He glanced at his cousin and at the young lady visitor; both were looking at him with a smile of approbation.

"Colonel Schubert of the Pavlogradsky regiment of hussars is going to dine with us to-night. He has been home on leave of absence, and is going to take Nikolaï

back with him. What's to be done about it?" asked
the count, shrugging his shoulders and affecting to treat
as a jest what had evidently occasioned him much
pain.

"I have already told you, pápenka," said the lad,
"that if you do not wish me to go, I will stay at home.
But I know that I am not good for anything except the
army ; I cannot be a diplomatist or a chinovnik, I can't
hide what I feel," and as he said this he glanced, with a
handsome young fellow's coquetry, at Sonya and the
young lady visitor.

The kitten feasted her eyes on him and seemed ready
at a second's notice to play and show all her kittenish
nature.

"Well, well, let it go," said the old count. "He's
all on fire ! This Bonaparte has turned all their heads;
they all think what an example he gave them in rising
from a lieutenant to be an emperor. Well, good luck
to them," he added, not noticing his visitor's sarcastic
smile.

They began to talk about Napoleon. Julie Karagina
turned to young Rostof : —

"How sorry I was that you didn't come last Thurs-
day to the Arkharofs'. It was a bore to be there without
you," said she, giving him an affectionate smile.

The young man, much flattered, drew his seat nearer
to her and engaged the smiling Julie in a confidential
conversation, entirely oblivious that this coquettish smile
cut as with a knife the jealous heart of poor Sonya, who
flushed and tried to force a smile.

In the midst of this conversation he happened to
glance at her. She gave him a look of passionate
anger, and, scarcely able to hold back her tears, but
with the pretended smile still on her lips, got up and
left the room. All Nikolaï's animation deserted him.
He availed himself of the first break in the conversation, and with a disturbed countenance left the room in
search of Sonya.

"How the secrets of these young folks are sewed
with white threads !" exclaimed Anna Mikháïlovna,

nodding in the direction of the vanishing Nikolaï.
"Cousinship's a risky relationship," she added.

"Yes," replied the countess, when, as it were, the
very light of the sun had departed from the room with
these young people, and then, as if she were answering
a question which no one had asked, but which was constantly in her mind : " How much suffering, how much
unrest, must be gone through with in order that at last
we may have some joy in them ! And even now ! truly
there's more sorrow than joy. You're always in apprehension, always in apprehension ! This is the age when
there are so many perils both for young girls and for
boys."

" It all depends upon the education," said the visitor.

" Yes, you are right," continued the countess. " So
far I have been, thank God, the friend of my children,
and enjoy their perfect confidence," declared the countess, repeating the error of many parents who cherish
the illusion that their children have no secrets in which
they do not share. " I know that I shall always be my
daughters' chief *confidante*, and that Nikolenka, if, with
his impetuous nature, even he plays some pranks, as all
boys will, will not be like those Petersburg young men!"

"Yes, they're splendid, splendid children," emphati-
cally affirmed the count, who always settled every question
too complicated for him by finding everything splendid.
" But what's to be done ! He wanted to go into the
hussars ! What would you have, my love ? "

" What a charming creature your youngest girl is ! "
said the visitor. " Like powder ! "

" Yes, like powder," said the count. "She resembles
me ! And what a voice she has ! Although she is my
daughter, yet I am not afraid to say that she is going to
be a singer, a second Salomoni. We have engaged an
Italian master to teach her."

"Isn't she too young yet? They say it is injurious for
the voice to study at her age."

"Oh, no! why do you consider it too early?" exclaimed
the count. " Didn't our mothers get married when they
were twelve or thirteen ? "

"And she's already in love with Borís! Just think of it!" said the countess, looking at the princess with a sweet smile; then apparently answering a thought which constantly occupied her, she went on to say:—

"Well, now, you see if I were too strict with her, if I were to forbid her .... God knows what they might be doing on the sly!" (she meant, they might exchange kisses) "but now I know everything they say. She comes to me herself every evening, and tells me all about it. Maybe, I spoil her, but indeed this seems to be the best plan. I kept a too strict rein over my eldest daughter."

"Yes, I was brought up in an entirely different way," said the oldest daughter, the handsome Countess Viera, smiling. But the smile did not add to the beauty of her face, as often happens; on the contrary it lost its natural expression and therefore became unpleasant. She was handsome, intelligent, well bred, well educated, her voice was pleasant, what she said was right and proper enough, and yet, strange to say, her mother and all the others looked at her, as if surprised at her saying such a thing, and regarded it as one of the things that had better have been left unsaid.

"People always try to be very wise with their eldest children,— try to accomplish something extraordinary," said the visitor.

"How naughty to prevaricate, my love! The little countess tried to be very wise with Viera," said the count. "Well, on the whole, she has succeeded splendidly," he added, winking approvingly at his daughter.

The visitors got up and took their departure, promising to return to dinner.

"What manners! they kept staying and staying," remarked the countess, after she had seen her visitors to the door.

CHAPTER XII

WHEN Natasha left the drawing-room, she ran only as far as the conservatory. There she paused, listening to the chatter in the drawing-room and expecting Borís to follow her. She was already beginning to grow impatient, and stamped her foot, on the very verge of crying because he did not follow her instantly, when she heard the young man's noisy, deliberate steps. Natasha hastily sprang between some tubs full of flowers and concealed herself.

Borís paused in the center of the room, looked around him, brushed some specks of dust from the sleeve of his uniform, and then going to the mirror, contemplated his handsome face. Natasha, holding her breath, peered out from her hiding-place and waited to see what he would do. He stood for some moments in front of the mirror, smiled with satisfaction, and went toward the entrance door.

Natasha was just about to call to him, but then she thought better of it. " Let him find me," she said to herself.

As soon as Borís had left the conservatory, Sonya came in from the other door, all flushed, and angrily muttering to herself. Natasha restrained her first impulse to run to her and kept in her hiding-place, as if under an invisible cap, looking at what was going on in the world. She was experiencing a new and peculiar enjoyment.

Sonya was still muttering something, and looked expectantly toward the drawing-room. Then Nikolaï made his appearance.

" Sonya ! what is the matter ? How can you do so ? " he asked, going up to her.

" No, no, leave me alone ! " and Sonya began to sob.

" Well, I know what the trouble is."

" If you know, so much the better ; go back to her, then."

" So-o-onya ! one word ! How can you torment me,

and torment yourself, for a mere fancy!" asked Nikolaï, taking her hand.

Sonya did not withdraw her hand and ceased weeping.

Natasha, not moving, and hardly breathing, with sparkling eyes peered from her concealment. "What will they do now, I wonder," she said to herself.

"Sonya! The whole world is nothing to me! Thou alone art all to me," said Nikolaï. "I will prove it to thee!"

"I don't like it when you talk so with ...."

"Well, I won't do so any more, only forgive me, Sonya!"

He drew her to him and kissed her.

"Ah! how nice!" thought Natasha, and when Sonya and Nikolaï had left the room, she followed them and called Borís to her.

"Borís! Come here," said she, with her face full of mischievous meaning. "I want to tell you something. Here, come here!" she said, and drew him into the conservatory, to the very place among the tubs where she had been in hiding. Borís, smiling, followed her.

"What may this *something* be?" he inquired.

She grew confused, glanced around her, and espying the doll which she had thrown on one of the tubs, she took it up.

"Kiss the doll," said she.

Borís looked down into her eager face, with an inquiring, gracious look, and made no reply.

"Don't you care to? Well, then come here," said she, and made her way deeper among the flowers, at the same time throwing away the doll. "Nearer, nearer," she whispered. She seized the officer's coat by the cuff, and her flushed face expressed eagerness and apprehension. "Then, will you kiss me?" she whispered, so low as hardly to be heard, looking up at him and smiling, and almost crying with emotion.

Borís reddened. "How absurd you are!" he exclaimed, but he bent over to her, reddening still more violently, but not quite able to make up his mind whether to do it or not.

Natasha suddenly sprang on a tub, so that she was taller than he, threw both slender bare arms around his neck, and by a motion of her head, tossing back her curls, kissed him full in the lips. Then she slipped away between the flower-pots, and hanging her head, stood still on the other side.

"Natasha," said he, "you know that I love you, but...."

"Are you in love with me?" asked Natasha, interrupting him.

"Yes, I am, but please let us not do this again. .... In four years, — then I will ask for your hand."

Natasha pondered.

"Thirteen, fourteen, fifteen, sixteen," said she, reckoning on her delicate fingers. "Good! Then it is decided?" And a smile of joy and satisfaction lighted up her animated face.

"Yes, it is decided," said Borís.

"Forever and ever," said the girl. "Till death itself!" And taking his arm, she went with a happy face into the divan-room with him.

CHAPTER XIII

THE countess was now so tired of receiving, that she gave orders not to admit any more visitors, and the Swiss was told to invite any one else who came, to return to dinner.

The countess was anxious to have a confidential talk with the friend of her childhood, the Princess Anna Mikhaïlovna, whom she had scarcely seen since her return from Petersburg. Anna Mikhaïlovna, with her tearful but pleasant face, drew her chair nearer to the countess.

"I will be perfectly frank with you," said she. "We have very few of our old friends left. And that's why I prize your friendship so highly!"

She glanced at Viera, and paused.

The countess pressed her hand; then she said, addressing her eldest daughter, who was evidently not her favorite : —

"Viera, haven't you any perception at all? Cannot you see that you are in the way? Go to your sisters, or ...."

The handsome Viera smiled scornfully, evidently not feeling the least offended.

"If you had only told me sooner, mámenka, I should have gone immediately," said she, and she left the room. But as she was going past the divan-room, she saw that two couples were snugly settled in the embrasures of the two windows. She paused and smiled satirically. Sonya was sitting close by Nikolaï, who was copying some verses in her honor, — the first he had ever written. Borís and Natasha were sitting in the other window, and stopped talking as Viera passed. Both of the girls looked up at her with guilty and yet happy faces.

It was both amusing and touching to see these two girls, so head over ears in love, but the sight of them evidently did not rouse pleasant thoughts in Viera's mind.

"How many times have I asked you not to take my things," said she; "you have your own room."

And she snatched the inkstand away from her brother.

"Wait a minute, wait a minute," said he, dipping his pen.

"You always succeed in doing things at just the wrong time," exclaimed Viera. "There you came running into the drawing-room, so that every one was mortified on your account."

In spite of the fact, or perhaps because what she said was perfectly true, no one made her any reply, and all four only exchanged glances among themselves. Viera lingered in the room, holding the inkstand in her hand.

"And how can such young things as Natasha and Borís and you two have 'secrets,' — it's all nonsense!"

"Well, what concern is it of yours, Viera?" asked Natasha, in a gentle voice, defending herself. She was evidently more than ordinarily sweet, and well disposed to every one on that day.

"It's very stupid," said Viera; "I blush for you. What sort of 'secrets'...."

"Every one has his own. We don't meddle with you and Berg," said Natasha, hotly.

"I suppose you don't," said Viera, "and because you can't find anything improper in my behavior. But I am going to tell mámenka how you and Borís behave."

"Natalya Ilyínishna behaves very well to me," said Borís; "I cannot complain of it."

"Stop, Borís, you are such a diplomat," — the word "diplomat" was in great vogue among the young people, with a special meaning which they gave to it, — "it's very annoying," said Natasha, in an offended, trembling voice. "Why should she worry me so? You will never understand such things," she added, turning to Viera, "because you never were in love with any one, you have no heart, you are only Madame de Genlis," — this was a nickname considered very insulting, which had been first applied to Viera by Nikolaï, — "and your chief pleasure is to cause other people annoyance. You may flirt with Berg as much as you please," she said spitefully.

"Well, at all events, you don't find me running after a young man in the presence of visitors."

"There, now, you have done what you wanted," interrupted Nikolaï, "you have said all sorts of unpleasant things, and disturbed us all. Let's go to the nursery."

All four, like a frightened bevy of birds, jumped up and flew out of the room.

"You are the ones who have been saying unpleasant things, but I haven't said anything to any one," cried Viera.

"Madame de Genlis! Madame de Genlis!" shouted the merry voices from the other room through the open door.

The handsome Viera, who found a sort of pleasure in doing these unpleasant and irritating things, smiled, evidently undisturbed by what was said of her, went to the mirror, and rearranged her sash and hair. As she caught a glimpse of her pretty face, she became, to all appearances, cooler and more self-satisfied.

Meantime, the ladies in the drawing-room continued their talk : —

"Ah, *chère*," said the countess, "in my life it is not all rose-color. I cannot help seeing that at the rate we are going, our property will not hold out much longer. And then his club, and his easy ways. Even if we live in the country, how much rest do we get? Theatricals, hunting, and heaven knows what all. But what's the use of my talking !.... Now tell me how you manage to get along. I often marvel at you, Annette ; how it is that you, at your time of life, fly about so in your carriage, alone, in Moscow, in Petersburg, to all the ministers, to all the notables, and succeed in getting around them all, I marvel at it ! Now tell me how you do it. I cannot understand it at all."

"Ah! my dear heart," replied the Princess Anna Mikhaïlovna, "may God forbid that you ever learn by experience what it is to be left a widow, and without any protector, with a son whom you adore. You get schooled to everything," she went on to say, with some pride. "My lawsuit has given me a great experience. If I need to see any 'bigwig,' I write a note : ' Princess so and so desires to see such and such a person,' and I myself go in a hired carriage, twice, three times, four times, until I get what I need. It is a matter of indifference to me what they think of me."

"Well now, how was it, — whom did you apply to for Bórenka," asked the countess. "There he is already an officer of the Guard, and my Nikolushka is going merely as a yunker. There was no one to work for him. Whom did you ask?"

"Prince Vasíli. He was very kind. He immediately consented to do all in his power, and he laid the matter before the emperor," said the Princess Anna Mikhaïlovna, entirely forgetting, in her enthusiasm, all the humiliation through which she had passed for the attainment of her ends.

"Prince Vasíli must have aged somewhat," queried the countess. "I have not seen him since our theatricals at the Rumyantsofs'. I suppose he has entirely forgotten me. He was very assiduous in his attention to me," she added, with a smile.

"He is just the same as ever," replied Anna Mikhaïlovna, "polite and full of compliments. His head hasn't been turned at all by all his elevation. 'I am grieved that I can do so little for you, my dear princess,' said he. 'You have only to command me.' Yes, he's a splendid man, and a lovely relative to have. But you know, Nathalie, my love for my boy. I don't know what I would not do for his happiness. But my means are so small for doing anything," continued the princess, in a melancholy tone, lowering her voice. "They are so small that I am really in a most terrible position. My unlucky lawsuit eats up all that I have, and is no nearer an end. I have nothing, you can imagine it, literally I haven't a kopek, and I don't know how I shall get Borís his uniform."

She drew out her handkerchief and began to weep.

"I must have five hundred rubles, and all I have is a twenty-five ruble bill. I am in such a position! I have only one hope now, — in Kírill Vladímirovitch Bezukhoï. If he will not help out his godson — for you see he stood sponsor to Borís — and grant him something for his support, then all my pains will have been lost. I shall not have enough to pay for his uniform."

The countess shed some sympathetic tears, and sat silently pondering.

"Maybe, it's a sin," said the princess, "but I often think: There is Count Kírill Bezukhoï, living alone.... that enormous fortune.... and, why does he live on? Life is a burden for him, while Borís is only just beginning to live."

"He will probably leave something to Borís," said the countess.

"God only knows, *chère amie!* These rich men and

grandees are so selfish! But, nevertheless, I am going right away to see him with Borís, and I am going to tell him plainly how things are. Let them think what they please of me, it is all the same to me, when my son's fate depends upon it." The princess got up. "It is now two o'clock and you dine at four. I shall have plenty of time to go there."

And with the decision of the true Petersburg lady of business, who knows how to make the best use of her time, she called her son and went with him into the anteroom.

"Good-by, dear heart," said she to the countess, who accompanied her to the door. "Wish me good luck," she added in a whisper, so that her son might not hear.

"So you are going to Count Kírill Vladímirovitch, *ma chère!*" said the count, coming out from the dining-room into the anteroom. "If he is better, ask Pierre to come and dine with me. You see he used to be here a great deal, and danced with the children. Be sure to bring him, *ma chère!* Now we shall see how splendidly Taras will do by us to-day. He declares that Count Orlof never had such a dinner as we are going to have!"

CHAPTER XIV

"My dear Borís," said the Princess Anna Mikhaïlovna to her son, as the Countess Rostova's carriage, in which they were riding, rolled along the straw-covered street and entered the wide court of Count Kírill Vladímirovitch Bezukhoï's residence. "My dear Borís," said the mother, stretching out her hand from under her old mantle and laying it on her son's with a timid and affectionate gesture, "be amiable and considerate. Count Kírill Vladímirovitch is your godfather, and your prospects depend upon him. Remember this, my dear; be nice as you can be."

"If I knew that anything would come from this except humiliation," replied the son, coldly. "But I have given you my promise, and I do it for your sake."

Though it was a respectable carriage which drove up

to the steps, the Swiss, noticing the lady's well-worn mantle, looked askance at mother and son (who without sending the footman to announce them had walked straight into the mirror-lined vestibule, between two rows of statues standing in niches) and asked them whom they wished to see, the young princesses or the count; and when they said the count, he told them that his excellency was worse and could not receive any one to-day.

"Then let us go," said the son, in French.

"My love!" exclaimed the mother, in a supplicating voice, again laying her hand on his arm, as if her touch had the effect of calming or encouraging him. Borís said no more, but without removing his cloak looked dubiously at his mother.

"My dear," [1] said the princess, in a wheedling tone, turning to the Swiss, "I know that the Count Kírill Vladímirovitch is very ill .... that's why I came. I am a relative of his. I do not wish to disturb him, my dear .... I only wanted to see Prince Vasíli Sergéyevitch; I understand that he is here. Be so good as to announce us."

The Swiss gave a hard pull at the bell-cord and turned away.

"Princess Drubetskaya for Prince Vasíli Sergeyevitch," he called to the footman in small-clothes, pumps, and dress coat, who ran to the head of the stairs and looked over from above.

The princess straightened the folds of her dyed silk dress, glanced at the massive Venetian mirror on the wall, and firmly mounted the carpeted staircase in her old worn shoes.

"My dear, you have given me your promise!" said she, turning round to her son and encouraging him with a touch of her hand. The young man, dropping his eyes, silently followed her.

They went into a hall which led into the suite of rooms occupied by Prince Vasíli. Just as the mother and son started to walk through this room, and were about to ask the way of an elderly footman, who on their approach

---

[1] In the original she calls him the pet name *golúbchik*.

had sprung to his feet, the bronze door-knob of one of the heavy doors turned, and Prince Vasíli himself, dressed in a velvet shubka with a single star, as if he were at home, came in, escorting a handsome, black-bearded man. This man was the celebrated Petersburg Doctor Lorrain.

"So then it is certain?" the prince was saying.

"*Prince*, '*errare humanum est*'; but...." replied the doctor, who swallowed his r's and spoke the Latin words, "To err is human," with a strong French accent.

"Very good, very good...."

Perceiving Anna Mikhaïlovna and her son, Prince Vasíli dismissed the doctor with a bow, and advanced in silence and with an inquiring look toward them. The son noticed that his mother's eyes suddenly took on an expression of deep concern and grief, and he smiled a little.

"Under what melancholy circumstances we meet again, prince. .... Well, how is our dear invalid?" said she, pretending not to notice the cold, insulting glance he gave her. Prince Vasíli, as if he were surprised to see them there, looked questioningly at her and then at Borís.

Borís bowed civilly. Prince Vasíli, entirely ignoring it, replied to Anna Mikhaïlovna's question by a significant motion of his head and lips, giving her to understand that there was very slim hope for the sick man.

"Is it possible?" cried Anna Mikhaïlovna. "Ah! this is terrible! Fearful to think. .... This is my son," she added, indicating Borís. "He was anxious to thank you in person."

Borís again bowed politely.

"Be assured, prince, that a mother's heart will never forget what you have done for us."

"I am glad if I have been able to be of service to you, my dear Anna Mikhaïlovna," said Prince Vasíli, adjusting his frill, and manifesting both in tone and manner, here in Moscow before Anna Mikhaïlovna, whom he had put under deep obligation, a far more consequential air than at Petersburg at Annette Scherer's reception.

"Do your best to serve with credit and prove yourself deserving," he added, turning to Borís. "I am glad. .... Are you here on leave of absence?" he asked, in his coldest tone.

"I am waiting for orders, your excellency, before setting out for my new position," replied Borís, manifesting not the slightest resentment of the prince's peremptory manner, nor any inclination to pursue the conversation, but bearing himself with such dignity and deference that the prince gave him a scrutinizing glance.

"Do you live with your mother?"

"I live at the Countess Rostova's," said Borís, again taking pains to add, "your excellency."

"It is that Ilya Rostof, who married Nathalie Shinshina," said Anna Mikhaïlovna.

"I know, I know," returned Prince Vasíli, in his monotonous voice. "I never could understand how Nathalie made up her mind to marry that unlicked bear. A perfectly stupid and absurd creature, and a gambler besides, they say."

"But an excellent man, prince," remarked Anna Mikhaïlovna, smiling with a touching smile, as if she, too, knew very well that Count Rostof deserved such an opinion of him, but did her best to say a good word for the poor old man.

"What do the doctors say?" asked the princess, after a short silence, and again allowing an expression of deep grief to settle upon her careworn face.

"Very little hope," said the prince.

"I wanted so much to thank my *uncle* once more, for all his kindnesses to me and Borís — he's his godson," she added in French, in such a tone as if this piece of information must be highly delightful to the prince.

Prince Vasíli sat pondering and knitting his brows. Anna Mikhaïlovna realized that he was apprehensive lest she were a rival for the count's inheritance. She hastened to reassure him.

"If it were not for my true love and devotion to my

uncle," said she, uttering the words *my uncle* with re-markable effrontery and unconcern — " I know his noble, straightforward character; but you see, he has only the young princesses with him : they are both so inex-perienced." She inclined her head and added, in a whisper : " Has he yet fulfilled the last duty, prince ? How precious are these last moments ! Things couldn't be worse, he should be prepared at once, if he is so ill. We women, prince," she smiled with self-importance, " always understand how to put these things. It's indis-pensable that I should see him, however hard it may be for me ; but then, I am accustomed to sorrow."

The prince evidently knew only too well, just as he had known at Annette Scherer's, that he would have no little difficulty in getting rid of Anna Mikhaïlovna.

" This interview might be very injurious for him, my dear Anna Mikhaïlovna; better wait till evening; the doctors have been expecting a crisis."

" But it is impossible to wait, prince, at such mo-ments. Just think, it concerns his soul's safety. Ah, it is terrible, the duties of a Christian."

A door opened, and from an inner chamber appeared one of the count's nieces, a young lady with a sour, cold face, and with a waist disproportionately long for her stature.

Prince Vasíli went toward her.

" Well, how is he ? "

" Just about the same ; but what could you expect — this noise," said the princess, staring at Anna Mikhaï-lovna as if she were a stranger.

" Ah, my dear, I did not recognize you," exclaimed Anna Mikhaïlovna, with a beaming smile and ambling lightly forward toward the count's niece. " I have just come, and I am at your service to help you take care of *my uncle*. I can imagine how much you have suffered," she added, still in French, and sympathetically turning up her eyes.

The count's niece made no reply, nor did she even smile, but immediately left the room. Anna Mikhaï-lovna took off her gloves and established herself in an arm-chair in a victorious attitude, and motioned to the prince to sit down near her.

"Borís," said she to her son, and with a smile, "I am going to see the count, my uncle; in the meantime, *mon ami*, you go and find Pierre, and don't forget to give him the invitation from the Rostofs. They ask him to dinner. I think very likely he may not wish to come," she suggested, turning to the prince.

"On the contrary," returned the prince, evidently very much annoyed, "I should be very glad to have him taken off my hands. He is staying here. The count has not asked for him once."

He shrugged his shoulders. A footman conducted the young man down-stairs and then up, by another flight, to Piotr Kiríllovitch's quarters.

CHAPTER XV

PIERRE had not succeeded in choosing a career for himself in Petersburg when he was sent to Moscow on account of his disorderly conduct. The story that had been related at Count Rostof's was correct: Pierre had been one of the young men who had tied the policeman on the bear's back.

He had arrived in Moscow a few days previous, and taken up his abode as usual in his father's house. Although he foresaw that the story would be noised abroad in Moscow, and that the ladies who formed his father's household and who were always hostile to him, would take advantage of this occurrence to irritate the count against him, nevertheless, on the very day of his arrival, he started to go to his father's apartments.

As he went into the drawing-room, where the princesses usually sat, he stopped to pay his respects to the ladies, who were there busy with their embroidery-frames and in listening to a book which one of them was reading aloud.

There were three of them. The oldest, a severely

prim old maid with a long waist, — the very one who had made the descent upon Anna Mikhaïlovna, — was the reader; the younger ones, both rosy-cheeked and rather pretty, and exactly alike, except that one of them had a little mole on her lip, decidedly adding to her beauty, were engaged with embroidery-frames.

Pierre was received like a ghost or a leper. The oldest princess ceased reading and silently looked at him with eyes expressive of alarm. The one without the mole did the same. The third, who had the mole and some sense of the ludicrous, bent over the embroidery to conceal a smile, caused by what she thought promised to be an amusing scene. She drew the thread down and bent over, as if studying the pattern, but could hardly keep from laughing.

"Good-morning, cousin," said Pierre, "don't you know who I am?"

"I know you very well, altogether too well."

"How is the count? May I see him?" asked Pierre, awkwardly as usual, but still not disconcerted.

"The count is suffering, both in body and in spirit, and it seems you have taken pains to cause him the greater part of his moral suffering."

"May I see the count?" repeated Pierre.

"Hm! If you desire to kill him, to kill him out and out, then you may see him. Olga, go and see if the bouillon is ready for dear uncle, it is high time," she added, making Pierre see by this that they were wholly absorbed in caring for his father, while he, on the contrary, was palpably bent on annoying him.

Olga left the room. Pierre stood still, looking at the sisters, and then said with a bow : —

"Well, I will go back to my room. As soon as·it is possible, you will please tell me."

He went out, and behind his back was heard the clear but subdued laughter of the sister that had the mole.

On the next day Prince Vasíli had come and put up at the count's. He called Pierre to him, and said : —

"My dear fellow, if you carry on here as you have

at Petersburg, you will come out very badly; that's all I have to say to you. The count is very, very ill; it is imperative that you should not see him."

From that time Pierre had been left severely alone, and spent his days in solitude, up-stairs in his own rooms.

When Borís appeared at the door, Pierre was walking up and down his room, occasionally pausing in the corners and making threatening gestures at the walls, as if trying to thrust his sword through some unknown enemy, and looking savagely over his spectacles and then again beginning his restless walking, muttering indistinct words, shrugging his shoulders, and spreading out his hands.

"England has outlived its glory," he was declaiming, with a frown, and pointing at some imaginary person with his finger. "Pitt, as a traitor to the nation and to the law of nations, is condemned to...."

He was imagining that he was at that instant Napoleon himself, and he pictured how his hero would make the perilous passage across from Calais, and take London by storm, but he had not completed his denunciation of Pitt when he caught sight of a handsome, well-built young officer coming toward him.

He stopped short.

Borís was a lad of fourteen when he had last seen him, and he did not recognize him at all; but, nevertheless, he seized him by the hand in his impulsive, cordial way, and smiled affectionately.

"Do you remember me?" asked Borís, calmly, with a pleasant smile. "I came with my mother to see the count, but it seems he is very ill."

"Yes, he is very ill. They keep him stirred up all the time," returned Pierre, striving to recollect who this young man was.

Borís was certain that Pierre did not recognize him, but he did not think it necessary to tell his name, and without manifesting the slightest awkwardness he looked him full in the face.

"Count Rostof invites you to dine with him this afternoon," said he, after a rather long silence which made Pierre feel uncomfortable.

"Ah! Count Rostof," exclaimed Pierre, joyfully. "Then you are his son Ilya. At the first instant I did not recognize you, as you can easily imagine. Do you remember how you and I and Madame Jaquot used to go out walking on the Sparrow Hills — years ago?"

"You are mistaken," said Borís, deliberately, and with a bold and rather derisive smile; "I am Borís, the son of the Princess Anna Mikhaïlovna Drubetskaya. Rostof's father is named Ilya, and his name is Nikolaï. And I never knew Madame Jaquot."

Pierre made a gesture with his hands and head, as if mosquitoes or bees were attacking him.

"Ah! is that so indeed? I have mixed everything all up. I have so many relatives in Moscow! So you are Borís — yes. Well, you and I seem to have begun with a misunderstanding. Well, what do you think of the Boulogne expedition? It will go pretty hard with the English if only Napoleon crosses the Channel, won't it? I think the expedition is very feasible! If only Villeneuve does n't fail him."

Borís knew nothing about the Boulogne expedition; he had not read the newspapers, and this was the first time he had ever heard of Villeneuve.

"We here in Moscow are more taken up with dinners and gossip than with politics," said he, in his calm, satirical tone. "I know nothing about such things, and I don't think about them. Moscow is given over to tittle-tattle more than anything else," he went on to say. "Now you and the count are the talk."

Pierre smiled his good-natured smile, as if fearing lest his companion might say something that he would regret. But Borís spoke with due circumspection, clearly and dryly, looking straight into Pierre's eyes.

"Moscow likes to do nothing better than talk gossip," he repeated. "All are solicitous about knowing to whom the count is going to leave his property; and yet, very possibly, he will outlive all of us. I hope so with all my heart."....

"Yes, this is all very trying," interrupted Pierre, — "very trying."

Pierre all the time was apprehensive lest this young officer should unexpectedly turn the conversation into some awkward channel.

"But it must seem to you," said Borís, flushing slightly, but not allowing his voice or his manner to vary, — "it must seem to you that all take an interest in this simply because they hope to get something from the estate."

"Here it comes," thought Pierre.

"I expressly wish to tell you, lest any misunderstanding should arise, that you are entirely mistaken if you consider me and my mother in the number of these people. We are very poor, but I at least say this on my own account for the very reason that your father is rich, that I do not consider myself a relative of his, and neither I nor my mother would ask or even be willing to receive anything from him."

Pierre for some time failed to comprehend, but when the idea dawned upon him, he leaped from the divan, seized Borís under the arm with characteristic impetuosity and clumsiness, and while he grew even redder than the other, he began to speak with a mixed feeling of vexation and shame : —

"Now, this is strange! I then .... indeed and who would have ever thought .... I know very well ...."

But Borís again interrupted him.

"I am glad that I have told you all. Perhaps it was disagreeable to you; you will pardon me," said he, soothing Pierre instead of letting himself be soothed by him. "I hope that I have not offended you. It is a principle with me to speak right to the point. What answer am I to give? Will you come to dinner at the Rostofs'?"

And Borís, having acquitted himself of a difficult explanation, and got himself out of an awkward position by putting another into it, again became perfectly agreeable.

"Now, look here, listen," said Pierre, calming down.

"You are a remarkable man. What you have just said is very good, very good. Of course you don't know me. We have not met for a long time.... not since we were children. .... You might have had all sorts of ideas about me. I understand you, understand you perfectly. I should not have done such a thing, I should not have had the courage, but it is excellent. I am very glad to have made your acquaintance. Strange," he added, after a short silence and smiling, — "strange that you should have had such an idea of me." He laughed. "Well, who knows? We shall get better acquainted, I beg of you."

He pressed Borís's hand.

"Do you know, I have not seen the count yet? He has not sent for me. It is trying to me as a man.... but what can I do about it?"

"And do you think that Napoleon will succeed in getting his army across?" asked Borís, with a smile.

Pierre understood that Borís wanted to change the conversation, and taking his cue he began to expound the advantages and disadvantages of the Boulogne expedition.

A footman came to summon Borís to his mother. The princess was ready to start. Pierre promised to come and dine with the Rostofs so as to get better acquainted with Borís, and he warmly pressed his hand, looking through his spectacles straight into his eyes.

After he had gone, Pierre still paced for a long time up and down the room, no longer threatening an invisible enemy with the sword, but smiling at the thought of this intelligent, clever, and decided young man. As often happens in early youth, and especially when one is lonely, he felt an inexplicable affection for the young man, and promised himself that they would become good friends.

Prince Vasíli escorted the princess to the door. The good lady held her handkerchief to her eyes, and there were tears on her cheeks.

"This is terrible, terrible!" she exclaimed. "But, so far as in me lay, I fulfilled my duty. I will come back

and spend the night. It is impossible to leave him
in such a state. Every moment is precious. I cannot
understand why the princesses have delayed about it.
Perhaps God will enable me to find some means of
preparing him. *Adieu*, prince, may the good God sus-
tain you."

" *Adieu*, my friend," replied Prince Vasíli, as he turned
away from her.

"Ah, he is in a frightful state," said the mother to
her son, after they had again taken their seats in the
carriage. " He scarcely knows any one."

" I cannot understand, mámenka, what his relations
are to Pierre; can you?" asked the son.

" Everything will be made clear by his will, my dear;
our fate also depends upon that." ....

" Why do you think he is going to leave us anything ? "

" Ah! my dear, he is so rich and we are so poor."

" Well, that is a most inconclusive reason, mámenka."

" Ah, my God, my God, how ill he is!" exclaimed the
mother.

CHAPTER XVI

AFTER Anna Mikhaïlovna and her son had gone to
Count Bezukhoï's, the Countess Rostova sat for some
time alone, applying her handkerchief to her eyes. At
last she rang the bell.

" What is the matter with you, my dear?" she demanded severely of the maid, who had kept her waiting
several minutes. " Don't you care to serve me? If
not, I can find another place for you."

The countess was greatly affected by her old friend's
grief and humiliation, and therefore she was out of
sorts, as could be told by her speaking to the maid by
the formal *vui*, "you," and the appellation *míliya*, "dear."

" Beg pardon," said the maid.

" Ask the count to come to me."

The count came waddling to his wife with a rather
guilty look, as usual.

"Well, little countess,[1] what a *sauté au madère* of woodcock we are going to have, my love. I have been trying it. Taras is well worth the thousand rubles that I gave for him. It was well spent."

He took a seat near his wife, with an affectation of bravery, leaning one hand on his knee, and with the other rumpling up his gray hair: "What do you wish, little countess?"

"See there, my love; how did you get that spot on you?" said she, pointing to his waistcoat. "It is evidently some of your *sauté*," she added, with a smile. "See here, count, I need some money."

His face grew mournful.

"Ah, little countess!"....

And the count made a great ado in getting out his pocket-book.

"I want a good deal, count; I want five hundred rubles." And she took her cambric handkerchief and began to rub her husband's waistcoat.

"You shall have it at once. Hey, there!" cried the count, in a tone used only by men who are certain that those whom they command will rush headlong at their call. "Send Mítenka to me!"

Mítenka, the nobleman's son whom the count had brought up and had now put in charge of all his affairs, came with soft noiseless steps into the room.

"See here, my dear," said the count to the deferential young man as he entered the door, "bring me," — he hesitated, — "yes, bring me seven hundred rubles, yes. And see here, don't bring such torn and filthy ones as you do sometimes, but clean ones; they are for the countess."

"Yes, Mítenka, please see that they are clean," said the countess, sighing deeply.

"Your excellency, when do you wish them?" asked Mítenka; "you will deign to know that.... however, don't allow yourself to be uneasy," he added, perceiving that the count was already beginning to breathe heavily and rapidly, which was always a sign of a burst of rage.

[1] *Graphinyushka.*

— "I had forgotten. Will you please to have them this instant?"

"Yes, yes, instantly; bring them. Give them to the countess."

"What a treasure that Mítenka is!" he added with a smile, as the young man left the room. "He never finds anything impossible. That is a thing I cannot endure. All things are possible."

"Ah! money, count, money; how much sorrow it causes in the world!" exclaimed the countess. "But this money is very important for me."

"Little countess, you are a terrible spendthrift," declared the count, and kissing his wife's hand he disappeared again into his own apartment.

When Anna Mikhaïlovna returned from her visit to Bezukhoï, the money, all in new clean bank-notes, was lying on a stand under a handkerchief in the countess's room. Anna Mikhaïlovna noticed that the countess was excited over something.

"Well, my dear?" asked the countess.

"Ah! he 's in a terrible state! you would never know him, he is so ill, so ill! I stayed only a short minute and didn't say two words." ....

"Annette, for heaven's sake don't refuse me," suddenly exclaimed the countess, taking out the money from under the handkerchief, while her old, thin, grave face flushed in a way that was strange to see.

Anna Mikhaïlovna instantly understood what she meant, and was already bending over so as to embrace the countess gracefully at the right moment.

"It is from me to Borís, for his outfit."

Anna Mikhaïlovna interrupted her by throwing her arms around her and bursting into tears. The countess wept with her. They wept because they were friends and because they were kind-hearted, and because, having been friends from childhood, they were now occupied with such a sordid matter as money, and because their youth had passed.

But theirs were pleasant tears.

CHAPTER XVII

THE Countess Rostova, with her daughters and a large number of guests, was sitting in the drawing-room. The count had taken the men into his cabinet and was showing them his favorite collection of Turkish pipes. Occasionally, he would go out and ask: "Has n't she come yet?"

They were waiting for Marya Dmítrievna Akhrosímova, called in society *le terrible dragon :* a lady who was distinguished not for her wealth or her titles, but for the honesty of her character, and her frank, simple ways. The imperial family knew her, all Moscow knew her, and all Petersburg, and both cities, while they laughed at her brusque manners on the sly and related anecdotes of her, nevertheless, without exception, respected and feared her.

The conversation in the cabinet, which was full of smoke, turned on the war which had just been declared through a manifesto and on the recruiting. No one had, as yet, read the manifesto, but all were aware that it had appeared.

The count was sitting on a low ottoman, between two of his friends, who were talking and smoking. He, himself, was not smoking or talking, but with his head bent now to one side, now to the other, he was looking with manifest satisfaction at those who did, and was listening to the conversation of his two friends, whom he had already set by the ears.

One of the men was a civilian, with a wrinkled, sallow, lean face cleanly shaven; though he was approaching old age, he was dressed in the height of style, like a young man; he was sitting with his feet on the ottoman, like a man thoroughly at home, and, holding the amber mouthpiece at one side of his mouth, was sucking strenuously at the smoke, and frowning over the effort. This was the old bachelor, Shinshin, the countess's own cousin, a "venomous tongue," as it was said of him in Moscow drawing-rooms. He seemed to be condescending to his opponent.

The other, a fresh, ruddy young officer of the Guard, irreproachably belted, buttoned, and barbered, held the mouthpiece in the middle of his mouth, and gently sucked the smoke through his rosy lips, sending it out in rings from his handsome mouth. This was Lieutenant Berg, an officer of the Semyonovsky regiment, with whom Borís was going to the army; the very person about whom Natasha had teased Viera by calling him her lover.

The count was sitting between these two and listening attentively. The occupation that the count enjoyed most, next to the game of Boston, of which he was very fond, was that of listener, especially when he had a chance to get two good talkers on the opposite sides of an argument.

"Well now, batyushka, my most honorable Alphonse Karlitch," said Shinshin, with a sneer, and, as his custom was when he talked, mixing up the most colloquial Russian expressions with the most refined French idioms, "your idea is to make money out of the state? you expect to get a nice little income from your company, do you?"

"Not at all, Piotr Nikolaitch, I only wish to prove that the advantages of serving in the cavalry are far less than in the infantry. You can now imagine my position, Piotr Nikolaitch."

Berg always spoke very accurately, calmly, and politely. His conversation invariably had himself as its central point; he always preserved a discreet silence when people were talking about anything that did not directly concern himself, and he could sit that way silently for hours without feeling or causing others to feel the slightest sense of awkwardness. But as soon as the conversation touched any subject in which he was personally interested, he would begin to talk at length and with evident satisfaction.

"Consider my position, Piotr Nikolaitch: if I were in the cavalry I should not receive more than two hundred a quarter, even with the rank of lieutenant, but now I get two hundred and thirty," said he, with a pleasant, joyful smile, glancing at Shinshin and the count, as if it were plain for him that his success would always be an object of interest to everybody else.

"Moreover, Piotr Nikolaitch," continued Berg, "by being transferred to the Guard, I am in sight; vacancies in the infantry occur far more often. Then, you can see for yourself, on two hundred and thirty rubles a quarter, how well I can live. I can lay up some and send some to my father, too," he went on to say, puffing out a ring of smoke.

"That's where the difference lies; a German can grind corn on the butt of his hatchet, as the proverb puts it," said Shinshin, shifting the mouthpiece of his pipe to the other side of his mouth and winking at the count.

The count laughed heartily. The other guests, seeing that Shinshin was engaged in a lively conversation, crowded round to listen. Berg, remarking neither the quizzical nor indifferent looks of the others, proceeded to explain how, by his transfer to the Guard, he would attain rank before his comrades of the Corpus; how, in time of war, the company commanders were apt to be killed; and he, if left the senior in the company, might very easily become a captain; and how everybody in the regiment liked him, and how proud of him his pápenka was.

Berg evidently took great delight in telling all this, and he never seemed to suspect that other people had also their interests. But all that he said was so suavely serious, the *naïveté* of his youthful egotism was so palpable, that he quite disarmed his auditors.

"Well, my lad,[1] whether you are in the infantry or in the Guard, you will get on; that I can predict," said Shinshin, tapping him on the shoulder and setting his feet down from the ottoman. Berg smiled with self-satisfaction. The count, followed by his guests, passed into the drawing-room.

It was the time just before dinner is announced when the assembled guests, in expectation of being summoned

[1] *Bátyushka*, little father.

to partake of the *zakuska*, are disinclined to entering any detailed conversation, and, at the same time, feel that it is incumbent upon them to stir about and say something, in order to show that they are in no haste to sit down at table.

The host and hostess keep watch of the door and exchange glances from time to time. The guests try to read in those glances for whom or for what they are waiting, — some belated influential connection, or for some dish that is not done in time.

Pierre came in just before the dinner-hour, and awkwardly sat down in the first chair that he saw, right in the middle of the drawing-room, so that he was in every one's way. The countess tried to engage him in conversation, but he merely answered her questions in monosyllables and kept looking naïvely around him through his spectacles, as if in search of some one. It was exceedingly annoying, but he was the only person who did not notice it. The majority of the guests, knowing about his adventure with the bear, looked curiously at this big, tall, quiet-looking man, and found it difficult to believe that one so burly and unassuming could have played such a trick on a police officer.

"Have you only just come?" asked the countess.

"*Oui, madame*," replied he, glancing around.

"You have not seen my husband?"

"*Non, madame.*"

And he smiled at absolutely the wrong time.

"You were in Paris lately, I believe. I think it is very interesting."

"Very interesting."

The countess exchanged glances with Anna Mikháïlovna, who perceived that she was wanted to take charge of this young man. She took a seat by his side and began to talk to him about his father, but he answered her, just as he had the countess, merely in monosyllables.

The other guests were all engaged in little groups: "Les Razoumovsky...." "That was charming...." "You are very good...." "The Countess Apráksina," were the broken phrases that were heard on all sides. The countess got up and went into the hall.

"Is that you, Marya Dmítrievna?" rang her voice through the hall.

"My own self," was the answer in a harsh voice, and immediately after Marya Dmítrievna entered the room. All the young ladies and even the married women, except those who were aged, rose. Márya Dmítrievna paused in the doorway, and from the height of her imposing stature and holding her head very erect with its ringlets showing the gray of fifty years, she took a deliberate survey of the guests and adjusted the wide sleeves of her gown as if they were disarranged. Marya Dmítrievna always spoke in Russian.

"Congratulations to the dear one and her children on this happy day," said she, in her loud, deep voice, which drowned all other sounds. "Well, you old sinner, how are you?" she said, addressing the count, who kissed her hand. "I suppose you are bored to death in Moscow? Hey? No chance to let out the dogs. Well, what's to be done, batyushka, when you have these birds already grown up?" She waved her hand toward the young ladies. "Whether you wish it or no, you have got to find husbands for them. Well, my Cossack," said she (Marya Dmítrievna always called Natasha the Cossack), patting Natasha as she came running up to kiss her hand gayly and without any fear. "I know that this little girl is a madcap, but I am fond of her all the same."

She took out of a monstrous reticule a pair of pear-shaped amethyst earrings, and gave them to the blushing Natasha in honor of her name-day; then she turned immediately from her and addressed Pierre.

"Hé! hé! my dear! come here, right here!" she cried in a pretendedly gentle voice. "Come here, my dear fellow." And she threateningly pulled her sleeve still higher.

Pierre went to her, ingenuously looking at her through his spectacles.

"Come here, come, my dear fellow. I have been the

only one who dared tell your father the whole truth when he required it, and now I shall do the same in your case. It 's God's will."

She paused. All held their breath, waiting for what was to come, and feeling that this was but the prologue.

" He's a fine lad, I must say, a fine lad! His father lying on his death-bed, and this young man amuses himself by tying a policeman on a bear's back! For shame, bátyushka, for shame. You would better have gone to the war."

She turned away from him and gave her hand to the count, who found it difficult to keep from laughing outright.

"Well, then, to dinner; it is ready, I believe," said Marya Dmítrievna.

The count led the way with Marya Dmítrievna, followed by the countess escorted by the colonel of hussars, a man of influence whose regiment Nikolaï was to join. Anna Mikhaïlovna went with Shinshin. Berg gave his arm to Viera. The smiling Julie Karagina went with Nikolaï to the table. Behind them followed the rest in couples, making a long line through the hall, and the rear was brought up by the tutors and governesses, each leading one of the children.

The waiters bustled about, chairs were noisily pushed back, an orchestra was playing in the gallery, and the guests took their places. The sounds of the count's private band were soon drowned in the clatter of knives and forks, the voices of the guests, and the hurrying steps of the waiters.

At the head of the table sat the countess, Marya Dmítrievna at her right, Anna Mikhaïlovna at her left; then the other ladies. At the other end of the table sat the count, with the colonel of hussars at his left, and Shinshin and the other men at his right.

At one side of the long table were the young gentlemen and ladies; Viera next to Berg, Pierre next Borís, on the other side the children and their tutors and governesses.

The count, from behind the crystal of bottles and

vases with fruits, looked across to his wife and her towering head-dress with its blue ribbons, and zealously helped his neighbors to wine, not forgetting himself. The countess also, not neglecting the duties of a hostess, cast significant glances at her husband over the tops of the pineapples, and it seemed to her that his bald forehead and face were all the more conspicuously rubicund from the contrast of his gray hair.

On the ladies' side there was an unceasing buzz of conversation. On the side of the men the voices grew louder and louder; and loudest of all talked the colonel of hussars, who ate and drank all that he could, his face growing more and more flushed, so that the count felt called upon to hold him up to the other guests as an example. Berg, with an affectionate smile, was talking with Viera on the theme of love being not an earthly but a heavenly feeling. Borís was enlightening his new friend Pierre as to the guests who were at the table, and occasionally exchanged glances with Natasha, whose seat was on the opposite side.

Pierre himself said little but ate much, while he scanned the faces of the guests. Having been offered two kinds of soups, he had chosen turtle, and from the fish-*kulebyáka* to the *sauté* of woodcock, he did not refuse a single dish, or any of the wines which the butler offered him, thrusting the bottle, mysteriously wrapped in a white napkin, over his neighbor's shoulder, murmuring: "Dry Madeira," or "Hungarian," or "Rhine wine." He held up the first that he happened to lay his hand upon of the four wine-glasses, engraved with the count's arms, that stood before each guest, and drank rapturously, and the face that he turned upon the guests grew constantly more and more friendly.

Natasha, sitting opposite, gazed at Borís, as young girls of thirteen only can on the lad with whom they have just exchanged kisses and are very much in love. Occasionally she let her eyes rest on Pierre, and this glance of the ridiculous little maiden, so lively in all her ways, almost made him feel like laughing, he could not tell why.

Nikolaï was seated at some distance from Sonya, and next to Julie Karagina, and was again talking with her with the same involuntary smile. Sonya also had a smile on her lips, but it was not natural, and she was evidently tortured by jealousy; first she turned pale, then red, and was doing her best to imagine what Nikolaï and Julie were talking about.

The governess was looking around nervously, as if ready to make resistance should any one presume to injure her young charges. The German tutor was endeavoring to fix in his memory all the different courses, desserts, and wines, so as to give a full description of it when he wrote home to Germany; he felt sorely grieved because the butler who had the bottle wrapped in the napkin passed him by. He frowned, and tried to make it appear that he had no wish to taste that wine and was only affronted because no one was willing to see that he needed the wine, not for allaying his thirst, or from greediness, but from motives of curiosity.

CHAPTER XVIII

At the men's end of the table, the conversation was growing more and more animated. The colonel was telling that the manifesto in regard to the declaration of war had already appeared in Petersburg, and that he had seen a copy of it which had been brought that day by a courier to the commander-in-chief.

"Why the deuce should it behoove us to fight with Bonaparte?" exclaimed Shinshin. "He has already lowered the crest of Austria. I fear that now it will be our turn."

The colonel was a stout, tall German of a sanguine temperament, but a thorough soldier and a patriot, nevertheless. He felt affronted at what Shinshin said.

"But why, my dear sir," said he, mispronouncing every word, "inasmuch as de emperor knows dat? In his mahnifest, he says dat he cahnnot looke with indeef-erence on de danjers treetening Russia, and dat de safety of de empire and de sanctity of de allies...." and he put a special emphasis on the word *allies*, as if it contained the whole essence of the matter.

And then with his infallible memory, trained by official life, he began to repeat the introductory clause of the manifesto : "'And as the emperor's wish and constant and unalterable aim is to establish peace in Europe on lasting foundations, he has determined to move a portion of his army across the frontier, and to make every effort for the attainment of this design.' And dat is de reason, my dear sir," said he, in conclusion, edifyingly draining his glass of wine and glancing at the count for encouragement.

"Do you know the proverb, ' Yerema, Yerema, you'd better stay at home and twirl the spindle?'" said Shinshin, frowning and smiling. "That fits us to a T. Even Suvorof was cut all to pieces, and where shall we find a Suvorof in these days? What do you think about it?" asked he, incessantly changing from Russian to French.

"Ve must fight to the last dr-r-rop of cur blood," said the colonel, thumping on the table ; "ve must be villing to per-r-r-rish for our emberor, and then all vill be vell. And arkue as leedle as po-oo-sible, as leedle as po-ossible," he repeated, giving a strong stress to the word "possible," and looking again at the count. "Dat's de vay ve old hussars look at it. And how do you look at it, young mahn and young hussar?" he added, turning to Nikolaï, who, quite neglecting his fair companion, now that the talk turned on the war, was looking with all his eyes at the colonel and drinking in all that he had to say.

"I agree with you entirely," returned Nikolaï, in a glow, and turning his plate round and rearranging his wine-glasses with a resolute and desperate face, as if at that very instant he were going to be called upon to face a great peril. "I am convinced that we Russians must either conquer or die," said he, and then instantly felt just as the rest did, after the words were out of his mouth, that he had spoken more enthusiastically and bombastically than the occasion warranted, and, there-fore, awkwardly.

"What you just said was splendid," said Julie, with a sigh. Sonya was all of a tremble, and blushed to her ears and even to her shoulders, while Nikolaï was speaking. Pierre listened to the colonel's speeches and nodded his head in approval.

"Now, that's splendid," said he.

"You're a real hussar, young mahn!" cried the colonel, again thumping on the table.

"What are you making such a noise about there?" suddenly spoke up Marya Dmítrievna, her deep voice ringing across the table. "Why are you pounding on the table?" she demanded of the hussar. "What are you getting so heated about, pray? One would really think that the French were right here before you!"

"I am delling the druth," said the hussar, smiling.

"Always talking about the war," cried the count, across the table. "You see I have a son who is going. Marya Dmítrievna, my son is going."

"Well, I have four sons in the army, but I don't mourn over it. God's will rules all. You may die at home lying on your oven, or God may bring you safe out of battle," rang Marya Dmítrievna's loud voice, without any effort, from the farther end of the table.

"That is so."

And the conversation again was confined among the ladies at their end of the table and among the men at theirs.

"You won't dare to ask it," said Natasha's little brother to her. "I tell you, you won't dare to!"

"Yes, I shall too," replied Natasha.

Her face suddenly kindled and expressed a desperate and mischievous resolution. She started up with a glance, causing Pierre who was sitting opposite to her to listen, and addressed her mother.

"Mamma," rang her childish contralto voice across the table.

"What is it you wish?" asked the countess, alarmed; but seeing by her daughter's face that it was some prank, she shook her finger sternly at her and made a warning motion with her head.

There was a lull in the conversation.

" Mamma! what sort of pastry is coming?" cried the little voice, even more clearly and without any hesitation.

The countess tried to look severe but could not. Marya Dmítrievna shook her stout finger at the girl.

" Cossack!" said she.

The majority of the guests looked at the old ladies and did not know what to make of this freak.

" You will see what I shall do to you," said the countess.

" Mamma! tell me what pastry are we going to have," cried Natasha again, all in a giggle, and assured in her own merry little heart that her prank would not be taken amiss. Sonya and the stout little Petya were struggling with suppressed laughter.

" There, I did ask," whispered Natasha to her little brother and to Pierre, on whom she again fastened her eyes.

" Ices; but you are not to have any," said Marya Dmítrievna.

Natasha saw that there was nothing to be afraid of, and therefore she had no fear even of Marya Dmítrievna.

" Marya Dmítrievna! what kind of ices? I don't like ice cream."

" Carrot."

" No! what kind? Marya Dmítrievna, tell me what kind," she almost screamed.

Marya Dmítrievna and the countess laughed, and the rest of the guests did the same. All laughed, not so much at Marya Dmítrievna's repartee, as at the incomprehensible bravery and cleverness of the little girl who could and dared treat Marya Dmítrievna so.

Natasha was made to hold her tongue only when she was told that they were to have pineapple sherbet. Before the ices were brought, champagne was handed around. Again the orchestra played, the count ex-

changed kisses with his "little countess," and the guests
standing, drank a health to the hostess, clinking their
glasses across the table with the count, with the children, and with each other. Again the waiters bustled
about, there was the noise of moving chairs, and in the
same order but with more flushed faces, the guests returned to the drawing-room and to the count's cabinet.

CHAPTER XIX (Maude 20)

THE card-tables were brought out, partners were
selected, and the count's guests scattered through the
two drawing-rooms, the divan-room, and the library.

The count, having arranged his cards in a fan-shape,
found it difficult to keep from indulging in his usual
after-dinner nap, and laughed heartily at everything.
The young people at the countess's instigation gathered
around the clavichord and the harp. Julie, first, by
general request, played a piece with variations on the
harp; and then she joined with the rest of the girls in
urging Natasha and Nikolaï, whose musical talent was
known to all, to sing something. Natasha was evidently
very much flattered by this request and at the same
time it filled her with trepidation.

"What shall we sing?" she asked.

"'The Fountain,'" suggested Nikolaï.

"Well, give me the music, quick; Borís, come here,"
said Natasha. "But where is Sonya?"

She looked around and seeing that her cousin was
nowhere in the room, she started to find her.

She ran into Sonya's room and not finding her there,
hastened to the nursery, but she was not there. Natásha then came to the conclusion that Sonya might be
in the corridor on the great chest. The great chest in
the corridor was the place of mourning for all the
young women of the house of Rostof. There in fact
Sonya was in her airy pink frock all crumpled, lying flat
on her face on a dirty striped pillow which belonged to
the nurse, and, hiding her face in her hands, was crying,

as if her heart would break, while her bare shoulders shook under her sobs.

Natasha's face, which had been so radiant all through her name-day, suddenly changed; her eyes grew fixed, then her throat contracted, and the corners of her mouth drew down.

"Sonya! what is the matter? Tell me what is it; what is the matter with you? Oo-oo-oo!"

And Natasha, opening her large mouth and becoming perfectly ugly, cried like a child, without knowing any reason for it except that Sonya was crying. Sónya tried to lift up her head, tried to answer, but found it impossible and hid her face again. Natásha sat down on the blue cushion and threw her arms around her dear cousin. At length Sonya put forth an effort, sat up, and began to wipe away her tears, saying: —

"Nikolenka is going away in a week.... his.... papers .... have come.... he himself told me so. But I should not have wept."…. She held out a piece of paper which she had been reading; it contained the verses that Nikolaï had written for her.…. "I should not have wept for that.... but you cannot understand.... no one can understand.... what a noble heart he has."

And once more her tears began to flow at the thought of what a noble heart he had.

"You are happy.... I do not envy you.... I love you and Borís too," said she, composing herself by an effort. "He is good.... for you there are no obstacles. But Nikolaï is my cousin.... we should have to.... the archbishop himself.... else it would be impossible. And then if mamenka"—Sonya always regarded the countess as her mother and called her so — "she will say that I am spoiling Nikolaï's career, that I am heartless and ungrateful, and she would be right too; but God is my witness"—she crossed herself—"I love her so and all of you, except only Viera.... and why is it? What have I done to her?.... I am so grateful to you, that I would gladly make any sacrifice for you.... but it's no use.... "
Sonya could say no more, and again she buried her face in the cushion and her hands. Natasha tried to calm

her, but it could be seen by her face that she understood all the depth of Sonya's woe.

"Sonya!" she exclaimed suddenly, as if surmising
the actual reason of her cousin's grief, "truly, didn't
Viera say something to you after dinner? Tell me!"

"Nikolaï wrote these verses himself, and I copied
off some other ones; and she found them on my table
and said that she was going to show them to mámenka,
and she said, too, that I was ungrateful, that mámenka
would never let him marry me, and that he was going
to marry Julie. You saw how he was with her all the
time. .... Natasha! why should it be so?"

And again she began to sob, more bitterly than before. Natasha tried to lift her up, threw her arms
around her, and smiling through her tears, began to
console her.

"Sonya, don't you believe her, dear heart; don't believe her. Don't you remember we three and Nikolenka
talked together in the divan-room, after lunch? Why,
we thought it all out, how it should be. I don't exactly
remember how it was, but you know it will be all right
and everything can be arranged. There was Uncle
Shinshin's brother married his *own* cousin, and we are
only second cousins. And Borís said that that was perfectly possible. You know I tell him everything. For
he is so clever and so kind," said Natasha. "Now,
Sonya, don't cry any more, dear dove, sweetheart,
Sonya," and she kissed her, and laughed merrily;
"Viera is spiteful, I 'm sorry for her! But all will be
well, and she won't say anything to mámenka; Nikolenka himself will tell her, and then again, he does n't
care anything about Julie," and she kissed her on her
hair.

Sonya jumped up, and again the kitten became lively,
its eyes danced, and it was ready, waving its tail, to
spring down on its soft little paws and to play with the
ball again, as was perfectly natural for it to do.

"Do you think so? Truly? Do you swear it?"
said she quickly, smoothing out her crumpled dress and
hair.

"Truly! I swear it!" replied Natasha, tucking an unruly tuft of curly hair back under her cousin's braid. "Well, now, let us go and sing 'The Fountain.'"

"Come on!"

"But do you know, that stout Pierre who sat opposite me is so amusing!" suddenly exclaimed Natasha, stopping short. "Oh, it is such fun!" and the girl danced along the corridor.

Sonya, shaking off some down, and hiding the verses in her bosom, her face all aglow, followed Natasha with light merry steps along the corridor, into the divanroom. According to the request of the guests, the young people sang the quartet, entitled "The Fountain," which was universally acceptable; then Nikolaï sang a new song which he had just learned: —

> " *The night is bright, the moon is sinking,*
> *How sweet it is to tell one's heart*
> *That some one in the world is thinking,*
> *'My own true only love thou art!'*
> *That she her lovely hand is laying*
> *Upon the golden harp to-night,*
> *While passionate harmonies are swaying*
> *Her soul and thine to new delight;*
> *One day, two days, then Paradise! —*
> *Alas! thy love on her death-bed lies!* "

He had hardly finished singing the last word, when preparations began to be made for dancing, and the musicians made their way into the gallery with a trampling of feet, and coughing.

Pierre was sitting in the drawing-room with Shinshin, who, knowing that he had recently returned from abroad, was trying to induce a political conversation that was exceedingly tedious to the young man; several others had joined the group. When the music struck up, Natasha went into the drawing-room, and going straight up to Pierre, said, laughing and blushing: —

"Mamma told me to ask you to join the dancers."

"I am afraid of spoiling the figures," said Pierre; "but if you will act as my teacher," and he offered his big arm to the dainty damsel, though he was obliged to put it down very low.

While the couples were getting their places, and the musicians were tuning up, Pierre sat down with his little lady. Natasha was perfectly delighted; she was going to dance with a *big man*, who had just come *from abroad*. She sat out in front of everybody, and talked with him, exactly as if she were grown up. In her hand she had a fan which some lady had given her to hold; and with all the self-possession of an accomplished lady of the world (God knows when and where she had learned it), she talked with her cavalier, flirting her fan and smiling behind it.

"Well, well! do look at her, do look at her," said the countess, as she passed through the ball-room and caught sight of Natasha. The girl reddened and laughed.

"Now what is it, mamma? what would you like? What is there extraordinary about me?"

In the midst of the third "*Écossaise*," the chairs in the drawing-room, where the count and Marya Dmítrievna were playing cards, were moved back, and a large number of the distinguished guests and the older people, stretching their cramped limbs after long sitting, and putting their porte-monnaies and wallets into their pockets, came into the ball-room.

First of all came the count and Marya Dmítrievna, both with radiant faces. The count, with farcical politeness, as if in ballet fashion, offered the lady his bended arm. Then he straightened himself, and his face lighted with a peculiarly shrewd and youthful smile, and, as soon as the last figure of the "*Écossaise*" was danced through, he clapped his hands at the musicians and called out to the first violin:—

"Semyon! Do you know 'Daniel Cooper'?"

This was the count's favorite dance, which he had danced when he was a young man (more particularly it was one of the figures of the *Anglaise*).

"Look at papa!" cried Natasha, loud enough to be heard all over the ball-room (entirely forgetting that she

was dancing with a grown-up man!). She bent her curly head over her knees, and let her merry laugh ring out unchecked. Indeed, all who were in the hall gazed with a smile of pleasure at the jolly little man standing with the dignified Marya Dmítrievna, who was considerably taller than her partner, holding his arms in a bow, straightening his shoulders, and turning out his toes, slightly beating time with his foot, while a beaming smile spread more and more over his round face, and gave the spectators an inkling of what was to follow. As soon as the merry, fascinating sounds of "Daniel Cooper" were heard, reminding one of the national dance, the *trepaká*, all the doors to the ball-room were suddenly filled; on one side by the serving-men belonging to the household, on the other with the women, all with smiling faces coming to look at their merry-hearted master.

"Oh! our little father! an eagle!" exclaimed a nurse, in a loud staccato, in one of the doors.

The count danced well, and he knew it, but his partner had absolutely no wish or ability to dance well. Her portentous form was erect, and her big hands hung down by her side; she had handed her reticule to the countess; only her stern but handsome face danced!

What was expressed in the whole rotund person of the count, was expressed in Marya Dmítrievna merely in her ever more and more radiantly smiling face and more loftily lifted nose!

But while the count, growing ever more and more lively, captivated the spectators by the unexpectedness of his graceful capers and the light gambols of his lissome legs, Marya Dmítrievna, by the slightest animation on her part, by the motion of her shoulders or the bending of her arms in turning about or beating time, produced the greatest impression; for the very reason that every one always felt a certain awe before her dignity of bearing and habitual severity.

The dance grew livelier and livelier. The other dancers could not for an instant attract attention to themselves and did not even try. All eyes were fastened on the count and Marya Dmítrievna. Natasha kept pulling at the sleeves and dresses of all who were near her to make them look at her pápenka, but even without this reminder they would have found it hard to take their eyes off the two dancers.

The count, in the intervals of the dance, made desperate efforts to get breath, waved his hands, and cried to the musicians to play faster. Quicker, quicker, and ever quicker, lighter, lighter, and ever more lightly, gambolled the count, now on his toes, now on his heels, pirouetting around Marya Dmítrievna, and, at last, having conducted the lady to her place, he made one last "*pas,*" lifting his fat leg up from behind in a magnificent scrape, and bowing his perspiring head low, at the same time with a smiling face sweeping his arm round amid rapturous applause and laughter, especially from Natasha.

Both of the dancers paused, breathing heavily, and wiping their heated faces with cambric handkerchiefs.

"That's the way we used to dance in our time, *ma chère,*" said the count.

"Good for 'Daniel Cooper'!" exclaimed Marya Dmítrievna, drawing a long breath and tucking back her sleeves.

CHAPTER XX

AT the very time when in the Rostofs' ball-room they were dancing the sixth "*Anglaise,*" and the musicians from weariness were beginning to play out of tune, and the tired servants and cooks were preparing for the supper, Count Bezukhoï received his sixth stroke of apoplexy. The doctors declared that there was not the slightest hope of his rallying from it. The form of confession and communion was administered to the dying man, and preparations were making for extreme unction, while the mansion was filled with the bustle and expectation usual in such circumstances.

Outside the house, around the doors, hidden by the throngs of carriages, gathered the undertakers, hoping to reap a rich harvest from the count's obsequies.

The military governor of Moscow, who had been assiduous in sending his adjutant to inquire for the count, this evening came himself to bid farewell to the famous grandee of Catherine's time.

The magnificent reception-room was crowded. All rose deferentially, when the governor, who had been closeted for half an hour with the sick man, came out, slightly bowing in reply to the salutations, and endeavoring to pass as rapidly as possible by the doctors, priests, and relatives who fixed their eyes upon him. Prince Vasíli, grown a trifle thinner and paler during these last days, accompanied the military governor, and was repeating something in an undertone.

Having seen the military governor to the door, Prince Vasíli sat down alone in the salon, threw one leg over the other, resting his elbow on his knee and covering his eyes with his hand. Having sat that way for some little time, he got up and with hasty irregular steps, looking around with startled eyes, he passed through the long corridor that led to the rear portion of the house, to the room occupied by the oldest of the three princesses.

The visitors in the dimly lighted reception-room talked among themselves in low whispers and relapsed into silence, looking with eyes full of curiosity or expectation when the door that led into the death-chamber opened to let any one pass in or out.

"The limit of his life," said a little old man, a priest, to a lady sitting near him and listening earnestly, "the limit is fixed, he will not live beyond it."

"It seems to me it is late for extreme unction, is it not?" asked the lady, adding the name of the priest. She affected to be unenlightened on this point.

"It is a great mystery, mátushka," replied the priest, passing his hand over his bald forehead, on which still lay a few carefully brushed locks of grayish hair.

"Who was that? The governor of Moscow?" some

one asked at the other end of the room. "What a young-looking man!"

"But he's seventy years old! They say, don't they, that the count doesn't recognize any one any longer? Are they going to give him extreme unction?"

"All I know is, he's had seven strokes."

The second princess just came out of the sick-chamber with weeping eyes, and sat down by Dr. Lorrain, who had assumed a graceful position under the portrait of the Empress Catherine and sat with his elbow resting on the table.

"Beautiful weather, princess, and this being in Moscow is like being in the country," said the doctor, in French.

"It is, indeed," said the princess, with a sigh. "Can he have a drink?"

Lorrain pondered a moment.

"Has he taken his medicine?"

"Yes."

"Take a glass of boiled water, and add a pinch" — he indicated with his slender fingers what he meant by a pinch — "of cream of tartar."

"I neffer haird of a gase vere a mahn surfifed more dan a dird stroke," said a German doctor to an adjutant.

"What a constitution the man must have had!" said the adjutant. "And who will get all his wealth?" he added, in a whisper.

"Some vun vill be fount to tek it," replied the German, with a smile.

Again they all looked at the door; it opened to let the young princess pass with the drink which Lorrain had ordered for the sick man. The German doctor went over to Lorrain: "Do you think he will last till to-morrow morning?" he asked, in atrocious French.

Lorrain thrust out his lips and made a motion of severe negation with his fingers, in front of his nose: —

"To-night, at latest," said he, in a low voice, with a slight smile of self-satisfaction at being able to understand and express the state of his patient; then he went out.

Meantime, Prince Vasíli had opened the door into the princess's apartment.

It was almost dark in the room; two little lamps were burning before the holy pictures, and there was a pleasant odor of incense and flowers. The whole room was furnished with small articles of furniture, chiffonniers, cabinets, and little tables. Behind a screen could be seen the white curtain of a high-post bedstead. A little dog came running out, and barking.

"Ah, is it you, cousin?"

She got up and smoothed her hair, which, as always, was so extraordinarily smooth that one would have thought it made of one piece with her head and then covered with varnish.

"What is it? What has happened?" she asked. "You startled me so!"

"Nothing! There is no change, I only came to have a talk with you, Katish — about business," said the prince, wearily sitting down in the chair from which she had just risen. "How warm you are here," he exclaimed. "However, sit down there; let us talk."

"I thought something must have happened," said the princess, and she took a seat in front of him, with her face hard and stony as usual and prepared to hear what he had to say. "I was trying to get a nap, cousin, and I could not."

"Well, my dear," said Prince Vasíli, taking the princess's hand and doubling it over in a way peculiar to himself.

It was evident that this "well, my dear," referred to a number of things, which, though unspoken, were understood by both of them.

The princess, with her long thin waist, so disproportionate to the rest of her body, looked the prince full in the face from her prominent gray eyes. Then she shook her head, and, with a sigh, glanced at the holy pictures. This action might have been taken as an expression of grief and resignation, or as an expression of weariness and hope of a speedy respite. Prince Vasíli explained this action as an expression of weariness.

"That's the way with me," said he. "Do you suppose it's any easier for me? I am as played out as a post-horse, but still, I must have a talk with you, Katish, and a very serious one."

Prince Vasíli became silent, and his cheeks began to twitch nervously, first on one side, then on the other, giving his face an unpleasant look such as it never had when he was in company. His eyes, also, were different from usual; at one moment they gleamed impudently malicious, at the next, a sort of fear lurked in them.

The princess, holding the little dog in her dry, thin hands on her lap, scrutinized the prince sharply, but it was plain to see that she did not intend to break the silence by asking any question, even though she sat till morning.

"Do you not see, my dear princess and cousin, Katerina Semyonovna," continued Prince Vasíli, evidently bringing himself, not without an inward struggle, to attack the subject; "at such moments as this, we must think about all contingencies. We must think about the future, about yourselves. .... I love all of you as if you were my own children ; you know that."

The princess gazed at him immovably, betraying no sign of her feelings.

"Finally, it is necessary, also, to think of my family," continued Prince Vasíli, averting his eyes from her and testily giving a small table a push. "You know, Katish, that you three Mamontof sisters and my wife are the count's only direct heirs. I know, I know how hard it is for you to speak and think about such things. And it is no easier for me; but, my dear, I am sixty years old, I must be ready for anything. Do you know that I had to send for Pierre? The count pointed directly at his portrait, signifying that he wanted to see him."

Prince Vasíli looked questioningly at the princess, but he could not make out whether she comprehended what he had said to her or was simply looking at him.

"Cousin, I do not cease to pray God for him," she replied, "that He will pardon him and grant his noble soul a peaceful passage from this...."

"**Yes**, of course," hastily interposed Prince Vasíli, rubbing his bald forehead and again testily drawing toward him the table that he had just pushed away, "but — but — to make a long story short, this is what I mean : you yourself know that last winter the count signed a will by which all his property was left to Pierre, and all the rest of us were left out in the cold."

"But think how many wills he has made!" replied the princess, calmly. "Besides, he can't leave his property to Pierre. Pierre is illegitimate."

"My dear girl," said Prince Vasíli, suddenly clutching the table in his excitement, and speaking more rapidly, "but supposing a letter has been written to the emperor, in which the count begs to have Pierre legitimatized ? Don't you understand that in view of the count's services his petition would be granted ?"....

The princess smiled that smile of superiority peculiar to people who think they know more about any matter than those with whom they are talking.

"I will tell you, moreover," pursued Prince Vasíli, seizing her by the hand, "the letter has been written, but it has not been sent yet, and the emperor knows about it. The question is merely this : has it been destroyed or not ? If not, then, as soon as *all is over*," — Prince Vasíli sighed, giving to understand what he meant to convey by the words "*all is over*," — "then the count's papers will be opened, the will and the letter will be handed to the emperor, and the petition will be undoubtedly granted. Pierre, as the legitimate son, will inherit all!"

"But our share ?" demanded the princess, smiling ironically, as if all things except this were possible.

"But, my poor Katish, it is as clear as day. Then he will be the only legal heir and will have the whole, and you will simply get nothing. You ought to know, my dear, whether the will and the letter have been written, or whether they have been destroyed. And if they have been forgotten, then you ought to know where they are and to find them, so that...."

"That's the last feather!" interrupted the princess,

smiling sardonically, and not varying the expression of her eyes. "I am a woman, and according to your idea, all of us women are stupid, but I know well enough that an illegitimate son cannot inherit .... *un bâtard !* " she added, with the intention of showing the prince, by this French term, conclusively how inconsistent he was.

"Why can't you understand, Katish! You are so clever! Why can't you understand that if the count has written a letter to the emperor begging him to legitimatize his son, of course Pierre will not be Pierre any longer, but Count Bezukhoï, and then he will inherit the whole according to the will? And if the will and the letter are not destroyed, then you will get nothing except the consolation of knowing that you were dutiful and brought on us all these results! That is one sure thing!"

"I know that the will has been signed, but I know also that it is not good for anything, and it seems to me, cousin, that you take me for a perfect fool," said the princess, with that expression that women assume when they think they have said something sharp and insulting.

"My dear Princess Katerina Semyonovna," impatiently reiterated Prince Vasíli, "I did not come with the intention of having a controversy with you, but to talk with you about your own interests as with a relative, — a kind, good, true relative. I tell you for the tenth time that if this letter to the emperor and the will in Pierre's favor are among the count's papers, then you, my dear little dove, will not inherit anything, nor your sisters either. If you don't believe me, then ask somebody who does know. I have just been talking with Dmítri Onufríyitch," — that was the count's lawyer, — "and he says the same thing."

A change evidently came over the countess's thoughts; her thin lips grew white (her eyes remained the same), and her voice when she spoke evidently surprised even herself by the violence of its gusty outburst.

"That would be fine!" said she. "I have never desired anything, and I would not now." She brushed the dog from her lap and straightened the folds of her dress. "Here is gratitude, here's recognition for all the sacrifices that people have made for him!" cried she. "Excellent! Admirable! I don't need anything, prince."

"Yes, but it is not you alone: you have sisters," replied Prince Vasíli.

The princess, however, did not heed him.

"Yes, I have known for a long time, but I had forgotten it, that I had nothing to expect in this house except baseness, deception, envy, intrigue; except ingratitude, the blackest ingratitude."....

"Do you know or do you not know where that will is?" asked Prince Vasíli, his cheeks twitching even more than before.

"Yes, I was stupid; I have always had faith in people, and loved them, and sacrificed myself. But those only are successful who are base and low. I know through whose intrigues this came about."

The princess wanted to get up, but the prince detained her by the arm. The princess's face suddenly took on the expression of one who has become soured against the whole human race; she looked angrily at her relative.

"There is still time enough, my love. You must know, my dear Katish, that all this may have been done hastily, in a moment of pique, of illness, and then forgotten. Our duty, my dear, is to correct his mistake, to soothe his last moments, so that he cannot in decency commit this injustice; we must not let him die with the idea that he was making unhappy those who...."

"Those who have sacrificed everything for him," interrupted the princess, taking the words out of his mouth. Again she tried to get up, but still the prince would not allow her. "And he has never had the sense to perceive it. No, cousin," she added, with a sigh, "I shall yet live to learn that it is idle to expect one's reward in this world; that in this world there is no such thing as honor or justice; in this world one must be shrewd and wicked."

"Well, well, now calm yourself; I know your good heart."

"No; I have a wicked heart."

"I know your heart," repeated the prince. "I prize your friendship, and I could wish that you had as high an opinion of me. Now calm yourself and let us talk sensibly. Now is the time.... perhaps a few hours, perhaps a few moments.... now tell me all you know about this will, and above all where it is; you must know. He has probably forgotten all about it. Now we must take it and show it to the count. Probably he has forgotten all about it, and would wish it to be destroyed. You understand that my sole desire is sacredly to carry out his wishes, and that is why I came here. I am here only to help him and you."

"Now I understand all. I know whose intrigues it was. I know," said the princess.

"That is not to the point, my dear heart."

"It is your *protégée*, your dear Princess Drubetskaya, Anna Mikhaïlovna, whom I would not take for my chambermaid, — that filthy, vile woman!"

"Let us not lose time," said the prince, in French.

"Akh! don't speak to me. Last winter she sneaked in here, and she told the count such vile things, such foul things, about all of us, especially about Sophie, — I cannot repeat them, — so that the count was taken ill, and for two weeks would not see any of us. It was at that time, I know, that he wrote that nasty, vile paper, but I supposed that it did not signify."

"That is just the point; why have n't you told me before?"

"In the mosaic portfolio which he keeps under his pillow. Now I know," again went on the princess. "Yes, if I have any sins on my soul, my greatest sin is my hatred of that horrid woman," almost cried the princess, her face all convulsed. "And why did she sneak in here? But I will tell her my whole mind, that I will. The time will come!"

CHAPTER XXI

WHILE these various conversations were going on in the reception-room and in the princess's apartment, the carriage with Pierre (who had been sent for) and with Anna Mikhaïlovna (who found it essential to accompany him) drove into Count Bezukhoï's courtyard. When the carriage wheels rolled noiselessly in on the straw scattered under the windows, Anna Mikhaïlovna turned to her companion with consoling words, but was surprised to find him asleep in the corner of the carriage. She awakened him, and he followed her from the carriage, and then for the first time he thought of the meeting with his dying father that was before him.

He noticed that they had drawn up, not at the state entrance, but at the rear door. Just as he stepped down from the carriage, two men in citizens' clothes skulked down from the doorway and hid in the shadow of the wall. Stopping a moment to look around, he saw several other similar figures on both sides in the shadow. But neither Anna Mikhaïlovna nor the lackey nor the coachman, though they could not have helped seeing these men, paid any attention to them.

"Why, of course it must be all right," said Pierre to himself, and followed Anna Mikhaïlovna.

Anna Mikhaïlovna with hurried steps tripped up the dimly lighted, narrow stone stairway, and beckoned to Pierre, who loitered behind her. He could not seem to realize why it was necessary for him to go to the count, and still less why they had to enter by the rear door, but concluding by Anna Mikhaïlovna's assurance and haste that it was absolutely necessary, he decided to follow her.

Half-way up the stairs they almost ran into some men with buckets, who came clattering down and pressed up close to the wall to let them pass, but showed not the slightest surprise to see them there.

"Is this the way to the princesses' apartments?" asked Anna Mikhaïlovna of one of them.

"Yes," replied the lackey, in a loud, insolent voice, as if now anything were permissible. "The door at the left, matushka."

"Perhaps the count did not call for me," said Pierre, when they reached the landing. "I would better go to my room."

Anna Mikhaïlovna waited till Pierre overtook her: —

"Ah, my dear," said she, laying her hand on his arm, just as she had done that morning to her son, "believe that I suffer as much as you, but be a man!"

"Really, had I better go?" asked Pierre, looking affectionately at Anna Mikhaïlovna through his spectacles.

"Ah, my dear," said she, still in French, "forget the wrongs that may have been done you; remember he is your father — perhaps even now dying." She sighed. "I have loved you from the very first, like my own son. Trust in me, Pierre. I will not forget your interests."

Pierre did not in the least comprehend, but again with even more force it came over him that all this must necessarily be so, and he submissively followed Anna Mikhaïlovna, who had already opened the door.

The door led into the entry of the rear apartments. In one corner sat an old man-servant of the princesses, knitting a stocking. Pierre had never before been in this part of the house; he was not even aware of the existence of such rooms.

Anna Mikhaïlovna spoke to a maid whom she saw hurrying along with a carafe on a tray, and calling her by various familiar terms of endearment, asked how the princesses were, and at the same time beckoned Pierre to follow her along the stone corridor.

The first door on the left led into the princesses' private rooms. The chambermaid with the carafe, in her haste (everything was done in haste at this time in this mansion), failed to close the door, and Pierre and Anna Mikhaïlovna, as they passed by, involuntarily glanced into the room, where sat the oldest of the nieces in close conference with Prince Vasíli. Seeing them passing, Prince Vasíli made a hasty movement and drew himself up; the princess sprang to her feet, and in her vexation slammed the door to with all her might.

This action was so unlike the princess's habitual serenity, the apprehension pictured on the prince's face was so contrary to his ordinary expression of self-importance, that Pierre paused and looked inquiringly at his guide through his spectacles. Anna Mikhaïlovna manifested no surprise; she merely smiled slightly and sighed, as if to signify that all this was to be expected.

"Be a man, my dear! I will watch over your interests," said she, in answer to his glance, and tripped along the corridor even more hastily than before.

Pierre did not comprehend what the trouble was and still less her words, "watch over your interests," but he came to the conclusion that all this must be so. They went from the corridor into a dimly lighted hall which adjoined the count's reception-room. It was one of those cold and magnificent front apartments Pierre knew so well. But even in this room, right in the middle, stood a forgotten bath-tub, from which the water was leaking into the carpet. A servant, and a clergyman carrying a censer, came toward them on their tiptoes, but paid no attention to them. Then they entered the reception-room, with its two Italian windows, its door leading into the "winter garden," and adorned with a colossal bust and a full-length portrait of the Empress Catherine.

The room was filled with the same people in almost the same attitudes, sitting and whispering together. They all stopped talking, and stared at Anna Mikhaïlovna as she entered with her pale, tear-stained face, followed by the stout, burly Pierre, submissively hanging his head.

Anna Mikhaïlovna's face expressed the consciousness that a decisive moment was at hand; and with the bearing of a genuine Petersburg woman of affairs, she marched into the room, not allowing Pierre to leave her, and showing even more boldness than in the morning.

She was conscious that, as she was bringing the person whom the dying count desired to see, her reception was assured. With a quick glance she surveyed all that were in the room, and perceiving the count's priest, she, without exactly courtesying but suddenly diminishing her stature, sailed with a mincing gait up to the confessor and respectfully received the blessing first of one and then of the other priest.

"Thank God! we are in time," said she to the priest; "we are his relatives and were so much alarmed lest we should be too late. This young man here is — the count's son." She added, in a lower tone — "A terrible moment."

When she had spoken these words, she went over to the doctor: —

"Dear doctor," said she to him, "this young man is the count's son. .... Is there any hope?"

The doctor, silently, with a quick movement shrugged his shoulders and cast his eyes upward. Anna Mikhaïlovna, exactly imitating him, also raised hers, almost closing them, and drew a deep sigh; then she went from the doctor to Pierre. She addressed him very respectfully and affectionately, with a shade of sadness.

"Have confidence in His mercy," said she in French, pointing him to a small divan where he should sit and wait for her, while she noiselessly directed her steps toward the door which was the attraction for all eyes, and, noiselessly opening it, disappeared from sight.

Pierre, making up his mind in all things to obey his guide, went to the divanchik which she had pointed out to him. As soon as Anna Mikhaïlovna was out of sight, he noticed that the eyes of all that were in the room were fastened on him with more curiosity than sympathy. He noticed that all were whispering together, nodding toward him with a sort of aversion and even servility. He was shown a degree of respect which he had never been shown before: a lady whom he did not know, the one that had been talking with the two priests, got up from her place and made room for him to sit down; the adjutant picked up a glove which he had dropped, and handed it to him; the doctors preserved a respectful silence as he passed by them, and fell back to make way for him.

At first, Pierre was inclined to sit down in another place so as not to disturb the lady, was inclined to pick up his own glove, and to turn out for the doctors, though they were not at all in his way; but on second thought, it suddenly occurred to him that this would not be becoming; he felt that this night he was a person expected to fulfil some terrible and obligatory ceremony, and therefore he was in duty bound to accept the services of all these people.

He silently received the glove from the adjutant, took the lady's place, laying his huge hands on his evenly planted knees in the naïve poise of an Egyptian statue, and saying to himself that all this was just as it was meant to be, and that, lest he should lose his presence of mind and commit some absurdity, it behooved him this evening above all to give up all idea of self-guidance, but commit himself wholly to the will of those who assumed the direction of him.

Not two minutes had passed, when Prince Vasíli in his kaftan, with three stars on his breast, carrying his head majestically, came into the room. He seemed thinner than when Pierre had last seen him; his eyes opened larger than usual when he glanced about the room and caught sight of Pierre. He went straight up to him, took his hand (a thing which he had never done before), and bent it down as if trying by experiment whether it had any power of resistance.

"Courage, courage, my dear fellow! he has asked to see you. That is good...." and he started to go away. But Pierre felt that it was suitable to ask: —

"How is he?" He stammered, not knowing exactly how to call the dying count; he was ashamed to call him father.

"He had another stroke half an hour ago. Courage, *mon ami*."

Pierre was in such a dazed condition of mind that at the word *coup* he imagined that some one had hit him.

He looked at Prince Vasíli in perplexity, and it was only after some time that he was able to gather that "*coup*" meant an attack of apoplexy.

Prince Vasíli, as he went by, said a few words to Lorrain, and went into the bedroom on his tiptoes. He was not used to walking on his tiptoes and his whole body jumped awkwardly as he walked. He was immediately followed by the oldest princess; then came the confessor and priests; some of the domestics also passed through the door. There was heard some stir in the next room, and finally Anna Mikhaïlovna, with the same pale countenance, firmly bent on the fulfilment of her duties, came running out, and, touching Pierre on the arm, said: "The goodness of God is inexhaustible; the ceremony of divine unction is about to begin. Come!"

Pierre passed into the room, treading on the soft carpet, and noticed that the adjutant and the strange lady and one more of the servants all followed him, as if now it were no longer necessary to ask permission to go in.

CHAPTER XXII

PIERRE well knew this great room, divided by columns and an arch, and all hung with Persian tapestries. The part of the chamber behind the columns, where on one side stood a high mahogany bedstead with silken curtains, and on the other a monstrous *kiot* or shrine with images, was all brightly and beautifully lighted, just as churches are usually lighted for evening service.

Under the glittering decorations of this shrine stood a long Voltaire reclining-chair, and in the chair, supported by snowy-white unruffled cushions, apparently only just changed, lay the majestic form of Pierre's father, Count Bezukhoï, with his hair heaped up on his lofty forehead like a lion's mane, as Pierre remembered it so well, and the same strong deep wrinkles on his handsome, aristocratic face, reddish yellow in color. He was wrapped to the waist in a bright green quilt, and lay directly under the holy pictures; both of his great stout arms were uncovered and lay on the quilt. In his right hand, which lay palm down, a wax taper was placed between the thumb and forefinger, and an old servant, bending over the chair, held it upright.

Around the chair stood the clergy in their magnificent glittering robes, with their long locks streaming down over their shoulders, with lighted tapers in their hands, performing their functions with slow solemnity.

A little back of them stood the two younger princesses with handkerchiefs in their hands, pressed to their eyes, and just in front of them was the oldest sister, Katish, with a spiteful resolute expression, not for a moment letting her eyes wander from the ikon, as if she were saying to all that she would not be responsible for her actions if she looked around.

Anna Mikhaïlovna, with an expression of sanctified grief and universal forgiveness on her face, stood near the door with the strange lady. Prince Vasíli, on the other side of the door, nearer the count, stood behind a carved chair, upholstered in velvet, which he had turned back to and was leaning on it his left hand with a taper, and crossing himself with his right hand, raising his eyes each time that his fingers touched his forehead. His face expressed calm devoutness and submission to the will of God. "If you cannot comprehend these feelings, so much the worse for you," his countenance seemed to say.

Behind him stood the adjutant, the doctors, and the men-servants; just as in church, the men and women took opposite sides. No one spoke; all kept crossing themselves; the only sound was the reading of the service, the low subdued chanting of the priests' deep bass, and during the intervals of silence the restless movement of feet and deep sighs.

Anna Mikhaïlovna, with that significant expression of countenance that showed she knew what she was doing, crossed the whole width of the chamber to where Pierre was and gave him a taper. He lighted it, and then, growing confused under the glances of those around him, began to cross himself with the hand that held the taper.

The youngest of the sisters, the rosy and fun-loving princess Sophie, the one with the mole, was looking at him. She smiled and hid her face in her handkerchief, and did not expose it for some time; whenever she caught sight of Pierre, her amusement again overcame her. Then, evidently feeling that she had not the self-control sufficient to allow her to look at him without smiling and that she could not keep from looking at him, she fled from temptation by quietly retreating behind a column.

In the midst of the service the voices of the clergy suddenly ceased, the priests whispered something to one another; the old waiting-man who held the candle in the count's hand straightened up and went over to the ladies' side. Anna Mikhaïlovna stepped forward, and bending over the sick man, beckoned to Dr. Lorrain without turning round. The French doctor had been standing without a lighted taper, leaning against one of the pillars, in that reverent attitude by which one who, though a stranger and belonging to a different communion, shows that he appreciates all the solemnity of the ceremony and even assents to it. With the noiseless steps of a man possessed of perfect vigor he answered Anna Mikhaïlovna's call, went over to the sick man, lifted in his white, slender fingers the hand that lay on the green quilt, and bending over, began to count the pulse and grew grave.

Something was given to the invalid to drink, there was a slight stir about him; then once more they all took their places and the service proceeded.

At the time of this interruption, Pierre noticed that Prince Vasíli left his position behind the carved chair, and, with an expression of countenance that seemed to say that he knew what he was doing, and that it was so much the worse for others if they did not understand him, went, not to the sick man, but past him, and being joined by the oldest of the princesses, retired with her into the depths of the alcove, to the high bedstead under the silken hangings. From there both the prince and the princess disappeared through a rear door, but before the end of the service both resumed their places, one after the other. Pierre gave this strange action no more thought than to anything else, having once for all made up his mind that all that took place that evening was absolutely essential.

The sounds of the church chant ceased, the voice of the priest was heard respectfully congratulating the sick man on his having received the mystery. The count lay as before, motionless, and apparently lifeless. Around him there was a stir; footsteps and a whispering were heard; Anna Mikhaïlovna's voice could be distinguished above the rest. Pierre listened, and heard her say : —

"He must be carried instantly to bed; it will never do in the world for him here to...."

The doctors, princesses, and servants crowded around the invalid so that Pierre could no longer see that reddish-yellow face with the gray mane of hair, which ever since the service began had constantly filled his vision to the exclusion of everything else. He surmised by the guarded movements of those who crowded around the arm-chair that they were lifting and carrying the dying man.

"Hold by my arm! You'll drop him so," said one of the servants in a frightened whisper. "Take him lower down!" "One more," said different voices, and the labored breathing, and shuffling of feet growing more hurried, seemed to indicate that the load that the men were carrying was beyond their strength.

As the bearers, among their number Anna Mikhaïlovna, came opposite the young man, he caught a momentary glimpse, over their heads and backs, of his father's strong, full chest uncovered, his stout shoulders, lifted above the people carrying him under their arms, and his leonine head with its curly mane. The face, with its extraordinary high forehead and cheek-bones, handsome, sensitive mouth, and majestic, cold eyes, was undisfigured by the nearness of death. It was just the same as when Pierre had seen it three months previously when the count sent him to Petersburg. But the head rolled helplessly under the uneven steps of the bearers, and the cold, indifferent eyes gave no sign of recognition.

There followed a few moments of bustle around the high bedstead; those who had been carrying the sick man withdrew. Anna Mikhaïlovna touched Pierre on the arm and said, "Come."

Pierre went with her to the bed whereon the sick man had been placed in solemn attitude, evidently in some manner connected with the sacrament just accomplished. He lay with his head propped high on pillows. His hands were placed side by side, palm downward, on the green silk quilt. As Pierre went to him, the count was looking straight at him, but his look had a meaning and significance which it is impossible for a man to read. Either that look had simply nothing to say and merely fastened upon him because those eyes must needs look at something, or they had too much to say.

Pierre paused, not knowing what was expected of him, and glanced inquiringly at his guide. Anna Mikhaïlovna made him a hasty motion with her eyes toward the sick man's hand, and with her lips signified that he should kiss it. Pierre bent over carefully so as not to disturb the quilt, and in accordance with her advice touched his lips to the broad, brawny hand. Neither the hand nor a muscle of the count's face moved. Pierre again looked questioningly at Anna Mikhaïlovna to find what he should do next. She signed to him with her eyes to sit down in an arm-chair which stood near the bed. Pierre submissively sat down, his eyes mutely asking if he were doing the right thing. Anna Mikhaïlovna approvingly nodded her head. Pierre again assumed the symmetrically simple attitude of the Egyptian statue, and evidently really suffered because his awkward, huge frame took up so much space, though he strove with all his might to make it seem as small as possible.

He looked at the count. The count was staring at the spot where Pierre had just been standing. Anna Mikhaïlovna showed by her actions that she realized the pathetic importance of this final meeting of father and son. This lasted two minutes, which seemed an hour to Pierre. Suddenly a tremor appeared in the deep, powerful muscles and lines of the count's face. It grew more pronounced; the handsome mouth was drawn to one side (this caused Pierre for the first time to realize how near to death his father was) and from the drawn mouth proceeded an indistinguishable hoarse sound.

Anna Mikhaïlovna looked anxiously into the sick man's eyes and tried to make out what he wanted, pointing first at Pierre, then at the tumbler; then she asked in a whisper if she should call Prince Vasíli, then pointed at the quilt. The sick man's face and eyes expressed impatience. He mustered force enough to look at the man-servant who never left his master's bedside.

"He wants to be turned over on the other side," whispered the servant, and proceeded to lift and turn the count's heavy body, face to the wall.

Pierre got up to help the servant.

Just as they were turning the count over, one of his arms fell back helplessly, and he made a futile effort to raise it. Did the count notice the look of terror in Pierre's face at the sight of that lifeless arm? or did some other thought flash across his dying brain at that moment? At all events, he looked at his disobedient hand, then at Pierre's terror-stricken face, and back to his hand again, and over his lips played a martyr's weak smile, out of character with his powerful features, and seeming to express a feeling of scorn for his own lack of strength.

At the sight of this smile, Pierre unexpectedly felt an oppression around the heart, a strange pinching in his nose, and the tears dimmed his eyes.

The sick man lay on his side toward the wall. He drew a long sigh.

"He is going to sleep," said Anna Mikhaïlovna, to one of the nieces who returned to watch. "Let us leave him."

Pierre left the room.

CHAPTER XXIII

THERE was no one in the reception-room except Prince Vasíli and the oldest princess, and these two were sitting under the empress's portrait, talking eagerly about something. As soon as they caught sight of Pierre and his guide, they stopped, and it seemed to the young man that the princess hid something and whispered : —

"I cannot abide the sight of that woman."

"Katish has had tea made in the little drawing-room," said Prince Vasíli in French, addressing Anna Mikhaïlovna. "Come, my poor Anna Mikhaïlovna, you had better take something to eat ; else you might be the worse for it."

He said nothing to Pierre, but gave his arm a sympathetic pressure just below the shoulder. Pierre and Anna Mikhaïlovna went into what he called *le petit salon.*

"There is nothing so refreshing as a cup of this excellent Russian tea, after a sleepless night," said Dr. Lorrain, with an expression of restrained liveliness, as he stood in the small, circular drawing-room, sipping his tea from a delicate porcelain cup. Just back of him was a table with the tea service and a cold supper. Around the table were gathered for refreshments all those who were spending this night in Count Bezukhoï's mansion.

Pierre well remembered this little circular drawing-room, with its mirrors and small tables. In days gone by, when the count gave balls, Pierre, who did not know how to dance, liked to sit in this little room of mirrors and watch the ladies in their ball toilets, with diamonds and pearls on their bare necks, as they passed through, glance at themselves in the brightly illuminated mirrors, which reflected back their beauties.

Now, the room was dimly lighted by a pair of candles, and at this midnight hour there stood on one of the small tables a disorderly array of tea-things, while a motley throng of people in anything but ball dresses were scattered about in it talking in whispers, by every motion, every word, evincing how little they could forget what was now taking place or going to take place in that chamber of death.

Pierre did not eat anything, though he was very hungry. He glanced inquiringly at his guide, and saw that she was tiptoeing back to the reception-room, where they had left Prince Vasíli and the oldest niece. Pierre took it for granted that this, also, was as it should be, and after waiting a little while, he followed her.

Anna Mikhaïlovna was standing in front of the young lady, and both were talking at once in angry undertones.

"Permit me, princess, to decide what is necessary and what is not necessary," the Princess Katish was saying, evidently still in the same angry frame of mind as she had been when she slammed the door of her room.

"But, my dear young princess," said Anna Mikhaïlovna, in a sweet but conclusive manner, barring the way to the count's chamber, and not allowing the young lady to pass, "will this not be too great an effort for poor uncle at this time, when he so much needs rest? At this time any conversation about worldly matters, when his soul has already been prepared...."

Prince Vasíli still sat in the arm-chair in his familiar posture, with one leg thrown over the other. His cheeks twitched violently, and seemed to grow flabbier than usual, but he preserved the attitude of a man to whom the altercation of the two women was of no consequence.

"Come, my good Anna Mikhaïlovna, let Katish have her way. You know how fond the count is of her."

"I don't even know what is in this paper," said the young princess, turning to Prince Vasíli, and pointing to the mosaic portfolio which she had in her hand. "I only know that his last will is in his bureau, but this is a paper which he has forgotten."

She tried to pass by Anna Mikhaïlovna, but Anna Mikhaïlovna, springing forward, again barred her way.

"I know, my dear good princess," said Anna Mikhaïlovna, grabbing the portfolio, and so firmly that it was evident she would not let go in a hurry. "My dear princess, I beg of you, I beseech you, have pity upon him. *Je vous en conjure.*"

The young princess said not a word. All that was heard was the noise of the struggle for the possession of the portfolio.

It was plain to see that if she had opened her mouth to speak, what she said would not have been flattering for Anna Mikhaïlovna. The latter clung to the portfolio unflinchingly, but nevertheless her voice preserved all its softness, sweetness, and gentleness.

"Pierre, my dear, come here. I think he will not be in the way in this family council, will he, prince?"

"Why don't you speak, cousin?" suddenly cried the young princess, so loud that those in the little drawing-room heard it, and were startled. "Why don't you speak, when this impertinent creature permits herself to meddle in matters that don't concern her, and make scenes on the very threshold of the death-chamber! *Intrigantka!*" she hissed in a loud whisper, and snatched at the portfolio with all her force; but Anna Mikhaïlovna took two or three steps forward so as not to let go her hold of it, and succeeded in keeping it in her hand.

"Oh!" cried Prince Vasíli, with a look of surprise and reproach. He stood up.

"It is absurd! Come, now, let go, I tell you!"

The Princess Katish obeyed. "You, also!"

Anna Mikhaïlovna paid no attention to him.

"Drop it, I tell you. I will assume the whole responsibility. I will go and ask him. I.... That ought to satisfy you."

"But, prince," said Anna Mikhaïlovna, "after this great mystery allow him a moment of rest. Here, Pierre, give us your opinion," said she, turning to the young man, who, coming close to them, looked in amazement at the young princess's angry face, from which all dignity had departed, and at Prince Vasíli's twitching cheeks.

"Remember that you will answer for all the consequences," said Prince Vasíli, angrily; "you don't know what you are doing."

"You vile woman," screamed the young princess, unexpectedly darting at Anna Mikhaïlovna, and snatching away the portfolio. Prince Vasíli hung his head and spread open his hands.

At this juncture the door, that terrible door at which Pierre had been looking so long, and which was usually opened so gently, was hastily and noisily flung back, so that it struck against the wall, and the second sister rushed out, wringing her hands.

"What are you doing?" she cried, in despair. "He is dying, and you leave me alone."

The Princess Katerina dropped the portfolio. Anna Mikhaïlovna hastily bent over, and, picking up the precious object, hastened into the death-chamber. The Princess Katerina and Prince Vasíli, coming to their senses, followed her. In a few moments Princess Katerina came out again, the first of all, with a pale, stern face, and biting her lower lip. At the sight of Pierre her face expressed uncontrollable hatred.

"Yes, now you can swell round," said she. "You have been waiting for this," and, beginning to sob, she hid her face in her handkerchief and ran from the room.

The princess was followed by Prince Vasíli. Reeling a little he went to the sofa on which Pierre was sitting, and flung himself on it, covering his face with his hands. Pierre noticed that he was pale, and that his lower jaw trembled and shook as if from an attack of ague.

"Ah, my friend," said he, taking Pierre by the elbow, and there was in his voice a sincerity and gentleness which Pierre had never before noticed in it. "How we sin and how we cheat and all for what? I am sixty years old, my dear. .... Look at me. .... Death is the end of all, all! Death is horrible!"

He burst into tears.

Anna Mikhaïlovna came out last of all. She went straight up to Pierre, with slow, quiet steps : —

"Pierre !" said she.

Pierre looked at her inquiringly. She kissed the young man on the forehead, which she wet with her tears. Then after a silence she added : —

"He is dead."

Pierre looked at her through his glasses.

"Come, I will lead you away. Try to weep. Nothing is so consoling as tears."

She led him into the dark drawing-room, and Pierre was relieved that no one was there to see his face. Anna Mikhaïlovna left him there, and when she returned he was sound asleep, with his head resting on his arm.

The next morning, Anna Mikhaïlovna said to Pierre in French : —

"Yes, my dear, it is a great loss for all of us. I am not speaking of you. But God will give you support; you are young, and at the head of an immense fortune, I hope. The will has not been opened yet. I know you well enough to believe that this will not turn your head, but new duties will devolve upon you, and you must be a man."

Pierre made no reply.

"Perhaps later I will tell you, my dear, that if I had not been here, ... God knows what might have happened. You know uncle, only the day before, promised me that he would not forget Borís. But he did not have the time ; I hope, my dear friend, that you will fulfil your father's desire."

Pierre entirely failed to see what she was driving at, and, without saying anything and reddening with mortification, looked at the Princess Anna Mikhaïlovna. Having thus spoken with Pierre, she drove back to the Rostofs' and lay down to rest. After her nap, that same morning, she began to tell the Rostofs and all her acquaintances the particulars of the death of Count Bezukhoï.

She declared that the count had died as she herself would wish to die, that his end had been not only pathetic but even edifying; the last meeting of father and son had been so touching that she could not think of it without tears, and that she could not tell which had borne himself with the more composure during these dreadful moments, the father who had had a thought for everything and every one during those last hours, and had spoken such affectionate and touching words to his son, or Pierre, whom it was pitiful to see, he was so overcome, and yet in spite of it struggled so manfully to hide his grief, so as not to pain his dying father.

"Such scenes are painful, but they do one good; it is elevating to the soul to see such men as the old count and his worthy son."

She also spoke of the actions of the Princess Katerina and Prince Vasíli, but in terms of reprobation, and under the promise of the strictest secrecy.

CHAPTER XXIV

THE arrival of the young Prince Andreï and his wife at Luísiya Gorui (Bald Hills), Prince Nikolaï Andreyevitch Bolkonsky's estate, was daily expected. But this made no break at all in the strenuous routine according to which life in the old prince's mansion was regulated. Prince Nikolaï Andreyevitch, a former general-in-chief, called in society *le roi de Prusse*, had been banished to his estates during the reign of the Emperor Paul, and had lived like a hermit there ever since with his daughter, the Princess Maríya, and her hired companion, Mlle. Bourienne.

Even after the new reign had begun, although he was free to go wherever he pleased, he still continued to live exclusively in the country, saying that if any one wanted him, it was only half a hundred versts from Moscow to Luísiya Gorui, and he himself wanted nothing and nobody.

He declared that there were only two sources of

human vice, idleness and superstition; and only two virtues, activity and intelligence.

He himself undertook his daughter's education, and in order to inculcate both these virtues he had given her lessons up to the age of twenty in algebra and geometry, and had apportioned her life into an uninterrupted system of occupations.

He was constantly engaged in writing his memoirs, or in solving problems in the higher mathematics, or in turning snuff-boxes on a lathe, or in working in his garden and superintending the erection of buildings which were always going up on his estate. As the chief condition of activity is order, order in his scheme of life was carried to the last degree of minuteness. His appearance at meals invariably took place under the same circumstances, and at not only the same hour but the same moment each day.

The prince was sharp and scrupulously exacting with the people around him, from his daughter to the humblest menial, and therefore, while he was not cruel, he inspired an awe and deference such as it would have been difficult for even the cruelest man to exact.

Although he was living in seclusion, and had now no influence in matters of state, every nachalnik of the government in which he lived considered it his duty to pay his respects to him, and, precisely the same as the architect or the gardener or the Princess Maríya, waited the designated hour for the prince's appearance in the lofty hall. And each one of those waiting in this hall experienced the same feeling of awe and fear as soon as the massive door of his cabinet swung open, and the form of the little old man appeared, in his powdered wig, with his small, dry hands and pendulous gray eyebrows, which sometimes when he frowned concealed the gleam of his keen and youthfully glittering eyes.

On the morning of the day when the young couple were expected, the Princess Maríya, as usual, at the regular hour, came down into the hall to wish her father good-morning, and with fear and trembling crossed herself and repeated an inward prayer. Each morning she came the same way, and each morning she prayed that their daily meeting might be propitious.

An aged servant in a powdered wig, who was sitting in the hall, got up quietly and addressed her in a respectful whisper: "I beg of you."

Beyond the door could be heard the monotonous hum of the lathe. The princess timidly opened the door, which moved easily and noiselessly on its hinges, and stood at the entrance. The prince was working at his lathe. He looked round and then went on with his work.

The great cabinet was full of things, apparently in constant use: a huge table, whereon lay books and plans; the lofty bookcases, with keys in the mirror-lined doors; a high reading-desk on which lay an opened copy-book; a cabinet-maker's lathe, with various kinds of tools and shavings and chips scattered around, — all this indicated a constant, varied, and regular activity.

By the motion of his small foot, shod Tatar fashion in a silver-embroidered boot, by the firm pressure of his sinewy, thin hand, it could be seen that the prince had still the tenacious and not easily impaired strength of a green old age.

Having made a few more turns, he took his foot from the treadle of the lathe, wiped his chisel, put it in a leather pocket attached to the lathe, and going to the table called his daughter to him. He never wasted caresses on his children, and therefore, merely offering his bristly cheek, which had not as yet been shaven for the day, he said, with a severe and at the same time keenly affectionate look : —

"Are you well?.... Now then, sit down."

He took a copy-book of geometrical work written out in his own hand, and pushed his chair along with his foot.

"For to-morrow," said he, briskly, turning the page, and marking the paragraphs with his stiff nail. The princess leaned over the table toward the note-book. "Wait, here's a letter for you," said the old man, abruptly, taking an envelope addressed in a feminine hand from the pocket fastened to the table, and tossing it to her.

The princess's face colored in blotches at the sight of the letter. She hastily picked it up and examined it intently.

"From your Heloïse?" asked the prince, with a chilling smile that showed his sound, yellow teeth.

"Yes, from Julie," said the princess, timidly glancing up and timidly smiling.

"I shall allow two more letters to pass, but I shall read the third," said the prince, severely. "I fear you write much nonsense. I shall read the third."

"You may read this, father," replied the princess, with a still deeper flush, and holding the letter toward him.

"The third, I said, the third," rejoined the prince, laconically, pushing away the letter; then, leaning his elbow on the table, he laid the note-book with the geometrical designs before her.

"Well, young lady,"[1] began the old man, bending over toward his daughter and laying one arm on the back of her chair, so that the young princess felt herself surrounded by that peculiar acrid odor of tobacco and old age which she had so long learned to associate with her father. "Well, young lady, these triangles are equal; if you will observe, the angle ABC...."

The princess gazed in dismay at her father's glittering eyes so near to her; the red patches again overspread her face, and it was evident that she had not the slightest comprehension of what he said, and was so overcome with fear that it really prevented her from comprehending any of her father's instructions, no matter how clearly they were expressed.

The teacher may have been at fault, or the pupil may have been, but each day the same thing recurred; the princess's eyes pained her; she could not see anything or hear anything; all that she felt was the consciousness of her stern father's withered face, the consciousness of his breath and peculiar odor, and her single

[1] *Nu suddruinya.*

thought was to escape as soon as possible from the cabinet and solve the problem by herself in peace. The old man would lose all patience; noisily push back the chair in which he was sitting, and then draw it forward again; then he would exert his self-control so as not to break out into a fury, but rarely succeed, and sometimes he would fling the note-book down on the floor.

The princess made a mistake in her answer.

"Now, how can you be so stupid!" stormed the prince, throwing aside the note-book and hastily turning away; then he rose to his feet, walked up and down, laid his hand on her hair, and again sitting down, drew close to her and proceeded with his instructions.

"No use, princess, no use," said he, as the young lady took the lesson-book, and closing it started to leave the room; "mathematics is a great thing, my girl, and I don't wish you to be like our stupid, silly women. By dint of perseverance one learns to like it," he patted her on the cheek; "the dulness will vanish from your brain."

She started to go; he detained her by a gesture, and took down from the high table a new book with uncut leaves.

"Here, your Heloïse has sent you something else; some 'Key to the Mystery,' a religious work. I don't interfere with any one's belief. I looked it over. Take it. Now, be off, be off."

He patted her on the shoulder and, as she went out, closed the door himself.

The young Princess Maríya returned to her chamber with the pensive, scared expression that rarely left her and rendered her plain, sickly face still more unattractive. She sat down at her writing-table, covered with miniature portraits and cluttered with note-books and volumes. The princess was just as disorderly as her father was systematic: she threw down her book of problems and hastily broke the seal of the letter, which was from her most intimate friend from childhood; this was no other than the Julie Karagina who was at the Rostofs' on the day of the reception.

Julie wrote as follows: [1] —

Chère et excellente amie: — What a terrible and frightful thing is absence ! It is in vain that I tell myself that half of my existence and happiness is in you, that, in spite of the distance that lies between us, our hearts are bound to each other by indissoluble ties ; mine rebels against my fate, and, notwithstanding all the pleasures and attractions that surround me, I cannot overcome a certain lurking sadness which I have felt in the depths of my heart ever since our separation. Why are we not together as we were this past summer in your great cabinet, on the blue sofa, — that *confidential-sofa !* Why can I not now, as I did three months ago, draw fresh moral strength from your eyes, so sweet, so calm, so penetrating, the eyes which I loved so much and which I imagine I see before me as I write.

Having read to this point, the Princess Maríya sighed and glanced at the pier-glass that stood over against her, reflecting her slight, homely form and thin face. Her eyes, which were generally melancholy, just now looked with a peculiarly hopeless expression at her image in the glass.

"She is flattering me," said the princess to herself, turning away and continuing her reading of the letter. Julie, however, had not flattered her friend : in reality, the princess's eyes were large, deep, and luminous; sometimes whole sheaves, as it were, of soft light seemed to gleam forth from them; and then they were so beautiful that they transformed her whole face, notwithstanding the plainness of her features, and gave her a charm that was more attractive than mere beauty.

But the young princess had never seen the beautiful expression of her own eyes, the expression which they had at times when she was not thinking of herself. Like most people, her face assumed an affectedly unnatural and ill-favored expression as soon as she looked into the glass.

She went on with the letter : —

All Moscow is talking of nothing but the war. One of my two brothers has already gone abroad ; the other is with the

----

[1] The letters in this chapter are in French in the original.

Guard, which is just about to set out for the frontier. Our beloved emperor has left Petersburg, and, according to what they say, is intending to expose his precious life to the perils of war. God grant that the Corsican monster, who is destroying the peace of Europe, may be laid low by the angel whom the Almighty, in His mercy, has sent to rule over us.

Not to speak of my brothers, this war has deprived me of one who is nearest and dearest to my heart; I mean the young Nikolaï Rostof, who was so enthusiastic that he was unable to endure inactivity, and has left the university to join the army. Ah, well, my dear Marie, I will confess to you that, notwithstanding his extreme youth, his departure for the army is a great grief to me. The young man — I told you about him last summer — has so much nobility, so much of that genuine youthfulness that we find so rarely in this age of ours, among our old men of twenty! He has really so much candor and heart! he is so pure and poetic, that my acquaintance with him, slight as it has been, must be counted as one of the sweetest enjoyments of my poor heart, which has already suffered so keenly. Some day I will tell you of our parting and what passed between us. As yet, it is still too fresh in my memory.

Ah! dear friend, how happy you are not to experience these joys and these pangs so keen! You are fortunate, because the latter are usually the keenest. I know very well that Count Nikolaï is too young ever to be anything to me more than a friend, but this sweet friendship, these relations, so poetic and so pure, have become one of the necessities of my heart. But enough of this!

The chief news of the day, which all Moscow is engaged in talking about, is the death of the old Count Bezukhoï and his inheritance. Just imagine: the three princesses get very little, Prince Vasíli nothing, and it is Monsieur Pierre who has inherited everything. He has, moreover, been declared legitimate, and is, therefore, Count Bezukhoï, and the possessor of the finest fortune in Russia. It is claimed that Prince Vasíli has played a very poor part in this whole business, and that he has gone back to Petersburg very much crestfallen.

I confess I have very little understanding of this matter of the bequests and the will; all I know is that since this young man whom we knew under the name of Monsieur Pierre, pure and simple, has become Count Bezukhoï and master of one of the greatest fortunes of Russia, I am greatly amused to notice the changed tone and behavior of mammas burdened with marriageable daughters, and even the young ladies themselves, toward this individual, who, parenthetically, has always seemed to me to be a poor specimen. As it has been the amusement of many people for the past few years to marry me off, and generally to men whom I do not even know, *la Chronique matrimoniale* of Moscow now makes me out Countess Bezukhova. You know perfectly well that I have no desire of acquiring that position !

Speaking of marriage, do you know that quite recently the Universal Auntie, Anna Mikhaïlovna, has confided to me, under the seal of the strictest secrecy, a marriage project for you ; this is neither more nor less than Prince Vasíli's son, Anatol, whom it is proposed to bring to order by marrying him to a young lady of wealth and distinction, and you are the one on whom the choice of the relatives has fallen. I know not how you will look upon the matter, but I felt that it was my duty to inform you. They say he is very handsome and a great scapegrace ; that is all that I have been able to find out about him.

But a truce to gossip like this. I am at the end of my second sheet, and mamma is calling me to go to dine at the Apraksins'. Read the mystic book which I send you, and which is all the rage with us. Although there are things in this book difficult for the feeble mind of man to fathom, it is an admirable work, the reading of which soothes and elevates the mind. Adieu. My respects to your father, and my compliments to Mlle. Bourienne. I embrace you with all my heart.

JULIE.

P.S. Tell me the news about your brother and his charming little wife.

The princess sat thinking, a pensive smile playing over her lips ; her face, lighted up by her luminous eyes, was perfectly transfigured ; then, suddenly jumping up, she walked briskly across the room to her table. She got out some paper and her hand began to fly rapidly over it. This was what she wrote in reply : —

Chère et excellente amie : — Your letter of the thirteenth caused me great delight. So then, you still love me, my poetic Julie. And absence, of which you say such hard things, has not had its usual effect upon you. You complain of absence — what should I have to say if I *dared* complain, bereft as I am of all those who are dearest to me? Ah! if we had not religion to console us, life would be very sad.

Why should you suspect me of looking stern, when you speak to me of your affection for the young man? In this respect, I am lenient to all except myself. I appreciate these sentiments in others, and if I cannot approve of them (never having myself experienced them), I do not condemn them. It only seemed to me that Christian love, love for our neighbor, love for our enemies, is more meritorious, and, therefore, sweeter and more beautiful, than those sentiments inspired in a poetic and loving young girl like you by a young man's handsome eyes.

The news of Count Bezukhoï's death reached us in advance of your letter, and my father was very much moved by it. He says that he was the last representative but one of the "*grand siècle*," and that now it is his turn, but that he shall do his best to put it off as long as possible. God preserve us from such a terrible misfortune!

I cannot agree with you in your judgment of Pierre, whom I knew as a boy. He always seemed to me to have an excellent heart, and that is the quality I most value in people. As to his inheritance and the *rôle* played by Prince Vasíli, it is very sad for both of them. Ah, dear friend! our divine Saviour's saying, that it is easier for a camel to pass through the eye of a needle than for a rich man to enter into the kingdom of God, is terribly true; I pity Prince Vasíli and I am still more sorry for Pierre. So young, and to be loaded down with this wealth; what temptations will he not have to undergo! If I were asked what I should desire most in this world, it would be to be poorer than the poorest of beggars.

A thousand thanks, dear friend, for the work which you send me and which is so much the rage with you in Moscow. However, as you say that while there are many good things in it, there are others which the feeble mind of man cannot fathom, it seems to me quite idle to waste one's time in reading what is unintelligible, and which, therefore, can be productive of no good fruit. I have never been able to understand the passion which some people have for disturbing their minds by devoting themselves to mystical books that arouse nothing but doubts, kindling their imaginations, and giving them a love for exaggeration utterly contrary to Christian simplicity. Let us read the Apostles and the Gospels. Let us give up trying to penetrate the mysteries they contain, for how should we, miserable sinners that we are, presume to investigate the terrible secrets of Providence, while we carry with us this garment of flesh which forms an impenetrable veil between us and the Eternal? Then let us confine ourselves to a studying of the sublime principles which our divine Saviour has left for our guidance here below; let us seek to conform to them and follow them, being persuaded that the less rein we give to our feeble human minds, the more pleasing it is to God, Who repudiates all knowledge not proceeding from Him; that the less we seek to explore what it has seemed best to Him to hide from our comprehension, the sooner He will grant us to discover it by His divine spirit.

My father has not said anything to me of a suitor; he has merely told me of having received a letter and of expecting a visit from Prince Vasíli. As far as the project of marriage concerns me, I will tell you, *chère et excellente amie*, that in my opinion, marriage is a divine institution to which it is necessary to conform. However painful it might be to me, if the Almighty should ever impose upon me the duties of a wife and mother, I shall endeavor to fill them as faithfully as I can, without disturbing myself by inquiring into the nature of my feelings toward him whom He shall give me as a husband.

I have had a letter from my brother, announcing his speedy arrival at Luísiya Goruí with his wife. This will be a joy of short duration, for he will leave us to take part in this unhappy war, into which we are dragged God knows why and how. Not alone with you, at the center of business and society, is the war the only topic of conversation, but here amid the labors of the fields, and that calm of nature which the inhabitants of cities ordinarily imagine to be peculiar to the country, the rumors of the war make themselves painfully heard and felt. My father can talk of nothing else but marches and countermarches, things of which I have no comprehension; and day before yesterday, while taking my usual walk down the village street, I witnessed a heartrending scene: it was a party of recruits, enlisted on our estate, and on their way to the army. You ought to have seen the state in which were the mothers, wives, and children of the men who were off, and to have heard their sobs. You should think that humanity had forgotten the precepts of their divine Saviour, Who taught love, and the forgiveness of offenses; one would think that they imputed their greatest merit to the art of killing one another.

Adieu, *chère et bonne amie!* May our divine Saviour and His Holy Mother keep you in their holy and powerful keeping.

MARIE.

"Ah, you are sending off a letter, princess; I have already sent mine; I have written to my poor mother," said the smiling Mlle. Bourienne, speaking rapidly and swallowing her R's, and altogether bringing into the Princess María's concentrated and melancholy atmosphere what seemed like the breath of another world, where reigned gayety, light-heartedness, and complacency.

"Princess, I must warn you," she added, lowering her voice, "the prince has had a quarrel with Mikhaïl Ivanof. He is in a very bad humor; very morose. I warn you, — you know."

"Ah, my dear friend," replied the Princess María, "I have asked of you never to speak to me of the humor in which my father happens to be. I do not allow myself to make remarks about him and I do not wish others to."

The princess glanced at her watch and noticing that she was already five minutes behind the time when it was required of her to practise on the clavichord, she hurried from the room with dismay pictured on her face. Between twelve o'clock and two the prince took his nap, and it was the immutable rule of the house that the princess then should practise.

CHAPTER XXV

THE gray-haired man-servant was sitting in the cabinet, dozing and listening to the prince's snoring. From a distant part of the house, through the closed doors, came the notes of a difficult phrase of a Dussek sonata, repeated for the twentieth time.

At this time, a coach and a britchka drove up to the entrance door, and from the coach descended Prince Andreï, who handed his little wife down and allowed her to pass ahead of him. The gray-haired Tikhon, in a wig, thrust his head out of the hall door and informed them in a whisper that the prince was asleep and then softly closed the door. Tikhon was well aware that not even the arrival of the son, or any other event, however out of the common, should be allowed to interrupt the order of the day. Prince Andreï knew this as well as Tikhon; he looked at his watch, as if to convince himself that there had been no change in his father's habits since he had seen him, and having satisfied himself on that score, turned to his wife.

"He will be awake in twenty minutes. Let us go to the Princess Maríya," said he.

The little princess had grown stouter, but her eyes, and her short, downy lip, and her sweet smile were just the same as ever as she exclaimed : —

"Why, it is a palace!"

And she looked around with an expression such as people have in congratulating a host on a ball : —

"Come along quick, quick!" .... She smiled at Tikhon and her husband and the footman who was leading the way.

"Is it Marie practising? let us go softly, so as to surprise her."

Prince Andreï followed her, with a civil but bored expression.

"You have grown older, Tikhon," said he to the old man-servant, who, as he passed by, kissed his hand.

Just before they reached the room where the clavichord was heard, the pretty little fair-haired Frenchwoman came tripping out from a side door. Mlle. Bourienne seemed overjoyed to see them.

"Ah! What a pleasure for the princess!" she cried; "you are here at last. I must go and tell her."

"No, no, I beg of you! You are Mlle. Bourienne; I know you already from the friendship which my sister-in-law has for you," said the princess, kissing her; "she is not expecting us?"

They went to the door of the divan-room, where the phrase was being repeated again and again. Prince

Andreï paused and frowned, as if he were expecting something disagreeable.

The princess went in. The phrase was broken off in the middle; a cry was heard, followed by the sound of hasty footsteps and kisses. When Prince Andreï went in, the two sisters-in-law, who had only met once for a short time, at Prince Andreï's wedding, were still locked in a fond embrace, just as at the first moment of their meeting. Mlle. Bourienne was standing near them, with her hand on her heart and a beatific smile on her lips, evidently as ready to cry as to laugh. Prince Andreï shrugged his shoulders and frowned, just as lovers of music frown when they hear a discord. Both the women stood apart; then once again, as if fearing that a moment would be lost, they seized each other by the hand and began to kiss them; and not satisfied with kissing each other's hands, they began to kiss each other in the face, and, to Prince Andreï's unqualified surprise, they both burst into tears and again began to kiss each other. Mlle. Bourienne was also melted; it was awkward enough for Prince Andreï, but to the women it seemed perfectly natural to weep; indeed, they could never have dreamed of a meeting without such an accompaniment.

"Ah, *chère !* " .... "Ah, Marie!" .... they kept exclaiming, amid laughter and tears. "I dreamed last night." .... "And so you were not expecting us?" .... "Ah, Marie, you have grown thin." .... "And you have grown so stout!"

"I knew the princess the moment I saw her," put in Mlle. Bourienne.

"And here was I not thinking of such a thing!" cried the Princess Maríya .... "Ah, Andreï, I did not see you!"

Prince Andreï kissed his sister's hand, and told her that she was as great a cry-baby as ever. The Princess Maríya turned to her brother, and through her tears, her eyes, now large and beautiful and luminous, rested on him with a fond, gentle, and sweet expression.

The young wife chattered incessantly. Her short,

downy upper lip every instant drew down and touched the rosy under lip, and then curled again with the brilliant smile that made her eyes and her teeth shine. She told about an accident at Spaskaya Gora which threatened to be seriously dangerous in her condition, and the next instant she informed them that she had left all her dresses in Petersburg and God knew what she should have to wear while here, and that Andreï had greatly changed, and that Kitty Oduíntsova had married an old man, and that she really had a husband for Marie, but that they would talk about that afterwards.

The Princess Maríya stood looking silently at her brother, and her lovely eyes beamed with affection and melancholy. It was evident that she was now following her own course of thought, quite independent of her sister-in-law's prattle. Right in the midst of a description of the last reception at Petersburg, she turned to her brother : —

"And are you really going to the war, André," she asked, with a sigh. Lise also sighed.

"Yes, and I must be off by to-morrow," replied her brother.

"He leaves me, and God knows why, when he might have been promoted."

The Princess Maríya paid no attention to this remark, but, following the thread of her thoughts, gave her sister-in-law a significant glance from her affectionate eyes.

"You are sure of it?"

The young wife's face changed. She sighed again.

"Certainly I am," said she. "Ah, it is terrible."

Her lip went down. She brought her face near to the young princess's, and again unexpectedly burst into tears.

"She needs to rest," said Prince Andreï, scowling; "don't you, Liza? Take her to her room and I will go to my father. How is he? Just the same as ever?"

"Just the same; but perhaps your eyes will see some change in him," replied the princess, cheerfully.

"The same regular hours, the same walks in the garden, the lathe?" asked Prince Andreï, with a barely perceptible smile, which proved that notwithstanding all his love and reverence for his father, he was not blind to his weaknesses.

"Yes, just the same hours, and the lathe, and the mathematics, and my geometry lessons," replied the princess, merrily, as if her geometry lessons were among the great delights of her life.

When the twenty minutes which remained for the prince's nap were over, Tikhon came to summon the young man to see his father. The old man allowed a variation in his mode of life in honor of his son; he commanded to have him come to him in his own room, while he was dressing (before dinner). The prince dressed in the old-time costume of a kaftan and powered wig. When Prince Andreï — not with the peevish face and manners which he assumed in society, but with a lively expression, such as he had when he was talking with Pierre — went into his father's room, the old man was at his toilet, sitting in a wide morocco-upholstered arm-chair in a wrapper, while Tikhon was putting the last touches to his head.

"Ah, my soldier! so you are going to conquer Bonaparte?" cried the old prince, and he shook his powdered head, so far as he was allowed by the pigtail which Tikhon was busy plaiting. "You do well to go against him; otherwise, he would soon be calling us his subjects! .... Are you well?" and he offered his son his cheek.

The old man awoke from his noon nap in an excellent frame of mind (he was accustomed to say that a nap after dinner was silver, but one before dinner was golden). He squinted cheerily at his son from under his thick, beetling brows. Prince Andreï went and kissed his father on the spot designated. He made no reply to his father's favorite topic of conversation or to his sarcasms on the military men of the present time and especially on Napoleon.

"Yes, I have come to you, batyushka, and with my wife, who expects to be confined soon," said Prince Andreï, watching with eager and reverent eyes all the play of his father's features. "How is your health?"

"Only fools and rakes ever need to be unwell, my boy, and you know me; busy from morning till night, and temperate, and of course I'm well."

"Thank God," said the son, smiling.

"God has nothing to do with it. Well," continued the old man, returning to his favorite hobby, "tell us how the Germans and Bonaparte have taught us to fight, according to this new science of yours, that you call 'strategy'?"

Prince Andreï smiled.

"Let me have time to collect my wits, batyushka," said he, and his expression showed that his father's foibles did not prevent him from reverencing and loving him. "Why, you see I have not even been to my room yet."

"Nonsense, nonsense," cried the old man, pulling at his little pigtail to assure himself that it was firmly plaited, and grasping his son by the arm. "The quarters for your wife are all ready. The Princess Maríya will take her there and show them to her, and they will chatter their three basketfuls! that's their woman's way. I'm glad to have her here. Sit down and talk. I understand Michelson's army and Tolstoï's, too. It's a simultaneous descent. But what's the Southern army going to do? Prussia remains neutral, I know that; but how about Austria?" he asked, as he got up from his chair and began to walk up and down the room, with Tikhon running after him to give him the various parts of his attire. "What's Sweden going to do? How will they get across Pomerania?"

Prince Andreï, perceiving the urgency of his father's inquiries, began, at first unwillingly, but gradually warming up more and more, to explain the plan of operations determined upon for the campaign. As he spoke, he involuntarily, from very force of habit, kept dropping from Russian into French. He explained how an army of ninety thousand was to threaten Prussia and force her to abandon her neutrality and take part in the war; how a portion of this army was to go to Stralsund and unite with the Swedish forces; how two hundred and twenty thousand Austrians, with a hundred thousand Russians, were to engage in active operations in Italy and on the Rhine; and how fifty thousand Russians and fifty thousand English were to disembark at Naples, and how this army, with a total of five hundred thousand men, was to make an attack simultaneously from different sides on the French.

The old prince did not manifest the least interest in the description, any more than if he had not heard it, and continued to dress himself as he walked up and down; though three times he unexpectedly interrupted him. Once he stopped him by crying, "The white one! the white one!"

That meant that Tikhon had not given him the waist-coat that he wished. The second time he stopped and asked, "And is the baby expected soon?" and reproachfully shaking his head, said, "That's too bad, — go on, go on!"

The third time, when Prince Andreï had finished his description, the old man sang in a high falsetto, with the cracked voice of age: —

> "*Malbroug s'en va-t-en guerre.*
> *Dieu sait quand reviendra.*"[1]

The son merely smiled.

"I don't say that I approve of this plan," said he; "I am only telling you what it is. Napoleon, of course, has his plan, which is probably as good as ours."

"Well, you haven't told me anything that is in the least new," and the old man thoughtfully continued to hum the refrain: "*Dieu sait quand il reviendra.*" — "Go into the dining-room."

CHAPTER XXVI

At the appointed hour, the prince, powdered and shaved, went to the dining-room, where his daughter-in-law, the Princess Maríya, and Mlle. Bourienne and the

---

[1] Marlborough is going to the war. God knows when he'll come back again.

architect were waiting for him. The latter was allowed at the table through a strange caprice of the prince, though from his position this insignificant man would never have been shown such an honor. The prince, who had a firm belief in the gradations of rank, and rarely admitted to his table even the important functionaries of the province, had suddenly selected Mikháïl Ivánovitch (who blew his nose in the corner on a checked handkerchief) as a living example of the theory that all men were equal, and more than once assured his daughter that the architect was as good as they were. At the table the prince was very apt to address his conversation mainly to the speechless Mikháïl Ivanovitch.

In the dining-room, tremendously lofty, like all the rest of the rooms in the mansion, the prince's butlers and serving-men, each standing behind a chair, were waiting his coming. The dvoretsky, or house-steward, with a napkin over his arm, glanced to see that the table was properly set, beckoned to the waiters, and constantly let his troubled eyes wander from the wall-clock to the door where the prince was expected to enter.

Prince Andreï was looking at a huge gilded frame, which he had never before seen, containing a representation of the genealogical tree of the Bolkonskys, which hung opposite a similar frame with a badly executed painting, evidently perpetrated by some domestic artist, and meant to be a portrait of a reigning prince, in a crown, showing that he was descended from Rurik, and was the originator of the house of Bolkonsky. Prince Andreï was studying this genealogical tree, and shaking his head and laughing, as if the portrait struck him as something ludicrous.

"How like him this all is!" he was saying to the Princess Maríya, as she came up to him.

The Princess Maríya looked at her brother in amazement. She could not understand what he could find to amuse him. All that her father did inspired in her a reverence which removed it beyond criticism.

"Every man has his Achilles' heel," continued Prince

Andreï. "With his tremendous intellect, the idea of going into this absurdity!"

The Princess Maríya could not approve of this audacious judgment of her brother's, and was just about to reprove him, when the steps which they were awaiting were heard coming from the cabinet. The prince came in briskly, even gayly, as was his universal custom, as if he meant by his lively ways to make a contrast with the stern routine of the house.

Just at the instant that the great clock struck two, and was answered by the feebler tone of another in the reception-room, the prince made his appearance. He paused. From under his thick, overhanging brows, his keen, flashing, stern eyes surveyed all who were present, and then rested on his son's young wife. The young princess instantly experienced that feeling of fear and reverence which this old man inspired in all those around him, — a feeling akin to that experienced by courtiers at the coming of the Tsar.

He smoothed the princess's head, and then, with a clumsy motion, patted her on the back of the neck.

"I am glad to see you, glad to see you," said he; and, after looking into her face steadily once more, he turned away and sat down in his place.

"Sit down, sit down! Mikhaïl Ivanovitch, sit down."

He assigned his daughter-in-law the place next him; the waiter pushed the chair up for her.

"Ho! ho!" said the old man, looking at her critically, "your time is coming! too bad!"

He smiled dryly, coldly, disagreeably, with his lips alone, as usual, and not with his eyes. "You must walk, walk, as much as possible; as much as possible," said he.

The little princess did not hear, or did not wish to hear, his words. She said nothing, and seemed dispirited. The prince asked after her father, and she replied and smiled. He asked about common acquaintances; the princess grew more animated, and began to deliver messages, and tell the prince the gossip of the town.

"The Countess Apraksina, poor woman, has lost her husband, and quite cried her eyes out," said she, growing still more lively.

The livelier she became, the more sternly the prince looked at her, and suddenly, as if he had studied her enough, and had formed a sufficiently clear idea of her mental caliber, he turned abruptly away and began to talk with Mikhaïl Ivanovitch.

"Well, now, Mikhaïla Ivanovitch, it is going to go hard with our Bonaparte. As Prince Andreï has been telling me," — he always spoke of his son in the third person, — "great forces are collecting against him. But then, you and I have always considered him to be a wind-bag."

Mikhaïl Ivanovitch really did not know when he and the prince had ever said any such things about Bonaparte, but perceiving that this was necessary as a preliminary for the prince's favorite subject of conversation, looked in surprise at the young prince, and wondered what would be the outcome of it.

"He is great at tactics," said the old prince to his son, referring to the architect; and again the conversation turned on the war, on Bonaparte, and the generals of the present day, and the great men of the reign. The old prince, it seemed, was persuaded in his own mind that all the men at the head of affairs at the present day were mere school-boys, who did not know even the *a b c* of war and civil administration, and that Bonaparte was an insignificant Frenchman, who had been successful simply from the fact that there were no Potemkins or Suvorofs to meet him; but he was persuaded, also, that no political complications, of any account, existed in Europe; that the war did not amount to anything, but was a sort of puppet-show, at which the men of the present day were playing, while pretending to do something great.

Prince Andreï took his father's sarcasms at the "new men" in good part, and with apparent pleasure led him on, and heard what he had to say.

"The past always seems better than the present,"

said the young man; "yet did n't that same Suvoróf fall
into the trap which Moreau laid for him, — fell in, and
had n't the wit to get himself out of it?"

"Who told you that? who told you?" cried the
prince. "Suvorof!" and he flung away his plate,
which Tikhon was quick enough to catch. "Suvorof!
.... Consider, Prince Andreï! Friedrich and Suvorof were
a pair; .... Moreau! Moreau would have been taken prisoner if Suvorof's hands had been free; but he had on his
hands a *Hofskriegswurstschnapsrath*.[1] The devil himself could not have done anything. Now if you go on
you will find out what these *Hofskriegswurstschnapsraths*
are like. Suvorof was no match for them; what chance
do you suppose Mikhaïl Kutuzof will have? No, my
dear young friend," he went on to say; "there's no
chance for you and your generals against Bonaparte;
you must needs take Frenchmen, so that birds of a
feather may fight together. You have sent the German Pahlen to New York, to America, after the
Frenchman Moreau," said he, referring to the over-
tures that had been made that same year to Moreau to
enter the Russian service. "It's marvelous! Were
the Potemkins, Suvorofs, Orlofs, Germans, pray? No,
brother, either all of you have lost your wits, or I have
gone into my dotage! God give you good luck! but
we shall see. Their Bonaparte a great general! hm!"

"I don't pretend to say that all our arrangements are
wise," returned Prince Andreï, "only I can't understand how you have such a low opinion of Bonaparte.
Laugh as much as you please, but Bonaparte is, nevertheless, a great general."

"Mikhaïla Ivanovitch," cried the old prince to the
architect, who was giving his attention to the roast, and
devoutly hoping that he was quite forgotten, "I have
told you, have I not, that Bonaparte was a great tacti-
cian? And he says so, too."

"How, your illustriousness?" replied the architect.
The prince again laughed his chilling laugh.

"Bonaparte was born with a silver spoon in his

[1] Court-War-Sausage-Schnaps-Council.

mouth. [1] His soldiers are excellent. And then again, he had the good luck to fight with the Germans first. Only a lazy man would fail to whip the Germans. Ever since the world began, the Germans have always been whipped. And they have never whipped any one. Oh, yes, one another! He made his reputation by fighting them."

And the prince began to expatiate on all the blunders that Napoleon, in his opinion, had made in all his wars, and even in his act of administration. His son did not dispute what he said, but it was evident that, whatever arguments were employed against him, he was just as little inclined to alter his opinion as the old prince himself. Prince Andreï listened, refraining from engaging in any discussion, and only smiling as he involuntarily wondered how it was possible for this old man, who had lived for so many years like a hermit in the country, to know so thoroughly and accurately all the military and political occurrences that had taken place in Europe during the last years, and was able to form such an opinion of them.

"You think, do you, that I am too old to understand the present state of affairs? Well, this is all there is of it: I can't sleep o' nights. Now, wherein is this general of yours so great? Where has he ever shown it?"

"It would take too long to tell," replied the son.

"Well, then, go off to your Bonaparte! Mlle. Bourienne, here, is another admirer of your clodhopper of an emperor," he cried, in excellent French.

"You know that I am not a Bonapartist, prince."

"*Dieu sait quand il reviendra*," hummed the prince, in his falsetto; and with a smile that was still more falsetto, he got up and left the table.

The little princess, during the whole time of the discussion and the rest of the meal, sat in silence, looking in alarm, now at her husband's father, now at the Princess Maríya. After they left the table she took her sister-in-law's arm and drew her into the next room.

[1] Russ : " Was born in his shirt."

"How bright your father is," said she; "that's probably the reason that he makes me afraid of him."

"Ah, he is so good!" exclaimed the princess.

CHAPTER XXVII

THE next evening Prince Andreï was about to take his departure. The old prince, not making any change in his routine, had gone to his room immediately after dinner. The young wife was with the Princess Maríya. Prince Andreï, having put on a traveling coat without epaulets, was engaged in his room, with his valet, in packing up. He himself had personally looked after the carriage, and the arrangement of his luggage, and ordered the horses to be put in. In the chamber remained only those things that he always took with him: his dressing-case, a huge silver bottle-holder, two Turkish pistols, and a saber which his father had captured at Ochakof and presented to him. All these appurtenances had been put in the most perfect order; all were bright and clean, in woolen bags, carefully strapped.

If men are ever inclined to think about their actions, the moment when they are about to go away and enter upon some new course of life is certain to induce a serious frame of mind. Generally, at such moments, the past comes up for review, and plans are made for the future.

Prince Andreï's face was very thoughtful and tender. With his hands behind his back, he was walking briskly, from corner to corner, up and down the room, with his eyes fixed, and occasionally shaking his head. Was it terrible for him to be going to the war, or was he a little saddened at the thought of leaving his wife? Perhaps there was a trifle of each feeling. However, hearing steps in the entry, and evidently not wishing to be seen in any such state, he hurriedly dropped his hands and paused by the table, as if engaged in fastening the cover of his dressing-case, and his face became, as usual, serene and impenetrable. The heavy steps that he heard were those of the Princess Maríya.

"I was told that you had ordered the horses put in," said she, panting, — she had evidently been running, — "and I did so want to have a little talk with you, all alone. God knows how long it will be before we see each other again. You are not angry with me for coming? You have changed very much, Andryusha," she added, as if in explanation of such a question.

She smiled as she called him by the pet diminutive, "Andryusha." Evidently it was strange for her to think that this stern, handsome man was the same Andryusha, the slender, frolicsome lad who had been the playmate of her childhood. A smile was his only reply to her question.

"Where is Lise?" he asked.

"She was so tired that she fell asleep on the divan in my room! Oh, André, what a treasure of a wife you have," she said, as she sat down on the sofa, facing her brother. "She is a perfect child, such a sweet, merry-hearted child. I have learned to love her dearly!"

Prince Andreï made no reply, but the princess noticed the ironical and scornful expression which her words called forth on his face.

"But you must be indulgent to her little weaknesses; who is there that is without them, André? You must not forget that she was educated and brought up in society. And besides, her position is now not all roses. We ought always to put ourselves in the place of another. To understand is to forgive. Just think how hard it is on the poor little woman, after the gay life to which she is accustomed, to be parted from her husband, and to be left alone in the country, and in her condition! It is very hard!"

Prince Andreï smiled and looked at his sister, as we smile when we look at people whose motives are perfectly transparent to us.

"You live in the country and don't find this life so horrible, do you?"

"I?—but that's another thing. Why should you speak about me? I have no desire for any other life, because I have never known any other life. But you think, André, what it is for a fashionable young woman to be buried for the best years of her life in the country, alone, too,—for pápenka is always busy, and I,—you know what poor company I am for a woman who has been accustomed to the best society. There's only Mlle. Bourienne."

"Your Bourienne does not please me very much," said Prince Andreï.

"Oh, how can you say so? She is very kind and good, and, what is. more, is greatly to be pitied. She has no one, no one at all. To tell you the truth, she is not at all necessary; if anything, she is in my way. You know that I have always been somewhat of a misanthrope, and now more than ever I love to be alone. *Mon père* is very fond of her. She and Mikhaïl Ivanovitch are two people to whom he is always polite and kind, because both of them are under obligations to him; as Sterne says, 'We do not love men so much for the good that they do us, as for the good that we do them.' *Mon père* took her in as an orphan from the street, and she is very good, and *mon père* loves her way of reading. She always reads aloud to him in the evening. She reads beautifully."

"Now truly, Marie, I am afraid father's temper must be very trying to you sometimes,—is n't it so?" asked Prince Andreï suddenly. The Princess Maríya was at first dumfounded, then terrified, at this question.

"To me—me—trying?" she stammered.

"He has always been harsh, but now he has become desperately trying, I should think," said Prince Andreï, speaking lightly of his father, apparently for the sake of perplexing or testing his sister.

"You're good to every one, André, but you have such pride of intellect," said the princess, following the trend of her own thoughts rather than the course of the conversation. "And that is a great sin. Have we any right to judge our father? And even if we had, what other feeling besides veneration could such a man as *mon père* inspire? And I am so happy and content to live with him. I only wish that all were as happy as I am."

Her brother shook his head incredulously.

"There is only one thing that is hard for me — I will tell you the truth about it, André — it is father's ways of thinking of religious things. I cannot understand how a man with such an immense intellect can fail to see what is as clear as day, and can go so far astray. This is the one thing that makes me unhappy. But even in this I have noticed lately a shade of improvement. Lately his sarcasms have not been quite so pronounced, and there is a monk whom he allowed to come in and have a long talk with him."

"Well, my dear, I am afraid that you and the monk wasted your powder," said Prince Andreï, in a jesting but affectionate way.

"Ah! my dear! All I can do is to pray to God and hope that he will hear me. André," she said timidly, after a moment's silence, "I have one great favor to ask of you."

"What is that, my dear?"

"Promise me that you will not refuse me. It won't be any trouble to you at all, and nothing unworthy of you in doing it; but it will be a great comfort to me. Promise me, Andryusha," said she, thrusting her hand into her reticule and holding something in it but not yet showing it, as if what she held constituted the object of her request, and she were unwilling to take this *something* from the reticule, until she were assured of his promise to do what she desired. She looked at her brother with a timid, beseeching glance.

"Even if it required great trouble, I would," replied Prince Andreï, evidently foreseeing what the request was.

"Think whatever you please, — I know that you are exactly like *mon père*, — think whatever you please, but do this for my sake. Please do! My father's father, our grandfather, wore it in all his battles." Not even now did she take from the reticule what she held in her hand. "So, will you promise me?"

"But what is it?"

"André, I give you this little picture with my blessing, and you must promise me that you will never take it off. Will you promise?"

"If it does not weigh two poods [1] and won't break my neck, I will do it if it will give you any pleasure," but at that instant, noticing the pained expression which passed over his sister's face at this jest, he regretted it. "With pleasure, really with pleasure, my dear," he added.

"He will save and pardon you against your own will; He will bring you to Himself, because in Him alone are truth and peace," she said, in a voice trembling with emotion, and with a gesture of solemnity held up before her brother, with both hands, an ancient oval medallion of the Saviour, with a black face in a silver frame, attached to a silver chain of delicate workmanship.

She made the sign of the cross, kissed the medallion, and held it out to Andreï.

"Please, André, for my sake."

Her large eyes were kindled by the rays of a soft and kindly light which transfigured her thin, sickly face and made it beautiful. Her brother was about to take the medallion, but she stopped him. He understood what she meant, and crossed himself and kissed the image. His face was both tender (for he was touched) and, at the same time, ironical.

"Thanks, my dear."

She kissed him on the brow and again sat down on the divan. Both were silent.

"As I was saying to you, André, be kind and magnanimous as you always used to be. Don't judge Lise harshly," she began after a little. "She is so sweet, so good! and her position is very hard just now."

"Why, Masha, I have not told you that I have found

---

[1] A pood is thirty-six pounds avoirdupois.

any fault with my wife, or been vexed with her. Why do you say such things to me?"

The Princess Maríya flushed in patches and was silent as if she felt guilty.

"I have not said anything to you, but some one has been talking to you. And I am sorry for that."

The red patches flamed still more noticeably on the Princess Maríya's forehead, neck, and cheeks. She tried to say something, but speech failed her. Her brother had guessed right; his little wife after dinner had wept, and confessed her forebodings about the birth of her baby, and how she dreaded it, and poured out her complaints against her fate and her father-in-law and her husband. And after she had cried, she fell asleep.

Prince Andreï was sorry for his sister.

"I wish you to know this, Masha, that I find no fault with my wife, I never have found fault with her and never shall, and there is nothing for which I can reproach myself; and this shall always be so, no matter in what circumstances I find myself. But if you wish to know the truth .... do you wish to know whether I am happy? I tell you, No. Is she happy? No! Why is it? I don't know." ....

As he said this, he got up, went over to his sister, and bending down kissed her on the forehead. His handsome eyes showed an unwonted gleam of sentiment and kindliness, though he looked not at his sister, but over her head at the dark opening of the door.

"Let us go to her, it is time to say good-by. Or, rather, you go ahead and wake her, and I will follow you. Petrushka," he cried to the valet, "come here; pick up those things. This goes under the seat; this at the right."

The Princess Maríya got up and directed her steps toward the door; then she paused: —

"André," said she, in French, "if you had faith, you would have implored God to give you the love which you do not feel, and your prayer would have been heard."

"Yes, perhaps so," said Prince Andreï. "Go on, Masha, I will follow immediately."

On the way to his sister's room, in the gallery which connected one part of the house with the other, Prince Andreï met the sweetly smiling Mlle. Bourienne. It was the third time that she had crossed his path that day in the corridor, and with the same enthusiastic and naïve smile.

"Ah, I thought you were in your own room," said she, blushing a little, and dropping her eyes.

Prince Andreï looked at her sternly. His face suddenly grew wrathful. He gave her no answer, but looked at her forehead and hair, not into her eyes, with such a scornful expression that the little Frenchwoman flushed scarlet and turned away without another word.

When he reached his sister's room, the princess, his wife, was already awake, and her blithe voice was heard through the open door. She was chattering as fast as her tongue would let her, as if she were anxious to make up for lost time, after long repression : —

"No, Marie, but just imagine the old Countess Zubova, with her false curls and a mouth full of false teeth, as if she were trying to cheat old age! ha! ha! ha!"

Prince Andreï had heard his wife get off exactly the same phrase about the Countess Zubova, and the same joke,[1] at least five times. He went quietly into the room. The princess, plump and rosy, was sitting in an easy-chair, with her work in her hands, and was talking an incessant stream, repeating her Petersburg reminiscences, and even the familiar Petersburg phrases. Prince Andreï went up to her, smoothed her hair, and asked if she felt rested from her journey. She answered him and went on with her story.

A coach with a six-in-hand was waiting at the front entrance. It was a dark, autumn night. The coachman could not see the pole of the carriage. Men with

[1] *Zub*, from which the name Zúbova is derived, means "tooth."

lanterns were standing on the door-steps. The great
mansion was alive with lights, shining through the lofty
windows. The domestics were gathered in the entry to
say good-by to the young prince; all the household were
collected in the hall: Mikhaïl Ivanovitch, Mlle. Bourienne, the Princess María, and her sister-in-law. Prince
Andreï had been summoned to his father's cabinet,
where the old prince wished to bid him good-by privately.
All were waiting for their coming.

When Prince Andreï went into the cabinet, the old
prince, with spectacles on his nose and in his white
dressing-gown, in which he never received any one
except his son, was sitting at the table and writing. He
looked around.

"Are you off?" and he went on with his writing.

"I have come to bid you good-by."

"Kiss me here." He indicated his cheek. "Thank
you, thank you."

"Why do you thank me?"

"Because you don't dilly-dally, because you don't
hang on to your wife's petticoats. Service before all!
Thank you! thank you!"

And he went on with his writing so vigorously that
the ink flew from his sputtering pen. "If you have
anything to say, speak. I can attend to these two
things at once," he added.

"About my wife — I am so sorry to be obliged to
leave her on your hands."

"What nonsense is that? Tell me what you want."

"When it is time for my wife to be confined, send to
Moscow for an *accoucheur*. Have him here early."

The old prince paused, and pretending not to understand, fixed his stern eyes on his son.

"I know that no one can help, if nature does not do
her work," said Prince Andreï, evidently confused; "I
am aware that out of millions of cases only one goes
amiss; but this is her whim and mine. They have been
talking to her, she had a dream, and she is afraid."

"Hm! hm!" growled the old prince, taking up his
pen again. "I will do so." He wrote a few more lines

suddenly turned upon his son, and said with a sneer,
"Bad business, hey?"

"What is bad, batyushka?"

"Wife!" said the old prince, with laconic significance.

"I don't understand you," said Prince Andreï.

"Well, there's nothing to be done about it, little
friend," said the prince; "they're all alike, there's no
way of getting unmarried. Don't be disturbed, I won't
tell any one, but you know 't is so."

He seized his son's hand in his small, bony fingers
and shook it, looking him straight in the face with his
keen eyes, which seemed to look through a man, and
then once more laughed his cold laugh.

The son sighed, thereby signifying that his father
read him correctly. The old man continued to fold and
seal his letters with his usual rapidity, and when he had
finished he caught up and put away the wax, the seal,
and the paper.

"What can you do? She's a beauty! I will see
that everything is done. Be easy on that score," said
he, abruptly, as he sealed the last letter.

Andreï made no reply: it was both pleasant and disagreeable to have his father understand him so well.
The old man stood up and handed a letter to his son.

"Listen," said he, "don't worry about your wife.
Whatever can be done, shall be done. Now listen:
give this letter to Mikhaïl Ilarionovitch.[1] I have written
him to employ you in the good places, and not keep you
too long as aide, — it's a nasty position. Tell him I
remember him with affection, and write me how he receives you. If all goes well, stay and serve him.
Nikolaï Andreyitch Bolkonsky's son must not serve any
one from mere favoritism. Now, come here."

He spoke so rapidly that he did not finish half of his
words, but his son understood him; he led him to a
desk, threw back a lid, opened a little box, and took out
a note-book, written in his own large, angular, but close
hand.

"I shall probably die before you do. Remember,

[1] Kutúzof.

these are my memoirs; they are to be given to the emperor, after my death. Now, see here, take this banknote and this letter: this is a prize for the one who shall write a history of the wars of Suvorof; send it to the Academy. Here are my notes; after I am gone you may read them, you will find them worth your while."

Andreï did not tell his father that he would probably live a long time yet. He felt that it was not necessary to say that.

"I will do it all, bátyushka," said he.

"Well, then, good-by." He offered him his hand to kiss, and then gave him an embrace. "Remember one thing, Prince Andreï; if you are killed it will be hard for me to bear; I am an old man...." He unexpectedly paused, and then as suddenly proceeded, in a tempestuous voice: "But if I should hear that you had behaved unworthy of a son of Nikolaï Bolkonsky, I should be — ashamed," he hissed.

"You should not have said that to me, batyushka," replied the son, with a smile.

The old man was silent.

"I have still another request to make of you," Prince Andreï went on to say. "If I should be killed, and if a son should be born to me, don't let him go from you, as I was saying last evening. Let him grow up under your roof, please."

"Not let your wife have him?" asked the old man, and tried to laugh.

Both stood in silence for some moments, facing each other. The old man's keen eyes gazed straight into his son's. There was a slight tremor in the lower part of the old prince's face.

"We have said good-by, now go!" said he, suddenly. "Go!" he cried in a stern, loud voice, opening his cabinet door.

"What is it? what's the matter?" asked Prince Andreï's wife and sister, as the young man came out, and they caught a momentary glimpse of the old prince, in his white dressing-gown, and without his wig, and in his spectacles, as he appeared at the door, screaming at his son.

Prince Andreï sighed, and made no answer.

"Well?" said he, turning to his wife, and this "well (*nu*)" sounded chillingly sarcastic, as if he had said, "Now begin your little comedy."

"André, already?" said the little wife, turning pale, and fixing her terror-stricken eyes on her husband. He took her in his arms; she gave a cry, and fell fainting on his shoulder.

He carefully disengaged himself from her form, looked into her face, and tenderly laid her in an arm-chair.

"Adieu, Marie," said he, gently, to his sister, kissed her hand, and hastened out of the room.

The fainting princess lay in the chair; Mlle. Bourienne chafed her temples. The Princess Maríya, holding her up, was still looking, with her lovely eyes dim with tears, at the door through which Prince Andreï had disappeared, and her blessing followed him.

In the cabinet the old prince was heard repeatedly blowing his nose, with sharp, angry reports, like pistol-shots. Prince Andreï had hardly left the room when the cabinet door was hurriedly flung open, and the prince's stern figure appeared in the white khalát.

"Has he gone?" he asked; "well, it is just as well," said he. Then, looking angrily at the unconscious little princess, he shook his head reproachfully, and clapped the door to after him.

PART SECOND

CHAPTER I

IN October, 1805, the Russian army were cantoned in certain villages and towns in the archduchy of Austria, making a heavy burden for the inhabitants, and still new regiments were on the way from Russia, and concentrating around the fortress of Braunau, where Kutuzof, the commander-in-chief, had his headquarters.

On the twenty-third of October of that year, one of the many regiments of infantry that had just arrived stopped about half a mile from the city, waiting to be reviewed by the commander-in-chief. Notwithstanding the un-Russian landscape — orchards, stone walls, tiled roofs, and mountains on the horizon — and the un-Russian aspect of the people, who gathered to look with curiosity at the soldiers, this regiment presented exactly the same appearance as every other Russian regiment getting ready for inspection anywhere in the center of Russia.

The evening before, during their last march, word had been received that the commander-in-chief would review the regiment. The words of the order had not seemed altogether clear to the regimental commander, and the question having arisen, how it was to be taken, — were they to be in marching order or not? — he called a council of officers, at which it was decided that the regiment should be presented in parade dress, on the principle that it is always better to go beyond than not to come up to the requirements. And the soldiers, after a march of three hundred versts, during which they had not once closed their eyes, were kept all night mending and cleaning; the aides and captains classified and enrolled their men, and by morning the regiment, instead of a straggling, disorderly mob, such as it had

155

been during the last stage of their march, presented a compact mass of two thousand men, each one of whom knew his place and his duty; every button and every strap were in order, and shining with neatness.

Not only were all the externals put into perfect order, but if the commander-in-chief should take it into his head to look under the uniforms, then he would have found that each man had on a clean shirt, and that in each knapsack were the required number of things, " *shíltse i míltse* " — awl and soap — as the soldiers express it.

There was only one particular in regard to which no one could be satisfied; that was the footwear. The shoes of more than half of the men were in tatters. But this lack was not the fault of the regimental commander, since, notwithstanding his repeated demands, the necessary goods had not been furnished by the Austrian commissariat, and, moreover, the regiment had marched a thousand versts.

The regimental commander was an elderly general, of sanguine complexion, with gray brows and side-whiskers; he was stout and broad; the distance from his chest to his back was greater than across his shoulders. He wore a brand-new uniform, which showed the creases caused by the garments having been folded, and on his shoulders were heavy gold epaulets, which raised his fat shoulders still higher.

The regimental commander had the aspect of a man who had happily accomplished one of the most important functions of life. He marched up and down in front of the line, and as he marched he shook at every step, slightly bending his back. It could be seen that the regimental commander was very fond of his regiment, and felt happy at the idea that all his mental faculties were absorbed in it. But, nevertheless, his pompous gait seemed to insinuate that over and above his military interests there was still left no small room in his heart for the affairs of society and the female sex.

" Well, batyushka, Mikhaïlo Mitritch," said he, turning to one of the battalion commanders, who stepped forward

with a smile (it was evident that they were all happy),
"we had a pretty tough tussle last night, did n't we?
However, according to my idea our regiment is n't one
of the worst, hey?"

The battalion commander appreciated the jocund
irony and laughed.

"No, we should not be driven off from the Empress's
Field." [1]

"What is it?" asked the commander, catching sight
of two horsemen galloping along the road to the city,
lined with signal men. It was an aide with a Cossack
riding behind him.

The aide had been sent from headquarters to explain
what had been enigmatical in the last evening's order,
and especially to insist upon it that the commander-in-
chief wished to review the regiment in exactly the condition in which it had arrived — in cloaks, gun-covers,
and without any preparations whatever!

The evening before, it had happened that a member
of the Hofkriegsrath had arrived from Vienna, asking
and urging that Kutuzof should make all haste to join
the allied armies under the Archduke Ferdinand and
General Mack; and Kutuzof, considering that this
junction was not advantageous, desired to exhibit in
support of his own theories, and to have the Austrian
general see for himself, the pitiable state in which the
army from Russia had arrived. With this end in view
he was anxious to find the regiment in marching order,
and therefore the worse the situation of the men the
more agreeable it would be to him. The aide knew
nothing about these reasons, but he transmitted to the
regimental commander the general-in-chief's urgent desire that the men should be in marching order, and
added that if it were otherwise the commander-in-chief
would be very much offended.

On hearing these words, the regimental commander
hung his head, silently shrugged his shoulders, and
spread his hands with a despairing gesture.

"This is great doings!" he cried. "It's what I told

[1] *Tsaritsuin Lug*, a famous parade ground near St. Petersburg. — TR.

you, Mikhařlo Mitritch — in marching order, in cloaks,"
said he, turning reproachfully to the battalion commander. "Akh! my God," he exclaimed, and stepped
resolutely forward. "Gentlemen! Company commanders!" he cried in a voice accustomed to command.
"Sergeants! — Will they be here soon?" he asked,
turning to the aide with an expression of deferential
politeness evidently proportioned to the dignity of the
personage of whom he was speaking.

"Within an hour, I think."

"Shall we have time to make the change?"

"I don't know, general."

The regimental commander, hastening into the ranks,
made the dispositions for changing back into marching
costume again. The company commanders ran to their
companies, the sergeants bustled about (the cloaks had
not yet been put in perfect order) and in an instant the
solid squares, which had just been standing silently and
orderly, stirred, stretched out, and began to buzz with
busy voices. Soldiers were running in every direction,
getting their knapsacks on their shoulders and over
their heads, taking down their cloaks and lifting their
arms high in the air, trying to get them into their
sleeves.

Within half an hour the whole regiment was in the
same order as before; only the squares were transformed
from black to gray. The regimental commander was
again walking up and down in front of the regiment
with the same tottering gait, and inspecting it from a
distance.

"What does that mean? What is that?" he cried,
suddenly halting. "Commander of the third company!"

"The general wants the commander of the third company...."

"The general wants the commander of the third!"....
"The general wants the commander of the third company!" cried various voices along the ranks, and an
aide hastened to discover the missing officer.

Even while the sounds of gruff voices commingling,
and some even crying "The company wants the gen-

eral," rang along the lines, the missing officer appeared from behind his company, and, although he was well on in years and not used to running, he came toward the general at an awkward dog-trot on his tiptoes.

The captain's face expressed such anxiety as a schoolboy feels when he is called upon to recite a lesson which has not been learned. His nose was red and covered with blotches (evidently caused by intemperance) and his mouth twitched nervously. The regimental commander surveyed the delinquent captain from head to foot, as he came up, panting, and slackening his pace as he approached.

"Do you let your men wear women's sarafans? What does that mean?" cried the regimental commander, thrusting out his lower jaw and pointing to a soldier in the ranks of the third company who wore a colored capote of broadcloth in violent contrast with the cloaks of the other soldiers. "Where have you been? The commander-in-chief is expected, and here you are out of your place!—Hey?—I will teach you to dress your men in Cossack coats for review!—Hey!"

The company commander, not taking his eyes from his chief, kept his two fingers at his visor, as if he found his salvation now in this one position alone.

"Well, why don't you speak? Whom have you there, in that Hungarian costume?" sternly demanded the regimental commander, with grim facetiousness.

"Your excellency...."

"Well, what of *your excellency?* 'Your excellency'! and 'your excellency'! But what does .... do you mean by 'your excellency'?[1] Nobody knows what you mean!"

"Your excellency, that is Dolokhof, cashiered," stammered the captain.

"Well, was he cashiered to be a field-marshal, or a private? If as a private, then he ought to be dressed like the others, in uniform!"

"Your excellency, you yourself allowed him to dress so on the march."

"Allowed him? Allowed him? That's always the

[1] *Váshe prevaskhodïyelstvo.*

way with you young men," said the regimental commander, cooling down a little. "Allowed him? We
tell you one thing and you...." The regimental commander paused. "We tell you one thing and you ....
well!" said he, with a fresh access of temper, "be
good enough to have your men dressed decently." ....

And the regimental commander glanced at the aide
and proceeded along the line with his faltering gait. It
could be seen that his outburst of temper had given him
great satisfaction, and that as he passed along the line
he wanted to find some excuse for further violence.
Berating one officer for not having a clean gorget, and
another for having his company "dressed" unevenly,
he proceeded to company three. "H-o-o-o-ow are you
standing? Where is your leg? Your leg! where is
it?" screamed the regimental commander, with a suggestion of keen suffering in his voice, passing by half a
dozen men to come to Dolokhof, who was dressed in a
blue cloak.

Dolokhof slowly straightened his bended leg, and,
with his keen, bold eyes, stared into the general's face.

"Why that blue cloak? Off with it! Sergeant!
strip him. The blun...."

He did not have time to finish.

"General, I am bound to fulfil orders, but I am not
bound to put up with ...." began Dolokhof, hastily.

"No talking in the ranks! No talking, no talking!"

"I am not bound to put up with insults," cried Dolokhof, in a loud, ringing voice. The eyes of the general
and the private met.

The general said no more, but angrily pulled down
his tight belt.

"Have the goodness to change your coat, I beg of
you," said he, as he turned away.

CHAPTER II

"He is coming," cried one of the signalmen.

The regimental commander, flushing scarlet, ran to his horse, adjusted the stirrup with trembling hands, threw himself into the saddle, straightened himself up, drew his saber, and, with a radiant, resolute face, drew his mouth to one side, ready to shout his order. A shiver ran through the regiment, as if it were a bird about to spread its wings; then it became motionless.

"Eyes fr-r-r-r-ront!" cried the regimental commander, in a voice trembling with emotion; pleasant as it sounded to himself, it was peremptory toward the regiment, and suggestive of welcome to the approaching chief.

Along the broad highway, unpaved, shaded with trees, came a high Viennese calash, painted blue, and swinging easily on its springs, as its six horses trotted briskly along. Behind it galloped the suite and an escort of Kroatians. Next Kutuzof sat the Austrian general, in a white uniform, contrasting strangely with the dark Russian ones. The calash drew up near the regiment. Kutuzof and the Austrian general were engaged in conversation in low tones, and Kutuzof smiled slightly, as he slowly and heavily stepped down from the carriage, exactly as if the two thousand men who were breathlessly gazing at him, and the regimental commander, did not exist.

The word of command rang out, again the regiment stirred into life, and presented arms. In the dead silence the commander-in-chief's weak voice was heard.

The regiment shouted, "Long life to your hi-i-ighness!" and again all was still.

At first Kutuzof stood where he was and watched the regiment go through its evolution; then, side by side with the general in the white uniform, and accompanied by his suite, he started to walk down the line.

By the way in which the regimental commander had saluted his chief, and kept his eyes fastened upon him, and now followed behind the two generals as they walked down the lines, and by the way that he drew himself up and bent forward to listen to every word that fell from their lips, it was evident that he fulfilled his duties as a subordinate with even greater satisfaction than he did those of a commander. The regiment, thanks to the commander's stern discipline and strenuous endeavors, was in excellent condition compared to the others which had come to Braunau at the same time; there were only two hundred and seventeen sick and stragglers; and all things were in excellent order, with the exception of the shoes.

Kutuzof proceeded down the ranks, occasionally stopping to say a few friendly words to officers or even privates whom he had known during the war with Turkey. Glancing at their shoes, he more than once shook his head mournfully and directed the Austrian general's attention to them with an expression which meant to imply that he would not blame any one for it, but that he could not avoid seeing how wretched it was.

The regimental commander, each time that he did so, pushed forward, fearing to lose a single word that his chief might speak regarding his regiment.

Behind Kutuzof, just near enough to be able to catch every word, however lightly spoken, that might fall from his lips, followed the twenty men of his suite, talking among themselves and occasionally laughing. Nearest to the commander-in-chief walked a handsome aide; this was Prince Bolkonsky. Next him went his messmate, Nesvitsky a tall and remarkably stalwart staff-officer, with a kindly, smiling, handsome face and liquid eyes. Nesvitsky could hardly refrain from laughing at the antics of a dark-complexioned officer of hussars who was walking near him. The hussar officer, without smiling, and not changing the serious expression of his eyes, was staring at the regimental commander's back and mimicking his every motion. Every time that the general tottered and pushed forward, the young hussar officer would, in almost precisely the same way, totter and push forward. Nesvitsky was amused, and nudged the others to look at the mimic.

Kutuzof walked slowly and lazily in front of the thousands of eyes that were starting from their sockets to follow the motions of the chief. As he came along to company three, he suddenly halted. The suite, not anticipating this halt, involuntarily crowded up close to him.

"Ah, Timokhin!" cried the commander-in-chief, recognizing the red-nosed captain, — the one who had been obliged to suffer on account of the blue cloak.

It would seem as if it were impossible for him to draw himself up higher than he had done during the scolding administered by the regimental commander. But now that the commander-in-chief stopped to speak to him, the captain put such a strain upon himself, that it seemed as if he could not stand it should the commander-in-chief stay a moment longer; and, accordingly, Kutuzof, evidently appreciating his position and being anxious to show every kindness to the captain, hastened to turn away, a scarcely perceptible smile flitting over his plump, scarred face.

"Another comrade of Izmaïlo!" said he. "A brave officer! Are you satisfied with him?" asked Kutuzof of the regimental commander.

The regimental commander, who, unknown to himself, was mimicked as in a mirror by the officer of hussars, started as if stung, sprang forward, and replied : —

"Very well satisfied, your high excellency." [1]

"We all of us have our weaknesses," continued Kutuzof, smiling and turning away. "His used to be his devotion to Bacchus."

The regimental commander was alarmed lest he were to blame for this and found no words to reply. The hussar at this instant caught sight of the captain with the red nose and rounded belly and perpetrated such an exact imitation of his face and pose that Nesvitsky laughed outright. Kutuzof turned around. It was evident that the young officer had perfect command of his features; for at the instant that Kutuzof turned round

[1] *Váshe vuisokoprevaskhodityelstvo.*

the officer's face had assumed the most serious, deferential, and innocent of expressions.

The third company was the last and Kutuzof paused, evidently trying to recollect something. Prince Andreï stepped out from the suite and said in French in an undertone:—

"You ordered me to remind you of Dolokhof, who was cashiered to this regiment...."

"Where is this Dolokhof?"

Dolokhof, who now wore the gray military cloak, did not wait to be summoned. Kutuzof saw a well-built soldier with light curly hair and bright blue eyes come forth from the ranks and present arms.

"A grievance?" asked Kutuzof, slightly frowning.

"That is Dolokhof," said Prince Andreï.

"Ah!" exclaimed Kutuzof, "I hope that you will profit by this lesson. Do your duty. The emperor is merciful. And I will not forget you, if you deserve well."

The clear blue eyes looked into the chief's face with the same boldness as at the regimental commander's, their expression seeming to rend the veil of rank that so widely separated the commander-in-chief from the private soldier.

"I should like to ask one favor, your high excellency," said he, deliberately, in his firm, ringing voice; "I beg that you give me a chance to wipe out my fault and show my devotion to his majesty the emperor, and to Russia."

Kutuzof turned away. The same sort of smile flashed over his face and through his eyes as at the time when he turned away from Captain Timokhin. He turned away and frowned, as if he wished to express by this that all that Dolokhof had said to him and all that he could possibly say to him he had known long, long ago, and that it was all a bore to him and that it was so much wasted breath. He turned away and went back to the calash.

The regiment broke up into companies and marched to the quarters assigned them not far from Braunau, where they hoped to get shoes and clothes and rest after their hard marches.

"You will not complain of me, will you, Prokhor Ignatyitch," asked the regimental commander, galloping after the third company, which was going to quarters, and overtaking Captain Timokhin, who rode at their head. The regimental commander's face shone with unrestrained delight at the successful outcome of the review. "The service of the Tsar....one can't help.... another time, if you happen to be out of line .... I am the first to apologize. You know me..... Thank you very much!"

And he held out his hand to the captain.

"I beg of you, general! how could I think of such a thing," replied the captain; his nose grew scarlet and he smiled, the smile betraying the lack of two front teeth which had been knocked out by the butt-end of a gun at Izmaïlo.

"And assure Mr. Dolokhof that I shall not forget him — let him rest easy on that score. And tell me, please, I have been wanting for some time to ask you, how does he behave? And always...."

"He is very regular in his duty, your excellency — but his temper...." said Timokhin.

"Well, what of his temper?" demanded the regimental commander.

"Some days, your excellency, he goes it," said the captain, "but otherwise he is intelligent and well-informed and quiet. And then again he is a wild beast. In Poland he almost killed a Jew; you must know...."

"Yes, yes," said the regimental commander. "We must always be easy on a young man in misfortune. You see he has influential connections.... so you had better...."

"I understand, your excellency," rejoined Timokhin, with a smile that showed that he understood his chief's desires.

"Yes, yes, just so!"

The regimental commander sought out Dolokhof in the ranks and reined in his horse.

"Epaulets at the first engagement!" said he.

Dolokhof looked up, but made no answer and did not alter the expression of the ironical smile that curled his lips.

"Well, this is very good," continued the regimental commander; "a glass of vodka to the men from me," he added, loud enough to be heard by the soldiers. "I thank you all! Slava Bohu — glory to God!" And he rode on and overtook the next company.

"Well, it's a fact, he's a good man and not hard to serve under," said Timokhin to a subaltern riding next him.

"In a word, very hearty," said the subaltern officer, laughing at his own joke. The regimental commander was nicknamed, "The King of Hearts."

The cheerful frame of mind felt by the officers after the review was shared also by the men. The regiment marched along merrily. On all sides were heard the voices of the soldiers talking.

"How is it? They say Kutuzof is blind of one eye?"

"Well, so he is, quite blind."

"Nay, brother, he can see better than you can. He inspected our boots and leg-wrappers and everything."

"How he looked at my legs! It seemed to me ...."

"And that other one, the *Avstriak* who was with him! I should think he was whitewashed! White as flour! Think what a job to clean that uniform!"

"Say, Fedeshou, did he say when we should begin to be on our guard? You were standing nearer to him! I was told that *Bunaparte* himself is at *Brunova*."

"Bunaparte here! what a lie, you fool! Don't you know anything? Now the *Prusak* is up in arms; and the *Avstriak*, of course, have got to put him down. And when he's put down then there'll be war with Bunaparte. And they say Bunaparte is here at Brunova! Anybody could see you was a fool! Keep your ears peeled, you idiot!"

"The devil! what sort of quartermasters these are! see! there's the fifth company turning off into the village; they'll have their kasha-pots boiling, and here we are n't in yet!"

"Give me a biscuit, you devil!"

"Did n't I gie you some tobacky, last evening? Too thin, brother! Well, then, God be with you!"

"Oh! I wish they'd call a halt! the idea of marching five versts more on an empty stomach!"

"What you'd like'd be for those Germans to give us a lift in their carriages. Then you'd go easy enough; that would be fine!"

"But here, brother, see all these beggarly people come out! We had back there the *Polyaks*, they belonged to the Russian crown, but here, brother, there's nothing but Germans come out."

"Singers to the front!" cried the captain.

A score of men from the different companies ran to their places at the head of the column. The drummer who led the singing faced the singers and waved his arm and struck up the drawling soldier's song beginning with the words: —

" Is it the dawn, and has the red sun risen ? "

and ending: —

" Well, boys, what glory we shall win with Father Kamyensky."

This song had been composed in Turkey, and was now sung in Austria, with simply this variation, that in place of " Father Kamyensky," Father Kutuzof was substituted.

The drummer, a stalwart, handsome fellow, forty years old, having sung these last words in a soldierly style, made a gesture with his hands as if he were throwing something to the ground, looked sternly at his singers, and frowned. Then, feeling the consciousness that all eyes were fastened upon him, he lifted his arms high above his head, as if he were carrying with the greatest care some invisible and precious object, and, holding them so for several moments, he suddenly flung it down with a despairing gesture, singing: —

" Akh vui séni, moï séni," [1]

while twenty voices took up the refrain, "my new cottage," and a spoonmaker, disregarding the weight of his equipment, friskily danced ahead and walked backwards before the company, shrugging his shoulders and making gestures of defiance with his spoons.

The soldiers, clapping their hands in time with the measure of the song, marched on in step.

Behind them were heard the rattle of wheels, the creaking of springs, and the trampling of horses' feet. It was Kutuzof and his suite, on their way back to the city. The commander-in-chief signified that the men should keep on as they were, and he and all his suite showed by their faces how much they enjoyed the music of the songs, the sight of the dancing soldier, and the bold and buoyant appearance of the company.

Conspicuous in the second file of the right flank, near which the calash passed, was Dolokhof, the blue-eyed soldier, who was marching along with an extraordinarily bold and graceful gait, keeping time to the song and looking into the faces of those who passed, with an expression as if he pitied all who did not march with his company. The cornet of hussars in Kutuzof's suite, who had mimicked the regimental commander, fell behind the calash and drew up alongside of Dolokhof.

Zherkof, this cornet of hussars, had at one time belonged to the same wild set in Petersburg of which Dolokhof was the leader. Here, abroad, Zherkof met Dolokhof in the ranks, but did not find it expedient to recognize him at first. Now, however, since Kutuzof had set the example by talking with the degraded officer, he went to him with all the cordiality of an old friend.

"My dear fellow, how are you?" said he, right in the midst of the song, as he walked his horse abreast of the company.

"How am I?" repeated Dolokhof, coldly. "As you see."

[1] Ah, my cottage, my cottage.

The military song gave a special significance to the tone of easy good fellowship in which Zherkof spoke, and the pronounced coolness of Dolokhof's answer.

" And how do you get along with your chiefs ? " asked Zherkof.

"All right; good fellows. How did you manage to get on the staff ? "

" I am attached — on duty."

Neither spoke.

> *"Vuipuskála sokolá*
> *Da iz právava rukavá"* [1]

rang out the song, involuntarily inspiring a bold, blithe feeling. Their talk would probably have been different, if they had not spoken while the singing was in progress.

"Is it true that the Austrians are beaten?" asked Dolokhóf.

" The devil only knows; so they say."

" I am glad of it," exclaimed Dolokhof, curtly and distinctly, as if the song demanded it of him.

" Say, come to us this evening. You 'll have a chance at faro," said Zherkof.

" Did you bring much money with you ? "

" Come."

" Can't. I 've sworn off. I neither drink nor play till I 'm promoted."

"Well, that 'll come the first engagement."

"We shall see."

Again they relapsed into silence.

" Look in, anyway; if you need anything, the staff will help you."

Dolokhof laughed.

" You 'd better not trouble yourself. If I need anything, I shall not ask for it; I 'll take it."

"Well, I mean.... "

"Well, and so do I mean."

" Good-by."

" Farewell."

---

[1] She unleashed the falcon, and from the right sleeve.

" I vuisokó i dalekó,
Na rodómu storanú." [1]

Zherkof put spurs to his horse, which pranced and danced not knowing with which foot to start, and then, with a spring, galloped off, leaving the company far behind, and overtook the calash, while still the rhythm of the song seemed to wing its feet.

CHAPTER III

On his return from the review, Kutuzof, accompanied by the Austrian general, went into his private room, and calling his aide bade him bring certain papers relating to the state of the troops, and some letters received from the Archduke Ferdinand, the commander of the army of the van. Prince Andreï Bolkonsky came into the commander-in-chief's office with the desired papers. Kutuzof and the member of the Hofkriegsrath were sitting at a table on which was spread a map.

"Ah," said Kutuzof, with a glance at Bolkonsky, signifying by this exclamation that the adjutant was to wait, while at the same time he went on in French with the conversation that he had begun.

"I have only one thing to say, general," proceeded Kutuzof, with a pleasing elegance of diction and accent which constrained one to listen to each deliberately spoken word.

It was evident that Kutuzof took pleasure in hearing himself.

"I have only one thing to say, general; if the matter depended solely on me, then the desire of his majesty the Emperor Franz would long ago have been fulfilled. I should long ago have joined the archduke. And I assure you, on my honor, that for me personally, I should have been rejoiced to give over the supreme command of the armies to a general so much more

---

[1] "High and far in our fatherland."

learned and more experienced than myself, — and such men abound in Austria, — and to be relieved of the heavy responsibility; but circumstances are often beyond our control, general."

And Kutuzof smiled, with an expression which seemed to say: 'You are at perfect liberty not to put any confidence in what I say, and it is absolutely of no consequence to me whether you believe me or not, but you have no need to tell me so. And that's all there is of it.'

The Austrian general looked dissatisfied, but could not do otherwise than reply in the same tone.

"On the contrary," said he, in a querulous and angry tone, that gave the lie to the flattering intention of his words, "on the contrary, his majesty highly appreciates the part that your excellency has taken in the common cause; but we think that the present delay will rob the brave Russian army and their generals of those laurels which they are in the habit of winning in war," he rejoined, in a phrase evidently prepared beforehand.

Kutuzof bowed, but still continued to smile.

"Well, such is my idea of it, and relying upon the last letter which his highness the Archduke Ferdinand has done me the honor of writing me, I have no doubt that the Austrian army, under the command of such an experienced coadjutor as General Mack, has already won a decisive victory and no longer needs our aid," said Kutuzof.

The general frowned. There was indeed no accurate information about the condition of the Austrians, yet there was a preponderating weight of circumstantial evidence in favor of the unfavorable rumors that were in circulation, and, therefore, Kutuzof's assumption of an Austrian victory seemed very much like a jest. But Kutuzof smiled blandly, with an expression which seemed to affirm his right to make this assumption. In fact, the last letter that he had received from Mack's army informed him of a probable victory, and of the very advantageous strategical position of his army.

"Give me that letter," said Kutuzof, addressing

Prince Andreï. " Have the goodness to listen to this,"
and Kutuzof, with an ironical smile hovering on his lips,
read in German to the Austrian general the following
passage from the Archduke Ferdinand's letter : —

"We have our forces perfectly concentrated — nearly seventy thousand strong — so that we can attack and defeat the
enemy should he attempt to cross the Lech. Since we are
masters of Ulm, we cannot lose the advantage of having control of both banks of the Danube ; moreover, should the enemy
not cross the Lech, we can at any moment take the other side
of the Danube, attack his line of communication, and, by re-
crossing the Danube lower down, instantly nullify his plans, if
he should think of turning the main body of his forces against
our faithful allies. Thus we can confidently wait the moment
when the imperial Russian army is ready to join us, and then
easily find an opportunity in common to inflict upon the enemy
the fate that he deserves." [1]

Kutuzof drew a long breath, when he had finished
this passage, and looked with a sympathetic and kindly
expression at the member of the Hofkriegsrath.

" But you know, your excellency, that the proverb
advises to be prepared for the worst," said the Austrian general, evidently anxious to have done with jokes
and take up serious business. He involuntarily glanced
at the aide.

" Excuse me, general," exclaimed Kutuzof, interrupting him and also turning to Prince Andreï. " See here,
my dear fellow, get from Kozlovsky all the reports from
our scouts. Here are two letters from Count Nostitz,
and here's a letter from his highness the Archduke
Ferdinand, — another still," said he, handing him several papers. " Have an abstract of these made out
neatly in French, as a memorandum, so that we can
see at a glance all the facts that we have in regard to
the doings of the Austrian army. Now then, when it
is done you will hand it to his excellency."

Prince Andreï inclined his head as a sign that he
comprehended from the very first word not only all that

[1] In German in the original.

Kutuzof had said, but all that he intended to say to him. He gathered up the papers and with a general salutation went into the reception-room, stepping noiselessly over the soft carpet.

Notwithstanding the fact that not much time had elapsed since Prince Andreï had left Russia, he had greatly changed. In the expression of his face, in his motions, in his gait, there was almost nothing to be recognized of his former affectation, lassitude, and laziness. He had the appearance of a man who has no time to think about the impression that he produces upon others, but who is occupied with pleasant and interesting work. His face showed more of contentment with himself and his surroundings; his smile and glance were more cheerful and attractive.

Kutuzof, whom he joined in Poland, had received him very warmly and promised not to forget him; treated him with more distinction than his other aides, and had taken him to Vienna with him and intrusted him with the most important duties. From Vienna Kutuzof sent a letter to his old comrade, Prince Andreï's father: —

"Your son," he wrote, "bids fair to become an officer who will be distinguished for his quickness of perception, his firmness, and his faithfulness. I count myself fortunate in having such an assistant."

Among the officers of Kutúzof's staff and in the army generally, Prince Andreï bore two diametrically opposite reputations, just the same as in Petersburg society. One party, the minority, regarded Prince Andreï as in some way different from themselves and all other people, and expected him to achieve the most brilliant success; they listened to him, praised him, and imitated him, and Prince Andreï was on pleasant and easy terms with these men. The other party, the majority, were not fond of Prince Andreï; they considered him haughty, cold, and disagreeable. But Prince Andreï had conducted himself toward these men in such a way as to win their respect and even their fear.

Coming into the reception-room from Kutuzof's cabinet, Prince Andreï took his papers to his colleague, the aide Kozlovsky, who was on duty and was sitting with a book at the window.

"Well, what is it, prince?" asked Kozlovsky.

"You are ordered to draw up a memorandum, to account for our not advancing."

"But why?"

Prince Andreï shrugged his shoulders.

"Any news of Mack?" asked Kozlovsky.

"No."

"If it were true that he is defeated, the news would have come by this time."

"Probably," rejoined Prince Andreï, and started for the outer door; but at that very instant the door was flung almost into his face, and a tall Austrian general, in an overcoat, and with his head swathed in a dark handkerchief, and with the ribbon of Maria Theresa around his neck, hurried into the room, having evidently just arrived from a journey.

Prince Andreï paused.

"General-in-chief Kutuzof?" hurriedly asked the newly arrived general, with a strong German accent, and, looking anxiously on all sides, started without delay for the door of the general's private room.

"The general-in-chief is engaged," said Kozlovsky, hastening toward the unknown general and barring the way to the cabinet. "Whom shall I announce?"

The unknown general looked scornfully down on the diminutive Kozlovsky, and seemed to be amazed that he was not recognized.

"The general-in-chief is engaged," repeated Kozlovsky, calmly.

The general's face contracted, his lips drew together and trembled.

He drew out a note-book, quickly wrote something in pencil, tore out the leaf, and handed it to the aide; then, with quick steps, he walked over to the window, threw himself into a chair, and surveyed those in the room, as if to ask why they stared at him so. Then the general lifted his head, stretched out his neck, as if he were about to say something, and then, affecting to hum to himself, produced a strange sound, instantly swallowed. The office door opened, and Kutuzof himself appeared on the threshold. The general with the bandaged head, who had apparently escaped from some peril, bowed, and hastened, with long swift strides of his thin legs, across the room, toward Kutuzof.

"You see the unfortunate Mack!" said he, in a broken voice.

Kutuzof's face, as he stood at his office door, remained perfectly unchangeable for several moments. Then a frown ran like a wave across his brow, and passed off, leaving his face as serene as before. He respectfully bent his head, shut his eyes, silently allowed Mack to pass in front of him into the office, and then closed the door behind him.

The rumor, already spread abroad, as to the defeat of the Austrians and the surrender of the whole army at Ulm, was thus proved to be correct. Within half an hour aides were flying about in all directions with orders for the Russian army, till now inactive, to prepare with all haste to meet the enemy.

Prince Andreï was one of those uncommon staff-officers who devote their chief interest to the general operations of the war. On seeing Mack, and learning the particulars of his defeat, he realized that half of the campaign was lost, realized the difficult situation of the Russian army, and vividly pictured the fate that was awaiting the army, and the part which he was about to play in it. In spite of himself he experienced a strong feeling of delight at the thought of the shame that Austria had brought upon herself, and that perhaps within a week he would have a chance to witness and take part in an encounter between the Russians and the French, the first since the time of Suvorof.

But he feared lest Bonaparte's genius should show itself superior to all the valor of the Russian troops, and at the same time he could not bear the thought of his hero suffering disgrace.

Agitated and stirred by these thoughts, Prince Andreï started for his room to write his father, to whom he sent a daily letter. In the corridor he fell in with his roommate, Nesvitsky, and the buffoon Zherkof; as usual, they were laughing and joking.

"Why are you so down in the mouth?" asked Nesvitsky, noticing Prince Andreï's pale face and flashing eyes.

"There's nothing to be gay about," replied Bolkonsky.

Just as Prince Andreï joined Nesvitsky and Zherkof, there came toward them from the other end of the corridor the Austrian general, Strauch, who was attached to Kutuzof's staff to look after the commissariat of the Russian army. He was with the member of the Hofkriegsrath, who had arrived the evening before.

There was plenty of room in the wide corridor for the generals to pass without incommoding the three officers; but Zherkof, giving Nesvitsky a push, exclaimed in a hurried voice:—

"They are coming!.... they are coming!.... Stand aside, please! Please make room!"

The generals came along, evidently desiring to avoid embarrassing etiquette. A stupid smile of pleasure spread over the buffoon Zherkof's face; it was plain that he could not repress it.

"Your excellency," said he, in German, as he stepped forward and addressed the Austrian general, "I have the honor of congratulating you."

He made a low bow, and, awkwardly, like a child learning to dance, began to scrape first with one foot, then with the other.

The member of the Hofkriegsrath gave him a stern look; but, concluding by his idiotic smile that he was in earnest, he was constrained to listen for a moment. He frowned, to show that he was listening.

"I have the honor of congratulating you! General Mack has come; he's perfectly well, save for a slight wound here," said he, with a radiant smile, pointing to his head.

The general frowned, and turned away,—and went on his way.

"Gott! what simplicity!" said he, angrily, after he had gone a few steps.

Nesvitsky, with a laugh, threw his arms around Prince Andreï; but the latter, paler than ever, and with a wrathful look on his face, pushed him aside, and turned to Zherkof. The nervous excitement induced by the sight of Mack, by the news of his defeat, and the thoughts of what was awaiting the Russian army, found its outlet in wrath at this ill-timed jest of Zherkof's.

"If you, my dear sir," he exclaimed scornfully, while his lower jaw twitched a little, "choose to be a buffoon, why, I cannot hinder you; but I assure you that if you *dare* a second time to act like a fool in my presence, I will teach you how to behave."

Nesvitsky and Zherkof were so amazed at this outburst that all they could do was to look in silence at Bolkónsky, with wide-open eyes.

"Why, I only congratulated them!" said Zherkof.

"I am not jesting with you; be good enough to hold your tongue!" cried Bolkonsky, and taking Nesvitsky by the arm he drew him away from Zherkof, who found nothing to say.

"Well, now, what's the matter, brother?" asked Nesvitsky, in a soothing tone.

"What's the matter?" repeated Prince Andreï, pausing in his excitement. "Why, you know well enough, either we are officers in the service of our Tsar and our country, rejoicing at our common success and grieving over our common failure, or we are 'lackeys,' who have no interest in our master's concerns. Forty thousand men massacred and the army of our allies destroyed, and still you find it something to laugh at!" said he, as if these last sentences, which were spoken in French, added to the effect of what he was saying. "It is well enough for a trifler like that fellow whom you have made your friend, but not for you, not for you. Only silly boys could find amusement in such things," said Prince Andreï, suddenly changing to Russian again, but pronouncing the Russian word for silly boys with a French accent. Noticing that Zherkof was still within hearing, he waited to see if the cornet had any answer to make. But Zherkof had turned away and was going down the corridor.

CHAPTER IV

THE Pavlograd regiment of hussars was encamped two miles from Braunau. The squadron in which Nikolaï Rostof served as yunker was quartered in the German village of Salzeneck. The squadron commander, Captain Denísof, who was known to the entire cavalry division as Vaska Denísof, had been assigned to the best house in the village. Yunker Rostof had shared the captain's quarters ever since he joined the regiment in Poland.

On the very same October day, when at headquarters all had been thrown into excitement by the news of Mack's defeat, the camp life of the squadron was going on in its usual tranquil course. Denísof, who had been playing a losing game of cards all night long, had not yet returned to his rooms, when Rostof early in the morning rode up on horseback from his foraging tour. He was in his yunker uniform, and, as he galloped up to the doorstep and threw over his leg with the agile dexterity of youth, he paused a moment in the stirrup, as if sorry to dismount, but at last sprang lightly from the horse and called the orderly.

"Hey! Bondarenko, my dear fellow," he shouted to the hussar who hurried forward to attend to the horse. "Lead him about a little, my friend," said he, with that fraternal geniality with which handsome young men are apt to treat everybody when they are happy.

"I will, your illustriousness," replied the little Russian,[1] gayly shaking his head.

"See that you walk him about well."

Another hussar also hastened up to attend to the horse, but Bondarenko had already taken the bridle. It was evident that the yunker gave handsome fees and that it was a pleasure to serve him. Rostof smoothed

[1] *Khokhól*, literally Topknot, a nickname of the Malo-Russians.

the horse's neck, then his flank, and turned and looked
back from the step.

"Excellent! He'll be a horse worth having!" said
he to himself, and then smiling and picking up his saber
he mounted the steps with clinking spurs.

The German who owned the house glanced up as he
worked in his shirt-sleeves and nightcap, pitching over
manure in the cow-house. The German's face always
lighted at the sight of Rostof. He gayly smiled and
winked : —

"Good-morning, good-morning!" he reiterated, evidently taking great satisfaction in giving the young
man his morning greeting.

"Busy already?" asked Rostof, with the same good-
natured, friendly smile, which so well became his animated face. "Hurrah for the Austrians! hurrah for
the Russians! hurrah for the Kaiser Alexander!" he
shouted, repeating the words which his German host was
fond of saying. The German laughed, came out from
the door of the cow-house, took off his nightcap, and
waving it over his head, cried, "Hurrah for the whole
world!"

Rostof, following the German's example, waved his
forage cap around his head, and with a merry laugh
shouted, *"Und vivat die ganze Welt !* — Long live the
whole world!"

Although there was no special reason for rejoicing,
either on the part of the German who was engaged in
pitching manure, or of Rostof, who had been on a long
ride with his men after hay, nevertheless both of these
men looked at each other with joyous enthusiasm and
brotherly love, nodded their heads to show that they
understood each other, and then separated with a smile,
the German to his cow-house, and Rostof to the cottage
which he and Denísof shared together.

"What is your master doing?" he asked of Lavrushka, Denísof's rascally valet, who was known to the
whole regiment.

"He hasn't been in since evening. Probably been
losing at cards," replied Lavrushka. "I have learned

that, if he has good luck, he comes in early and in high spirits, but if he does not get in before morning, it means he 's been losing, and he 'll come in mad enough. Will you have coffee ? "

"Yes, give me some."

In less than ten minutes, Lavrushka brought the coffee. "He 's coming," said he, "now we 'll get it ! "

Rostof glanced out of the window and saw Denísof meandering home. He was a little man, with a red face, brilliant black eyes, and black mustache, and hair all in disorder. He wore a hussar's pelisse unbuttoned, wide, sagging pantaloons, and a hussar's cap, crumpled on the back of his head. He came up the steps in a gloomy mood, with hanging head.

"Lav'ushka," he cried in a loud, surly voice, "here, you blockhead — take this off ! "

"Don't you see I am taking it off ? " replied Lavrushka's voice.

"Ah, you are up alweady ? " asked Denísof, as he came into the cottage.

"Long ago ! " replied Rostof. "I have been after hay and I saw Fräulein Mathilde ! "

"So ho ! and there I have been, bwother, losing howibly all night, like a son of a dog ! " cried Denísof, swallowing his R's. "Such howid bad luck ! Peffectly howid ! The moment you left, luck changed. Hey there, tea ! "

Denísof snarled with a sort of smile, which showed his short, sound teeth, and began to run the short fingers of both hands through his thick, black hair, that stood up like a forest.

"The devil himself dwove me to that Wat" (the officer's nickname was the Rat), said he, rubbing his forehead and face with both hands. "Just imagine ! Did n't have a single cahd, not one, not a single one ! "

Denísof took the pipe which had been handed to him already lighted, grasped it in his fist, and knocked it on the floor, scattering the fire, shouting all the time : —

"Simple stakes, lose the doubles, simple stakes, lose the doubles." He scattered the fire, broke his pipe in two, and flung it away. Then, after a silence, he suddenly looked up at Rostof with his bright, black eyes full of merriment : —

"If there were only some women here. But here there's nothing to do but dwink. If we could only have a wound of fighting! .... Hé! who's there?" he cried, going to the door, on hearing the sound of heavy boots and the jingling of spurs in the next room.

"The quartermaster," announced Lavrushka. Denísof frowned still more portentously.

"Dwat it," he exclaimed, flinging his friend a purse containing a few gold pieces. "Wostof, count it, chicken! see how much is left, then put it under my pillow," said he, and went out to see the quartermaster.

Rostof took the money, and mechanically making little heaps of the new and old coins, according to their denominations, began to count them.

"Ah! Telyanin! How d'e? Got done up last night!" Denísof was heard saying in the next room.

"Where? At Buikof's — at the Rat's — I heard about it," said a second, thin voice, and immediately after, Lieutenant Telyánin, a young officer of the same squadron, came into the room.

Rostof thrust the purse under the pillow and pressed the little moist hand that was held out to him. Telyanin had been removed from the Guards, shortly before the campaign, for some reason or other. He now conducted himself very decently in the regiment, but he was not liked, and Rostof, especially, could not conquer, or even conceal, his unreasonable antipathy to this officer.

"Well, young cavalier, how does my Grachik suit you?" (Grachik, or Young Rook, was a saddle-horse which Telyanin had sold Rostof). The lieutenant never looked the man with whom he was talking straight in the eye ; his eyes were constantly wandering from one object to another. "I saw you riding him this morning."

"First-rate, he's a good horse," said Rostof, in spite of the fact that the animal, for which he had given seven hundred rubles, was worth only half the price he had paid. "He's begun to go lame of the left fore leg."

"Hoof cracked! That's nothing. I will teach you or show you what kind of a rivet to put on."

"Yes, show me, please," said Rostof.

"I will show you, certainly I will; it's no secret. And you will thank me for the horse."

"I'll have him brought right round," said Rostof, anxious to get rid of Telyanin, and went out to give his orders.

In the entry, Denísof, with a pipe in his mouth, was sitting cross-legged on the threshold in front of the quartermaster, who was making his report. When he saw Rostof, Denísof made up a face and, pointing with his thumb over his shoulder into the room where Telyanin was, scowled still more darkly, and shuddered with aversion.

"Okh! I don't like that young fellow," said he, undeterred by the quartermaster's presence.

Rostof shrugged his shoulders, as much as to say, 'Nor I, either, but what is to be done about it,' and, having given his orders, returned to Telyanin.

The latter was still sitting in the same indolent position in which Rostof had left him, rubbing his small, white hands.

"What repugnant people one has to meet," said Rostof to himself, as he went into the room.

"Well, did you order the horse brought round?" asked Telyanin, getting up and carelessly looking around.

"I did."

"Come on, then. I just went out to ask Denísof about to-day's orders; that was all. Have they come yet, Denísof?"

"Not yet. Where are you going?"

"Oh, I am just going to show this young man how to have his horse shod," replied Telyánin.

They went out down the front steps to the stable. The lieutenant showed Rostof how to have a rivet made, and then went home.

When Rostof returned, he found Denísof sitting at

the table with a bottle of vodka and a sausage before him, and writing with a sputtering pen. He looked gloomily into Rostof's face.

"I 'm witing to her," said he.

He leaned his elbow on the table, with his pen in his hand, and told his friend what his letter was to be, evidently taking real delight in the chance of saying faster than he could write all that he had in his mind to put on the paper.

"Do you see, my fwiend," said he, "we are asleep when we are not in love. We are childwen of the dust; but when you are in love, then you are like God, you are as pure as on the first day of kweation. — Who is there now? Send him to the devil. I have no time!" he cried to Lavrushka, who came up to him, not in the least abashed.

"What can I do? It's your own order. It's the quartermaster come back for the money."

Denísof scowled, opened his mouth to shout something, but made no sound.

"Nasty job," he muttered to himself. "How much money was there left in that purse?" he asked of Rostof.

"Seven new pieces and three old ones."

"Akh, dwat it! — Well, what are you standing there for like a booby; fetch in the quartermaster," cried Denísof to Lavrushka.

"Please, Denísof, take some of my money; you see I have plenty," said Rostof, reddening.

"I don't like to bowow of my fwiends, I don't like it," declared Denísof.

"But if you don't let me lend you money, comrade fashion, I shall be offended!" insisted Rostof. "Truly, I have plenty."

"No, indeed, I shan't," and Denísof went to the bed to get the purse from under the pillow.

"Where did you put it, Wostof?"

"Under the bottom pillow."

"It is n't here." Denísof flung both pillows on the floor. There was no purse there. "That's stwange."

"Hold on, did n't you throw it out?" asked Rostof, picking up the pillows and shaking them, and then hauling off the bedclothes and shaking them. But there was no purse.

"I could not have forgotten it, could I? No, I remember very well thinking how you kept it like a treasure trove, under your pillow. — Where is it?" he demanded, turning to Lavrushka.

"I have n't been into the room. It must be where you put it."

"But it is n't."

"That is always the way with you. You throw it down, and then forget all about it. Look in your pockets."

"No, if I had not thought about the treasure trove" .... said Rostof, "and I remember putting it there."

Lavrushka tore the whole bed apart, looked under it, under the table, searched everywhere in the room, and then stood still in the middle of the room. Denísof silently followed all his motions, and when Lavrushka in amazement spread open his hands, he glanced at Rostof.

"Wostof, stop your school-boy twicks....."

Rostof, conscious of Denísof's gaze fixed upon him, raised his eyes and instantly dropped them again. All the blood, till then contained somewhere below his throat, rushed in an overmastering flood into his face and eyes. He could not get a breath.

"There has been no one in the room except the lieutenant and yourselves. It 's nowhere to be found," said Lavrushka.

"Now, you devil's puppet, fly awound, hunt for it," suddenly cried Denísof, growing livid, and starting toward the valet with a threatening gesture. "Find me that purse or I 'll soak you! I 'll soak you all!"

Rostof, avoiding Denisof's glance, began to button up his jacket, adjusted his saber, and put on his cap.

"I tell you, give me that purse," cried Denísof, shaking his man by the shoulders and pushing him against the wall.

"Denísof, let him go, I know who took it," said Rostof, going toward the door and not lifting his eyes.

Denísof paused, considered a moment, and evidently perceiving whom Rostof meant, he seized him by the arm. "Wubbish!" he cried, the veins on his face and neck standing out like cords. "I tell you, you are beside yourself and I won't have it. The purse is here. I 'll take the hide off this waskal and I 'll get it."

"I know who took it," repeated Rostof, in a trembling voice, and went to the door.

"But I tell you, don't you dare to do it!" cried Denísof, throwing himself on the yunker, to hold him back. But Rostof freed his arm, and, with as much anger as if Denísof were his worst enemy, gave him a direct and heavy blow right between the eyes.

"Do you realize what you are saying?" he cried in a trembling voice. "He is the only person besides myself who has been in the room. Of course if it was not he, then...."

He could not finish, and rushed from the room.

"Akh! the devil take you and all the west," were the last words that Rostof caught.

He went straight to Telyanin's rooms.

"My master 's not at home; he went to headquarters," said Telyanin's man. "Why, has anything happened?" he added, surprised at the yunker's distorted face.

"No, nothing!"

"You just missed him," said the man.

Headquarters were three versts [1] from Salzeneck. Rostof, without returning home, took a horse and galloped off to headquarters. In the village occupied by the staff was a tavern where the officers resorted. Rostof went to this tavern; at the doorsteps he saw Telyanin's horse.

The lieutenant himself was sitting in the second room of the tavern with a plate of sausages and a bottle of wine.

[1] A verst is 3500 feet, 1067 kilometers.

"Ah! so you have come too, young man," said he, smiling and lifting his brows.

"Yes," said Rostof, though it required the greatest effort to speak this monosyllable; and he sat down at the next table.

Neither said more; two Germans and a Russian officer were the other occupants of the room. All were silent, and the only sounds were the rattle of knives and forks and the lieutenant's munching.

When Telyanin had finished his breakfast, he pulled out of his pocket a double purse, and, with his delicate white fingers which turned up at the ends, slipped up the ring, took out a gold piece, and, lifting his brows, gave it to the waiter.

"Please make haste," said he.

The gold piece was new. Rostof got up and went to Telyanin.

"Allow me to look at your purse," said he, in a quiet, almost inaudible voice.

With wandering eyes and still lifted brows, Telyánin handed him the purse.

"Yes, it's a handsome little purse, is n't it? Yes...." said he, and suddenly turned pale. "Look at it, youngster," he added.

Rostof took the purse into his hand and looked at it and at the money that was in it and at Telyanin. The lieutenant glanced around in his usual way, and apparently became suddenly very merry.

"If we ever get to Vienna I shall leave all this there, but there's nothing to get with it in these filthy little towns," said he. "Well, give it back to me, youngster, I must be going."

Rostof said nothing.

"And you? Are n't you going to have some breakfast? Pretty good fare," continued Telyanin. "Give it to me."

He stretched out his hand and took hold of the purse. Rostof let it go. Telyanin took the purse and began to let it slip into the pocket of his riding-trousers and his brows went up higher than usual, and his mouth slightly parted as much as to say: 'Yes, yes, I will put my purse in my pocket, and it is a very simple matter, and it is no one's business at all.'

"Well, what is it, youngster," said he, sighing and glancing into Rostof's eyes from under his raised brows. Something like a swift electric flash darted from Telyanin's eyes into Rostof's and was darted back again and again and again all in a single instant.

"Come here with me," said Rostof, taking Telyanin by the arm. He drew him almost to the window. "This money is Denísof's! You took it," he whispered in his ear.

"What?.... What?.... How do you dare? What?".... exclaimed Telyanin. But his words sounded like a mournful cry of despair and a prayer for forgiveness. As soon as Rostof heard this note in his voice it seemed as if a great stone of doubt had fallen from his heart. He was rejoiced, and at the same time felt sincere pity for the unhappy man standing before him; but he was obliged to carry the matter to the end. "There are men here; God knows what they will think," stammered Telyanin, seizing his cap and starting for a small unoccupied room. "We must have an explanation. ....."

"I know this and can prove it," said Rostof.

"I...."

All the muscles of Telyanin's scared pale face began to tremble, his eyes kept wandering, though they were fixed on the floor, and never once raised to Rostof's, and something like a sob escaped from him.

"Count!.... don't ruin a young man. Here's that wretched money, take it." He threw it on the table. "I have a father who's an old man; I have a mother!"

Rostof took the money, avoiding Telyanin's gaze, and, not saying a word, started to leave the room. But at the door he paused and turned back. "My God!" said he, with tears in his eyes; "how could you have done it?"

"Count!" said Telyanin, coming toward the yunker.

"Don't touch me," cried Rostof, drawing himself up. "If you need this money, take it." He tossed him the purse, and hurried out of the tavern.

CHAPTER V

ON the evening of the same day a very lively discussion took place in Denísof's rooms among some of the officers of the squadron.

"But I tell you, Rostof, that it's your business to apologize to the regimental commander," said the second cavalry-captain, a tall man, with grayish hair, enormous mustache, and big features and a wrinkled skin.

This Captain Kirsten had twice been reduced to the ranks for affairs of honor, and twice promoted again.

"I will not allow any one to call me a liar," cried Rostof, who flushed crimson and was in a great state of excitement. "He told me that I lied, and I told him that he lied. And there the matter rests. He may keep me on duty every day; he may put me under arrest; but neither he nor any one else can force me to apologize. If he, as regimental commander, considers it improper to give me satisfaction, then...."

"Yes, yes, calm yourself, bátyushka, listen to me," interrupted Captain Kirsten, in his deep bass voice, calmly twirling his mustaches. "You told the regimental commander, in the *presence of other officers*, that an officer had stolen...."

"It wasn't my fault that the conversation took place before other officers. Maybe it was not best to have spoken before them, but I am not a diplomat. That's why I joined the hussars; I thought that here, at least, such fine distinctions were not necessary, and he told me that I lied.... So let him give me satisfaction....."

"That's all very good; no one thinks that you are a coward, but that is n't the point. Ask Denísof — put it to any one — if a yunker can demand satisfaction of his regimental commander."

Denísof, chewing his mustache, was listening to the discussion with a gloomy expression of countenance, evidently not wishing to take any part in it. In reply to the captain's question, he shook his head.

"In the presence of other officers, you spoke to the

regimental commander about this rascality," continued the second captain. "Bogdanuitch"[1] (so the regimental commander was called), "Bogdanuitch shut you up."

"He did not shut me up; he told me that I was telling a falsehood."

"Well, have it so, but you said foolish things to him and you ought to apologize."

"Not for the world!" cried Rostof.

"I did not think that of you," said the captain, seriously and sternly. "You are unwilling to apologize, and yet, batyushka, you are in fault, not only toward him, but toward the whole regiment, toward all of us. This is the way of it: if you had only thought, if you had only taken advice as to how to move in this matter, but no; you out with it, — right before other officers too. Well, then, what can the regimental commander do? Must he bring the officer before a court-martial and disgrace the whole regiment? Insult the whole regiment on account of a single rogue? Is that your idea of it? Well, it is n't ours! And Bogdanuitch was a brave fellow; he told you that you were not telling the truth. Disagreeable, but what else could he do? You found your match. And now, when we want to hush it up, you — out of sheer obstinacy and pride — are n't willing to apologize, but want to have everybody know about it. You are offended because you are put on extra duty, because you are required to apologize to an old and honored officer! Even if it were not Bogdánuitch, our honorable and brave old colonel, even then you would be offended and would be willing to insult the whole regiment, would you?" The captain's voice began to tremble. "Yes, batyushka, you, who will perhaps not be in the regiment a year from now, to-day here, to-morrow transferred somewhere as aide, you don't care a fig if it is said: *thieves* among the Pavlograd officers. But it is n't all the same to us. What do you say, Denísof? It is n't a matter of indifference, is it?"

---

[1] Karl Bogdánovitch Schubert, sportively called, in imitation of peasant usage, by the diminished form of the patronymic, Bogdánuitch, son of Bogdan (Deodat or Theodore).

Denísof had kept silent all the time, and did not move, though he occasionally glanced at Rostof from his brilliant black eyes.

"Your pride is so dear to you that you are n't willing to apologize," continued the captain. "We old men who have grown up and are going to die, if God grant, in the regiment, guard its honor dearly, and Bogdanuitch knows it. Oh! how we love it, batyushka! And this is not good of you, not good at all! Get mad if you please, but I shall always stick to mother truth. You 're all wrong."

And the captain got up and turned his back on Rostof.

"Wight! Devil take it!" screamed Denísof, jumping up. "Now then, Wostof, now then!"

Rostof, flushing and turning pale, looked first at one and then at the other officer.

"No, gentlemen, no .... you do not think .... I see that you are perfectly mistaken in your opinion of me .... I .... for my own sake .... for the honor of the regiment — what am I saying? And I will prove it, that for my own sake also honor is dear. — Well, it 's all the same, you 're right, I was to blame!" Tears stood in his eyes. "I was to blame, to blame all round. .... Now what more do you want?" ....

"That 's the way to do it," cried the captain, turning round and slapping him on the shoulder with his big hand.

"I tell you!" cried Denísof, "he 's a glowious young fellow!"

"That 's the best way, count," repeated the captain, as if giving him his title was a reward for his concession. "Go and apologize, your illustriousness,[1] that 's it."

"Gentlemen, I will do anything. No one shall ever hear another word from me," declared Rostof in a low, supplicating voice, "but I cannot apologize; by God, I cannot! how can you expect it? How can I apologize like a little boy, begging forgiveness?"

Denísof laughed.

[1] *Vashe siydtelstvo.*

"So much the worse for you. Bogdánuitch is spite-ful. You will pay for your stubbornness," said Kirsten.

"By God! 't is not stubbornness! I cannot describe to you what my feelings are, I assure you, I cannot."

"Well, do just as you please," said the captain. "By the way, what has become of that worthless scamp?" asked he, of Denísof.

"He weported himself ill. He's to be stwuck off the list in to-mowow's orders," replied Denísof.

"Well, it is a kind of illness, there's no other way of explaining it," said the captain.

"Whether illness or not, he'd better not come into my sight, I'd kill him," cried Denísof, in a most bloodthirsty manner.

At this instant, Zherkof came into the room.

"How come you here?" exclaimed the officer, ad-dressing the newcomer.

"Active service, gentlemen. Mack and his army have surrendered; it's all up with them."

"Nonsense!"

"I saw him myself."

"What! you saw Mack alive — with his hands and his feet?"

"Active service! active service! give him a bottle, for bringing such news! — But how come you here?"

"I am sent back to my regiment on account of that devil of a Mack! The Austrian general complained of me. I congratulated him on Mack's arrival. .... How are you, Rostof? just out of a bath?"

"My dear boy, we've been having such a stew here, these two days!"

The regimental adjutant came in and confirmed the news brought by Zherkof. The regiment was ordered to break camp the next day.

"Active service, gentlemen."

"Well, glory to God for that, we've lain here long enough!"

CHAPTER VI

KUTUZOF was retreating toward Vienna, destroying
the bridges behind him over the river Inn (at Braunau),
and over the river Traun at Linz. On the fourth of
November, the Russian army were crossing the river
Enns. At noon, the baggage-wagons, the artillery, and
the columns of the army stretched through the city of
Enns, at both ends of the bridge. It was a mild autumn
day, but showery. The wide prospect, commanded by
the height where stood the Russian batteries protecting
the bridge, was now suddenly veiled by a muslin-like curtain of slanting rain, then again was suddenly still further
broadened so that distant objects stood out distinctly,
gleaming in the sunlight as if they were varnished.

At their feet lay the little city, with its white houses
and red roofs, its cathedral, and the bridge, on both ends
of which the Russian troops could be seen, pouring
along in dense masses. Down the bend of the Danube,
where it was joined by the waters of the Enns, could be
seen boats and an island with a castle and park ; farther still was the left bank of the river, with bold rocks
and overgrown with evergreens, while in the mysterious
distance arose green mountains with purplish ravines.
The turrets of a nunnery stood out above the wild and
apparently impenetrable pine forest, and far away, on
a height in front, on the same side of the river Enns,
the enemy's scouts could be discerned.

On the brow of the hill, among the field-pieces, stood
the general in command of the rear-guard, with an
officer of his suite, making observations of the landscape with a glass. A little behind them, astride of a
gun-carriage, sat Nesvitsky, who had been sent to the
rear-guard by the commander-in-chief. The Cossack
who accompanied him was handing out a lunch-bag and
flask, and Nesvitsky was inviting the officers to share
his tarts and genuine doppel-kümmel. The officers
gayly crowded around him, some on their knees, others
sitting Turkish fashion on the wet grass.

"Certainly that Austrian prince was no fool in building his castle there. Glorious place! — You are not eating anything, gentlemen," said Nesvitsky.

"Thank you cordially, prince," returned one of the officers, glad of the chance to exchange a word with such an important member of Kutuzof's suite. "Yes, it's a splendid place. We rode by that very park, saw a couple of deer — and it's a magnificent house!"

"Look, prince," said another, who would very gladly have accepted another tart, but was ashamed to do so, and was, therefore, pretending to examine the landscape. "Look yonder, our infantry have got in already. Look there, on that meadow, behind the village, three men are dragging something along. They'll clear out that little place, quick enough!" said he, with evident approval.

"Yes, that's so," said Nesvitsky. "Ah! but what I should like," he added, stuffing a tart into his handsome moist mouth, "I should like to get in yonder!"

He pointed to the turreted convent which could be seen on the mountain side. He smiled, and his eyes contracted and flashed. "That would be some fun, gentlemen!"

The officers laughed.

"How I should like to frighten those little nuns! Italians, they say, and some of them young and pretty. Truly, I would give five years of my life!"

"Well, they must find it a bore," said an officer, bolder than the rest, with a laugh.

Meantime, the officer of the suite, standing on the brow of the hill, was pointing out something to the general, who scrutinized it with his field-glass.

"Yes, that is so, that is so," said the general, gravely, taking the glass from his eyes and shrugging his shoulders. "You are right, they are going to fire at them as they cross the river. Why do they dawdle so?"

In that direction, even with the naked eye, could be seen the enemy and his battery, from which arose a milk-white puff of smoke. After a while followed the distant report, and it could be seen how the Russian troops were hastening to get across the river.

Nesvitsky, having got his breath, dismounted from the cannon and, with a smile, went up to the general : —

"Would n't your excellency like to have a bite of luncheon?" he asked.

"It 's all wrong," said the general, not answering him. "Our men are so slow."

"Shall I not go down to them, your excellency?" asked Nesvitsky.

"Yes, do go down, please," replied the general, reiterating orders which he had already given. "And tell the hussars to cross last and burn the bridge, as I commanded, and see to it that they collect combustible materials on it."

"Very good," said Nesvitsky.

He called the Cossack to bring up his horse, bade him pack up the bag and flask, and lightly swung his heavy body into the saddle.

"Truly, I 'm going to that nunnery," said he to the officers, who were looking at him with a smile, and then galloped off down the path that skirted the hill.

"Now, then, captain, try if you can reach them — take good aim," said the general, turning to the artillery officer. "You 'll relieve the monotony by a little fun."

"Serve the guns," commanded the officer, and in a minute the gunners were running with a will from their bivouac fires, and beginning to load.

"Number one," rang the command.

"Number one" rushed spitefully away. With a deafening metallic ring, the cannon resounded and the whizzing, whirling shell flew far away over the head of the Russians in the valley, and then a spurt of smoke showed where it had fallen and burst long before it reached the enemy.

The faces of officers and men grew radiant at the noise of it; all leaped to their feet and watched with intense curiosity the motions of their troops in the valley below them, and the approach of the enemy, all spread out before them "as on the palm of the hand."

At the moment the gun had been fired, the sun came out entirely from under the clouds, and the report of the cannon and the brilliancy of the unclouded sun mingled in one single martial and joyous impression.

CHAPTER VII

Two of the enemy's shots had already been fired at the men as they crossed the river, and on the bridge there was a jam. Half way across stood Prince Nesvitsky, who had dismounted from his horse, and was leaning with his stout body against the parapet. Laughing, he looked back at his Cossack, who stood a short distance behind him, holding the bridles of their two horses. As soon as Prince Nesvitsky tried to force his way forward, the throng of soldiers and baggage-wagons crowded him and forced him up against the parapet, and nothing was left for him but to wait.

"Look out there, my boy!" cried the Cossack to a soldier who was driving a baggage-wagon and forcing his way right into the infantry, as they thronged under the horses' feet and among the wheels. "Look out there! Have a little patience, don't you see the general wants to pass?"

But the driver, paying no heed to the title of general, only cried to the soldiers who blocked his way: "Hey there, boys! keep to the left, hold on!"

But the Russian soldiers, crowding shoulder to shoulder, and clutching their bayonets, moved on across the bridge in one unbroken mass.

As Nesvitsky looked down over the parapet, he could see the swift babbling ripples of the Enns chase one another along as they bubbled, curled, and foamed around the piers of the bridge. Looking at the bridge he saw the almost incessant living waves of soldiery, tassels, shakoes with covers, knapsacks, bayonets, and long muskets, and under the shakoes, faces with wide cheek-bones, sunken cheeks, and careless weary eyes, and legs trampling through the sticky mud that covered the planks of the bridge.

Sometimes among the monotonous waves of the infantry, like a spurt of white foam on the ripples of the Enns, an officer in riding-cloak would force his way through, his face noticeable for its refinement in contrast to the men. Then again, like a chip borne along on the river, a hussar on foot, an officer, a servant, or a civilian, would be carried across the bridge by the tide of troops; and sometimes, like a log floating downstream, an officer, a company, or a baggage-wagon loaded to the top and covered with leather, would roll across the bridge, submerged in the throng.

"See, it's like a freshet breaking through a dyke," said the Cossack, hopelessly blocked. "Say! are there many more of you to come?"

"A million, minus one," replied a jolly soldier in a torn overcoat, winking as he passed. In an instant he was carried by; behind him came an old soldier.

"When *he*" (*he*, that is the enemy) "takes to making it hot for us on the bridge," said the old soldier, glumly, in his Tambof dialect, addressing a comrade, "we shan't stop to scratch ourselves." And the Tambof soldier and his comrade passed beyond.

Following them, came a soldier riding on a baggage-wagon.

"Where the devil did I put my leg wrappers?" exclaimed a servant, hurrying behind the wagon and rummaging into the rear of it. And he in turn was borne past with the wagon.

Behind them came a jovial band of soldiers, who had evidently been drinking. "My dear fellow, he hit him with the butt-end of his gun, right in the teeth," gayly said one of the soldiers, who wore the collar of his overcoat turned up and was eagerly gesticulating.

"Good for him, a regular milksop!"[1] said the other, with a loud laugh. And they too passed by. So that Nesvitsky did not find out who was struck in the teeth and to whom the epithet applied.

[1] Russ: the sweet ham.

"Bah! they 're in such a hurry! Because he fired a blank cartridge one would think they were all in danger of being killed," said a non-commissioned officer, in an angry, reproachful tone.

"When it flew by me — that round shot," said a young soldier with a monstrous mouth, " I thought I was dead. Fact! I was that frightened, by God," added the soldier, scarcely restraining himself from laughing outright with pleasure at the thought of being so frightened. And he too passed on.

Behind him came a vehicle unlike any that had passed so far. This was a German *Vorspann*, loaded apparently with the effects of a whole household; behind the cart, which was drawn by a pair of horses driven by a German, was a handsome brindled cow, with an enormous udder. On a pile of feather-beds sat a woman with a baby at the breast, an old granny, and a young, healthy-looking German girl, with flaming red cheeks. Evidently these natives were availing themselves of the general permission to remove with all their possessions. The eyes of the soldiers were fixed upon the women, and as the cart moved forward at a slow pace, step by step, all sorts of remarks were directed at the two young women. Almost all the faces wore the peculiar smile suggested by unseemly thoughts concerning them.

"Look ye, that sausage there! she 's moving too."

" Sell me the little woman," cried another soldier to the German, who with downcast eyes walked with long strides, frightened and solemn.

"Eh! ain't she gay! They 're fine little devils!"

"There 's a chance for you to make up to 'em, Fyedotof!"

" Did you ever see anything like it, old fellow?"

"Where are you going?" asked an infantry officer, who, as he munched an apple, looked up at the pretty German girl with a half-smile.

The German shut his eyes, signifying that he did not understand.

"If you 'd like it, take it," said the officer, giving the girl an apple. She took it and thanked him with a smile.

Nesvitsky, like all the rest who were on the bridge, kept his eyes on the women till they vanished from sight. After they had passed beyond, came the same kind of soldiers with the same interchange of repartee, and then at length they all came to a halt. As often happens, the horses attached to some company's baggage-wagon became entangled at the end of the bridge, and the whole line was obliged to halt.

"What are they waiting for? There's no order," said the soldiers. "Don't crowd!" — "The devil!" "Why can't you have patience!" — "It will be worse than this when *he* sets the bridge on fire." — "You're crushing that officer!"

Such were the remarks made on all sides among the halting columns, as the men looked at one another and still kept trying to push forward toward the outlet.

As Nesvitsky looked under the bridge at the water of the Enns, he suddenly heard a sound that was new in his ears — of something swiftly approaching him, ... of something huge, and something that splashed into the water.

"Did you see where that flew to?" gravely asked a soldier who was standing near and trying to follow the sound.

"They are encouraging us to move a little faster," said another uneasily. Again the throng began to move along. Nesvitsky realized that it had been a cannon-ball.

"Hé! Cossack! bring me my horse!" he said. "You there! make way, get out of the way! Clear the road!"

By main force he managed to swing himself on his horse. By shouting constantly, he succeeded in forcing his way forward. The soldiers crowded together so as to let him pass, but immediately after pressed on his heels so that they squeezed his leg, and those who were nearest could not help themselves because they were pushed on from behind.

"Nesvitsky! Nesvitsky! is it you, you old fwight?" cried a hoarse voice just behind him.

Nesvitsky turned round and saw, twenty paces away but separated from him by this living mass of hurrying infantry, the handsome Vaska Denísof, shaggy as ever, with his cap on the back of his head, and with his hussar's pelisse jauntily flung back over his shoulder.

"Tell these devils, these fiends, to give us woom," cried Denísof, going into a paroxysm of rage, his coal-black eyes, with their bloodshot whites, rolling and flashing while he brandished his unsheathed saber, in his bare little hand, as red as his face.

"Hé! Vasya," replied Nesvitsky, delighted, "is that you?"

"Can't get thwough the sqwadwon," cried Vaska Denísof, angrily, showing his shining teeth and spurring on his handsome coal-black Bedouin, which pricked back his ears at the touch of the bayonets, and, snorting and scattering around him the froth from his bit, was pawing impatiently the planks of the bridge, apparently ready to leap over the parapet, if only his rider gave the permission. "What does this mean? Like sheep! Just like sheep! Out of the way!—give us woom to pass! Hold on there, you man dwiving that wagon! dwat it! I'll cut you into mince-meat," he cried, actually drawing his saber and beginning to flourish it.

The soldiers, with frightened faces, crowded closer together, and Denísof managed to reach Nesvitsky.

"So you are n't drunk to-day?" said Nesvitsky, as Denísof joined him.

"They don't give us time to get dwunk," replied Vaska. "The wegiment has been wunning this way and that way all day long. If we're going to fight, then let us fight. But the devil knows what all this means."

"How fine you are these days!" said Nesvitsky, glancing at his new pelisse and housings.

Denísof smiled, took his scented handkerchief from his sabretash, and held it to Nesvitsky's nose.

"Can't help it! I'm going into action, pe'haps! and so I shaved, bwushed my teeth, and perfumed myself!"

Nesvitsky's imposing figure, with his Cossack in attendance, and Denísof's determination, as he flourished his saber and shouted at the top of his voice, enabled them to get to the farther end of the bridge and halt the infantry. Nesvitsky there found the colonel, to whom he was obliged to deliver the message, and having accomplished his errand he rode back.

After the way was cleared, Denísof reined up his horse at the exit of the bridge. Carelessly holding in his stallion, which stood pawing with one hoof anxious to join his fellows, he gazed at the squadrons that were moving in his direction. The hoof-beats of the eager horses sounded hollow on the flooring of the bridge, and the squadrons, with the officers riding in advance, hastened across the bridge, four men abreast, and began to pour off from the other end.

The infantry, which had halted in the mud and were packed together, gazed at the neat, jaunty hussars, riding by in good order, with that peculiar malevolent feeling of jealousy and scorn with which different branches of the service are apt to regard each other.

"Very tidy lads! but only fit for the Podnovinskoye."

"What 's the use of them? They 're merely for show," said another.

"You infantrymen, don't kick up such a dust!" jestingly shouted a hussar, whose horse playfully spattered the foot-soldier with mud.

"If you 'd been forced to march two stages with a knapsack, your gold lace would be tarnished," said the infantryman, wiping the mud from his face with his sleeve. "You 're not a man, but a bird, on that horse!"

"Well now, Zikin, if they should put you on a horse, you 'd have an easy time of it; you 'd make a graceful rider," jestingly remarked the corporal, aiming his jest at the lean little soldier who was bent almost double under the weight of his knapsack.

"Take a broomstick between your legs; that would be a good enough horse for you," retorted the hussar.

CHAPTER VIII

THE rest of the infantry hurriedly marched across the bridge, though they were crowded in the tunnel-like passage at the end. At last all the baggage-wagons had crossed, the crush became less, and the last battalion marched upon the bridge.

Only the hussars of Denísof's command were left at the end of the bridge toward the enemy. The enemy, though plainly visible from the heights opposite, could not as yet be seen from the level of the bridge, since from the valley, through which flows the river Enns, the horizon is bounded by an eminence lying about half a verst distant.

Directly in front was a plot of waste land, over which here and there moved bands of Cossack patrols.

Suddenly, on the height opposite the road, appeared troops in blue capotes and accompanied by artillery.

It was the French!

A patrol of Cossacks came galloping down the road. All the officers and men of Denísof's squadron, though they tried hard to talk of different things and to look in other directions, nevertheless were unable to keep out of their thoughts what was there before them on the hill, and their eyes constantly turned to those patches which were moving against the horizon, and which they knew were the troops of the enemy.

It was now afternoon, and the weather had cleared; the sun was sinking brilliantly over the Danube and the forest-clad mountains that walled him in. There was no wind, and occasionally from that hilltop rang the notes of bugles and the shouts of the enemy. Between the squadron and the enemy there was now no one except the scattered scouts. The space between them was only a little more than two thousand feet. The enemy had ceased to fire, and all the more distinctly was felt that solemn, ominous gap, unapproachable and inexorable, that divides two hostile armies.

"One step beyond that line, which is like the bourn that divides the living from the dead, and there is the Unknown of suffering and of death. And what is there? Who is there? there, beyond that field, beyond that tree, and that roof, glittering in the sun? No one knows, and no one wishes to know, and it is terrible to pass across that line, and I know that sooner or later I shall have to cross it, and shall then know what is there on that side of the line, just as inevitably as I shall know what is on the other side of death. And yet I am strong, full of life, joy, and exuberant spirits, and surrounded by other men, just as full of health and exuberant spirits."

Thus every man feels, even if he does not formulate it in his thought, when he comes in sight of the enemy, and this feeling lends a peculiar vividness and distinctness of impression to everything that occurs at such moments.

On the hill where the enemy were arose a puff of smoke, and a cannon-ball, whistling, flew over the heads of the squadron of hussars. The officers, who had been standing together, scattered to their posts; the hussars began to get their horses into regular line. No one spoke in the ranks. All looked intently at the enemy and at the commander, and awaited the word of command.

A second, a third shot flew over them. Evidently, the enemy were firing at the hussars, but the cannon-balls, whistling as they flew swiftly by, went far over their heads and fell somewhere in the rear.

The hussars did not look up, but each time that they heard the whizz of the ball, the whole squadron, with their monotonously diverse faces, holding their breaths until the cannon-shot had passed over, raised themselves in their stirrups as if by orders, and then settled back again. The soldiers, not turning their heads, looked at one another out of the corners of their eyes, each curious to know what impression was produced upon his neighbor. On every face, from Denísof's to the trumpeter's, there was around the lips and chin a common expression of internal struggle, excitement, and agitation. The quartermaster frowned, and looked at the men as if he meditated inflicting punishment upon them. The yunker, Mironof, ducked his head each time that the ball flew over. Rostof, posted on the left flank, on his prancing Grachik, had the delighted look of a school-boy called out before a great audience to pass his examination, in which he believes that he is going to distinguish himself. He looked at every one with a face unclouded and bright, as if asking them to bear him witness that he was perfectly calm under fire. But in even his face, the same expression, indicative of something new and solemn, showed itself around his mouth, against his will.

"Who's that making a bow, there? Yunker Miwonof, you? It is n't wight, look at me!" cried Denísof, who could not keep still, but kept riding up and down in front of the squadron.

Vaska Denísof, with his snub nose and black hair, his little bent figure, his sinewy hand with short, hairy fingers, grasping the hilt of his drawn sword, was just the same as usual, or, rather, just the same as he was apt to be in the evening, after he had been drinking a couple of bottles. Only he was a trifle ruddier than ordinary, and, carrying his head very high, like a bird when it is drinking, he pitilessly plunged the spurs into the flanks of his good Bedouin, and galloped back to the other flank of the squadron, and cried out in a hoarse voice his orders that they should examine their pistols.

Then he rode off toward Kirsten, the second captain, who came up to meet Denísof, walking his broad and steady-going mare. The captain, with his long mustaches, was as grave as usual, but his eyes flashed with unwonted brilliancy.

"Well, how is it?" said he to Denísof. "It won't come to a fight. You'll see, we shall be ordered back."

"The deuce only knows what they'll do," replied Denísof.

"Ah! Wostof!" he cried to the yunker, noticing his radiant face. "Well, now's your chance!" and he smiled approvingly, evidently feeling proud of the yunker.

Rostof felt perfectly happy. At this moment, an officer of high rank appeared on the bridge. Denísof spurred off to meet him.

"Your excellency, let us áttack 'em! I will dwive 'em back!"

"Attack them!" cried the officer, showing his annoyance in his voice, and frowning as if at a persistent fly. "And why are you delaying here? Don't you see the flankers are withdrawing. Order your squadron back."

The squadron crossed the bridge and retired beyond reach of the shots, not having lost a single man. Behind them came a second squadron which had formed the rear-guard, and, last of all, the Cossacks crossed to the farther side.

The two squadrons of the Pavlograd regiment, crossing the bridge, one after the other, galloped up the road. The regimental commander, Karl Bogdanovitch Schubert, overtook Denísof's squadron, and walked his horse along, not far from Rostof, but without giving him the slightest notice, although it was the first time that they had met since their quarrel about Telyanin.

Rostof, who realized, now that he was in line, that he was in the power of the man toward whom he felt guilty, did not take his eyes from the colonel's athletic back, the light hair at the back of his head, and his red neck. Sometimes, it seemed to Rostof that Bogdanuitch was merely pretending not to notice him, and that his whole aim now was to try the yunker's courage, and he straightened himself up and looked around him gayly; then, again, it seemed to him that Bogdánuitch rode close to him to display his own courage. Now, it occurred to him that his opponent was going to send the squadron into some forlorn hope, in order to punish him. And then again, it occurred to him that after the affray he would come to him and magnanimously extend to him the hand of reconciliation, in honor of the wound which he should receive.

The high-shouldered Zherkof, well-known to the Pavlograd boys, having not long since been in their regiment, came riding up to the regimental commander.

Zherkof, after his dismissal from the general's staff, had not remained in the regiment, saying that he was not such a fool as to put on the "tugging-collar" in the ranks, when, by serving on the staff and having nothing to do, he could gain greater rewards, and so he had succeeded in getting himself appointed as special orderly to Prince Bagration. He now came up to his former chief with a message from the commander of the rear-guard.

"Colonel," said he, with his most melancholy assumption of gravity, turning to Rostof's opponent, and glancing at his comrades, "you are ordered to halt and burn the bridge."

"Who orders it?" asked the colonel, testily.

"Well, I don't know, colonel, who orders it," replied the cornet, gravely, "but the prince said to me: 'Go and tell the colonel that the hussars are to return as quickly as possible and burn the bridge.'"

Immediately after Zherkof, an officer of the suite rode up to the colonel of hussars, with the same order. And immediately after the officer of the suite, came the stout Nesvitsky, galloping up with all his might, on his Cossack's horse, which could hardly carry him.

"How is it, colonel," he cried, while still at a distance. "I told you to burn the bridge, but now some one has mistaken the order; everybody here has lost his wits, and there's nothing done right."

The colonel took his time in halting the regiment, and turned to Nesvitsky: —

"You told me to burn up the combustibles," said he, "but as to burning that, you did not say a word."

"What's that, batyushka," exclaimed Nesvitsky, reining in his horse, taking off his cap, and with his fat hand brushing back his hair, dripping with perspiration. "How's that? Didn't I say that the bridge was to be burned, when you burned all the combustibles?"

"I won't be called batyushka by you, Mister Staff Officer, and you did not tell me to burn the bridge. I know my duties, and I am accustomed faithfully to carry out what I am commanded to do. You said the bridge was to be burned, but who was to do it, by the Holy Ghost, I could not tell." ....

"Well, that's always the way," cried Nesvitsky, with a wave of the hand. "What are you doing here?" he asked, turning to Zherkof.

"Exactly the same thing as you are! but how wet you are! let me wring you out!"

"You said, Mister Staff Officer" .... proceeded the colonel, in an offended tone.

"Colonel," interrupted the officer from the suite, "you must make haste, or else the enemy will be pouring grape-shot into us."

The colonel silently looked at the officer from the suite, at stout Prince Nesvitsky, and at Zherkof, and frowned.

"I will burn the bridge," said he, in a solemn voice, as if to express by it that in spite of all the disagreeable things that happened to him, he was always prepared to do his duty.

Spurring his horse with his long, muscular legs, as if the animal were to blame for everything, the colonel started forward, and ordered the second squadron, in which Rostof served, to return, under the command of Denísof, and burn the bridge.

"Well, that's the way it is," said Rostof to himself. "He wants to try me." His heart beat and the blood rushed to his face. "Let him see if I am a coward," he thought.

Once more, over all the happy faces of the men in the squadron appeared that same serious expression which they had worn at the time that they were under fire. Rostof, not taking his eyes from his opponent, the regimental commander, tried to discover in his face a confirmation of his suspicions; but the colonel did not once look at Rostof, but as usual gazed sternly and solemnly along the line. The word of command was heard.

"Lively! lively!" cried voices around him. With their sabers catching in the reins, with rattling spurs, the hussars dismounted in all haste, not knowing what

they were to do. They crossed themselves. Rostof
now looked no more at the colonel, he had no time.
He was afraid, afraid with a real sinking of the heart,
lest he should be left behind by the hussars. His hand
trembled as he turned his horse over to the groom, and
he felt how the blood was rushing back to his heart.
Denísof, on his way back, shouted something to him
as he passed. Rostof saw nothing except the hussars
running by his side, with impeding spurs and rattling
sabers.

"The stretchers!" cried some voice behind him, but
Rostof did not stop to think what that demand for
stretchers meant; he ran on, striving only to be in
advance of the others, but at the very bridge, not looking where he stepped, slipped in the slimy, sheeted
mud, stumbled, and fell on his hands and knees. The
others dashed ahead of him.

"At both sides, captain," shouted the regimental commander, who, having ridden ahead, had reined in his
horse not far from the bridge, and sat looking on with
a triumphant and radiant expression.

Rostof, wiping his soiled hands on his riding-trousers,
glanced at his opponent and determined to go on, thinking that the farther forward he went, the better it would
be. But Bogdanuitch, without looking at him, or even
noticing that it was Rostof, cried to him: —

"Who is that in the middle of the bridge? Take the
right side! Yunker, come back!" he shouted testily,
and then turned to Denísof, who, making a show of
his foolhardiness, was riding upon the bridge.

"Why run such risks, captain? You'd better dismount," cried the colonel.

"Hé! he always finds some one in fault," replied
Vaska Denísof, turning in his saddle.

Meantime, Nesvitsky, Zherkof, and the staff-officer
stood in a little group, out of range, and watched now
the little band of hussars, in yellow shakoes, dark-green
roundabouts embroidered with gold lace, and blue trousers, who were swarming over the bridge; and now, in

the other direction, looked at the blue capotes marching down from the distant hill, and the groups with
horses, which could easily be recognized as field-
pieces.

"Will they get the bridge burnt, or not?" — "Who
is ahead?" — "Will they have time to set the bridge
on fire, or will the French turn grape on them and
drive them back?"

Such questions as these, every man in the great band
of soldiers that was stationed near the bridge involuntarily asked himself, as he looked that bright afternoon
at the bridge, and at the hussars, and then again, on
the other side, at the blue-coats approaching with bayonets and field-pieces.

"Okh! the hussars will catch it!" exclaimed Nesvitsky. "They're within range of grape now."

"It was useless to send so many men," said the staff-
officer.

"That's a fact," returned Nesvitsky. "If he'd only
sent two smart young fellows, it would have been just
as well."

"Akh! your illustriousness," remarked Zherkof, not
taking his eyes from the hussars, but still speaking in
his own peculiar fashion, which left it in doubt whether
he were serious or in earnest, "akh! your illustriousness,
how can you think so! The idea of sending two men!
How then would we get the Vladímir and the ribbon?
Even if they do have a little thrashing, there'll be a
chance for the colonel to report the squadron and get
a ribbon for himself. Our Bogdánuitch knows a thing
or two."

"Now there," said the staff-officer, "that's grape!"
He pointed at the French field-pieces, which they
were unlimbering and bringing into range.

In the direction of the French, from the groups which
had been recognized as the artillery, they saw a puff of
smoke arise, then a second, a third, almost simultaneously, and by the time the report of the first had reached
their ears, a fourth puff arose. Two reports one after
the other, and then a third.

"O! okh!" groaned Nesvitsky, as if from excruciating agony, and seizing the staff-officer's arm. "Look, one fell, fell, one fell!"

"Two, I should think."

"If I were Tsar, there should be no more war," said Nesvitsky, turning away.

The French guns were again quickly loaded. The infantry in the blue capotes came dashing at double-quick toward the bridge. Again, at different distances, puffs of smoke appeared, and the grape pattered and rattled on the bridge. But this time Nesvitsky could not see what took place on it. A thick smoke poured up from it. The hussars had succeeded in setting fire to it, and the French field-pieces were fired at it, not, indeed, to prevent it, but because they were loaded, and there was nothing else to shoot at.

The French had succeeded in sending three charges of grape before the hussars returned to their grooms. Two of the volleys had been wildly aimed, and the grape had gone afield, but the last discharge struck into the middle of the group, and hit three hussars.

Rostof, preoccupied by his relations with Bogdanuitch, remained on the bridge, not knowing what he had to do. There was no one to cut down — he had always imagined a battle to consist of cutting down — and he could not help set fire to the bridge either, because he had not provided himself with wisps of straw, as the others had. He was standing there and looking on, when suddenly there was a rattling on the bridge as if some one had been scattering hazelnuts, and one of the hussars who happened to be nearest to him fell against the parapet with a groan. Rostof and several others ran to him. Again there was a cry for stretchers. Four men grasped the wounded hussar, and started to bear him away.

"O-o-o-o! Let me alone for Christ's sake," shrieked the wounded man, but nevertheless they took him up and bore him off. Nikolaï Rostof turned away, and, as if he were searching for something, began to gaze into the distance, at the water of the Danube, at the sky, at the sun. How beautiful the sky seemed, how blue, how calm, how profound! How bright and magnificent the sinking sun! How caressingly brilliant the waters of the distant Danube gleamed! And still more lovely were the far purpling mountains beyond the Danube, the nunnery, the mysterious defiles, the pine forests, veiled to the top in a transparent mist. There it was, full of peace and happiness.

"I should wish for nothing, wish for nothing, for nothing in the world, if only I were there," thought Rostof. "How much happiness I might have there in this sunshine, while here — groans, suffering, terror, and confusion and hurry. There again some one shrieks, and here we are all running for our lives, and I am running with the rest, and here it is, here is death, all above me and around me. A moment, and perhaps never again shall I see this sun, this river, those defiles."

At that instant the sun went into a cloud; Rostof saw several stretchers being carried before him. And the terror of death and of the stretchers, and love for the sun and for life, all mingled in one painfully disturbing impression.

"O Lord God! Thou who art there in yonder heaven, save, pardon, and defend me!" whispered Rostof in his heart.

The hussars hastened back to their grooms, their voices grew louder and more confident; the stretchers were now out of their sight.

"Well, bwother! so you 've smelt powder!" rang Vaska Denísof's voice in his ear.

"It 's all over, but I 'm a coward, yes, I 'm a coward," thought Rostof, and with a heavy sigh he took the bridle from the hands of his groom and mounted his Grachik, which was waiting for him.

"What was it, grape-shot?" asked he of Denísof.

"That 's just what it was!" shouted Denísof. "We worked like hewoes. And it was waskally work. A charge is ware sport, you hew down the dogs; but here, the devil only knows what it is, they shoot at you as if you were a target."

And Denísof rode off and joined the colonel, Nesvitsky, Zherkof, and the staff-officers, who were talking together a short distance from Rostof.

"One thing's evident, no one noticed it," thought Rostof. And in truth no one had noticed it, because each and every one shared in the sensation which the yunker experienced at being under fire for the first time.

"We shall have a splendid report sent," Zherkof was saying. "Do you know, they may give me a lieutenancy."

"Inform the prince that I burned the bridge," said the colonel, with a gay and triumphant expression.

"But suppose it is asked about our loss?"

"A mere trifle," said the colonel, in his deepest tones; "two hussars wounded and one dead," said he, with apparent joy, and scarcely refraining from a contented smile, as he brought out with ringing emphasis the happy phrase, *dead*.[1]

CHAPTER IX

THE Russian army of thirty-five thousand men, under command of Kutuzof, pursued by the French, a hundred thousand strong, under Bonaparte himself, meeting with unfriendly-disposed natives, no longer having confidence in their allies, suffering from a lack of provisions, and obliged to act in a manner opposed to all preconceived conditions of war, was in hasty retreat down the Danube, halting when the enemy overtook them, and fighting them off by skirmishes at the rear-guard, but fighting no more than was necessary to insure their retreat without losing any of their baggage.

Actions had taken place at Lambach, Amstetten, and Melck, but, notwithstanding the bravery and fortitude displayed by the Russians, as even their enemy acknowledged, these actions did not prevent their movement from being a retreat, conducted with all possible celerity.

[1] *Na-poval*, literally: without exception, totally.

The Austrians who had escaped from the surrender at Ulm, and had joined Kutuzof at Braunau, had now separated from the Russians, and Kutuzof was left only with his weakened, famished forces.

It was impossible any longer to think of defending Vienna. In place of the offensive warfare so craftily elaborated in accordance with the laws of the new science of strategy, the plan of which had been communicated to Kutuzof by the Hofkriegsrath while he was in Vienna, the only thing that was left him now, unless he were to sacrifice his army, as Mack had sacrificed his at Ulm, was to effect a juncture with the troops on their way from Russia, and even this was almost an impossibility.

On the eighth of November, Kutuzof and his army crossed to the left bank of the Danube, and, for the first time, halted, having now put the river between himself and the main body of the French. On the tenth, he attacked and defeated the division under Mortier, which was stationed on the left bank of the Danube. In this engagement, for the first time, some trophies were captured: a stand of colors, cannon, and two of the enemy's generals. For the first time, after a fortnight's retreat, the Russian army halted, and at the end of the battle not only held the field of battle, but had driven off the French.

Although the army was exhausted and in rags, and reduced a third by the killed, wounded, sick, and stragglers; although the sick and wounded had been left on the other side of the Danube, with a letter from Kutuzof commending them to the magnanimity of the enemy; although the regular hospitals and the houses of Krems, which had been turned into lazarettoes, were unable to receive all the sick and wounded remaining — still, in spite of all this, the halt at Krems and the victory over Mortier signally raised the spirits of the army.

The most gratifying but improbable reports were in circulation throughout the troops and even at headquarters, concerning imaginary reinforcements from

Russia being at hand, concerning some great victory won by the Austrians and the retreat and panic of Bonaparte.

During the battle, Prince Andreï had been near by when the Austrian general, Schmidt, was killed. His own horse had been wounded under him, and he himself had been slightly grazed by a bullet on the hand. As a sign of special favor from the commander-in-chief, he was sent to carry the news of this victory to the Austrian court, which had left Vienna, now threatened by the French, and was established at Brünn. On the evening of the victory, Prince Andreï, excited, but not weary, for, in spite of his apparently delicate constitution, he could endure physical fatigue far better than much stronger men, having brought Dokhtúrof's report to Kutúzof, was despatched that same evening as a special courier to Brünn. Such an errand insured the courier not only a decoration, but pointed infallibly to promotion.

The night was dark, but starry; the road made a black line across the snow which had been falling during the engagement. Now recalling the impressions of the battle through which he had passed, now joyfully imagining the impression which he should cause by the news of the victory, recollecting the parting words of the commander-in-chief and his comrades, Prince Andreï drove on at a furious pace in his post-carriage, experiencing the feelings of a man who has long waited and at last is about to attain his wished-for joy. As soon as he closed his eyes, his ears were filled with the roar of musketry and cannon, mingling with the rumble of the wheels and the details of the victory.

Now it seemed to him that the Russians were flying, and that he himself was killed. But he would awake with a start, feeling a strange delight in the realization that nothing of the sort had taken place, and that, on the contrary, it was the French who had been defeated. Then, again, he would recall all the details of the victory, his own serene manliness during the engagement, and his recollections would lull him to sleep again.

The dark, starry night was followed by a bright, joyous day. The snow gleamed in the sunshine, the horses sped swiftly along, and on both sides new woods, fields, and villages in never ending variety kept flying by.

At one of the post-houses he overtook a train of Russian wounded. A Russian officer in charge of the convoy was stretched out in the foremost cart, and shouting at the top of his voice, and scolding the soldiers in coarse language.

The long German vorspanns, each containing six or more wounded, pale and bandaged and dirty, jolted heavily along over the rough, paved road. Some of them were talking (Prince Andreï overheard their Russian speech), others were munching bread, while those who were most seriously hurt gazed with the good-natured and childish curiosity of sickness at the courier hurrying by them.

Prince Andreï ordered the driver to stop, and asked one of the soldiers where they had been wounded.

"Day before yesterday on the Danube," replied the soldier.

Prince Andreï took out his purse and gave the soldier three gold pieces.

"For them all," he added, turning to the officer in command. "Get well as fast as you can, boys," said he to the soldiers, "there's still much to be done."

"Well, Mister Aide, what's the news?" asked the officer, evidently taking a fancy to have a talk.

"Good news! — Forward," he cried to his driver, and he was borne swiftly on.

It was already quite dark when Prince Andreï reached Brünn and found himself surrounded by lofty houses, lighted shops, and street lamps, handsome carriages rumbling over the wooden pavements, and by all that atmosphere of a large, lively city which is always so fascinating to a soldier after camp-life.

Prince Andreï, notwithstanding the celerity of his journey and his sleepless night, felt as he drove up to the palace even more excited than he had the evening before. His eyes gleamed with a feverish light, and his thoughts rushed through his mind with extraordinary rapidity and clearness. Vividly all the details of the battle came into his mind, not with any confusion, but in due sequence, word for word, as he imagined he should render his account to the Emperor Franz.

Vividly he imagined the circumstantial questions which might be asked him, and the answers which he should make to them. He supposed that he should be immediately summoned before the emperor. But at the principal entrance of the palace he was met by an official who, discovering that he was only a courier, sent him around to another entrance.

"Take the corridor at the right, *Euer Hochgeboren*, there you will find the Flügel-adjutant, who is on duty," said the official. "He will take you to the minister of war."

The Flügel-adjutant, coming to meet Prince Andreï, asked him to wait while he went to the minister. In five minutes he returned, and, bowing with unusual deference and allowing Prince Andreï to pass in front of him, directed him through a corridor into a private office occupied by the minister of war. The Flügel-adjutant, by his extravagant politeness, seemed to be trying to defend himself from any attempt at familiarity on the part of the Russian courier. Prince Andreï's exultant feeling was decidedly cooled down the moment he entered the door into the minister's private office. He felt humiliated, and this feeling of wounded pride changed instantly, but imperceptibly, into a feeling of contempt which had no reasonable cause. His fertile mind at the same moment began to search for a point of view according to which he might be justified in scorning both the Flügel-adjutant and the minister of war.

"It's probably very easy for them to show how to gain victories, though they have never smelt gunpowder," he said to himself.

His eyes contracted contemptuously; he walked into the war minister's private office with all the deliberation in the world. The feeling was still further intensified when he caught sight of that dignitary sitting between two candles at a great table, and not even glancing at his visitor for the first two minutes.

The war minister's bald head with its fringe of gray hair was bent over some papers which he was reading and marking with a lead-pencil. He finished reading them, not even lifting his head when the door opened to admit his visitor, though he must have heard the steps.

"Take this and deliver it at once," said the minister of war to his secretary, handing him some papers, and not even yet recognizing the existence of the courier.

Prince Andreï came to the conclusion that, out of all the affairs that preoccupied the minister of war, the feats of Kutuzof's army either interested him the least, or else he felt obliged to give this impression to the Russian courier. "Well, it's all the same to me," said he to himself.

The minister of war assorted the rest of his papers, placing them in regular order, and then at last lifted his head. He had an intelligent and determined face, but at the instant that he turned to Prince Andreï, this intelligent and firm expression seemed to change as if by purpose and consciously, and in its place came a dull, hypocritical smile, in which there was no pretence even of hiding its hypocrisy, — the habitual smile of a man accustomed to receiving many petitioners one after the other.

"From General Field Marshal Kutuzof?" he asked. "I hope it is good news. So he's had an encounter with Mortier? A victory? It was time!"

He took the despatch which was directed to him and began to read it with a melancholy expression.

"Ach, mein Gott! mein Gott! Schmidt!" said he, in German. "What a misfortune! what a misfortune!" Having run through the paper, he laid it on the table and glanced at Prince Andreï, evidently weighing something in his mind. "Ach! what a misfortune! The affair, you say, was decisive? But Mortier was not taken." He pondered. "I 'm very glad that you have brought this good news, although the death of Schmidt is a costly price to pay for the victory. His majesty will probably desire to see you, but not this evening. I thank you; go and get rested. To-morrow be at the levee after the parade. However, I will give you due notice."

The dull smile, which had disappeared during this conversation, again appeared on the war minister's face.

"Good-by. *Auf wiedersehen* — I thank you very much. His majesty the emperor will no doubt wish to see you," he repeated, and inclined his head.

When Prince Andreï had left the palace he felt that all the interest and happiness which the victory had brought him had deserted him, and had been left behind in the indifferent hands of the war minister and of the polite Flügel-adjutant. The whole course of his thoughts had instantly changed; the battle seemed to him like the recollection of something that had happened long before.

CHAPTER X

PRINCE ANDREÏ put up at Brünn at the residence of his friend, the diplomat Bilibin.

"Ah! my dear prince, no one could be more welcome," said Bilibin, coming down to greet him. "Franz, take the prince's luggage into my sleeping-room," he added, turning to the valet that had admitted the visitor. "So you 're bringing news of a victory. Excellent! But I 'm under the weather, as you can see."

Prince Andreï, having washed and changed his dress, joined the diplomat in his luxurious study, and sat down to the dinner which had been prepared for him. Bilibin drew up comfortably before the fire.

After his hurried journey, and indeed after this whole campaign, during which he had been deprived of all the comforts and elegances of life, Prince Andreï experienced a pleasant feeling of repose amid these luxurious conditions of existence, to which he had been accustomed since childhood. Moreover, it was pleasant after his reception by the Austrians to talk, not indeed in Russian, for they spoke in French, but with a Russian who, as he supposed, shared the general Russian aversion, now felt with especial keenness, for the Austrians.

Bilibin was a man of thirty-five, unmarried, and belonging to the same set as Prince Andreï. They had been acquaintances long before in Petersburg, and had become more intimate during Prince Andreï's last visit to Vienna, in company with Kutuzof. Just as Prince Andreï was a young man who promised to make a brilliant career in the military profession, so Bilibín, with even greater probability, was on the road to success in diplomacy. He was still a young man, but he was not a young diplomat, since he had begun his career at the age of sixteen, had been in Paris and in Copenhagen, and now held a very responsible post in Vienna. Both the chancellor and the Russian ambassador at the court of Vienna knew him and prized him highly. He was not one of those diplomats who are considered to be very good because they have merely negative qualities, do nothing but their perfunctory duties, and are able to speak French. He was rather one of those who work *con amore*, and with intelligence; notwithstanding his natural indolence, he sometimes spent the whole night at his writing-table. He put in good work, no matter what was the nature of the work in hand. It was the question "how," not the question "why," that interested him.

It was a matter of indifference to him what the diplomatic business was about, but he took the greatest satisfaction in artistically, accurately, and elegantly composing circulars, memorials, or reports.

Bilibin's services were prized, not only because of his skill in inditing letters, but also and still more because of his faculty for shining in society and carrying on conversation in the highest spheres.

Bilibin liked to talk just as he liked to work, but it **was** essential that the topic should let him display his delicately polished wit. In society, he was constantly on the watch for a chance to say something remarkable, and he never mingled in conversation except under such conditions. His talk was plentifully begemmed with keen and polished phrases, original with himself, and yet having an interest for all. These phrases were prepared in Bilibin's internal laboratory, as a sort of portable property which even the dullest members of society might easily remember and carry from drawing-room to drawing-room. And, in fact, Bilibín's witticisms made the rounds of the *salons de Vienne* — and often had an effect on so-called important events.

His thin, weary-looking sallow face was covered with deep wrinkles, which always seemed clean and par-boiled, like the ends of the fingers after a bath. The play of these wrinkles constituted the principal variations in his expression.

Now, it was his forehead that was furrowed with broad lines and his eyebrows were lifted high; again his brows were contracted and deep lines marked his cheeks. His deep-set little eyes looked always frank and cheerful.

"Now, then, tell us your exploits," said he.

Bolkonsky, in the most modest manner, without once referring to himself, told him of the combat and of the ministers' behavior.

"They received me and the news that I brought like a dog in a game of ninepins," he said, in conclusion.

Bilibin smiled, and the wrinkles in his face relaxed.

"However, my dear fellow," said he, "in spite of the high esteem that I profess for the Orthodox Russian army, I confess that your victory is not one of the most victorious."

Thus he went on, all the time speaking in French, and introducing Russian words only when he wished to give them a scornful emphasis.

"It was this way, was n't it? You fell with all your overwhelming numbers upon that unhappy Mortier, who had only one division, and yet Mortier slipped be-tween your hands? Where was the victory in that?"

"Well, speaking seriously," replied Prince Andreï, "we can, at least, say without boasting that it was rather better than Ulm."

"Why didn't you take one, at least one, marshal prisoner?"

"Because things are n't always done as they are forecast, nor can they be arranged with all the regularity of a parade. We expected, as I told you, to turn their flank at seven o'clock in the morning, and we did not succeed till five in the evening."

"Why did n't you succeed by seven in the morning? You ought to have outflanked them by seven in the morning," said Bilibin, smiling, "you ought to have done it at seven in the morning."

"Why did n't you suggest to Bonaparte, through diplomatic agency, that he 'd better abandon Genoa," asked Prince Andreï, in the same tone.

"I know," interrupted Bilibin, "as you sit on your sofa before the fire you think that it is very easy to capture marshals. It is, indeed, but why did n't you capture him? And don't be surprised that neither the minister of war, nor his most august majesty, the emperor, nor King Franz is very grateful for your victory, and I myself, the unfortunate secretary of the Russian legation, feel no special impulse to express my delight by giving my Franz a thaler and letting him take his Lieb-chen for a walk in the Prater. To be sure, there 's no Prater here!"

He looked straight at Prince Andreï, and suddenly smoothed out the wrinkled skin upon his forehead.

"Now, my dear, it is my turn to ask you why," said Bolkonsky. "I assure you, I cannot understand, — perhaps there are diplomatic subtleties here that are above my feeble mind, but I cannot understand: Mack has destroyed a whole army, the Archduke Ferdinand and the Archduke Karl are giving no signs of life, and are making one blunder after another; finally, Kutuzof is the only one who really gains a victory, destroys the spell of the French, and the minister of war is n't interested enough to inquire after the details!"

"This is the very reason, my dear. You, see, my dear fellow! hurrah for the Tsar! for Russia, the faith! all that's very well and good! but what do we, I mean the Austrain Court, care for your victories! Only bring them your fine news about a victory won by the Archduke Karl, or Ferdinand, — one archduke is as good as another, — as you know well, a victory, even though it were only over a squad of Bonaparte's firemen, and that would be another thing; we should proclaim it with the thunder of cannon. But this, as a matter of course, can only vex us. The Archduke Karl is doing nothing, the Archduke Ferdinand covers himself with disgrace! You desert Vienna, you no longer defend it, as if you said, 'God is with us, may God be with you and your capital.' One general, whom we all loved, Schmidt, you allowed to be killed by a bullet, and you congratulate us on the victory! Confess that nothing could be imagined more exasperating than this news that you bring. It seems as if it were all cut and dried, cut and dried. Moreover, even if you had won the most brilliant victory, even if the Archduke Karl should, what change would that make in the course of events? It's too late now, for Vienna has been occupied by the French army."

"What, occupied! Vienna occupied!"

"Not only occupied, but Bonaparte is at Schönbrunn, and the count, our dear friend, Count Vrbna, has gone there to him for orders."

Bolkónsky, after his fatigue and the impressions of his journey, and his reception, and especially since his dinner, felt that he did not grasp the full meaning of the words which he heard.

"This morning, Count Lichtenfels was here," continued Bilibin, "and showed me a letter containing a circumstantial account of the parade of the French in Vienna. *Le Prince Murat et tout le tremblement* .... you can see that your victory is not such an immense delight, and you can hardly be regarded as our saviors."

"Truly, as far as I am concerned, it is a matter of indifference, absolute indifference," said Prince Andreï,

beginning to comprehend that his tidings about the en-
gagement at Krems was of really little importance com-
pared with such an event as the occupation of the
Austrian capital. "How came Vienna to be occupied?
How about the bridge and that famous *tête de pont*, and
Prince Auersperg? It was reported among us that
Prince Auersperg was defending Vienna," said he.

"Prince Auersperg is on this side, on our side of the
Danube, and will defend us, defend us very wretchedly,
I think, but still, he will defend us. And Vienna is on
the other side. No, the bridge is not taken yet, and I
hope it will not be. It has been mined, and the order
is to blow it up. If it were not for that, we should
have been long ago in the mountains of Bohemia, and
you and your army would have spent a wretched quarter of an hour between two fires."

"But still this does not mean that the campaign is at
an end, does it?" asked Prince Andreï.

"Well, it's my impression that it is. And so think
the bigwigs here, but they dare not say so. What I
said at the beginning of the campaign will come true:
that your skirmish near Dürenstein will not settle the
affair, nor gunpowder, in any case, but those who contrived it," said Bilibin, repeating one of his *mots*, while
he puckered his forehead and paused a moment. "The
question simply depends on this: What is to be the outcome of the meeting of the emperor with the Prussian
king at Berlin? If Prussia joins the alliance, Austria's
hand is forced — and there will be war. But if not,
then all they have to do is arrange for the preliminaries
of a second Campo Formio."

"But what an extraordinary genius," suddenly cried
Prince Andreï, doubling his small fist and pounding the
table with it. "And what luck that man has!"

"Who? Buonaparte?" queried Bilibin, knitting his
brow, and thereby signifying that he was going to get
off a witticism. "Buonaparte," he repeated, laying a
special emphasis on the *u*, "I certainly think that now
when he is laying down the laws for Austria from
Schönbrunn, he must be spared that *u*. .... I am firmly

resolved to make the innovation, and I shall call him Bonaparte."

"No, but joking aside," said Prince Andreï, "is it possible that you think the campaign is finished?"

"This is what I think: Austria has been made a fool of and she is not used to that. And she will take her revenge. And she has been made a fool of because in the first place her provinces have been pillaged (it is said the Orthodox are terrible pillagers), her army is beaten, her capital is taken, and all this on account of the handsome eyes on the Sardinian throne. And in the second place, between us, my dear, I suspect that we are being duped, I suspect dealings with France, and a project of peace, a secret peace, separately concluded."

"That cannot be," said Prince Andreï; "that would be too base."

"*Qui vivra, verra*, you will see," said Bilibin, scowling, this time in a way which signified that the conversation was at an end.

When Prince Andreï went to the chamber that had been prepared for him, and stretched himself between clean sheets on a soft down mattress, and on warm perfumed pillows, he felt that the battle, the report of which he had brought, was far, far away. The Prussian alliance, the treachery of Austria, Bonaparte's new triumph, the parade and levee, and his reception by the Emperor Franz the next day, filled his mind.

He closed his eyes, but instantly his ears were deafened by the cannonading, the musketry, the rumble of the carriage-wheels, and now once more the musketeers came marching in scattered lines down the hillside, and the Frenchmen were firing, and he felt how his heart thrilled, and he galloped on ahead, with Schmidt at his side, and the bullets whistled merrily around him, and he experienced such a feeling of intensified delight in life as he had not felt since childhood. He awoke with a start. ....

"Yes, it was all so!" said he, smiling to himself, a happy, childlike smile, and he fell asleep with the sound sleep of youth.

CHAPTER XI

HE awoke the next morning, late. Recalling the impressions of the previous day, he remembered, first of all, that he was to be presented that day to the Emperor Franz, he remembered the minister of war, the officiously polite Flügel-adjutant, Bilibin, and the conversation of the evening before.

Putting on his full-dress uniform, which he had not worn for a long time, to go to court, he went down to Bilibin's private room. His hand was bandaged, but he was fresh, full of spirits, and handsome. Four young gentlemen connected with the diplomatic corps were gathered in the cabinet. Bolkonsky was already acquainted with Prince Ippolit Kuragin, who was secretary of the legation; Bilibin introduced him to the others.

The gentlemen at Bilibin's were gay, rich young men of fashion, who formed, both in Vienna and here in Brünn, an exclusive circle, which Bilibin, the leader of it, called "ours," *les nôtres*. This clique, composed almost exclusively of diplomats, were occupied with the doings of society, their relations to certain women, and their duties as secretaries; war and diplomacy did not much concern them. The gentlemen apparently took to Prince Andreï, and adopted him as one of themselves — an honor which they did not confer upon every one.

From politeness, and as a topic for beginning conversation, they asked him a few questions about the army and the battle, and then conversation quickly drifted into inconsequential but jovial sallies of wit and gossip.

"But this is especially good," said one, relating the misfortunes of a colleague. "Especially good, when the chancellor himself told him to his face that his transfer to London was a promotion, and that he was so to regard it. Can you imagine his looks at hearing that?" ....

"But what is worse than all, gentlemen, I must expose Kuragin : a man is in trouble, and this Don Juan, this terrible man, must needs take advantage of it ! "

Prince Ippolit was stretched out in a Voltaire chair, with his legs thrown over the arm.   He laughed : —

"Tell me about it," said he.

"Oh, you Don Juan ! " — "Oh, you snake ! " said various voices.

"You don't know, Bolkonsky," said Bilibin, turning to Prince Andreï, "that all the atrocities committed by the French army (I almost said the Russian army) are nothing in comparison with what this man has been doing among the ladies ! "

"Woman is man's helpmeet," said, Prince Ippolit, sententiously, and he began to stare through his lorgnette at his elevated feet.

Bilibin and " our fellows " roared, as they looked at Prince Ippolit.   Prince Andreï saw that this young man, of whom (it must be confessed) he had almost been jealous, was the butt for this circle.

"I must give you a little sport with Kuragin," whispered Bilibin to Bolkonsky.   "It's rich to hear him talk about politics !   You must see what an important air he assumes."

He took a seat near Ippolit and, wrinkling his brows portentously, began to draw him into a conversation on political affairs.

Prince Andreï and the others gathered around the two.

"The cabinet of Berlin cannot express any thought of an alliance," began Ippolit, looking significantly from one to another, "without expressing .... as in its last note .... *vous comprenez* .... *vous comprenez* .... and then if his majesty the emperor does not go back on his principles, our alliance ....   Wait, I have not finished," said he to Prince Andreï, seizing him by the arm, "I suppose that intervention will be stronger than non-intervention, and .... "   He was silent for a moment, — "the non-receipt of our despatch of the twenty-eighth of November cannot be charged as intentional.   That is the way it will all end."

And he let go of Bolkonsky's arm, signifying that now he was entirely done.

"Demosthenes, I recognize thee by the pebble which thou hast concealed in thy golden mouth," said Bilibin, his cap of hair moving on his head with satisfaction.

All laughed. Ippolit laughed louder than the rest. It evidently hurt him; he choked but he was unable to refrain from the laugh that distorted his usually impassive face.

"Now, then, gentlemen," said Bilibin, "Bolkonsky is a guest at my house here in Brünn, and I am anxious to treat him well and give him a taste of all of our pleasures here so far as possible. If we were in Vienna this would be easy, but here — in this beastly Moravian hole — it will be harder, and I beg you all to lend me your aid. We must do him the honors of Brünn. You undertake the theatres; I will introduce him to society; you, Ippolit, of course, the ladies."

"You must show him Amélie, she's a beauty!" said one of the circle, kissing the ends of his fingers.

"All in all, this bloodthirsty soldier," said Bilibin, "must be brought to more humane views."

"It is doubtful if I can take advantage of your hospitality, gentlemen, for now it is time for me to go out," said Bolkonsky, looking at his watch.

"Where?"

"To the emperor."

"Oh! — oh! — oh!"

"Well, *au revoir*, Bolkonsky. Good-by, prince; come back to dinner as early as you can," shouted several voices. "We will look out for you."

"Try to say as much as you can in praise of the commissariat and the roads, when you speak to the emperor," said Bilibin, as he accompanied Bolkonsky into the entry.

"I wish I could say flattering things, but I cannot," said Bolkonsky, with a smile.

"Well, then, do just as much of the talking as you can. His passion is for audiences, but he does not like to talk, and he does not know how, as you will see for yourself."

CHAPTER XII

AT the levee, Prince Andreï, who stood in the place appointed among the Austrian officers, merely received a long fixed stare from the Emperor Franz, and a slight inclination of his long head. But, after the levee, the Flügel-adjutant of the evening before politely communicated to Bolkonsky the emperor's desire to give him an audience. The Emperor Franz received him standing in the middle of his room. Before beginning the conversation, Prince Andreï was struck by the evident confusion of the emperor, who reddened and did not know what to say.

" Tell me when the action began," he asked hurriedly. Prince Andreï told him.

This question was followed by others, no less simple : —

"Is Kutuzof well? How long ago did he leave Krems?" and so on.

The emperor spoke as if his whole aim were to ask a certain number of questions. The answers to these questions, as he made only too evident, did not interest him.

" At what hour did the engagement begin ? " asked the emperor.

" I cannot tell, your majesty, at what hour the fighting began on the front, but at Dürenstein, where I happened to be, the army made the first attack at six o'clock in the evening," said Bolkonsky, eagerly, for he supposed that now he had a chance to enter into the carefully prepared and accurate description of all that he had seen and knew. But the emperor smiled and interrupted him : —

" How many miles is it ? "

" From where and to where, your majesty ? "

" From Dürenstein to Krems ? "

" Three miles and a half, your majesty."

" Have the French abandoned the left bank ? "

" According to the reports of our scouts, the last of them crossed that same night on rafts."

" Plenty of provender at Krems ? "

" Provender was not furnished in that abundance which .... "

But the emperor interrupted him : —

" At what hour was General Schmidt killed ? "

" At seven o'clock, I should think." ....

" At seven o'clock ! Very sad ! very sad ! "

Then the emperor thanked him and made him a bow. Prince Andreï left the audience chamber and was immediately surrounded by courtiers coming from all sides. From all sides flattering glances rested on him and flattering words were heard around him. The Flügel-adjutant reproached him for not having put up at the palace and offered him the use of his rooms. The minister of war came and congratulated him on having received the order of Maria Theresa of the third degree, which the emperor had conferred upon him. The empress's chamberlain invited him to wait upon her majesty. The grand duchess also desired to see him. He did not know whom to answer first, and it took him several seconds to collect his wits. The Russian ambassador put his hand on his shoulder, drew him into a window, and began to talk with him.

In spite of Bilibin's prognostications, the news brought by Bolkonsky was joyfully hailed. A thanksgiving Te Deum was ordained, Kutuzof was decorated with the grand cross of Maria Theresa, and all the army was rewarded. Bolkonsky was overwhelmed with invitations, and was obliged to spend the whole morning in making calls upon the principal dignitaries of Austria.

Having finished his calls, about five o'clock in the afternoon Prince Andreï, thinking over what he should write his father about the engagement and his visit to Brünn, returned to Bilibin's lodgings. At the door of the house occupied by Bilibin stood a britzska half full of luggage, and Franz, Bilibin's valet, was just coming out, laboriously dragging another trunk.

On his way back to Bilibin's, Prince Andreï had stepped into a bookstall, to lay in a store of books for his campaign, and had spent some time there.

"What does this mean?" asked Bolkónsky.

"Alas! your excellency!" said Franz, with difficulty tumbling the trunk into the britzska, "we're going farther off. The rascal is after us again."

"What do you say? tell me!" asked Prince Andreï. Bilibin came out to meet Bolkonsky. His usually tranquil face showed traces of excitement.

"Well, well, confess that it's delightful," said he, "this story of the Thabor bridge [the bridge at Vienna]. They crossed it without meeting any resistance!"

Prince Andreï still failed to understand. "Where have you been that you don't know what every coachman in the city has heard long since."

"I have just come from the grand duchess's. I heard nothing of it there."

"And haven't you noticed that everywhere they're packing up?"

"No, I haven't. But what is the trouble?" asked Prince Andreï, impatiently.

"What is the trouble? The trouble is that the French have crossed the bridge which Auersperg was defending, and the bridge was not blown up, so that Murat is now hastening down the road to Brünn, and they will be here to-day or to-morrow."

"Be here? But why was the bridge not blown up, when it was mined?"

"Well, that's what I ask you. No one, not even Bonaparte, knows that."

Bolkonsky shrugged his shoulders.

"But if the bridge is crossed, the army is destroyed; of course it will be cut off," said he.

"That's the joke of the thing," rejoined Bilibin. "Listen! The French enter Vienna, just as I told you. All very good. On the next day, — that is yesterday, — Messrs. Marshals Murat, Lannes, and Belliard mount their horses and ride down to the bridge (notice, all three of them are Gascons). 'Gentlemen,' says one of them, 'you know that the Thabor bridge is mined and countermined, and that in front of it is a terrible *tête de pont* and fifteen thousand men, who are commanded to blow up the bridge and not allow us to pass. But our master, the Emperor Napoleon, would be pleased if we took that bridge. Let us three go therefore and take that bridge.' 'Yes, let us go,' say the others, and they go to it and take it and cross it, and now they are on this side of the Danube with their whole army, and are in full march against us and against your communications."

"A truce to jesting," said Prince Andreï, in a melancholy and serious tone. This news was sad, and at the same time pleasant to him. As soon as he knew that the Russian army was in such a hopeless situation, it occurred to him that he himself was the one called upon to rescue it from this situation, — that this was his Toulon, destined to lift him from the throng of insignificant officers and open to him the straight path of glory! Even while he was listening to Bilibín, he was picturing himself going back to the army, and there, in a council of war, proposing a plan which alone might save them, and that to him alone it was granted to accomplish this plan.

"A truce to jesting," said he.

"I am not jesting," insisted Bilibin. "Nothing is more veracious or more melancholy. These gentlemen ride on the bridge without escort, displaying their white handkerchiefs; they assert that there is an armistice, and that they, the marshals, have come over to talk with Prince Auersperg. The officer on guard lets them into the *tête de pont*. They give him a thousand choice specimens of gasconade; they say that the war is ended, that the Emperor Franz has decided on a conference with Bonaparte, that they wanted to see Prince Auersperg, and a thousand other trumpery lies. The officer sends for Auersperg; these gentlemen embrace the officers, jest, sit astride the cannon, and meantime a French battalion quietly crosses the bridge and flings the bags with the combustibles into the water, and enters the *tête de pont*. At last the lieutenant-general, our dear Prince Auersperg von Mautern himself, appears on the scene. 'Our dear enemy! Flower of the

Austrian army, hero of the Turkish wars! Our enmity is at an end, we can shake hands. The Emperor Napoleon is dying with anxiety to make the acquaintance of Prince Auersperg!'

"In one word, these gentlemen, who are not Gascons for nothing, so bejuggle Auersperg with fine words, he is so ravished by this rapidly instituted intimacy with the French marshals, so dazzled by the sight of Murat's mantle and ostrich feathers, that he doesn't see the point, and quite forgets what he himself ought to be pointing at the enemy." [1]

Notwithstanding the vehemence of his remarks, Bilibín did not fail to pause after this pun, so as to allow Bolkónsky time to appreciate it.

"The French battalions run into the *tête de pont*, spike the cannon, the bridge is theirs! But this is best of all," he went on to say, allowing the fascination of his narrative to keep him calm, "this, — that the sergeant who had charge of the cannon, the discharge of which was to explode the mines and blow up the bridge, this sergeant, I say, seeing the French soldiers running over the bridge, was just going to fire his gun, but Lannes pulled away his hand. The sergeant, who evidently had more sense than his general, hastens to Auersperg and says, 'Prince, you are imposed upon, here are the French!'

"Murat sees that their game is played if the sergeant is allowed to speak further. With pretended surprise (true Gascon that he is) he turns to Auersperg: 'I don't see in this anything of your world-renowned Austrian discipline,' says he. 'Do you allow a man of inferior rank to speak to you so?' It was a stroke of genius. Prince Auersperg prides himself on punctilio and has the sergeant put under arrest. But you must confess that all this story of the Thabor bridge is perfectly delightful. It was neither stupidity nor cowardice." ....

"Perhaps it is treason, though," said Prince Andreï,

---

[1] *Qu'il n'y voit que du feu, et oublie celui qu'il devait faire faire sur l'ennemi*. The French pun turns on the idiom *ne voir que du feu*, to be dazzled, not to understand; but *feu* means fire.

his imagination vividly bringing up before him the gray cloaks, the wounds, the gunpowder smoke, the sounds of battle, and the glory which was awaiting him.

" Not at all. This puts the court in a most stupid position," continued Bilibin; " it is neither treason nor cowardice nor stupidity, it 's just the same as at Ulm." He paused, as if trying to find a suitable expression : "*C'est — c'est du Mack. Nous sommes Mackés* — we are Macked !" he said, at last satisfied that he had coined *un mot*, and a brilliant *mot*, such an one as would be repeated. The wrinkles that had been deeply gathering on his forehead quickly smoothed themselves out, in token of his contentment, and with a slight smile on his lips, he began to contemplate his finger-nails.

" Where are you going ? " he asked, suddenly turning to Prince Andreï, who had got up and was starting for his chamber.

" I 'm off."

"Where ? "

" To the army ! "

" But you intended to stop two days longer, didn 't you ? "

" Yes, but now I 'm going immediately."

And Prince Andreï, having given his orders for the carriage, went to his room.

" Do you know, my dear fellow ? " said Bilibin, coming into his room, " do you know, I have been thinking about you. — Why are you going ? "

And in testimony of the irrefragability of his argument against it, all the wrinkles vanished from his face.

Prince Andreï looked inquiringly at his friend, and made no reply.

" Why are you going ? — I know ; you think that it is your duty to hurry back to the army, now, when it is in danger. I understand it, my dear ; it is heroism in you ! "

" Not at all," said Prince Andreï.

" But you are a philosopher ; be one absolutely ; look at things from the other side, and you will see that your duty, on the contrary, is to preserve yourself. Leave this to others who are not fit for anything else. .... You have had no orders to return, and you won't be allowed to go from here, so of course you can stay, and go with us wherever our unhappy lot carries us. They say we are going to Olmütz. Now Olmütz is a very nice little city. And you and I can make the journey very comfortably in my calash."

"Cease your jesting, Bilibin," said Bolkonsky.

"I am speaking to you sincerely, and as your friend. Judge for yourself. Where, and for what purpose, are you going now, when you can remain here? One of two things will happen to you," — here he managed to gather a fold of wrinkles over his left temple, — "either peace will be concluded before you reach the army, or else defeat and disgrace await you with all of Kutuzof's force."

And Bilibin smoothed the skin again, feeling that the dilemma was unavoidable.

"Of that I cannot judge," said Prince Andreï, coldly; but he thought in his own mind, "I am going to save the army."

"My dear, you are a hero!" said Bilibin.

CHAPTER XIII

THAT same night, having taken his leave of the minister of war, Bolkonsky set out for the army, not knowing where he should find it, and fearing lest he should be captured by the French, on the road to Krems.

At Brünn all the court were engaged in packing, and the heavy luggage had already been despatched to Olmütz.

Near Etzelsdorf Prince Andreï struck the highway over which the Russian army was moving in the greatest haste and the greatest disorder. The road was so encumbered with teams that it was impossible for a carriage to make its way along. Having secured from the head of the Cossack division a horse and Cossack, Prince Andreï, hungry and tired, managed to get past the teams, and at last drove on in search of the commander-in-chief and his own train. The most ominous reports of the condition of the army had reached him on his way, and these reports were confirmed by the sight of the army hurrying on in disorder.

"This Russian army, which English gold has brought together from the ends of the universe, we shall make it suffer the same fate (the fate of Ulm)."

Bolkonsky remembered these words from Bonaparte's general orders to his army at the beginning of the campaign, and these words inspired in him an admiration for the genius of his hero, together with a sense of wounded pride and a hope of glory.

"But suppose nothing be left me but to die!" he said to himself. "Well, then, be it so, if it is necessary. I shall not die more shamefully than others."

Prince Andreï looked contemptuously at the endless confusion of detachments, baggage-wagons, field-pieces, and gun-carriages, and again baggage-wagons, baggage-wagons, baggage-wagons, of every possible description, trying to outstrip one another, and getting in one another's way, as they toiled along over the muddy road, three and four abreast. In all directions, in front as well as behind, wherever the ear listened, were heard the creaking of wheels, the rumbling of vehicles, carts and gun-carriages, the trampling of horses' feet, the cracking of whips, the shouts of drivers, the cursing of soldiers, servants, and officers.

Along the borders of the highway were everywhere seen the carcasses of horses that had fallen, and been left, either flayed or not flayed, as the case might be; then broken-down wagons, by which solitary soldiers sat waiting for something; then, again, he saw little detachments of troops straying from the main column and hastening to scattered villages, or coming back from them, with hens, sheep, hay, or bags filled with various objects.

On the slopes and rises the groups crowded together still more densely, and there was an uninterrupted tumult of noises. Soldiers plodding through mud up to their knees helped to drag, by main force, the field-pieces and wagons. Whips cracked, hoofs slipped, traces strained, and throats were split with shouting. The officers who directed the retreat galloped back and forth among the wagons. Their voices were hardly distinguishable above the general uproar, and it could be seen by their faces that they were in despair at the possibility of reducing this chaos into order.

"Here is our dear Orthodox army," said Bolkonsky to himself, quoting Bilibin's words.

Wishing to inquire of some of these men where the commander-in-chief was to be found, he galloped up to the train. Directly opposite to him was an odd equipage, a sort of cross between a cart, a cabriolet, and a calash, drawn by one horse, and evidently constructed out of some soldier's domestic belongings. This vehicle was driven by a soldier, and under the leather cover, behind the apron, sat a woman all wrapped up in shawls.

Prince Andreï rode up and was just going to question the soldier, when his attention was attracted by the despairing shrieks of the woman sitting in the vehicle. An officer, who had charge of the train, had set to beating her driver because he attempted to pass ahead of the others, and the blows of the whip fell on the apron. The woman was screaming desperately. Seeing Prince Andreï, she thrust her head out from under the hood, and waving her thin arms, freed from the shawls, she cried : —

"Aide ! Mr. Aide ! .... for God's sake .... protect me ! What will become of us ? .... I am the doctor's wife, of the Seventh Jägers. .... They won't let us pass, we are left behind, and have lost our friends."

"I will knock you flatter than a pancake ! turn back!" cried the officer, angrily, to the soldier; "back with you, and take your jade !"

"Mr. Aide, help me ! What can I do ?" cried the doctor's wife.

"Please let this team pass. Don't you see that it is a woman?" said Prince Andreï, riding up to the officer.

The officer glanced at him, and, without saying a word, turned to the soldier again. "I'll teach you.... back!"

"Let them pass, I tell you," repeated Prince Andreï, compressing his lips.

"Who are you, anyway?" suddenly cried the officer, turning to Prince Andreï, in a drunken fury. "Who are you?" (he addressed him insolently, with a special emphasis on the insulting word). "Are you commander here? I'm the commander here, and not you! Back with you, I'll knock you flatter'n a pancake."

This expression had evidently pleased the officer.

"He gave the little aide a capital rating," said a voice behind.

Prince Andreï saw that the officer had got into one of those paroxysms of drunken fury in which a man is not responsible for what he says. He saw that his interference in the troubles of the doctor's wife was attended with what he feared more than aught else in the world, — being made ridiculous, but instinct immediately came to his aid. The officer had not time to finish what he was saying before Prince Andreï, his face distorted by rage, rode close to him and held up his whip: "Have the goodness to let them pass!"

The officer shook his fist in his face and hastily rode off. "It all comes from them, from these staff-officers, all this disorder does," he muttered. "Do as you please."

Prince Andreï hastily rode away, without looking up or heeding the thanks of the doctor's wife, who called him her preserver; and, recalling with disgust the particulars of this humiliating scene, he galloped toward the village where he had been told that the commander-in-chief was to be found.

When he reached this village, he dismounted and started for the first house, intending to rest, if only for a minute, and get something to eat, and try to banish all the humiliating thoughts that tortured him. "This is a troop of footpads and not an army," he was saying to himself, when, just as he happened to look up at the window of the first house, a well-known voice called him by name.

He looked up and saw Nesvitsky's handsome face thrust out of the window. Nesvitsky, vigorously chewing something in his moist mouth, was waving his hand and calling him to come in.

"Bolkonsky! Bolkonsky! don't you hear me? Come quick!" he cried.

Entering the house, Prince Andreï found Nesvitsky and another aide having some luncheon. They turned eagerly to Bolkonsky, with the question whether he had brought anything new. Prince Andreï read in their well-known faces an expression of alarm and uneasiness. This expression was especially noticeable on Nesvitsky's usually jolly face.

"Where is the commander-in-chief?" asked Bolkonsky.

"Here, in yonder house," replied the aide.

"Tell us, is it true there is peace and a capitulation?" demanded Nesvitsky.

"I should have to ask you that! I know nothing, except that I had great trouble in finding you."

"And what sort of a plight do you find us in! It's horrible, my dear fellow; I plead guilty for having laughed at Mack, but here we are in a far worse position, brother," said Nesvitsky. "But sit down and have something to eat.

"Now, prince, you won't find your luggage, or anything, and only God knows where your man, Piotr, is," said the other aide.

"Where's the headquarters?"

"We are to spend the night at Znaim."

"And I had everything I needed packed on two horses," said Nesvitsky, "and they made me some splendid pack-saddles. Even though we should have to worry through the mountains of Bohemia. It's a bad state of things, brother. What's the matter? Are n't you well, you shake so?" asked Nesvitsky, noticing that a sudden tremor ran over Prince Andreï, as if from the discharge of a Leyden jar.

"Nothing is the matter," replied Prince Andreï. He happened at that instant to remember his recent encounter with the doctor's wife and the officer of the baggage-train.

"What's the commander-in-chief doing here?" he went on to ask.

"I have n't the least idea," replied Nesvitsky.

"All I know is that it is all a nasty, nasty, nasty business," said Prince Andreï, and he started for the house where the commander-in-chief was.

Passing by Kutuzof's carriage, the jaded saddle-horses of his suite, and the vociferating Cossacks, he went into the cottage. Kutuzof himself, as Prince Andreï had been told, was in the cottage with Prince Bagration and Weirother. Weirother was the Austrian general who had succeeded to the place of Schmidt, who had been killed.

In the entry, the little Kozlovsky was squatting on his heels before a clerk. The clerk, with his cuffs rolled up, was hastily writing, with a tub turned over for a desk. Kozlovsky's face looked pinched and wan; he had evidently not slept the night before. He glanced up as Prince Andreï came in, but he did not even nod to him.

"Second line..... Have you written it?" said he, proceeding with what he was dictating to the clerk: "The Kief grenadiers, the Podolian...."

"Don't go so fast, your honor,"[1] said the clerk in a disrespectful and surly manner, looking up at Kozlovsky.

Kutuzof's animated and impatient voice was at this moment heard in the room beyond, answered by another which Prince Andreï did not recognize. By the sound of these two voices, by the preoccupied way in which Kozlovsky glanced up at him, by the surly disrespect shown by the clerk, by the fact that the clerk and Kozlovsky were sitting on the floor by a tub, and so handy to the commander-in-chief, and finally, because the Cossacks holding the saddle-horses were laughing so noisily in front of the windows, — by all of this, Prince Andreï

---

[1] *Vashe vuisokoblagoródie: high-well-born, Hochwohlgeboren.*

was impressed with the idea that something grave and disagreeable must have occurred.

Prince Andreï, with urgency, turned to Kozlovsky with questions.

"In a moment, prince," said Kozlovsky. "These are the dispositions for Bagration."

"But the capitulation?"

"There's no such thing. Preparations are making for a battle."

Prince Andreï started for the room where he heard the talking. But, just as he was going to open the door, the voices in the room became silent, the door was flung open, and Kutuzof, with his eagle nose and puffy face, appeared on the threshold. Prince Andreï stood directly in front of him; but from the expression of the commander-in-chief's one available eye it could be seen that he was so absolutely absorbed by his work and idea that he did not see anything at all. He looked straight into his aide's face and yet did not recognize him.

"How now! Finished?" he inquired of Kozlovsky.

"In one second, your excellency."

Bagration, a short, slender man, still in the prime of life, and with a firm and impassive face of the Oriental type, followed the commander-in-chief.

"I have the honor of presenting myself," said Prince Andreï, in a pretty loud tone, and at the same time extending an envelope.

"Ah? From Vienna? Good! Wait, wait!"

Kutuzof and Bagration went out on the step.

"Well, prince, good-by," said he to Bagration. "Christ be with you! I give you my best wishes for the great task."

Kutuzof's face unexpectedly softened, and the tears came into his eyes. With his left hand he drew Bagration to him, and with his right, on which flashed a ring, he made the sign of the cross over him in a manner peculiar to himself, and offered him his puffy cheek to kiss, instead of which Bagration kissed him on the neck.

"Christ be with you," repeated Kutuzof, and went to his calash. — "Come with me," said he to Bolkonsky.

"Your high excellency, I should like to be employed in this movement. Let me stay in Prince Bagration's division."

"Come with me," again said Kutuzof, and, noticing that Bolkonsky hesitated, he added: "I myself need good officers, I need them myself."

They took their seats in the calash and drove in silence for some minutes.

"There is still much, very much, before us," said he, with an old man's keenness of perception, as if he clearly read all that was passing in Bolkonsky's mind. "If a tenth part of his division returns to-morrow, I shall thank God," added Kutuzof, evidently talking to himself.

Prince Andreï looked at Kutuzof, and his eyes were involuntarily attracted by the deep scar on his temple, where the Turkish bullet had crashed through his head at Izmaïlo, and by his extravasated eye.

"Yes, he has a right to speak thus calmly of the destruction of these men," thought Prince Bolkonsky.

"That was the very reason why I asked you to let me go with that division," said he, aloud.

Kutuzof made no reply. It seemed as if he had already forgotten what he had just said, and he sat absorbed in thought. Five minutes later Kutuzof, comfortably rocking on the easy springs of the calash, turned to Prince Andreï. His face showed not a sign of emotion. With gentle irony he began to ask Prince Andreï after the details of his interview with the emperor, the court gossip concerning the Krems engagement, and concerning certain women with whom both of them were acquainted.

CHAPTER XIV

KUTUZOF had learned on the thirteenth of November, through one of his scouts, that the army under his command was in an almost inextricable position. The scout had brought word that the French, in overwhelming numbers, had crossed the bridge at Vienna, and were marching to cut off the communication between Kutúzof and the reinforcements coming to him from Russia.

If Kutuzof decided to remain at Krems, then Napoleon's army of one hundred and fifty thousand men would cut him off from all his communications, would outflank his exhausted army of forty thousand, and then he would be in the same position as Mack at Ulm.

If Kutuzof decided to abandon the road leading to his point of communication with his reinforcements, then he would be obliged to penetrate into the unknown and pathless region of the Bohemian mountains, defending his rear from the constant attacks of the enemy on his trail, and giving up all hope of effecting a junction with Buxhövden.

If Kutuzof determined to take the highway from Krems to Olmütz, so as to meet the reinforcement from Russia, then he ran the risk of being anticipated on this route by the French, who had crossed the Danube at Vienna and would be likely to force him to fight in the middle of the march, burdened with all the luggage and train baggage, and to deal with an enemy double his own number, and surrounding him on two sides.

Kutuzof had decided on this last alternative.

The French, according to the report of the scout, had crossed the bridge at Vienna, and were in full march upon Znaim, which lay in the line of Kutuzof's projected retreat, more than a hundred versts — about sixty miles — ahead of him. If they could reach Znaim before the French, they were in a fair hope of saving the army; but if the French were given a chance of getting to Znaim first, it surely meant the disgrace of a surrender, like that at Ulm, or else the general destruction of the army. It was certainly impossible to anticipate the French with all the troops. The road which the French would traverse from Vienna to Znaim was both shorter and better than the road which the Russians had from Krems to Znaim.

On the night after receiving this information, Kutuzof sent four thousand men of Bagration's vanguard over the mountains to occupy the road from Vienna to Znaim. Bagration was ordered to make this short cut without pausing to rest; he was to face Vienna and turn his back on Znaim, and if he succeeded in getting there before the French did, he was to do his best to hold them in check. Kutuzof himself, with all the baggage, would hasten on toward Znaim.

Bagration, crossing the mountains, marching without a road, forty-five versts on a stormy night, losing a third part of his forces in stragglers, came out with his famished, shoeless men at Hollabrunn, on the road from Vienna to Znaim, a few hours before the French reached it from Vienna. It was necessary for Kutúzof to travel a whole day and night with his baggage-wagons before reaching Znaim, and, therefore, in order to save the army, Bagration, with only four thousand soldiers, hungry and tired out, was obliged to engage the entire force of the enemy during the course of the twenty-four hours; this was manifestly impossible.

But a strange chance made the impossible possible.

Having been successful in the piece of finesse which had given the French the bridge at Vienna without a blow, Murat thought that it would be fine to try a similar deception on Kutuzof. Meeting Bagration's feeble contingent on the road to Znaim, he supposed that it was Kutuzof's whole army. In order that there might be no question of his crushing this army, he determined to wait the arrival of all the forces that had started out from Vienna, and, with this end in view, he proposed an armistice for three days, with the condition that both armies should not change their positions, or move from their places.

Murat asserted that negotiations for peace were already in progress, and that, therefore, in order to avoid the useless shedding of blood, he had proposed the armistice. The Austrian general, Count Nostitz, who was posted in the van, placed credence in the words of Murat's emissary, and retired, exposing Bagration. Another emissary came to the Russian line to make the same assurances about negotiations of peace, and to propose three days' armistice. Bagration answered that he was not authorized either to refuse or accept an armistice, and he sent his adjutant back to Kutuzof, to carry the proposition that had been made to him.

The armistice was, for Kutuzof, the only means of gaining time, of giving Bagration's toil-worn division a chance to rest, and of sending the baggage-wagons and other things (the movements of which were concealed from the French) by a roundabout way to Znaim. The proposal for an armistice offered the only possibility, and one most unexpected, of saving the army.

On the receipt of this news, Kutuzof promptly sent his adjutant-general, Winzengerode, who happened to be present, over to the hostile camp. Winzengerode was not only to accept the armistice, but also even to propose terms of capitulation, while, in the meantime, Kutuzof sent his aides back to expedite the movements of the baggage-train of the whole army along the road from Krems to Znaim. The weary, famished contingent under Bagration was to cover this operation of the baggage-train and of the whole army, and to maintain a firm front against an enemy eight times as strong.

Kutuzof saw that by discussing terms of capitulation, which did not bind him to anything, time would be gained for sending around at least a portion of the heavy baggage, but he also saw that Murat's blunder would be quickly detected. Both of these anticipations were realized.

As soon as Bonaparte, who was at Schönbrunn, twenty-five versts from Hollabrunn, read Murat's report and his scheme for an armistice and capitulation, he saw through the hoax, and wrote the following letter to him : —

SCHÖNBRUNN, Nov. 16, 1805, 8 o'clock A.M.

TO PRINCE MURAT : — I cannot find words to express my displeasure. You merely command my van, and have no right to conclude an armistice without orders from me. You are making me lose the advantage of a campaign. End the armistice instantly, and march on the enemy. Explain to him that the general who signed this capitulation had no right to do so, — that only the Emperor of Russia has this right.

However, if the Russian emperor should ratify the proposed agreement, I also would ratify it. But it is only a trick. March! Destroy the Russian army! You are in a position to capture their baggage and artillery.

The Russian emperor's adjutant-general is a —— Officers are of no account when they are not endowed with any powers ; this one had none. The Austrians let themselves be duped about the crossing of the Vienna bridge ; you have allowed yourself to be duped by the Russians.

NAPOLEON.[1]

Bonaparte's aide galloped off at headlong speed, to carry this angry letter to Murat. Bonaparte himself, not feeling confidence in his generals, moved toward the field of battle with all his guards, fearing lest he should be cheated of his prey ; and the four thousand men under Bagration, gayly building bivouac fires, dried and warmed themselves and for the first time in three days cooked their kasha, and not one of the detachment knew or dreamed of what was threatening them.

---

[1] SCHÖNBRUNN, 25 *Brumaire, en* 1805, *à huit heure du matin.*

AU PRINCE MURAT : — *Il m'est impossible de trouver des termes pour vous exprimer mon mécontentement. Vous ne commandez que mon avant-garde, et vous n'avez pas le droit de faire d'armistice sans mon ordre. Vous me faites perdre le fruit d'une campagne. Rompez l'armistice sur le champ, et marchez sur ennemi. Vous lui ferez déclarer que le général qui a signé cette capitulation n'avait pas le droit de le faire, qu'il n'y a que l'empereur de Russie qui ait ce droit.*

Toutes les fois cependant que l'Empereur de Russie ratifierait la dite convention, je la ratifierai ; mais ce n'est qu'une ruse. Marchez, détruisez l'armée russe. Vous êtes une position de prendre son bagage et son artillerie.

L'aide de campe de l'Empereur de Russie est un —— Les officiers ne sont rien quand ils n'ont pas de pouvoirs : celui-ci n'en avait point. Les Autrichiens se sont laissé jouer pour le passage du pont de Vienne, vous-vous laissez jouer par un aide de camp de l'empereur.

NAPOLEON.

CHAPTER XV

IT was four o'clock in the afternoon, when Prince Andreï, having through his urgency been granted his request by Kutuzof, reached Grund, and reported to Bagration. Bonaparte's aide had not yet reached Murat's division, and the battle had not begun. Nothing was known in Bagration's detachment about the general course of events; they talked about a peace, but did not believe in its possibility. They talked also about an engagement, but neither did they believe in the imminence of any engagement. Bagration, knowing that Bolkonsky was the commander-in-chief's favorite and trusted adjutant, received him with all the marks of respect and condescension possible to a commander, assured him that either that day or the next an engagement would probably take place, and granted him free choice to be present with him during the battle, or to remain in the rear and superintend the retreat, "which," he said, "would be a very important position."

"However, it is most likely that nothing will be done to-day," said Prince Bagration, as if to relieve Prince Andreï's anxieties.

At the same time he thought: "If this is only one of the ordinary jack-a-dandies of the staff, sent out to win a cross, he will get it just as well by staying in the rear; but if he desires to be with me, let him. .... He will be useful if he is a brave officer."

Prince Andreï gave no decided answer, but asked the prince's permission to reconnoiter the position and learn the disposition of the forces, so that in case of necessity he might know where he was. The officer on duty, a handsome man, faultlessly attired and with a diamond ring on his index finger, who spoke French badly but fluently, offered to be Prince Andreï's guide.

On all sides were to be seen wet and melancholy-looking officers, apparently searching for something, and soldiers lugging from the village doors, benches, and fences.

"Here, prince, we cannot get rid of such men as these," said the staff-officer, pointing to the soldiers. "The officers let them leave their places. And here again!" the officer pointed to a sutler's tent pitched near them, "they gather around and loaf. This morning I drove them all out, and look! it's all full again. I must go and disperse them. One minute!"

"Let us go, and I will get some cheese and a loaf of bread of him," said Prince Andreï, who had not yet had anything to eat.

"Why did n't you tell me, prince? I should have been delighted to have shared my bread and salt with you."

They dismounted and went into the sutler's tent, where a few men and a number of officers with flushed and weary faces were sitting around a table, eating and drinking.

"Now what does this mean, gentlemen?" said the staff-officer in a tone of vexation, like a man who has been iterating the same thing again and again. "You know it is forbidden to absent yourselves from your posts in this way. The prince has forbidden any such thing. — And here you are, Mr. Captain!" said he, turning to a little, lean, dirty artillery officer, who without boots (he had given them to the sutler to dry), in his stocking-feet, stood up as the others entered, and greeted them with a not altogether natural smile. "Well, are n't you ashamed of yourself, Captain Tushin?" continued the staff-officer. "One would think that as an officer you would set a good example, and here you are with your boots off! If an alarm were sounded, you would make a fine show without boots!" The staff-officer smiled satirically. "Please go to your places, gentlemen, all, all of you," he added, in a tone of command.

Prince Andreï could not help smiling as he looked at Captain Tushin, who, silent and smiling, stood first on one bare foot and then on the other, and looked inquiringly with his large, intelligent, and good-natured eyes from Prince Andreï to the officer of the day.

"The soldiers say: 'It's easier to go barefooted,'" said Captain Tushin, timid and still smiling, evidently anxious to escape from his awkward predicament by assuming a jesting tone; but he did not say anything further, as if he felt that his joke was not appreciated and was not a success. He grew confused.

"Please go to your places," repeated the staff-officer, trying to preserve his gravity.

Prince Andreï once more glanced at the diminutive form of the artillery officer. There was something about it peculiar, utterly unmilitary, and rather comical, but still extraordinarily attractive.

The officer of the day and Prince Andreï remounted their horses and rode on.

Having passed beyond the village, constantly overtaking or meeting soldiers and officers of different divisions, they came in sight of the new entrenchments at their left, made of reddish clay freshly dug up. Several battalions of soldiers in their shirt-sleeves, in spite of the cold wind, and looking like white ants, were busy digging at these fortifications. Behind the breastworks, shovelfuls of red clay were constantly tossed up by men hidden from sight. They rode up to the earthworks, examined them, and then proceeding, mounted the opposite slope. From the top of it they could see the French. Prince Andreï reined in his horse and began to look around.

"There's where our battery is stationed," said the staff-officer, indicating the highest point, — "under command of that droll fellow whom we saw without his boots. From the top there, you can get a bird's-eye view of everything; let us go to it, prince."

"I thank you cordially, but now I can make my way alone," said Prince Andreï, wishing to get rid of the staff-officer. "Do not trouble yourself, I beg of you."

The staff-officer turned back, and Prince Andreï rode on alone.

The farther toward the front he rode, and the nearer to the enemy he came, the more orderly and admirably disposed seemed to be the army. The greatest disorder and despondency were in that division of the baggage-train before Znaim which Prince Andreï had overtaken that morning and which was at least ten versts from the French. In Grund also there was a certain atmosphere of apprehension and fear of something.

But the nearer Prince Andreï came to the French out-posts, the more satisfactory seemed to be the condition of the Russian forces. The soldiers in their cloaks stood drawn up in line, and a sergeant and a captain were counting the men, laying a finger on the breast of the last soldier of each division and directing him to lift his hand. Others, scattered over the whole space, were dragging sticks and brushwood and constructing rude huts, while they gayly laughed and chatted; around the bivouac fires, some dressed and others stripped were drying their shirts and leg-wrappers, mending their boots and cloaks, crowding around the kettles and kasha-pots. In one company, dinner was ready and the soldiers with eager faces gazed at the steaming kettle and waited while the *kaptenarmus* or sergeant carried a wooden cupful to be tasted by the officer who was sitting on a log in front of his hut.

In another company, more fortunate, since not all were provided with vodka, the soldiers stood in a throng around a pock-marked broad-shouldered sergeant, who, tilting the keg, filled in turn the covers of the cans which eager hands extended toward him. The soldiers, with reverent faces, lifted the can-covers to their lips, drained them, and, rinsing the vodka in their mouths and wiping them on their coat-sleeves, went off with contented faces. All the faces were as free from care as if the enemy were miles away and there were no probability of a battle in which at least half their division might be left on the field, — as if indeed they were somewhere in their native land anticipating undisturbed repose.

Having ridden past the regiment of jägers, Prince Andreï reached the Kief grenadiers, gallant young fellows, occupied all with the same peaceful pursuits; but not far from the regimental commander's hut, dis-tinguished only by its height from the others, he saw a platoon of the grenadiers, in front of whom lay a man, stripped. Two soldiers held him down, and two, flourishing supple rods, were giving him measured strokes on his naked back.

The man who was undergoing the punishment screamed unnaturally. A stout major walked up and down in front of the line, and, without heeding the man's shrieks, kept saying : —

"It's scandalous for a soldier to steal; a soldier ought to be honest, noble, and brave, and if he steals from his comrade, he has no honor in him; he's a mean fellow. More! more!"

And still resounded the swishing of the rods and the despairing but pretendedly piteous cries. "More! more!" repeated the major. A young officer, who was just turning away from the scene of the punishment with a mixed expression of incredulity and compassion, looked up questioningly at the aide, as he rode by.

Prince Andreï, passing to the extreme front, rode along by the outposts. The Russian pickets and those of the French were separated by a considerable distance at each flank, but at the center, on that space where the emissaries had crossed in the morning, the lines were so close that they could see one another's faces and exchange remarks. Besides the soldiers who were stationed as pickets in this place, there stood on both sides many sight-seers, who, laughing and jesting, stared at the hostile troops as if they were strange and foreign curiosities.

Ever since early morning (notwithstanding the orders forbidding their presence), the officers had been unable to rid themselves of these inquisitive persons within the lines. The soldiers, standing in the lines, like men who had come out to see something rare, no longer paid any attention to the French, but made observations on the new-comers, or, bored to death, waited to be relieved. Prince Andreï reined in his horse to reconnoiter the French.

"Look you, look!" said one soldier to his comrade, pointing to a musketeer, who, in company with an officer had gone up to the line of sentries, and was talking earnestly and hotly with a French grenadier. "See, how glib he jabbers! The Frenchman [1] can't begin to keep up with him. That beats you, Sidorof!"

"Wait! listen. He's clever!" replied Sidorof, who considered himself a master in the art of speaking French.

The soldier whom the jesters were remarking was Dolokhof. Prince Andreï recognized him, and listened to what he was saying. Dolokhof, with his captain, had gone up to the sentry on the left flank, where their regiment was stationed.

"There, once more, once more," urged the captain, leaning forward and trying not to miss a word, albeit it was perfectly unintelligible to him! "Please make haste! What does he say?"

Dolokhof did not answer his captain; he had got drawn into a heated discussion with the French grenadier. Naturally, they were talking about the campaign. The Frenchman, confusing the Austrians with the Russians, contended that it was the Russians who had surrendered and run away from Ulm. Dolokhof contended that the Russians had not surrendered, but had beaten the French. "And here, if they tell us to clear you out, we will do it," said Dolokhof.

"You look out that we don't take you and all your Cossacks with us," retorted the Frenchman.

The spectators and the Frenchmen, who were listening, laughed.

"We'll teach you to dance Russian fashion, as we did in the time of Suvorof," said Dolokhof.

"What's that tune he's giving us?" asked another Frenchman.

"Ancient history," said another, perceiving that the reference was to some past war. "The emperor will teach your *Souvára*, the same as he has taught others."

"Bonaparte," began Dolokhof, but the Frenchman interrupted him: —

"We have no Bonaparte. We have the emperor! *Sacré nom!*" .... cried the other, excitedly.

---

[1] *Khrantsus* instead of *Frantsus*, a Frenchman.

"The devil skin your emperor!"

And Dolokhof began to pour out a string of oaths, in Russian soldier fashion, and, shouldering his musket, walked off. "Let us be going, Ivan Lukitch," said he to his captain.

"He 's stopped talking French," cried the soldiers in the line. "Now it 's your turn, Sidorof!"

Sidorof winked, and, addressing the Frenchmen, began to jabber a perfect stream of meaningless words: "*Kari, mala, tafa, safi, muter, kaská*," he jabbered, trying to give great expression to the inflexions of his voice.

"Ho! ho! ho! ha! ha! ha! ukh! ukh!" rang among the soldiers with such a hearty and jovial laughter, that the Frenchmen across the line were irresistibly infected, and one would have thought, after this, that all that was necessary was for them all to fire off their muskets, explode their cartridges, and scatter to their homes as soon as possible; but the guns remained loaded, the barbicans in the huts and earthworks looked out just as threateningly as ever, and the unlimbered cannon remained as before, pointing at each other.

CHAPTER XVI

AFTER riding along the entire line, from the right flank to the left, Prince Andreï made his way to the battery, from which, according to the staff-officer, the whole field was visible. Here he dismounted and leaned against the last one of four unlimbered field-pieces.

An artilleryman, who was pacing up and down in front of the guns, as sentry, started to give Prince Andreï the military salute, but at a sign desisted, and once more began his monotonous, tedious march.

Behind the guns were the gun-carriages; still farther back the horses were picketed, and the bivouac fires of the gunners were burning. At the left, at a little distance from the outermost gun, was a new, wattled hut, in which could be heard the lively voices of officers, talking together.

From the battery was really disclosed a view of almost all the disposition of the Russian forces, and of a large part of the enemy's. Directly in front of the battery, on the slope of another hill, lay the village of Schöngraben. Farther, both to the left and to the right, could be distinguished in three places, through the smoke of their bivouac fires, the masses of the French troops, the greater part of which were evidently stationed in the village itself, and behind the hill.

At the left of the village, in the smoke, something that resembled a battery could be made out, but by the naked eye it was impossible to distinguish it clearly. The Russian right flank was distributed along a rather steep elevation, which commanded the position of the French. Here were stationed the Russian infantry, and at the very end could be seen the dragoons.

In the center, where Tusnin's battery was posted, and where Prince Andreï was studying the lay of the land, there was a very steep and direct descent and approach to a brook separating the Russians from Schöngraben.

At the left of the Russian position, the infantry were engaged in cutting wood in the forest, and there also arose the smoke of their bivouac fires.

The French lines were much more extended than the Russians, and it was plain that the French could easily outflank them on both sides. Back of the Russian position was a steep and deep ravine, along which it would be difficult for artillery or cavalry to retreat.

Prince Andreï, leaning on the cannon, took out a note-book and drew a plan of the disposition of the armies. At two places he indicated with a pencil certain observations to which he intended to draw Bagration's attention. In the first place, it was his idea that the artillery should be concentrated in the center, and, in the second place, to transfer all the cavalry to the other side of the ravine.

Prince Andreï, having been constantly thrown with the commander-in-chief, and occupied with the movements of masses and general arrangements, and having diligently studied descriptions of historical engagements, found himself involuntarily trying to forecast the course of the action, but only in its general features. He imagined that the engagement would probably occur somewhat as follows : —

"If the enemy attack the right flank," said he to himself, "the Kief grenadiers and the Podolian jägers will be obliged to hold their position until the reserves from the center are sent to their aid. In this case, the dragoons may attack the flank and cut them to pieces. In case the attack is made on the center, we must place on this elevation our central battery, and under its protection we can draw back the left flank, and let them retreat down the ravine *en échelon*."

Thus he reflected.

All the time that he was in the battery by the cannon, he had constantly heard the voices of the officers, talking in the hut, but, as often happens, he had not noticed a single word that they said. Suddenly he was so struck by the note of sincerity in the tone of their voices, that he involuntarily began to listen.

"No, my dear," [1] said a pleasant voice, which somehow seemed very familiar to Prince Andreï. "I say that if it were possible to know what was to be after death, then none of us would have any fear of death. That's so, my dear."

Another voice, evidently that of a younger man, interrupted him : —

"Well, whether we're afraid of it or not, it's all the same, there's no escaping it."

"But all men are afraid of it."

"Yes, you know so much," said a third lusty voice, breaking in upon the others. "You artillerymen know so much because you can take with you, everywhere you go, your tipples of vodka and your rations."

And the possessor of the lusty voice, evidently an infantry officer, laughed.

"Yes, all men are afraid of it," continued the first familiar voice. "We are afraid of the unknown; that's it. It's no use saying the soul goes up to heaven ; why,

[1] *Galúbchik.*

we know very well that up yonder there's no heaven, but only the atmosphere."

Again the lusty voice interrupted the artilleryman : —

"Come, now, Tushin, let us have some of your travnik." [1]

"So that is the very same captain that was at the sutler's tent, in his stocking-feet," said Prince Andreï to himself, glad to recognize the pleasant voice of the philosopher.

"The travnik you can have," said Tushin, "but all the same, as to comprehending the life to come ...."

He did not finish his sentence.

At that instant a whizz was heard in the air; nearer and nearer, swifter and louder, louder and swifter, and a cannon-ball, as if unable to say all that it wanted to say, plunged into the earth not far from the hut, tearing up the ground with superhuman violence.

The ground seemed to groan with the terrible shock.

In a moment the little Tushin came running out of the hut ahead of the others, with his after-dinner pipe at the side of his mouth; his kind, intelligent face was rather pale. He was followed by the possessor of the lusty voice, a young infantry officer, who hurried off to his company, buttoning his coat as he ran.

CHAPTER XVII

PRINCE ANDREÏ mounted his horse, but remained in the battery, trying to distinguish, by the smoke, the cannon that had sent the projectile. His eyes wandered over the whole landscape. All that he could make out was that the till now motionless masses of the French were beginning to stir, and that there really was a battery at the left. The smoke above it had not yet dispersed. Two French riders, apparently aides, were spurring down the hill. At the foot of the hill, a small but clearly distinguishable column of the enemy were moving, evidently for the purpose of strengthening the lines.

[1] A strong beer made of herbs (*travui*).

The smoke of the first gun had not blown away when another puff arose, followed by the report.

The action had begun.

Prince Andreï turned his horse and galloped back to Grund, to find Prince Bagration. Behind him he heard the cannonade, growing more frequent and louder. It was plain that our side had begun to reply. Below, in the space where the envoys had met, musket-shots were heard.

Lemarrois, with Bonaparte's angry letter, had just dashed up to Murat, and Murat, ashamed of himself, and anxious to retrieve his blunder, had immediately begun to move his army against the center, and at the same time around both flanks, hoping, before night and the arrival of the emperor, to demolish the insignificant division that opposed him.

"It has begun! Here it is!" said Prince Andreï to himself, feeling his heart beat more violently. "But where — how shall I find my Toulon?"

Riding among the companies which had been eating their kasha gruel and drinking vodka only a quarter of an hour before, he everywhere found the soldiers hastily moving about, getting into line, and examining their guns; on all faces there was the same feeling of expectancy as he had in his heart.

The face of every soldier and officer seemed to say : '*It has begun! Here it is! How terrible! How glorious!*'

Before he reached the unfinished earthworks, he saw in the twilight of the gloomy autumn day some horsemen riding toward him. The foremost, in a felt burka and a lamb's-wool cap, rode a white horse. This was Prince Bagration. Prince Andreï stopped and waited for them. Prince Bagration reined in his horse, and, recognizing Prince Andreï, nodded to him. He kept his eyes straight ahead all the time, while Prince Andreï was reporting to him what he had seen. The thought, *it has begun; here it is!* could also be read on Bagration's strong, brown face with the half-closed, dull eyes, that seemed to show the lack of sleep. Prince Andreï, with uneasy curiosity looked into his impassive face, and tried to read whether he had any thoughts or feelings, and if so, what the thoughts and feelings of this man were at this moment. "Is there anything remarkable behind that impassive face?"

Prince Bagration nodded his head in approval of what Prince Andreï reported, and said, "Good!" as if all that had taken place and all that he heard was exactly what he had already anticipated. Prince Andreï, all out of breath from his swift gallop, spoke hurriedly. Prince Bagration pronounced his words with his Eastern accent, and with especial deliberation, as if to give the impression that there was no haste. However, he put his horse to the trot in the direction of Tushin's battery.

Prince Andreï and his suite followed him. His suite consisted of an attaché, Zherkof, the prince's personal aide, an orderly, the staff-officer of the day on a handsome English cob, and a civil chinovnik serving as auditor, who, out of curiosity, had asked permission to come out to the battle. The auditor, a fat man with a fat face, with a naïve smile of delight, glanced around, as he jolted on his horse, presenting a strange figure, in his camelot cloak on a pack-saddle, among the hussars, Cossacks, and aides.

"This man here wanted to see a battle," said Zherkof to Bolkonsky, pointing to the auditor. "Why, he 's got a pain in the pit of his stomach already!"

"Come, now, that 'll do," exclaimed the auditor with a radiant, naïve and at the same time shrewd smile, as if he enjoyed being made the butt of Zherkof's jokes, and as if he purposely made himself out to be duller than he really was.

"*Très drôle, mon monsieur prince*," said the staff-officer of the day. He remembered that in French there was some peculiar way of speaking the title of prince, but he could not get it quite right.

By this time they had all reached Tushin's battery; a cannon-ball fell a short distance in front of them.

"What was that fell?" asked the auditor, with his naïve smile.

"French pancakes," replied Zherkof.

"Such things kill, I suppose?" mused the auditor. "How shocking!" And it was evident that he took great delight in witnessing the whole scene.

The words were hardly out of his mouth, when again unexpectedly came the same terrible whistle, interrupted suddenly by striking into something alive, and with a strange thud a Cossack, riding only a few steps behind, and at the right, plunged off his horse to the ground. Zherkof and the staff-officer of the day crouched down in their saddles, and drew their horses to one side. The auditor reined up near the Cossack, and looked at him with eager curiosity. The Cossack was dead, the horse was still struggling.

Prince Bagration, blinking his eyes, glanced around and, seeing the cause of the confusion, turned his head again indifferently, as much as to say: 'It isn't worth while to bother with trifles.' He reined in his horse with the skill of a good rider, bent over a trifle, and adjusted his sword, which had got entangled in his burka. The sword was an old one, unlike those worn at the present time. Prince Andreï remembered having heard it said that Suvorof had given his sword to Bagration in Italy, and this recollection was peculiarly agreeable to him at this time.

They reached the very same battery where Bolkonsky had been when he made his reconnoissance of the battle-field.

"Whose company?" asked Prince Bagration of the gunner who was standing by the caissons.

He asked, "Whose company," but his question seemed really to imply: 'Are n't you all frightened, you men here?' And the gunner understood it so.

"Captain Tushin's, your excellency," cried the freckled, red-headed gunner, in a jocund voice, and saluting.

"So, so," exclaimed Bagration absent-mindedly, and he passed by the limbers toward the last gun. Just as he reached it, this cannon rang out, with a report which deafened Bagration and his suite, and in the smoke that spread round could be seen the gunners, seizing the cannon and slowly bringing it back to its first place.

Gunner number one, a huge soldier with broad shoulders, holding the sponge, leaped back with a long stride to the wheel, and number two, with trembling hand, forced the charge down the muzzle. A little round-shouldered man, the officer Tushin, stumbling over the tail of the carriage, hastened forward, without heeding the general, and gazed into the distance from under his small hand.

"Raise it two lines more; there, there! that'll do," he cried, in his little, thin voice, to which he tried to impart a vigor ill-suiting his stature. "Number two!" he whined. "Let 'em have it, Medvyedef!"

Bagration beckoned to the officer, and Tushin, with an awkward and timid gesture, absolutely unlike those used by military men, and more like a priest when giving a blessing, raised three fingers to his visor and went to the general. Although it had been intended for Tushin's field-pieces to sweep the valley, he had begun to send red-hot balls at the village of Schöngraben, in front of which heavy masses of the French could be seen concentrating.

No one had directed Tushin where and how to fire, and so, having consulted with his sergeant Zakharchenko, in whom he had great confidence, he decided that it would be a good plan to set the village on fire.

"Good," said Bagration, in reply to the officer's scheme, and then began to scan the field of battle before him, and seemed to be lost in thought.

On the right, in the foreground, the French were advancing. Below the height on which the Kief regiment was stationed, in the ravine through which flowed the brook, could be heard the soul-stirring roll and rattle of musketry, and, just at the right, the attaché pointed out to the prince the column of the French trying to outflank the Russian wing. At the left, the horizon was bounded by dense forest.

Prince Bagration ordered two battalions from the center to strengthen the right wing. The attaché ventured to remark to the prince that, if these battalions were withdrawn, the artillery would be uncovered. Prince Bagration turned to the attaché and without replying looked at him through his lifeless eyes. It seemed to Prince Andreï that the attaché's criticism was correct, and that in fact no reply could be made to it. But at this instant an aide came galloping up from the regimental commander who was in the valley, with the report that overwhelming masses of the French were marching down upon them, and that his regiment was demoralized, and was falling back upon the Kief grenadiers. Prince Bagration inclined his head in token of assent and approval. He walked slowly toward the right, and then sent the aide to order the dragoons to charge the French. But, after the aide had been gone half an hour with this order, he returned with the report that the commander of the dragoon regiment had retired to the other side of the ravine, so as to escape the destructive fire brought to bear upon him and to avoid useless loss of life, and therefore he had despatched sharpshooters into the woods. "Good," said Bagration.

Just as he was leaving the battery, at the left also, the reports of rifles in the forest began to be heard, and as it was too far for him to reach the left wing in time, Prince Bagration sent Zherkof thither to tell the old general — the very one who had exhibited his regiment before Kutuzof at Braunau — to retreat as soon as possible to the other side of the ravine, since, probably, the right wing would not be strong enough to withstand the enemy any length of time. Tushin and the battalion covering him were quite forgotten.

Prince Andreï listened attentively to Prince Bagration's conversation with his subordinates, and to the orders that he issued, and to his amazement discovered that in reality he did not give any orders at all, but that the prince only tried to give the impression that all that was done by his various officers either through necessity, chance, or volition, was done, if not exactly by his orders, at all events in accordance with his design. Prince Andreï noticed that, owing to the tact displayed by Prince Bagration, in spite of the fortuitousness of events and their absolute independence of the general's will, his presence was of great importance. The subordinates, with distracted faces, who kept galloping up to the prince, instantly became calm; soldiers and officers received him with enthusiasm, and were animated by his presence and evidently took pride in displaying their courage.

CHAPTER XVIII

PRINCE BAGRATION, having ridden up to the highest point of the Russian right flank, began to make the descent, toward a spot where the continual rattle of musketry was heard and nothing could be seen through the gunpowder smoke. The nearer they approached the valley, the less they could see what was going on, but the more evident it became that they were near an actual battle-field. They began to meet with wounded. One man, with a bleeding head, and without his cap, was being dragged along in the arms of two soldiers. He was gurgling and spitting. The bullet had apparently entered his mouth or throat. Another whom they met was stoutly marching off by himself, without his musket, groaning loudly and shaking his injured hand with the keenness of the smart, while the blood was slowly dripping down on his cloak. His face appeared more frightened than hurt. He had only just been wounded. Crossing the road, they rode down a steep incline and on the slope they saw a number of men lying; then they met a crowd of soldiers, none of whom were wounded. These soldiers were hurrying up the slope, breathing heavily, and though they saw the general they were talking in loud voices and gesticulating.

Farther forward in the smoke could now be seen the ranks of gray cloaks, and an officer, recognizing Bagration, dashed after the retreating throng of men, shouting to them to return. Bagration rode up to the lines, along which, here and there, could be heard the swift cracking of musket-shots, suppressed remarks, and the shouts of command. The whole atmosphere was dense with gunpowder smoke. The faces of all the soldiers were blackened with powder, and full of animation. Some were ramming the charge home, others putting powder in the pan, or taking wads from their pouches; still others were firing. But it was impossible to make out what they were aiming at through the dense cloud of smoke which hung in the motionless air. Quite often could be heard the pleasant sounds of buzzing and whistling bullets.

"What does this mean?" Prince Andreï asked himself, as he rode up to this throng of soldiers. "It cannot be a charge, because they are not moving; it cannot be a square, for that is not the way they form."

The regimental commander, a rather spare, slender old man, with eyelids which more than half concealed his aged-looking eyes, giving him a benignant aspect, rode up toward Prince Bagration with a pleasant smile, and received him as a host receives a welcome guest. He explained to Prince Bagration that the French had made a cavalry charge against his regiment; but that, though the charge had been repelled, it had cost him half of his men. The regimental commander declared that the charge had been repulsed, meaning to express, by this military term, what had happened to his forces; but in reality he himself did not know what had taken place during the preceding half-hour, in the army entrusted to his command, and was unable to say with absolute certainty whether the charge had been repulsed or whether his regiment had been worsted in the attack. At the beginning of the engagement he simply knew this: that along his whole line, cannon-balls and shells began to fly and to kill his men, that next, some one had cried "The cavalry!" and our men had begun to fire. And they had been firing till that time, not at the cavalry, which was out of sight, but at the French infantry showing themselves in the valley and shooting down our men.

Prince Bagration inclined his head, to signify that this was just as he had wished and anticipated. Turning to his aide, he ordered him to bring down from the hill the two battalions of the Sixth Jägers, which they had just ridden past. At this moment Prince Andreï was struck by the change which had taken place in Bagration's face. It expressed that concentrated and joyful resolution which is shown by a man ready on a hot day to leap into the water, and who is taking the final run. That impression of dullness and lethargy covering a pretense of deep thoughts had vanished quite away. His hawk's eyes, round and determined, looked straight ahead with an enthusiastic and rather contemptuous expression, and wandered restlessly from one object to another, although his motions were as slow and deliberate as before.

The regimental commander turned to Prince Bagration, and begged him to retire to the rear, on the ground that it was very perilous where they were. "Please, your illustriousness, for God's sake," said he, looking for confirmation to the attaché, who was turning away from him. "Be kind enough to notice."

He was calling his attention to the bullets which were constantly whizzing, singing, and whistling around them. He spoke in a questioning, reproachful tone, such as a joiner might use to a gentleman trying to use an ax: "This is our work and we 're used to it, but you will callous your dainty hands." He spoke as if there was no possibility of these bullets killing him, and his half-closed eyes gave his words a still more persuasive effect.

The staff-officer joined his entreaties to those of the regimental commander, but Prince Bagration did not deign to answer him, and merely gave his orders to have the men cease firing and to open ranks so as to give room for the two battalions that were on their way to join them. Just as he issued his command, a breeze sprang up and the canopy of smoke which covered the valley from right to left was lifted as if by an invisible hand, and the opposite height, with the French marching down, was brought into full view. All eyes were involuntarily fixed on this column of the enemy moving toward them, and winding like a serpent down the escarpment of the hill. Already, the soldiers' bearskin shakoes could be seen; already, the officers could be distinguished from the ranks, and their banner, as it clung around the staff.

"They march superbly," said some one in Bagration's suite.

The head of the column was now just entering the valley. The collision would necessarily take place on this side of the ravine. ....

The remains of the regiment that had been in the action before hastily reformed and went toward the right; behind them, driving in the stragglers, came the two battalions of the Sixth Jägers, in good order. They had not yet reached the position where Bagration was, but their heavy, measured step could be heard, as the whole body kept perfect time. On the left wing, nearest of all to Bagration, marched the company commander, a round-faced, stately man, with a stupid, happy expression of face. He was the very man that had been in Tushin's hut. It was evident that his only thought at this moment was that he was marching bravely past his superiors.

With the self-satisfaction of one attracting notice, he marched by lightly on his muscular legs; he almost seemed to fly, without the slightest effort keeping his back straight, and distinguishing himself by his grace from the heavy march of the men who pressed on in step with him.

He held down by his leg a slender, delicate sword, unsheathed, a sort of curving simitar, not like a weapon, and looking now at the commander, now back at his men, not once losing step, he gallantly hastened on, with all the energy of his gigantic frame. It seemed as if all the strength of his mind were directed toward going past his commander in the best possible form; being conscious that he was doing this, he was happy. *Left! .... left! .... left!* .... It seemed as if he said this inwardly at every instant, and, taking the same step, the wall of soldiers marched by with heavy knapsacks and equipment, as if each one of these hundreds of different soldiers, with their grave faces, said to himself in thought, *left! .... left! .... left! ....*

A stout major had to turn out, puffing, and losing step, for a bush which was in his way; a straggler, gasping for breath, his face expressing terror at his being out of his place, came at a double-quick to overtake his company; a cannon-ball, condensing the air before it, flew over the heads of Bagration and his suite, and, accenting the beat, *left !* .... *left !* .... plunged through the column.

"Close up the ranks!" rang the intrepid voice of the company commander. The soldiers made a bend around the place where the shot had made the gap; an old cavalryman, a non-commissioned officer, who had remained behind to care for the wounded, regained the ranks, with a hop and a skip fell into step, and looked around sternly. *Left !* .... *left !* .... *left !* .... seemed to resound from the threatening silence, and from the monotonous trampling of feet beating simultaneously on the ground.

"Keep up your courage, boys!" said Prince Bagration.

"Glad-ad-ad," [1] ran the reply down the line. A morose-looking soldier, as he passed at the left, shouting at the top of his voice, turned his eyes on Bagration, his expression seeming to say, 'We know'; another, not looking up, and evidently afraid of having his attention distracted, with wide-open mouth, shouted and went by.

The command was given to halt and unstrap knapsacks.

Bagration rode up to the ranks that had just marched past him, and got down from his horse. He gave the bridle to a Cossack, took off his burka and handed it to him, stretched his legs, and adjusted his leather cap on his head. The head of the French column, with officers at the front, now appeared at the foot of the hill.

"*S Bogom !* — God be with you!" shouted Bagration, in a firm, loud, ringing voice, and instantly taking the lead, and lightly waving his arm, led them himself, with the awkward and apparently laborious gait of a cavalryman, across the first half of the field. Prince Andreï

[1] Glad of the trouble.

felt as if some irresistible impulse dragged him forward, and he experienced a great sense of happiness.[1]

Already the French were near at hand, already Prince Andreï, rushing on side by side with Bagration, saw the belts, the red epaulets, even the faces of the French. (He clearly distinguished one elderly French officer, who, with feet turned out and wearing gaiters, was struggling up the hill.)

Prince Bagration gave no new orders, and marched on in silence at the head of his forces. Suddenly, from among the French, rang out one discharge, then a second, a third! and along the whole extent of the enemy's lines spread smoke and the rattle of musketry. A few of the Russians fell; in the number, that round-faced officer who had marched by so gallantly and in such good form. But at the very instant that the first discharge had taken place, Bagration turned round and shouted "hurrah."

"Hurrah-ah-ah," rang in a protracted yell down the line, and, outstripping Bagration and one another, in a broken but joyous and animated line, the Russians dashed down the slope after the enemy, who had given way.

CHAPTER XIX

THE charge of the Sixth Jägers secured the retreat of the right wing. In the center, the action of Tushin's forgotten battery, which had succeeded in setting the village of Schöngraben on fire, retarded the advance of the French. They stopped to put out the conflagration, which the wind was spreading, and thus gave time to retreat. The retirement of the center through the

[1] Here followed that charge of which Taine says: "The Russians behaved gallantly, and, a rare thing in war, two masses of infantry were seen marching resolutely against each other, neither giving way before they came within reach of each other. (*Les Russes se conduisèrent vaillament, et chose rare à la guerre on vit deux masses d'infanterie marcher resolument l'une contre l'autre sans qu'aucune des deux ceda avant d'être abordé.*)" And Napoleon said at Saint Helena: "*Quelques bataillons russes montrèrent de l'intrépidité.*"— AUTHOR'S NOTE.

ravine was accomplished hastily and noisily, but there was no sign of demoralization.

But the left wing, consisting of the infantry of the Azof and Podolian regiments, and the Pavlograd hussars, which was attacked simultaneously, and outflanked by overwhelming numbers of the French, under the command of Lannes, was defeated.

Bagration had sent Zherkhof to the general in command of the left wing, with orders to retreat slowly. Zherkof, raising his hand to his cap, struck spurs into his horse and swiftly dashed off. But he had not more than got out of Bagration's sight than his courage began to fail him. Irresistible fear came over him, and he could not make up his mind to go where it seemed to him so perilous.

He rode over to the army of the left wing, but he did not dare press forward to the front, where there was firing, and he began to search for the general and the officers where there was no possibility of finding them, and therefore the order was not delivered.

The command of the left wing fell by order of seniority to the regimental commander of that same brigade which had been reviewed at Braunau by Kutuzof, and in which Dolokhof served as a private. The command of the extreme left wing was intrusted to the colonel of the Pavlograd regiment, in which Rostof served. This led to a serious misunderstanding. The two commanders had become involved in a violent quarrel, and at the very time when the right wing was in the thick of the battle, and the French had already begun to retreat, the two commanders were absorbed in a dispute, each doing his best to affront the other.

The troops, both infantry and cavalry, were very far from being prepared for the work before them. The men, from private to general, were not expecting an engagement, and were calmly occupying themselves with the ordinary pursuits of peace, — the cavalrymen engaged in feeding their horses, the infantry in collecting firewood.

"He's my senior, however, in rank," the German

colonel of hussars was saying, flushing and addressing the aide who had just ridden up to him, "so let him do as he pleases. I cannot sacrifice my hussars. Bugler, sound the retreat!"

But the battle came upon them in hot haste. Cannonade and musketry, all in confusion, thundered and rattled at their right and center, and the capotes of Lannes's sharpshooters were already crossing the mill-dam and forming on this side, two gunshots away. The infantry general, with his tottering gait, went to his horse, and, mounting and drawing himself up very straight and tall, rode off to the Pávlograd commander. The two men met with polite bows, and with concealed hatred in their hearts.

"Once for all, colonel," said the general, "I cannot leave half of my men in the woods. I beg of you, I really beg of you," he repeated the word, "to draw up in position, and meet the charge."

"I beg of you not to meddle in what does not concern you," replied the colonel, angrily. "If you were a cavalryman...."

"I am not a cavalryman, colonel, but I am a Russian general, and if you don't know this...."

"I know it very well, your excellency," cried the colonel, suddenly starting up his horse and turning purple with rage. "Would n't you like to come to the line, and then you can see that this position is as bad as it could be? I do not care to destroy my regiment for your gratification."

"You forget yourself, colonel. I am not seeking my own gratification, and I will not permit this to be said."

The general, accepting the colonel's invitation as a challenge of courage, swelled out his chest, and, frowning, rode forward with him in the direction of the outposts, as if all their dispute were to be settled there, at the front, under the fire of the enemy. They reached the outposts; a few bullets flew over them, and they paused and were silent. There was no reason for inspecting the outposts, since, from the place where they had been before, it was perfectly evident that there was no chance for cavalry to manœuver among the bushes and gullies, and that the French were outflanking the left wing.

The general and colonel looked at each other with fierce and significant eyes, like two game-cocks all ready for battle, and each waited vainly for the other to show sign of cowardice. Both stood the test. As there was nothing for them to say, and as neither wished to give the other a chance to assert that he had been the first to retire from exposure to the enemy's fire, they would have stood there a long time, each manifesting his bravado, if at this time they had not heard in the forest, almost directly behind them, the crackling of musketry and a dull, confused yell.

The French had fallen on the soldiery scattered through the forest gathering firewood. It was now impossible for the hussars to retreat at the same time with the infantry. They were already cut off by the French line at the left. Now, although the locality was most unpropitious, it was absolutely necessary to fight their way through to reach the road beyond.

The squadron in which Rostof served had barely time to mount their horses, before they found themselves face to face with the enemy. Again, as at the bridge over the Enns, between the squadron and the line of the enemy there was no one, and between them lay that terrible gap of the unknown and the dreadful, like the bourn that divides the living from the dead. All the men felt conscious of that gap, and were occupied by the question whether they should pass beyond it or not, and how they should cross it.

The colonel came galloping along the front, and angrily replied to the questions of his officers, and, like a man who in despair insists on his own way, thundered out some command. No one said anything definitely, but something had given the squadron an idea that there was to be a charge. The command to fall in was given, then sabers were drawn with a clash. But as yet no one stirred. The army of the left wing and the infantry and the hussars felt that their leaders did not know what to do, and the indecision of the commanders communicated itself to the soldiers.

"If they would only hurry, hurry," thought Rostof, feeling that at last the time was at hand for participating in the intoxication of a charge of which he had heard so much from his comrades, the hussars.

"*S Bogom !* Fohwahd, children," rang out Denísof's voice, "twot!"

In the front rank, the haunches of the horses began to rise and fall. Grachik began to pull on the reins, and dashed ahead. At the right, Rostof could see the forward ranks of his hussars, but farther in front there was a dark streak, which he could not make out distinctly, but supposed to be the enemy. Reports were heard, but in the distance.

"Charge!" rang the command, and Rostof felt how his Grachik broke into a gallop and seemed to strain every nerve. He realized that his division was dashing forward and it became more and more exciting to him. He noticed a solitary tree just abreast of him. At first this tree had been in front of him, in the very center of that line which seemed so terrible. But now he had passed beyond it and there was not only nothing terrible about it, but everything seemed ever more and more jolly and lively.

"Okh! how I will slash at them!" thought Rostof, as he grasped the handle of his saber.

"Hurrah-ah-ah-ah!" rang the cheers in the distance.

"Now let us be at them if ever," thought Rostof, striking the spurs into Grachik; and, overtaking the others, he urged him to the top of his speed. The enemy were already in sight before him. Suddenly, something like an enormous lash cracked all along the squadron. Rostof raised his saber, in readiness to strike, but just at that instant Nikitenko, a hussar galloping in front of him, swerved aside from him, and Rostof felt, as in a dream, that he was being carried with unnatural swiftness forward, and yet was not moving from the spot. A hussar whom he recognized as Bandarchuk was galloping behind him and looked at him gravely. Bandarchuk's horse shied and he dashed by him.

"What does it mean? Am I not moving? Have I fallen? Am I dead?" These questions Rostof asked and answered in a breath. He was alone in the middle of the field. In place of the galloping horses and backs of the hussars, he saw all around him the solid earth and stubble. Warm blood was under him. "No, I am wounded, and my horse is killed."

Grachik raised himself on his fore legs, but fell back, pinning down his rider's foot. From the horse's head a stream of blood was flowing. The horse struggled but could not rise. Rostof tried to get to his feet, but likewise fell back. His sabretash had caught on the saddle. Where our men were, where the French were, he could not tell. There was no one around him.

Freeing his leg, he got up.

"Where, in which direction, is now that line which so clearly separated the two armies?" he asked himself, and could find no answer. "Has something bad happened to me? Is this the way things take place, and what must be done in such circumstances?" he asked himself again, as he got to his feet; and at this time he began to feel as if something extra were hanging to his benumbed left arm. His wrist seemed to belong to another person. He looked at his hand, but could find no trace of blood on it. "There now, here are our fellows," he exclaimed mentally, with joy, perceiving a few running toward him. "They will help me."

In front of these men ran one in a foreign-looking shako and in a blue capote. He was dark and sunburnt, and had a hooked nose. Two or three others were running at his heels.

One of them said something in a language that was strange and un-Russian. Surrounded by a similar set of men, in the same sort of shakoes, stood a Russian hussar. His hands were held; just behind him they were holding his horse.

"Is our man really taken prisoner? Yes! And will they take me too? Who are these men?" Rostof kept asking himself, not crediting his own eyes. "Can they be the French?"

He gazed at the on-coming strangers, and, in spite of the fact that only a second before he had been dashing forward solely for the purpose of overtaking and hacking down these same Frenchmen, their proximity now seemed to him so terrible that he could not trust his own eyes!

"Who are they? Why are they running? Are they running at me? And why? Is it to kill me? *Me*, whom every one loves so?"

He recollected how he was beloved by his mother, his family, his friends, and the purpose of his enemies to kill him seemed incredible.

"But perhaps .... they may .... " For more than ten seconds he stood, not moving from the spot and not realizing his situation.

The foremost Frenchman, with the hooked nose, had now come up so close to him that he could see the expression of his face. And the heated foreign-looking features of this man, who was coming so swiftly down upon him with fixed bayonet and bated breath, filled Rostof with horror. He grasped his pistol, but, instead of discharging it, flung it at the Frenchmen, and fled into the thicket with all his might. He ran, not with any of that feeling of doubt and struggle which had possessed him on the bridge at Enns, but rather with the impulse of a hare trying to escape from the dogs. One single fear of losing his happy young life took possession of his whole being. Swiftly gliding among the heather, with all the intensity with which he had ever run when playing *gorelki*,[1] he flew across the field, occasionally turning round his pale, kindly young face, while a chill of horror ran down his back.

"No, I'd better not look round," he said to himself, but, as he reached the shelter of the bushes, he glanced round once more. The Frenchmen had slackened their pace, and at the very minute that he glanced round, the foremost runner had just come to a stop and was start-

[1] A kind of Russian popular game, something like tag.

ing to walk back, shouting something in a loud voice to his comrade behind him. Rostof paused. "It cannot be so," he said to himself. "It cannot be that they wish to kill me." But meantime his left arm became as heavy as if a hundredweight were suspended to it. He could not run another step. The Frenchman also paused, and aimed. Rostof shut his eyes and ducked his head. One bullet, then another, flew humming by him. He collected his last remaining energies, took his left arm in his right hand, and hurried into the thicket. Here in the bushes were the Russian sharpshooters.

CHAPTER XX

THE infantry regiments, taken unawares in the forest, had rushed out, and the companies, becoming confused with one another, had formed a demoralized mob. One soldier, in his panic, had shouted the senseless words so terrible in war: "Cut off!" and these words, with the accompanying panic, had spread through the whole troop. "Surrounded!".... "Cut off!".... "Lost!" cried the voices of the fugitives.

The regimental commander, the moment he heard the musketry and the shouting behind him, comprehended that something awful had happened to his regiment, and the thought that he, who had been during many years of service an exemplary officer, never guilty of any breach, might now be accused of negligence or faulty arrangements, came on him so keenly, that, for the moment entirely forgetting the recalcitrant colonel of cavalry and his own importance as a general, and, above all, forgetting the peril and the impulse of self-preservation, he seized the saddle-bow, and, spurring on his horse, dashed back toward the regiment under a shower of bullets falling all around him, but fortunately sparing him. He had only one desire: to find out what had occurred, to bring aid, and to repair the blunder, if it were in any way to be attributed to him, and to escape all censure after his twenty-two years' service,

in which his record as an officer had been blameless.

Having fortunately spurred through the line of the
French unharmed, he came upon his regiment on the
other side of the same forest through which the Russians had been running and scattering down the ravine,
not heeding the word of command.

That moment of moral vacillation had arrived which
decides the fate of a battle: would these scattered
throngs of soldiers heed their commander's voice, or
would they merely look at him and pursue their way?

Notwithstanding the despairing shouts of their general, which had hitherto been so terrible to them, notwithstanding his infuriated, purple face, so unlike its
ordinary appearance, and notwithstanding his brandished sword, the soldiers still persisted in their flight,
shouted, fired their guns into the air, and paid no heed
to the command. The moral balance, which decides
the destiny of battles, had evidently kicked the beam
on the side of panic.

The general coughed, choking with the violence of
his shouts and the gunpowder smoke, and reined in his
horse in despair. All seemed lost.

But at this moment the French, who had fallen upon
our lines, suddenly, without any apparent reason, fell
back and vanished behind the edge of the forest, and
the Russian sharpshooters made their appearance. This
was Timokhin's company, the only one in the woods
which had preserved any semblance of order; entrench-
ing themselves in the ditch near the forest, they had unexpectedly attacked the French. Timokhin had thrown
himself upon the enemy with such a desperate cry, and,
flourishing his rapier, had dashed after them with such
frantic and rash energy, that the French, before they
had time to collect their wits, flung away their muskets
and fled.

Dolokhof, dashing on abreast of Timokhin, killed one
Frenchman point blank, and was the first to seize the
officer by the collar and make him surrender. The fugitives turned back, the battalions formed again, and the

French, who had cut the left wing in two, were driven back in a trice. The reserves succeeded in uniting their forces; the fugitives were brought to a halt.

The regimental commander was standing with Major Ekonomof by the bridge, watching the retreating companies file past him, when a soldier approached him, seized his stirrup, and almost leaned against him. This soldier wore a blue cloak of broadcloth, without knapsack or shako; his head was bound up, and over his shoulder he carried a French cartridge-pouch. In his hand he held an officer's sword. This soldier was pale; his blue eyes looked boldly into the general's face, and a smile parted his lips. Although the general was engaged in giving directions to Major Ekonomof, he could not help noticing this soldier.

"Your excellency, here are two trophies," said Dolokhof, showing the French cartridge-pouch and sword. "I took an officer prisoner with my own hand. I stopped the company."

Dolokhof was all out of breath with fatigue. He spoke in broken sentences. "The whole company can bear me witness. .... I beg of you to remember it, your excellency!"

"Very good, very good," said the regimental commander, and he turned to Major Ekonomof. But Dolokhof did not pass on. He untied his handkerchief, pulled him by the sleeve, and called his attention to the clotted blood on his hair: —

"A bayonet wound; I was in the front. Remember, your excellency!"

Tushin's battery had been entirely forgotten, and only at the very end of the engagement, Prince Bagration, still hearing cannonading at the center, sent thither the first staff-officer of the day, and then Prince Andreï, to order the battery to retire as speedily as possible.

The covering forces, which had been stationed near Tushin's cannon, had been withdrawn during the heat of the engagement by some one's orders; but the battery still continued to blaze away, and had not been taken by the French, simply because the enemy could not comprehend the audacity of four guns continuing to fire, after the supporting columns had been withdrawn. On the contrary, they supposed, from the energetic activity of this battery, that the principal forces of the Russians were here concentrated in the center, and twice they attempted to storm this point, and both times they were driven back by discharges of grape from these four cannon, standing alone on the hill.

Shortly after Prince Bagration's departure, Tushin had succeeded in setting Schöngraben on fire.

"See, see them scatter!".... "It burns! see the smoke!" .... "Cleverly done!" ...: "Splendid!" .... "The smoke! the smoke!" cried the gunners, growing excited.

All the cannon had been directed, without special orders, in the direction of the fire. As if by one impulse the soldiers would cry out after every shot, "Cleverly done!" .... "That's the way to do it!" .... "See! see there! admirable!"

The fire, fanned by the wind, quickly spread. The French columns, retreating behind the village, fell back, but as if for a punishment for this misfortune, the enemy established a battery of ten guns a little to the right of the village and began to reply to Tushin's fire.

In their childish delight at setting the village on fire and at their successful onslaught upon the French, our gunners did not notice this battery until two cannonballs, followed by four at once, fell among the guns; one of them knocked over two horses, and the other carried away the leg of the powder-master. The animation of the men, once aroused, was not dampened, however, but only changed in character. The horses were replaced by two others from the reserve; the wounded were removed, and the four cannon were turned against the ten-gun battery.

An officer, Tushin's comrade, had been killed at the beginning of the action, and, during the course of the hour, out of forty men serving the guns, seventeen were disabled; but still the gunners were jolly and full of energy. Twice they noticed that below and not far away from them the French were beginning to appear, and they had loaded with grape.

The little captain, with his weak, awkward gestures, kept calling upon his servant for "just one more little pipe," which he called *tríbotchka*, instead of *trúbotchka;* and then, knocking the ashes out, he would leap forward and look from under his little hand at the enemy.

"Let 'em have it, boys!" he would exclaim, and, himself seizing the cannon by the wheel, he would bring it back into position, or he would clean out the bore. In the smoke, stunned by the incessant firing, though he jumped every time a gun went off, Tushin, keeping his "nose-warmer" between his teeth, ran from one gun to another, now aiming, now counting the charges left, now making arrangements for the change or removal of the killed or wounded horses, and shouting his orders in his weak, delicate, irresolute voice. His face kept growing more and more animated. Only when his men were killed or wounded did he frown, and, turning away from the unfortunate, shout sternly to the others, who, as usual, pressed forward, ordering them to carry away the wounded or the dead.

The soldiers, for the most part handsome young heroes, — as always happens in the artillery, a couple of heads taller than their officer, and twice as broadly built, — looked at their commander with the inquiring look of children in trouble, and the expression which happened to be in his face was immediately reflected in theirs.

As a consequence of the terrible din and roar, and the necessity for oversight and activity, Tushin felt not the least unpleasant qualm of fear, nor did the thought that he might be killed or painfully wounded enter his head. On the contrary, he kept growing happier and happier. It seemed to him that it was very long ago, not even that same afternoon, since the moment when he first caught sight of the advancing enemy, and had fired the first gun, and that the little scrap of ground where he stood had been long, long known and familiar to him. Although he remembered everything, took everything into consideration, did everything that the best of officers could have done in his position, still he was in a state bordering on the delirium of fever, or the condition of a drunken man.

In the midst of the stunning sounds of his own guns roaring on every side of him, in the midst of the enemy's shells, whistling and striking around him, seeing his sweating, flushed men serving the guns, seeing the blood of men and horses, seeing the puffs of smoke in the direction of the enemy, followed always by the swift flight of the cannon-ball, striking into the ground, on a human being, on the guns, or among the horses — seeing all these various sights, still his mind was filled with a fantastic world of his own, which at this moment constituted a peculiar delight to him. The enemy's guns were, in his imagination, not guns, but pipes, from which, from time to time, a viewless smoker puffs out wreaths of smoke.

"See there, he gave another puff!" said Tushin, in a half-whisper, to himself, just as a wreath of smoke leaped away from the hill and was borne to the left in a ribbon by the wind.

"Now let us catch the little ball and send it back!"

"What is your order, your honor?" asked a gunner who stood near him and noticed that he muttered something.

"Nothing, send a shell," he replied.

"Now then, our Matveyevna!" said he to himself. It was the great, old-fashioned howitzer that Tushin personified under the name of Matveyevna, *Daughter of Matthew*.

The French around their guns reminded him of ants. Gunner "Number one," of the second field-piece, a handsome fellow, too much given to drink, was *dyadya*, uncle, in his world; Tushin looked at him oftener than at the others, and delighted in all his movements. The sound of the musketry in the valley, now dying away and then increasing in violence, seemed to him like some one drawing long breaths. He listened to the intermittent rising and falling of these sounds.

"Hark! she's breathing again, breathing hard!" he said to himself.

He imagined himself a mighty giant of monstrous size, seizing the cannon-balls with both hands and hurling them at the French.

"Well, Matveyevna — *Matushka !* — little mother! don't betray us," he was just saying, and starting away from the cannon, when back of him was heard a voice which he did not know : —

"Captain Tushin! Captain!"

Tushin looked around in alarm. It was the same staff-officer who had sent him out of Grund. In a quavering voice, the officer cried : —

"Are you beside yourself? Twice you have been ordered to retire and you .... "

"Now, why do they bother me?" exclaimed Tushin to himself, looking with dread at the officer. "I .... I'm all right," he returned, raising two fingers to his visor. "I .... "

But the colonel did not say all that he meant to say. A cannon-ball, flying close to him, made him cower down close to his horse. He paused and was just going to repeat his order, when still another cannon-ball interrupted him. He wheeled his horse round and galloped away.

"Retire! all of you retire!" he cried from the distance.

The soldiers laughed. In a minute an aide came with the same order.

This was Prince Andreï. The first thing he saw, as he reached the little space occupied by Tushin's cannon, was an unharnessed horse, with a broken leg, neighing near the horses that were still hitched up. From his leg the blood was spurting as from a fountain. Among the limbers lay a number of the killed. One cannon-ball after another flew over him as he galloped up, and he was conscious of a nervous tremor running down his back. But the mere thought that he was afraid again roused his courage. "I cannot be afraid," he said to himself, and he deliberately dismounted among the field-pieces. He delivered his message and still lingered in the battery. He resolved that the guns should be removed from their position and brought in under his direction. He and Tushin, stepping among the dead bodies, made the arrangements for limbering the cannon, even while the French were pouring a murderous fire upon them.

"An officer just dashed up here, but he made himself scarce in no time," remarked a gunner to Prince Andreï. "He wasn't like your honor."

Prince Andreï exchanged no words with Tushin. They were both so occupied that it seemed as if they did not see each other. When at last they succeeded in getting two of the four field-pieces limbered, they started to descend the hill, leaving one field-piece dismounted, together with the howitzer. Prince Andreï turned to Tushin. "Well, good-by," said he, offering him his hand.

"Good-by, my dear," returned Tushin, "dear heart, farewell, my dear fellow!"[1] exclaimed Tushin, the tears springing to his eyes though he knew not why.

CHAPTER XXI

THE breeze had died down; dark clouds hung low over the battle-field, mingling on the horizon with the smoke of gunpowder. It had grown dark, and therefore with all the more clearness the blaze of two burning villages stood out against the sky. The cannonade had slackened, but still the rattle of musketry at the rear, and at the right, was heard with ever increasing frequency and distinctness.

As soon as Tushin and his field-pieces, jolting and constantly meeting wounded men, got out of range and

---

[1] "*Da sviddnya, galúbchik! prashchdïte, galúbchik!*" There is a delicate distinction in these two forms of farewell. *Prashchdïte* hints that the farewell may be forever.

descended into the ravine, he was met by the commander and his aides, among whom were both the staff-
officer and Zherkof, who had been twice sent but had
not once succeeded in reaching Tushin's battery. All
of them gave him confused orders and counter-orders,
as to how and where to go, and overwhelmed him with
reproaches and criticisms.

Tushin made no arrangements, but rode toward the
rear on his artillery jade, not saying a word for fear he
should burst into tears, which, without his knowing why,
were ready to gush from his eyes. Although the order
was to abandon the wounded, many dragged themselves
after the troops and begged for a ride on the gun-carriages. That very same gallant infantry officer who,
before the beginning of the engagement, had darted so
energetically from Tushin's hut, was stretched out on
the carriage of the Matvéyevna, with a bullet in his
belly. At the foot of the hill, a pale yunker of hussars,
holding one arm in his hand, came to Tushin and asked
for a seat!

"Captain, for God's sake, my arm is crushed," said
he, timidly. "For God's sake, I can't walk any longer.
For God's sake!"

It was evident that this yunker had more than once
repeated this request and been everywhere refused.
He asked in an irresolute and piteous voice. "Give me
a place for God's sake!"

"Climb on, climb on!" said Tushin. "Spread out a
cloak, uncle," he added, turning to his favorite gunner.
"But where is the wounded officer?"

"We took him off; he died," replied some one.

"Climb on! Sit there, sit down, my dear fellow, sit
there! Spread out the cloak, Antonof!"

The yunker was Rostof. He held his left arm in
his right hand; his face was pale, and his teeth chattered with fever. He was assisted to climb on the
Matveyevna, to the very same spot from which they
had removed the dead officer. There was blood on the
cloak which Antonof spread out, and it stained Rostof's
riding-trousers and hands.

"What! are you wounded, my dear?"[1] asked Tushin, approaching the gun on which Rostof was riding.

" No, only a bruise."

" But where did that blood come from, on the gun-cheek?" asked the other.

"That is the officer's, your honor," replied a gunner, wiping away the blood with the sleeve of his cloak, as if he were apologizing for the stain on the gun.

By main force and with the help of the infantry, the guns were dragged up the slope, and when they reached the village of Gunthersdorf, they halted. By this time it was quite dark, so that it was impossible at ten paces to distinguish the uniforms of the soldiers; the musketry fire was beginning to slacken.

Suddenly shouts and the rattle of shots were heard again near by at the right. The darkness was lighted up by the flashes of the guns. This was the last attack of the French, and the soldiers replied to it as they intrenched themselves in the houses of the village. Once more all hands rushed out from the village, but Tushin's field-pieces could not be moved, and the gunners and Tushin and the yunker, silently exchanging glances, awaited their fate.

Then the firing began to die away once more, and out from a side street came a party of soldiers, engaged in lively conversation.

"Safe and sound, Petrof?" asked one.

"We gave it to them hot and heavy, brother. They won't meddle with us again," returned the other.

" Can't see a thing. How was it? Warmed 'em up a little, hey? Can't see a thing, it's so dark, fellows! Anything to drink?"

The French had been driven back for the last time. And once more, through the impenetrable darkness, Tushin's field-pieces moved forward, surrounded by the rumbling infantry as by a frame.

Something seemed to be flowing on through the darkness, like an invisible, gloomy river, ever pushing for-

[1] *Galúbchik.*

ward in one direction, with a murmur of voices, and the clinking of bayonets, and the rumble of wheels.

And above the general turmoil, clear and distinguishable above all other sounds, arose the groans and cries of the wounded in the blackness of the night. Their groans seemed to coincide with the pitchy blackness which surrounded the army. Their groans and this darkness of the night seemed to be one and the same thing. After a while, a wave of excitement ran through this onward struggling mass. Some one had come from headquarters on a white horse and shouted something as he rode along by.

"What's that he says?".... "Where now?".... "Is it to halt?".... "Did he express any gratitude?" Such were the eager questions heard on all sides, and then the whole moving mass, as it moved forward, recoiled on itself. Evidently, the van had halted, and the report spread that orders were to bivouac there. All hands settled down where they were in the middle of the muddy road.

Fires were lighted, and voices began to grow animated. Captain Tushin, having made his arrangements for his company, sent one of his men to find the temporary hospital, or at least a surgeon for the yunker, and sat down in front of the fire which his soldiers had built by the roadside.

Rostof also dragged himself up to the fire. The fever, caused by his pain, the cold, and the dampness, shook his whole frame. An irresistible inclination to drowsiness overcame him, but still he could not sleep, owing to the tormenting pain which he felt in his arm; it ached, and he found no position that relieved it. Sometimes he closed his eyes; then, again, he gazed into the fire, which seemed to him angrily red; then, again, at the round-shouldered, slender figure of Tushin, sitting Turkish fashion near him. Tushin's large, intelligent, kindly eyes were fastened upon him with sympathy and compassion. He saw that Tushin with all his soul desired, and yet was totally unable, to help him.

On all sides were heard the steps and voices of the

infantry passing by, coming up, and settling down
around them. The sounds of voices, of steps, and
trampling of horses, stamping their hoofs in the mud,
the echo of axes far and near, all mingled in one pul-
sating roar.

Now, it was no longer like a viewless river rolling
onward through the darkness, but rather like a gloomy
sea, roaring and breaking, after a storm. Rostof, half
dazed, looked and listened to what was going on around
him, and before him.

A foot-soldier came up to the bivouac fire, squatted
down on his heels, rubbed his hands over the fire, and
turned his face around.

"Any harm, your honor?"[1] he asked, turning to
Tushin with an inquiring expression. "Here I've lost
my company, your honor, I don't know where it is!
Hard luck."

At the same time with the soldier, an infantry officer
with a bandaged cheek came to the fire, and begged
Tushin to order his field-pieces to be moved a trifle, so
as to allow the baggage-train to pass. The company
commander was followed by two soldiers. They were
quarreling desperately, reviling each other, and almost
fighting over a boot.

"You lie! You didn't pick it up! Oh! you villain!"
one of them was crying, in a hoarse voice.

Then came a lean, pale soldier, with his neck done
up in blood-stained bandages, and, in an irascible voice,
asked the artillerymen for a drink of water.

"What, must I die like a dog?" he grumbled.

Tushin ordered the men to give him a drink. Then
came a jolly soldier, asking for some fire for the
infantry.

"A little fire, from a red-hot man, for the infantry!
Good luck to you, fellow-countrymen! Thank you for
the fire; we'll return it with interest," said he, as he
disappeared into the darkness, with a flaming brand.

---

[1] "*Nitchevo, váshe blagoróbdie?*" *Nitchevo*, literally *nothing*, is in every
Russian's mouth, and means everything and anything, according to the
context.

After this soldier came four, carrying something heavy wrapped up in a cloak, and went past the fire. One of them stumbled. "Oh, bah! the devils! they've been spilling firewood," cried one of them.

"He's dead! what's the use of lugging him?" exclaimed another.

"Well, I tell you...."

And they vanished in the darkness with their burden.

"Say, does it hurt?" asked Tushin, in a whisper.

"Yes, it hurts."

"Your honor, the general wants you. He's at the cottage, yonder," said one of the gunners, coming up to Tushin.

"In a moment, my boy."[1]

Tushin arose, and, buttoning his cloak and straightening himself up, he left the fireside.

In a cottage which had been made ready for him, not far from the artillerist's fire, Prince Bagration was still sitting at the dinner-table, talking with a number of high officers, who had called in for consultation.

There was a little, old man, with half-closed eyes, greedily gnawing a mutton-bone; and the general of twenty-two years' blameless service, his face flushed from his vodka and his dinner; and the staff-officer with the birthday ring; and Zherkof, uneasily looking at the others; and Prince Andreï, with compressed lips and feverishly shining eyes.

In the corner of the cottage leaned the standard taken from the French, and the auditor, with his innocent face, was fingering the stuff of which the standard was made, shaking his head doubtfully, perhaps because he was really interested in the standard, and possibly because, being hungry, it was hard to see the dinner-table, at which no place had been set for him.

In the next cottage was a captured colonel of dragoons, with the Russian officers crowding around him, with curiosity in their eyes.

Prince Bagration thanked the officers of the various

[1] *Galúbchik.*

divisions, and made inquiries about the details of the engagement, and the losses.

The regimental commander who had commanded the review at Braunau explained to the prince that, as soon as the action began, he had withdrawn from the woods, collected the men engaged in gathering firewood, and, sending them back, had charged with two battalions, and simply carried the French at the point of the bayonet.

"When I saw that the first battalion was giving way, your illustriousness, I stood on the road and said to myself, 'I will let them get by first, and then order a running fire,' and that was the way I did."

The regimental commander had been so anxious to do this, and so sorry that he had not been successful in doing it, that it now seemed to him that he actually had done so. Indeed, may it not have been so? How was it possible to decide, in the general confusion, what had happened and what had not happened?

"By the way, I ought to observe, your illustriousness," he went on to say, remembering Dolokhof's conversation with Kutuzof, and his last meeting with the young man, "that the cashiered private, Dolokhof, took a French officer prisoner, under my very eyes, and distinguished himself notably."

"It was there I saw the charge of the Pavlograd hussars, your illustriousness," remarked Zherkof, looking around uneasily, for he had not that day seen a single hussar, and had only heard about them from an infantry officer! "They broke two squares, your illustriousness."

A few, hearing Zherkof's words, smiled, because a joke was always expected from him; but, perceiving that what he said also redounded to the glory of our arms, and of the day's doings, they grew serious again, though they knew very well that what Zherkof said was a lie without even a semblance of foundation. Prince Bagration turned to the elderly colonel.

"I thank you all, gentlemen; all parties have worked like heroes, infantry, cavalry, and artillery. But how

was it two field-pieces were abandoned in the center?"
he demanded, looking round for some one. — Prince
Bagration made no inquiries for the cannon of the left
wing; he knew by this time that all the cannon there
had been abandoned at the very beginning of the
action. — "I believe I asked you about them?" he
said, turning to the staff-officer of the day.

"One was dismounted," replied the staff-officer; "but
the other — as to that I myself cannot understand; I
was there all the time and gave orders for it to be retired, and immediately I was called away. It was hot
there, to be sure," he added modestly.

Some one remarked that Captain Tushin was right
here in the village, and that he had already been sent
for.

"Ah, but you were there, were you not?" asked
Prince Bagration, of Prince Andreï.

"Certainly, we almost met there," said the staff-
officer, giving Prince Andreï an affable smile.

"I did not have the pleasure of seeing you," declared
Prince Andreï, coolly and curtly. All were silent.

Tushin now appeared on the threshold, modestly
making his way behind the backs of the generals.
Passing around the generals in the narrow room, and
confused, as always, in the presence of his superiors,
Tushin did not see the flagstaff, and stumbled over it.
Several laughed.

"How is it the guns were abandoned?" asked Bagration, frowning, but not so much at the captain as at
those who were rude enough to laugh, among whom
Zherkof's voice was distinguished above the rest.
Tushin now, for the first time, at the sight of the stern
commander, realized with horror his crime and disgrace at having lost two guns, while he himself was left
alive.

He had been so agitated that, till this moment, he
had not had time to think of this incident. The laughter of the officers still more threw him off his balance.
He stood in front of Bagration with his lower jaw
trembling, and could hardly stammer: —

"I .... I .... don't know .... your illustriousness .... I had no men, your illustriousness." ....

"You might have had them from the forces that covered you."

Tushin did not reply that there were not forces covering him, though this would have been the unvarnished truth. He was afraid that he might compromise some of his superior officers, and so in silence, with staring eyes, he gazed into Bagration's face, as a schoolboy looks in confusion into his master's.

A rather long silence ensued. Prince Bagration, evidently not wishing to be too severe, knew not what to say; the others did not venture to interfere in the conversation. Prince Andreï looked askance at Tushin, and his fingers twitched nervously.

"Your illustriousness," said Prince Andreï, breaking the silence, in his clear voice, "you were pleased to send me to Captain Tushin's battery. I went there and found two-thirds of his men and horses disabled, two of his guns dismounted, and no forces to cover him!"

Prince Bagration and Tushin kept their eyes fixed on Bolkonsky, who was speaking under the influence of restrained excitement.

"And if your illustriousness will permit me to express my opinion," he went on to say, "we are indebted more than all for the success of this day to the action of this battery, and the heroic steadfastness of Captain Tushin and his company," said Prince Andreï; and, without waiting for any reply, he got up and left the table.

Prince Bagration looked at Tushin, and evidently not wishing to show any disbelief in Prince Bolkonsky's stiff judgment, and at the same time not feeling himself prepared to acquiesce entirely with it, he inclined his head and told Tushin that he might go. Prince Andreï followed him.

"Thank you, my boy,[1] you have saved me," said Tushin to him.

Prince Andreï looked at Tushin, and, without saying

[1] *Galúbchik.*

anything, turned away from him. His heart was heavy and full of melancholy. It was all so strange, so unlike what he had anticipated.

"Who are they? why do they come here? what do they want? and when will all this end?" Rostof asked himself, as he gazed at the shadows which unceasingly passed before him. The pain in his arm grew worse and worse. Unconquerable drowsiness oppressed him. Red circles danced before his eyes, and the impression of these voices and these faces, and the sense of his loneliness, mingled with the sense of his agony. These soldiers, wounded and not wounded, they all did the same thing — they pressed upon him, crushed him, tore his muscles, and roasted the flesh in his crushed arm and shoulder.

To rid himself of them he closed his eyes.

He lost himself for one moment, but during that brief interval of forgetfulness he saw in his dream a countless collection of objects. He saw his mother, with her large white hand; he saw Sonya's thin shoulders, Natasha's eyes and smiling lips, and Denísof, with his voice and mustache, and Telyanin, and his whole encounter with Telyanin and Bogdanuitch. All this story was one and the same thing with what this soldier with the shrill voice said, and all this story and this soldier so cruelly, so constantly crushed, twitched, and pulled his arm in one direction! He struggled to escape from them, but they would not for a single second let go of his shoulder, or in the least relax their hold. It would not have hurt, it would have been all right, if they would cease pulling him; but it was impossible to get rid of them.

He opened his eyes and looked up. A black strip of the night, an arshin wide, hung over the glowing coals. Across this strip of light flew the powdery snow as it fell. Tushin did not return; the surgeon had not come. He was alone; a little soldier now sat on the other side of the fire, stripped, and warming his thin, sallow body.

"I'm of no use to any one!" thought Rostof. "No

one helps me or takes pity on me! But if I were only at home, strong, happy, beloved!"

He sighed and his sigh involuntarily changed into a groan.

"Aï! does it hurt?" asked the little soldier, shaking his shirt over the fire, and, without awaiting his answer, quacking like a duck, he added, "Good many men knocked to pieces this day! terrible!"

Rostof did not heed the soldier. He gazed at the snowflakes fluttering down into the fire, and he recalled what winter would be at home in Russia, his warm, bright home, with his downy furs, swift sledges, his strong, healthy body, and the love and care of his family.

"And why did I come here?" he asked himself.

On the following day the French did not renew their attack, and the remains of Bagration's division effected a conjunction with Kutuzof's army.

VOL. I. — 19

END OF VOL. I.

SHE LOOKED STRAIGHT INTO HIS HANDSOME FACE.

Original Drawing by E. H. Garrett.

WAR AND PEACE

VOL. II

CONTENTS

PART III (1806)

PART IV (1806–1811)

CONTENTS ix

PART V

CONTENTS

CONTENTS

WAR AND PEACE

PART THIRD

CHAPTER I

PRINCE VASILI was not in the habit of forecasting his plans. Still less did he ever think of doing people harm for the sake of his own advantage. He was merely a man of the world, who had been successful in the world, so that success had become a sort of second nature to him. He was always accustomed to allow circumstances and his relations to other men to modify his various plans and projects; but he rarely gave himself a very scrupulous account of them, though they constituted his chief interest in life. He managed to have not merely one and not merely two, but a dozen, such plans and projects on the docket at one and the same time, and thus some only formulated themselves, some came to something, while others fell through.

He never said to himself, for example: "This man is now in my power, I ought to gain his confidence and friendship, and thereby secure myself the advantage of his assistance;" or this: "Here, Pierre is rich, I ought to induce him to marry my daughter, and thus get the forty thousand rubles that I need." But if, by chance, he met the man in power, instinct immediately whispered to him that this man might be profitable to him, and Prince Vasíli struck up a friendship with him, and at the first opportunity, led by instinct, flattered him, treated him with easy familiarity, and finally brought about the crucial conversation.

Pierre was under his tutelage at Moscow, and Prince Vasíli procured for him an appointment as gentleman-in-waiting, which at that time conferred the same rank as Councillor of State, and he insisted on the young man accompanying him to Petersburg and taking up his residence in his own mansion.

Without making any exertion, and at the same time taking it absolutely for granted that he was on the right track, Prince Vasíli was doing all in his power to marry Pierre to his daughter.

If Prince Vasíli had formulated his plans beforehand, he could not have been so natural in his conversation, so simple and unaffected in his relations with all men, not only those above him, but those who stood below him. There was something that ever attracted him to men richer or more powerful than himself, and he was endowed with the rare art of seizing exactly the right moment for profiting by people.

Pierre, who had unexpectedly succeeded to Count Bezukhoï's wealth and title, found himself, after his late life of loneliness and inaction, surrounded and occupied to such a degree that only when he was in bed could he have a moment entirely to himself. He was obliged to sign letters, to show himself at the court-house in regard to matters of which he had no clear comprehension, to ask questions about this and that, of his chief overseer, to ride out to his estate in the suburbs of Moscow, and to receive many people who hitherto had ignored his very existence, but who would now be offended and insulted if he refused to see them.

All these various individuals — business men, relatives, acquaintances — were all, with one accord, disposed to treat the young heir in the most friendly and flattering manner; they were all indubitably persuaded of Pierre's distinguished merits. He was constantly hearing such phrases as: "With your extraordinary goodness;" or, "Considering your kind heart;" or, "You are so upright, count;" or, "If he were as clever as you are;" and so on, until he actually began to believe in his extraordinary goodness and his extraordinary intelligence, all the more because always, in the depths of his heart, it had seemed to him that he was really very good and very clever.

Even people who before had been cross to him and showed him undisguised hatred, now became sweet and affectionate toward him.

For example, the sharp-tempered elder sister, the princess with the long waist and the phenomenally smooth hair, like a doll's, came into Pierre's room after the funeral.

Dropping her eyes and flushing deeply, she assured him how sincerely she regretted the misunderstandings that had arisen between them, and asked him as a special favor, though she felt that she had no right to do so, that she might be allowed, after the blow that had befallen her, to remain for a few weeks longer in the house which she had loved so well, and where she had borne so many sacrifices. She could not restrain her tears, and wept freely at these words.

Touched by the change that the statuesque princess had undergone, Pierre took her by the hand and begged her forgiveness, though he could not have told for what. From that day the princess began to knit Pierre a striped scarf, and became entirely different to him.

"Do this for her, my dear fellow, for she had much to put up with on account of the late count's whims," said Prince Vasíli, giving him a paper to sign for the princess's benefit. Prince Vasíli had made up his mind that he must cast this die, and get this check of thirty thousand rubles for the poor princess, in order that it might not enter her head to talk about the part which he had taken in the matter of the mosaic portfolio.

Pierre signed the check, and from that time forth the princess became still more affectionate to him. The younger sisters also were very flattering in their behavior to him; especially the youngest one — the beauty with the mole — who often embarrassed Pierre with her smiles and her own embarrassment at the sight of him.

It seemed to Pierre so natural that everybody should like him, it seemed to him so unnatural that any one should not like him, that he could not help believing in the sincerity of those who surrounded him. In the first place, he had no time to question the sincerity or lack of sincerity. He had no time for anything, but was constantly in a state of delicious intoxication, as it were. He was conscious that he was the center of an important social mechanism, felt that something was constantly expected of him, that if he failed to accomplish this he would offend many, and disappoint their expectations. But if he did this thing and that, all would be well, and he did whatever was asked of him, and always imagined that better things lay in store for him.

During this first part of the time, Prince Vasíli, more than any one else, undertook the management of Pierre and his affairs. After Count Bezukhoï's death, he scarcely let Pierre out of his sight. Prince Vasíli acted like a man who, though overburdened with business, wearied, and careworn, was so filled with sympathy that he found it impossible to leave this helpless young man, the son of his old friend, and the possessor of such an enormous fortune, to the play of fate and the designs of knaves.

During the few days which he spent in Moscow after Count Bezukhoï's death, he kept calling Pierre to him or going himself to Pierre, and instructed him on his duties in a tone of such weariness and assurance that he seemed to say each time: 'You know that I am overwhelmed with business; but it would be heartless in me to leave you now; and you know that what I tell you is the only thing feasible.'

"Well, my dear fellow, to-morrow we will start at last," said he one day, closing his eyes and touching Pierre's elbow with his fingers, while his voice had a tone which seemed to imply that this had long, long ago been decided on and was now perfectly beyond question.

"To-morrow we start; I will give you a place in my carriage. I am glad. We have done everything necessary here, and I ought to have been at home long ago. Here's what I got from the chancellor. I asked him for it for you : you have a place in the diplomatic corps, and are appointed gentleman-in-waiting. The diplomatic career is now open to you."

Notwithstanding the tone of weariness and assurance in which these words were spoken, Pierre, who for some time had been thinking about his future, began to make an objection. But Prince Vasíli interrupted him and spoke on in that low, persuasive tone which effectually prevents any one from breaking into a man's discourse, and which he employed in cases where it was absolutely necessary to meet a final objection.

"But, my dear fellow, I did this for my own sake, to satisfy my own conscience, and there is nothing to thank me for. No one ever complained of being too well loved; but then, you are free; you can leave to-morrow. Then you can see for yourself in Petersburg. It is high time that you left these scenes of painful recollections." Prince Vasíli sighed. "Well, well, my dear. And let my valet follow in your carriage. Oh, yes, I had almost forgotten," added Prince Vasíli. "You know, my friend, we had some accounts with the late lamented, and so I have collected and kept the money from your Riazan property; you don't need it. We will settle it up afterwards."

What Prince Vasíli called "from the Riazan" property was a few thousand rubles of obrok, or peasants' quit-rent, which he had appropriated for his own use.

In Petersburg, just the same as in Moscow, Pierre found himself surrounded by an atmosphere of affection and love. He could not decline the office, or rather sinecure, — for he had nothing to do, — which Prince Vasíli had procured for him, but he was so engrossed with acquaintances, invitations, and social duties, that he felt, even more than in Moscow, the sense of confusion, hurry, and of happiness ever beckoning but never becoming realized.

Many of the set of gay young bachelors with whom he had formerly been intimate were now absent from Petersburg. The Guard were away on the campaign;

Dolokhof was serving in the ranks; Anatol had joined the army, and had been sent into the province; Prince Andreï was abroad, and therefore Pierre had no chance to spend his nights as he had once liked to do, or in occasionally engaging in confidential talks with his old and treasured friend. All his time was spent in dinners and balls, and preëminently at Prince Vasíli's, in the society of the portly princess, his wife, and the beautiful Ellen.

Anna Pavlovna Scherer, like everybody else, made Pierre feel the change which had come over society in regard to him.

Hitherto, Pierre, in Anna Pavlovna's presence, had constantly felt that whatever he said was unbecoming, wanting in tact, unsuitable; that his speeches, however sensible they might seem while he was getting them ready in his mind, were idiotic as soon as he spoke them aloud; while, on the other hand, Ippolit's most stupid utterances were regarded as wise and witty. Now, however, everything that he said was greeted with the epithet 'charming.' Even if Anna Pavlovna did not say this, still he was made to see that she meant it, and that she refrained from saying it only out of regard for his modesty.

At the beginning of the winter of 1805–1806, Pierre received from Anna Pavlovna the usual pink note of invitation, and with this postscript: "The beautiful Ellen will be with us, whom one is never tired of looking at."

On reading this sentence, Pierre for the first time realized that a peculiar bond had sprung up between him and Ellen, recognized by other people, and this thought alarmed him because it seemed to place him under some sort of an obligation which he could not fulfil, and at the same time it pleased him as an amusing situation.

Anna Pavlovna's reception was exactly like the former one, except that the dessert with which she regaled her guests was not Montemart as before, but a diplomat who had just arrived from Berlin, bringing the freshest details about the visit of the Emperor Alexander at Potsdam, and how the two most august friends had there sworn an oath of eternal alliance to protect the cause of right against the enemy of the human race.

Pierre was received by Anna Pavlovna with a shade of melancholy, evidently having reference to the recent loss which the young man had undergone in the death of Count Bezukhoï, — every one constantly felt it their duty to assure Pierre that he was greatly afflicted by his father's taking off, although he could hardly be said to have known him, — and in Anna Pavlovna's case this melancholy was almost equal to that high degree of melancholy which she always manifested at the mention of the most august Empress Maria Feodorovna. Pierre felt himself quite overwhelmed by this.

Anna Pavlovna, with her usual art, arranged the circles of her drawing-room. The largest, in which Prince Vasíli and the generals were conspicuous, was enjoying the diplomat's conversation. Still another group was gathered about the tea-table. Pierre was anxious to join the former, but Anna Pavlovna, who was in the excitable state of a great captain on the field of battle, when a thousand new and brilliant ideas are struggling almost hopelessly for a successful accomplishment, — Anna Pavlovna, seeing Pierre's motion, laid her finger on his sleeve.

"Wait, I have designs on you for this evening."

She glanced at Ellen, and gave her a smile.

"My dear Ellen, you must be good to my poor aunt, who has conceived a perfect adoration for you. Go and spend ten minutes with her. And lest it should be very tiresome to you, here is our dear count, who certainly will not fail to follow you."

The beauty went over to *ma tante*, but Anna Pavlovna detained the young man, pretending that she had still some indispensable arrangement to complete.

"Charming! isn't she?" said she to Pierre, referring to the stately beauty who was sailing away. "And so self-possessed, and so much tact for a young girl, such wonderful capability and dignity. It all comes natural

to her. Fortunate will be the man who secures her!
With her a man, even of the humblest position in
society, could not fail to attain the most brilliant position. Isn't that so? I only wanted to know your
opinion."

And Anna Pavlovna released Pierre.

Pierre had honestly replied in the affirmative to her
question about Ellen's art of self-reliance. Whenever
he thought of Ellen, he thought of her beauty, and of
her extraordinary ability at appearing grave and dignified in society.

Ma tante received the two young people in her
corner, but it seemed as if she were trying to hide her
adoration for Ellen, and make rather a show of awe for
Anna Pavlovna. She glanced at her niece as if asking
how she should behave toward these people. As Anna
Pávlovna turned away, she again touched Pierre's sleeve
with her finger, and said: —

"I hope that you won't say another time that you are
bored at my house," and she glanced at Ellen.

Ellen smiled back with a look which seemed to say
that she could not admit the possibility of any one seeing her and not being delighted. The aunt coughed,
swallowed down the phlegm, and said in French that
she was very glad to see Ellen; then she turned to
Pierre with the same compliment and the same look.
During their tedious and desultory conversation, Ellen
glanced at Pierre, and smiled upon him with the same
bright and radiant smile that she bestowed upon all
people. Pierre was so accustomed to this smile, that it
made little impression on him, and he gave it no special
attention. The aunt happened at that moment to be
speaking about a collection of snuff-boxes, which had
belonged to Pierre's late father, Count Bezukhoï, and
she showed him her own snuff-box. The Princess Ellen
asked to see the portrait of her husband painted in miniature on the cover.

"That is apparently the work of Vinnes," remarked
Pierre, mentioning the name of a distinguished miniature painter. He leaned over the table to take up the

snuff-box, but all the time he was listening to the conversation at the other table. He got up, intending to pass around; but the aunt handed him the snuff-box, passing it directly behind Ellen. Ellen moved aside to give room, and, as she looked up, she smiled. In accordance with the custom of the day, she wore a dress cut very low both in front and behind. Her bust, which always reminded Pierre of marble, was so near to him that even with his near-sighted eyes he could not help seeing the exquisite beauty of her neck and shoulders, and if he had stooped but a little, his lips would have touched her neck. He was conscious of the warmth of her body, the faint breath of some perfume, and the rustle of her corset as she moved. He saw not the statuesque beauty which agreed so well with the color of her dress, he saw and felt the whole charm of her form, concealed, as it was, only by her drapery. And having once seen this, his eyes refused to see her in any other way, just as it is impossible for us to recall an illusion which has once been explained.

'And so you have not noticed before how charming I am?' Ellen seemed to say; 'have you not noticed that I am a woman? Yes, I am a woman, whom any man might win, — even you,' her look seemed to say. And at that instant, Pierre was conscious that Ellen not only might be, but that she must be, his wife, that it could not be otherwise.

He knew this at this instant just as surely as he would have known it had he been standing with her under the bridal crown.

How would this be? and when would it be?

He could not tell, he was not sure that it would be the best thing for him; he even had a dim consciousness that somehow it would not be for the best, but still he knew that it would be. Pierre dropped his eyes, then raised them, and tried once more to see that beauty so far off and foreign to him, as it were, which he had seen every day before; but he found it impossible. He no more could recall his former thought of her than a man who, having seen a blade of steppe grass in the mist and mistaken it for a tree, could ever be deceived into taking the blade of grass for a tree again. She was terribly near to him; already she had begun to wield her power over him. And between him and her there was no longer any impediment except the impediment of his own will.

"Excellent! I leave you in your quiet corner. I see you are getting along very well there," said Anna Pavlovna's voice.

And Pierre, coming to his senses with a start of terror lest he had been guilty of something reprehensible, reddened and glanced around. It seemed to him that all knew as well as he himself did, what had happened to him.

After a little while, when he had joined the large circle, Anna Pavlovna said to him, "I hear that you are refitting your Petersburg house."

This was true; the architect had told him that it was needful to be done, and Pierre, though he did not know why, allowed the huge mansion to be improved. "That's a good plan, but I would n't give up your quarters at Prince Vasíli's. It is a good thing to have a friend like the prince," said she, smiling at Prince Vasíli. "I know something about it, do I not? And you are still so young. You need some one to advise you. You are not angry with me for exercising the prerogative of an old woman, I hope?" She added this in Russian, and paused as women always pause, expecting something complimentary, when they have been mentioning their age. "If you marry, that would be a different thing." And she united them in one significant glance. Pierre did not look at Ellen, but she looked at him. But all the time she was terribly close to him. He stammered something and reddened.

After he returned home, Pierre was long unable to sleep, for thinking of what had happened to him.

What had happened to him?

Nothing!

All he knew was that a woman whom he had known as a child, of whom he had often heedlessly said, "Yes, she 's pretty," when he was told that Ellen was a beauty, might be his.

"But she is stupid; I myself have declared that she is stupid," he said to himself. "There is something revolting in the feeling that she stirs in me, — something repulsive. I have been told that her own brother Anatol was in love with her, and that she loved him in return; that there was quite a scandal about it, and that was the reason why Anatol was sent away. Ippolit is her brother. Her father — Prince Vasíli.... it 's all ugly," he went on thinking, and even while he came to this decision, — such considerations are endless, — he found himself to his surprise indulging in a smile, and acknowledged that another series of considerations were arising in his mind; that while he was thinking of her faults he was at the same time dreaming how she would be his wife, how she might be in love with him, how she might be quite different, and how all that he had heard and thought about her might be untrue. And again he saw her, not as Prince Vasíli's daughter, but as a woman, her form concealed merely by her gray gown.

"But no, why has this idea never entered my mind before?" And again he assured himself that it was impossible, that there would be something shameful, contrary to nature, something, as it seemed, dishonorable to him, in this marriage. He recalled her words and glances, and the words and glances of those who had seen them together. He remembered Anna Pavlovna's words and looks when she spoke to him about his house; he remembered a thousand similar insinuations on the part of Prince Vasíli and others; and a sense of horror came over him, lest he had bound himself by the very undertaking of such a project, a project which was evidently wrong, and which he ought not to have undertaken. But at the very time that he came to this decision, in the other half of his mind arose her form in all its womanly beauty.

CHAPTER II

In November, 1805, Prince Vasíli was obliged to go to four governments on a tour of inspection.[1] He had secured this commission for himself so as to visit one of his ruined estates, and it was his intention, having picked up his son Anatol, who was with his regiment at one of the places on his route, to go with him on a visit to Prince Nikolaï Andreyevitch Bolkonsky, so as to marry this same son to the daughter of this wealthy old man.

But before starting on this journey and undertaking these new duties, Prince Vasíli felt called upon to bring Pierre's little affair to a crisis. The truth was, Pierre, during these latter days of his visit at Prince Vasíli's, had lately been spending whole days at home, that is to say, at Prince Vasíli's, where he was staying, and was absurd, agitated, and moping in Ellen's presence, — the proper condition of a man in love, — but still he had not made his declaration.

"All this is very well and good, but it must be decided," said Prince Vasíli one morning, with a melancholy sigh, confessing to himself that Pierre, considering under what obligations he was to him ("though Christ be with him!"), was not behaving very nicely in this matter. "Youth .... fickleness. Well, God bless him!" .... said Prince Vasíli, with a feeling of satisfaction at his own benevolence; "but it must be decided. Day after to-morrow is Lyolya's birthday; I will have a little party for her, and if he does not come up to the point in seeing what his duty is, then it will be my affair. Yes, my affair. I am her father."

A fortnight after Anna Pavlovna's reception, and the sleepless, agitated night that followed it, when he had made up his mind that to marry Ellen would lead to unhappiness, and that it was his duty to flee from her, and go away, Pierre, in spite of this decision, was still

[1] Russia is divided into *gubérnie*, or governments; these again into *uyézdi*, districts.

at Prince Vasíli's, and felt with a sort of horror that each day he was becoming, in the eyes of the world, more and more attached to her; that he could not return to his former way of looking upon her; could not tear himself from her; that it was abominable, but still he must link his fate with hers. Perhaps he might have kept away, but scarcely a day passed without Prince Vasíli's having company — though formerly he had so rarely given receptions — and Pierre was obliged to be present, unless he were willing to disturb the general contentment, and disappoint the expectation of all.

Prince Vasíli, during those rare moments when he was at home, as he passed by Pierre, would draw his head down, carelessly offer him his shaven, wrinkled cheek to kiss, and say: " Till to-morrow," or "We'll meet at dinner, or else I shall not see you," or, " I stay at home for your sake," or the like.

But, notwithstanding the fact that Prince Vasíli, according to his own account, stayed at home for Pierre's sake, he did not exchange two words with him, and yet, Pierre did not feel himself strong enough to disappoint him. Each day he said to himself ever the same thing: " I must in the end understand her and explain her — what is she? Was I mistaken in her before, or am I mistaken now? No, she is not stupid. No, she is a beautiful girl," he said to himself from time to time. Never did she make a single error; never, by any chance, did she say anything stupid. She spoke little, but what she said was always simple and clear. So she could not be stupid. Never was she agitated or confused. She could not be a vile woman!

Often it chanced that he began to discuss with her, or to utter his thoughts in her hearing, but every time she replied in some brief but appropriately worded remark, showing that she was not interested, or else with a silent smile and look, which more palpably than anything else proved to Pierre her superiority. She was in the right, for she made it evident that all arguments and reasonings were rubbish in comparison with this smile.

She always treated him with a radiant, confiding, and confidential smile, which was meant for himself alone, as though there were in it something more significant than there was in that smile which she wore for the world in general. Pierre knew that all were waiting for him at last to speak the one word needful, to step over the certain line, and he knew that, sooner or later, he should cross it; a strange and invincible horror seized him at the mere thought of this momentous step. A thousand times in the course of this fortnight, during which he felt himself all the time drawn deeper and deeper into the terrible gulf, he said to himself: "What does it mean? What I need is decision! Why do I lack it?"

He was anxious to come to a decision, but felt with horror that, in this matter, he was not displaying the strength of will which he knew he had, and which he really had.

Pierre belonged to the number of those who are strong only when they have the consciousness of being perfectly pure. But ever since he had begun to be overmastered by the feeling of sensual desire that came upon him at Anna Pavlovna's, during the scene with the snuffbox, an undefined sense of guilt had paralyzed his willpower.

On the evening of Ellen's name-day, a small party of friends and relatives, — "Our nearest and dearest," as the princess expressed it, — took supper at Prince Vasíli's. All these friends and relatives were given to understand that, on this day, the young lady's fate was to be decided. The guests were seated in the dining-room. The Princess Kuragina, a portly, imposing woman, who had once been famous for her beauty, sat at the head of the table. On each side of her were placed the more important guests, — an old general, his wife, and Anna Pavlovna Scherer; at the other end of the table were the younger and less honored guests; and there, also, sat the various members of the household — Pierre and Ellen side by side.

Prince Vasíli did not sit down with the rest; he walked around the table, in a jocund mood, stopping to chat now with one, now with another of his guests, speaking some light and pleasant word to all, except Pierre and Ellen, whose presence he seemed entirely to ignore.

Prince Vasíli was the very life of the company.

The wax candles burned brightly, the silver and cut glass gleamed, the jewels of the ladies and the gold and silver epaulets of the officers glistened. The clatter of knives and plates and glasses, and the hum of lively conversation, were heard around the table. An aged chamberlain, at one end, was heard assuring an aged baroness of his passionate love for her, while her laugh in reply rang out. At the other end some one was telling of the misfortune that had befallen a certain Marya Viktorovna. Near the center of the table, Prince Vasíli had attracted a little circle of auditors, and was telling the ladies, with a facetious smile on his face, of the last meeting, on Wednesday, of the Imperial Council, at which Sergyeï Kuzmitch Vyazmitínof, the new military governor-general of Petersburg, received and read the then famous rescript àddressed to him from the army headquarters, by the Emperor Alexander Pavlovitch.

The emperor declared that he was receiving from all sides proofs of the devotion of the people, and that the demonstration of Petersburg was particularly delightful to him, that he was proud of being the head of such a nation, and would do all in his power to prove himself worthy of the honor. This rescript began with these words: "*Sergyeï Kuzmitch: From all sides, reports reach me....*"

"And so he could not get further than '*Sergyeï Kuzmitch*'?" asked a lady.

"No, not a hair's breadth," replied Prince Vasíli, laughing. "'*Sergyeï Kuzmitch: from all sides.... Sergyeï Kuzmitch! from all sides.*' Poor Vyazmitínof could not get any farther. Several times he began the letter over again, but could only say, '*Sergyeï....*' then sobs, ... '*Ku....zmi....tch,*' — tears, and then the words, — '*from all sides*' were drowned in sobs, and he could not get any further. And again his handkerchief, and again, '*Sergyeï Kuzmitch from all sides*' and more tears, until at last he had to get some one else to read it for him."

"'Kuzmitch .... from all sides'.... and tears," repeated some one with a laugh.

"Don't be naughty," exclaimed Anna Pavlovna, from the other end of the table, and raising her finger threateningly, "our good Vyazmitínof is such a dear, excellent man."

This greatly amused the company. At the upper end of the table, where sat the honorary guests, all were apparently in jovial spirits, and under the influence of the most varied and lively emotions; but Pierre and Ellen sat silent, side by side, at the lower end of the table; on the faces of each hovered a radiant smile, not evoked by the story about Sergyeï Kuzmitch, but rather a smile of bashfulness at their own thoughts. The others might chatter and laugh and jest, they might with good appetite enjoy the Rhine wine and the *sauté* and the ices, they might let their eyes avoid resting on that couple, they might seem tò be quite indifferent and even to ignore their existence; nevertheless, there was something in the very atmosphere which made it evident by the furtive glances bent upon them, that the anecdote about Sergyeï Kuzmitch and the laugh that it evoked, and the dinner, and everything were but merely pretense; and that the energies of the whole company were, in reality, devoted to this young couple, Pierre and Ellen, even while Prince Vasíli was imitating the lachrymose Sergyeï Kuzmitch. All the time his glance sought his daughter, and, even when he was laughing his heartiest, the expression of his face seemed to say: "Yes, yes, it is going all right; it will be decided this evening."

Anna Pavlovna, when she threatened him with *our good Vyazmitínof*, let Prince Vasíli read in her eyes, as they flashed for a moment in Pierre's direction, a congratulation for his daughter's coming marriage and good fortune.

The old princess, as she offered a glass of wine to her neighbor with a melancholy sigh, and glanced gravely toward her daughter, seemed to say by this sigh : —

'Yes, my dear, now there is nothing left for us but to sip sweet wine; now it is the young people's turn to be so insolently, defiantly happy.'

"And what melancholy rubbish, all that I have to say is! As if it meant anything!" thought the old diplomat, as he gazed at the happy faces of the lovers; "yonder is true happiness!"

Amid these mean, petty, and artificial interests uniting this company, there arose the natural feeling of attraction felt for each other by a handsome and healthful young man and woman. And this human feeling put to naught and soared above all their artificial babble. The jests were not amusing, the news was not interesting, the liveliness was only counterfeited. Not only they, but also the servants, waiting on the table, seemed to feel the same thing, and forget the proprieties of the service, as they gazed on beautiful Ellen, with her radiant face, and on Pierre's comely, stout face, so happy and so uneasy. It even seemed as if the light from the candles were all concentrated on these two happy faces. Pierre was conscious that he was the center of everything, and this position both pleased him and made him uncomfortable. He found himself in the position of a man plunged in some sort of absorbing occupation. He saw nothing, heard nothing, understood nothing clearly. Only occasionally, through his consciousness, flashed fragmentary thoughts and expressions of the reality.

"And so it is all over," he said to himself. "How in the world did it ever happen? It was so sudden! Now I know that not for her sake alone, nor for my own sake alone, but for the sake of all, *this* must be accomplished without fail. They all expect *this* so confidently, they are so certain that it will take place, that I cannot, I cannot disappoint them. But how will it take place? I know not; but it will be, it infallibly must be!" thought Pierre, as he glanced at those shoulders gleaming so near him.

Then suddenly a feeling of humiliation mingled in his thoughts. He felt embarrassed to be the object of general attention, to be "a lucky man" in the eyes of all others, to be another, though homely, Paris, possessing his Helen of Troy.

"But, to be sure, this has always been, and therefore it must be so," he said, trying to comfort himself. "And, besides, what have I done to bring it about? When did it begin? I came from Moscow with Prince Vasíli. There was certainly nothing in that. Then what harm was there in my staying at his house? And so I played cards with her, and picked up her reticule, and went to drive with her. When did it begin, when did it all begin?"

And now here he is sitting by her in the quality of accepted suitor, hearing, seeing, feeling her presence, her breathing, her every motion, her beauty. Then suddenly it seemed to him that it was not she who was the beauty, but he himself, and to such an extraordinary degree that all had to look at him, and that he, delighting in this universal admiration, swelled out his chest, raised his head high, and rejoiced in his own happiness. Suddenly he heard a voice, a well-known voice, speaking, and saying something for the second time. But Pierre was so absorbed, that he did not comprehend what was said to him.

"I asked you when you heard last from Bolkonsky," said Prince Vasíli for the third time. "How absent-minded you are, my dear fellow!"

Prince Vasíli smiled. And Pierre saw that all, all were smiling at him and at Ellen. "Well, suppose you all do know!" said Pierre to himself. "What then? It is true," and he himself smiled his sweet, childlike smile, and Ellen also smiled.

"When did you get the letter? Was it from Olmütz?" repeated Prince Vasíli, who pretended that he wished to know in order to decide a dispute.

"How can one talk and think about such trifles?" was Pierre's mental exclamation. "Yes, from Olmütz," he replied, with a sigh.

After supper Pierre gave his arm to Ellen, and led her to the drawing-room in the wake of the others. The guests began to disperse, and some went away without bidding Ellen farewell. Others, as if unwilling to tear her away from serious concerns, went up to her for a minute and then hurried away, without allowing her to accompany them to the door. The diplomat preserved a mournful silence as he left the drawing-room. The utter futility of his diplomatic career presented itself in comparison with Pierre's good fortune. The old general growled out a surly reply to his wife when she asked him about the gout in his foot. "Eka! the old fool!" he said to himself, "here's Elena Vasílyevna; and she'll be just as much of a beauty at fifty!"

"It seems as if I may congratulate you," said Anna Pavlovna, in a whisper to the old princess, and gave her a resounding kiss. "If I hadn't a sick headache, I would stay a little longer."

The princess made no answer; she was tormented by jealousy at her daughter's good fortune.

While the guests were taking their departure, Pierre was left for some time alone with Ellen in the little sitting-room where they often sat. During the past fortnight he had been often alone with Ellen, but he had never said a word to her about love. Now he felt that this was indispensable, but still he found it impossible to make up his mind to undertake this last step. He felt abashed; it seemed that here in Ellen's presence he occupied a place that belonged to some one else. 'Not for thee is this good fortune,' some internal voice seemed to whisper. 'This happiness is for those who have not what thou hast.'

But it was essential to say something, and he tried to talk. He asked her if she had enjoyed the evening. She replied, with her usual simplicity, that this name-day had been one of the pleasant events of her life.

One or two of the nearest relatives still remained. They were gathered in the great drawing-room. Prince Vasíli with leisurely steps came to Pierre. Pierre got up and remarked that it was already late. Prince Vasíli looked at him with a gravely questioning face, as much as to imply that what he said was too strange to be heard. But instantly this expression of sternness vanished, and Prince Vasíli laid his hand on Pierre's sleeve, made him sit down again, and gave him a flattering smile. "Well, Lyolya," he asked, turning instantly to his daughter, in that easy-going tone of habitual affection, peculiar to parents who have lived on terms of especial affection with their children ever since their childhood, but which in Prince Vasíli's case had been acquired only through having observed other parents. And then he turned again to Pierre: "*Sergyeï Kuzmitch, from all sides*" .... he repeated, nervously unbuttoning the upper button of his waistcoat.

Pierre smiled, but his smile made it evident how well he understood that Prince Vasíli was not interested now in this anecdote about Sergyeï Kuzmitch, and Prince Vasíli understood that Pierre understood this. Prince Vasíli suddenly muttered some excuse, and left the room. It seemed to Pierre that even Prince Vasíli was embarrassed. The appearance of embarrassment in this old society man deeply affected Pierre. He glanced at Ellen, and she, it seemed, was also embarrassed, and her glance said: "Well, it is all your fault!"

"It is absolutely indispensable for me to take this step, but I cannot, I cannot!" said Pierre to himself, and once more he began to talk about irrelevant things, about "Sergyeï Kuzmitch," asking what was the point of this anecdote, as he had not caught it. Ellen with a smile confessed that she also knew nothing about it.

When Prince Vasíli returned to the drawing-room, the princess was engaged in talking in low tones with an elderly lady about Pierre. "Of course, it is a very brilliant match, but happiness, my dear," said she, in the usual mixture of French and Russian.

"Marriages are made in heaven," returned the old lady. Prince Vasíli, pretending not to hear what she said, went to the farthest table and sat down on the sofa. He closed his eyes and appeared to be dozing. His head sank forward and then he woke with a start.

"Alína," said he to his wife, "go and see what they are doing."

The princess went to the door, passed by it with a significant but indifferent look, and glanced in. Pierre and Ellen were still sitting and talking.

"Just the same," she said, in reply to her husband. Prince Vasíli scowled, and screwed his mouth to one side, and his cheeks began to twitch with that unpleasant, coarse expression so characteristic of him; then with a sudden impulse he sprang to his feet, threw his head back, and with decided steps strode past the ladies into the little sitting-room. Swiftly, and with a great assumption of delight, he went straight up to Pierre. His face was so unusually triumphant that Pierre, in seeing him, rose to his feet in dismay.

"Slava Bohu! glory to God!" he cried, "my wife has told me all." He threw one arm round Pierre, the other round his daughter. "My dear boy! Lyolya! I am very, very glad;" his voice trembled. "I loved your father.... and she will make you a good wife.... God bless you." He embraced his daughter, then Pierre again, and kissed him with his malodorous mouth. Tears actually moistened his cheeks. "Princess, come here!" he cried.

The princess came and wept. The elderly lady also wiped her eyes with her handkerchief. They kissed Pierre, and he kissed the lovely Ellen's hand several times. After a little they were left alone again.

"All this had to be so, and could not be otherwise," thought Pierre, "and there is no need to ask if it be good or evil. Good at least in that it is decided, and I am no longer tortured by suspense."

Pierre silently held the hand of his betrothed, and looked at her fair bosom as it rose and fell.

"Ellen!" said he aloud, and then paused. He was aware that something of this sort must be said under such circumstances, but he could not for the life of him remember what was the proper thing to say. He looked into her face, she came nearer to him. Her face grew a deep crimson.

"Akh! take them off. How they...." she pointed to his glasses.

Pierre took them off, and his eyes had a scared and entreating look in addition to that strange expression which people's eyes assume when they remove their glasses suddenly. He was about to bend over her hand, and kiss it, but she with a quick and abrupt motion of her head intercepted the motion, and pressed her lips to his. Her face disturbed Pierre by its changed and unpleasantly passionate expression.

"Now it is too late, it is all decided; yes, and I love her," thought Pierre.

"I love you," he said, at last remembering what was necessary in these circumstances; but these words sounded so meager that he was ashamed of himself.

At the end of a fortnight he was married, the fortunate possessor, as they say, of a beautiful wife and of millions, and settled in the enormous Petersburg mansion of the Counts Bezukhoï, newly refitted for them.

CHAPTER III

The old Prince Nikolaï Andreïtch Bolkonsky, in December, 1805, received a letter from Prince Vasíli, announcing his coming with his son on a visit.

"I am making a tour of inspection, and of course the hundred versts' distance across the country shall not keep me from coming to see you, venerated benefactor," he wrote, "and my Anatol accompanies me; he is on his way to the army, and I hope you will permit him to show you the deep respect which he, in emulation of his father, has conceived for you."

"Well, there's no need of bringing Marie out, if suitors come to us of their own accord," said the little princess, indiscreetly, when this was mentioned to her. Prince Nikolaï Andreïtch frowned and made no reply. Two weeks after the receipt of the letter, Prince Vasíli's servants made their appearance in advance of him, and on the next day he and his son arrived.

The old Prince Bolkonsky had a low opinion of Prince Vasíli's character, and this had been intensified of late by the great advances which he had made in rank and honors under the Emperors Paul and Alexander. Now especially, from the letter, and the insinuations made by the little princess, he saw what was in the wind, and his low opinion of Prince Vasíli was transmuted in his heart into a feeling of really malevolent contempt. He snorted whenever he mentioned his name. On the day that Prince Vasíli was expected, Prince Nikolaï Andreïtch was especially surly and out of sorts. Whether he were out of sorts because Prince Vasíli was coming, or whether he was dissatisfied with Prince Vasíli's visit because he was out of sorts, it did not alter the fact that he was out of sorts, and Tikhon early in the morning advised the architect not to come near the prince with his plans.

"Listen! Hear him walking up and down," remarked Tikhon, calling the architect's attention to the sounds of the prince's tramp. "He stamps his heels, and we all know what that means."

However, at the usual hour of nine o'clock, the prince came out for his morning walk, dressed in his velvet shubka with its sable collar, and in a cap of the same fur. The night before there had been a snowstorm. The path along which the prince walked to the orangery had been swept; traces of the broom were still to be seen on the snow, and the shovel was driven into a light embankment of snow, heaped high on both sides of the path. The prince went the round of the greenhouses, the yard, and the various buildings, frowning and silent.

"Can sleighs come up?" he asked of his overseer, a man who was his image in face and actions, and was accompanying him with great deference back to the house.

"The snow is deep, your illustriousness; I have already given orders to have the snow shoveled away from the preshpekt." The prince bent his head, and started to go up the steps. "Glory to thee, O Lord," was the overseer's mental exclamation, "the cloud has passed."

"It was hard to approach, your illustriousness," added the superintendent, "when I heard, your illustriousness, that your illustriousness was expecting a minister."....

The prince turned round toward his overseer, and fastened his gloomy eyes upon him.

"What? A minister. What minister? Who commanded you?" he exclaimed, in his shrill, harsh voice. "The road is cleared, not for the princess, my daughter, but for a minister, is it? We have no ministers at my house."

"Your illustriousness, I supposed...."

"You supposed," screamed the prince, uttering the words more and more hastily and incoherently. "You supposed.... cutthroats, blackguards! I will teach ye to suppose," and, raising his cane, flourished it over Alpatuitch, and would have struck him had not the overseer instinctively dodged the blow. "You supposed.... blackguard!" screamed the prince, but, notwithstanding the fact that Alpatuitch, alarmed at his audacity in avoiding the blow, hastened up to the prince, and humbly bent before him his bald pate, or possibly for this very reason, the prince continued to scream, "Blackguards! have the snow shoveled back again," but did not raise the cane a second time, and hastened into his room.

The Princess Maríya and Mlle. Bourienne, knowing that he was in a bad humor, stood waiting for him to come to dinner, Mlle. Bourienne with a beaming face, which said, "Oh! I know nothing about it; as for me, I am always the same." And the princess pale and scared, with downcast eyes. Hardest of all was it for the Princess Maríya to know that in these circumstances she ought to imitate Mlle. Bourienne, but she could not do so. She said to herself, "If I should pretend not to pay any attention, he would think that I had no sympathy for him; and if I show him that I am melancholy and out of sorts myself, he will say (as he always does), that I'm in the blues."

The prince looked at his daughter's scared face and snorted.

"Goo.... or fool!" he muttered. "And the other one not here? Can they have been tattling to her?" he wondered, when he saw that the little princess was not in the dining-room.

"Where is the princess?" he asked. "Is she hiding herself?"

"She is not feeling very well," said Mlle. Bourienne, with á radiant smile, "she won't come down. That is natural in her condition."

"Hm! hm! kh! kh!" grumbled the prince, and took his seat at the table. His plate seemed to him not quite clean; he pointed to a spot, and flung it away. Tikhon caught it and handed it to the butler.

The little princess was not ill, but she was so invincibly afraid of the old prince that when she learned that he was in a bad humor she resolved not to leave her room.

"I am afraid for my baby," said she to Mlle. Bourienne; "God knows what might happen if I were frightened."

The little princess lived at Luisiya Gorui the larger part of the time, with a sense of fear and antipathy for her father-in-law, whom she did not understand because her terror so overmastered her that she could not. The prince reciprocated this antipathy for his daughter-in-law, but it was not so strong as his contempt for her. The princess, since her residence at Luisiya Gorui, had taken a special fancy to Mlle. Bourienne, spent whole days with her, often begged her to sleep with her, and talked about the old prince with her and criticised him.

"So some visitors are coming to see us, prince," said Mlle. Bourienne, as she unfolded her white napkin with her rosy fingers. "His excellency, Prince Kuragin, I understand?" she said, with a questioning inflection.

"Hm — this 'excellency,' as you call him, is a puppy. I secured him his appointment," said the prince, disdainfully, "but why his son is coming is more than I know. Possibly the Princess Lizavieta Karlovna and the Princess Maríya know, but I don't know what he's bringing his son here for; I don't want him." And he looked at his blushing daughter. "So she is n't very well to-day? From fear of the 'minister,' I suppose, as that block-head of an Alpatuitch called him to-day."

"No, *mon père!*"

Though Mlle. Bourienne had been particularly unfor-tunate in her choice of a subject of conversation, she was not at all put out of countenance, but rattled on about the greenhouses, and about the beauty of some new flower that had just blossomed, and the prince, after his soup, melted and became more genial.

After dinner he went to see his daughter-in-law. The little princess was sitting by a little table and chatting with Masha, her maid. She turned pale at the sight of her father-in-law. The little princess had very much altered. One would now much sooner call her ugly than pretty. Her cheeks were sunken, her lip was raised, her eyes had a drawn look.

"Yes, a little headache," she replied to the prince's question how she felt.

"Do you need anything?"

"No, thank you, *mon père.*"

"Well, then, very good, very good."

He left the room and went to the office. Alpatuitch, with drooping head, was waiting for him there.

"Is the snow shoveled back?"

"It is, your illustriousness; forgive me, for God's sake, this one piece of stupidity."

The prince interrupted him and smiled his unnatu-ral smile. "Well, then, very good, very good." He stretched out his hand for Alpatuitch to kiss, and then he went to his cabinet.

Prince Vasíli arrived in the evening. He was met on the preshpekt (as they called the prospekt or high-road) by the coachmen and stable hands, who with loud shouts dragged his covered sledge and sleigh up to the entrance, over snow which had been purposely heaped on the driveway. Separate chambers had been prepared for Prince Vasíli and Anatol.

Anatol, in his shirt-sleeves, and with his arms akimbo,

was sitting before a table on one corner of which he stared absent-mindedly with his large, handsome eyes, while a smile played over his lips. He looked on his life as one unbroken round of gayety which it was fated should be prepared for his amusement. And even now he looked in the same way on this visit to a churlish old man and a rich and monstrously ugly heiress. According to his theory, all this might lead to something very good and amusing. And why should he not marry her, if she were so very rich? "That never comes amiss," thought Anatol.

He shaved, perfumed himself carefully and coquettishly, and, with an expression of indifference which was innate in him, and holding his head high, like a young conqueror, he went to his father's chamber. Two valets were engaged in getting Prince Vasíli dressed; he himself looked around him with much animation, and gave a nod to his son as he came in, as much as to say, "Good, that's the way I want you to look!"

"No, but tell me, batyushka, without joking, is she monstrously ugly? — say," he asked, as if continuing a subject which had been more than once broached during the course of their journey.

"That'll do!.... Nonsense! The main thing is to try to be respectful and prudent towards the old prince."

"If he's going to say unpleasant things to me, I shall go right away," said Anatol. "I can't abide these old men. Hey?"

"Remember, your whole future depends on this."

Meantime, in the maidservant's room, not only was it known that the minister and his son had arrived, but every detail of their personal appearance had been circumstantially discussed. But the Princess Maríya sat alone in her room, and vainly struggled to conquer her inward agitation.

"Why did they write me? Why has Liza spoken to me about this? Why, of course this cannot be!" she said to herself, looking into her mirror. "How can I go down to the drawing-room? Even if he pleased me, I could not now be sure of myself in his presence."

The mere thought of her father's eyes filled her with horror. The little princess and Mlle. Bourienne had, by this time, received all necessary information from the maid Masha, who told them what a handsome young man, with rosy cheeks and dark eyebrows, the minister's son was; and how, when his pápenka had been scarcely able to drag his feet up the stairs, he had flown up like an eagle, three steps at a time. After hearing this news, the little princess and Mlle. Bourienne hastened to the Princess Maríya's room, filling the corridor with the lively sound of their voices as they went.

"They've come, Marie; did you know it?" said the little princess, waddling along, and dropping heavily into an arm-chair.

She was no longer in the dressing-sack which she had worn in the morning, but had put on one of her best gowns. Her hair was carefully brushed, and her face was full of animation, which, however, did not make one forget her sunken and livid features. In the finery in which she was accustomed to appear in Petersburg society, it was still more noticeable that her beauty had sadly faded. Mlle. Bourienne had also taken pains to make some improvement in her dress, and this made her pretty, fresh face still more attractive.

"What? and you intend to appear as you are, dear princess?" she exclaimed. "They will be here in a moment to bring word that the gentlemen are in the drawing-room; we must go down; so won't you make just a little change in your toilet?"

The little princess got up out of the arm-chair, rang for the maid, and hastily and merrily began to devise some adornment for her sister-in-law, and get it materialized. The Princess Maríya felt humiliated in her own sense of dignity by the excitement which the coming of her suitor stirred in her, and still more humiliated because both of her friends did not seem to imagine that it was possible to be otherwise. To tell them how ashamed she was for herself and for them would have been to betray her agitation; moreover, to have refused to put on the adornment which they were getting ready for her would have entailed endless jests and reproaches. She grew red, her lovely eyes lost their brilliancy, her face became covered with patches; and with the unlovely expression, as of a victim, coming more and more frequently in her face, she surrendered herself into the power of Mlle. Bourienne and Liza. But the ladies labored in perfectly good faith to render her handsome. She was so homely, that neither of them could ever dream of entering into rivalry with her; therefore, being perfectly sincere in that naïve and firm conviction peculiar to women, that ornaments can make a face beautiful, they busied themselves with her adornment.

"No, it's a fact, *ma bonne amie*, that dress is n't becoming," said Liza, looking critically at her sister-in-law from some little distance. "Try that dark-red *masaka* that you have. Truly! you know your whole fate, perhaps, depends on this matter. This one is too light; it won't do! no, oh, no! it won't do!"

It was not that the dress was unbecoming, but the princess's face and whole figure were at fault; and yet neither Mlle. Bourienne nor the little princess realized this. It seemed to them that if they put a blue ribbon in her hair, and combed it up, and then added a blue scarf to her cinnamon-colored dress, and made some other such additions, all would be well. They forgot that her scared face and her figure could not be altered, and, therefore, no matter how much they might vary the frame and adornment, the face itself would remain pitiful and unattractive. At last, after two or three experiments, to which the Princess Maríya patiently submitted, when her hair had been combed up high from her forehead (a mode of dressing the hair which absolutely changed her face, and that for the worse), and she was dressed in the *masaka* dress with the blue scarf, the little princess walked around her twice in succession, adjusted with her dainty fingers some of the folds in the skirt, pulled out

the   arf, looked at her with her head bent now on this
sid   now on that : —

No, that is impossible," said she, decidedly, clasping
hands.   " No, Marie, decidedly, this does not do at
. I like you better in your little, every-day, gray dress.
ow, please do this for me.   Katya," she said to the
aid, "bring the princess her grayish dress, and .... see,
Mlle. Bourienne, how I am going to arrange it," she
added, with a thrill of anticipation in her artistic pleasure.   But when Katya brought the desired garment, the
Princess Maríya sat motionless before the mirror, looking at her face, and the mirror gave back the reflection
of eyes full of tears, and a mouth trembling with the
premonition of a storm of sobbing.

" Now, dear princess," said Mlle. Bourienne, " just one
more little experiment ! "

The little princess, taking the dress from the maid,
went to Princess Marie.

" Well, now we will try something that is simple and
becoming," said she.   The three voices, hers, Mlle. Bourienne's, and Katya's, who was laughing, mingled into
one merry chatter, like the chirping of birds.

" *Non*, let me be," said the princess, and her voice
sounded so serious and sorrowful that the chirping of
the birds ceased instantly.   They looked at her large,
beautiful eyes, full of tears and of melancholy, and they
knew from their wide and beseeching expression that it
was useless, and even cruel, to insist.

" At least, change the style of your hair," said the
little princess.   " I told you so ! " said she, reproachfully, to Mlle. Bourienne.   " Marie has one of those
faces that can't stand this way of dressing the hair.   Not
at all, not at all.   Change it, please do."

" Let me be, let me be ; it 's all absolutely the same to
me," replied the young princess, in a weary voice, and
scarcely refraining from tears.

Mlle. Bourienne and the little princess were obliged
to acknowledge to themselves that the Princess Maríya,
as they had dressed her, was very homely, more so than
usual; but now it was too late.   She looked at them with

that expression which they had learned to know so well,
— an expression of deep thought and melancholy. It
did not inspire them with any sense of awe of her (for
that feeling she never could inspire), but they knew that
when her face had this expression, she was silent and
immovable in her resolutions.

"You will make the change, won't you?" asked Liza,
but when the Princess Maríya made no reply, Liza left
the room.

The Princess Maríya was left alone. She did not
comply with Liza's request, and not only did she not
change the style of her hair, but did not even look at
herself in the glass. Dropping her eyes, and letting
her hands fall nervously, she sat and pondered. She
saw in her imagination what her husband should be: a
man, a strong, commanding, and strangely attractive being, who should suddenly carry her off into his own
world, so different from hers, so full of happiness. She
imagined herself pressing to her bosom her own child,
just such a baby as she had seen the evening before at
her old nurse's daughter's. Her husband stands looking affectionately at her and at their baby; "But no,
this is impossible, I am too homely," she said to herself.

"Please come to tea. The prince will be down in a
moment," said the voice of the chambermaid outside the
door. She started up from her day-dream, and was hor-
ror-struck at her own thoughts. And before she went
down-stairs she got up, went into the oratory, and pausing before the blackened face of the great "image" of
the Saviour, lighted by the beams of the tapers, she stood
there for several moments with folded hands. Her heart
was filled with painful forebodings. Could it be that for
her there was the possibility of the joy of love, of earthly
love for a husband? In her imaginings concerning marriage, the Princess Maríya dreamed of family happiness
and children, but her principal dream, predominating
over all others, though unknown to herself, was that of
earthly love. The feeling was all the stronger, the more
she tried to hide it from others, and even from herself.

"My God," she cried, "how can I crush out in my

heart these thoughts inspired by the devil? How can I escape once and for all from evil imaginings, and calmly fulfil Thy will?"

And she had hardly offered this prayer ere God gave an answer in her own heart.

"Desire nothing for thyself, seek not, disturb not thyself, be not envious. The future and thy fate must needs be hidden from thee; but live so as to be ready for anything. If it please God to try thee in the responsibilities of marriage, be ready to fulfil His will."

With this consoling thought — but still with a secret hope that her forbidden, earthly dream might be realized — the Princess María, with a sigh, crossed herself, and went down-stairs, thinking not of her dress, or of her hair, or of how she should make entrance, or of what she should say. What did all that signify in comparison with the preordination of God, without whose will not a hair can fall from a man's head.

CHAPTER IV

WHEN the Princess María came down, Prince Vasíli and his son were already in the drawing-room, talking with the little princess and Mlle. Bourienne. When she came in with her heavy gait, treading on her heels, the gentlemen and Mlle. Bourienne stood up, and the little princess exclaimed, "Here is *Marie!*" The Princess María saw them all, and saw them distinctly. She saw Prince Vasíli's face becoming for an instant serious at the sight of her, instantly resume its smiling expression, and the little princess watching curiously the impression which her entrance would produce upon their guests. She saw also Mlle. Bourienne, with her ribbon and her pretty face, and her eyes more sparkling than usual, fixed on *him;* but she could not bring herself to see *him;* all she could see was something tall, brilliant, and magnificent coming toward her as she entered the room.

Prince Vasíli was the first to greet her, and she kissed the bald forehead, bending over her hand, and answered his question by assuring him, "that, on the contrary, she remembered him very well."

Then Anatol came to her. She could not see him as yet at all. She was only conscious of a soft hand holding hers, while she lightly touched with her lips a white brow under a thatch of beautiful brown hair perfumed with pomade. When she looked at him his beauty dazzled her.

Anatol, hooking the thumb of his right hand behind one button of his uniform, stood with his chest thrust out, and his back bent in, resting his weight on one leg, and slightly inclining his head, and looked at the princess cheerily, but without speaking. He was evidently not thinking of her at all. Anatol was not quick-witted or a ready talker, but, on the other hand, he had that gift of composure which is so invaluable in society, and a self-confidence which nothing could disturb. If a man lacking self-confidence is silent at a first introduction, and betrays a consciousness of the impropriety of such a silence, and attempts to escape from it, it makes a bad matter worse; but Anatol, swaying a little on one leg, had nothing to say, and gazed with an amused look at the princess's hair. It was evident that such ease of manner would enable him to preserve silence any length of time. His look seemed to say: 'If this silence is awkward for any one, then speak; but as for me, I have no desire to say anything.'

Moreover, Anatol had in his behavior toward women that manner which strongly piques curiosity, and excites fear, and even love in them, — a sort of scornful consciousness of his own superiority. His look seemed to say to them: 'I know you, I know what is disturbing you. Ah, how happy you would be if....' possibly he did not think any such thing when he met women (and there is considerable ground for such a supposition, because he thought very little), but this was what was expressed by his look and manner. The princess felt it, and apparently wishing to show him that she did not venture to do such a thing as engage his attention, she turned to his father.

The conversation became general, and rather lively, thanks to the merry voice of the little princess, who kept lifting up her downy lip and showing her white teeth.

She met Prince Vasíli with that peculiarly vivacious manner which is often employed by people of merrily loquacious mood, and consists in the interchange between you and your acquaintance of the regulaı stock witticisms of the day, and of pleasant and amus. ing reminiscences which it is taken for granted are noᴛ understood by all people, comical reminiscences of things that they have never experienced together, and so it was with the little princess and Prince Vasíli.

Prince Vasíli willingly adapted himself to this spirit; the little princess managed **to** include Anatol as well, though she scarcely knew him, and soon found herself sharing with him in recollections of ridiculous occurrences, events which in some cases had never happened at all. Mlle. Bourienne also took part in these general recollections, and even the Princess Maríya had a sort of satisfaction in feeling herself drawn into this light gossip.

"Here at least we shall have the benefit of your com pany all to ourselves, dear prince," said the little princess — in French of course — to Prince Vasíli. "It won't be as it used to be at our receptions at Annette's, where you always made your escape, you know — *cette chère* Annette!"

"Ah, but of course you won't oblige me to talk about politics as Annette does?"

"But our tea-table?"

"Oh, yes!"

"Why were you never at Annette's?" asked the little princess, of Anatol. "Oh! but I know, I know," said she, with a sly expression. "Your brother Ippolit told me all about your doings — oh!" she exclaimed, threatening him with her finger. "And then again in Paris, I know about your pranks!"

"And has n't Ippolit told you?" asked Prince Vasíli, addressing his son and seizing Princess Liza by the arm, as if there were danger of her running away, and hᴇ wished to prevent it while yet there was time, "has n't he ever told you how he himself was dead in love with our dear princess here, and how she would n't have anything to say to him?"

"Oh, she is a pearl among women, princess!"[1] said he, addressing the Princess Maríya.

Mlle. Bourienne, on her part, when she heard the word "Paris," did not lose the opportunity of also adding her recollections to the general conversation. She allowed herself to inquire of Anatol if he had been long in Paris, and how that city pleased him.

Anatol took evident pleasure in answering the French-woman's questions, and with a smile talked with her about her native land. Seeing how pretty la Bourienne was, Anatol decided that, after all, it would not be so very stupid here at Luisiya Gorui. "Not at all bad looking," he said to himself, as he looked at her; "very far from it. I hope that when she marries me she will take this *demoiselle de compagnie* with her, she's a pretty little girl!"

The old prince took his time about dressing, and he frowned, as he thought what he should do. The coming of these guests annoyed him.

"What are Prince Vasíli and his son to me? Prince Vasíli is an empty swaggerer, and his son must be a fine specimen," he grumbled to himself. He was annoyed because the coming of these guests aroused in the depths of his soul an unsettled and constantly avoided question, a question in regard to which the old prince was always deceiving himself. The question was this: whether he could make up his mind to part with his daughter and let her marry. The old prince could never bring himself to ask the question directly, know-ing beforehand that if he should answer it honestly, his honesty would come into open antagonism, not merely with his feelings, but with the whole order and system of his life. For Prince Nikolaï Andreyevitch, life with-out his daughter, little as he outwardly seemed to ap-preciate her, was out of the question.

---

[1] *Oh, c'est la perle des femmes, princesse.*

"And why should she get married?" he asked himself. "Probably to be unhappy. Here is Liza — certainly it would be hard to find a better husband than Andreï — and yet is she contented with her lot? And who would take her from mere love? She is homely, awkward! They would marry her for her connections, for her wealth! And can't girls live unmarried? They'd be much happier."

Thus thought Prince Nikolaï Andreyevitch, as he performed his toilet in his cabinet, and still at the same time the ever-procrastinated question now demanded an immediate solution. Prince Vasíli had brought his son, evidently with the intention of making a proposal, and therefore this very day or the next he should have to give a direct answer. His name, his position in the world, were excellent.

"Well, I've no objection," said the prince to himself. "But let him prove himself worthy of her. Well, we shall see. Yes, we shall see!" he exclaimed aloud, "yes, we shall see how it is," and with his usual firm tread he went into the drawing-room, took in all present with a sweeping glance, noticed even the change that the little princess had made in her dress, and la Bourienne's ribbon, and the Princess Maríya's ugly head-dress, and her isolation in the general conversation, and Bourienne and Anatol's exchange of smiles.

"She is dressed up like a fool," he said to himself, giving his daughter a wrathful glance. "She has no sense of shame, and he — he does not care anything about making her acquaintance."

He went straight to Prince Vasíli: "Well, how are you, how are you? Glad to see you!"

"Friendship laughs at distance,"[1] exclaimed Prince Vasíli, quoting the familiar proverb with ready wit, and with his usual self-confident familiarity. "Here is my second son; grant him your friendship, I beg of you."

Prince Nikolaï Andreyevitch surveyed Anatol.

"Fine young fellow! Fine young fellow," said he. "Now come, give me a kiss," and he offered him his

[1] Literally: For a dear old friend even seven versts is not a roundabout.

cheek. Anatol kissed the old man and looked at him
curiously, but with perfect composure, expecting soon
to hear one of those droll remarks of which his father
had told him. Prince Nikolaï Andreyevitch sat down
in his usual place, in one corner of the divan, drew up
an arm-chair for Prince Vasíli, pointed him to it, and
began to ask him about the news in the political world.
He listened with apparent attention to what Prince
Vasíli had to say, but he kept glancing at the Princess
Maríya.

"So that's what they write from Potsdam, is it?"
said he, repeating Prince Vasíli's last words; and then
suddenly getting up, he went over to his daughter.
"So this is how you dress before company, hey?"
exclaimed he. "Excellent, admirable! You appear
before folks with your hair done up in this new-fangled
way, and I tell you, in the presence of these same folks,
never again, without my leave, to rig yourself up in such
a fashion!"

"It was my fault, *mon père*," said the little princess,
blushing, and coming to her sister-in-law's rescue.

"You may do as you please," said Prince Nikolaï
Andreyevitch, making a low bow before his son's wife.
"But she has no right to disfigure herself; she's ugly
enough without that." And he once more resumed his
place, paying no further heed to his daughter, who was
ready to weep.

"On the contrary, that way of dressing her hair is
very becoming to the princess," said Prince Vasíli.

"Well, batyushka — my young prince — what is his
name?" said Prince Nikolaï Andreyevitch, turning to
Anatol, "come here. Let us have a little talk, and get
acquainted."

"Now the sport begins," thought Anatol, and with a
smile he took a seat by the old prince.

"Well, now, my dear, you have been educated abroad,
somewhat different from your father and me, who had
the parish dyachok[1] teach us our *a b c*'s. Tell me, my
dear, you serve in the Horse Guards, don't you?"

[1] Precentor or sexton.

asked the old prince, scrutinizing Anatol closely and keenly.

"No, I have been transferred to the Line," replied Anatol, scarcely able to keep from laughing.

"Ah, excellent thing! So that you can serve the Tsar and your country. It's war-time. Such fine young men as you ought to be in the service. At the front, I suppose?"

"No, prince; our regiment has gone, but I was detached. What was I detached for, papa?" asked Anatol, turning to his father with a laugh.

"Famous way of serving, I must confess. 'What am I detached for?' ha! ha! ha!" roared Prince Nikolaï Andreyevitch, and Anatol joined in still more vociferously. Suddenly Prince Nikolaï Andreyevitch began to scowl. "Well, get you gone," said he to Anatol.

Anatol with a smile went and rejoined the ladies.

"And so you have had him educated abroad, hey, Prince Vasíli?" asked the old prince, of Kuragin.

"I did the best I could for him, and I must say that the schools there are far better than ours."

"Well, everything is changed, all new-fangled notions. He's a fine young man, a fine lad. Now let's go into my room." He took Prince Vasíli by the arm, and carried him off to his cabinet.

Prince Vasíli, finding himself alone with the old prince, immediately began to unfold to him his wishes and hopes.

"What kind of an idea have you?" exclaimed the old prince, savagely, "that I keep her tied, and cannot part with her? What notions people have!" he exclaimed angrily. "To-morrow, as far as I'm concerned, — I merely tell you that I want to know my daughter's husband better. You know my principles: *all above board*. To-morrow I will ask her in your presence if she will have him; if she will, then let him stay. Let him stay, I will study him." The prince snorted, "Or let him go, it's all the same to me," he cried, in the same piercing tone in which he had uttered his farewell when his son took his departure.

"I will tell you frankly," said Prince Vasíli, in the tone of a cunning man who is convinced of the uselessness of trying to be shrewd toward such a sharp-eyed opponent. "You see, your eyes read through men. Anatol is no genius, but he is an honorable, kind-hearted boy, and an excellent son."

"Very good, we shall see."

As usually happens in the case of women who have been long deprived of the society of men, all three of the women at Prince Andreyevitch's, now that they had Anatol in their midst, felt that hitherto life had not been life for them. The powers of feeling, thinking, loving, were instantly multiplied tenfold in each one of them, so that their existence, which had been till now, as it were, spent in darkness, was suddenly filled by a new light, full of rich significance.

The Princess Maríya no longer gave a thought to her looks, or the dressing of her hair. Her whole attention was absorbed by the handsome open face of the man who perhaps would be her husband. He seemed to her good, brave, resolute, manly, and noble. She was quite convinced of this. A thousand dreams of the family life which she should enjoy in the future persisted in rising in her mind. She tried to banish them, and keep them out of her imagination.

"But was I too cool toward him?" queried the Princess Maríya. "I try to be reserved, because I feel in the depths of my soul that he is already too near to me; but, of course, he cannot know all that I think about him, and he may imagine that I do not like him."

And the Princess Maríya strove, and yet was unable to be amiable to her new guest.

"Poor girl! she is devilishly ugly!" Such was Anatol's uncomplimentary thought of her.

Mlle. Bourienne, whom Anatol's arrival had brought into a high state of excitement, allowed herself to have quite different thoughts. Of course, being a pretty young girl, without any stated position in society, without relatives and friends, and far from her native land,

she had no intention of devoting her whole life to the
service of Prince Nikolaï Andreyevitch, reading books
to him, and playing the part of companion to the Princess Maríya.　Mlle. Bourienne had been long waiting
for the Russian prince who should immediately have
wit enough to appreciate her superiority to these homely,
unbecomingly dressed, and awkward Russian princesses,
should fall in love with her, and elope with her; now,
at last, the Russian prince had come.

Mlle. Bourienne knew a story which her aunt had
once told her, and which, in imagination, she liked to
repeat to the end, with herself in the heroine's place.
The story was about a young girl who had been seduced,
and whose poor mother, finding where she was, came
and covered her with reproaches because she had gone
to live with a man to whom she was not married.　Mlle.
Bourienne was often melted to tears by imagining herself telling *him*, her seducer, this story.　And now this
he, this genuine Russian prince, had made his appearance.　He would elope with her, then *sa pauvre mère*
would appear, and he would marry her.

Thus in Mlle. Bourienne's fertile brain the whole
romance evolved itself, from the moment that she began
to talk with him about Paris.　Not that Mlle. Bourienne
conceived of all the details — what she was going to do
did not once occur to her — but still all the materials
were long ago ready in her, and now they merely grouped
themselves around Anatol, whom she was anxious and
determined to please as much as possible.

The little princess (forgetting her situation instinctively), and like an old war-horse at the sound of the
trumpet, made ready to flirt at headlong speed, without
meaning anything by it, but with her usual naïve and
light-hearted spirit of fun.

In spite of the fact that Anatol in the society of
women generally affected the position of a man who
considers it a bore to have them running after him, still
he felt a consciousness of gratified vanity to see his
power over these three women.　Moreover, he began
to feel for the pretty and enticing Bourienne a real

animal passion, such as sometimes overcame him with extraordinary rapidity, and impelled him to commit the coarsest and most audacious actions.

After tea, they all went into the divan-room, and the Princess Maríya was invited to play on the clavichord. Anatol leaned on his elbows, in front of her, near Mlle. Bourienne, and, with eyes full of mirth and gayety, looked at Maríya, who, with a painful and at the same time joyous emotion, felt his gaze resting on her. Her favorite sonata bore her away into a most genuinely poetic world, and the consciousness of that glance endowed this world with even more poetry. In reality, however, Anatol, though he looked in her direction, was not thinking of her, but was occupied with the motion of Mlle. Bourienne's foot, which he was at this moment pressing with his under the piano. Mlle. Bourienne was also looking at the princess, but her beautiful eyes had an expression of frightened happiness and hope, which the Princess Maríya had never seen in them before.

"How fond she is of me," thought the Princess Maríya. "How happy I am now, and how happy I might be with such a friend and such a husband! Husband! Can it be possible?" she asked herself, not daring to look at him, but, nevertheless, feeling his gaze fixed on her face.

In the evening, when after supper they were about to separate for the night and Anatol kissed the young princess's hand, she herself knew not how she dared to do such a thing, but she looked straight into his handsome face as it approached her short-sighted eyes.

Turning from the princess, he went and kissed Mlle. Bourienne's hand. This was contrary to etiquette, but he did everything with such confidence and simplicity! Mlle. Bourienne flushed and glanced in dismay at the princess.

"How considerate of him," thought the princess. "Can it be that Amélie" — so she called Mlle. Bourienne — "thinks that I should be jealous of her, and do not appreciate her affection and devotion to me?"

She went straight over to Mlle. Bourienne, and gave her an affectionate kiss. Anatol was about to kiss the little princess's hand also.

"*Non! non! non!* when your father writes me that you are behaving beautifully, then I will let you kiss my hand. Not before."

And, shaking her finger at him, she left the room, with a smile.

CHAPTER V

ALL had gone to their rooms, but, with the exception of Anatol, who went to sleep as soon as he got into bed, it was long before any one could close an eye that night.

"Is he really to be my husband, this handsome stranger, who seems so good; ah, yes, above all, so good!" thought the Princess María, and a feeling of fear, such as she had scarcely ever experienced before, came upon her. She was afraid to look round; it seemed to her as if some one were standing there behind the screen in the dark corner. And this some one was *he* — the devil — and *he* was this man with the white forehead, the black eyebrows, and the rosy lips.

She called her maid, and begged her to sleep in her room.

Mlle. Bourienne, that same evening, walked for a long time up and down the winter garden, vainly expecting some one, now smiling at her own thought, now stirred to tears by imagining the words which *sa pauvre mère* would say in reproaching her after her fall.

The little princess scolded her maid because her bed was not comfortable. It was impossible for her to lie on her side, or on her face. Any position was awkward and uncomfortable. She felt more than ever tried to-day, especially because Anatol's presence brought back so vividly the days before she was married, when she was light-hearted and merry. She reclined in her easy-chair, in her dressing-jacket and nightcap.

Katya, half asleep, and with her hair hanging down in a braid, was turning for the third time and shaking up the heavy mattress, muttering to herself.

"I told you that it was all humps and hollows," insisted the little princess, "I should like to go to sleep myself; I'm sure it isn't my fault," and her voice trembled as if she were a child getting ready to cry.

The old prince, also, could not sleep. Tikhon, as he napped, heard him stamping wrathfully up and down, and snorting. It seemed to the old prince that he had been insulted through his daughter. The insult was painful, because it was directed not to himself, but to another, to his daughter, whom he loved better than himself. He kept telling himself that he would calmly think the whole matter over, and decide how in justice to himself he must act; but, instead of so doing, he grew more and more vexed with himself.

"Let the first young man come along, and she forgets father and all! and she runs up-stairs, combs up her hair and prinks, and is no longer like herself. Glad to throw her father over. And she knew that I noticed it. Fr! — fr! — fr! and then, haven't I eyes to see that that simpleton has no eyes for any one except *Burienka* (I must get rid of her!). And how is it she hasn't enough pride to see it herself? If not for her own sake, she might at least show some for mine. I must show her that this booby doesn't think of her at all, but stares only at Bourienne. She has no pride, but I'll prove this for her."

The old prince knew that if he told his daughter that she was laboring under a delusion, that Anatol was bent on flirting with Bourienne, he would in this way touch his daughter's pride, and his game would be played; for he was anxious not to part with his daughter. This consideration served to quiet him. He summoned Tikhon, and began to undress.

"The devil take 'em!" he said to himself, as Tikhon slipped the night-shirt over his master's thin old body, the chest overgrown with gray hairs.

"I did not invite 'em. They have come to upset my

whole life. And my life will soon be come to an end. To the devil with 'em!" he muttered, while his head was still hidden by the shirt. Tikhon knew the prince's habit of sometimes thinking aloud, and therefore he met with unflinching eyes the prince's wrathfully scrutinizing gaze, as his head came out from the night-shirt.

"Have they gone to bed?" asked the prince.

Tikhon, after the manner of all well-trained valets, knew by intuition what his barin was thinking about. He judged that the question referred to Prince Vasíli and his son.

"They have deigned to go to bed, and their lights are out, your illustriousness."

"No reason why they should n't," briskly exclaimed the prince, and, thrusting his feet into his slippers and his arms into his dressing-gown, he went to the sofa where he usually slept.

Although but few words had been exchanged by Anatol and Mlle. Bourienne, they thoroughly understood each other as to the first chapters of the romance, up to the appearance of the poor mother; they understood that they had much to say to each other in secret, and therefore early in the morning they both sought an opportunity for a private interview. While the young princess was going at the usual hour to meet her father, Mlle. Bourienne and Anatol met in the winter garden.

The Princess Maríya on this particular day went with unusual trepidation to the door of her father's cabinet. It seemed to her that every one knew that this day her fate was to be decided, but also knew what she herself felt about it. She read this expression on Tikhon's face, and on the face of Prince Vasíli's valet, as he met her in the corridor on his way with hot water for the prince, and made her a low bow.

The old prince this morning was thoroughly affectionate and kind in his behavior to his daughter. The Princess Maríya well knew this expression of kindness. It was the expression his face generally wore when his nervous hands doubled up with vexation because she did not understand her arithmetical examples, and he would spring to his feet, walk away from her, and then repeat the same words in a low, gentle voice.

He immediately addressed himself to the business in hand, and began to explain it to her, all the time using the formal *vui*, you.

"I have received an offer for your hand in marriage," said he, with an unnatural smile. "I suppose you did not imagine," he went on to say, "that he came here and brought his pupil " — for some inexplicable reason, Prince Nikolaï Andreyevitch called Anatol *vospítannik*, pupil — "for the sake of ' my handsome eyes.' Last evening he proposed for your hand. And, as you know my principles, I refer it to you."

"How am I to understand you, *mon père?*" she exclaimed, turning pale and then blushing.

"How understand me! " cried her father, wrathfully, "Prince Vasíli is satisfied with you for a daughter-in-law, and has proposed for your hand in behalf of his pupil. That 's what it means. ' How understand it! ' That I ask you."

"I do not know so well as you, *mon père*," whispered the princess.

"I ? I ? what have I to do with it ? Consider me out of the question. *I 'm* not the one who is going to be married. What 's *your* opinion ? That is what must be known."

The princess saw that her father did not regard the matter very favorably, but at the same time the thought occurred to her that now or never the whole destiny of her life hung in the balance. She dropped her eyes, so as not to see his face, because she knew that she could not think if she were under its dominion but even then could only be subject to him, and she said : —

"I desire only one thing, to fulfil your will; but if it be necessary for me to express my desire .... "

She had no time to finish her sentence. The prince interrupted her.

"That 's admirable," he cried. "He will take you for your fortune, and, by the way, hook on Mlle. Bourienne ! She will be his wife, and you " .... the prince paused. He noticed the effect produced on his daughter by his words. She hung her head, and was ready to burst into tears.

"Well, well, I was only jesting," said he. "Remember this one thing, princess; I stick to my principles that a girl has a perfect right to choose for herself. I give you your freedom. Remember this, though, the happiness of your whole life depends upon your decision. Leave me out of the consideration."

"But I do not know.... *mon père.*"

"There's nothing to be said. He will marry as he is bid, whether it be you or somebody else, but *you* are free to choose. Go to your room; think it over, and at the end of an hour come to me and tell me in his presence what your decision is, yea or no. I know that you'll have to pray over it. Well, pray if you please. Only you'd better use your reason. Get you gone. .... Yes or no, yes or no, yes or no!" cried he, as the princess, still as if in a mist, left the room with tottering step.

Her fate was already decided, and happily decided. But what her father said about Mlle. Bourienne, — that insinuation was horrible. False, let us hope, but still it was horrible, and she could not keep it out of her thoughts. She started directly to her room through the winter garden, seeing nothing and hearing nothing, when suddenly Mlle. Bourienne's well-known chatter struck her ear and woke her from her dreaming. She raised her eyes and, two paces away, saw Anatol with the Frenchwoman in his arms, and whispering something in her ear. With a terrible expression on his handsome face he looked at the Princess Maríya, and at first did not release Mlle. Bourienne, who had not seen the princess at all.

"Who is here? what is the trouble? Just wait a little," Anatol's face seemed to say. The Princess Maríya silently gazed at them. She could not comprehend it. Then Mlle. Bourienne uttered a cry and fled. Anatol, with an amused smile, gave the princess a bow, as if asking her to look on the ridiculous side of this strange behavior, and, shrugging his shoulders, disappeared through the door that led to his own quarters.

At the end of an hour, Tikhon came to summon the Princess Maríya. He conducted her to her father's room, and told her that Prince Vasíli was also there. When Tikhon came for her, the princess was sitting on a sofa in her room, with her arm around Mlle. Bourienne. The latter was weeping, and the princess was softly stroking her hair. The princess's beautiful eyes, with all their usual calmness and brilliancy, gazed with affectionate love and sympathy into Mlle. Bourienne's pretty face.

"No, princess, my place is forever gone from your heart," said Mlle. Bourienne.

"Why, I love you more than ever," replied the Princess Maríya, "and I will try to do all that is in my power for your happiness."

"But you despise me! You, who are so pure, will never understand this frenzy of passion. Ah! my poor mother!"

"I understand it all," replied the princess, with a melancholy smile. "Compose yourself, my friend, I am going to see my father," said she, and left the room.

Prince Vasíli, — with one leg thrown across his knee, and holding his snuff-box in his hand, — excited to the last degree, and appearing as if he felt a sort of pity for himself and yet amused at his own emotion, was sitting with an anxious smile on his face as the Princess Maríya entered the room. He hastily applied a pinch of snuff to his nose.

"*Ah! ma bonne, ma bonne!*" he exclaimed, rising and seizing her by both hands. He sighed, and added, "My son's fate is in your hands. *Decide, ma bonne, ma chère, ma douce Marie!* I have always loved you as if you were my own daughter." He turned away. Genuine tears stood in his eyes.

"Fr!.... fr!"....snorted Prince Nikolaï Andreyitch. "The prince in the name of his pupil.... I mean his son ....makes you an offer. Will you or will you not be the wife of Prince Anatol Kuragin? Speak: yes or no," cried he. "And then I reserve to myself the right of giving my opinion also. Yes, my opinion, and my opinion only," added Prince Nikolaï Andreyitch, in reply to Prince Vasíli's beseeching expression. "Yes or no?"

"My desire, *mon père*, is never to leave you, never to part from you as long as we live. I do not wish to marry," said she with firm deliberation, fixing her lovely eyes on Prince Vasíli and on her father.

"Folly! nonsense! nonsense! nonsense!" cried Prince Nikolaï Andreyitch, frowning; he drew his daughter to him, yet he did not kiss her, but merely brought his forehead close to hers, and squeezed her hand, which he held in his, so that she screamed out with pain. Prince Vasíli arose: —

"My dear, I will tell you that this is a moment that I shall never forget, never! but, my dear, can't you give us a little hope of ever touching your kind and generous heart? Say that perhaps .... the future is so long. Only say 'perhaps.'"

"Prince, what I have told you is all that my heart can say. I thank you for the honor, but I can never be your son's wife."

"Well, that ends it, my dear fellow. Very glad to have seen you. Very glad to have seen you. Go to your room, princess, go to your room," said the old prince. "Very, very glad to have seen you," he reiterated, embracing Prince Vasíli.

"My vocation is different," said the Princess Maríya to herself, "my vocation is to be happy in the happiness of others; a different sort of happiness, the happiness of love and self-sacrifice. And as far as within me lies, I will bring about the happiness of poor Amélie. She loves him so passionately. She repents her conduct so bitterly. I will do everything to bring about a marriage between them. If he is not rich, I will give her the means, I will petition my father, I will ask Andreï. And I shall be so happy when she becomes his wife. She is so unfortunate, lonely, and helpless in a strange land. And *Bozhe moï!* how passionately she must love him, if she can so far forget herself. Maybe, I myself should have done the same thing!" .... thought the Princess Maríya.

CHAPTER VI

THE Rostofs had not heard for a long time from their Nikolushka, and it was near the middle of winter when a letter was handed to the count, on the envelope of which he recognized his son's handwriting. On receipt of the letter, the count hastily and anxiously stole off to his own cabinet, walking on his tiptoes, so as to escape observation, and shut himself in, and began to read it. Anna Mikhaïlovna, learning about the arrival of the letter, — for she knew everything that took place in the house, — quietly followed the count, and found him with the letter in his hands, sobbing and laughing at the same time.

Anna Mikhaïlovna, notwithstanding the improvement in her affairs, still continued to live at the Rostofs.

"*My dear friend*," exclaimed Anna Mikhaïlovna, with a tone of pathetic inquiry in her voice, and prepared to give him sympathy to any extent.

The count sobbed still more violently: "Nikolushka .... a letter .... wounded .... he wa-wa-was w-wounded .... *ma chère* .... wounded, my darling boy [1] .... the little countess .... he's been .... made an officer .... glory to God, *slava Bohu!* .... how can I tell the little .... countess?" ....

Anna Mikhaïlovna sat down by him, wiped the tears from his eyes with her handkerchief, and from the letter, for they were dropping on it, and then from her own eyes, read the letter herself, soothed the count, and decided that she would use the time till dinner, and even tea, for preparing the countess, and then after tea she would break the news to her, if God would only aid her.

During dinner-time, Anna Mikhaïlovna talked about the events of the war and about Nikolushka, and asked twice when they had received the last letter from him — though she herself knew perfectly well, and remarked that very likely they might have a letter from him, perhaps that day. Every time when, at such in-

[1] *Galúbchik.*

sinuations, the countess began to grow uneasy, and glance anxiously first at the count and then at Anna Mikhaïlovna, Anna Mikhaïlovna most adroitly led the conversation to insignificant topics.

Natasha more than the rest of the family was endowed with peculiar sensitiveness to shades of intonation, to the looks and expressions of faces, and, as soon as dinner began, she pricked up her ears, and came to the conclusion that there was some secret between her father and Anna Mikhaïlovna, and that it was something referring to her brother, and that Anna Mikhaïlovna was trying to "prepare" some one. Notwithstanding all her audacity, she dared not ask any questions during dinner-time, for she knew too well how sensitive her mother was in regard to all that related to her son; but her curiosity was so great that she ate nothing, and kept turning and twisting in her chair, in spite of the reproaches of her governess. After dinner, she rushed precipitately after Anna Mikhaïlovna, and threw herself into her arms. "Aunty darling,[1] tell what it is!"

"Nothing, my dear."

"Yes, there is, dearest, sweet one, you old pet,[2] and I shan't let you go till you tell me, for I know that you know."

Anna Mikhaïlovna shook her head: "You 're a little witch, child," said she.

"A letter from Nikolenka? Truly, is n't that it?" cried Natasha, reading an affirmative answer in Anna Mikhaïlovna's face.

"Yes, but for heaven's sake be more cautious; you know how this might trouble your *maman.*"

"I will, I will, but tell me all about it! — You won't tell me? Well, then, I 'm going right to tell her!"

Anna Mikhaïlovna in few words told Natasha the contents of the letter, under the conditions of secrecy.

"My true, true word of honor," said Natasha, crossing herself, "I won't tell any one," and she immediately went to Sonya.

---

[1] *Tyótenka, galúbushka.*
[2] *Dúshenka* (little soul) *galúbchik, milaya* (dear), *pérsik* (peach).

" Nikolenka .... wounded .... a letter," she exclaimed, triumphantly and joyously.

" Nicolas ! " cried Sonya, turning pale.

Natasha, seeing the impression produced on Sonya by the news that her brother was wounded, realized for the first time all the sorrowful side of this news.

She ran to Sonya, threw her arms around her neck, and burst into tears.

" He is not badly wounded, and has been promoted to be an officer; he 's all well again, for he wrote the letter himself," cried she, through her tears.

" That 's the way ! All you women are milksops ! " exclaimed Petya, marching with long, gallant strides up and down the room. " I am very glad, indeed, I am very glad, that my brother has distinguished himself so ! You are all cry-babies. You have n't any sense at all."

Natasha smiled through her tears : —

" You have n't read the letter, have you ? "

" No, I have n't read it, but she said the worst was over, and that he was already an officer."

" Glory to God ! " cried Sonya, crossing herself. " But maybe she was deceiving you. Let us go to *maman !* "

Petya walked silently up and down the room.

" If I had been in Nikolushka's place, I should have killed still more of those Frenchmen," said he, after a little; " what nasty brutes they are ! I would have killed such a lot of them that it would have made a pile so high," continued Petya.

" Hush, Petya ! what a goose you are ! "

" I am not a goose, but you are geese to cry over mere trifles ! " said he.

" Do you remember him ? " suddenly asked Natasha, after a moment's silence.

Sonya smiled : " Do I remember Nicolas ? "

" No, Sonya. Do you remember him perfectly, so that you can recall everything about him ? " asked Natasha, with an emphatic gesture, evidently wishing to give her words the most serious meaning. " Well, now, I remember Nikolenka, I remember him well; but I don't remember Borís. I don't remember him at all."

"What? You don't remember Borís!" exclaimed Sonya, in amazement.

"No, I don't really remember him. I have a general idea how he looked, but I can't bring him up before me, as I can Nikolenka. If I shut my eyes I can see, but it is not so with Borís." She shut her eyes. "That way, no, not at all."

"Oh, Natasha," said Sonya, looking at her friend, with enraptured earnestness, as if she considered her unworthy to hear what she had in mind to say, and as if she were saying it to some one else, with whom it was impossible to jest. "I love your brother, and whatever might happen to him or to me, I should never cease to love him as long as I live!"

Natasha looked at Sonya with wondering inquisitive eyes and made no answer. She felt convinced that what Sonya had said was true; that what Sonya talked about was real love; but Natasha had never experienced anything like it. She believed that it was in the realm of the possible, but she did not understand it.

"Shall you write him?" she asked.

Sonya deliberated.

The question how to write to Nicolas, and whether it were her duty to write to him, and what she should write to him, tormented her. Now that he were already an officer, and a wounded hero, it was a question of doubt in her mind, whether it would be right for her to remind him of herself, and of the promise which he had made her.

"I do not know. I think if he writes to me, then I will answer it," she replied, blushing.

"And shan't you feel ashamed to write him?"

Sonya smiled:—

"No."

"Well, I should feel ashamed to write to Borís, and I am not going to."

"Why should one feel ashamed?"

"There now, I'm sure I don't know. It's awkward; anyway, I should be ashamed."

"Well, I know why she would be ashamed," said

Petya, affronted at Natasha's first remark, — "because she fell in love with that fat fellow with the glasses " — he meant by this his namesake, Pierre, the new Count Bezukhoï — " and now she's in love with that singer " — Petya now referred to an Italian, who was giving Natasha singing lessons — "and that's why she would be ashamed ! "

" Petya, you're too silly."

" I'm no sillier than you are, matushka !" said the ten-year-old lad, exactly as if he were an elderly brigadier.

The countess had been " prepared " during dinner-time by means of Anna Mikhaïlovna's hints. Going to her own room, she sat down on her sofa, not taking her eyes from a miniature picture of her son, painted on her snuff-box, and her eyes quickly filled with tears. Anna Mikhaïlovna, with the letter, came into the countess's room on her tiptoes and remained standing. " Don't you come in," said she to the old count, who was following her. She closed the door behind her. The count applied his ear to the keyhole and tried to listen.

At first all that he heard was a monotonous sound of voices ; then Anna Mikhaïlovna, making a long speech without interruption ; then a shriek ; then silence ; then, again, both voices speaking together with joyful inflections, and then steps, and Anna Mikhaïlovna opened the door. Anna Mikhaïlovna's face wore the proud expression of a surgical operator, who has just accomplished a difficult amputation and allows the public to enter and appreciate his skill.

" It's all right," said she to the count, pointing with an enthusiastic gesture to the countess, who held in one hand the snuff-box with the portrait, in the other the letter, and was pressing her lips first to the one and then to the other. Seeing the count, she stretched out her arms toward him, threw them round his bald head, and over his bald head looked at the letter and the portrait, and then, in order to press them to her lips again, gently pushed the bald head away.

Viera, Natasha, Sonya, and Petya came into the room, and the reading of the letter began. It contained

a brief description of the campaign, and the two engagements in which Nikolushka had taken part; he announced his promotion, and said that he kissed *maman's*
and papa's hands, asking for their blessing, and kissed
Viera, Natasha, and Petya. Moreover, he made his
respects to Mr. Schelling and Madame Chausse, and
his old nurse, and then he begged them to kiss his dear
Sonya, whom he had always loved so, and whom he
had remembered so affectionately.

When Sonya heard this, she blushed so that the tears
came into her eyes. And, not able to endure the
glances fastened on her, she ran into the drawing-parlor,
whirled round it at full speed, her dress flying out like
a balloon, and then plumped down on the floor, all
flushed and smiling. The countess was weeping.

"What makes you cry, *maman?*" asked Viera.
"Everything that he writes seems to me a cause for
rejoicing, and not for weeping!"

This was perfectly true, but, nevertheless, the count
and the countess, and Natasha, all looked at her reproachfully.

"Whom is she like, I wonder!" said the countess, to
herself.

Nikolushka's letter was re-read a hundred times, and
those who felt themselves entitled to hear it had to go
to the countess, who would not let it out of her hands.
The tutors came, and the nurses, and Mítenka, and ever
so many acquaintances, and the countess read the letter
to them each time with new delight, each time discovering new virtues in her Nikolushka. How strange,
marvelous, and beautiful it was to her that her son —
that son, the almost imperceptible motions of whose
tiny limbs she had felt twenty years before, that son
over whom she had quarreled with the count for spoiling him, that son who had learned to say *grusha* first
and then *baba* — that this same son was now far away
in a foreign land, in foreign surroundings, a heroic
soldier, alone, without help or guidance, performing
there his part in the deeds of heroes. The universal
experience of the world in all ages, going to show that

children by imperceptible steps march from the cradle into manhood, was not realized by the countess. The attainment of manhood by her son was at every step as extraordinary as if there had not been millions upon millions of men who had gone through exactly the same process. Just as twenty years before it had been almost impossible for her to believe that the mysterious little being that was living and moving somewhere under her heart would ever wail and nurse and learn to talk, so now, it was incredible that this same being had become a strong, gallant man, the paragon of sons and of men, such as he was now, judging by his letter.

"What a style he has! How elegantly he expresses himself," said she, as she read over the descriptive portions of the letter. "And how much soul! Nothing about himself, nothing at all! Something about that Denísof, but he himself must have been braver than all the rest! He writes nothing at all about his sufferings! How much heart he has! How well I know him! And how kindly he remembered all the household! He did not forget a single one! But I always said it of him, even when he was ever so little — I always said it." ....

For more than a week rough drafts of letters to Nikolushka were prepared and written and copied out on white paper by the whole family under the superintendence of the countess and the zealous care of the count, all sorts of necessary articles were made into a parcel, together with money for the new uniform and the installation of the newly appointed officer.

Anna Mikhaïlovna, a practical woman, had been shrewd enough to secure for her son a protector in the army, even for the better forwarding of correspondence. She had managed to find the opportunity of sending her letters in care of the Grand Duke Konstantin Pavlovitch, who commanded the Guards. The Rostofs had supposed that *Russkaya Gvardiya za Granitsei* — the Russian Guard on service abroad — was a sufficiently definite address, and that if a letter reached the grand duke commanding the Guards, then there was no reason why it should not reach the Pavlograd regiment, which must be somewhere near; and therefore it was decided to be best to send the packet and the money by the grand duke's courier to Borís, and Borís would see to it that it was put in Nikolushka's hands. There were letters from the old count, from the countess, from Petya, from Viera, from Natasha, from Sonya, and finally six thousand rubles for his outfit, and various things which the count wished to send his son.

CHAPTER VII

On the twenty-fourth of November, Kutuzof's fighting army, bivouacked near Olmütz, made ready to be reviewed on the following day by the emperor of Russia and the emperor of Austria. The Imperial Guards which had just arrived from Russia encamped about fifteen versts from Olmütz, and on the next day were to proceed directly to the review, which would take place about ten o'clock in the morning, on the parade-ground at Olmütz.

Nikolaï Rostof on that day had received a note from Borís informing him that the Izmaïlovsky regiment was going to encamp about fifteen versts away, and that he wanted to see him to give him some letters and some money. The money came particularly handy to Rostof just now, when, after the toils of the campaign, the army had settled down at Olmütz, and well-provided sutlers and Austrian Jews, offering all sorts of enticements, infested the camp. The Pavlograd warriors enjoyed banquet after banquet, celebrated in honor of promotions won during the campaign, as well as excursions into town where Karolina, called *Vengerka*, or the Hungarian, had recently opened a tavern, at which all the waiters were girls.

Rostof had just celebrated his promotion from yunker to cornet, had bought Denísof's horse Bedouin, and was in debt to his comrades and the sutlers on every side. On receipt of the note from Borís, Rostof rode into

Olmütz with some comrades, dined there, drank a bottle of wine, and rode off alone to the Guard's camp to find the friend and companion of his youth.

Rostof had not as yet had a chance to procure his new uniform. He wore a yunker's jacket well soiled, with a private's cross, his ordinary much-worn leather-seated riding trousers, and an officer's saber with the sword-knot; the horse he rode was a Don pony which he had bought during the campaign, of a Cossack; his crumpled cap was rakishly set sidewise on the back of his head.

When he reached the camp of the Izmaïlovsky regiment, he thought how much he should surprise Borís and all his comrades of the Guard by appearing before them like a veteran who had been under fire.

The Guard had made the whole campaign like a picnic, making a great display of their neatness and discipline. Their marches had been short, their knapsacks had been transported on the baggage-wagons, and the officers had been given splendid entertainments at every halting-place by the Austrian authorities. The regiments entered and left the cities with music playing, and during the whole campaign, much to the pride of the Guard, the men had marched in serried ranks, keeping step, while the officers, mounted, rode in their places of assignment.

Borís during the whole campaign had marched and halted with Berg, who had now risen to be *rotnui komandír*, or captain. Berg having been given a company, had succeeded by his promptness and punctuality in winning the good-will of his superiors, and his financial affairs were now in very good shape. Borís had made many acquaintances with men who might be of service to him, and by means of a letter of introduction given him by Pierre, had become acquainted with Prince Andreï Bolkonsky, through whom he hoped to obtain a place on the staff of the commander-in-chief.

Berg and Borís, neatly and elegantly dressed, were resting after their day's journey, and, seated in a neat room which had been made ready for them, were playing checkers at a small round table. Berg held between his knees the pipe which he was smoking. Borís, with the carefulness characteristic of him, had piled up the checkers in pyramidal form with his delicate white fingers, and was waiting for Berg's move, and looking at his opponent's face, evidently thinking only of the game, just as he always thought only of what occupied him at the moment.

"There now, how will you get out of that?" he asked.

"We'll do our best," replied Berg, touching a king, and then dropping his hand again.

At this moment the door opened.

"Ah, there he is at last," cried Rostof. "And Berg here too! Ah, you 'petizanfan ale kushe dormir!'"[1] he cried, quoting the words of their old nurse, in which he and Borís always found great amusement.

"Batyushki! How you have changed!"

Borís arose to meet Rostof, but as he did so he took pains to pick up and replace the checkers that had fallen, and he was about to embrace his friend, but Nikolaï slipped out of his grasp. With that feeling peculiar to youth, which suggests the avoidance of beaten paths, and the expression of feelings like every one else, and especially that often hypocritical fashion which obtains with our elders, Nikolaï wanted to do something unusual and original, on the occasion of meeting his friends; he wanted to give Borís a pinch or a push, anything except kiss him, as was universally done.

Borís, on the contrary, threw his arns around Rostof in a composed and friendly fashion, and kissed him three times. They had not met for almost six months, and in such an interval, when young men have been taking their first steps on the pathway of life, each finds in the other immense changes, due to surroundings so entirely different from those in which they had taken the first steps of life. Both had changed greatly since they had last met, and each was equally anxious to show the other the changes that they had undergone.

"Oh! you cursed dandies! Spruce and shiny, just in from a promenade! Not much like us poor sinners

[1] *Petits enfants, allez coucher, dormir!* Little children, go to sleep!

of the Line!" exclaimed Rostof, with baritone notes in his voice, and with brusque army manners, quite new to Borís, and he exhibited his own dirty and bespattered trousers. On hearing Rostof's loud voice, the German mistress of the house put her head in through the door.

"Rather pretty, hey?" cried Nikolaï, with a wink.

"What makes you shout so? You will scare them!" said Borís. "I was n't expecting you to-day," he added. "It was only this afternoon that I sent my note to you through an acquaintance of mine, Kutuzof's aide, Bolkonsky. I did n't think of its reaching you so soon. Well, how are you? So you 've been under fire already, have you?" asked Borís.

Rostof said nothing in reply, but shook the Georgievsky cross on the lace of his coat, and, pointing to his arm which he carried in a sling, looked at Berg with a smile.

"As you see," said he.

"Well, well, so you have!" returned Borís with a smile, "and we also have had a glorious campaign. You know his imperial highness was most of the time near our regiment, so that we had all sorts of privileges and advantages. What receptions we had in Poland, what dinners and balls! I can't begin to tell you! and the Tsesarevitch [1] was very courteous to all of us officers."

Then the two friends related their experiences; the one telling of the jolly good times with the hussars, and his campaign life; the other of the pleasures and advantages of serving under the direct command of men high in authority and so on.

"Oh, you guardsmen!" cried Rostof. "But come now, send out for some wine."

Borís scowled. "Certainly, if you really wish it," and going to his couch he took out from under the clean pillow a purse, and ordered his man to bring wine. "Oh, yes; and I will deliver over to you some letters and your money," he added.

[1] The crown prince.

Rostof took his packet and, flinging the money on the sofa, leaned both elbows on the table and began to read. He read a few lines and then gave Berg a wrathful glance. Berg's eyes, fastened upon him, annoyed him, and he shielded his face with the letter.

"Well, they've sent you a good lot of money," exclaimed Berg, glancing at the heavy purse, half buried in the sofa. "And here we have to live on our salaries, count! Now I will tell you about myself."

"Look here, Berg, my dear fellow," said Rostof, "whenever I find you with a letter just received from home, and with a man with whom you want to talk about all sorts of things, I will instantly leave you so as not to disturb you. Hear what I say, get you gone anywhere, anywhere; to the devil," he cried, and then seizing him by the shoulder and giving him an affectionate look full in the face, evidently for the purpose of modifying the rudeness of his words, he added, "Now see here, don't be angry with me, my dear heart,[1] I speak frankly because you are an old acquaintance."

"Akh! for heaven's sake, count! I understand perfectly," said Berg, getting up and swallowing down his throaty voice.

"Go and see our hosts; they have invited you," suggested Borís.

Berg put on his immaculate, neat, and dustless coat, went to the mirror, brushed the hair up from his temples, after the style of the emperor, Alexander Pávlovitch, and, being persuaded by Rostof's looks that his coat was noticeable, left the room with a smile of satisfaction.

"Akh! what a brute I am, though!" exclaimed Rostof, reading the letter.

"What now?"

"Akh! what a pig I am, that I did not write them sooner, and frightened them so! Akh! what a pig I am!" he repeated, suddenly reddening. "Well, you've sent Gavrílo for wine, have you? Very good, we'll have a drink!" said he.

[1] *Galúbchik.*

Among the home letters, there was inclosed a note of recommendation to Prince Bagration, which the old countess at Anna Mikhaïlovna's suggestion had obtained from some acquaintance and sent to her son, urging him to present it and get all the advantage that he could from it.

"What nonsense! Much I need this!" said Rostof, flinging the letter on the table.

"Why did you throw it down?" asked Borís.

"Oh! it was a letter of recommendation; what the deuce do I want of such a letter!"

"Why do you say that?" asked Borís, picking up the letter and reading the inscription; "this letter might be very useful to you."

" I don't need anything, and I don't care to become any one's aide!"

"Why not, pray?" asked Borís.

"It's a lackey's place!"

"You still have the same queer notions, I see," rejoined Borís, shaking his head.

"And you 're the same old diplomat. However, that 's not to the point. How are you?" asked Rostof.

"Just exactly as you see! So far, all has gone well with me. But I confess I should very much like to be made an aide, and not stick to the Line."

"Why?"

" Because, having once entered upon the profession of arms, it is best to make one's career as brilliant as possible."

"Yes, that 's true," said Rostof, evidently thinking of something else. He gave his friend a steady, inquiring look, evidently trying in vain to find in his eyes the answer to some puzzling question.

Old Gavrílo brought the wine.

"Had n't we better send now for Alphonse Karluitch," asked Borís. "He will drink with you, for I can't."

"Yes, do send for him! But who is this Dutchman?" asked Rostof, with a scornful smile.

"He 's a very, very nice, honorable, and pleasant man," explained Borís.

Rostof once more looked steadily into Borís's eyes and sighed. Berg came back, and over the bottle of wine the conversation between the three officers grew more lively. The two guardsmen told Rostof of their march, and how they had been honored in Russia, Poland, and abroad. They told about the sayings and doings of their commander, the grand duke, together with anecdotes about his goodness and irascibility.

Berg, as usual, kept silent when there was nothing that specially concerned himself, but when they began to speak about the goodness and irascibility of the grand duke, he told with great gusto how, in Galicia, he happened to have a talk with the grand duke. The grand duke was making the tour of the regiment, and became very angry at the disorderly state of the division. With a smile of complacency on his face, Berg told how the grand duke, in a great state of vexation, came up to it and shouted: "*Arnautui*,[1] villains," being a favorite term of abuse when he was vexed, and called the company commander.

"Would you believe it, count, I was not in the least scared, because I knew that I was all right. And, count, I may say without boasting, that I knew all the regulations by heart, and the standing orders as well; knew them just as well as 'Our Father in Heaven.' And so, count, in my company, there was no complaint to be made of negligence. And that was the reason of my being so composed and having such an untroubled conscience. I stepped forward,"— here Berg stood up and represented in pantomime how he had raised his hand to his visor as he stepped forward; really it would have been hard to imagine a face more expressive of deference and self-sufficiency. — "Oh! how he scolded me, rated me, you might say, rated and rated and rated mortally — 'not for life, but for death,' as the Russians say, and

---

[1] *Arnautka* is the South Russian name for a kind of hard wheat, probably derived from an Albanian tribe, *Arnaut*, which is also the name of a portion of the army in Turkey, composed of Christians; hence a term of reproach: "abortion," "a savage," "a bursurman (Mussulman, unbeliever)."

called me an Arnaut and a devil, and threatened me with Siberia," proceeded Berg, with a shrewd smile. "But I knew that I was in the right, and so I made no reply; was n't that best, count? 'What! are you dumb?' he cried. Still I held my tongue. What do you think, count? On the next day, there was nothing at all about it in the general orders; that 's what comes of not losing one's wits. That 's so, count," said Berg, lighting his pipe, and sending out rings of smoke.

"Yes, that 's splendid," said Rostof, with a smile; but Borís, perceiving that Rostof was all ready to poke fun at Berg, adroitly changed the conversation. He asked Rostof to tell them how and where he had been wounded.

This was agreeable to Rostof, and he began to give a circumstantial account of it, growing more and more animated all the time.

He described his action at Schöngraben exactly in the way those who take part in battles always describe them; that is, in the way they would be glad to have had them happen, so that his story agreed with all the other accounts of the participants, but was very far from being as it was.

Rostof was a truthful young man; not for anything in the world would he have deliberately told a falsehood. He began with the intention of telling it exactly as it happened, but imperceptibly, involuntarily, and unavoidably, as far as he was concerned, he fell into falsehood. If he had told the truth to these listeners of his, who had already heard from others, just as he himself had many times, the story of the charge, and had formed a definite idea of how the charge was made, and expected a substantially similar account of it from him, either they would not have believed him, or, what would have been worse, they would have come to the conclusion that Rostof was himself to blame for it, and that he had not experienced what he claimed to have experienced, since it did not agree with what is usually related of cavalry charges.

He could not tell them, in so many words, that they had all started on the trot, that he had fallen from his horse, sprained his arm, and run away from the French man with all his might and main, into the forest. Moreover, in order to tell the story in its grim reality, he would have been obliged to exercise much self-control to tell only what had occurred. To tell the truth is very hard, and young men are rarely capable of it. It was expected of him to tell how he grew excited under the fire, and, forgetting himself, had dashed like a whirlwind against the square, how he had cut and slashed with his saber right and left, as a knife cuts cheese, and how at length he had fallen from exhaustion, and the like. And that was what he told them.

In the midst of his tale, just as he was saying the words, "You can't imagine what a strange sensation of frenzy you experience during a charge," Prince Andreï Bolkonsky, whom Borís had been expecting, came into the room.

Prince Andreï, who liked to bear a patronizing relationship toward young men, was flattered by having Borís consigned to his protection, and was very well disposed toward him. Borís had succeeded in making a pleasant impression upon him, and he had made up his mind to have the young man's desire gratified. Being sent with despatches from Kutuzof to the Tsesarevitch, he had looked up his young *protégé*, expecting to find him alone. When he came in and found there a hussar of the Line, relating his military experiences, a sort of individual whom Prince Andreï could not endure, he gave Borís an affectionate smile, scowled at Rostof, half closing his eyes, and, with a stiff little bow, took his seat wearily and indifferently on the sofa.

He was disgusted at finding himself in uncongenial society.

Rostof, feeling this instinctively, instantly grew angry. But it was all the same to him; it was a stranger. He looked at Borís, and saw that he seemed to be ashamed of being in company with a hussar of the Line.

Notwithstanding Prince Andreï's disagreeable, mocking tone, notwithstanding the general scorn which, from his point of view, as a hussar of the Line, Rostof shared for staff aides, to which number evidently belonged the gentleman who had just entered, Rostof felt overwhelmed with confusion, reddened, and grew silent. Borís asked what was the news at headquarters, and whether it were indiscretion for him to inquire about future movements.

"Probably we shall advance," replied Bolkonsky, evidently not wishing to commit himself further in the presence of strangers. Berg took advantage of his opportunity to ask, with his usual politeness, whether it were true, as he had heard, that double rations of forage were to be supplied to captains of the Line.

At this Prince Andreï smiled, and replied that he could not give an opinion in regard to such important questions of state, and Berg laughed heartily with delight.

"In regard to that matter of yours," said Prince Andreï, turning to Borís again, "we will talk about it by and by," and he glanced at Rostof. "You come to me after the review; we will do all that is in our power." And glancing around the room, he addressed himself to Rostof, pretending not to notice his state of childish confusion, which was rapidly assuming the form of ill-temper. Said he:—

"I suppose you were telling about the affair at Schöngraben? Were you there?"

"I was there," replied Rostof, curtly, as if he desired by his tone to insult the aide. Bolkonsky noticed the hussar's state of mind, and it seemed to him amusing. A slightly scornful smile played over his lips.

"Yes, there are many stories afloat now about that affair!"

"Stories, indeed!" exclaimed Rostof, in a loud voice, turning his angry eyes on Borís and Bolkonsky. "Yes, many stories; but the stories we tell are the accounts of those who were under the hottest fire of the enemy. Our accounts have some weight, and are very different from the stories of those staff-officers, milk-suckers, who win rewards by doing nothing."

"Do you mean to insinuate that I am one of them?"

asked Prince Andreï, with a calm and very pleasant smile.

A strange feeling of anger and at the same time of respect for the dignity of this stranger were at this moment united in Rostof's mind.

"I was not speaking of you," said he. "I do not know you, and I confess I have no desire to know you. I merely made a general remark concerning staff-officers."

"And I will say this much to you," said Prince Andreï, interrupting him, a tone of calm superiority ringing in his voice. "You wish to insult me, and I am ready to have a settlement with you, it being very easy to bring about, if you have not sufficient self-respect; but you must agree with me that the time and place are exceedingly unpropitious for any such settlement. We are all soon to take part in a great and far more serious duel, and moreover, Drubetskoï here, who says that he is an old friend of yours, cannot be held accountable for the fact that my face was unfortunate enough to displease you. However," he went on to say, as he got up, "you know my name, and you know where to find me; but don't forget," he added, "that I consider that neither I nor you have any ground for feeling insulted, and my advice, as a man older than you, is not to let this matter go any further. Well, Drubetskoï, on Friday, after the review, I shall expect you; Da Svidanya!" cried Prince Andreï, and he went out with a bow to both of them.

It was only after Prince Andreï had left the room that Rostof remembered what reply he should have made. And he was still more out of temper because he had not had the wit to say it. He immediately ordered his horse brought round, and, bidding Borís farewell rather dryly, rode off to his own camp. "Should he go next day to headquarters and challenge this captious aide, or should he follow his advice and leave things as they were?" That was the question that tormented him all the way. At one moment he angrily imagined how frightened this little, feeble, bumptious man would look when covered by his pistol; the next, he confessed with amazement, that of all the men whom he knew, there was none whom he should be more glad to have as his friend than this same aide whom he detested!

CHAPTER VIII

On the day following the meeting of Borís and Rostof occurred the review of the Austrian and Russian troops, including those who had just arrived from Russia as well as those who had made the campaign with Kutuzof. Both the emperor of Russia, with the Tsesarevitch, and the emperor of Austria, with the archduke, reviewed this army, aggregating eighty thousand men.

Early in the morning the soldiers, elegantly spruced and attired, began to move, falling into line in front of the fortress. Here thousands of legs and bayonets moved along with streaming banners, and at the command of their officers halted or wheeled, or formed into detachments, passing by other similar bodies of infantry, in other uniforms.

There, with measured hoof-beats and jingling of trappings, came the cavalry, gayly dressed in blue, red, and green embroidered uniforms, with gayly dressed musicians ahead, riding coal-black, chestnut, and gray horses.

Yonder, stretching out in a long line, with their polished shining cannon, jolting with a brazen din on their carriages, and with the smell of linstocks, came the artillery between the infantry and cavalry, and drew up in the places assigned them. Not only the generals in full-dress uniform, with slender waists or stout waists, tightened in to the last degree, and with red necks tightly clasped by their collars, and wearing their scarfs and all their orders; not only the officers, pomaded and decked with all their glories, but all the soldiers, with shining, clean-washed, and freshly shaven faces, with all their appurtenances polished up to the highest luster, and all the horses gayly caparisoned, and groomed so that their coats were as glossy as satin, and every individual hair in their manes in exactly its proper place, had the consciousness that something grave, significant, and solemn was taking place. Every general and every soldier felt his own insignificance, counting himself as merely a grain of sand in this sea of humanity, and at the same time felt his power, when regarded as a part of this mighty whole.

By means of strenuous efforts and devoted energy, the preparations which had begun early in the morning were completed by ten o'clock, and everything was in proper order. The ranks were drawn up across the broad parade-ground. The whole army was arranged in three columns; in front the cavalry, then the artillery, and in the rear the infantry.

Between each division of the army was a space like a street. The three divisions of this army were sharply contrasted with one another; Kutuzof's war-worn veterans — among whom on the right flank in the front row stood the Pavlogradsky hussars — the troops of the Line that had just arrived from Russia, and the regiments of the Guard and the Austrian army. But all stood in one line under one commander, and in identical order.

Like the wind rustling the leaves, a murmur agitated the lines: "They are coming! They are coming!" Anxious voices were heard, and throughout all the troops, like a wave, ran the bustle of the final preparations.

Far away in front of them, near Olmütz, appeared a group coming toward them. And at this moment, though the day was calm, a gentle breeze stirred the army, and seemed to shake the pennoned pikes, and the loosened standards clinging to their staffs. It seemed as if the army itself by this slight tremor expressed its gladness at the approach of the emperors. One voice was heard — "Smirno, eyes front!" Then, like the answering of cocks at daybreak, many voices repeated this command from point to point, and all grew still.

In the death-like silence the only sound heard was the trampling of horses' feet. This was the suite of the emperors. The two monarchs rode along the left wing, and the bugles of the First Cavalry Regiment burst forth with the general-marsch. It seemed as if it were not the bugles which played this march, but as if the army itself, in its delight at the approach of the emperors, emitted these sounds. Their echoes had not died away, when the Emperor Alexander's affable young voice was distinctly heard addressing the men. He uttered the usual welcome, and the first regiment gave forth one huzza, so deafening, so long drawn out and expressive of joy, that the men themselves were amazed and awe-struck at the magnitude and strength of the mass which they constituted : —

" Hurrah ! "

Rostof, standing in the front rank of Kutuzof's army, which the emperor first approached, shared the feeling experienced by every man in that army, a feeling of self-forgetfulness, a proud consciousness of invincibility and of passionate attachment to him on whose account all this solemn parade was prepared. He felt that only one word from this man was needed for this mighty mass, including himself as an insignificant grain of sand, to dash through fire and water, to commit crime, to face death, or perform the mightiest deeds of heroism, and therefore he could not help trembling, could not help his heart melting within him at the sight of this approaching Word.

" Hurrah ! Hurrah ! Hurrah ! " was roared on all sides, and one regiment after another welcomed the sovereigns with the music of the general-marsch, then renewed huzzas, the general-marsch and huzzas on huzzas, which, growing louder and louder, mingled in one overpowering, deafening clamor.

Until the sovereign came quite close, every regiment in its silence and rigidity seemed like a lifeless body ; but, as soon as the sovereign came abreast of it, the regiment woke to life and broke out into acclamations which mingled with the roar extending down the whole line past which the sovereign rode. Amid the tremendous deafening clamor of these thousands of voices, through the midst of the armies, standing in their squares as motionless as if they had been carved out of granite, moved easily, carelessly, but symmetrically, and above all with freedom and grace, the hundreds of riders constituting the suites, and in front of all — two men, the emperors! On them, and on them alone, were concentrated the suppressed but eager attention of all that mass of men.

The handsome young Emperor Alexander in his Horse Guards' uniform and three-cornered hat worn point forward, with his pleasant face and clear but not loud voice, was the cynosure of all eyes.

Rostof stood not far from the buglers, and his keen glance recognized the emperor while he was still far off, and followed him as he drew near. When the sovereign had approached to a distance of twenty paces, and Nikolaï could clearly distinguish every feature of his handsome and radiant young face, he experienced a sense of affection and enthusiasm such as he had never before felt. Everything, every feature, every motion, seemed to him bewitching in his sovereign.

Pausing in front of the Pavlograd regiment, the monarch said something in French to the emperor of Austria and smiled.

Seeing this smile, Rostof himself involuntarily smiled also, and felt a still more powerful impulse of love toward his sovereign. He felt a burning desire to display this love in some way. He knew that this was impossible and he felt like weeping.

The sovereign summoned the regimental commander and said a few words to him.

"*Bozhe moï!* what would happen to me if the sovereign were to address me!" thought Rostof. "I should die of happiness!"

The emperor also addressed the officers : —

"Gentlemen," said he. And Rostof listened as to a voice from heaven. How happy would he have been now could he only die for his Tsar! "I thank you all from my heart! You have won the standards of the George, prove yourselves worthy of them!"

"Only to die, to die for him!" thought Rostof.

The sovereign said a few words more, which Rostof did not catch, and the soldiers, straining their throats, cried "Hurrah! hurrah!"

Rostof also joined with them, leaning forward in his saddle and shouting with all his might, willing to burst his lungs in his efforts to express the full extent of his enthusiasm for his sovereign.

The emperor stood a few seconds in front of the hussars as if he were undecided.

"How can the sovereign be undecided?" mused Rostof; but immediately even this indecision seemed to him a new proof of majesty and charm, like everything else that the sovereign did.

The emperor's indecision lasted only a moment. His foot, shod in a narrow, sharp-pointed boot, such as were worn at that time, pressed against the flank of the English-groomed bay mare on which he sat. The sovereign's hand, in a white glove, gathered up the reins, and he rode off, accompanied by a disorderly tossing sea of aides.

As he kept riding farther and farther down the line, he kept halting in front of the different regiments, and at last only his white plume could be seen by Rostof, distinguishing him from the suite that accompanied the emperors.

In the number of those who accompanied the emperor, he noticed Bolkonsky, lazily and indifferently bestriding his steed. The yesterday evening's quarrel with him came into his mind, and the question arose whether or no he ought to challenge him.

"Of course it is out of the question now," thought Rostof. "Is it worth while to think or to talk about such a thing at such a moment as this? At a time when one feels such impulses of love, enthusiasm, and self-renunciation, what consequence are our petty quarrels and provocations? I love the whole world, I forgive every one now!" said Rostof to himself.

After the sovereign had ridden past almost all the regiments, the troops began to move in front of him in the "ceremonial march," and Rostof, on his Bedouin, which he had recently bought of Denísof, rode at the end of his squadron, that is, alone, and in a most conspicuous position before his sovereign.

Just before he came up to where the emperor was, Rostof, who was an admirable horseman, plunged the spurs in Bedouin's flanks, and urged him into that mad, frenzied gallop which Bedouin always took when he was excited. Pressing his foaming mouth back to his breast, arching his tail, and seeming to fly through the air, and spurning the earth, gracefully tossing and interweaving his legs, Bedouin, also conscious that the emperor's eyes were fastened on him, dashed gallantly by.

Rostof himself, keeping his feet back, and sitting straight in his saddle, feeling himself one with his horse, rode by his sovereign with disturbed but beatific face, — "a very devil," as Denísof expressed it.

"Bravo! Pavlogradsui!" exclaimed the emperor.

"*Bozhe moï!* how happy I should be if he would only bid me to dash instantly into the fire!" thought Rostof.

When the review was ended, the officers that had just come from Russia and those of Kutuzof's division began to gather in groups and talk about the rewards of the campaign, about the Austrians and their uniforms, about their line of battle, about Bonaparte, and what a desperate position he had got himself into now, especially if Essen's corps should join them, and Prussia should take their side.

But more than all else in each of these circles, the conversation ran on the sovereign Alexander, and every word that he had spoken was repeated, and everything that he had done was praised, and all were enthusiastic over him.

All had but one single expectation: under the personal direction of the sovereign, to go with all speed against the enemy. Under the command of the emperor himself, it would be an impossibility not to win the victory over any one in the world: so thought Rostof and the majority of the officers.

After this review, all were more assured of victory than they could have been after the gaining of two battles.

CHAPTER IX

ON the day following the review, Borís, dressed in his best uniform, and accompanied by the wishes of his comrade, Berg, for his success, rode off to Olmütz to find Bolkonsky, anxious to take advantage of his good-will and secure a most brilliant position, especially the position of aide to some important personage, as this seemed to him the most attractive branch of the service.

"It's fine for Rostof, whose father sends him ten thousand at a time, to argue that he would not accept favors of any one, or be any one's lackey; but I, who have nothing except my brains, must pursue my career and not miss opportunities, but take advantage of them."

He did not find Prince Andreï in Olmütz that day. But the sight of the town where the imperial headquarters were situated, where the diplomatic corps were established, and both emperors were quartered with their suites, and courtiers, and intimates, only inspired the more desire in the young man's heart to belong to this exalted world.

He had no acquaintances, and, notwithstanding his elegant uniform of the Guards, all these superior people crowding the streets in handsome equipages, plumes, ribbons, and orders, these courtiers and warriors, seemed to stand so immeasurably above him that not only they would not but moreover they could not recognize the existence of such an insignificant officer of the Guards as he was. At the establishment of the commander-in-chief, Kutuzof, where he inquired for Bolkonsky, all the aides, and even the servants, looked at him as if it were their wish to inspire him with the idea that there was a great abundance of officers like him there, and that all were very much annoyed by their presence.

In spite of this, or rather in direct consequence of this, on the very next day, the twenty-seventh, immediately after dinner, he went to Olmütz again, and going to the house occupied by Kutuzof, inquired for Bolkonsky.

Prince Andreï was at home, and Borís was ushered into a great drawing-room, where probably in times gone by balls had been given, but which was now occupied by five beds, and a heterogeneous medley of furniture, tables, chairs, and a clavichord. An aide, in a Persian khalat, was sitting at a table near the door and writing. Another, the stout handsome Nesvitsky, lay on his bed with his hands supporting his head, and laughing and talking with an officer who was sitting near him. A third was at the clavichord playing a Viennese waltz; a fourth leaned on the clavichord and was humming the air.

Bolkonsky was not in the room. Not one of these gentlemen, though they glanced at Borís, paid him the slightest attention. The one who was writing, and whom Borís ventured to address, turned round with an air of annoyance and told him that Bolkonsky was on duty, and that he would find him by passing through the door on the left, and going to the reception-room if he wanted to see him. Borís thanked him and went to the reception-room. He found there ten or a dozen generals and other officers.

At the moment that Borís came in, Prince Andreï, with a contemptuous frown on his face and that peculiar look of well-bred weariness which says louder than words that "if it were not my duty, I should not think of wasting any more time talking with you," was listening to an old Russian general with orders on his breast, who was standing upright, almost on his tiptoes, and, with the servile expression characteristic of the military on his purple face, was laying his case before Prince Andreï.

"Very good, be kind enough to have patience," he was saying to the general in Russian, but with that French accent which he affected when he wished to speak rather scornfully; then, catching sight of Borís, and making no further reply to the general, who hastened after him with his petition, begging him to let him say just one thing more, Prince Andreï with a radiant smile and waving his hand to him went to meet Borís.

Borís at this instant clearly understood what he had suspected before, that in the army there was, above and beyond the subordination and discipline taught by the code, and which they in the regiments knew by heart, and which he knew as well as any one else, — there was another still more essential form of subordination, one which compelled this anxious general with the purple face respectfully to wait, while Captain Prince Andreï, for his own satisfaction, found it more interesting to talk with Ensign Drubetskoï. More than ever Borís decided henceforth not to act in accordance with the written law, but with this unwritten code. He now felt that merely through the fact of having been sent to Prince Andreï with a letter of recommendation he was allowed to take precedence of this old general, who in other circumstances, at the front, for instance, might utterly humiliate him — a mere ensign of the Guards.

Prince Andreï came to meet him and took him by the hand.

"Very sorry that you missed me yesterday. I spent the whole day with the Germans. Weirother and I went to inspect the disposition of the troops. What fellows these Germans are for accuracy; there's no end to it!"

Borís smiled exactly as if he understood to what Prince Andreï referred. He affected to see in it a piece of generally known information, but really this was the first time that he had heard Weirother's name, and even the word *dispozítsiya*.

"Well, now, my dear, so you would like to become an aide, would you? I was just thinking about you."

"Yes," replied Borís, in spite of himself, reddening at the very thought, "I was thinking of calling on the commander-in-chief; he has had a letter in regard to me from Prince Kuragin; I wanted to ask it," he added, as if by way of apology, "because I was afraid the Guards would not take part in any action."

"Very good, very good! We will talk it all over,'

said Prince Andreï. "Only let me finish up this gentleman's business and I will be at your service."

While Prince Andreï went to report on the business
of the purple-faced general, this general, evidently not
sharing Borís's comprehension in regard to the advantages of the unwritten code, glared so fiercely at the
audacious young ensign who had interrupted his conversation with the aide, that Borís grew uncomfortable.
He turned away and waited impatiently for Prince
Andreï's return from the commander-in-chief's private
room.

"Well, my dear fellow, as I said, I was just thinking
of you," said Prince Andreï, as they went into the big
room where the clavichord was. "There is no use in
your going to call on the commander-in-chief," he went
on to say; "he will make you pleasant enough speeches,
he will have you invited to dinner," ("That would not
be so bad according to this other code," thought Borís,
in his own mind), "but nothing more would come of it;
if it did, there would soon be a whole battalion of us
aides and orderlies. But I tell you what we'll do; I
have a good friend, who is general adjutant, and a splendid man, Prince Dolgorukof, — and perhaps you may
not know this, but it is a fact, that just now Kutuzof
and his staff and all of us are of mighty little consequence; everything at the present time is centered on
the emperor, — so let us go to Dolgorukof; I have an
errand to him anyway, and I have already spoken to
him of you, so we will see whether he can't find the
means of giving you a place on his own staff, or somewhere even nearer to the sun."

Prince Andreï always showed great energy when he
had the chance to lend a young man a hand and help
him to worldly success. Under cover of the assistance
granted another, and which he would have been too
proud to accept for himself, he came within the charmed
circle which was the source of success, and in reality a
powerful attraction for him. He very readily took Borís
under his wing and went with him to Prince Dolgorukof.

It was already quite late in the afternoon when they

reached the palace of Olmütz, occupied by the emperors and their immediate followers.

On this very day there had been a council of war in which all the members of the Hofkriegsrath and the two emperors had taken part. In the council it had been decided, contrary to the advice of the old generals, Kutuzof and Schwartzenberg, to act immediately on the offensive and offer Bonaparte general battle.

The council had only just adjourned when Prince Andreï, accompanied by Borís, entered the palace in search of Prince Dolgorukof. Already the magic impression of this war council, which had resulted in victory for the younger party, could be seen in the faces of all whom they met at headquarters. The voices of the temporizers who advised further postponement of the attack had been so unanimously drowned out and their arguments confuted by such indubitable proofs of the advantage of immediate attack, that the subject of their deliberations — that is, the impending engagement and the victory which would doubtless result from it — seemed to be a thing of the past rather than of the future.

All the advantages were on our side. The enormous forces of the allies, doubtless far outnumbering Napoleon's forces, were concentrated at one point; the armies were inspired by the presence of the emperors, and eager for action; the "strategical point" where the battle was to be fought was known, in its minutest details, to the Austrian General Weirother who would take the direction of the army; it happened also, by a fortunate coincidence, that the Austrian army had manœuvered the previous year on these very plans where now it was proposed that they should meet the French in battle; all the features of the ground were well known and accurately delineated on the maps, and Bonaparte, evidently weakened, was making no preparations to meet them.

Dolgorukof, one of the most fiery partisans in favor of immediate attack, had only just returned from the council, weary and jaded, but full of excitement and proud of the victory won. Prince Andreï introduced

the young officer, whom he had taken under his protection, but Prince Dolgorukof, though he politely and
even warmly pressed his hand, said nothing to him, and
being evidently unable to refrain from expressing the
thoughts that occupied him at this time to the exclusion
of everything else, turned to Prince Andreï and said in
French : —

"Well, my dear fellow, what a struggle we 've been
having! May God only grant that the one which will
result from it will be no less victorious! One thing, my
dear fellow," said he, speaking eagerly and brusquely,
"I must confess my injustice to these Austrians, and
especially to Weirother! What exactness and care for
minutiæ! what accurate knowledge of the localities! what
foresight for contingencies! what thoughts for all the
minutest details! No, my friend, nothing more advantageous than the condition in which we find ourselves
could possibly be imagined. Austrian accuracy and
Russian valor combined! What more could you desire?"

"So an engagement has been actually determined
on?" asked Bolkonsky.

"And do you know, my dear, it seems to me that
really Bonaparte 'has lost his Latin.' Did you know a
letter was received from him to-day addressed to the
emperor?"

Dolgorukof smiled significantly.

"What 's that? What did he write?" asked Bolkonsky.

"What could he write? Tradiridira and so forth,
merely for the sake of gaining time; that 's all. I tell
you, he 's right in our hands; that 's certain! But the
most amusing thing of all," said he, with a good-natured
smile, "was this, that no one could think how it was
best to address the reply to him! Not as 'consul' and
still less as emperor, of course; I supposed it would be
to General Bonaparte."

"But there is considerable difference between not
recognizing him as emperor and addressing him as
General Bonaparte," said Bolkonsky.

"That 's the very point," said Dolgorukof, interrupting him with a laugh, and speaking rapidly. "You know Bilibin — he's a very clever man — he proposed to address him as 'Usurper and Enemy of the Human Race.'"

Dolgorukof broke into a hearty peal of laughter.

"Was that all?" remarked Bolkonsky.

"But in the end it was Bilibin who invented a serious title for the address. He's a shrewd and clever man!"

"What was it?"

"'Head of the French Government,' — *au chef du gouvernement français*," replied Prince Dolgorukof, gravely, and with satisfaction. "Say, now, was n't that good?"

"Very good, but it won't please him much," replied Bolkonsky.

"Oh, not at all! My brother knows him; he's dined with him more than once, — with the present emperor at Paris, and told me that he never saw a more refined and cunning diplomat! French *finesse* combined with Italian astuteness, you know! You've heard the anecdotes about him and Count Markóf, have n't you? Count Markóf was the only man who could meet him on his own ground. You know the story of the handkerchief? It's charming!"

And the loquacious Dolgorukof, turning now to Borís, now to Prince Andreï, told how Bonaparte, wishing to test Markóf, our ambassador, purposely dropped his handkerchief in front of him and stood looking at him, apparently expecting Markóf to hand it to him, and how Markóf instantly dropped his handkerchief beside Bonaparte's and stooping down picked it up, leaving Bonaparte's where it lay.

"*Charmant!*" exclaimed Bolkonsky. "But prince, I have come as a petitioner in behalf of this young man here. Do you know whether" — but before Prince Andreï had time to finish, an adjutant came into the room with a summons for Prince Dolgorukof to go to the emperor.

"Akh! what a nuisance!" exclaimed Dolgorukof, hurriedly rising and shaking hands with Prince Andreï and Borís. "You know I should be very glad to do all in my power either for you or for this charming young man." Once more he pressed Borís's hand with an expression of good-natured frankness and mercurial heedlessness. "But we'll see about it. .... See you another time!"

Borís was greatly excited by the thought of being so near to such exalted powers. He felt that here he was almost in contact with the springs which set in motion all these enormous masses of which he and his regiment appeared to be a small, humble, and insignificant part.

They followed Prince Dolgorukof into the corridor. Just then, from out the door leading into the sovereign's apartments, through which Dolgorukof was going, came a short individual in civil attire, with an intellectual face and a strongly pronounced and prominent lower jaw, which without disfiguring him lent especial energy and mobility to his expression. This short man nodded to Dolgorukof as to a friend, and came along straight toward Prince Andreï with a fixed cold stare, evidently expecting him to make a bow, or to stand out of the way for him. Prince Andreï did neither; a wrathful expression came into his face, and the young man, turning about, went down the corridor in the other direction.

"Who was that?" asked Borís.

"That is one of the most remarkable, and to me most detestable, of men, — the minister of foreign affairs, Prince Adam Czartorisky. Those are the men," said Bolkonsky, with a sigh which he could not stifle, as they left the palace, "those are the men that decide the fate of nations."

On the next day the armies were set in motion, and Borís had no opportunities, until the battle of Austerlitz itself, to meet either Prince Bolkonsky or Dolgorukof, and remained for the time being in the Izmaïlovsky regiment.

CHAPTER X

At dawn, on the twenty-eighth, Denísof's squadron, in which Nikolaï Rostof served, and which belonged to Prince Bagration's division, marched out from its bivouac to battle, as it was said, and after proceeding about a verst, behind the other columns, was halted on the highway.

Rostof saw the Cossacks riding forward past them; then the first and second squadron of hussars, and battalions of infantry and artillery; and then the generals, Bagration and Dolgorukof, and their adjutants also rode by.

All the fear which, just as at the previous battles, he had experienced before the action, all the internal conflict, by means of which he had overcome this fear, all his dreams of how he would distinguish himself, hussar fashion, in this action were wasted. Their squadron were stationed in the reserve, and Nikolaï Rostof spent that day bored and anxious.

About nine o'clock in the morning, he heard at the front the sounds of musketry firing, huzzas, and shouting; he saw some wounded men carried to the rear (there were not many of them), and at last he beheld a whole division of French cavalrymen conducted by in charge of a *sótnya* of Cossacks. Evidently, the action was at an end, and though it appeared to have been of small magnitude, it was attended with success. The soldiers and the officers, as they returned, narrated the story of their brilliant victory, resulting in the occupation of the city of Wischau and the capture of a whole squadron of the French.

The day was clear and sunny, after the nipping frost of the night before, and the joyful brilliancy of an autumn day seemed to harmonize with the news of the victory, which was confirmed not only by the narratives of those who had taken part in it, but still more by the enthusiastic faces of the soldiers, officers, generals, and adjutants, passing this way and that before Rostof.

Nikolaï's heart was the heavier for having suffered to no purpose all the pangs of fear anticipatory of the battle, and then being obliged to spend this glorious day in inaction.

"Wostof, come here! Let us dwown our sow'ow in dwink!" cried Denísof, seated on the edge of the road, with a flask and lunch spread before him. The officers gathered in a circle around Denísof's bottle-case, eating their lunch and chatting.

"Here they come, bringing another!" exclaimed one of the officers, pointing to a French dragoon who had been made prisoner and was walking along under guard of two Cossacks. One of them was leading by the bridle a large, handsome French horse which had been taken from the prisoner.

"Sell us the horse?" cried Denísof to the Cossack.

"Certainly, your nobility."

The officers sprang up and crowded around the Cossacks and the prisoner. The French dragoon was a young Alsatian, speaking French with a German accent. He was quite out of breath with emotion; his face was crimson. Hearing the officers talking French, he began to speak with them eagerly, turning to one and another of them. He told them that he ought not to have been taken, and that it was not his fault he was taken, but the fault of *le caporal*, who had sent him to get some caparisons, and that he told him the Russians were already there. And at the end of every sentence, he added: "But don't let any harm come to my little horse!" at the same time patting his coat.

It was evident that he didn't understand very well what had happened to him. Now he apologized for having been captured, then, as if he imagined himself in the presence of his own superiors, he vaunted his strict attention to the duties of a soldier and his zeal in the service. He brought with him to our rear-guard in all its freshness the very atmosphere of the French army, which was so foreign to our men.

The Cossacks sold the horse for two ducats, and Rostof, who was just now possessed of money in plenty, and was the richest of the officers, bought it.

"But don't let any harm come to my little horse!" said the Alsatian, good-naturedly, to Rostof, when the horse was handed over to the hussar.

Rostof, with a smile, reassured the dragoon, and gave him some money.

"*Allee! allee!*" said the Cossack, attempting to speak in French, and touching the prisoner's arm to make him move on.

"*Gosudar! gosudar!* — the emperor! the emperor!" was suddenly heard among the hussars. All was hurry and confusion as the officers scattered, and Rostof distinguished down the road a number of horsemen with white plumes in their hats riding toward them. In a moment's time, all were in their places and waiting.

Rostof did not remember and had no consciousness of how he got to his place and mounted his horse. Instantly his disappointment at not being present at the skirmish, the mutinous frame of mind that he had felt during the hours of inaction, passed away; every thought about himself instantly vanished; he was perfectly absorbed in the sense of happiness arising from the proximity of his sovereign! He felt himself compensated by the mere fact of his presence for all the loss of the day. He was as happy as a lover, in expectation of the wished-for meeting! Not daring to look down the line, and not glancing around, he felt *his* approach by a sense of rapture. And he felt this, not alone by the mere trampling of the horses' hoofs as the cavalcade rode along, but he felt it because in proportion as they drew near everything around him grew brighter, more radiant with joy, more impressive and festive. Nearer and nearer came what was the sun for Rostof, scattering rays of blissful and majestic light, and now at last he realized that he was enveloped by these rays; he heard his voice, that affable, serene, majestic, and at the same time utterly unaffected voice. A dead silence ensued, just as Rostof felt ought to be the case, and this silence was broken by the sound of his sovereign's voice : —

"The Pavlograd hussars?" he asked in French.

"The reserves, your majesty," replied some other voice, a merely human voice, after the superhuman voice which had asked if they were the Pavlograd hussars.

The emperor came up near where Rostof was and reined in his horse. Alexander's face was still more beautiful than it had been three days before at the time of the parade. It fairly beamed with delight and youthful spirits, — such innocently youthful spirits that it reminded one of the sportiveness of a fourteen-year-old lad ; and yet, nevertheless, it was the face of a majestic emperor! Chancing to glance down the squadron, the sovereign's eyes met Rostof's and for upward of two seconds gazed into them. Maybe the sovereign read what was passing in Rostof's soul ; it certainly seemed to Rostof that he must know it ; at all events, he fixed his blue eyes for the space of two seconds on Rostof's face. A sweet and gentle light seemed to emanate from them. Then suddenly his eyebrows contracted, and with a brusque movement of his left foot he spurred his horse and galloped forward.

The young emperor could not restrain his desire to be present at the battle, and in spite of all the objections of his courtiers, he managed about twelve o'clock to leave the third column, under whose escort he had been moving, and spurred off to the front. But before he reached the hussars he was met by some of his aides with the report of the happy issue of the skirmish.

The engagement, which was merely the capture of a squadron of the French, was represented as a brilliant victory, and consequently the sovereign and the whole army after this, and especially before the smoke had cleared away from the field of battle, were firmly convinced that the French were conquered and were in full retreat.

A few minutes after the passing of the sovereign, the division of the Pavlograd hussars were ordered to ad-

vance.   In the little German town of Wischau, Rostof
saw the emperor yet a second time.   In the town square,
where, just before the sovereign's arrival, there had been
a pretty lively interchange of shots, still lay a number
of men, killed and wounded, whom they had not as yet
had time to remove.

The sovereign, surrounded by his suite of military and
civil attendants, and riding a chestnut mare, groomed in
English style, though not the same one which he had
ridden at the parade, leaning over and gracefully holding a gold *lorgnette* to his eye, was looking at a soldier
stretched out on the ground, without his shako, and with
his head all covered with blood.

The soldier was so filthy, rough, and disgusting that
Rostof was quite affronted that he should be so near
his majesty.   Rostof saw how the sovereign's stooping
shoulders contracted, as if a chill ran down his back,
and how his left heel convulsively pressed the spur into
the horse's side, and how the admirably trained animal
looked around good-naturedly, and did not stir from his
place.

An adjutant dismounted, and taking the soldier under
the arm assisted to lift him to a stretcher which had
just been brought.

The soldier groaned.

"Gently, gently! can't you lift him more gently!"
exclaimed the sovereign, apparently suffering more
keenly than the dying soldier, and he rode away.

Rostof saw the tears that filled his monarch's eyes,
and heard him say in French to Czartorisky as he rode
away : —

"What a terrible thing war is, what a terrible thing!
— *Quelle terrible chose que la guerre !*"

The vanguard had been stationed in front of Wischau,
in sight of the enemy's pickets, who had abandoned to
the Russians the place after desultory firing that had
lasted all day.   The vanguard had been personally congratulated and thanked by the emperor, rewards had
been promised, and a double portion of vodka had been
dealt out to the men.   The bivouac fires crackled even

more merrily than the night before, and the soldiers' songs rang out with still greater gusto.

Denísof that night gave a supper in honor of his promotion as major, and Rostof, who had already taken his share of wine, at the end of the merrymaking proposed a toast to the sovereign's health : —

"Not the sovereign emperor, the *gosudar-imperator*, as he is called in official circles," said he, "but the health of the sovereign, as a kind-hearted, lovable, and great man, — let us drink to his health, and to our probable victory over the French. If we fought well before," he went on to say, "and gave no quarter to the French at Schöngraben, will not this be the case now when he himself leads us ? We will all die, gladly die for him ! Is n't that so, gentlemen ? Perhaps I do not express myself very well, for I have been drinking a good deal, but that 's what I feel, and so do you all ! To the health of Alexander the First ! Hurrah !"

"Hurrah ! hurrah !" rang the hearty voices of the officers. And the old Captain Kirsten shouted just as heartily and no less sincerely than the twenty-year-old Rostof.

When the officers had drunk the toast and broken their glasses, Kirsten got a fresh one and filled it, and in his shirt-sleeves and riding-trousers, with the glass in his hand, went to the camp-fire of some of the soldiers, and assuming a majestic pose, waving his hand over his head, stood with his long gray mustache and white chest visible under his unbuttoned shirt, in the firelight.

"Boys ! to the health of the sovereign emperor, to victory over our enemies ! Hurrah !" he cried in his youthful-old hussar's baritone.

The hussars crowded around, and answered in friendly wise with a tremendous shout.

Late that night, when all had separated, Denísof laid his stubby hand on his favorite Rostof's shoulder : —

"In the field, no woom for love affairs, when one's so much in love with the Tsar !" said he.

"Denísof ! don't jest on this subject !" cried Rostof. " This is such an exalted, such a noble feeling, that...."

" I agwee with you, I agwee with you, my fwiend, I understand, I appwove...."

" No, you can't understand it ! "

And Rostof got up and began to wander among the watch-fires, and dreamed of what bliss it would be to die — as to losing his life, he did not dare to think of that ! — but simply to die in the presence of his sovereign. He was really in love, not only with the Tsar, but also with the glory of the Russian arms and the hope of impending victory. And he was not the only one who experienced this feeling on the memorable days that preceded the battle of Austerlitz : nine-tenths of the men composing the Russian army were at that time in love, though perhaps less ecstatically, with their Tsar and the glory of the Russian arms.

CHAPTER XI

On the following day, the sovereign remained in Wischau. His body physician Villiers was several times called to see him, and not only at headquarters, but in the various corps, the report was spread abroad that the emperor was ill. He had eaten nothing that day, and had slept badly the night before, so those who were in his counsels reported. This indisposition proceeded from the powerful impression produced upon his sensitive soul by the sight of the wounded and the killed.

At daybreak, on the twenty-ninth, a French officer with a flag of truce passed the sentinels, and was brought into Wischau, demanding a personal interview with the Russian emperor.

This officer was Savary.

The sovereign had just fallen asleep, and therefore Savary was obliged to wait. At noon he was admitted into the emperor's presence, and at the end of an hour came out and rode, accompanied by Prince Dolgorukof, back to the pickets of the French army.

It was soon reported that the purpose of Savary's mission was a proposal for a meeting of the emperor with Napoleon.   This personal meeting was refused, much to the gratification and delight of the whole army, and in the sovereign's place Prince Dolgorukof, the conqueror of Wischau, was delegated to confer with Napoleon, if, contrary to anticipation, these conferences had for their object a genuine desire for peace.

In the evening, Dolgorukof returned, went directly to the sovereign, and was closeted a long time with him alone.

On the thirtieth of November and the first of December, the armies moved forward two more stages, and the advanced pickets of the enemy, after slight skirmishes, retired.   Before noon of December first, there began in the upper circles of the army a vigorous, stirring, and exciting movement, which continued until the morning of the second of December, when was fought the world-renowned battle of Austerlitz.

Up to the afternoon of the first, the movement, the excited conversations, the galloping about and carrying of messages, was confined to the headquarters of the two emperors; in the afternoon of the same day the excitement was communicated to Kutuzof's headquarters and to the staffs of the division commanders.   By evening this movement had spread, by means of the aides, to all the remotest parts of the army, and during the night that followed the first of December the enormous mass of eighty thousand men, comprising the allied armies, arose from their bivouacs with a hum of voices, and stirred and wavered like a mighty fabric ten versts in length.

The concentrating movement, beginning in the morning at the headquarters of the emperors and finally giving its impulse to the whole, even to the remotest parts, was analogous to the first movement of the central wheel of a great tower clock.   The one wheel moves slowly, it starts another, — a third; and ever more and more swiftly the wheels, pulleys, pinions, begin to revolve, the chimes of bells to play, the figures to go through their evolutions, the hands to move in measured time, showing the results of the motions.

As in the mechanism of the clock, so in the mechanism of this military movement; no less irresistibly they move even to the last resultant, when once the impulse is given and just as impassively immovable, up to the moment when the movement is started, are the parts of the mechanisms as yet unstirred by their work. The wheels whizz on their axles, the cogs catch, the revolving sheaves hiss in their rapid motion, but the next wheel is as yet as calm and immovable as if it had before it a century to remain in immobility; and then its moment comes, the cog has caught, and becoming subject to the motion the wheel begins to whir as it revolves and takes part in an activity, the results and aim of which are incomprehensible to it.

Just as in the clock, the result of the complicated motions of numberless and different wheels and pulleys is merely to move the hands slowly and in measured rhythm so as to tell the time, so the result of all the complicated human motions of these one hundred and sixty thousand Russians and French — all the passions, desires, regrets, humiliations, sufferings, transports of pride, panic, enthusiasm of all these men was merely the loss of the battle of Austerlitz, called the Battle of the Three Emperors, — in other words, the measured forward motion of the hand of universal history on the dial of humanity.

Prince Andreï was on duty this day and constantly by the side of the commander-in-chief.

About six o'clock in the evening, Kutuzof came to the headquarters of the emperors, and, after a short audience with his sovereign, went to see Count Tolstoï, the Ober-hofmarshal, master of supplies.

Bolkonsky took advantage of this time to run into Dolgorukof's to find out about the impending engagement. Prince Andreï felt that Kutuzof was dissatisfied and out of sorts for some reason or other, and that he was out of favor at headquarters, and that all whom he met at the emperor's headquarters behaved toward him like men who know more than others know, and it was for this reason that he was anxious for a talk with Dolgorukof.

"Well, how are you, my dear?" exclaimed Dolgorukof, who was drinking tea with Bilibin. "The celebration comes to-morrow! — What's the matter with your old man? Is he out of sorts?"

"I should not say that he was out of sorts, but I think that he would like to have been listened to."

"Well, he was listened to at the council of war, and he will be when he is willing to talk business; but to be temporizing and waiting for something, now that Bonaparte fears a general engagement more than anything else, is impossible."

"And so you've seen him, have you?" asked Prince Andreï. "Well, what sort of a man is this Bonaparte? What impression did he produce upon you?"

"Yes, I have seen him, and I am convinced that he is more afraid of a general engagement than of anything else in the world," replied Dolgorukof, evidently putting great importance on this general conclusion drawn from his interview with Napoleon. "If he were not afraid of a general battle, why should he have demanded this interview, and entered into negotiations, and above all retreated, when retreating is contrary to his entire method of carrying on war? Believe me, he is afraid — afraid of a general engagement; his hour is at hand! Mark my words!"

"But tell me about him, what kind of a man is he?" insisted Prince Andreï.

"He is a man in a gray overcoat, very anxious for me to address him as 'your majesty,' and very much affronted because I gave him no title at all. That's the kind of a man he is, and that's all I can say!" replied Dolgorukof, looking at Bilibin with a smile. "In spite of my perfect confidence in old Kutuzof," he went on to say, "we should all be in a fine state if we kept on waiting for something to happen, and thereby giving him the chance to outflank us or play some trick upon us, now when he's right in our hands evidently. No, it's not a good thing to forget Suvorof and his rule:

'It's a better policy to attack than to be attacked.' Believe me, in war the energy of young men often points out the way more wisely than all the experience of old tacticians."

"But in what position are we going to attack him? I was at the advanced posts to-day, and it is impossible to make out where his main force is stationed," said Prince Andreï. He was anxious to explain to Dolgorukof a plan of attack of his own which he had devised.

"Oh, it is of absolutely no consequence," replied Dolgorukof, hastily getting up and spreading a map on the table. "All contingencies are foreseen. If he is posted at Brünn...."

And Prince Dolgorukof rapidly and not very clearly unfolded Weirother's plan for a flank movement.

Prince Andreï hastened to raise objections and to expound his own plan. Perhaps it was fully as good as Weirother's, but it had one serious fault — that Weirother's had been approved instead. As soon as Prince Andreï began to point out the disadvantages of Weirother's, and the excellences of his own plan, Prince Dolgorukof ceased listening to him and looked absently, not at the map, but at Prince Andreï's face.

"Well, there is to be a council of war this evening at Kutuzof's; there you will have a chance to deliver your views," said Dolgorukof.

"I certainly shall," said Prince Andreï, pushing the map aside.

"And what are you wrangling over, gentlemen?" asked Bilibin, who until now had been listening to their discussion with a gay smile, and had at last made up his mind to get some sport out of it. "Whether we have a victory or a defeat to-morrow, the glory of the Russian arms is assured. Except our Kutuzof, there is n't a single Russian division commander. The heads are Herr Général Wimpfen, le Comte de Langeron, le Prince de Lichtenstein, le Prince de Hohenlohe et enfin Prscz — Prscz — and all the rest of the alphabet, like all Polish names."

"Hush, Impudence!" said Dolgorukof, — "it is n't so, for here are two others, Russians, Miloradovitch and Dokhturof, and we might count Count Arakcheyef as a third, but he has weak nerves."

"Well, I think Mikhaïl Iliaronovitch must have come out," said Prince Andreï. "I wish you all happiness and success, gentlemen," he added, and after shaking hands with Dolgorukof and Bilibin went in search of Kutuzof.

On the way back to their quarters, Prince Andreï could not refrain from asking Kutuzof, who sat in moody silence beside him, what he thought of the approaching engagement.

Kutuzof looked sternly at his aide, and after a moment of silence replied: —

"I think that the battle will be lost, and so I told Count Tolstoï, and begged him to repeat it to the sovereign, and what do you think was the answer he gave me? 'Ah, my dear general, rice and cutlets occupy me; you attend to the affairs of war!'[1] Yes, that's the way they answer me!"

CHAPTER XII

At ten o'clock that evening Weirother came with his plans to Kutuzof's headquarters, where the council of war was to convene. All the division commanders had been summoned to meet at the commander-in-chief's, and with the exception of Prince Bagration, who excused himself, all appeared at the appointed hour.

Weirother, who was the chief promoter of the proposed engagement, presented by his eagerness and vehemence a sharp contrast to the dissatisfied and sleepy-looking Kutuzof, who in spite of himself was obliged to preside as chairman over the council of war.

---

[1] *Eh, mon cher général, je me mêle de riz et des cotelettes, mêlez vous des affaires de la guerre.*

Weirother evidently felt that he was the head center of the movement which had already become irresistible. He was like a horse harnessed into a loaded team and going downhill. He knows not whether he is pulling it or whether it is forcing him onward; but he is borne down with all possible rapidity, and has no time to forecast the outcome of this downward motion.

Weirother twice that afternoon had been out personally to inspect the enemy's pickets, and had twice called on the Russian and Austrian emperors with his reports and explanations, and had been to his own chancellery, where he had dictated his dispositions in German. And now, all worn out, he came to Kutuzof's.

He was evidently so full of his own ideas that he forgot to be civil to the commander-in-chief; he interrupted him, spoke rapidly and incoherently, not looking into the face of his colleague, not replying to the questions asked him, and he was spattered with mud and had a woebegone, haggard, distracted, but at the same time self-conceited and haughty appearance.

Kutuzof occupied a small manor-house near Austerlitz. In the large drawing-room, which had been converted into an office for the commander-in-chief, were gathered Kutuzof, Weirother, and all the members of the council of war. They were drinking tea. They were only waiting for Bagration in order to open the council session. Shortly after ten o'clock, Bagration's orderly rode over with the message that the prince was unable to be present. Prince Andreï came in to report this to the commander-in-chief, and improving the permission previously granted by Kutuzof to be present at the council remained in the room.

"Well, then, as Prince Bagration is not to be here, we may as well begin," exclaimed Weirother, hastily jumping up from his seat and going over to the table whereon was spread a large map of the environs of Brünn.

Kutuzof with his uniform unbuttoned, apparently to give greater freedom to his stout neck clasped by his collar, was sitting in a Voltaire chair, with his plump, aged-looking hands symmetrically placed on the arms, and was almost asleep. At the sound of Weirother's voice he with difficulty opened his one eye.

"Yes, yes, please, else it will be late," said he; nodding his head he let it sink, and again closed his eye.

If, at first, the members of the council supposed that Kutuzof was only pretending to sleep, this time the sounds that proceeded from his nose during the course of the subsequent reading were sufficient proof that what occupied the commander-in-chief was vastly more serious to him than his desire to express scorn for the plan of battle, or anything else: what concerned him at that moment was the invincible requirement of human nature, sleep. He was actually napping!

Weirother, with the action of a man too much occupied to waste a moment of time, glanced at Kutuzof, and though he perceived that he was asleep, took his paper, and in a loud, monotonous tone began to read his plan for the disposition of forces for the impending engagement, under the heading, which he also read, "Distribution of the forces for the attack on the enemy's position behind Kobelnitz and Sokolnitz, November 30, 1805."

The "disposition" was very complicated and difficult to comprehend. In the original German, it was to the following effect:[1]—

"Since the enemy rests his left wing on the wooded mountains, and his right wing stretches along by Kobelnitz and Sokolnitz, behind the ponds that are there; while we, on the other hand, far outnumber his right wing with our left — it is, therefore, for our advantage to attack the enemy's right wing, espe-

---

[1] *Da der Feind mit seinem linken Flügel an die mit Wald bedeckten Berge lehnt, und sich mit seinen rechten Flügel längs Kobelnitz und Sokolnitz hinter die dort befindlichen Teiche zieht, wir im Gegentheil mit unserem linken Flügel seinen rechten sehr debordiren, so ist es vortheilhaft letzeren Flügel des Feindes zu attakiren, besonders wenn wir die Dörfer Sokolnitz und Kobelnitz im Besitze haben wodurch wir dem Feind zugleich in die Flanke fallen und ihn auf der Fläche zwischen Schlapanitz und dem Thürassa-Walde verfolgen können, indem wir die Defileen von Schlapanitz und Bellowitz ausweichen, welche die feindliche Front decken. Zu diesem Endzwecke ist es nothig: .... Die erst Kolonne marschirt .... die zweite Kolonne marschirt .... die dritte Kolonne marschirt .... u. s. w.*

cially if we are in possession of the villages of Sokolnitz and Kobelnitz, because we should immediately fall upon the enemy's flanks, and be able to drive him across the plain between Schlapanitz and the Thuerass forest, and avoid the defiles of Schlapanitz and Bellowitz, which protect the enemy's front. To this end it is necessary: the first column must march — the second column must march — the third column must march" — and so on.

Thus read Weirother. The generals found it hard to listen to the tedious details of the scheme. The tall, fair-haired General Buxhövden stood leaning against the wall, and, resting his eyes on one of the lighted candles, seemed neither to listen nor to wish it to be supposed that he was listening. Directly opposite Weirother sat Miloradovitch, with his brilliant, wide-open eyes, ruddy face, and elevated mustache and shoulders. In soldierly attitude, resting his hands on his knees, with the elbows turned out, he preserved a stubborn silence, gazing directly into Weirother's face, and taking his eyes from him only when the Austrian commander paused. Then, Milorádovitch looked significantly at the other generals. But it was utterly impossible to tell by this significant look whether he agreed or disagreed, whether he was satisfied or dissatisfied, with the proposed plan.

Nearest of all to Weirother, sat the Count de Langeron, and with a shrewd smile, which did not once during the reading vanish from his Southern French countenance, he gazed at his slender fingers, rapidly twirling by the corners his gold snuff-box adorned with a miniature portrait. In the midst of one of the longest sentences, he stopped this whirling of his snuff-box, raised his head, and, with a disagreeable show of politeness carried to extremes, he interrupted him, and started to make some remark; but the Austrian general, not pausing in his task, frowned angrily, and made a gesture with his elbows, as much as to say: 'Wait, wait, you shall tell me your ideas by and by; now be good enough to look at the map and follow me!"

Langeron threw up his eyes with an expression of

perplexity, glanced at Miloradovitch, as if he were seeking for an explanation; but meeting Miloradovitch's significant but enigmatical glance, he looked away gloomily, and began once more to twirl his snuff-box.

"A geography lesson!" he exclaimed, as if to himself, but loud enough to be heard by the others.

Prsczebiszewsky, with respectful but dignified politeness, held one hand to the ear nearest Weirother, and had the appearance of a man whose attention is perfectly absorbed.

Dokhturof, small in stature, sat opposite Weirother with attentive and modest mien, and leaned over the map unrolled before him, and conscientiously followed the scheme as it was evolved, studying the places which he did not know. Several times he begged Weirother to repeat some word that he had failed to understand, or the names of villages that were hard for him to catch. Weirother complied with his request, and Dokhturof wrote them down in his note-book.

When the reading, which had lasted upward of an hour, was completed, Langeron, again laying down his snuff-box, and without looking at Weirother, or any one in particular, began to discourse on the difficulties in the way of carrying out such a plan of battle, even where the position of the enemy was known, and particularly when the position of the enemy could not be known, owing to their constant changing from one place to another.

Langeron's objections were well taken, but it was evident that their *animus* came from a desire to show General Weirother, who had been reading his plan of attack in the most conceited manner, as if to a pack of school-boys, that he was dealing not with dunces but with men who were able to give even him lessons in the art of waging war.

When Weirother's monotonous voice ceased, Kutúzof opened his eyes, like a miller who wakes the moment the soporific sounds of his mill-wheels are interrupted; he listened to what Langeron said, and then, as much as to say, "Well, what nonsense you all are capable of uttering," hurriedly closed his eyes again, and let his head sink even lower on his breast.

Langeron, endeavoring to wound Weirother as cruelly as possible in his self-love as an author and soldier, went on to show that Bonaparte might easily attack instead of waiting to be attacked, and, consequently, make all this elaborate plan of battle perfectly nugatory. Weirother replied to all these objections with a steady, scornful smile, which was evidently prepared beforehand against everything that might be said to him : —

"If he had been able to attack us, he would have done so to-day," said he.

"You think that he is weak, do you?" asked Langeron.

"He is well off if he has forty thousand men," replied Weirother, with the smile of a regular practitioner to whom a woman doctor wishes to suggest some remedy.

"In that case, he is rushing on his own ruin by waiting for us to attack him," said Langeron, with a slight, ironical smile, looking to Miloradovitch again for confirmation. But Miloradovitch was apparently thinking least of all of what the generals were contending about : —

"*Ma foi!*" said he, "to-morrow we shall find out all about it on the battle-field!"

Weirother again indulged in that smile which said that to *him* it was absurd and strange to meet the objections of the Russian generals toward what not only he himself, but the sovereign emperors, had had faith in.

"The enemy have quenched their fires, and a constant rumble has been heard in their camp," said he. "What does that signify? Either he is retreating, which is the only thing that we have to fear, or he is changing his position." He smiled. "But even if he should take up his position in Thürassa, he is merely saving us great trouble, and all our arrangements, even to the minutest details, would remain the same."

"How so?" asked Prince Andreï, who had been watching for some time for an opportunity to express his doubts. Kutuzof here woke up, coughed severely, and looked around on the generals.

"Gentlemen, the arrangements for to-morrow — or rather for to-day — for it's already one o'clock — cannot be changed," said he. "You have heard them, and we will all perform our duty. But before a battle there is nothing more important" — he paused a moment — "than to have a good night's rest."

He made a motion to arise. The generals bowed and separated. It was already after midnight. Prince Andreï went to his quarters.

The council of war at which Prince Andreï was not given a chance to express his opinion as he had hoped, left a dubious and disturbing impression on his mind. He did not know who was right, Dolgorukof and Weirother, or Kutuzof and Langeron, and the others who did not approve of the plan of attack. "But is it possible that Kutuzof cannot communicate his ideas directly with the emperor? Can't this be done even now? Can it be that for mere court or private considerations thousands of lives must be imperiled — and mine, *mine?*" he asked himself.

"Yes, it is very possible," he thought, "that I may be killed to-morrow." And suddenly at this thought of death, a whole series of most remote and most sincere recollections began to arise in his mind; he recalled his last parting with his father and his wife; he remembered the early days of his love toward her! He remembered the baby that she was to bear him, and he began to feel sorry for her and for himself, and so in a nervously tender and agitated frame of mind he left the cottage where he lodged with Nesvitsky, and began to walk up and down in front of the house.

The night was cloudy, but the moonbeams mysteriously gleamed through the clouds. "Yes, to-morrow, to-morrow!" he thought. "To-morrow, perhaps all will be ended as far as I am concerned, all these recollections will have vanished, all these recollections will be for me as a mere nothing. To-morrow perhaps, indeed most probably, — to-morrow — I am convinced of it I shall have an opportunity for the first time at last of showing all that I can do."

And he began to picture to himself the battle, the loss of it, the concentration of the fighting at one single point, and the confusion and bewilderment of all the leaders. And now comes the blessed moment, that Toulon, for which he had been waiting so long, offering itself to him! He resolutely and clearly tells his opinion to Kutuzof and Weirother and the emperors. All his plans are honored with their approval, but no one offers to carry them out, and so he selects a regiment, a division, imposes the condition that no one shall interfere in his arrangements, and he leads his division to the decisive point, and alone wins the victory!

"But death and suffering?" says another voice.

Prince Andreï, however, paid no heed to this voice, and continued to dream of his triumphs. The arrangements of the next battle are intrusted to him alone. He is still nothing but an officer of the day in Kutuzof's army, but still he does everything by his own unaided efforts. The next battle is gained by him alone. Kutuzof is removed, he is called to fill his place.

"Well, but what then," whispered the other voices; "what then? supposing you are not wounded ten times, before all this, or killed, or cheated, well, then, and what next?"

"I am sure I know not," replied Prince Andreï to himself, "I know not what will come next, I cannot know and I have no wish to know. But if I wish this, if I wish to win glory, if I wish to be a famous man, if I wish to be loved by men, then I am not to blame because I desire it, because this is the only thing that I desire, the only thing for which I live. Yes, the only thing. I never will confess this to any one! But my God! what can I do, if I love nothing except glory only, and devotion to humanity? Death, wounds, loss of family, nothing is terrible to me. And yet dear to me, precious to me as many people are, — father, sister, wife, the dearest of all, — yet strange and unnatural as it may seem, I would instantly sacrifice them all for one minute of glory, of triumph, for the affection of men whom I do not know and never shall know, even for the love of those men there," said he to himself, as he listened to the sounds of voices talking in Kutuzof's courtyard.

In Kutuzof's courtyard the *denshchiks* were busy packing up and talking; one voice, apparently that of the coachman, who was teasing Kutuzof's old cook, whom Prince Andreï knew, and whom they called Tit, kept saying, "Tit, I say, Tit!"

"There, now," replied the old man.

"Tīt, Tīt, grind the wheat."[1]

"Tfu! go to the devil," rang the voice, which was drowned by the shouts of laughter of the *denshchiks* and other servants.

"And yet I love and prize the victory over them all, I prize this mysterious strength and glory which seems here to hover above my head in this fog."

CHAPTER XIII

ROSTOF that same night was with his platoon in the line of scouts stationed in front of Bagration's division. His hussars were posted two and two along the line; he himself kept riding his horse the whole length of the line, struggling to overcome his irresistible inclination to drowsiness.

Behind him he could see the long line of the watchfires of our army dimly gleaming through the fog; in front of him was the misty darkness. Though he strained his eyes to penetrate this misty distance, he could see nothing; now it seemed to brighten up a little, then there seemed to be some black object; then he imagined that he saw a light which he thought must be the watch-fires where the enemy were, and then again he told himself that his eyes had deceived him.

He closed his eyes and his imagination presented now his sovereign, now Denísof, now his recollections of Moscow, and again he would open his eyes and see right before his face the head and ears of his horse, and

---

[1] "*Tit, stupaï molotit!*"

here and there the dark forms of hussars as he came within six paces of them, while everywhere there was the same misty darkness veiling the distance.

"Why not? It might very possibly come to pass," thought Rostof, "the emperor might meet me and give me an order, just as to any other officer; might say: 'Ride off yonder and find out what is there.' I have heard many stories about his finding just merely by chance an officer like me, and taking him into his personal service. What if he should take me into his personal service! oh! how I should watch over him, how I should tell him the whole truth, how I should unmask his deceivers!" and Rostof, in order to give greater color to the love and devotion which he felt for his sovereign, imagined that he had before him an enemy whom he was killing, or a German traitor whose ears he was roundly boxing, in presence of his sovereign.

Suddenly, a distant shout startled him. He awoke and opened his eyes.

"Where am I? Oh, yes, at the outposts. Countersign and password are 'cart-pole' and 'Olmütz.' What a shame that our squadron is going to be held in reserve to-morrow," he said to himself. "I will beg to take part. That is probably the only chance I shall have of seeing the emperor. It won't be long before I am relieved. I will ride up and down once more, and then I will go and ask the general."

He straightened himself up in the saddle, and turned his horse, once more to inspect his hussars. It seemed to him that it had grown lighter. Toward his left, he could see a slope, the gleam of a declivity, and, lying opposite to him, a dark knoll which seemed as steep as a wall. On the top of this knoll was a white spot. Rostof could not clearly make out whether it was a clearing in the woods, lighted by the moon, or a patch of snow, or white houses. It even seemed to him that there was something moving on that white spot.

"It must be snow, that spot; spot — *une tache*," said Rostof, first in Russian, then in French. "How absurd; it's no *tache* — Natasha .... my sister .... has black eyes.

Na—tashka (how amazed she will be when I tell her I have seen the emperor!). Na—tasha. My sabre-*tash* — take it."

"Farther to the right, your nobility, there are bushes here!" said the voice of the hussar, by whom Rostof was passing, half asleep. Rostof raised his head, which had fallen over almost down to the horse's mane; he drew up near the hussar. The sleep of youth, of childhood, irresistibly overcame him.

"O dear me, what was I thinking of? I must not forget. How shall I speak to the emperor? No, that's not it; that's for to-morrow. Oh, yes, yes! that spot — *cette tache!* they'll be attacking us! Us?.... who?.... The hussars! But the hussars and — and a pair of mustaches. — Along the Tverskaya, this hussar was riding, and I was thinking about him, — right opposite Hurief's house — the old man Hurief — ekh! splendid little Denísof! Ah! this is all nonsense. The main thing: the emperor is here now! How he looked at me and wanted to say something to me, but he did not venture. No, it was I who did not venture! This is all mixed up! but the main thing is that I must not forget that I had something important on my mind; so I had! Natashka — Na—tasha — *la tache* — yes, that's a good joke!" and again his head sank forward on the horse's mane.

Suddenly, it seemed to him that the enemy were firing at him.

"What? What, what's that; speak! what is it?" cried Rostof, waking.

At the instant Rostof opened his eyes, he heard in front of him, in the direction of the enemy, the prolonged shouts of thousands of voices. His horse and the hussars' stationed near him pricked up their ears at these sounds. On the spot from which the cries proceeded, one point of fire after another flashed and died, and along the whole line of the French army, stretching up the hills, gleamed those fires, while the shouts grew louder and louder. Rostof made out that it was French, but could not distinguish the words.

There was too great a roar of voices. All that it sounded like was a confused a-a-a-a! and rrrrrrr!

"What's that? What do you think it is?" asked Rostof, turning to his neighbor, the hussar. "It's from the enemy, is n't it?"

The hussar made no reply.

"What! did n't you hear anything?" asked Rostof, after waiting for some time for the hussar to speak.

"How can anybody tell, your nobility," replied the hussar, in a non-committal way.

"Judging from the direction, it must be the enemy, must n't it?" inquired Rostof.

"Maybe 't is, and maybe 't is n't," exclaimed the hussar. "You see it's night. There now, steady," he cried to his horse, who was growing restive. Rostof's horse also became excited, and pawed the frozen ground, as he listened to the shouting and glanced at the flashing fires.

The shouts of the voices constantly increased in volume, and mingled in a general roar, such as could have been produced only by an army of many thousand men. The fires stretched out more and more, until at last they seemed to extend throughout the French camp. Rostof had now lost all inclination to sleep. The joyful, enthusiastic huzzas in the enemy's army had a most stimulating effect upon him. *Vive l'empereur! l'empereur!* were the words that Rostof could now clearly distinguish.

"Well, they can't be far away; must be just beyond the brook," said he to the hussar by his side.

The hussar only sighed, without vouchsafing any answer, and coughed sullenly.

Along the line of the hussars was heard the sound of a horseman, coming at full gallop, and out of the darkness of the night suddenly loomed up a shape apparently larger than a colossal elephant: it was a non-commissioned officer of hussars.

"The generals, your nobility!" cried the subaltern, riding up to Rostof. Rostof, still looking in the direction of the shouting and the lights, joined the subaltern and rode back to meet several horsemen who were riding along the line. One was on a white horse. It was Bagration, who, together with Prince Dolgorukof and several aides, came down to see what they could make out of the strange phenomenon of the fires and shouting in the enemy's army. Rostof rode up to Bagration, reported, and took his place among the aides, who were listening to what the generals might say.

"Believe me," said Prince Dolgorukof, addressing Bagration, "this is nothing but a ruse; he is retreating, and has ordered the rear-guard to light fires and make a noise, so as to deceive us."

"It is not likely," said Bagration. "Last evening I saw them on that knoll; if they were retreating, they would have abandoned it. Mr. Officer," turning to Rostof, "are his scouts still there?"

"They were there last evening, but I can't tell now, your illustriousness. If you would like, I will take some of the hussars and find out," replied Rostof.

Bagration hesitated, and making no answer, tried to peer into Rostof's face. "Well, all right, go and reconnoiter," said he, after a short pause.

"I will do so."

Rostof applied spurs to his horse, called Subaltern Fadchenko and two other hussars, ordered them to follow him, and galloped off down the slope in the direction of the prolonged shouts. Rostof felt both sad and glad to be riding thus alone with three hussars yonder into that mysterious and terrible misty distance where no one had preceded him. Bagration called to him from the crest not to go farther than the brook, but Rostof pretended not to hear what he said, and without pausing they rode farther and farther, constantly finding himself subject to illusions, mistaking bushes for trees, gullies for men, and constantly rectifying his impressions.

After they had reached the bottom at a rapid trot, they no longer saw any fires either on our side or on the enemy's, but the shouts of the French began to sound louder and clearer. In the ravine he saw before him what he took to be a river, but when he approached it, he recognized that it was a highway over which he had once ridden. When he reached the highway, he reined in his horse in some uncertainty; should he ride along the road, or cross it, or strike into the dark field on the other side? To ride along the road which shone through the fog was less perilous, because he could distinguish men at a greater distance.

"Follow me," he cried, crossing the road, and he began to gallop up the hill toward a place where a French picket had been standing the afternoon before.

"Your nobility, there he is!" exclaimed one of the hussars, and before Rostof had a chance to look at what was beginning to loom up black in the fog, there came a flash of fire, the report rang out, and the bullet, as if winged with pity, buzzed[1] high over their heads through the fog, and sped out of hearing. The second musket did not go off, the powder merely flashed in the priming-pan. Rostof turned his horse about and rode back at a gallop. Again from different points four musket-shots rang out, and the bullets with various tones whistled by and buried themselves in the darkness. Rostof reined in his horse, which, like himself, felt a thrill of joy at the firing, and proceeded at a walk. "Well, there it is again, there it is again," whispered some inspiriting voice in his heart. But there were no more shots.

As soon as he neared Bagration, Rostof again urged his horse to a gallop, and held his hand to his visor as he approached.

Dolgorukof still clung to his opinion that the French were retreating, and had kindled the fires merely for the sake of deceiving us. "What does this signify?" he asked, as Rostof rode up to them. "They might retreat and still leave pickets."

"It is evident they have not all gone, prince," said Bagration. "To-morrow morning, to-morrow, we shall know for a certainty."

"There is a picket, your illustriousness, in just the

[1] *Zazhuzhdla.*

same place as yesterday," reported Rostof, bending forward, still holding his hand at his visor, and unable to refrain from a smile of delight at his ride, and especially at the sound of the bullets.

"Very good, very good," replied Bagration. "Thank you, Mr. Officer."

"Your illustriousness," said Rostof, "allow me to ask a favor."

"What is it?"

"To-morrow our squadron is to be left in reserve; allow me to be transferred to the first squadron."

"What's your name?"

"Count Rostof."

"Ah, good. Stay with me as orderly."

"Son of Ilya Andreyitch?" asked Dolgorukof. But Rostof made him no answer.

"So I may expect it, your illustriousness?"

"I will see to it."

"To-morrow, very likely, I may be sent with some message to the sovereign," said Rostof to himself. "Glory to God!"

The shouts and cries in the enemy's army arose from the circumstance that at the time Napoleon's general order was being read throughout the army, the emperor himself came on horseback to inspect the bivouacs. The soldiers, seeing the emperor, lighted trusses of straw and followed him with cries of *vive l'empereur!*

Napoleon's order was as follows: —

"Soldiers! The Russian army has come against us in order to avenge the Austrian army of Ulm. These are the same battalions which we defeated at Hollabrünn, and which, since that time, we have been constantly following up.

"The position which we occupy is paramount, and as soon as they attempt to outflank my right they will expose their own flank.

"Soldiers! I myself will direct your battalions. I will keep out of range of the firing, if you, with your usual gallantry, carry confusion and consternation into the ranks of the enemy; but if the combat becomes for one instant doubtful, you will see

your emperor exposing himself at the front to the blows of the
enemy, since there can be no hesitation in the victory, especially
to-day when the honor of the French infantry, in whose hands
lies the honor of the nation, is at stake. Do not break the
ranks under pretext of carrying away the wounded. Let each
man be animated by the thought that we must conquer these
mercenaries of England, filled with such hatred against our nation. This victory will bring the campaign to an end, and we
can retire to winter quarters where we shall be joined by the
fresh troops that are mobilizing in France. And then the
peace which I shall conclude will be memorable for my people,
for you, and for me.   NAPOLEON."

CHAPTER XIV

AT five o'clock in the morning it was still perfectly
dark. The troops of the center, of the reserves, and
the right wing, under Bagration, were as yet motionless;
but on the left wing the columns of infantry, cavalry,
and artillery, ordered to be the first to descend from
the heights and attack the enemy's right flank, and
drive him back into the mountains of Bohemia, according to the "disposition," were already stirring and beginning to rise from where they lay. The smoke from
the fires, into which they were throwing everything
superfluous, made their eyes smart. It was cold and
dark. The officers were hastily drinking their tea and
breakfasting; the soldiers were munching their biscuits,
kicking the round shot to warm their feet, and crowding
about in front of the fires, throwing in the remains of
their huts, chairs, tables, wheels, buckets, and everything that could not be taken with them.

The Austrian guides were wandering about among
the Russian troops, and serving as starters of the forward movement. As soon as an Austrian officer made
his appearance near the quarters of a regimental commander, the regiment began to stir: the soldiers
hastened from the fires, thrust their pipes into their
boot-legs, their bags into the baggage-wagons, put their
guns in order, and fell into line.

Officers were buttoning themselves up, putting on their swords and pouches, and inspecting the lines, scolding as they went; the trainmen and officers' servants were hitching up horses, packing in various articles, and loading the wagons.

Aides, battalion commanders, and colonels were mounting their horses, crossing themselves, and issuing their last instructions, orders, and commissions to the train-hands left in charge of the baggage; then was heard the monotonous trampling of thousands of feet.

The columns were set in motion, but they knew not whither they were going, and owing to the throngs that surrounded them, and the smoke, and the thickening fog, they could not see either the place that they were leaving, or that to which they were sent.

The soldier in a military movement is as much surrounded, limited, and fettered by his regiment as a sailor is by the ship on which he sails. However far he goes, into whatever strange, unknown, and terrible distances he is sent, around him are always and everywhere the same comrades, the same ranks, the same sergeant, Ivan Mítrich, the same company dog, Zhutchka, the same officers; just as for the sailor there are the same decks, the same masts, the same cables.

The sailor rarely cares to know the distances over which his ship has sailed; but on the day of a military movement God knows how, or whence, or in what world of mystery the soldiers hear a stern note, which is the same for all, and which signifies the nearness of something decisive and solemn, and invites them to dream of what they are not usually wont to think about. The soldiers on the day of a military movement are excited, and strive to get beyond the petty interests of their own regiment; they are all ears and eyes, and greedily ask questions about what is going to take place before them.

The fog was so dense that, though it had grown lighter, it was impossible to see ten paces ahead. Bushes seemed like huge trees, level places gave the impression of being precipices and slopes. Anywhere, at any moment, they might meet the enemy, who would be utterly invisible within ten paces. But the columns marched for a long time in the same fog, up hill and down dale, skirting gardens and orchards, along by places where none of them had ever been before, and still they found no enemy. On the other hand, in front of them, behind them, on all sides of them, the soldiers were made conscious that our Russian columns were all marching in the same direction. Each soldier felt a thrill at the heart at the knowledge that many, many others of our men were going where he was going: that is, he knew not whither.

"See there! The Kursk men have started," said various voices in the ranks.

"Terrible lot of our troops collected here, messmates! Last evenin' I looked around when the fires were lit; could n't see the end of 'em! Like Moscow, in one word!"

Although not one of the division nachalniks came near the ranks or had anything to say to the soldiers, — the division nachalniks, as we saw in the council of war, were out of sorts and dissatisfied with the work in hand, and, consequently, merely carried out the general orders and did nothing to inspirit the men, — still the soldiers marched on cheerfully, as is usually the case when they are going into action, and particularly into offensive action.

But after they had been marching for about an hour, all the time in thick fog, they were ordered to halt, and an unpleasant consciousness of disorder and confusion in the operations spread through the ranks. It would be very difficult to explain how such a consciousness got abroad; but there was no doubt that it was transmitted and spread with extraordinary rapidity: the uncertainty became certainty, gaining with irresistible force, as water rushes down a ravine. If the Russian army had been alone by itself, without allies, then possibly it would have taken much longer time for this consciousness of confusion to grow into a general certainty;

but, as it was, all took a natural satisfaction in attributing the cause of the disorder to the stupid Germans, and were convinced that the pernicious snarl was due to the sausage-makers!

"Why are we halting? What? Have we got blocked? We can't have come afoul of the French, can we?"

"No! We should have heard from them. They'd have begun to fire at us."

"They hurried us off so, and now here we are, all in a muddle in the middle of the field; that's the way with those cursed Germans; they muddle everything all up!"

"What stupid devils! If I'd had anything to do with them, I'd have put 'em to the front. But instead, you may be sure of that, they are pressing us from behind. And here we are without having anything to eat!"

"Well, I wonder if we shall be planted here all day? The cavalry, they say, is what is blocking the road," exclaimed an officer.

"Ekh! these damned Germans don't know their own country," said another.

"What division are you?" cried an aide, riding up to them.

"The Eighteenth."

"Then why are you here? You should have been at the front long since; you won't get there now before afternoon."

"Here's a stupid piece of confusion; they themselves don't know what they're up to," said the officer, and he rode off.

Then a general passed, and angrily shouted some order in a language that was n't Russian.

"Tafa-lafa! what sort of stuff is he jabbering? can't make out a thing he says," remarked a soldier, mimicking the general as he rode off. "I'd have had them all shot down, the scoundrels!"

"We were ordered to be in position by nine o'clock, and now we have not got half-way there! What stupid arrangements!" And this was heard on all sides, and the feeling of energetic ardor with which the army had started out, began to be wasted in vexation and anger against the arrangements and the Germans.

The cause of the confusion was this : after the Austrian cavalry on the left wing had set forward, those who had charge of it came to the conclusion that the Russian center was too widely separated from the right, and all the cavalry was commanded to cross over to the right side. Several thousands of cavalrymen rode across in front of the columns of infantry, and the infantry had to wait till they passed.

At the front a dispute had risen between the Austrian guide and a Russian general. The Russian general shouted angrily, demanding that the cavalry should stop. The Austrian insisted that he was not to blame, but his superior officers. Meantime the army was obliged to halt, and was growing impatient and losing spirit. At last, after an hour's delay, the troops began to move forward once more, and found themselves descending into the valley. The fog, which had been scattering on the heights, was as thick as ever on the lower lands where they were now marching. In front of them in the fog, one shot, then a second, was fired, incoherently and at different points, *tratta tat;* and then the firing became more regular and rapid, and the engagement fairly began over the brook called Holdbach.

As the troops had no expectation of falling in with the enemy so far down in the valley as the brook, and then met them unexpectedly in the fog; as they had no words of encouragement from their commanding officers, and the idea was widespread among them that it was too late; and, moreover, as they could not see any one either in front of them or anywhere near them, owing to the density of the fog, they apathetically and lazily exchanged shots with the enemy, slowly moved forward, and then came to a halt again, failing to receive in time the word of command from their officers or the aides, who wandered at haphazard through the fog in places with which they were unacquainted, and in search of their own divisions.

Thus began the action for the first, second, and third columns which had gone down into the valley. The fourth column, which Kutuzof himself had under his own command, was stationed on the heights of the Pratzer.

In the lowlands, where the battle had already begun, the fog seemed thicker than ever, but on the heights it was clear; still nothing could be seen of what was going on at the front. Until nine o'clock no one could tell whether the enemy was in his full strength, as the Russians supposed, ten versts in advance, or was down there in that impenetrable fog.

It was now nine o'clock. The fog like a fathomless sea spread over the valley, but on the height in front of the village of Schlapanitz on the height, where Napoleon stood surrounded by his marshals, it was perfectly bright. Over them was the blue bright heaven, and the mighty sun, like a gigantic, hollow purple balloon, was just rising above the milk-white sea of fog. The French troops and Napoleon himself with his staff were not on the farther side of the brooks and the hollows of Sokolnitz and Schlapanitz behind which we had expected to take up our position and begin the engagement, but they had all come over to the hither side and were so near our troops that Napoleon with his naked eye could distinguish in our army a horseman from an infantry soldier.

Napoleon, mounted on his little gray Arab and wearing the same blue cloak in which he had made the whole Italian campaign, was standing a little in advance of his marshals. He was silently gazing at the summits of the hills that emerged like islands from the fog and was watching the Russian troops as they moved along in the distance, and listening to the sounds of firing in the valley. Not a muscle of his face — it was still thin — moved, his glittering eyes were steadfastly fixed on one spot. His anticipations seemed to be justified.

The Russian troops had already in part defiled down into the ravine toward the ponds and lakes, and part of them were evacuating the heights of the Pratzer, which he considered the key of the situation and intended to attack. He could see, through the fog, how down into the hollow formed by the two high hills near the village of Pratz, the Russian columns with glittering bayonets were steadily moving in one direction toward the valley, and disappearing one after another into the sea of fog. By the reports which had been brought him the evening before, by the sounds of wheels and footsteps that had been heard during the night along the vanguard, by the disorderly movements of the Russian columns, by all the indications, he clearly saw in fact that the allied armies supposed him to be posted a long distance from them, that the columns moving near in the vicinity of Pratz constituted the center of the Russian army, and that this center was weak enough to justify him in giving it attack.

But not even yet did he begin the battle.

That was a solemn day for him, the anniversary of his coronation. Just before morning he had taken a nap for a few hours, and then waking, healthy, jovial, fresh, and in that happy frame of mind in which everything seems possible, success certain, he mounted his horse and rode out into the field. He stood motionless, gazing at the hills becoming visible through the fog, and into his cold face there came that peculiar shade of self-confident, well-deserved happiness, such as is sometimes seen on the face of a young lad who is happy and in love.

His marshals were grouped behind him and did not venture to distract his attention. He gazed now at the heights of the Pratzer, now at the sun swimming out from the fog.

When the sun had risen clear above the fog, and his dazzling radiance gushed over the fields and the fog, as if this were the signal for which he was waiting to begin the affair, he drew off his glove from his handsome white hand, beckoned his marshals, and gave the order for beginning the battle. The marshals, accompanied by their aides, galloped off in different directions, and within a few minutes the chief forces of the French army were in rapid motion toward those same heights of the Pratzer which the Russian troops were abandoning more and more as they filed to the left and into the vale.

CHAPTER XV

At eight o'clock that morning, Kutuzof had ridden up toward the Pratzer, at the head of the fourth division, — Miloradovitch's, — which was to take the place of the columns of Prsczebiszhewsky and De Langeron, which were now on their way down into the valley. He greeted the men of the foremost regiment and gave the word of command, thereby signifying that he intended to lead that column in person. When he reached the village of Pratz, he halted. Prince Andreï, forming one of his large staff, stood just behind him. Prince Andreï felt stirred and excited, and at the same time self-confident and calm, as is apt to be the case with a man at the arrival of the moment which he has been anxiously awaiting. He was firmly convinced that this day was to be his Toulon, or his bridge of Arcola.[1]

How it would come about he had not the faintest idea, but he was firmly convinced that it would be. The lay of the land and the position of our forces were well known to him, so far as they could be known to any one in the Russian army. His own strategical plan, which now seemed to be doomed never to be carried into effect, had been forgotten. Having made himself master of Weirother's scheme, Prince Andreï wondered what possibilities might rise before him, and began to make new combinations according to which his presence of mind and firmness might be called into request.

Toward the left, in the valley below, where the fog lay, could be heard the musket fires of the unseen opponents. There, so it seemed to Prince Andreï, the fighting would be hottest, there the obstacles would be met with ; "and there I shall be sent," he said to himself, "with a brigade or division, and with the standard in my hand, I shall rush on and conquer everything before me."

Prince Andreï could not look at the standards of the

[1] The desperate battle by which Napoleon became master of Italy, November 14-17, 1796.

battalions passing before him without a thrill. As he looked at one he kept saying to himself: "Maybe that is the very standard that I shall seize when I lead the army to the front!"

The nocturnal fog now remained on the heights only in the form of hoar frost, which was rapidly changing into dew; in the hollows, however, it still spread out like a milk-white sea. Nothing could be discerned in that fog toward the left, where our troops were descending, and where the musketry firing was heard. Over the heights stretched the clear, bright sky, and at the right hung the monstrous orb of the sun. Far away, toward the front, on the other shore of the sea of fog, could be seen high wooded hills, on which the enemy must be stationed, and there some objects could be distinguished.

At the right, the Guards, with echoing tramp, and rattling wheels, and occasionally the glint of bayonets, were passing down into the dominion of the fog. At the left, beyond the village, similar masses of cavalry were filing down and disappearing from view in the sea of fog.

In front, and behind, the infantry were debouching.

The commander-in-chief stationed himself at the entrance of the village, and allowed the troops to file past him. Kutuzof that morning appeared fatigued and irritated. The infantry, filing by him, came to a halt without any orders, apparently because they had come in contact with some obstacle ahead of them.

"Go and tell them to form into battalions and get outside the village," said Kutuzof to a general who came riding along. "How is it, you do not understand, your excellency, my dear sir,[1] that it's impossible to open ranks so, along a village street, when we are moving against the enemy?"

"I proposed to form behind the village, your eminence," replied the general.

Kutúzof gave him a saturnine smile.

[1] "*Vàshe privoskhoditelstvo, milostivui gosudàr.*"

"You'd be in a fine condition, deploying your front in presence of the enemy; very fine idea!"

"The enemy are still a long way off, your eminence. According to the plan ...."

"The plan!" cried Kutuzof, bitterly, "and who told you that? Be good enough to do as I bid you."

"I obey."

"My dear," whispered Nesvitsky to Prince Andreï, "the old man is as surly as a dog."

An Austrian officer, in a white uniform, with a green plume in his hat, galloped up to Kutuzof, and asked him, in the name of the emperor, if the fourth column was taking part in the action.

Kutuzof, without answering him, turned around, and his glance fell accidentally on Prince Andreï, who was stationed near him. When he noticed Bolkonsky, the vicious and acrimonious expression of his face softened, as if to signify that he was not to blame for what was taking place. And still without answering the Austrian aide, he turned to Bolkonsky, and said in French: "Go and see, my dear, if the third division has passed the village yet; command them to halt and await my orders."

As soon as Prince Andreï started, he called him back : —

"And ask if the skirmishers are posted, and what they are doing. What they are doing," he repeated to himself, still paying no attention to the Austrian.

Prince Andreï galloped off to execute this order.

Outstripping the battalions, which were all the time pressing forward, he halted the third division, and convinced himself that no skirmishers had been thrown out in front of our columns. The general in command of the foremost regiment was greatly amazed at the order from the commander-in-chief to throw out sharp-shooters. The regimental commander was firmly assured in his own mind that other troops were in front of him and that the enemy could not be less than ten versts distant. In reality, nothing could be discerned in front of them except waste ground which sloped down, and was shrouded in fog. . After giving him the commander-in-chief's orders to repair his negligence, Prince Andreï galloped back. Kutuzof was still in the same place, and with his fat body sitting in a dumpy position in his saddle was yawning heavily, with his eyes closed. The troops had not yet moved, but stood with grounded arms.

"Good, very good," said he to Prince Andreï, and turned to the general, who, holding his watch in his hand, said that it must be time to move, since all the columns had already gone down from the left wing.

"Time enough, your excellency," said Kutuzof. "We shall have time enough," he repeated.

At this time, behind Kutuzof, were heard the sounds of the regiments in the distance cheering, and these voices quickly ran along the whole extent of the line of the Russian columns under march.

It was evident that the one whom they were greeting was approaching rapidly. When the soldiers of the regiment at whose head Kutuzof was stationed began to cheer, he rode a little to one side and glanced around with a frown. Along the road from Pratz came what appeared to be a squadron of gay-colored horsemen. Two of them at a round gallop rode side by side ahead of the others. One was in a black uniform with a white plume, on a chestnut horse groomed in the English style; the other in a white uniform on a coal-black steed. These were the two emperors with their suite.

Kutuzof, with an affectation of "the thorough soldier" found at his post, shouted "*Smirno*, Eyes front," to the soldiers halting near him, and saluting rode toward the emperor. His whole figure and manner had suddenly undergone a change. He had assumed the mien of a subordinate, of a man ready to surrender his own will. With an affectation of deference which evidently was not pleasing to the Emperor Alexander, he came to meet him and saluted him.

This impression crossed the young and happy face of the emperor, and disappeared like the mist wreaths in the clear sky. After his indisposition he **was a trifle**

thinner that day than he had been on the field of
Olmütz where Bolkonsky had for the first time seen
him abroad.   There was the same enchanting union of
majesty and sweetness in his beautiful gray eyes, and
on his thin lips the same possibility of varied feelings,
and the same predominating expression of beneficent,
innocent youth.

At the review at Olmütz he had been more majestic;
here he was happier and more full of energy.   His
face was a trifle flushed after his gallop of three versts,
and as he reined in his horse he drew a long breath
and glanced around into the faces of his suite, all young
men like himself, and like himself all full of life.   Czartorisky and Novosiltsof and Prince Volkonsky and
Stroganof and many others, all richly dressed, jovial
young men on handsome, well-groomed, fresh-looking
and slightly sweating horses, chatting and laughing
together, formed a group behind the sovereign.

The Emperor Franz, a florid young man with a long
face, sat bolt upright in his saddle on his handsome
black stallion, and slowly glanced around him with an
anxious expression.   He beckoned to one of his white-
uniformed aides and asked him some question.   "Probably he asked at what hour they started," thought Prince
Andreï, gazing at his old acquaintance with a smile
which he could not repress at the thought of his audience.   The emperors' suite was composed of young
orderlies, Austrian and Russian, selected from the
regiments of the Guards and of the Line.   Grooms
had brought with them handsome reserve horses in embroidered caparisons for the emperors.

Just as when a fresh breeze from the fields breathes
through an open window into a stuffy chamber, so these
brilliant young men brought with them to Kutuzof's
dispirited staff the sense of youth and energy and confidence in victory.

"Why don't you begin, Mikhaïl Larionovitch?" impatiently demanded the Emperor Alexander, turning to
Kutuzof, at the same time looking courteously toward
the Emperor Franz.

"I was waiting, your majesty," replied Kutuzof, deferentially bowing low. The emperor leaned toward him, frowning slightly, and giving him to understand that he did not hear.

"I was waiting, your majesty," repeated Kutuzof, and Prince Andreï noticed that Kutuzof's upper lip curled unnaturally when he repeated the words, "I was waiting." — "The columns have not all assembled, your majesty."

The sovereign heard, but the answer evidently displeased him; he shrugged his drooping shoulders, glanced at Novosiltsof, who was standing near him, and his glance seemed to imply a certain compassion for Kutuzof.

"We are not on the Empress's Field, Mikhaïl Larionovitch, where the review is not begun until all the regiments are present," said the emperor, again glancing into the Emperor Franz's eyes, as if to ask him if he would not take part so that he might listen to what he might say; but the Emperor Franz, who was still gazing about, did not heed him.

"That's the very reason I do not begin, sire," said Kutuzof, in a ringing voice, seeming to anticipate the possibility that the emperor might not see fit to hear him, and again a peculiar look passed over his face. "That's the very reason that I do not begin, sire, because we are not on parade and not on the Empress's Field," he repeated, clearly and distinctly.

The faces of all those composing the emperor's suite expressed annoyance and reproach, as they hastily exchanged glances on hearing these words. 'No matter if he is old, he ought not, he never ought to speak in that way,' the faces seemed to say.

"However, if you give the order, your majesty," said Kutuzof, raising his head and again assuming that former tone of a general ready to listen to orders and to obey. He turned his horse, and beckoning to Division-Commander Miloradovitch he gave him the order to attack.

The troops were again set in motion, and two battalions of the Novgorodsky regiment and one battalion of the Apsheron regiment filed forward past the emperor. While this Apsheron battalion was passing, the florid Miloradovitch, without his cloak and with his uniform covered with orders, and his hat decorated with an immense plume and set on one side with the point forward, galloped forward and gallantly saluting reined in his horse in front of the sovereign.

" *S Bogom*, God be with you, general," exclaimed the emperor.

" Faith, we will do our best, your majesty," replied the other, cheerily; nevertheless the gentlemen of the suite could not refrain from smiling contemptuously at the execrable way in which he pronounced his French.

Miloradovitch turned his horse sharply round and remained a short distance behind the emperor. The Apsheron boys, inspirited by the presence of their sovereign, marched by the emperors and their suite with lively, gallant strides, keeping perfect time.

" Children !" cried Miloradovitch in a loud, self-confident, and cheering voice, evidently roused by the sounds of the firing, the expectation of the battle, and the sight of the Apsheron soldiers, who had been his comrades in the campaigns with Suvorof, and were now briskly marching past the emperors, and roused to such a pitch that he forgot that the sovereign was present: " Children ! this is not the first village that you have had to take," he cried.

" We 'll do our best," cried the soldiers. The emperor's mare started at the unexpected shout. This mare which the emperor had ridden before during other reviews in Russia, here on the battle-field of Austerlitz carried her rider, not noticing the captious thrusts of his left heel, pricking up her ears at the sound of the musketry firing, just as she did on the Field of Mars,[1] not realizing the significance of those reëchoing volleys, nor of the neighborhood of the Emperor Franz's black stal-

[1] The *Tsáritsuin Lug*, Tsaritsa or Empress's Field is also called *Marsovoye póle*.

lion, nor of what the man who on that day sat upon her back said, thought, felt.

The sovereign with a smile turned to one of his immediate suite and pointing to the Apsheron lads made some remark.

CHAPTER XVI

KUTUZOF, accompanied by his aides, rode slowly after the carabiniers. After riding half a verst, he caught up with the rear end of the column, and halted at a single deserted house — it had apparently been a drinking house — near the junction of two roads. Both roads led down into the valley, and both were crowded with troops.

The fog began to disperse and already, two versts away, could be seen, though as yet indistinctly, the ranks of the enemy on the heights opposite. Down in the valley at the left, the firing was growing more violent. Kutuzof halted, discussing some point with the Austrian general. Prince Andreï, sitting on his horse a little distance behind, gazed at them, and then, wishing to obtain the use of a field-glass, turned to one of the aides who had one.

"Look! look!" exclaimed this aide, turning his glass not at the distant host, but to the hill nearly in front of them, "look, there are the French!"

The two generals and the adjutants reached after the glass, one taking it from the other. All the faces suddenly changed, and an expression of dismay came into them.

They expected to find the French two versts away, and there they were unexpectedly appearing right at hand.

"Is that the enemy?" .... "It can't be!" .... "Yes, look, they ...." "Certainly it is." .... "What does it mean?" exclaimed various voices.

Prince Andreï with his naked eye could see a dense mass of the French moving up at the right to meet the

Apsheron boys, not more than five hundred paces from the very spot where Kutuzof was standing.

"Here it is! the decisive moment is at hand! my chance has come!" said Prince Andreï, and starting up his horse he approached Kutuzof. "The Apsheron men ought to be halted, your eminence," he cried.

But at that very instant all became veiled in smoke; the rattle of musketry sounded near them, and a naïvely terrified voice only two steps from Prince Andreï cried: "Well, brothers, it's all up with us!" and this voice seemed to be a command. At this voice all started to run.

Confused but still constantly increasing throngs ran back by the very same place where five minutes before the troops had filed so proudly past the emperors. Not only was it hard to arrest these fugitives, but it was even impossible not to be borne back by the mob. Bolkonsky could only struggle not to let them pass him, and he gazed around, finding it quite out of the question to understand what was taking place at the front. Nesvitsky, with angry face, flushed and quite unlike himself, cried to Kutuzof that if he did not instantly come away, he would be probably taken prisoner. Kutuzof still stayed in the same place, and without answering took out his handkerchief. A stream of blood was trickling from his face. Prince Andreï forced his way through to where he was.

"You are wounded?" he asked, scarcely controlling the trembling of his lower jaw.

"The wound is not here, but yonder," said Kutuzof, pressing his handkerchief to his wounded cheek, and pointing to the fugitives. "Halt them!" he cried, and at the same time, evidently convinced that it was an impossibility to bring them to a halt, he gave spurs to his horse and rode off to the right. New masses of fugitives came pouring along like a torrent, engulfed him, and bore him along with them.

The troops were pouring back in such a dense throng, that when one was once entangled in the midst of it, there was great difficulty in extricating one's self. Some shouted: "He's coming, why don't you let him pass?" Others turned around and fired their muskets into the air; others struck the horse on which Kutuzof rode, but by the exercise of supreme force Kutuzof — accompanied by his staff, diminished by more than half — struggled through to the left and rode off in the direction of cannonading heard not far away.

Prince Andreï, also forcing his way through the throng of fugitives and endeavoring not to become separated from Kutuzof, could make out through the reek of gunpowder smoke a Russian battery on the side of the hill, still blazing away vigorously, while the French were just marching against it. A little higher up stood the Russian infantry, neither moving forward to the aid of the battery, nor back in the same direction with the fugitives. A general spurred down from this brigade of infantry and approached Kutuzof. Out of Kutuzof's staff only four men were left, and all were pale and silently exchanged glances.

"Stop those poltroons!" cried Kutuzof, all out of breath, as the regimental commander came up to him, and pointing to the fugitives; but at that very second, as if for a punishment for those words, like a bevy of birds a number of bullets flew buzzing over the heads of the regiment and of Kutuzof's staff. The French were charging the battery, and when they caught sight of Kutuzof they aimed at him.

At this volley, the regimental commander suddenly clapped his hand to his leg; a few soldiers fell, and an ensign standing with the flag dropped it from his hand; the flag reeled and fell, catching on the bayonets of the soldiers near him. The men began to load and fire without orders.

"O-o-o-okh!" groaned Kutuzof, with an expression of despair, and glanced around. "Bolkonsky," he whispered, his weak old man's voice trembling with emotion, "Bolkonsky!" he whispered, pointing to the demoralized battalion and at the enemy, "what does this mean?"

But before he had uttered these words, Prince Andreï,

conscious of the tears of shame and anger choking him, had already leaped from his horse and rushed toward the standard.

"Children, follow me!" he cried in his youthfully penetrating voice. "Here it is," thought Prince Andreï, as he seized the flagstaff; and he listened with rapture to the whizz of the bullets that were evidently directed straight at him. A number of the soldiers fell.

"Hurrah!" cried Prince Andreï, instantly seizing the flag and rushing forward with unfailing confidence that the whole battalion would follow him.

In fact he ran on only a few steps alone. Then one soldier was stirred, and then another, and the whole battalion with huzzas dashed forward and overtook him. A non-commissioned officer of the battalion, darting up to him, seized the standard, which from its weight shook in Prince Andreï's hand, but he was instantly shot down. Prince Andreï again grasped the flag and, dragging it along by the staff, hurried on with the battalion.

In front of him he saw our artillerymen, some fighting, others abandoning the guns and running toward him; he also saw the French infantry, who had seized the artillery horses, and were reversing the field-pieces.

Prince Andreï and the battalion were now only twenty paces distant from the battery. He heard the incessant *ping* of the bullets over his head, and the soldiers constantly groaning and falling at his left hand and at his right. But he did not look at them; his eyes were fastened only on what was going on in front of him, where the battery was. He now saw distinctly the figure of a red-headed artilleryman, with his shako half knocked off, and dragging with him an artillery sponge, while a French soldier was trying to pull it away from him. Prince Andreï distinguished clearly the distorted and angry faces of these two men, who evidently were not aware of what they were doing.

"What are they up to?" queried Prince Andreï, as he looked at them. "Why doesn't the red-headed artillerist run, if he has no weapons, and why doesn't the Frenchman finish him? He wouldn't have time to get any distance, though, before the Frenchman would recollect his musket, and put an end to him."

In point of fact another Frenchman, clubbing his musket, ran up to the combatants, and the fate of the red-headed artillerist, who had no idea of what was coming upon him, and had just triumphantly made himself master of the sponge, must have been sealed. But Prince Andreï did not witness the end of the struggle. It seemed to him that one of the approaching soldiers struck him in the head with the full weight of a heavy cudgel. It was rather painful, but his chief sensation was that of displeasure because this pain distracted his attention and prevented him from seeing what he had been looking at.

"What does this mean? Am I falling? Surely my legs are giving way," he said to himself, and he fell on his back. He opened his eyes, hoping to see how the struggle between the artilleryman and the Frenchman ended, and anxious to know whether the red-headed artillerist was killed or not, and the cannon saved or captured. But he could see nothing of it. Over him he could see only the sky, the lofty sky; not clear, but still immeasurably lofty, and with light gray clouds slowly wandering over it.

"How still, calm, and solemn! How entirely different from when I was running," said Prince Andreï to himself. "It was not so when we were all running, and shouting, and fighting; how entirely different it is from when the Frenchman and the artilleryman, with vindictive and frightened faces, were struggling for possession of the sponge: the clouds then were not floating over those infinite depths of sky as they are now. How is it that I never before saw this lofty sky? and how glad I am that I have learned to know it at last! Yes! all is empty, all is deception, except these infinite heavens. Nothing, nothing at all besides! And even that is nothing but silence and peace! And glory to God!...."

CHAPTER XVII

At nine o'clock the right wing, under Bagration, had not as yet begun to fight. Unwilling to acquiesce in Dolgorukof's urgency to begin the battle, and anxious to escape the responsibility, Prince Bagration proposed to the latter to send and make inquiries of the commander-in-chief. Bagration knew that, as the distance separating the two wings was almost ten versts, the messenger, if he were not killed, which was very probable, and even if he found the commander-in-chief, which would be extremely difficult, would not have time to return till late in the afternoon.

Bagration glanced over his staff with his great, expressionless, sleepy eyes, and was involuntarily attracted by Rostof's boyish face, full of excitement and hope. He chose him for the messenger.

"And if I should meet his majesty first, before I found the commander-in-chief, your illustriousness?" asked Rostof, touching his cap visor.

"You can give the message to his majesty," said Dolgorukof, taking the words out of Bagration's mouth.

After he was relieved at the outposts, Rostof had been able to catch a few hours' sleep before morning, and felt happy, daring, and resolute, with that elasticity of motion and confidence in his own good fortune, and in that state of mind, when everything seems easy, bright, and possible.

All his desires had been fulfilled that morning: a general engagement was to be fought; he was to take part in it; moreover, he had been made orderly on the staff of one of the bravest generals; nay, more, he was intrusted with a message to Kutuzof, and might have to deliver it to the sovereign himself!

The morning was clear and bright; the horse he rode was excellent. His heart was full of joy and courage. Having received his instructions, he struck in the spurs and galloped off along the line. At first, he passed in front of Bagration's forces, which had not as yet engaged, and were ranged in motionless ranks. Then he rode into the space occupied by Uvarof's cavalry, and here he began to remark some excitement and indications of readiness for battle; after passing Uvarof's cavalry he began to distinguish clearly the sounds of cannonading and musketry in front of him. The firing kept growing more violent.

In the fresh, clear morning air the sound of the firing was no longer, as at first, desultory at irregular intervals, two or three shots at a time, and then one or two cannon shots; but along the declivities of the hills in front of Pratzer was heard the crackling of musketry, dominated by such frequent reports from the heavy guns, that often a number of them could not be distinguished apart, but mingled in one general thunderous roar.

It could be seen how, over the mountain side, the puffs of smoke from the muskets seemed to run along, chasing one another, and how the great clouds of smoke from the cannon rolled whirling up, spread and mingled in the air. By the glint of bayonets through the smoke, the masses of infantry could be seen moving along, and the narrow ribbons of artillery with their green caissons.

Rostof reined in his horse on a hilltop for a moment, in order to watch what was going on; but in spite of the closeness of his scrutiny, he could not make out or decide for himself from what he saw what men were moving in the smoke, or what bodies of the troops were hurrying this way and that, back and forth.

"But why? Who are they? Where are they going?" It was impossible to tell.

This spectacle did not arouse in him any melancholy or timid feelings; on the contrary they filled him with new energy and zeal.

"Well, then, give it to them again!" said he, mentally replying to these sounds, and again he started on a gallop along the lines, making his way farther and farther within the domain of the troops already now entering into the action.

"How this is going to turn out yonder I do not know, but it will be all right!" thought Rostof.

Having passed by some of the troops of the Austrian army, Rostof noticed that the portion of the Line next — they were the Guards — were already moving to the attack.

"So much the better, I can see it close at hand!" he said to himself.

He was now riding along almost at the very front. A number of horsemen were galloping in his direction. These were our Leib-Uhlans, who, with broken and disorderly ranks, were returning from the charge. Rostof passed them and could not help noticing that one of them was covered with blood, but he galloped on.

"That's of no consequence to me," he said to himself.

He had ridden only a few hundred paces farther when he perceived at his left, cutting him off, an immense body of cavalry on coal-black horses and in brilliant white uniforms. They extended the whole length of the field and were galloping straight at him.

Rostof spurred his horse at full speed so as to get out of the way of these cavalrymen, and he would easily have distanced them had they kept on at the same pace all the time, but they rode faster and faster, and some of the horses were almost upon him. Rostof distinguished more and more clearly the trampling of their hoofs and the jingling of their arms, and could see more and more distinctly their horses, their figures, and their faces. These were our "Cavalier-guards" on their way to charge the French cavalry who were deploying to meet them.

The Cavalier-guards came galloping along, but still kept their horses under restraint. Rostof could already see their faces and hear the word of command, — *Marsch! marsch!* — spoken by the officer who was urging on his blooded charger.

Rostof, afraid of being crushed or carried away into the charge against the French, spurred along the front with all the speed that he could get out of his horse,

and still it seemed as if he were going to fail of it.
The last rider in the Line, a pock-marked man of giant
frame, frowned angrily when he saw Rostof in front
of him, knowing that they must infallibly come into
collision. This Guardsman would surely have over-
thrown Rostof, — for Rostof himself could not help
seeing how small and slight he and Bedouin were in
comparison with these tremendous men and horses, —
if he had not had the presence of mind to shake his
riding-whip in the eyes of the Guardsman's horse.

The charger, black as a coal, heavy and tall, shied,
cropping back his ears, but the pock-marked rider plunged
his huge spurs into his side with all his might, and the
charger, arching his tail and stretching out his neck,
rushed onward faster than ever. Rostof was hardly out
of the way of the Guardsmen when he heard their
hurrah, and glancing around saw that their front ranks
were already mingling with strange horsemen with red
epaulets, apparently the French. Farther away it was
impossible to see anything, because immediately after
this, on the other side, the cannon began to belch forth
smoke, and everything was shrouded.

At the moment the Guardsmen dashed past him and
were lost to view in the smoke, Rostof was undecided in
his own mind whether he should gallop after them or
go where his duty called him.

This was that brilliant "Charge of the Cavalier-guards"
which the French themselves so much admired. It was
terrible for Rostof when he heard afterward, that out of
all that throng of handsome young giants, out of all
those brilliant, rich young men, officers and yunkers
mounted on splendid chargers who galloped past him,
only eighteen were left alive after the charge.

"Why should I envy them? My turn will come,
and perhaps I shall see the sovereign very soon now,"
thought Rostof, and he galloped on.

When he came up to the infantry of the Guards, his
attention was called to the fact that shot and shell were
flying over them and around them, not so much because
he heard the sounds of the missiles as because he saw

dismay on the faces of the soldiers and an unnatural martial solemnity on the faces of the officers.

As he was riding behind one of the infantry regiments of the Guard, he heard a voice calling him by name:—

"Rostof!"

"What is it?" he replied, not seeing that it was Borís.

"What do you think of this? We were put in the front line. Our regiment has been in a charge," said Borís, smiling with the happy smile that young men wear when they have been for the first time under fire.

Rostof drew up.

"Have you, indeed!" said he, "and how was it?"

"We drove them back," said Borís, eagerly, and becoming talkative. "You can imagine."

And Borís began to relate how the Guards, as they stood in their places and saw troops in front of them, at first mistook them for Austrians, and then suddenly, by the shots that came flying over from these same troops, recognized that they were in the front line and unexpectedly engaged in the conflict. Rostof, not stopping to hear Borís to the end of his story, started his horse.

"Where are you bound?"

"To his majesty, with a message."

"There he is," said Borís, who supposed that Rostof wanted his highness instead of his majesty, and therefore directed him to the grand duke, who was standing not a hundred paces away. Dressed in a helmet and a Cavalier-guard *kolet*, or jacket, with elevated shoulders and frowning face, he was shouting something to a pale Austrian officer in a white uniform.

"No! that's the grand duke, but my errand is to the commander-in-chief or to the emperor," said Rostof, and was just getting his horse under way.

"Count! count!" cried Berg, who, no less excited than Borís had been, came running up from the other side, "count, I have been wounded in my right arm," said he, pointing to his wrist, which was bloody and wrapped up in a handkerchief, "and I stayed at the **front**. Count, I shall have to hold my sword in my left hand. In the Von Berg family, count, all of us have been knights!"

Berg was saying something more, but Rostof, not stopping to listen to him, was already far away.

Passing by the Guards and across a vacant space, Rostof in order not to get into the front again, as he had been, when he was caught by the charge of the Cavalier-guards, rode along the line of the reserves, making a considerable detour of the place where the most violent cannonade and musketry firing was heard. Suddenly he heard loud volleys of musketry before him and behind our troops, in a place where he would never have suspected the presence of the enemy.

"What can that mean?" wondered Rostof. "Can the enemy have outflanked us? It cannot be," said he to himself, and a horror of fear for himself and for the success of the battle suddenly came over him. "Whatever it is, however," he thought, "now there's no avoiding it. I must find the commander-in-chief here, and if all is lost, then it is my place to perish with the rest."

The gloomy presentiment which had suddenly come over him was more and more made certainty the farther he rode into the fields behind the village of Pratz, occupied by throngs of demoralized troops.

"What does this mean? What can this mean? At whom are they firing? Who is firing?" he inquired, as he overtook Russian and Austrian soldiers running in confused throngs across his path.

"The devil only knows! He has beaten us all. All is lost," answered the throngs of the fugitives in Russian, in German, and in Bohemian, and they could tell no better than he himself could what was going on there.

"Hang the Germans!" cried one.

"The devil take 'em, the traitors!"

"*Zum Henker diese Russen* — to the devil with these Russians," stammered some German.

A number of wounded were wandering down the road. Curses, cries, groans, mingled in one general uproar. The firing ceased; as Rostof afterward heard, Russian and Austrian soldiers had fired at each other.

"*Bozhe moï!*— My God, what does this mean? thought Rostof. "And here where any minute the emperor might see them. But no! these were apparently only a few cowards. This is only transient, this is nothing! it cannot be," he said to himself; "I must get by them as soon as possible."

The idea of a defeat and of a total defeat could not enter Rostof's head. Although he could see the French cannon and troops on the Pratzer, on the very place where he had been commanded to find the commander-in-chief, he could not and would not believe this.

CHAPTER XVIII

ROSTOF had been told that he should find Kutuzof and the emperor somewhere in the vicinity of the village of Pratz. But they were not to be found there, nor was a single officer in sight, but everywhere throngs of fleeing troops of all nationalities.

He spurred on his horse, which was already growing fagged, so as to pass by these fugitives as quickly as possible; but the farther he went, the more demoralized he found the forces. Along the highroad where he was riding, carriages and equipages of all sorts were crowded together, Russian and Austrian soldiers of all the different branches of the service, wounded and not wounded. All this mass hummed and confusedly swarmed under the dispiriting sounds of the shells fired from French batteries posted on the heights of the Pratzer.

"Where is the emperor? Where is Kutuzof?" asked Rostof of every one whom he could bring to a stop, but not one would answer his question.

At last seizing a soldier by the collar, he obliged him to reply.

"Eh! brother! They've all been yonder this long time — all cut sticks!" said the soldier, laughing for some reason and breaking away.

Releasing this soldier, who was evidently drunk, Rostof managed to stop the denshchik, — or groom of some person of consequence, — and began to ply him with questions. The denshchik told Rostof that the emperor had been driven by an hour before at full speed in a carriage along this same road, and that the emperor had been wounded.

"It cannot be," said Rostof; "it must have been some one else."

"I myself saw him," said the denshchik, with a self-satisfied laugh, "I ought to know the sovereign by sight; I should like to know how many times I have seen him in Petersburg! He leaned back in the carriage and was pale, very pale. Heavens! what a rate those four black horses thundered by us here; I should think I might know the Tsar's horses, and Ilya Ivanuitch! I guess Ilya, the coachman, would n't be very likely to drive by with any one less than the Tsar!"

Rostof gave his horse the spur and started to ride farther. A wounded officer passing by turned to him.

"Who was it you wanted?" asked the officer; "the commander-in-chief? He was killed by a cannon-ball; hit him in the chest, right at the head of our regiment."

"Not killed! only wounded," said another officer.

"Who? Kutuzof?" asked Rostof.

"No, not Kutuzof, but what do you call him — ah, well, it 's all the same. Not many are left alive. If you go down yonder, yonder to that village, you 'll find all the commanders gathered," said this officer, pointing to the village of Gostieradeck, and he passed on.

Rostof walked his horse, not knowing now where to go or whom to seek. The sovereign wounded! the battle lost! Even now it was impossible to believe that. Rostof rode away in the direction indicated by the officer; in the distance could be seen towers and a church. What need was there of his hurrying? What had he now to say to the sovereign or to Kutuzof, even if they were alive and not wounded?

"That road; take that road, your nobility, else they 'll shoot you down, yonder!" cried a soldier to him. "They 'll shoot you!"

"Oh, what are you talking about?" cried another. "That's the nearest way to where he is going."

Rostof considered a moment and then rode in exactly the direction where they said that he would be killed.

"Now it's all the same to me; if the sovereign is wounded, why should I try to save my life?" he asked himself. He rode out on the open space where there had been the heaviest slaughter of the men escaping from Pratz. The French had not yet occupied this place, and the Russians — that is those who were alive or only slightly wounded — had long before abandoned it. On the ground, like shocks of corn on a fertile field, lay men in tens, in dozens, killed or wounded, on every rood of the place.

The wounded had crawled together, two or three at a time, and their cries and groans could be heard most gruesomely, though it seemed to Rostof that they were often simulated. He put his horse at a trot, so as not to see all these suffering men, and a great horror came over him. He was not afraid for his own life; but lest he should lose the manliness, which he felt was essential to him, he knew that he could not endure the spectacle of those unfortunate wretches.

The French had ceased to fire on this field strewn with dead and wounded, because there was no longer any sign of life on it; but when they caught sight of the adjutant riding across, they turned one of their cannon on it, and sent a few balls after him. The sensation caused by these terrific whistling sounds, and the spectacle of the dead around him, aroused in Rostof's mind an impression of horror and self-commiseration. He recalled his mother's last letter. "How would she feel," he asked himself, "if she should see me now, here in this field, with those cannon pointed at me?"

At the village of Gostieradeck the Russian troops were retiring from the field of battle in good order, though the regiments were mixed together. This was out of range of the French cannon-balls, and the firing sounded more distant. Here all clearly saw and openly confessed that the battle was lost. No one to whom

Rostof applied for information could tell him where the emperor or Kutuzof was. Some declared that the report about the sovereign being wounded was correct, others denied it and explained this false though widespread rumor by the fact that the Ober-hofmarshal, Count Tolstoï, who had gone out in company of others of the suite to see the battle, had dashed away, pale and frightened, from the field of battle in the emperor's carriage.

One officer told Rostof that in the rear of a village, over toward the left, he had seen some officials of high rank, and Rostof started in that direction, not indeed with the expectation of finding any one, but merely for the sake of clearing his conscience.

After riding three versts and passing beyond the last of the Russian troops, Rostof reached an orchard protected by a ditch, and saw two riders standing near the ditch. One, with a white plume in his hat, had a familiar look; the other rider, whom he did not know, was mounted on a handsome chestnut charger, — this charger somehow seemed familiar to Rostof, — and rode up to the ditch, put spurs to his horse, and giving him his head easily leaped the ditch into the orchard. The earth merely crumbled away a little from the embankment under the horse's hind hoofs. Turning his horse short, he leaped back over the ditch again, and addressed himself respectfully to the rider with the white plume, apparently urging him to do the same thing. The rider, whose figure Rostof seemed to recognize, and had therefore involuntarily attracted his attention, shook his head and made a gesture of refusal with his hand, and Rostof immediately, by this gesture, knew that it was his idolized, lamented sovereign.

"But it cannot be that he is left alone in this bare field!" thought Rostof. Just then Alexander turned his head, so that he had a good view of those beloved features so sharply graven on his memory. The sovereign was pale, his cheeks sunken, and his eyes cavernous, but there was all the more charm, all the more sweetness, in his features. Rostof was delighted to be convinced that the rumor of the sovereign's wound was false. He was happy to have seen him. He knew that he might, nay, that he ought to, go straight up to him and deliver the message that had been intrusted to him by Dolgorukof.

But just as a young man in love trembles and loses his presence of mind, not daring to say what he has been dreaming about night after night, and timidly looks around, in search of help or the possibility of postponing it, when the wished-for moment has at last arrived and he is alone with her; so also with Rostof, now that he had attained what he had yearned for more than all else in the world: he did not know how to approach his sovereign, and devised a thousand excuses for finding it untimely, improper, and impossible.

"What! I might seem to be taking advantage of his being alone and dejected. An unknown face at this moment of sorrow might seem unpleasant and troublesome; besides, what could I say to him now, when one glance from him makes my heart swell within me and seem to leap into my mouth."

Not one of those innumerable speeches which he had so carefully prepared in case he should meet the emperor now recurred to his mind. Those speeches were, for the most part, composed under different conditions; they were to be spoken at the moment of victory and triumph; above all on his death-bed, when, as he sank under the wounds that he had received, his sovereign would come to see him, and thank him for his heroic conduct, and he would thus show him his love sealed by his death.

"Besides, what now could I ask the emperor in regard to his commands to the left wing when now already it is four o'clock in the afternoon, and the battle is lost. No, really, I ought not to trouble him. I ought not to break in upon his reflections. It would be better to die a thousand times than to receive an angry look or an angry word from him."

Such was Rostof's decision, and melancholy and with despair in his heart he rode away, constantly glancing back at the emperor, still remaining in the same unde-

cided attitude. While Rostof was making these reflections, and sadly rode away from his sovereign, Captain
von Toll galloped up to the same place, and seeing the
emperor went straight up to him, offered him his services,
and helped him to cross the ditch on foot. The emperor, wishing to rest and feeling ill, sat down under
an apple tree, and Toll stood near him. Rostof looked
from afar, and saw with jealousy and regret how Von
Toll talked long and eagerly to the sovereign, and how
the sovereign, apparently weeping, covered his eyes
with one hand and with the other pressed Von Toll's.

"And I might have done that in his place," thought
Rostof, and with difficulty restraining the tears of sympathy for his sovereign, he rode away in utter despair,
not knowing now where he should go or for what reason.

His despair was all the more bitter because he felt
that his own weakness was the cause of his misfortune.

He might — not only might, but he ought to — have
ridden up to the emperor. And this was his only
chance of exhibiting to the sovereign his devotion. And
he did not take advantage of it. "Why did I do so?"
he asked himself, and he turned his horse about and
galloped back to the same place where the emperor had
been sitting; but there was no one any longer on the
other side of the ditch. Only a train of baggage-wagons and carriages was winding along.

From one of the wagoners, Rostof learned that Kutuzof's staff were not very far away, at the village where
the wagons were bound. Rostof followed them.

The foremost in the train was Kutuzof's groom, leading a horse with his trappings. The wagons followed
behind the groom, and behind the wagon walked an
old man, a household serf with bandy legs, wearing a
cap and a short shuba.

"Tīt! ah! Tīt!" cried the groom.

"What is it?" asked the old man, heedlessly.

"Tīt! Tīt! grind the wheat!"

"E! durak! tfu!" said the old man, angrily spitting.
Some time passed in silence, as they moved onward, and
then the same joking rhyme was repeated.

By five o'clock in the evening the battle was lost at every point.   More than a hundred cannon had already fallen into the hands of the French.   Prsczebiszewsky and his battalion had laid down their arms.   The other columns, having lost more than half their efficient, were retreating in disorderly, demoralized throngs.

The relics of Langeron and Dokhturof's forces, all in confusion, were crowded together around the ponds, on the dikes and banks of the village of Augest.

By six o'clock the only cannonading that was any longer heard was directed at the dike of Augest by some of the French, who had established a large battery on the slopes of the Pratzer, and were trying to cut down our men as they retreated.   At the rear, Dokhturof and some others, having collected their battalions, made a stand against the French, who were pursuing our troops.

It had begun to be entirely dark.   On the narrow dike of Augest, where for so many years the little old miller had peacefully sat with his hook and line, while his grandson with shirt-sleeves rolled up played in the water-can with the flapping silver fish ; on that dike, over which the Moravians, in shaggy caps and blue blouses, had driven their two-horse teams loaded down with spring wheat, and returned dusted with flour and with whitened teams ; along this same dike, this narrow dike, among vans and field-pieces, under the feet of horses, and between the wheels, crowded a throng of men, their faces distorted with fear of death, pushing one another, expiring, trampling on the dying and dead, and crushing one another, only to be themselves killed a few steps farther on.

Every ten seconds a cannon-ball, compressing the air, flew by, or a shell came bursting amid this dense throng, dealing death and spattering with blood those who stood near by.   Dolokhof, wounded in the arm, on foot, with ten men of his company — he was now an officer again — and his regimental commander, on horseback, con stituted the sole survivors of the whole regiment.   Car. ried along in the throng, they were crowded together at the very entrance of the dike, and, pressed on all sides, were obliged to halt, because a horse attached to a field-piece had fallen, and the throng were trying to drag it along.

One cannon-ball struck some one behind them, another struck just in front, and spattered Dolokhof with blood. The crowd, in desperation, pressed on, squeezing together, and then, after advancing a few steps, halted again.

"If we could only make those hundred paces, and safety is sure; if we stay here two minutes longer, our destruction is certain!" said each one to himself.

Dolokhof, standing in the midst of the throng, forced his way through to the edge of the dike, knocking down two soldiers, and sprang out on the glare ice that covered the pond.

"Turn out this way!" he cried, sliding along on the ice, which bent under his weight. "Turn out," he cried to the gunner, "it will hold! it will hold!"

The ice held him, but it yielded and cracked, and it was evident that it would immediately give way, if not under his weight alone, certainly under that of the field-piece or the throng of men. They looked at him, and crowded along the shore, not venturing to step upon the ice. The commander of the regiment, sitting on horse-back at the entrance, was just raising his hand and opening his mouth to speak to Dolokhof, when suddenly a cannon-ball flew so close over the men that they all ducked their heads. There was a dull thud as if something soft were struck, and the general fell from his horse in a pool of blood. No one looked at the general or thought of picking him up.

"Come on the ice!" .... "Cross the ice!" .... "Come on!" .... "Move on! Don't you hear? Come!" was heard suddenly from innumerable voices, after the cannon-ball had struck the general, though the men knew not what or why they were crying.

One of the last field-pieces that was just entering on the dike ventured on the ice. A throng of soldiers started down from the ground on the frozen pond. One of the rearmost soldiers broke through, one leg slumping down into the water. He tried to save himself and sank up to his belt. The men who stood nearest held back; the driver of the field-piece drew in his horses, but still behind them were heard the shouts: —

"Take to the ice!".... "What are you stopping for?" .... "Take to the ice!".... "Take to the ice!" and cries of horror were heard among the throng. The soldiers surrounding the gun gesticulated over their horses, and beat them to make them turn and go on. The horses struck out from the shore. The ice, which might have held the foot-soldiers, gave way in one immense sheet, and forty men who were on it threw themselves, some forward and some back, trampling on one another.

All the time the cannon-balls kept regularly whistling by and falling on the ice, into the water, and, more frequently than all, into the mass of men that covered the dike, the pond, and the banks.

CHAPTER XIX

On the Pratzer hill, in the same spot where he had fallen with the flagstaff in his hand, lay Prince Andreï Bolkonsky, his life-blood oozing away, and unconsciously groaning, with light, pitiful groans, like an ailing child.

By evening, he ceased to groan, and lay absolutely still. He did not know how long his unconsciousness continued. Suddenly, he became conscious that he was alive, and suffering from a burning and tormenting pain in his head.

"Where is that lofty heaven which I had never seen before, and which I saw to-day?" That was his first thought. "And I never knew such pain as this, either," he said to himself. "Yes, I have never known anything, anything like this, till now. But where am I?"

He tried to listen, and heard the trampling hoofs of several horses approaching, and the sounds of voices, talking French. He opened his eyes. Over him still stretched the same lofty heavens, with clouds sailing over it in still loftier heights, and beyond them he could see the depths of endless blue. He did not turn his head or look at those who, to judge from the hoof beats of the horses and the sounds of the voices, rode up to him and paused.

These horsemen were Napoleon, accompanied by two aides. Bonaparte, who had been riding over the field of battle, had given orders to strengthen the battery that was cannonading the dike of Augest, and was now looking after the killed and wounded left on the battle-field.

"Handsome men!" said Napoleon, gazing at a Russian grenadier, who lay on his belly with his face half buried in the soil, and his neck turning black, and one arm flung out and stiffened in death.

"The ammunition for the field-guns is exhausted, sire!"

"Have that of the reserves brought," said Napoleon, and then a step or two nearer he paused over Prince Andreï, who lay on his back with the flagstaff clutched in his hands (the flag had been carried off by the French as a trophy).

"*Voilà, une belle mort,*" said Napoleon, gazing at Bolkonsky. Prince Andreï realized that this was said of him, and that it was spoken by Napoleon. He heard them address the speaker as "sire." But he heard these words as if they had been the buzzing of a fly. He was not only not interested in them, but they made no impression upon him, and he immediately forgot them. His head throbbed as with fire; he felt that his life-blood was ebbing, and he still saw far above him the distant, eternal heavens. He knew that this was Napoleon, his hero; but at this moment, Napoleon seemed to him merely a small, insignificant man in comparison with that lofty, infinite heaven, with the clouds flying over it. It was a matter of utter indifference to him who stood looking down on him, or what was said about him at that moment. He was merely conscious of a feeling of joy that people had come to him, and of a desire for these people to give him assistance and bring him back to life, which seemed to him so beautiful: because he understood it so differently now. He collected all his strength to move and make some sound. He managed to move his leg slightly, and uttered a weak, feeble, sickly moan which stirred pity even in himself.

"Ah! he is alive!" said Napoleon. "Take up this young man, and take him to the temporary hospital."

Having given this order, Napoleon rode on to meet Marshal Lannes, who, removing his hat and smiling, rode up and congratulated him on the victory.

Prince Andreï recollected nothing further; he lost consciousness in consequence of the terrible pain caused by those who placed him on the stretcher, and by the jolting as he was carried along, and by the probing of the wound. He recovered it again only at the very end of the day, as he was carried to the hospital together with other Russians wounded and taken prisoner. At this time, he felt a little fresher and was able to glance around and even to speak.

The first words he heard after he came to were spoken by a French officer in charge of the convoy, who said: —

"We must stop here; the emperor is coming by immediately; it will give him pleasure to see these prisoners."

"There are so many prisoners to-day, — almost the whole Russian army, — I should think it would have become a bore to him," said another officer.

"Well, at all events, this man here, they say, was the commander of all the Emperor Alexander's Guards," said the first speaker, indicating a wounded Russian officer in a white Cavalier-guards uniform. Bolkonsky recognized Prince Repnin, whom he had met in Petersburg society. Next him was a youth of nineteen, an officer of the Cavalier-guard also wounded.

Bonaparte coming up at a gallop reined in his horse.

"Who is the chief officer here?" he asked, looking at the wounded.

They pointed to Colonel Prince Repnin.

"Were you the commander of the Emperor Alexander's Horse-guard regiment?" asked Napoleon.

"I commanded a squadron," replied Repnin.

"Your regiment did its duty with honor," remarked Napoleon.

"Praise from a great commander is the highest reward that a soldier can have," said Repnin.

"It is with pleasure that I give it to you," replied Napoleon. "Who is this young man next you?"

Prince Repnin named Lieutenant Sukhtelen.

Napoleon glanced at him and said with a smile: "He is very young to oppose us."

"Youth does not prevent one from being brave," replied Sukhtelen in a broken voice.

"A beautiful answer," said Napoleon. "Young man, you will get on in the world."

Prince Andreï, who had been placed also in the front rank, under the eyes of the emperor, so as to swell the number of those who had been taken prisoner, naturally attracted his attention. Napoleon evidently remembered having seen him on the field, and turning to him he used exactly the same expression, "young man," as when Bolkonsky had the first time come under his notice.

"*Et vous, jeune homme.* — Well, and you, young man?" said he, addressing him. "How do you feel, *mon brave?*"

Although five minutes before this Prince Andreï had been able to say a few words to the soldiers who were bearing him, now he fixed his eyes directly on Napoleon, but had nothing to say..... To him at this moment all the interests occupying Napoleon seemed so petty, his former hero himself, with his small vanity and delight in the victory, seemed so sordid in comparison with that high, true, and just heaven which he had seen and learned to understand; and that was why he could not answer him.

Yes, and everything seemed to him so profitless and insignificant in comparison with that stern and majestic train of thought induced in his mind by his lapsing strength, as his life-blood ebbed away, by his suffering and the near expectation of death. As Prince Andreï looked into Napoleon's eyes, he thought of the insignificance of majesty, of the insignificance of life, the meaning of which no one could understand, and of the still greater insignificance of death, the thought of which no one could among men understand or explain.

The emperor, without waiting for any answer, turned away, and as he started to ride on, said to one of the officers : —

"Have these gentlemen looked after and conveyed to my bivouac; have Doctor Larrey himself look after their wounds. *Au revoir*, Prince Repnin," and he touched the spurs to his horse and galloped away.

His face was bright with self-satisfaction and happiness.

The soldiers carrying Prince Andreï had taken from him the golden medallion which the Princess Maríya had hung around her brother's neck; but when they saw the flattering way in which the emperor treated the prisoners, they hastened to return the medallion.

Prince Andreï did not see how or by whom the medallion was replaced, but he suddenly discovered on his chest, outside of his uniform, the little image attached to its slender golden chain.

"It would be good," thought Prince Andreï, letting his eyes rest on the medallion which his sister had hung around his neck with so much feeling and reverence, "it would be good if everything were as clear and simple as it seems to the Princess Maríya. How good it would be to know where to find help in this life, and what to expect after it, — beyond the grave! How happy and composed I should be, if I could say now, 'Lord have mercy on me!' But to whom can I say that! Is it force — impalpable, incomprehensible, which I cannot turn to, or even express in words; is it the great All or nothingness," said he to himself, "or is it God which is sewed in this amulet which the Princess Maríya gave me? Nothing, nothing is certain, except the insignificance of all within my comprehension, and the majesty of that which is incomprehensible but all-important."

The stretcher started off. At every jolt he again felt the insufferable pain, his fever grew more violent, and he began to be delirious. The dreams about his father, his wife, his sister, and his unborn son, and the feeling of tenderness which he had experienced on the night before the battle, the figure of the little insignificant Napoleon, and above all the lofty sky, formed the principal content of his feverish imaginations.

He seemed to be living a quiet life amid calm, domestic happiness at Luisiya Gorui. He was beginning to take delight in this blissful existence, when suddenly the little Napoleon appeared with his unsympathetic, shallow-minded face, expressing happiness at the unhappiness of others, and once more doubts began to arise and torment him, and only the skies seemed to promise healing balm.

Toward morning all his imaginations were utterly confused and blurred in the chaos and fogs of unconsciousness and forgetfulness, which much more likely, according to the opinion of Doctor Larrey, Napoleon's physician, would end with death than recovery.

"He is of a nervous and bilious temperament — he won't recover."

Prince Andreï, together with other prisoners hopelessly wounded, was turned over to the care of the natives of the region.

PART FOURTH

CHAPTER I

AT the beginning of the year 1806, Nicholaï Rostof went home on furlough. Denísof was also going to his home in Voronezh, and Rostof persuaded him to accompany him to Moscow and make him a visit. At the next to the last post station, Denísof fell in with a comrade, and drank three bottles of wine with him; and on the way to Moscow, in spite of the cradle-holes on the road, did not once wake up, but lay stretched out in the bottom of the post-sledge, next Rostof, who, in proportion as they approached the city, grew more and more impatient.

"Faster! faster! oh, these intolerable streets, shops, kalatchi,[1] lanterns, cab-drivers!" thought Rostof, when, having left their names at the city gates, as visitors on furlough, they had fairly entered the city.

"Denísof! we are here! — He's asleep!" he exclaimed, leaning forward with his whole body, as if by this motion he could hope to increase the speed of the sledge. Denísof made no answer.

"There is the cross street, where Zakhar, the izvoshchik, used to stand; and there is Zakhar himself, and the same horse! And here's the shop where we used to buy gingerbread! Can't you hurry, there?"

"Which house?" asked the postilion.

"That one yonder, on the corner, that big one, can't you see? That's our house!" said Rostof. "There that's our house! — Denísof! Denísof! we shall be there in a moment!"

Denísof lifted his head, coughed, and made no answer.

---

[1] *Kalatch:* a sort of wheaten bread, made of thin dough, peculiar to Russia.

"Dmitri," said Rostof, calling to his valet on the coachman's seat, "there's a light in our house, is n't there?"

"Certainly there is; there's a light in your father's room."

"They can't have gone to bed yet? Hey? What do you think? See here! Don't you forget it, I want my new Hungarian coat taken out," he added, stroking his young mustache. "Now, then, a little farther," he cried to the postilion. "Here, wake up, Vasha," turning to Denísof, who had again let his head fall back. "Come, now, get along, three silver rubles for vodka, get on!" shouted Rostof, when the sledge was within three doors of his own entrance. It seemed to him that the horses did not move. At last the sledge drew up at the entrance at the right. Over his head, Rostof saw the well-known cornice, with the peeling stucco, the front doorsteps, the curbstone. He leaped out before the sledge had stopped, and rushed into the entry. The house stood as cold and motionless as if it had no concern with the one who was entering its portals. There was no one in the entry.

"My God! has anything happened?" thought Rostof, with a sinking at the heart, standing still for a minute, and then starting to run along the entry and up the well-known winding stairs. There was still the same old door handle, the untidiness of which always annoyed the countess, as loose and as much askew as ever. In the anteroom burned a single tallow candle.

The old Mikháïla was asleep on the chest. Prokófi, the hall boy, who was so strong that he could lift a coach by the back, was sitting making shoes out of selvage. As the door opened he looked up, and his sleepy, indifferent expression of countenance suddenly changed to one of awe and even fright.

"Heavens and earth! The young count!" he cried, as soon as he recognized his young master. "How does it happen, my dear boy?" [1]

And Prokófi, trembling with emotion, rushed through

[1] *Galúbchik.*

the door into the drawing-room, evidently with the intention of announcing the good news; but then, on second thought, he came back and fell on the young barin's neck.

"All well?" asked Rostof, drawing away his arm.

"Yes! glory to God, glory to God! Only just done dinner! Let us have a look at you, your illustriousness!"

"Are they all perfectly happy?"

"Glory to God! glory to God!"

Rostof, entirely forgetting about Denísof, and not wishing any one to announce his arrival, pulled off his fur shuba, and ran on his tiptoes into the great dark drawing-room. Everything was the same: the same card-tables, the chandelier still in its covering. But some of the family must have seen the young barin, and hardly had he entered the drawing-room before something flew out from one of the adjoining rooms like a tornado, hugged him and began to kiss him. Then a second, and still a third object came leaping out of a second and third side door; more embraces more kisses, more shouts, tears of joy! He could not tell which was papa, or which was Natasha, or which was Petya! All were shouting, talking, and kissing him at one and the same time. Suddenly, he discovered that his mother was not among them.

"And here I knew nothing about it, ... Nikolushka, ... my darling!"

"Here he is .... ours again .... my darling, Kolya. .... How you have changed! .... There are no lights! Bring tea!"

"Now kiss me!"

"Dushenka, dear heart, ... and me too!"

Sonya, Natasha, Petya, Anna Mikhaïlovna, Viera, the old count, were all embracing him; and the servants and the maids, crowding into the room, were exclaiming and oh-ing and ah-ing.

Petya, clinging to his legs, kept crying, "Me, too!"

Natasha, after having thrown her arms around him and kissed him repeatedly all over his face, ran behind him, and seizing him by the tail of his coat, was jumping up and down like a goat, in the same spot, and squealing at the top of her voice.

On all sides of him were eyes gleaming with tears of joy and love; on all sides were lips ready to be kissed.

Sonya, red as kumatch,[1] also held him by the hand, and all radiant with affection, gazed into his eyes which she had been so longing to see. Sonya was now just past sixteen, and was very pretty, especially at this moment of joyous, triumphant excitement. She looked at him, without dropping her eyes, smiling, and almost holding her breath. He looked at her gratefully, but still he was all the time waiting and looking for some one else. The old countess had not yet made her appearance.

And now steps were heard at the doorway — steps so quick that they could not be his mother's.

But it was his mother in a gown which he had never seen before, one that had been finished since he was gone. All made way for him, and he ran to her. When they met, she fell on his heart, sobbing. She could not lift her face, and only pressed it against the cold silver braid of his Hungarian coat. Denísof, coming into the room unobserved by any one, stood there also, and as he looked at them, he wiped his eyes.

"Vasíli Denísof, the fwiend of your son," said he, introducing himself to the count, who looked at him with a questioning expression.

"I beg your pardon. I know, I know," said the count, embracing Denísof and kissing him. "Niko-lushka wrote. .... Natasha, Viera, here is Denísof."

The same happy, enthusiastic faces were turned upon Denísof's shaggy figure, and crowded around him.

"My dear[2] Denísof," screamed Natasha; and forgetting herself in her excitement and running to him, she threw her arms around him and kissed him. All were abashed at Natasha's escapade. Denísof also reddened, but smiled, and taking Natasha's hand, kissed it.

Denísof was conducted to the room that had been

[1] A kind of fustian. [2] *Galúbchik.*

prepared for him, but the Rostofs all collected in the divan-room around Nikolushka.

The old countess not letting go his hand, which she kept kissing every minute, sat next him. The others standing around them watched his every motion, word, glance, and could not take from him their enthusiastically loving eyes.

The brother and sisters quarreled and disputed with each other for places next him, and vied with each other in bringing him his tea, his handkerchief, his pipe.

Rostof was very happy in the love which they showed him, but the first moment of the meeting had been so beatific that his present happiness seemed a little tame, and he kept desiring and expecting something more and more, and yet more.

The next morning the travelers slept straight on till ten o'clock.

In the adjoining room there was a confusion of sabers, valises, sabretashes, opened trunks, muddy boots. Two pairs of boots cleaned and with brightened spurs had just been brought up and set along the wall. Servants were carrying wash-hand basins, hot water for shaving, and well-brushed clothes.

There was an odor of tobacco and of *men*.

"Hey! Gwishka! bwing my pipe!" cried Vaska Denísof, in his hoarse voice. "Wostof, wouse yourself!"

Rostof, rubbing his sleepy eyes, lifted his disheveled head from his warm pillow.

"What is it? late?"

"Late! It's after ten o'clock," cried Natasha's voice in answer to his question, and in the next room was heard the rustling of starched dresses, the whispering and giggling of the girls, and through the crack of the door could be seen a flash of something blue — ribbons, dark locks, and bright faces. This was Natasha with Sonya and Petya, who came to find out whether their friends were up.

"Nikolenka! get up!" again was heard in Natasha's voice at the door.

"Directly!"

But at this instant Petya in the first room, having spied and appropriated a saber, and experiencing that enthusiasm which little lads usually feel at the sight of their elder brothers of the army, and forgetting that it was unbecoming for the girls to see men undressed, pushed open the door.

"Is this your saber?" he cried. The maidens sprang away. Denísof, with startled eyes, hid his hairy legs under the counterpane, looking at his comrade for help.

The door let Petya through, and then closed on him. A sound of giggling was heard behind it.

"Nikolenka, come out in your dressing-gown!" said Natasha's voice.

"Is this your saber," insisted Petya, "or is it yours?" addressing with deepest respect the dark-mustached Denísof.

Rostof hastily put on his shoes and stockings, threw his dressing-gown over his shoulders, and went out. Natasha had put on one of his spurred boots and was just slipping her foot into the other. Sonya, as he came in, was whirling round and trying to make a balloon of her skirts and then squat down. Both were dressed alike in new blue dresses, and were fresh, rosy, full of spirits. Sonya ran away, but Natasha, putting her arm in her brother's, drew him into the divan-room and the two began to talk. They immediately began an endless series of questions and answers in regard to a thousand trifles that would interest no one else but themselves. Natasha laughed at every word that he said and that she said, not because there was anything to laugh at, but because she was happy, and because she had not the ability to restrain the joy that expressed itself in laughter.

"Akh! how nice! how delightful!" she kept exclaiming. Rostof was conscious that under the influence of these warm rays of love, for the first time in a year and a half, his heart and his face were lighted up by the childlike smile which he had not smiled since he had left his home.

"No, listen, you are now a grown-up man, are n't you? I am *awfully* glad that you are my brother!" She touched his mustache. "I should like to know what you men are like! Are you like us? No?"

"What made Sonya run away?" asked Rostof.

"Yes, that is a whole long story! How are you going to speak to her, — *thou* or *you?*"

"Just as it happens," said Rostof.

"Call her *you*, please! I will tell you why some other time. Well, then, I will tell you now. You know that Sonya is my dearest friend, such a friend that I have burnt my arm for her sake. Just look here!" She turned up her muslin sleeve and showed him a red spot on her long, thin, delicate arm below the shoulder and considerably above the elbow, in a place where it would be hidden even by a ball dress.

"I burnt that spot so as to prove how much I loved her! I simply heated a ruler in the fire and held it there!"

As he sat in what had formerly been his classroom, on the sofa with the cushion on the arms, and gazing into Natasha's desperately lively eyes, Rostof again fell back into that old world of his childhood, of his home, which no one besides himself could understand, but which appeared to him replete with some of the sweetest joys of life. And the burning of the arm with the ruler, for the sake of exhibiting love, seemed to him not so senseless; he understood it, and was not surprised.

"So that was the way you did? was that all?" he asked.

"We are such friends, such friends! All that matter of the ruler was a mere trifle; but we are to be friends forever. When she loves any one it is forever; but I can't understand that; I forget right away."

"Well, what then?"

"Well, she loves you just as she does me." Natasha suddenly blushed. "Well, you remember what happened just before you went away. And so she says that you have forgotten all about it — she says: 'I shall love him always, but he must be left to his own free choice.' That is a fact, and is n't it splendid and noble of her? Now, is n't it? very noble! Is n't it?" asked Natasha, so seriously and full of emotion that it could be seen that what she said now she had spoken of before with tears.

Rostof was lost in thought.

"I will not retract the words that I have given," said he. "And, besides, Sonya is so charming that any one would be a fool, a durak, to refuse such happiness."

"No, no!" cried Natasha, "she and I have already discussed that. We knew that you would say so. But it is impossible, because, you understand, if you say so, you will consider yourself bound by your word: it would seem as if she had said this on purpose. It would seem as if you had married her under compulsion, and that would n't do at all."

Rostof saw that all this had been well decided by them. Sonya had struck him the evening before by her beauty. To-day, just catching a glimpse of her, she seemed to him still prettier. She was a charming girl of "sweet sixteen," evidently passionately in love with him; of that he did not doubt for a single instant. "Why should n't he love her, and even marry her?" thought Rostof. "But just now there are so many pleasures and occupations still before me! — yes, they have made a wise decision," said he to himself, "I must remain free."

"Well, all right," said he, after their talk. "Akh! But how glad I am to see you!" he added. "Well, and tell me, have you changed toward Borís?" asked he.

"Oh, that 's all nonsense," cried Natasha, laughing. "I don't trouble myself about him, or any one else, and I don't want to hear about it."

"Hear the girl! Then who is it that you —?"

"I?" asked Natasha in her turn, and a smile of happiness spread over her face, "have you ever seen Duport?"

"No."

"Never saw Duport, the famous dancer! Then you can't understand. Well, that 's what I am going to be!" Natasha picked up her skirt as dancers do, and curving her arms, ran off a few steps, turned around, cut a caper, whirled one leg around the other, and standing on the very tips of her toes glided forward several feet. "See how I can pose! That's the way," said she. But she did not, could not, keep herself on her tiptoes. "That's what I'm going to be. I am never going to marry any one, but I am going to be a ballet-dancer! but don't you tell any one!"

Rostof laughed so loud and merrily that Denísof in his room really envied him, and Natasha could not help joining in with him.

"What, isn't that a good idea?" she asked.

"Excellent, and so you don't want to marry Borís?"

Natasha grew red in the face.

"I don't want to marry any one! And I will tell him the same thing when I see him."

"What an idea!" said Rostof.

"Ah, well, but this is all nonsense," said Natasha, continuing to chatter. "But tell me: is Denísof nice?" she asked.

"Yes, indeed, he is."

"Well, good-by, now; go and finish dressing. And isn't he, isn't Denísof, terrible?"

"Why should he be terrible?" inquired Nicolas. "No! Vaska is a splendid fellow."

"Do you call him Vaska? how funny! And so he's very nice, is he?"

"Yes, very nice."

"Well, then, come down to tea as quick as you can. We shall all be together."

And Natasha stood on her tiptoes and glided from the room after the manner of a ballet-dancer, but smiling all the time, just as happy young girls of fifteen are wont to smile.

When Rostof met Sonya in the drawing-room, he reddened. He did not know how to behave toward her. The evening before, they had kissed each other, in the first joyful moment of meeting again; but to-day they both felt that it was impossible to do so; he imagined that every one, his mother and his sisters, were looking inquisitively at him, and wondering how he would conduct himself toward her. He kissed her hand, and called her by the formal *vui*, you — Sonya. But their eyes met, and said to each other the tender, *tui*, thou, and expressed the kisses that were not exchanged. Her glance seemed to ask forgiveness for having, through the mediation of Natasha, dared to remind him of his promise, and thanked him for his love. He, with his glance, in turn, thanked her for offering him his freedom, and assured her that he should never cease to love her, since it was impossible not to love her.

"But how funny it is," said Viera, breaking the general silence. "Sonya and Nikolenka meet as if they were strangers, and call each other 'you.'"

Viera's remark was true enough, like all her remarks, but, like most of her remarks, it was awkward for all concerned, and not only Sonya, Nikolaï, and Natasha, but the old countess also, who dreaded lest her son should fall in love with Sonya and thus fail to make a brilliant marriage, blushed like a girl.

Denísof, to Rostof's amazement, made his appearance in the drawing-room in a new uniform, pomaded and scented, with as much ceremony as if he were going out to battle, and showed himself so polite to the ladies and gentlemen present that Rostof could hardly believe his eyes.

CHAPTER II

NIKOLAÏ ROSTOF, on his return to Moscow from the army, was welcomed by the home circle as the best of sons, as a hero, and their darling Nikolushka; by his relatives, as a fine, attractive, and distinguished young man; by his acquaintances, as a handsome lieutenant of hussars, a graceful dancer, and one of the best matches in town.

Every one in Moscow knew the Rostofs. This year the old count had plenty of money, having mortgaged all his possessions, and consequently Nikolushka, who kept his own fast trotter, and wore the most stylish riding trousers, of the latest cut, such as had never before been seen in Moscow, and likewise the most fashionable boots, with very pointed toes and little silver spurs, was enabled to spend his time very agreeably.

Now that he was at home again, after a considerable lapse of time, he experienced the pleasant sensation of accommodating himself to the old conditions of life. It seemed to him that he had grown to be very much of a man. His despair at not having been able to pass his examination in the catechism, his borrowing of money from Gavrílo for an izvoshchik, his clandestine kisses with Sonya, all came back to him as remembrances of a childhood from which he was now immeasurably separated. Now he was a lieutenant of hussars, in a silver-laced jacket, with the cross of Saint George, and he could enter his own racer, together with well-known, experienced, and respected amateurs. There was a lady of his acquaintance on the boulevard, with whom he liked to spend his evenings. He took the lead of the mazurka at the Arkharofs', discussed war with Field-Marshal Kamiensky, was an habitué of the English Club, and was on "thou" terms with a colonel of forty years, to whom Denísof had introduced him.

His passion for his sovereign had somewhat cooled since his return to Moscow, since he did not see him and had no opportunity of seeing him; but he often talked about him, and of his love for him, giving people to understand that he did not tell all, that there was something in his feeling toward the emperor that was not comprehensible to all men, and with his whole soul he entered into the sentiment, general at that period in Moscow, of devotion to the Emperor Alexander Pavlovitch, who was called then *angel vo ploti*, an angel in the flesh, or an angel on earth.

During Rostof's short stay in Moscow, before he returned to the army, instead of growing nearer to Sonya he rather drifted away from her. She was very pretty and sweet, and was evidently deeply in love with him;

but he had reached that period of young manhood when there seem to be so many things to do that no time is left for this, and the young man is afraid of binding himself irrevocably, and learns to prize his freedom, since it is necessary to him for other things. When he thought of Sonya during these days of his visit at home, he would say to himself : —

"Eh! there are many, many more as good as she is, whom I have not had a chance to see as yet. I shall have time enough whenever I want to engage myself and fall in love, but now I will have none of it."

Moreover, it seemed to him that there was something rather derogatory to his manhood to spend his time in the society of the ladies. If he went to balls and into the society of women, he pretended that he did so against his will. Races, the English Club, junketing with Denísof, and visits *there* were quite a different affair : such things were becoming to a gay young hussar !

About the middle of March, the old Count Ilya Andreyevitch Rostof was occupied with the preparations for a dinner to be given at the English Club in honor of Prince Bagration.

The count in his dressing-gown was walking up and down his drawing-room, giving orders to the club steward and the famous Feoktist, the old cook of the English Club, in regard to asparagus, fresh cucumbers, strawberries, veal, and fish for the dinner to the prince.

The count, ever since the founding of the club, had been a committeeman and the leading spirit. He had been appointed by the club to oversee the entertainment for Prince Bagration, because no one knew so well as he did how to organize a banquet on a broad and hospitable scale, and especially because no one else could or would spend his own money if it were necessary to make it a success. The cook and steward of the club listened to the count's orders with happy faces, because they knew that for their advantage there was no better person for them to have to manage a dinner costing several thousand rubles.

"Now see here, put esparcet in the turtle soup, esparcet, you know."

"Must there be three kinds of cold dishes?" asked the cook.

The count pondered: "Certainly not less than three — mayonnaise, one...." said he, beginning to count them on his fingers.

"Do you wish me to order some large sterlet?" interrupted the steward.

"What shall we do if there are no good ones? Yes, bátyushka, certainly — I came near forgetting. See here, we must have another *entrée* on the table. O dear me!" he put his hands to his head. "Now who is going to get me flowers?.... Mítenka! ah! Mítenka — hurry off, Mítenka!" he cried to his overseer, who came in at his call, "hurry off to my estate pod-Moskovnaya,[1] and tell Maksimka, the gardener, to get up the decorations. Tell him to have all the greenhouses stripped, and the flowers sent up, well wrapped in felt. Let him have two hundred flower-pots here by Friday."

Having given a profusion of various other orders, he was just going to the "little countess's" room to rest, but remembering some important item he turned round, called back the steward and cook, and began to give still further orders.

Just then in the doorway were heard the light steps of a man, the jingling of spurs, and the young count, handsome, ruddy-faced, with dark mustache, came into the room; it was evident that the lazy, easy-going life in Moscow agreed with him.

"Akh! my dear boy,[2] how my head whirls!" said the old man, smiling at his son with a sort of humiliated expression. "Come now, if you 'd only help me! We really must have some more singers. I shall have my own orchestra, but what should you think of getting the gypsies? Your brotherhood of military men like them."

"It 's a fact, pápenka! I think that Prince Bagration, when he was getting ready for the battle of Schöngra-

---

[1] Any estate in the suburbs of Moscow.   [2] *Brátets moï.*

ben, did not make such hard work of it as you are doing now," said the young man with a smile.

The old count pretended to be angry : —

"Yes, you talk, just try it yourself !"

And the count turned to the cook, who with an intelligent and respectful face was looking on, with friendly and flattering eyes, at the father and son.

"That's the way with the young men, hey, Feoktist?" said he. "Always making sport of us old fellows!"

"That's so, your illustriousness, all they want is to have good things to eat and drink, but how it's got and served is no concern of theirs."

"That's it, that's it," cried the count, and gayly seizing his son's two hands, cried : " Now this is what I want, since I have you. Take the sledge and pair and hurry off to Bezukhoï's and tell him that the count, that is Ilya Andreyitch, sent to ask for some fresh strawberries and pineapples. No one else has any at all. If he himself is not there, then find the princesses and ask them ; and from there, mind you, drive to the Razgulyai — Ipatka, the coachman, will know the way — and there find Ilyushka the Tsigan, the one who danced and sang in a white kazakin at Count Orlof's, you remember, and bring him with you to me here."

"Shall I bring some of the Tsigan girls with him too?" asked Nikolaï, laughing. "There! there!"

At this moment, with noiseless steps, and with her indefatigable and anxious, and at the same time sweet and Christian, expression, which never deserted her, Anna Mikhaïlovna came into the room. In spite of the fact that Anna Mikhaïlovna every day discovered the count in his dressing-gown, each time he was much abashed, and offered her apologies for his costume.

"No matter, count, my dear," said she, blandly closing her eyes. "I myself am going to the Bezukhoïs'. Pierre has come, and now we can get anything from his greenhouses. I have been wanting to see him. He sent me a letter from Borís. Glory to God ! — Borya is now on the staff."

The count was delighted to have one part of his commission undertaken by Anna Mikhaïlovna, and bade her make use of the coupé.

"You tell Bezukhoï to come. I will write him a note. How are he and his wife getting along?" asked the count.

Anna Mikhaïlovna rolled up her eyes, and her face expressed deep affliction.

"Akh, my dear! he's very unhappy," said she; "if it is true, what we have heard, it is terrible! And could we have dreamed of such a thing, when we rejoiced so in his happiness! And such a lofty, heavenly soul this young Bezukhoï is! Yes, I pity him from the bottom of my heart! and I mean to do all that within me lies, to give him consolation."

"Tell us, what is it?" asked both the Rostofs, elder and younger.

Anna Mikhaïlovna drew a deep sigh.

"Dolokhof, Márya Ivanovna's son," said she, in a mysterious whisper, "has, so they say, absolutely compromised her. Pierre introduced him to her, took him to his own house in Petersburg, and now.... she came here and that madcap fellow followed her," said Anna Mikhaïlovna, trying to express her sympathy for Pierre, but involuntarily, by the inflections of her voice and by the half-smile on her face, showing more sympathy for the "madcap fellow," as she called Dolokhof. "They say Pierre is perfectly broken by his trial."

"Well, then, be sure to tell him to come to the club. It will help to distract him. It will be a stunning banquet!"

On the next day, the fifteenth of March, at two o'clock in the afternoon, two hundred and fifty members of the English Club and fifty guests were waiting for their distinguished guest, Prince Bagration, the hero of the Austrian campaign.

At first the news of the battle of Austerlitz had been received at Moscow with incredulity. The Russians had been so accustomed to victory, that when they heard of the defeat, some simply refused to believe it, others sought explanations for such a strange circumstance in extraordinary causes. In the month of December, when the news was fully confirmed, at the English Club, which was a rendezvous for all men of note, or who had trustworthy sources of information, and everywhere else, nothing was said about the war and the recent defeat, just as if there had been common consent to hush the matter up. Men who were apt to give the cue to conversation — for instance Count Rostopchin, Prince Yuri Vladímirovitch Dolgoruky, Valuyef, Count Markóf, Prince Vyazemsky — did not show themselves at the club at all, but met at their own houses in their own intimate circles, and the rest of the Moscovites, who never had any opinions of their own, — and in this number we must reckon also Ilya Andreyitch Rostof, — remained for a short time without any definite opinion in regard to the war, and without their natural leaders.

These Moscovites had a dim idea that something was wrong, and that it was hard to arrive at a proper judgment in regard to this bad news, and therefore they preferred to keep silent.

But after some time, when the bigwigs who directed opinion at the club came back like jurors after a consultation in the jury-room, then all was made clear and definite. Reasons were found for this incredible, unheard-of, and impossible circumstance, that the Russians were beaten. It now became perfectly clear, and one and the same thing was said in all the corners of Moscow. These were the reasons: The treachery of Austria, the wretched victualing of the troops, the treason of the Pole Prsczebiszewsky and the Frenchman Langeron, the incapacity of Kutuzof, and — spoken with bated breath — the youth and inexperience of the sovereign, who had placed his confidence in inefficient and insignificant men.

But the army, the Russian army, — and all agreed in regard to this, — was extraordinary, and had accomplished prodigies of valor. Soldiers, officers, generals, all were heroes. But the hero of heroes was Prince Bagration, who had won imperishable glory by his victory of Schöngraben and his retreat at Austerlitz, where he alone had led off his division unbroken, and had fought the livelong day against an enemy double his numbers. What added still more *éclat* to his repute as a hero was the fact that he had no kin in Moscow, and was a foreigner. He was considered as the representative of the simple heroic Russian soldier, who had won his way without connections and intrigues, and was moreover associated with recollections of the Italian campaign, and the name of Suvorof. And then again, by showing him such distinguished honors, it was felt that there could be no better way of showing Kutuzof ill-will and disapprobation.

"If there were no Bagration, we should have to manufacture one," said the jester Shinshin, with a parody on Voltaire's witticism. Scarcely any one spoke of Kutuzof, and those who did abused him under their breath, calling him the court weathercock and an old satyr.

Prince Dolgorukof's witticism was repeated all over Moscow: "Stick to the plaster, and you'll become a master;" thus he consoled himself for our defeat by the remembrance of former victories. Men likewise freely quoted Rostopchin's clever saying, that "you have to spur the French soldier to battle with high-sounding phrases; the Germans must have it logically proved to them that it is more dangerous to run away than it is to advance; while the Russian soldier, on the contrary, must be held back and urged to go gently."

On all sides were heard new and ever new tales of individual examples of heroism shown by our officers and soldiers at Austerlitz. This man saved a standard, that one killed five Frenchmen, the other alone loaded five cannons. They spoke of Berg, even those who did not know him, and told how, when he was wounded in his right arm, he took his sword in his left hand and dashed forward. Nothing was heard of Bolkonsky, and only those who knew him intimately lamented his premature death, and pitied his wife with her unborn child, and his whimsical old father.

CHAPTER III

On the fifteenth of March, in all the rooms of the English Club, was heard the hum of busy voices, and, like bees at the spring swarming-time, the members and guests of the club, dressed in uniforms, dress-coats, and some even in powder and kaftans, roamed back and forth, sat down, stood up, met and parted. Powdered and liveried footmen in small-clothes and slippers stood at each door, and strove eagerly to anticipate each motion of the guests and members, so as to offer their services. The majority of those present were well on in years, men of distinction, with broad, self-satisfied faces, plump fingers, resolute gestures and voices. The guests and members of this class occupied the well-known places of honor, and were surrounded by little circles of well-known and distinguished men.

Those that formed the minority were chance guests, preëminently young men, among whom were Denísof, Rostof, and Dolokhof, the last being now an officer of the Semyonovsky regiment once more. The faces of these young men, especially those that belonged to the army, wore that expression of contemptuous deference toward their elders, which seemed to say to the older generation: 'We are ready to respect and honor you, but remember that nevertheless the future is ours.'

Nesvitsky was there, also, in the capacity of a former member of the club.

Pierre, who, by his wife's advice, had let his hair grow, renounced his spectacles, and dressed in the height of style, wandered through the rooms with a melancholy and dismal mien. As usual, he was surrounded by that atmosphere of worship offered by those who bow before riches, and he, having now become accustomed to this dominion, treated such sycophants with careless scorn.

In years he should have associated with the young men, but by his wealth and importance he gravitated toward the circles of the older and more influential guests, and consequently he drifted from one group to another. Central circles were formed by some of the most distinguished old men, around whom respectfully gathered many of the less conspicuous, for the purpose of listening to the great ones. Such groups were formed around Count Rostopchin, Valuyef, and Naruishkin. Rostopchin was telling how the Russians were caught by the fugitive Austrians and obliged to force their way through at the point of the bayonet.

Valuyef confidentially announced that Uvarof had been sent from Petersburg to learn the opinion of the Moscovites in regard to Austerlitz.

In the third great circle, Naruishkin was telling about a session of an Austrian council of war at which Suvorof crowed like a cock in answer to the absurdities spoken by the Austrian generals. Shinshin, who formed one of the group, tried to raise a laugh by saying that evidently Kutuzof had not been able to learn of Suvorof even such a simple thing as to crow like a cock; but the elderly men looked sternly at the jester, giving him thereby to feel that on such a day, and in such a place, it was so unseemly to speak of Kutuzof!

Count Ilya Andreyitch Rostof, in his soft boots, hovered, full of anxiety and solicitude, between the dining-room and the parlors, giving always the same hasty greeting to every one he met, whether men of mark or not men of mark, his acquaintance including every one, without exception, occasionally looking around for his handsome young son, at whom he would look with delight and a nod of satisfaction. Young Rostof was standing in the embrasure of a window, with Dolokhof, whose acquaintance he had recently made and felt to be congenial.

The old count came up to them and shook hands with Dolokhof : —

"I beg of you to come and see us; since you and my young man here are friends.... you and he played the heroes together, yonder. .... Ah! Vasíli Ignatyitch! Good afternoon, old friend," cried he, turning to welcome a little old man, just entering.

But he did not have time to add the usual greeting; there was a stir, and a footman with awestruck face announced : —

"He has come."

The bell rang; the elders hastened forward; the guests, scattered in the different rooms, like rye gathered up by the shovel, congregated in a throng, and stood in the great drawing-room at the door of the hall.

At the entrance appeared Bagration, without his hat and sword, which, according to the club custom, he had left in care of the Swiss. He was dressed not in his lambskin cap with his whip over his shoulder, as Rostof had seen him the night before the battle of Austerlitz, but in a new and tight-fitting uniform, with Russian and foreign orders, and with the star of the George on his left breast. He had evidently just had his hair and whiskers trimmed, and this did not change his appearance for the better.

His face had a naïvely festive look, which, being inappropriate to his firm, manly features, gave him a rather comical expression.

Bekleshof and Feodor Petrovitch Uvarof, who came together with him, paused at the doorway, waiting for him, as the guest of honor, to precede them. Bagration was confused, not wishing to take advantage of their politeness; there was a little pause at the entrance, and finally Bagration, after all, led the way. He walked across the inlaid floor of the reception-room, awkwardly and bashfully, not knowing what to do with his hands; it would have been much more to his mind, and much easier for him, to cross a ploughed field under a rain of bullets, as, for instance, he had done when leading the Kursk regiment at the battle of Schöngraben.

The older gentlemen met him at the door, said a few words expressive of their delight at seeing such an illustrious guest, and, without waiting for his reply, seized him, as it were, and dragged him off into the drawing-room. Around the doors of the drawing-room there was such a crowd that it was impossible to pass. Members and guests crushed one another, and tried to look over one another's shoulders for a glimpse of Bagration, as if he were some wild beast.

Count Ilya Andreyitch, laughing and talking more energetically than all the rest, pushed through the throng, crying, "Make way, *mon cher*, make way, please, make way," and led the guests into the drawing-room, and placed them on the central divan, where now all the bigwigs and the most distinguished members of the club gathered in an eager throng.

Count Ilya Andreyevitch, again pushing his way through the crowd, left the room, but quickly reappeared with another of the directors, bearing a huge silver salver, which he presented to Prince Bagration. On the salver lay some verses composed and printed in the hero's honor.

Bagration, seeing the salver, looked around in alarm, as if seeking for refuge. But all eyes demanded his submission, and Bagration, feeling that he was in their power, seized the salver resolutely with both hands, and looked gravely and reproachfully at the count, who brought it to him. Some one gallantly relieved the prince of the salver — for otherwise, he would have evidently felt it incumbent upon him to hold it in his hands till evening, and even gone out to dinner with it — and directed his attention to the ode. 'Well, I will read it,' Prince Bagration seemed to say, and fastening his weary eyes on the parchment, tried to read it with serious and concentrated attention. But the composer of the ode took it and began to read it aloud: *Slav tako Alèksandra vyek.* Prince Bagration bent his head and listened: —

> " Pride of Alexander's age !
> Be of our Titus' throne the stern defender !
> At once the mighty chief and humble sage:
> At home, a Ripheus, Cæsar, 'mid the battle's splendor !
> Yes ! e'en victorious Napoleon
> By sad experience knows Bagration !
> Now justice to the Alcide Russians he must render
> And fear ...."

But even while he was in the midst of his ode, the stentorian majordomo proclaimed "Dinner is served!"

The door was flung open, and from the dining-room were heard the resounding notes of the polonaise: "Roll, ye thunder tones of victory, gallant Russian hearts rejoice," and Count Ilya Andreyitch, giving the author a severe look for still continuing to read his verses, came and made a low bow before Bagration.

All rose to their feet, feeling that the dinner was of more consequence than poetry, and again Bagration was obliged to lead the way to the dining-room. He was assigned to the seat of honor between the two Alexanders, Bekleshof and Naruishkin, which was meant as a delicate allusion to the name of the sovereign. Three hundred men sat down at table, according to their ranks and stations, those most distinguished being nearest to the guest of honor, just as naturally as water flows deepest where it is narrowest.

Just before the dinner began, Count Ilya Andreyitch presented his son to the prince. Bagration, recognizing him, mumbled a few words, awkward and incoherent, like everything else that he said that day. Count Ilya Andreyitch looked around gleefully and proudly on all while Bagration was talking to his son.

Nikolaï Rostof, with Denísof and his new acquaintance, Dolokhof, sat together almost at the center of the table. Opposite to them sat Pierre, next to Prince Nesvitsky. Count Ilya Andreyitch's seat was opposite Bagration, with the other directors, and he did the honors to the prince, personifying in himself the hospitality of Moscow.

His labors were not spent in vain. The dinner, which was served both for those who were keeping Lent and for those who were not, was magnificent, but still he could not feel perfectly at ease until the very end. He kept beckoning to the butler, whispering directions to the waiters, and, not without agitation, looked for the arrival of each course which he knew so well. All passed off admirably.

At the second course, when they brought on the gigantic sterlet, at the sight of which Ilya Andreyevitch flushed with joy and modesty, the waiters began to uncork the bottles and pour out the champagne.

After the fish, which produced a great impression, Count Ilya Andreyitch glanced at the other directors. "There are so many toasts, it is time to begin," he said in a whisper, and taking his wine-cup in his hand, he got up. All grew still, and waited what he should have to say.

"To the health of our sovereign, the emperor," he cried, and at the same time his kindly eyes were dimmed with tears of pleasure and enthusiasm. At the same time the band broke out with the polonaise again: "Roll, ye thunder tones." All arose in their places and cried "Hurrah!" and Bagration also joined in shouting with the same voice which had cried "Hurrah!" on the field of Schöngraben.

Young Rostof's enthusiastic voice was heard above all the other three hundred. He could hardly refrain from tears.

"Hurrah for the emperor!" he cried, "hurrah!" Draining his glass at one draught, he smashed it on the floor. Many followed his example. And the deafening shouts continued for a long time. When silence was restored the servants swept up the broken glass, and all, having resumed their seats, began to converse and laugh again.

Then Count Ilya Andreyitch arose once more, and proposed the health of the hero of our last campaign, Prince Piotr Ivanovitch Bagration, and again the count's blue eyes grew tender with tears. "Hurrah!" again rang out the three hundred voices; but this time, instead of the band, the choir of singers struck up a cantata composed by Pavel Ivanovitch Kutuzof:—

> "Obstacles are naught to Russians;
>   Courage wins the victor's crown!
> If Bagration leads our columns,
>   We shall hew the foemen down."

As soon as the singers had finished, fresh toasts kept following, at which Count Ilya Andreyitch grew more and more sentimental, and more and more glasses were smashed, and the shouts grew ever more boisterous. They drank to the health of Bekleshof, Naruishkin, Uvarof, Dolgorukof, Apraksin, Valuyef, to the health of the directors, to the health of the committeemen, to the health of all the members of the club, to the health of all the guests of the club, and finally, as a special honor, to the health of the master of ceremonies, Count Ilya Andreyitch. At this toast the count took out his handkerchief and, hiding his face, actually wept.

CHAPTER IV

PIERRE sat opposite Dolokhof and Nikolaï Rostof. He ate much and greedily, and, as usual, drank much. But those who knew him intimately observed that day that a great change had come over him. He said nothing all the time of the dinner; scowling and frowning, he looked about him; or, with downcast eyes and a look of absolute abstraction, picked at his nose with his finger. His face was gloomy and dismal. Apparently he did not see or hear anything that was going on around him, and was absorbed in some disagreeable and unsolvable problem.

This unsolvable problem which tormented him was caused by the hints of the princess in Moscow in regard to Dolokhof's intimacy with his wife, and by an anonymous letter received that very morning, wherein it was said, in that dastardly mocking tone characteristic of anonymous letters, that his spectacles did him very little good, and that his wife's criminal intimacy with Dolokhof was a secret for him alone.

Pierre resolutely refused to heed the princess's insinuations or the letter, but it was terrible for him to look now at Dolokhof, sitting opposite him. Every time that his glance fell accidentally upon Dolokhof's handsome, insolent eyes, he was conscious of something awful and ugly arising in his soul, and he would quickly turn away. Involuntarily remembering all his wife's past, and her behavior toward Dolokhof, Pierre saw clearly that what was expressed so brutally in the letter might very well be true, might, at least, seem true, did it not concern *his wife !*

Pierre could not help recalling how Dolokhof, on being restored to his rank after the campaign, had returned to Petersburg and come to him. Taking advantage of the friendship arising from their former sprees together, Dolokhof had come straight to his house, and Pierre had taken him in and lent him money. Pierre remembered how Ellen, with her set smile, had expressed her discontent at having Dolokhof living under their roof; and how Dolokhof had cynically praised before him his wife's beauty, and how, from that time forth until his coming to Moscow, he had not budged from their house.

"Yes, he is very handsome," thought Pierre, "I know him. In his estimation it would be admirable sport to besmirch my name and turn me into ridicule, just for the very reason that I was doing so much for him, and taking care of him and helping him. I know, I understand, what spice it would add in his estimation to his villany, if this were true! Yes, if it were true; but I don't believe it! I have no right to believe it, and I cannot!"

He remembered the expression which Dolokhof's face had borne at times when he was engaged in his acts of deviltry, as for instance when they had tied the policeman to the bear and flung them into the river, or when, without any provocation, he had challenged men to fight duels, or shot the post-driver's [1] horse dead with his pistol. This expression he had often noticed lately on Dolokhof's face.

"Yes, he 's a bully," said Pierre to himself; "he would think nothing of killing a man; it is essential for him to think that every one is afraid of him; this must be pleasant to him. He must think that I am afraid of him. And in fact I am afraid of him," thought Pierre, and again at these suggestions the awful and ugly *something* arose in his mind.

Dolokhof, Denísof, and Rostof were still sitting oppo-

---

[1] *Yámshchik,* driver or postilion.

site to Pierre, and seemed to be very lively. Rostof was gayly chatting with his two friends, one of whom was a clever hussar, the other a well-known bully and madcap, and occasionally he glanced rather mockingly at Pierre, who had impressed him by the concentrated, abstracted, and stolid expression of his countenance. Rostof looked at Pierre with a malevolent expression, in the first place because Pierre, in the eyes of a hussar like him, was merely a millionaire civilian, the husband of a pretty woman, and moreover was a *baba* — an old woman! in the second place, because Pierre, in his abstracted state of mind, did not recognize Rostof, or return his bow. When they stood up to drink the toast to the emperor, Pierre was so lost in his thoughts that he forgot to get up with the others, and did not lift his wine-glass.

"What's the matter with you?" shouted Rostof, his eyes flashing with righteous indignation, as he looked at him, "why don't you pay attention; the health of our sovereign, the emperor!"

Pierre, with a sigh, humbly got to his feet, drained his glass, and then, after they had all sat down, he turned to Rostof with his good-natured smile: "Ah! I did not recognize you," said he.

But Rostof was engaged in shouting "Hurrah!" so that this was lost on him. "Are n't you going to renew the acquaintance?" asked Dolokhof of Rostof.

"Curse the fool!"[1]

"One must cawess a pwetty woman's husband," said Denísof. Pierre did not catch what they said, but he knew that they were talking about him. He reddened, and turned away.

"Well, now to the health of the pretty women!" said Dolokhof, and with a serious expression, though a smile lurked in the corners of his mouth, he lifted his glass to Pierre. "To the health of the pretty women, Pétrusha, and — their lovers!" he added.

Pierre, dropping his eyes, sipped his glass, not looking at Dolokhof or making him any reply.

[1] *Bog s nim, durak:* literally, "God be with him, fool or idiot."

A lackey, who was distributing copies of Kutuzof's cantata, handed one of the sheets to Pierre as being among the more distinguished guests. Pierre was going to take it, but Dolokhof leaned over, snatched the sheet from his hand, and began to read it. Pierre stared at Dolokhof; his pupils contracted; that awful and ugly something that had been tormenting him all the dinner-time, now arose in him and overmastered him. He leaned his heavy frame across the table.

"Don't you dare to take it!" he cried.

Nesvitsky and his right-hand neighbor, hearing him speak in such a tone of voice, and seeing whom he was dealing with, were filled with alarm and hastily tried to calm him.

"That's enough!" .... "Be careful!" .... "Think what you're doing!" whispered anxious voices.

Dolokhof stared at Pierre with his bright, merry, insolent eyes, and with that smile of his that seemed to say, "This is what I like."

"I will not give it back," he said, measuring his words.

Pale, with twitching lips, Pierre snatched back the sheet of paper. "You .... you .... blackguard! .... I shall call you to account for this!" he cried, and pushing away his chair, rose from the table.

At the very instant that Pierre did this, and pronounced these words, he felt that the problem of his wife's guilt, which had been torturing him for the past twenty-four hours, was finally and definitely settled beyond a peradventure. He hated her, and the breach between them was widened irrevocably.

In spite of Denísof's urgency that Rostof should not get mixed up in this affair, Rostof consented to act as Dolokhof's second, and after dinner he arranged with Nesvitsky, Bezukhoï's second, in regard to the conditions of the duel. Pierre went home, and Rostof, together with Denísof and Dolokhof, stayed at the club till late, listening to the gypsies and the singers.

"Well, then, till to-morrow, at Sokolniki," said Dolokhof, taking his leave of Rostof on the club steps.

"And you are confident?" asked Rostof.

Dolokhof paused.

"Now, see here, I will give you in two words the whole secret of dueling. If you are going to fight a duel, and write your will and affectionate letters to your father and mother, if you get it into your head that you are going to be killed, then you are an idiot — a durák — and deserve to fall; but if you go with firm intention to kill him as quickly and certainly as you can, then you are all right, as our Kostroma bear-driver told me. 'How can you help being afraid of the bear?' says he; 'yes, but when you once see him, your only fear is that he will get away.' Well, that's the way it is with me! *À demain, mon cher!*"

On the next morning, at eight o'clock, Pierre and Nesvitsky drove to the woods of Sokolniki, and found there Dolokhof, Denísof, and Rostof waiting for them. Pierre had the aspect of a man entirely absorbed in his reflections and absolutely incognizant of the affair before him. His countenance was haggard and yellow. He had evidently not slept the night before. He glanced around him vaguely, and frowned as if he were blinded by the bright sun. Two considerations exclusively occupied him: his wife's guilt, of which, after his sleepless night, he had no longer the slightest doubt; and the innocence of Dolokhof, who had no reason to guard the honor of a stranger.

"Maybe I should have done the same thing, if I had been in his place," said Pierre to himself; "I am perfectly certain that I should; why then this duel, this homicide? Either I shall kill him, or he will put a bullet through my head, in my elbow, or my knee. Can't I get out of it somehow, run away, hide myself somewhere?"

This thought came into his mind. But at the very instant that these suggestions were offering themselves to him, he, with his usual calm and absent-minded expression, — which aroused the respect of those who saw him, — was asking if all were ready and they should begin soon?

When all had been arranged, and the swords stuck upright in the snow, to mark the limits for them to advance, and the pistols had been loaded, Nesvitsky went up to Pierre.

"I should not be doing my duty, count," said he, in a faltering voice, "or be worthy of the confidence and honor which you confide in my hands, at this moment, this most serious moment, if I did not tell you the whole truth. I consider that this affair has not sufficient reason, and does not warrant the shedding of blood. You were in the wrong, absolutely, you were in a passion." ....

"Oh, yes, it was horribly foolish," said Pierre.

"Then allow me to offer your regrets, and I am sure that your opponent will be satisfied to accept your apologies," said Nesvitsky, who, like the other participants, and like all men in similar affairs, did not believe even now that it would actually come to a duel. — "You know, count, that it is far more noble to acknowledge one's fault, than to carry an affair to its irrevocable consequences. The insult was not wholly on one side. Let me confer."

"No! there's nothing to be said about it," said Pierre. "It's all the same to me. .... Is everything ready?" he asked. "Do you only tell me where I am to stand, and where to fire," he added, with an unnaturally sweet smile. He took the pistol and began to ask about the working of the trigger, for he had never before held a pistol in his hands, though he was unwilling to confess it. "Oh, yes, that's the way .... I know .... I had only forgotten," said he.

"No apologies, decidedly not," said Dolokhof to Denísof, who also on the other side proposed to effect a reconciliation, and he also went to the designated place.

The place selected for the duel was a small clearing in the fir woods, covered with what remained of the snow after the recent thaw, and about eighty paces from the road where the sledges were left. The opponents stood about forty paces apart on the border of the clearing. The seconds, while measuring off the distance, had trampled down the deep, wet snow between the place where they stood and Nesvitsky's and Denísof's sabers, stuck upright ten paces apart, to mark the bounds. It was thawing, and the mist spread around; nothing could be seen forty paces away. For three minutes, all had been ready, and still they hesitated about beginning; no one spoke.

CHAPTER V

"WELL, begin," said Dolokhof.

"All right," said Pierre, still smiling as before.

It was a solemn moment. It was evident that the affair, which at first had been so trivial, could no longer be averted, but was now bound to take its course to the very end, irrespective of the will of the men. Denísof first went forward to the barrier and announced : —

"As the adve'sawies have wefused to agwee, we may pwoceed. Take your pistols, and at the word thwee, advance and fire."

"U— one ! — two ! — thwee !" cried Denísof, sternly, and stepped to one side. The two men advanced along the trodden path, coming closer and closer, their faces growing more and more distinct to each other in the fog. The antagonists had the right to fire at any moment before reaching the barrier. Dolokhof advanced slowly, not raising his pistol, but fastening his bright, glittering blue eyes on his opponent's face. His lips as usual wore what seemed like a smile.

"So it seems I can fire when I please," said Pierre to himself, and at the word "three," he advanced with quick strides, leaving the beaten path, and pushing through the untrodden snow. He held the pistol in his right hand out at arm's length, apparently afraid of killing himself with it. His left hand he strenuously kept behind his back, because he felt such a strong desire to support his right arm with it, which he knew was out of the question.

After he had gone six steps, and had left the trodden path, he looked down at his feet, then gave a quick glance at Dolokhof, and, pulling the trigger, as he had been told to do, fired. Not anticipating such a loud report, Pierre jumped, and then, smiling at his own sensations, stood stock still. The smoke, made heavier by the misty atmosphere, prevented him from seeing anything at first; but there was no second report, as he had expected. All he could hear was Dolokhof's hasty steps, and then his form loomed up through the smoke. He was holding one hand to his left side; with the other he clutched the pistol, which he did not raise. His face was pale. Rostof had rushed up to him, and was saying something.

"N .... no," hissed Dolokhof through his teeth. "No, I'm not done yet," and, making a few tottering, staggering steps toward the saber, he fell on the snow, near it. His left arm was covered with blood. He wiped it on his coat and supported himself with it. His face was pale and contracted, and a spasm passed over it.

"I beg of you...." began Dolokhof, but he could not speak coherently. "Please...." said he, with difficulty.

Pierre, hardly restraining his sobs, started to run to Dolokhof, and was just crossing the line, when Dolokhof cried, "Stop at the barrier;" and Pierre, realizing what he meant, paused near the saber. They were only ten paces apart. Dolokhof bent his head over to the snow, greedily ate a mouthful, lifted his head again, straightened himself up, tried to get to his feet, and sat down, in his effort to recover his equilibrium. He swallowed the icy snow and sucked it; his lips twitched; but he still smiled, and his eyes gleamed with concentrated hatred, as he tried to collect his failing strength. He raised the pistol and tried to aim.

"Stand sidewise; protect yourself from the pistol," cried Nesvitsky.

"Pwotect yourself," instinctively cried Denísof, though he was the other's second.

Pierre, with his sweet smile of compassion and regret, helplessly dropping his arms and spreading his legs, stood with his broad chest exposed directly to

Dolokhof, and looking at him mournfully. Denísof, Rostof, and Nesvitsky shut their eyes.

They heard the report, and simultaneously Dolokhof's wrathful cry.

"Missed!" cried Dolokhof, and lay back feebly on the snow, face down. Pierre clutched his temples, and turning back, went into the woods, trampling down the virgin snow and muttering incoherent words.

"Folly! Folly! Death! Lies!" .... he kept repeating, with scowling brows. Nesvitsky called him back and took him home.

Rostof and Denísof lifted the wounded Dolokhof. They put him in the sledge, where he lay with closed eyes and without speaking or making any reply to their questions; but, when they reached Moscow, he suddenly roused himself, and, with difficulty raising his head, seized Rostof's hand, who was sitting next him. Rostof was struck by the absolutely changed and unexpectedly softened expression of Dolokhof's face.

"Well? How do you feel now?" asked Rostof.

"Wretchedly; but that is no matter. My dear," said Dolokhof, in a broken voice, "where are we? We are in Moscow, I know it. It's no matter about me, but I have killed her, killed her; she won't get over this. She won't survive."

"Who?" asked Rostof.

"My mother. My mother, my good angel, my adored angel, my mother," and Dolokhof burst into tears, pressing Rostof's hand. When he had grown a little calmer, he explained to Rostof that he lived with his mother, and that if his mother should see him dying, she would not survive it. He begged Rostof to go and break the news to her.

Rostof rode on ahead to attend to this, and to his great surprise discovered that Dolokhof, this insolent fellow, this bully, Dolokhof, lived with his old mother and a hunchbacked sister, and was a most affectionate son and brother.

CHAPTER VI

PIERRE had rarely of late seen his wife alone by themselves. Both in Petersburg and Moscow, their house was constantly full of company.

On the night that followed the duel he did not go to his sleeping-room, but, as was often the case, stayed in the vast cabinet where his father, the Count Bezukhoï, had died.

He stretched himself out on the sofa, with the idea of forgetting all that had taken place; but this he could n't do. Such a tornado of thoughts, feelings, recollections, suddenly arose in his mind, that not only he could not sleep, but could not keep still, and he was compelled to spring up from the sofa and walk the room with rapid strides.

Now she seemed to come up before him as she was during the first few weeks after their marriage, with her bare shoulders, and her languid, passionate eyes; and then immediately he would see Dolokhof by her side — Dolokhof, with his handsome, impudent, mocking face, as he had seen it at the banquet, and then the same face, pale, convulsed, and agonized, as it had been when he reeled and fell on the snow.

"What was it?" he asked himself. "I have killed her *paramour!* yes, I have killed my wife's *paramour.* Yes, that was it. Why? How did it come to this?"

"Because you married her," replied an inward voice.

"But wherein was I to blame?" he asked again.

"Because you married her without loving her; because you deceived yourself and her."

And then he vividly recalled the moment after the dinner at Prince Vasíli's, when he had murmured those words, "*Je vous aime*— I love you," that had come with so much difficulty.

"It was all from that. Even then I felt," said he to himself, "even then I felt that this was wrong, that I had no right to do it, and so it has proved."

He recalled their honeymoon, and reddened at the

recollection. Extraordinarily vivid, humiliating, and shameful was the recollection of how one time, shortly after their marriage, he had gone in his silk dressing-gown, at twelve o'clock in the daytime, from his sleeping-room to his library, and found there his head overseer, who, with an obsequious bow, glanced at Pierre's face and at his dressing-gown, while a shadow of a smile passed over his face, as if he thereby expressed his humble sympathy in the happiness of his master.

"And yet how many times I have been proud of her, — proud of her majestic beauty, of her social tact," he went on thinking, — "proud of my house, where she received all Petersburg, — proud of her inaccessibility and radiance. Yes, how proud I was of it all! then I thought that I did not understand her. How often, when pondering over her character, I said to myself that I was to blame, that I did not understand her, did not understand her habitual repose, self-satisfaction, and lack of all interests and ambition, and now I have found the answer in that terrible expression: she is a lewd woman. Now I have said to myself that terrible word, all has become clear!

"Anatol came to her to borrow some money, and kissed her on her naked shoulder. She did not let him have the money, but she was willing for him to kiss her. Her father, in jest, tried to make her jealous, and she, with her calm smile, replied that she was not so stupid as to be jealous: 'Let him do as he pleases,' said she about me. I asked her once if she saw no signs of approaching maternity. She laughed scornfully, and replied that she was not such a fool as to wish to have any children, and that I should never get any children by her."

Then he recalled the coarseness and frankness of her thoughts, the vulgarity of the expressions that came natural to her, in spite of her education in the highest aristocratic circles. "I am no such fool," "Go and try it on yourself," "*Allez vous promener*," and such like slang she was fond of using.

Pierre, witnessing her success in the eyes of old and

young, men and women, had often found it hard to understand why he did not love her.

"Yes, and I have never really loved her," said Pierre
to himself. "I knew that she was a lewd woman," he
kept repeating to himself, "but I did not dare to acknowledge it to myself. And now there is Dolokhof
sitting in the snow, and trying to smile, and dying
maybe, and responding to my repentance with pretended bravado!"

Pierre was one of those men who, notwithstanding
his affectionate nature, which some would call weakness of character, would never seek a confidant for
his troubles. He worked out his sufferings alone by
himself.

"She is to blame, the only one to blame for all," said
he to himself. "But what was back of that? That I
married her, that I said to her, 'I love you,' which was
a lie, and even worse than a lie," said he to himself.
"I am to blame and must suffer .... what? The be-
smirching of my name? the unhappiness of my life?
eh! that's all nonsense," he continued, "the disgrace
to my name and honor, all that is conditional, absolutely independent of me.

"Louis XVI. was executed because *they* said that he
was a guilty offender," thus Pierre reasoned, "and they
were right from their point of view, just as they also
were right from theirs who died a violent death after
him, and who reckoned him among the saints. Then
Robespierre was beheaded because he was a tyrant.
Who was right? who was to blame? No one! But
live while we live; to-morrow we die, just as I might
easily have died an hour ago. And is it worth tormenting one's self about, when life counts only as a moment
in comparison with eternity?"

But even while he was trying to reason himself into
calmness by such a train of thought, suddenly *she* again
rose before his imagination, and at one of those moments
when he had expressed to her more violently than ever
his insincere love, and he felt how the blood poured back
to his heart, and he was obliged again to get up, move

about, and break and smash whatever things came within reach of his hands.

"Why did I tell her that I loved her? why did I say 'I love you'?" he kept asking himself. And after he had asked himself this question a dozen times, the phrase of Molière came into his head, "*Mais que diable allait il faire dans cette galère?*"[1] and he had to laugh at himself.

At night he summoned his valet and ordered him to pack up in readiness to go to Petersburg. He could not imagine himself having anything more to say to her. He had decided to take an early departure the next day, leaving her a letter in which he should explain his intention of living apart from her for evermore.

The next morning, when the valet, bringing him his coffee, came into the cabinet, Pierre was lying on an ottoman, asleep, with an open book in his hand.

He aroused himself, and looked around for some time with a startled expression, wholly unable to understand where he was.

"The countess commanded to ask if your illustriousness were at home," said the valet.

But before Pierre had time to decide what answer to give, the countess herself, in a morning-gown of white satin embroidered in silver, and with her hair dressed in the simplest style — two enormously long braids wound twice, *en diadème*, around her graceful head — came into the room calmly and majestically; only on her marble forehead, which was a little too prominent, there was a deep frown of fury. With thoroughly masterful self-restraint, she did not say a word in the valet's presence. She had heard of the duel, and had come to speak about it. She waited until the valet had set down the coffee and left the room. Pierre looked at her timidly over his spectacles, and, like a hare surrounded by dogs, which lays back its ears and crouches motionless before its enemies, so he also pretended to take up his reading again; but he was conscious that this was a senseless and impossible thing to do, and again he looked at her.

[1] "What business had he there?"

She did not sit down, but with a scornful smile stared at him, waiting until the valet should be out of the room.

"Well, now, what's this latest? What have you been doing? I demand an answer!" said she, sternly.

"I.... what have I....?" stammered Pierre.

"Playing the bravado, hey? Come now, answer me; what about this duel? What did you mean to imply by it? What? I demand an answer!"

Pierre turned heavily on the sofa, opened his mouth, but could not make a sound.

"If you won't answer, then I will tell you," continued Ellen. "You believe everything that is told you: you were told," Ellen laughed, "that Dolokhof was my paramour," said she in French, with her uncompromising, explicit manner of speech, pronouncing the word *amant* like any other word. "And you believed it! And what have you proved by it? What have you proved by this duel? That you are a fool, a *durak*, that you are *un sot!* And that's what every one calls you! What will be the result of it? This! — that you have made me the laughing-stock of all Moscow; this! that every one will say that you, while in a drunken fit, and not knowing what you were about, challenged a man of whom you were jealous without any reason," — Ellen kept raising her voice and growing more and more excited, — "a man superior to you in every sense of the word...."

"Hm.... hm," bellowed Pierre, scowling, but not looking at her or stirring.

"And why did you believe that he was my paramour? Why was it? Because I liked his society! If you had been brighter and more agreeable, I should have preferred yours."

"Do not speak to me, I beg of you," whispered Pierre, hoarsely.

"Why shouldn't I speak to you? I have a right to speak, and I tell you up and down that it's rare to find a woman with a husband like you, who doesn't console herself with lovers, and that is a thing that I haven't done," said she.

Pierre started to say something, looked at her with strange eyes, the expression of which she could not understand, and again threw himself back. At that moment he was suffering physical pain; his chest was oppressed, and he could not breathe. He knew that it behooved him to do something to put an end to his torment, but what he wanted to do was too horrible.

"We had better part," he exclaimed in a broken voice.

"By all means, part, provided only you give me enough," said Ellen. "Part! That's nothing to scare one!"

Pierre sprang from the sofa, and staggered toward her.

"I will kill you!" he cried, and seizing from the table a marble slab, with a force such as he had never before possessed, rushed toward her brandishing it in the air.

Ellen's face was filled with horror; she screamed and sprang away from him. His father's nature suddenly became manifest in him. Pierre experienced the rapture and fascination of frenzy. He flung down the marble, breaking it in fragments, and with raised arms flew at her, crying, "Away!" with such a terrible voice that it rang through the whole house and filled every one with horror. God knows what Pierre would have done at that moment if Ellen had not escaped from the room.

At the end of a week, Pierre had given to his wife a power of attorney for the control of all his Great Russian possessions, which amounted to a large half of his property, and returned alone to Petersburg.

CHAPTER VII

Two months had elapsed since news of the battle of Austerlitz and the death of Prince Andreï had been received at Luisiya Gorui, and, in spite of all the letters sent through the diplomatic service, and all inquiries, his body had not been recovered, and his name was not on the lists of prisoners. Worse than all for his relatives was the very hope that still remained that he had been picked up on the battle-field by some of the natives, and might be even now convalescing or dying somewhere alone, among strangers, and unable to send them any word.

In the newspapers from which the old prince had first learned of the battle of Austerlitz, it was stated, as usual, in the briefest and vaguest terms, that the Russians, after brilliant deeds of arms, had been compelled to retreat, and had accomplished this with the greatest order possible.

The old prince understood from this official bulletin that our troops had been defeated. A week after the receipt of the newspapers which informed him of the battle of Austerlitz, a letter came from Kutuzof, who announced the fate that had befallen his son.

"Your son," wrote Kutuzof, "before my eyes, fell at the head of his regiment, with the standard in his hands, like a hero worthy of his father and his fatherland. To the universal regret of all the army, including myself, it is as yet uncertain whether he is alive or dead. I flatter myself with the hope that your son is still alive, for, in the contrary case, he would certainly have been mentioned among the officers found on the field of battle, the list of which was brought me under flag of truce."

Receiving this news late in the afternoon when he was alone in his cabinet, the old prince as usual went the next day to take his morning promenade, but he had nothing to say to the overseer, the gardener, or the architect, and, though his countenance was lowering, there was no outbreak of wrath.

When, at the accustomed time, the Princess Maríya went to him, he was standing at his bench and driving his lathe, but he did not glance up at her as usual when she entered the room.

"Ah! Princess Maríya," suddenly said he, in an unnatural tone, and threw down his chisel. The wheel continued to revolve from the impetus. The Princess Maríya long remembered this dying whir of the wheel, which was

associated for her with what followed. The Princess
María approached him, looked into his face, and suddenly something seemed to pull at her heartstrings.
Her eyes ceased to see clearly. By her father's face,
which was not melancholy or downcast, but wrathful
and working unnaturally, she saw that now, now some
terrible misfortune was threatening to overwhelm her,
a misfortune than which none is worse in life, none
more irreparable and incomprehensible, a misfortune
such as she had never yet experienced, — the death of
one she loved.

" *Mon père!* André!" said the princess, and she
who was ordinarily so clumsy and awkward became
endowed with such inexpressible charm of grief and
self-forgetfulness that her father could not endure her
glance, and, with a sob, turned away.

"I have had news. He's not among the prisoners,
he's not on the list of the dead. Kutuzof has written
me," he cried in a shrill voice, as if he desired by this
cry to drive the princess away. "He is killed!"

The princess did not fall; she did not even feel faint.
She was pale to begin with, but when she heard these
words her face altered and a light seemed to gleam in
her beautiful, lustrous eyes. Something like joy, a
supernatural joy, independent of the sorrows and joys
of this world, took the place of this violent grief that
filled her heart. She forgot all her fear of her father,
and went up to him, took him by the hand, and drew
him to her, and threw her arm around his thin, sinewy
neck.

" *Mon père!* " said she, " do not turn away from me;
let us weep together!"

"Villains! scoundrels!" cried the old man, averting
his face from her. "To destroy the army, to destroy
men! What for? Go, go and tell Liza."

The princess fell back feebly in the arm-chair near
her father, and burst into tears. She could now see
her brother as he looked at the moment when he bade
her and Liza farewell, with his affectionate and at the
same time rather haughty face. She could see him as

he tenderly and yet scornfully hung the medallion round his neck. Did he come to believe? Had he repented of his unbelief? Was he yonder now, yonder in the mansions of eternal calm and bliss?

These were the questions that filled her thoughts.

"*Mon père*, tell me how it happened?" said she, through her tears.

"Go, go; he was killed in that defeat where the best men of Russia and Russian glory were led out to sacrifice. Go, Princess Maríya. Go and tell Liza. I will follow."

When the Princess Maríya left her father, she found the little princess sitting at her work, with that expression of inward calm and happiness peculiar to women in her condition. She looked up as her sister-in-law came in. It was evident that her eyes did not see the Princess Maríya, but were rather profoundly searching into the tremendous and blessed mystery that was taking place within her.

"Marie," said she, turning from her embroidery-frame, and leaning back, "let me have your hand."

She took the princess's hand and laid it just below her heart. Her eyes smiled with anticipation, the short, downy lip was raised in a happy, childlike smile.

The Princess Maríya knelt down before her, and buried her face in the folds of her sister-in-law's dress.

"There! there, do you perceive it? It is so strange. And do you know, Marie, I am going to love him very dearly," said Liza, looking with shining, happy eyes at her husband's sister.

The Princess Maríya could not raise her head; she was weeping.

"What is the matter, Masha?"

"Nothing; only I felt sad, sad about Andreï," she replied, wiping away her tears on her sister-in-law's knee.

Several times in the course of the morning the Princess Maríya attempted to break the news to her sister-in-law, and each time she had to weep. These tears, the cause for which the little princess could not understand, alarmed her, unobservant as her nature was. She made no remark, but she looked around in some alarm, as if searching for some one. Before dinner the old prince came into her room and went right out again without saying a word; she was always afraid of him, but now his face was so disturbed and stern that she gazed at the Princess Maríya, then fell into a brown study, with her eyes, as it were, turned inward with that expression so characteristic of women in her condition, and suddenly burst into tears.

"Have you heard anything from Andreï?" she asked.

"No, you know that it is n't time yet to get news, but *mon père* is anxious, and it frightens me."

"Then there's nothing?"

"Nothing," replied the Princess Maríya, letting her lustrous eyes rest unflinchingly on her sister-in-law.

She had made up her mind not to tell her, and had persuaded her father to conceal the terrible tidings from her until her confinement, which would be now before many days. The Princess Maríya and the old prince, each according to their own nature, bore and hid their grief. The old prince was not willing to indulge in hopes; he had made up his mind that Prince Andreï was killed, and, although he sent a chinovnik to Austria to make diligent search for traces of his son, he commanded him to order in Moscow a gravestone to be erected in his garden, and he told every one that his son was dead. He himself aged rapidly; he unchangeably carried out the rigorous routine of his life, but his strength failed him; he took shorter walks, ate less, slept less, and each day grew weaker.

The Princess Maríya still hoped. She prayed for her brother, as if he were alive, and all the time was on the lookout for news of his return.

CHAPTER VIII

"*Ma bonne amie,*" said the little princess, after break-fast on the morning of the thirty-first of March, and her downy upper lip was lifted out of mere habit, for a certain sense of melancholy had affected not only the talk, but the footsteps, of all in this house ever since the receipt of the terrible news, so that even the little princess had come under the influence of it, and she smiled in such a way that it reminded one even more of the general depression.

"My dear girl, I am afraid my *frühstück* this morn-ing, as Foka, the cook, calls it, did n't agree with me."

"What 's the matter, sweetheart? You are pale. Akh! you are very, very pale," said the Princess María, alarmed, and going toward her sister-in-law with her heavy but gentle steps.

"Your illustriousness, shan't we call María Bogdá-novna?" inquired one of the maids, who happened to be present. (Marya Bogdanovna was the midwife from the district capital, who had now been living at Luisiya Gorui for a fortnight.)

"It certainly may be necessary," replied the Princess María. "I will go. Courage, *mon ange!*" She kissed Liza and started to leave the room.

"Ah, no, no!"

And over and above the pallor arising from physical suffering, the little princess's face showed a childish fear of unendurable agony.

"No, it is indigestion, tell me it is indigestion, Marie," and the princess wept, childishly, capriciously, and perhaps rather hypocritically, wringing her hands. The young princess went from the room in search of Marya Bogdanovna.

"*Mon Dieu! Mon Dieu!*"

"Oh!" was heard behind her.

Rubbing her plump, small, white hands, the midwife came to meet her, with a significant but perfectly com-posed expression of countenance.

"Marya Bogdanovna! I think it is beginning," said the Princess Maríya, looking at the midwife, with terrified, wide-open eyes.

"Well, then, glory to God for that, princess," said Marya Bogdanovna, not quickening her steps. "You young ladies have no need to know anything about it."

"But what shall we do if the doctor from Moscow has not come yet?" asked the princess.

By Liza and Prince Andreï's desire they had sent to Moscow for an obstetrician, and he was expected at any moment.

"No matter, princess, don't be alarmed," said Marya Bogdanovna; "it will come out all right even without a doctor."

In the course of five minutes the young princess heard, as she sat in her room, the sound of men carrying something heavy. She looked out and saw the servants, for some reason or other, carrying into the sleeping-room the leather divan which had always stood in Prince Andreï's study. There was an expression of gentleness and solemnity on the faces of the men who were lugging this.

The Princess Maríya sat alone in her room, listening to the various sounds in the house, and occasionally opening the door when any one passed, and trying to make out what was going on in the corridor. A number of women with light steps were moving hither and thither, and they gave a glance at the young princess and turned away. She did not venture to ask any questions, but shut her door, went back to her own bedroom, sat down for a little in her arm-chair, then hastened to her oratory, and bent on her knees before the *kiot*, or shrine of images. To her dismay and surprise, she found that prayer did not aid her in calming her agitation.

Suddenly the door of her room was softly opened, and on the threshhold appeared her old nurse Praskovya Savishna, with a kerchief tied over her head; she almost never came to the princess's room, as her father had expressly forbidden it.

"God be with you, Mashenka, I have come to sit a little while," said the nurse; "and here, my angel, are the prince's wedding tapers I 've brought to light before the saint," she added, with a sigh.

"Akh! how glad I am, nurse."

"God is merciful, my dove."[1]

The old nurse lit the tapers in the golden candlesticks before the shrine, and then sat down by the door with her knitting. The Princess María took a book and began to read. Only when steps or voices were heard the princess would glance up with frightened, anxious face, and the nurse would look at her with a soothing expression.

In all parts of the house every one was dominated by the same feelings which the Princess María experienced as she sat in her room. In accordance with the old superstition that the fewer people know of the sufferings of a woman in labor, the less she suffers, all pretended to be ignorant of what was going on; no one spoke about it, but every one, over and above the habitual gravity and respectful propriety that obtained in the prince's household, evidently shared the general anxiety, tender-heartedness, and consciousness that something great, incomprehensible, and solemn was taking place at that moment.

There was no sound of laughing heard in the great room devoted to the maidservants. In the offitsialnaya all the men sat silent, as if awaiting something. The servants kept pine knots and candles burning, and did not think of going to sleep. The old prince, walking on his heels, strode up and down his cabinet, and at last ordered Tikhon to go to Marya Bogdanovna: — "Merely say, 'The prince has sent to ask,' and come and tell me what she says."

"Inform the prince that labor has begun," said Marya Bogdanovna, giving the messenger a significant look. Tikhon went and reported to the prince.

"Very good," exclaimed the prince, closing the door behind him, and Tikhon heard not the slightest sound

[1] *Galúbka.*

in the cabinet. After waiting some time Tikhon went into the cabinet, pretending that it was to snuff the candles, and, seeing the prince lying on the sofa, he looked at his agitated face, shook his head, then silently stepping up to him and kissing him on the shoulder, he left the room forgetting to snuff the candles and not saying why he had gone in.

The most solemn mystery in the world was in process of consummation. The evening passed; the night wore away, and the sense of expectancy and solemnified thought at the presence of the ineffable grew intenser rather than grew weaker. No one slept.

It was one of those March nights when winter seems determined to resume his sway, and scatters with rage and despair his last snows and gusts of wind. A relay of horses had been sent along the highway to meet the German doctor from Moscow, who was every moment expected, and horsemen with lanterns were sent out to the junction of the cross-road, to guide him safely by the pitfalls and watery hollows.

The Princess Maríya had long since laid down her book; she was sitting in perfect silence, with her lustrous eyes fastened on her old nurse's wrinkled face, every line of which she knew so well; on the little tuft of gray hair that had escaped from under her kerchief, and on the loose flesh hanging under her chin.

Nyanya Savishna, with her unfinished stocking in her hand, was telling in a low voice, without heeding her own words, the story that she had told a hundred times about the late princess, and how she had been delivered of the Princess Maríya in Kishenef, with an old Moldavian peasant woman for a midwife.

"God is merciful; dokhtors are never needed," she was saying.

Suddenly a gust of wind beat violently against the window-frame (it was always a whim of the princess to have the double windows taken off from at least one of the windows in each room, as soon as the larks made their appearance) and burst the carelessly pushed bolt,

while a draught of cold air laden with snow shook the silken curtains and puffed out the light.

The princess shuddered. The old nyánya, laying down her stocking, went to the window, and, leaning out, tried to shut it to again. The cold wind fluttered the ends of her kerchief and the gray locks of her disheveled hair.

"Princess! matushka! some one's coming up the preshpekt," cried she, getting hold of the window, but not closing it, "with lanterns! It must be the dokhtor!"

"Akh! glory to God, *Slava Bohu*," exclaimed the Princess Maríya. "I must go and meet him; he won't be able to speak Russian."

The Princess Maríya wrapped her shawl around her and hastened down to meet the new-comer. When she reached the anteroom she looked through the window and saw a team and lanterns standing at the front door-steps. She went out on the landing. On the foot of the balustrade flamed a tallow candle, guttering in the wind. The groom Filipp, with terrified face, and with another candle in his hand, stood lower down on the first landing of the staircase. Still lower down at the turning of the staircase were heard advancing footsteps in thick boots. And a voice which struck the Princess Maríya as strangely familiar was saying something.

"Thank God, — *Slava Bohu!*" said the voice "and my father?"

"He has gone to bed," replied the voice of Demyan, the steward, who had by this time come down.

Then the well-known voice asked something, and Demyan answered, and the steps in the thick boots came swifter up the stairs and nearer to the princess, out of sight around the turn.

"It is Andreï!" said the princess to herself. "No, it cannot be! It would be too extraordinary," she thought, and at the very moment that this thought occurred to her, on the landing where stood the servant with the candle, appeared Prince Andreï's form, enveloped in a fur shuba, the collar all powdered with snow.

Yes, it was he; but pale and thin, and with an altered

and strangely gentle but anxious expression. He ran up the stairs and clasped his sister in his arms.

"You didn't receive my letter?" he asked, and not waiting for her reply, which, indeed, he would not have received, for the princess was too much moved to speak, he turned back, and joined by the obstetrician, who had come with him (he had overtaken him at the last post station), with hasty steps flew up the stairs again, and again embraced his sister.

"What luck!" he cried, "dear Masha!" and flinging off his shuba and boots, he went to his wife's room.

CHAPTER IX

THE little princess, in a white cap, was lying on the pillows. (For the moment she was a little easier.) Her dark locks fell in disorder over her flushed cheeks, wet with perspiration; her rosy, fascinating mouth, with its downy upper lip, was open, and she wore a smile of joy.

Prince Andreï went into the room and paused in front of her, at the foot of the sofa on which she lay. Her brilliant eyes, looking at him with childish trepidation and anxiety, rested on him without change of expression.

'I love you all; I haven't done any one any harm; why must I suffer so? Help me!' her expression seemed to say.

She saw her husband, but seemed to have no comprehension of the significance of his appearing just at this time before her.

Prince Andreï went round to the side of the sofa, and kissed her on the forehead.

"My darling heart — *dúshenka moyá*," he said. He had never called her by this endearing term before. "God is merciful...."

She looked at him with a questioning, childishly offended expression.

'I expected help from thee, and none comes, none comes!' her eyes seemed to say. She was not surprised at his coming; she did not even realize that he had come. His appearance had nothing to do with her agony and the assuagement of it.

The pains began again, and Marya Bogdanovna advised Prince Andreï to leave the room. The obstetrician entered the room. Prince Andreï went out, and meeting his sister he again joined her. They began to talk in a whisper, but the conversation was constantly interrupted by silences.

They kept waiting and listening.

"*Allez, mon ami*," said the Princess Maríya. Prince Andreï again went to his wife, and then sat down in the adjoining room waiting. Some woman or other came out of her room with a terrified face and was confused when she saw Prince Andreï.

He covered his face with his hands and sat thus for some minutes. Pitiful, heartbreaking groans were heard in the other room. Prince Andreï stood up and went to the door, and was about to open it. Some one held it to.

"You can't come in! it's impossible," said a terrified voice on the other side. He began to pace up and down the room. The cries had ceased; a few seconds more passed, when suddenly a terrible cry — it could not be his wife's, she could not cry like that — rang through the next room. Prince Andreï hastened to the door; this cry ceased; a baby's wailing was heard.

"What have they brought a baby in there for?" was Prince Andreï's query at first. "A baby? What baby?.... Why a baby there?.... Or can my baby have been born?"

Then he suddenly realized all the joyful significance of this cry; the tears choked him, and, leaning both his elbows on the window-seat, he wept and sobbed as children weep.

The door opened. The doctor, with his shirt-sleeves rolled up, without his coat, pale, and with trembling jaw, came from the room. Prince Andreï went to him, but the doctor looked at him with a strange expression of confusion, and, without saying a word, passed by him. A woman came running out, but when she saw Prince

Andreï, stopped short on the threshold.   He went into his wife's room.

She was dead, lying in the same position in which he had seen her five minutes before, and, notwithstanding the fixity of her eyes, and the pallor of her cheeks, that charming, little, childish face, with the lip shaded with dark hairs, wore the same expression as before.

"I love you all, and I have done no one any harm, and what have you done to me?" said her lovely face, pitifully pale in death.   In the corner of the room a small, red object was yelping and wailing in the trembling, white hands of Marya Bogdanovna.

Two hours later, Prince Andreï, with noiseless steps, went to his father's cabinet.   The old prince had already been informed of everything.   He was standing by the very door, and, as soon as it was thrown open, the old man, without speaking, flung his rough, aged hands around his son's neck, and held him as in a vise and sobbed like a child.

Three days later, the little princess was buried, and Prince Andreï went up the steps to the coffin to take his last farewell.   And there also in the coffin lay the same face, though with closed eyes.

'Akh! what have you done to me?' it all seemed to say.   Prince Andreï felt that his heartstrings were torn within him, that he had done a wrong that could never be repaired or forgotten.   He could not weep.

The old prince also came and kissed her waxen hand, placidly folded on her breast, and to him her face seemed to say: —

'Akh! and why have you done this to me?'

And the old man, after looking into her face, abruptly turned away.

Then, again, five days later, they christened the baby prince Nikolaï Andreyitch.   The wet-nurse held up the swaddling-clothes against her chin, while the priest, with a goose-quill, anointed with holy oil the infant's wrinkled little pink palms and soles. His grandfather, who acted as sponsor, with tottering steps, and afraid of dropping him, carried the little prince around the tin-lined font, and handed him over to his godmother, the Princess Maríya.

Prince Andreï, in deadly apprehension lest they should drop the child, sat in the next room, waiting for the conclusion of the sacrament. He looked joyfully at his baby when the nurse brought him to him, and nodded his head with great satisfaction when the nurse confided to him that the lump of wax with some of the infant's hairs on it, when thrown into the font, did not sink, but floated.[1]

CHAPTER X

THE part played by Rostof in the duel between Dolokhof and Bezukhoï was ignored through the old count's efforts, and the young man, instead of being cashiered as he anticipated, was appointed aide to the governor-general of Moscow. In consequence of this, he was unable to go to the country with the rest of the family, but was kept in Moscow all summer, engaged in his new duties.

Dolokhof recovered, and he and Rostof became great friends during the time of his convalescence. He had been carried to the residence of his mother, who loved him passionately and devotedly. The old lady, Marya Ivanovna, becoming attached to Rostof on account of his friendship for her Fedya, often talked with him about her son.

"Yes, count, he is too noble and high-souled for this corrupt world of ours. No one loves goodness; it serves as a reproach to every one. Now tell me, count, tell me honestly, was it fair and honorable on Bezukhoï's part? And Fedya, with all his noble nature, always liked him,

---

[1] It is part of the Russian baptismal service for the priest to cut the infant's hair. The superstition considers it unlucky for the bit of wax with a few of these hairs attached to sink if placed in the waters of the baptismal font, and lucky for it to float.

and now never says hard things about him at all.   And
in Petersburg, they played all those tricks on the policeman; they did it together, did n't they?   Well, Bezukhoï went scot free, and my Fedya had to bear the whole
brunt of it on his shoulders!   Yes, he had to bear it all!
To be sure, he has been restored to his rank, but why
should n't he have been?   I don't believe the fatherland
has many braver sons than he is!....   And now this duel!
Have such men any feeling, any honor?   Knowing that
he was an only son, to challenge him to fight a duel, and
then to fire right at him!   Fortunately, God helped us.
And what was it all about?   Who is there in our day
who does n't engage in intrigues?   Why should he have
been so jealous?   I should think he might have given
some signs of it before, and here a year has gone by!
And so he challenged him, supposing that Fedya would
not accept because he owed him some money.   How
nasty of him!   I know you appreciate Fedya, my dear
count, and so I love you with my whole heart, believe
me.   There are n't many who understand him.   He has
such a lofty, heavenly nature."

Dolokhof himself, during his convalescence, often said
things to Rostof that no one would ever have expected
from him.

"I am supposed to be a bad man, I know," said he,
"and let them think so.   I don't care anything about
the opinions of men, unless I am fond of them; but if I
am fond of people, I am so fond of them that I would
give my life for them, and as for the rest, if they stood
in my way, I would push them to the wall.   My mother
is a dear, precious woman, and I have two or three
others — you among the number — and as for the rest,
I only heed them as so many who may be able to be
useful or injurious to me.   And almost all are injurious,
especially the women.   Yes, my dear, — *dúsha moyá*"
— he went on to say, "among men I meet many who
are lovable, noble, elevated, but among women I have
yet to meet one who is not to be bought — all are alike,
countess and cook!   I have yet to find that celestial
purity, devotion, which I look for in woman.   If I were

ever to find such a woman, I would give my life for her. But these!"…. he made a depreciatory gesture. "And you may not believe me, but if I prize my life still, it is simply because I hope some day to find one of these heavenly creatures who would regenerate me, purify me, and elevate me. But you do not understand this."

"Indeed, I understand perfectly," replied Rostof, who was coming more and more under the influence of his new friend.

In the autumn the Rostof family returned to Moscow. Early in the winter Denísof also came back and stayed with the Rostofs. The first months of this winter of 1806, which Nikolaï Rostof spent in Moscow, could not have been happier or gayer for him and for all his family. Nikolaï brought home with him to his parents' home many young men. Viera was a pretty young lady of twenty summers. Sonya was just sixteen, and had all the charm of an opening flower. Natasha, half child and half maiden, was now at one moment full of innocent merriment, at the next showing all the fascination of a maiden.

The house of the Rostofs at this time seemed to be full of the peculiar atmosphere of loveliness characteristic of homes where there are very pretty and very young ladies. Every young man who came there and saw these bright, impressionable, girlish faces, smiling apparently from very happiness, and the merry running to and fro, and heard that continual chattering of maiden's voices, inconsequential, illogical, kindly to every one, ready for anything, and full of hope, and listened to these inconsequential sounds, now of singing, now of instrumental music, must have experienced one and the same feeling of predisposition for love and coming happiness, which the young people of the Rostof household themselves experienced.

Among the young men and one of the first whom Rostof introduced at home was Dolokhof, and every one, with the exception of Natasha, was pleased with him. She almost quarreled with her brother concerning him. She insisted that he was a bad man, that Pierre was in the right in his duel with Dolokhof, and the other in the wrong; and that he was disagreeable and insincere.

"There's nothing for me to understand," cried Natasha, with stubborn self-will; "he is bad, and lacks feeling. Now, here, I like your Denísof; he may be a spendthrift, and all that, but still I like him, and I certainly understand him. I don't know how to express it to you, but everything that *he* does has some ulterior object, and I don't like him; but Denísof...."

"There now, Denísof is quite another matter," replied Nikolaï, giving her to understand that, in comparison with Dolokhof, Denísof was of no consequence. "You ought to know what a tender heart this Dolokhof has, you ought to see him with his mother! what a warm-hearted fellow he is!"

"Well, I don't know anything about that, but I'm ill at ease with him. And do you know, he's in love with Sonya?"

"What nonsense!"....

"I'm certain of it, you can see for yourself."

Natasha's prognostication was justified. Dolokhof, though he did not like the society of ladies, had begun to be a frequent visitor at the Rostofs', and the problem what brought him there was quickly solved, though no one ventured to remark upon it. He came on account of Sonya. And Sonya, though she would never have dared to acknowledge such a thing, knew it very well, and every time that Dolokhof was announced blushed as red as kumatch.

Dolokhof often came to dinner at the Rostofs'; he never missed an entertainment where they were to be found, and frequented the *adolescentes* balls given by Iogel, which the Rostofs always attended. He paid preëminent attention to Sonya, and looked at her with such eyes, that not only the girl herself could not endure his glances without blushing, but even the old countess and Natasha flushed if they caught sight of him looking at her.

It was plain to see that this powerful, strange man was coming under the irresistible influence of this gracious, dark-eyed maiden, who, all the time, was in love with some one else.

Rostof perceived that there was something new between Dolokhof and Sonya, but he could not make out what this relationship was.

"Everybody here is in love with some one," he said to himself, referring to Sonya and Natasha. But he was no longer at his ease in the company of Sonya and Dolokhof, as before, and he began to be absent from home more frequently.

In the autumn of 1806 there had been continual talk about war with Napoleon, and with even greater heat than the year before. A conscription of ten men in a thousand, and of nine militiamen to a thousand, in addition, was ordered. Everywhere anathemas were heaped upon Bonapartism, and nothing was talked about in Moscow except the coming war.

For the Rostof family, all interest in these preparations for war were centered on the fact that Nikolushka would not hear of such a thing as remaining at home, and was only waiting for the end of Denísof's furlough in order to return with him to his regiment after the holidays. The approaching departure did not in any way prevent him from having a good time; it rather only seemed still more to spur them all on to enjoyment. The larger part of his time he spent away from the house, at dinners, receptions, and balls.

CHAPTER XI

On the third day of the Christmas holidays, Nikolai dined at home — a thing which he had rarely done of late. It was a sort of farewell dinner, as he and Denísof were going to start for their regiments after Epiphany. There were about twenty who sat down at table, among the number Dolokhof and Denísof.

Never at the Rostofs' had that delicious breath of

passion and that atmosphere of love made itself felt with such force as during these days of the Christmas-tide.

"Seize these moments of happiness; let yourself drift into love; become enamoured yourself. This is the only genuine bliss in the world; everything else is dross. And with this alone all of us here are exclusively occupied," said this atmosphere.

Nikolaï, as always, tired out two spans of horses, and yet had not had time enough to go to all the places where he was needed and summoned; he came home just before dinner-time. As soon as he came in, he noticed and felt this atmosphere so charged with the electrical tension of love, but more especially he remarked a strange embarrassment existing among several of those who were gathered in the drawing-room. Peculiarly agitated were Sonya, Dolokhof, and the old countess, and, to a certain extent, his sister Natasha. Nikolaï perceived that something must have happened between Sonya and Dolokhof, and, in accordance with his impulsive nature, and the genuine tact characteristic of him, he showed himself very affectionate and considerate toward these two.

That evening of the third day of the Christmas-tide, there was to be one of the balls which Iogel, the dancing-master, used to give during the holidays to all the young men and women who were his pupils.

"Nikolenka, you will go to Iogel's, won't you? Please do!" said Natasha to him. "He invited you especially, and Vasíli Dmítritch is going." (By Vasíli Dmítritch, she meant Denísof.)

"Where would n't I go at the countess's wequest!" exclaimed Denísof, who, in a joking way, occupied in the Rostof household the position of knight to Natasha. "I am weady to dance even the *pas de châle!*"

"I will if I have time. I promised to go to the Arkharofs', who have a party this evening," said Nikolaï.

"And you?" he asked, turning to Dolokhof. But the moment the words had left his lips, he perceived that he had committed a blunder.

"Yes, perhaps so," replied Dolokhof, coolly and laconically, glancing at Sonya, frowning, and giving Nikolaï exactly the same sort of a look that he had given Pierre, the night of the dinner to Bagration at the club.

"There must be something up," said Nikolaï to himself, and he was still further confirmed in this impression by the fact that Dolokhof took his departure immediately after dinner. He called Natasha to him, and asked what the matter was.

"And I was just looking for you," exclaimed Natasha, running to him. "I told you so, but you would not believe me," said she, triumphantly. "He has proposed for Sonya."

Little as Sonya had occupied Nikolaï's thoughts during these last weeks, still he felt a sort of pang when he learned this. Dolokhof was a suitable, and in some respects a brilliant, match for the dowerless orphan, Sonya. From the old countess's standpoint, and that of society, it was simply madness to refuse him. And, therefore, Nikolaï's first feeling on hearing this piece of news was that of indignation against the girl.

He had it on his tongue's end to say, "And it is an excellent thing, of course, for her to forget her old promises, and accept this first proposal," but before he spoke, Natasha went on : —

"And can you imagine it, she refused him ? — absolutely refused him ! She told him that she loved some one else," she added, after a moment's silence.

"Yes, and could my Sonya have done anything else ! " thought Nikolaï.

"In spite of all mamma's arguments, she refused him, and I know that she won't change her decision if she said that."

"And mamma tried to persuade her ? " he asked reproachfully.

"Yes," said Natasha. "And now, Nikolenka — and don't be vexed — but I know you will never marry her. I am sure of it, God knows why, but I am perfectly certain that you will never marry her."

"Well, you know nothing about it at all," said

Nikolaï. "But I must have a little talk with her. How charming she is! our Sonya," he added, with a smile.

"Charming! indeed she is. I will send her to you."

And Natasha, kissing her brother, ran away.

In a moment Sonya came in, alarmed and abashed, as if she had been doing something wrong. Nikolaï went to her and kissed her hand. This was the first opportunity that they had enjoyed for some time of being alone together, and talking about their love.

"Sophie," said he, timidly, and then growing more and more confident. "If you have seen fit to refuse an offer not only so brilliant, but so very advantageous .... he is a splendid, noble fellow; and he is a friend of mine."

Sonya interrupted him.

"I have already refused him," said she, hastily.

"If you have refused him for my sake, then I am afraid that I...."

Sonya again interrupted him. She looked at him with beseeching, frightened eyes.

"Nicholas, don't speak of that, please," said she.

"Nay, but I must. Maybe it is unbounded conceit on my part, but it is better to speak. If you have refused him for my sake, then I ought to tell you the whole truth. I love you, I think, more than all...."

"That is all I want," said Sonya, with a sigh.

"No! but I have fallen in love a thousand times, and I shall fall in love again, and I shall never find any one so friendly, so true, so lovely as you. But then, I am young. *Maman* does not approve of this. So, then, simply I can't make any promises. And I beg of you to reconsider Dolokhof's proposal," said he, finding it hard to speak his friend's name.

"Don't mention such a thing. I have no desires at all. I love you as if you were my brother, and shall always love you, and that is quite enough for me."

"You are an angel! I am not worthy of you, but what I am afraid is that I might give you a wrong impression!" Nikolaï once more kissed her hand.

CHAPTER XII

"IOGEL has the jolliest balls in Moscow."

This was what the mammas said, as they looked at their *adolescentes*, practising the steps which they had just been learning; this was said also by the grown-up girls and young men, who came to these balls with just a shade of condescension, and, nevertheless, found there the very best amusement.

This very same year, two engagements had resulted from these balls. The two pretty Princesses Gorchakova found husbands there, and thus these balls came into still greater vogue. Their peculiarity was the lack of any host or hostess: they merely had the good-natured Iogel, light as flying down, bowing and scraping, according to the rules of his art; and almost all of his guests were those from whom he had received bank-notes in payment for dancing lessons. The fact was only those came to these balls that liked to dance and have a good time with the zest of thirteen or fourteen year old maidens wearing a long dress for the first time in their lives.

All, with rare exceptions, were pretty, or at least seemed to be. How enthusiastically they all smiled, and how eloquent were their sparkling eyes! Sometimes even the *pas de châle*, or shawl figure was danced by his most advanced pupils, and of these Natasha was the best, as she was distinguished for her grace; but at this, the last of the season, they danced only English schottisches, and the mazurka, which was now beginning to be fashionable.

Iogel engaged for the ball the large drawing-room in the Bezukhoï mansion, and the ball was a great success, as every one confessed. Many were the pretty girls, and the Rostof maidens were among the prettiest. Both of them were remarkably happy and gay. That evening, before she started, Sonya, proud of Dolokhof's proposal, of her refusal of him, and of her explanation with Nikolaï, whirled around the house, scarcely giving her maid a chance to comb her hair, and now she was perfectly transfigured with impetuous delight.

Natasha, not less proud of going to this ball, for the first time in a long dress, was even more radiant. Both wore muslin gowns with pink ribbons.

The moment they entered the ball-room, Natasha began to be enamoured of every one. She was not enamoured of any one in particular, but of all! Whomever her eyes happened to fall upon, with him she was deeply in love for the time being.

"Akh! how nice it is!" she kept saying, whenever she met Sonya.

Nikolaï and Denísof strolled through the rooms, looking graciously and condescendingly on the dancers.

"How pwetty she is! She will be a waving beauty!"

"Who?"

"The Countess Natasha," replied Denísof.

"And how charmingly she dances! What gwace!" he said once more, after a little pause.

"Whom are you talking about?"

"I was refe'wing to your sister," said Denísof, testily. Rostof smiled.

"My dear count, you are one of my best pupils, you must dance," said the little Iogel, coming up to Nikolaï. "Just see what a lot of pretty girls."

And with the same request he turned to Denísof, who also had been one of his pupils.

"No, my dear, I pwefer to be a wall-flower," replied Denísof. "Don't you wemember how illy I pwofited by your lessons?"

"Oh, no," said Iogel, hastening to reassure him. "You were only somewhat inattentive, but you had the ability; oh, yes, you had the ability."

The band now began to play the newly introduced mazurka. Nikolaï could not refuse Iogel, and invited Sonya as his partner. Denísof sat down with some of the elderly ladies, and, leaning his elbows on his sword and beating time with his foot, told jolly stories and made the old ladies laugh, while his eyes followed the young people dancing.

Iogel led the mazurka with Natasha, who was his pride and his best pupil. Noiselessly, skilfully shuffling his feet, shod in pumps, Iogel flew around the hall with Natasha, rather timid, but, nevertheless, performing all the steps with the utmost care.

Denísof did not take his eyes from her, and thumped his sword in time, with an expression that said clearly that he was not dancing simply because he did not care to, and not because he was not able. In the midst of the figure he saw Rostof passing, and called him to him.

"That's no way at all," said he; "do you call that the Polish mazurka? But she dances admiwably though!"

Knowing that Denísof in Poland had won great reputation for his skill in dancing the genuine Polish mazurka, Nikolaï glided over to Natasha:—

"Go ahead," said he, "choose Denísof! He dances splendidly! It's wonderful!"

When it came Natasha's turn again, she got up and, swiftly *chasséeing* across the hall in her dainty slippers trimmed with rosettes, she blushingly made her way to the corner where Denísof was sitting. She saw that all were looking at her and waiting. Nikolaï noticed that Denísof and Natasha were having a playful quarrel, and that the former refused, but smiled with gratification. He went up to them.

"Please, Vasíli Dmitritch," said Natasha. "Come, please do!"

"I pway you, let me off, countess."

"There, there, that's no excuse, Vasya!" said Nikolaï.

"Just like two kittens persuading Vaska," said Denísof, jestingly.

"I will sing a whole evening for you," pleaded Natasha.

"The enchantwess can do anything with me!" exclaimed Denísof, and he laid aside his sword. He made his way out from among the chairs, firmly grasped his partner's hand, threw back his head, and put his feet in position, waiting to catch the beat of the music.

Only on horseback, or while dancing the mazurka, was Denísof's small stature lost sight of, and he appeared to be the gallant young hero that he felt himself to be. While waiting to get the time, he glanced askance at his partner triumphantly and mischievously, then suddenly stamped with one foot, and, like a tennis-ball, bounded up elastically, and sped out into the middle of the room, carrying his lady with him. Noiselessly, he flew half across the hall on one foot, and, apparently, not seeing the chairs ranged in front of him, was like to have run right into them; but, suddenly clinking his spurs and spreading his legs, he stopped on his heels, stood so for a second, then with a clanking of his spurs, making a sort of double shuffle, quickly turned about, and, with his left heel clicking against the right, he again flew around the circle.

Natasha realized by a sort of intuition what he intended to do, and herself not knowing how, simply followed him, and gave herself up to his guidance.

Now he would whirl around her from left to right, then from right to left; now falling on his knee cause her to pirouette around him, and then, again, he would spring up and dart off in a straight line with such impetuosity, without even taking breath, that it seemed as if they were going straight through all the rooms; then suddenly he would come to a pause again, and execute some other new and unexpected evolution. When at last, swiftly whirling his lady about in front of her own seat, and jingling his spurs, he made her a low bow, Natasha forgot to perform a courtesy. In perplexity, she fixed her eyes upon him, smiling as if she did not know him. "What does this mean?" she asked herself.

Although Iogel refused to acknowledge such a dance as a proper mazurka, all were in raptures over Denísof's skill; he was in constant requisition as a partner, and the old people, smiling, began to talk about Poland, and about the good old times. Denísof, flushed from the exertion of the mazurka, and wiping his face with his handkerchief, sat down next Natasha, and through the rest of the evening did not leave her side.

CHAPTER XIII

For two days, Rostof had not seen Dolakhof at his house, or found him at home; on the third day he received a note from him : —

"As I intend never to visit your house again, from reasons which you may appreciate, and as I am about to rejoin my regiment, I am going to give to my friends a farewell supper this evening. Come to the English hotel."

At ten o'clock that evening, after the theater, where he had been with Denísof and his family, Rostof repaired to the place which Dolokhof had designated. He was immediately shown into the handsomest room of the hotel, which Dolokhof had engaged for the occasion. A score of men were gathered around the table, at the head of which sat Dolokhof, between two candles. There was a pile of gold and bills on the table, and Dolokhof was keeping the bank.

Since Dolokhof's proposal and Sonya's refusal, Nikolaï had not seen him, and he felt a slight sense of confusion at the thought of their meeting.

Dolokhof's keen, cold eyes met Nikolaï's the moment he entered the room, as if he had been waiting for him for some time.

"We have not met for several days," said Dolokhof, "thank you for coming. Here, I will only finish this hand. Ilyushka and his chorus are coming."

"I have called at your house," said Rostof, reddening.

Dolokhof made him no answer.

"You may bet," he said.

Rostof recalled a strange conversation which he had once had with Dolokhof. "Only fools play on chance," had been Dolokhof's remark at the time.

"But perhaps you are afraid to play with me," said

Dolokhof now, as if he read Rostof's thought, and he smiled.

By his smile, Rostof could plainly see that he was in the same frame of mind as he had been at the time of the dinner at the club, or, one might say, at any of those times when Dolokhof, bored by the monotony of life, felt the necessity of escaping from it by some strange and usually outrageous action.

Rostof felt ill at ease. He racked his brain, but was unable to find an appropriate repartee for Dolokhof's words. But before he had a chance to reply, Dolokhof, looking straight into Rostof's face, said slowly, with deliberate intervals between the words, so that all might hear : —

"Do you remember you and I were talking once about gambling?.... 'It's a fool, a durak, who is willing to play on chance. One ought to play a sure hand,' but I am going to try it."

"Try the chance or the sure thing — I wonder which," thought Rostof.

"Well, you'd better not play," he added, and springing the freshly opened pack of cards, he cried: —.

"Bank, gentlemen!"

Pushing the money forward, Dolokhof prepared to start the bank. Rostof took a seat near him, and at first did not play. Dolokhof glanced at him.

"What? Won't you take a hand?" and strangely enough Nikolaï felt it incumbent upon him to select a card, and stake an insignificant sum on it, and thus begin to play.

"I have no money with me," he said.

"I will trust you."

Rostof staked five rubles on his card and lost; he staked again, and again he lost. Dolokhof trumped, in other words took Rostof's stake ten times running.

"Gentlemen," said he, after he had been keeping the bank some time, "I beg of you to lay your stakes on the cards, otherwise, I may become confused in the accounts."

One of the players ventured the hope that he was to be trusted.

"I trust you, certainly, but I am afraid of getting the accounts mixed. I beg of you to lay your money on the cards," replied Dolokhof. "Don't you worry yourself, you and I will settle our accounts afterwards," he added, turning to Rostof.

The game went on; the servant kept filling their glasses with champagne.

All Rostof's cards failed to be matched, and his losses amounted to eight hundred rubles. He was just writing down on the back of a card eight hundred rubles, but, as it happened that at that moment a glass of champagne was handed him, he hesitated, and once more staked the sum that he had been risking all along, that is, twenty rubles.

"Make it that," said Dolokhof, though he was apparently not looking at Rostof. "You'll win it back all the quicker. The others win but you keep losing. Or are you afraid of me?" he insisted.

Rostof acquiesced, staked the eight hundred which he had written down on a seven of hearts with a bent corner, which he had picked up from the floor. He remembered it well enough afterwards. He laid down this seven of hearts, after writing on the broken part, the figures eight hundred, in large, distinct characters; he drank the glass of foaming champagne handed him by the waiter, smiled at Dolokhof's words, and, with a sinking at the heart, while hoping that a seven would turn up, watched the pack of cards in Dolokhof's hands.

The gain or loss dependent on this seven of hearts would have very serious consequences for Rostof. On the preceding Sunday, Count Ilya Andreyitch had given his son two thousand rubles, and, although he generally disliked to speak of his pecuniary difficulties, had told him that he could not have any more till May, and therefore begged him, for this once, to be rather economical. Nikolaï had told him that that would be amply sufficient, and gave him his word of honor not to ask for any money till spring.

And now, out of that sum, only twelve hundred rubles were left. Of course that seven of hearts, if he lost on it, would signify not only the loss of sixteen hundred rubles, but also the necessity of breaking his word to his father. With a sinking of the heart, therefore, he watched Dolokhof's hands, and said to himself : —

"Now let him hurry up and give me this card, and I will put on my cap and go home to supper with Denísof, Natasha, and Sonya, and truly I will never, as long as I live, take a card into my hands again."

At that instant his home life, his romps with Petya, his talks with Sonya, his duets with Natasha, his game of piquet with his father, and even his peaceful bed in his home on the Pavarskaya, came over him with such force and vividness and attraction, that it seemed to him like an inestimable bliss, which had passed and been destroyed forever.

He could not bring himself to believe that stupid chance, by throwing the seven of hearts to the right rather than to the left, might deprive him of all this just comprehended and just appreciated happiness, and plunge him into the abyss of a wretchedness never before experienced, and of which he had no adequate idea. It could not be so, and yet, with a fever of expectation, he watched every motion of Dolokhof's hands. Those coarse reddish hands with wide knuckles and hairy wrists, showing from under his shirt bands, laid down the pack of cards, and took up the champagne glass that had been handed him, and put his pipe in his mouth.

"And so you are not afraid to play with me ?" repeated Dolokhof, and, as if for the purpose of telling some humorous story, he laid down the cards, leaned back in his chair, and with a smile deliberately began to speak : —

"Yes, gentlemen, I have been told that there is a report current in Moscow, that I am a sharper, and so I advise you to be on your guard against me."

"Come now, deal ahead !" said Rostof.

"Okh! these Moscow grannies!" exclaimed Dolokhof, and with a smile he took up the cards.

"Aaaakh!" almost screamed Rostof, clasping his head with both hands. The seven which he needed already lay on top, the very first card in the pack. He had lost more than he could pay.

"Now, don't ruin yourself!" said Dolokhof, giving Rostof a passing glance, and proceeded to deal the cards.

CHAPTER XIV

During the next hour and a half, the majority of the gamblers watched with much amusement their own play.

The whole game centered on Rostof alone. Instead of the sixteen hundred rubles against him there was already a long column of figures which he had reckoned to be at least ten thousand rubles, and which he now vaguely imagined to be perhaps fifteen thousand. In reality the sums footed up to more than twenty thousand rubles.

Dolokhof no longer listened to stories or told them himself; he watched each motion of Rostof's hands, and occasionally cast hasty glances at the paper containing Rostof's indebtedness. He had made up his mind to keep him playing until his losses should reach forty-three thousand rubles. He had selected this number because forty-three represented the sum of his and Sonya's ages.

Rostof, supporting his head in both hands, sat in front of the table, now all written over, wet with wine, and littered with cards. One painful impression filled his mind: those wide-jointed, red hands with the hairy wrists, those hands which he loved and which he also hated, held him in their power.

"Six hundred rubles, ace, quarter-stakes, nine spot.... impossible to win it back .... and how gay it would be at home! — Knave on five — it cannot be. — And why is he treating me so?" said Rostof to himself, mingling his thoughts and recollections.

Sometimes he staked on a card a large sum, but Dolokhof refused to accept it, and himself named the stake. Nikolaï would submit, and then pray God, just as he had prayed on the battle-field at the bridge of Amstetten; then it would occur to him that perhaps the first card that he should draw from the pile of rejected cards on the table would save him; then he would count up the number of buttons on his jacket, and select a card with the same number on which to stake the double of what he had already lost; then, again, he would look for aid to the other players, or glance into Dolokhof's face, now so cold, and try to read what was passing in his mind.

"Of course he knows what this loss means for me. It cannot be that he desires me to lose like this. For he was my friend. For I loved him..... But of course it isn't his fault; how can he help it if luck favors him? And neither am I to blame," said he to himself. "I have done nothing wrong. Have I killed any one, or insulted any one, or wished any one evil? Why, then, this horrible misfortune? And when did it begin? It was only such a short time ago that I came to this table with the idea of winning a hundred rubles, so as to buy for mamma's birthday that jewel-box, and then go home. I was so happy, so free from care, so gay! And I did not realize then how happy I was! When did it all end, and when did this new, this horrible state of things begin? What does this change signify? And here I am, just the same as before, sitting in the same place at this table, choosing and moving the same cards, and looking at those wide-knuckled, dexterous hands. When did this take place, and what is it that has taken place? I am well, strong, and just the same as I was, and in the selfsame place! No, it cannot be! Surely, this cannot end in such a way!"

His face was flushed, he was all in a perspiration, in spite of the fact that it was not warm in the room. And his face was terrible and pitiable, especially on account of his futile efforts to seem composed.

The list of his losses was nearing the fatal number

of forty-three thousand. Rostof had in readiness a card with the corner turned down as the quarter-stakes for three thousand rubles, which he had just won, when Dolokhof, rapping with the pack, flung it down, and taking the lump of chalk began swiftly to reckon up the sum total of Rostof's losses, with his firm, legible figures, breaking the chalk as he did so.

"Supper, it's time for supper, and here are the Tsigans!"

It was a fact; at that moment a number of dark-skinned men and women came in, bringing with them a gust of cold air, and saying something in their gypsy accent. Nikolaï realized that all was over; but he said, in an indifferent tone: —

"What, can't we play any more? Ah, but I had a splendid little card all ready!"

Just as if the mere amusement of the game was what interested him the most!

"All is over! I have lost!" was what he thought. "Now a bullet through my brains — that's all that's left," and yet he said, in a jocund tone, "Come now, just this one card!"

"Very well," replied Dolokhof, completing the sum total, "very good! Make it twenty-one rubles then," said he, pointing to the figures twenty-one, which was over and above the round sum of forty-three thousand; and, taking up the pack of cards, he began to shuffle them. Rostof obediently turned back the corner, and, instead of the six thousand which he was going to wager, carefully wrote twenty-one.

"It's all the same to me!" said he, "all I wanted to know was whether you would give me the ten or not."

Dolokhof gravely began to deal. Oh, how Rostof at that moment hated those red hands, with the short fingers and the hairy wrists emerging from his shirt bands, those hands that had him in their grasp!

The ten-spot fell to him.

"Well, you owe me just forty-three thousand, count," said Dolokhof, getting up from the table and stretching himself. "One gets tired sitting still so long," he added.

"Yes, and I am used up, also," said Rostof.

Dolokhof, as if to remind him that it was not seemly to jest, interrupted him : —

"When do you propose to pay me this money, count?"

Rostof, coloring with shame, drew Dolokhof into another room. "I cannot pay you at such short notice, you must take my note," said he.

"Listen, Rostof," said Dolokhof, with a frank smile, and looking into Nikolaï's eyes, "you know the proverb : 'Lucky in love, unlucky at cards.' Your cousin is in love with you, I know."

"Oh! how horrible it is to be in this man's power," thought Rostof. He realized what a blow it would be to his father, to his mother, to learn that he had been gambling and losing so much. He realized what happiness it would be if he could only have avoided doing it, or could escape confessing it, and he realized that Dolokhof knew how easily he might save him from this shame and pain, and yet, here he was playing with him as a cat plays with a mouse.

"Your cousin .... " Dolokhof started to say ; but Nikolaï interrupted him.

"My cousin has nothing to do with this, and there is no need of bringing her in," he cried, in a fury.

"Then when will you pay me?" demanded Dolokhof.

"To-morrow," replied Rostof, and he left the room.

CHAPTER XV

To say "to-morrow," and to preserve the conventional tone of decency, was not hard ; but to go home alone, to see his brother and sisters, his father and mother, to confess his fault and ask for money to which he had no right, after giving his word of honor, was horrible.

When Nikolaï reached home, the family were still up. The young people on their return from the theater had had supper, and were now sitting at the clavichord.

As soon as he entered the music-room he felt himself surrounded by that poetical atmosphere of love which had reigned all winter in that home, and which, now, after Dolokhof's proposal and Iogel's ball, had seemed to condense especially around Sonya and Natasha, like the air before a thunderstorm. Sonya and Natasha were in the blue gowns which they had worn to the theater. Pretty, and realizing that fact, they stood happy and smiling around the clavichord. Viera and Shinshin were playing checkers in the drawing-room. The old countess, waiting for her son and husband, was laying out a game of patience with the aid of an old noblewoman who made her home in their family. Denísof, with shining eyes and bristling hair, sat at the clavichord with one leg thrust out behind him, and, while drumming out the accompaniment with his little, short fingers, was singing in his thin, hoarse, but true voice some verses which he had composed under the title "The Enchantress," and to which he was trying to suit the music: —

> " Enchantress, tell by what strange charm compelling
>   Thou draw'st me back to long unwonted chords !
> What magic flames within my heart are swelling !
>   What rapture thrills me, all too deep for words ! "

He sang in a passionate voice, and fixed his bright, black, agate-colored eyes on Natasha.

"Lovely! delightful!" cried she. "Still another verse," she urged, not yet perceiving Nikolaï.

"With them it is just the same," said Nikolaï to himself, looking into the drawing-room, where he saw Viera, his mother, and the old lady.

"Ah! and here is Nikolenka!" cried Natasha, running to him.

"Is pápenka at home?" he demanded.

"How glad I am you have come!" exclaimed Natasha, not answering his question. "We are having such a jolly time; Vasíli Dmitritch is going to stay another day, just for my sake; did you know it?"

"No, papa hasn't come home yet," said Sonya.

"Koko, have you come? Come here, dear!" cried the countess, from the drawing-room. Nikolaï went to his mother, kissed her hand, and, without saying a word, took a seat near her table and began to watch her hands as she laid out the cards. From the music-room they could hear the sounds of laughter, and merry voices trying to persuade Natasha.

"Well, very good, very good," exclaimed Denísof. "Now there's no good your refusing; it's your turn! Give us the barcarole, I beg of you!"

The countess noticed her son's silence.

"What's the matter with you?" she asked.

"Akh, nothing," said he, as if he had heard the same question till he was weary of it. "Will pápenka be back soon?"

"I think so."

"They are the same as ever. They know nothing about it. Where can I hide myself?" thought Nikolaï, and he went again into the music-room, where the clavichord stood.

Sonya was sitting at it, and playing the introduction to the barcarole which was Denísof's especial favorite. Natasha was preparing to sing. Denísof was looking at her with enthusiastic eyes.

Nikolaï began to pace up and down the room.

"Now, why should they want to make her sing? What can she sing? There's nothing here to make a fellow feel happy!" said Nikolaï to himself.

Sonya struck the first chord of the prelude.

"My God, I am a ruined, dishonorable man! A bullet through my brain, that is the only thing left for me, and not singing!" his thoughts went on. "Go away? But where? Very well, let them sing!"

Nikolaï continued gloomily striding up and down the room, glancing at Denísof and the girls, but avoiding their eyes.

'Nikolenka, what is the matter?' Sonya's eyes, fixed on him, seemed to ask. She had immediately seen that something unusual had happened to him.

Nikolaï turned away from her. Natasha also, with

her quickness of perception, had instantly noticed her brother's preoccupation. She had observed it, but she felt so full of merriment at that time, her mood was so far removed from grief, melancholy, and reproaches, that (as often happens in the case of young girls) she purposely deceived herself.

"No, I'm too happy now to disturb my joy by trying to sympathize in the unhappiness of another," was her feeling, and she said to herself: "No, of course I am mistaken. It must be that he is as happy as I am myself. Now, Sonya," said she, and she started to go to the very middle of the music-room, where, in her opinion, her voice would have the most resonance. Lifting her head, and letting her hands hang easily by her side, just as ballet-dancers do, Natasha, with a fine display of energy, skipping from her little heels to her tiptoes, flew out into the middle of the room, and there paused. "See what a girl I am!" she seemed to say, in answer to Denísof's enthusiastic eyes following her.

"Now, what is she so happy about, I wonder?" queried Nikolaï, as he glanced at his sister. "And how can it be that she isn't tired to death of it all?"

Natasha took the first note, her throat swelled, her bosom rose, her eyes assumed a serious expression. She thought of no one, of nothing in particular at that moment, and from the smiling mouth gushed the sounds, those sounds which may proceed in the same *tempo* and with the same rhythm, but which a thousand times leave you cold and unmoved, and the thousand and first time make you tremble and weep.

Natasha this winter had for the first time begun to take singing seriously; this was especially because Denísof had been so enthusiastic over her voice. She sang now not like a school-girl, nor was there in her singing anything of that ludicrous, childish effort which had formerly been characteristic of her. She still sang far from well, as all the connoisseurs who had heard her declared. "Not developed yet, but still a lovely voice; she ought to cultivate it," said every one. But this was said generally some time after the sounds of her voice had entirely died away. While this, as yet, untrained voice, breathing in the wrong places, and finding it difficult to conquer rapid runs, was ringing out, even connoisseurs found nothing to say, but felt themselves unexpectedly moved by it, and only anxious to hear it again. In her voice there was a girlish sensitiveness, an unconsciousness of its own powers, and an untrained velvetiness, which were combined with the lack of knowledge of the art of singing in such a way that it seemed as if it would be impossible to change anything in that voice without ruining it.

"What does this mean?" queried Nikolaï, as he listened to her voice and opened his eyes wide. "What has come over her? How she sings to-night!" he said to himself. And suddenly all the world for him was concentrated on the expectation of the following note, the succeeding phrase, and everything in the world was divided into those three beats: "*Oh mio crudele affetto*" .... one, two, three; one .... two .... three; one .... two! "*oh mio crudele affetto*" .... one .... two .... three .... one — "Ekh! how foolish our life all is!" said Nikolaï to himself. "All of it and our unhappiness and money and Dolokhof and anger and honor; it is all rubbish, and this is the only real thing! There, Natasha, there, galubchik! there, matushka! Will she take that *si?* Yes, she's taken it. Glory to God — *Slava Bohu!*" and he himself, without noticing that he was singing, struck in the second a third below, in order to support that *si*.

"Good heavens! how nice! Did I take it right! How splendid!" he said to himself.

Oh! how that accord vibrated! and how all that was best in Rostof's soul came up to the surface. And this was something independent of all in the world, and higher than all in the world. What, in comparison with this, were his losses, and such men as Dolokhof and his word of honor! All rubbish. One might kill and rob and still be happy! ....

CHAPTER XVI

IT was long since Rostof had experienced any such delight from music as he did that night. But, as soon as Natasha had finished her barcarole, the grim reality again came back to him. Without saying a word to any one, he left the room and went up to his own chamber. A quarter of an hour later the old count came in from the club, gay and satisfied. Nikolaï, finding that he had come, went to his room.

"Well, have you been having a pleasant day?" asked Ilya Andreyitch, smiling gayly and proudly at his son. Nikolaï wanted to say "yes," but he found it impossible; it was as much as he could do to keep from bursting into tears. The count began to puff at his pipe, and did not perceive his son's state of mind.

"Ekh! it can't be avoided," said Nikolaï to himself, for the first and last time. And suddenly, in a negligent tone which seemed to himself utterly shameful, he said to his father, just as if he were asking for the carriage to drive down town:—

"Papa, I came to speak to you about business. I had forgotten all about it. I need some money."

"What's that?" said the father, who had come home in a peculiarly good-natured frame of mind. "I told you that you would n't have enough. Do you need much?"

"Ever so much," said Nikolaï, reddening, and with a stupid, careless smile which it was long before he could pardon himself for. "I have been losing a little; that is, considerable; I might say a great deal — forty-three thousand ...."

"What? To whom? You are joking!" cried the count, flushing, just as elderly men are apt to flush, with an apoplectic rush of blood coloring his neck and the back of his head.

"I promised to pay it to-morrow," continued Nikolaï.

"Well!"…. said the old count, spreading his hands and falling helplessly back upon the divan.

"What's to be done? It's what might happen to any

one!" said the son, in a free and easy tone of banter,
while all the time in his heart he was calling himself a
worthless coward, who could not atone by his whole life
for such a thing.   He felt an impulse to kiss his father's
hands, to fall on his knees and beg his forgiveness, but
still he assured his father in that careless and even
coarse tone, that this was a thing liable to happen to
any one!

Count Ilya Andreyitch dropped his eyes when he
heard his son's words, and fidgeted about, as if he were
trying to find something.

"Yes, yes," he murmured, "it'll be hard work, I am
afraid.... hard work to raise so much.... it happens to
every one, yes, yes, it happens to every one."

And the count, with a swift glance at his son's face,
started to leave the room.

Nikolaï was prepared for a refusal, but he had never
expected this.

"*Pápenka! pá....penka!*" he cried, hastening after
him with a sob, "forgive me!" and, seizing his father's
hand, he pressed it to his lips and burst into tears.

While father and son were having this conversation,
a no-less-important confession was taking place between
the mother and daughter.   Natasha, in great excitement, had run in where her mother was.

"Mamma!.... mamma!.... He has done it!"

"Done what?"

"He has done it! He has made me an offer; mamma!
mamma!" she cried.

The countess did not believe her ears.   Denísof made
a proposal!   To whom?   To this little chit of a Natasha,
who only a short time since was playing with her dolls,
and even now was only a school-girl?

"Natasha! Come now! No nonsense!" said she,
still hoping that it was a joke.

"Why do you say 'nonsense'?   I tell you just as it
is," said Natasha, indignantly.   "I came to ask you
what I should do about it, and you call it 'nonsense.'"

The countess shrugged her shoulders.   "If it is true

that *Monsieur* Denísof has made you an offer, then tell him that he is a fool, and that's all there is of it!"

"No, he is not a fool," replied Natasha, in a grave and offended tone.

"Well, then, what do you wish? It seems to me that these days all of you are falling in love. Well, if you love him, then marry him," exclaimed the countess, with an angry laugh. "Good luck to you!"

"No, mamma, I'm not in love with him; it can't be that I am!"

"Well, then, go and tell him so!"

"Mamma, are you annoyed? Don't be annoyed, sweetheart;[1] now wherein, I should like to know, was I to blame?"

"No, but what do you wish, my dear? Shall I go and tell him?" asked the countess, smiling.

"Certainly not, I will answer him myself, only tell me what to say. Everything comes so easy to you," she added, with an answering smile. "And if you had only seen how he said it to me! For, do you know, I am sure that he did not mean to say it, but it came out accidentally."

"Well, it behooves you, at all events, to refuse him."

"No, not refuse him! I feel so sorry for him! He is such a nice man!"

"Well, then, accept his proposal. Indeed, it is time you were married," exclaimed her mother, in a sharp, derisive tone.

"No, mamma, I pity him so. I don't know how to tell him!"

"Well, then, if you can't find anything to say, I myself will go and speak with him," said the countess, stirred to the soul that any one should dare to look upon her little Natasha as already grown up.

"No, not for anything; I will tell him myself, and you may listen at the door," and Natasha started to run through the drawing-room into the music-room, where Denísof was still sitting on the same chair by the clavi-

[1] *Galúbushka.*

chord with his face in his hands. He sprang up the moment he heard her light steps.

"Natalie," said he, going toward her with quick steps, "decide my fate. It is in your hands."

"Vasíli Dmitritch, I am so sorry for you. .... No! but you are so splendid. .... But it cannot be .... it is .... but I shall always, always love you."

Denísof bent over her hand, and she heard strange sounds which she could not understand. She kissed him on his dark, curly, disordered hair. At this instant was heard the hurried rustle of the countess's gown. She came toward them.

"Vasíli Dmitritch, I thank you for the honor," said the countess, in a troubled tone of voice, though it seemed to Denísof to be stern. "But my daughter is so young, and I should have thought that you, as a friend of my son's, would have addressed me first. In that case you might not have forced me to an unavoidable refusal."

"Countess," said Denísof, with downcast eyes and a guilty look, and vainly trying to stammer something more.

Natasha could not look with any composure upon him, it was so pitiable to see him. She began to sob aloud.

"Countess, I have done w'ong," at last he managed to articulate, in a broken voice. "But pway believe me, I adore your daughter and all your family, and I would gladly sacwifice my life twice over for you." He looked up at the countess, and, seeing her stern face, "Well, good-by, countess," he added, and kissing her hand and not even looking at Natasha, left the room with quick, resolute steps.

Rostof spent the next day making calls with Denísof, who would not hear to staying any longer in Moscow. All his Moscow friends gave him a send-off at the gypsies', and he had no recollection of how he was packed into his sledge, or how he rode the first three stages.

After Denísof's departure, Rostof spent a fortnight longer at home, waiting for the money which the old count was unable to raise at such short notice; he did not leave the house, and spent most of the time with the girls.

Sonya was more affectionate and devoted to him than ever. It seemed as if she were anxious to show him that his gambling losses were quite an exploit, for which she could only love him the more, but Nikolaï now felt that he was unworthy of her.

He filled the girls' albums with verses and music, and at last, toward the end of November, after paying over the forty-three thousand rubles, and receiving Dolokhof's receipt for it, he started away without taking leave of any of his acquaintances, to rejoin his regiment, which was now in Poland.

PART FIFTH

CHAPTER I

AFTER his explanation with his wife, Pierre went to Petersburg. At the post-station at Torzhok, there were no horses, or the station-master was unwilling to furnish them. Pierre was obliged to wait. Without undressing, he stretched himself out on the leather divan before a circular table, put his big feet in warm boots on it, and pondered.

"Do you order the trunks brought in? Shall I make up a bed? Do you wish tea?" asked his valet.

Pierre made no answer, for the reason that he heard nothing and saw nothing. He had begun to ponder while at the last station, and still he went on, propounding the same questions, quite too important for him to pay any attention to what was going on around him. He was not in the least interested whether he reached Petersburg sooner or later, or whether or not they found him a place to sleep that night at the station; everything indeed was immaterial in comparison with the thoughts that were now occupying his mind, and it made no difference whether he spent a few hours or his whole life at this station.

The station-master, the station-master's wife, his valet, an old woman who sold Torzhok embroidery, came into the room and offered their services.

Pierre, not changing the elevated position of his feet, looked at them over his spectacles, and did not comprehend what they could want, or how they could live without having decided the questions which were troubling him. He had indeed been occupied by the same questions perpetually ever since that day when, after his duel, he had returned home from Sokolniki, and spent the first painful, sleepless night; but now, in his solitary journey, they took possession of him with inexorable force. Whatever he began to think about, still his mind reverted to these problems which he could not solve and could not help asking himself. It was as if the principal screw on which his whole life depended had got sprung. The screw stays where it is; it does not give way, but it turns without the thread catching, always in the same fillet, and it is impossible to stop turning it.

The station-master came in and began obsequiously to ask his illustriousness to deign to wait only two "little hours," and then he could have for his illustriousness, come what would, post-horses for his service. The station-master was evidently lying, and his sole idea was to get as much money as possible from the traveler.

"Is this right, or is it wrong?" Pierre asked himself. "As far as I am concerned, it is good, but it is bad for the next traveler; but the station-master can't help himself doing so, because he has nothing to eat; he told me that some officer had given him a thrashing because of it. But perhaps the officer thrashed him because it was necessary for him to hasten away. And I shot at Dolokhof because I considered myself insulted, and Louis XVI. was beheaded because he was convicted as a criminal; but within a year those who had beheaded him were also put to death for something or other. What is wrong? What is right? What must one love? What must one hate? What is the object of life, and what am I? What is life, and what is death? What is the Power that directs all things?" he asked himself. And there was no answer to any one of the questions, except the one, the illogical answer which did not in reality fit any of these questions.

This answer was: "Thou shalt die — all will come to an end! Thou shalt die and know all, or else cease to question."

But the mere thought of death was terrible to him.

The Torzhok peddler woman, in her piping voice,

offered her wares, and called especial attention to her goatskin slippers.

" I have hundreds of rubles which I don't know what to do with, and she in her ragged shuba stands there and looks at me timidly," thought Pierre. " And what good would this money do her? Would this money of mine add the value of a single hair to her happiness, to her peace of mind? Can anything on earth make her or me in the least degree less susceptible to evil and death? Death, which ends all, and which may come to-day or to-morrow; everything becomes of equally little importance in comparison with eternity."

And once more he tried to screw up the screw that would not hold, and the screw, as before, kept turning around in the selfsame way.

His servant brought him the half-cut volume of a romance, in the form of letters by Madame de Souza. He began to read of the sufferings and virtuous resistance of the heroine, Amélie de Mansfeld. " And why did she resist her seducer if she loved him?" he asked himself. " God could not have put into her soul a desire which was contrary to His will. My former wife made no struggle, and maybe she was right. Nothing has ever been discovered, nothing ever invented," said Pierre again to himself. " The only thing that we can know is that we know nothing, and this is the highest degree of human wisdom!"

Everything within him and around him seemed confused, incoherent, loathsome. But, nevertheless, in this very loathing of everything, Pierre found a peculiar sense of exasperating delight.

" May I venture to ask your illustriousness to make a little room for this gentleman here?" asked the station-master, coming into the room and introducing another traveler, delayed also by the lack of horses. The new-comer was a thick-set, big-boned, little old man, yellow and wrinkled, with gray, beetling brows which shaded glittering eyes of indefinable grayish hue.

Pierre took his feet from the table, got up, and threw himself down on the bed that had been made ready for him, occasionally glancing at the stranger, who, with an air of moroseness and fatigue, without paying any heed to Pierre, allowed his servant to help him lay off his wraps.

The old man sat down on the divan. He had on a well-worn, nankeen-lined sheepskin jacket, and felt boots on his thin, bony legs; his head was large, and very broad in the temples, and his hair was closely cropped. Sitting thus, and leaning back against the sofa, he glanced at Bezukhoĭ. The grave, intelligent, and penetrating expression of his glance struck Pierre. He felt an inclination to converse with the stranger, but when he had made up his mind to address him with some question about the state of the roads, the old man had already closed his eyes, and was sitting motionless, with his wrinkled old hands folded, — on one finger he wore a heavy, cast-iron ring with a death's head for a seal, — and was either dozing, or, as it seemed to Pierre, meditating calmly and profoundly.

The stranger's servant was also a little old man, all covered with wrinkles, without mustache or beard, not because they had been shaven, but because they seemed never to have grown. This agile old servant opened the traveling-case, prepared the tea-table, and brought in the boiling samovar. When all was ready, the stranger opened his eyes, drew up to the table, and, after pouring out a glass of tea for himself, filled another for his beardless servant, and handed it to him.

Pierre began to feel uneasy; it seemed to him that it was unavoidable, and even inevitable, that he should enter into conversation with this traveler.

The servant brought back his empty glass, turned bottom side up, and with the lump of sugar untasted, and asked his master if he needed anything.

"Nothing. Hand me my book," said the stranger. The servant handed him a book which Pierre took to be a religious work, and the traveler buried himself in his reading. Pierre looked at him. Suddenly, the stranger laid down his book, put a mark in it and closed it, and, again shutting his eyes and leaning back, assumed his former position. Pierre gazed at him, but he had no time to look away before the old man opened his eyes and fastened his firm, steady, stern gaze directly on Pierre's face.

Pierre felt confused, and anxious to escape from that searching gaze, but the brilliant eyes of the old man irresistibly attracted him to them.

CHAPTER II

"If I am not mistaken, I have the pleasure of addressing Count Bezukhoï," said the stranger, in a loud and deliberate voice.

Pierre, without speaking, gave his neighbor an inquiring look over his spectacles.

"I have heard of you," continued the traveler, "and of the misfortune that has befallen you, my dear sir."

He seemed to lay a special stress on the word "misfortune," as much as to say: ' Yes, misfortune, whatever you may call it, for I know that what happened to you in Moscow was a misfortune.' "I have a great sympathy for you, my dear sir."

Pierre flushed, and, hastily putting down his legs from the bed, bent toward the old man, smiling with a timid and unnatural smile.

"Not from mere curiosity do I speak to you of this, my dear sir, but for a much more important reason."

He paused, though his eyes were still fixed on Pierre, and he moved along on the divan, signifying by this action that Pierre should sit down by his side.

It was not particularly agreeable for Pierre to enter into conversation with this old man, but, involuntarily submitting, he came and sat down by his side.

"You are unhappy, my dear sir," pursued the stranger. "You are young, I am old. I should like, as far as in me lies, to help you."

"Akh! yes!" replied Pierre, with the same unnatural smile. "I am very grateful to you. Have you been traveling far?"

The stranger's face was not genial, on the contrary, it was even cold and stern; but, nevertheless, his face and his speech had an irresistible attraction for Pierre.

"Now, if for any reason it is disagreeable for you to talk with me," said the old man, "tell me frankly, my dear sir."

And he suddenly smiled, an unexpected, a paternally affectionate smile.

"Akh! no, not at all; on the contrary, I am very happy to make your acquaintance," said Pierre, and, glancing once more at his new acquaintance's hand, he looked more carefully at the ring. He perceived on it the death's head, the symbol of Masonry.

"Allow me to ask," said he, "are you a Mason?"

"Yes, I belong to the Brotherhood of the Freemasons," said the traveler, looking deeper and ever deeper into Pierre's eyes. "And on my own account and that of the craft, I offer you the hand of fellowship."

"I fear," said Pierre, smiling, and hesitating between the confidence inspired in him by the Freemason's personality and the current disapprobation of the doctrines of the order.... "I fear that I am very far from being able to express myself; I fear that my whole system of thought in regard to the world in general is so opposite to yours, that we should not understand each other."

"I know your system of thought," replied the Freemason, "and this system which you mention, and which seems to you the product of your brain, is that common to most men; it is uniformly the fruit of pride, idleness, and ignorance. Excuse me, my dear sir; if I had not known this, I should not have addressed you. Your system of thought is a grievous error."

"In exactly the same way, I can imagine that it is you who are in error," said Pierre, with a feeble smile.

"I never venture to assert that I know the truth," said the Mason, impressing Pierre more and more by the precision and assurance of his discourse. "No one can alone attain to the truth; it must be stone upon stone, all lending their aid, millions of generations, from the first Adam even down to our day, building the temple which is destined to be the suitable abiding-place for the Most High God," said the Mason, and he shut his eyes.

"I must tell you, I do not believe .... do not believe in God," said Pierre, with an effort, and a sense of regret, but feeling it indispensable to confess the whole truth.

The Mason looked earnestly at Pierre and smiled, much as a rich man who had millions in his hands might smile upon a poor man who should tell him that he had nothing and that five rubles would make him the happiest of men.

"Yes, you do not know Him, my dear sir," said the Mason. "You cannot know Him — you cannot know Him; therefore, you are unhappy."

"Yes, yes, I am unhappy," repeated Pierre. "But what am I to do?"

"You do not know Him, my dear sir, and therefore you are very unhappy. You do not know Him, but He is here; He is in me, He is in my words; He is in thee, and even in those blasphemous words that thou hast just uttered," said the Mason, in his stern, vibrating voice.

He paused and sighed, evidently trying to master his emotion.

"If He did not exist," said he, gently, "you and I would not be speaking about Him, my dear sir. Of what, of whom, have we been speaking? Whom didst thou deny?" he suddenly asked, with a tone of enraptured sternness and power in his voice. "Who would have invented Him, if He did not exist? How camest thou to have the hypothesis that such an incomprehensible being exists? How came you and all the world to suppose the existence of an incomprehensible being, — a being omnipotent, eternal, and infinite in all His attributes?"

He paused, and remained silent for some time.

Pierre could not and would not break in upon his silence.

"He is, but it is hard to comprehend Him," said the Mason at last, looking not into Pierre's face, but straight ahead, while his aged-looking hands, which he could not keep quiet, owing to his internal excitement, kept turning over the leaves of his book.

"If it were a man whose existence thou disbelieved, I could bring this man to thee, I would take him by the hand and show him to thee. But how can I, an insignificant mortal, show all His omnipotence, all His infinity, all His goodness to him who is blind, or to him who shuts his eyes, in order not to see, not to comprehend Him, and not to see and not to comprehend all his own vileness and depravity?"

He paused again.

"Who art thou? What art thou? Thou imaginest that thou art heroic because thou canst utter those blasphemous words," said he, with a saturnine and scornful laugh. "And thou art stupider and less intelligent than a little child, which, playing with the artistically constructed parts of a clock, should dare to say that because it did not understand the clock, it did not believe in the artificer who made it. To comprehend Him is hard. For ages, since our first ancestor Adam even down to our own days, we have been striving to comprehend Him, and we are still infinitely far from the attainment of our purpose; but, while we cannot comprehend Him, we see only our feebleness and His majesty."

Pierre, with agitated heart and burning eyes, looked at the Mason, listening to his words, not interrupting him or asking him any questions; but with all his soul he believed in what this strange man told him. Whether it was that he was convinced by the reasonable arguments that the Mason employed, or was persuaded, as children are, by the conviction, by the sincerity expressed by the Mason's intonations, by the trembling voice which sometimes almost failed him, or by the brilliant eyes that had grown old in this conviction, or by that calmness, security, and belief in his own mission, which radiated from his whole being, and which especially impressed him when he compared it with his own looseness of belief and hopelessness, — he could not tell; at all events, he desired with all his soul to believe, and he did believe, and experienced a joyous sense of calmness, regeneration, and restoration to life.

"It is not by the intellect that He is comprehended, but by life," said the Mason.

"I do not understand," said Pierre, finding with dread his doubts arising in him again. He was afraid lest he might detect some weakness and lack of clearness in his new friend's arguments; he was afraid not to believe in him. "I do not understand," said he, "how the human mind can attain that knowledge of which you speak."

The Mason smiled his sweet, paternal smile.

"The highest wisdom and truth is like the purest ichor, which we should wish to receive into our very selves," said he. "Can I, an unclean vessel, accept this pure ichor and judge of its purity? Only through the cleansing of my inner nature can I, to a certain extent, receive this baptismal consecration."

"Yes, yes, that is so," said Pierre, joyfully.

"The highest wisdom is established, not on reason alone, not on those worldly sciences, physics, history, chemistry, and the like, on which intellectual knowledge stumbles. The highest wisdom is one. The highest wisdom has one science, the science of the All, the universal science which explains all creation, and the place which man occupies in it. In order to absorb this science, it is absolutely essential to purify and renovate the inner man, and, therefore, before one can know it one must believe and accomplish perfection. And to attain this end, our souls must be filled with that divine light which is called conscience."

"Yes, yes," cried Pierre.

"Look with the eyes of your spirit at your inner man, and then ask yourself if you are content with your life. What do you attain when you put yourself under the guidance of the intellect alone? What are you? You are young, you are intelligent, and educated, my dear sir. What have you been doing with all those blessings that have been put into your hands? Are you content with yourself and your life?"

"No, I detest my life," exclaimed Pierre, with a scowl.

"If you detest it, then change it, undergo self-purification, and in accordance as you accomplish it, you will learn wisdom. Examine into your life, my dear sir. What sort of a life have you been leading? Wild revels and debauchery! Receiving everything from society, and giving nothing in return. You have become the possessor of wealth, — how have you been employing it? What have you been doing for your neighbor? Have you had a thought for your tens of thousands of slaves? Have you helped them, physically or morally? No! You have taken advantage of their labor to lead a dissipated life. That is what you have been doing! Have you chosen a life-work which might enable you to be of help to your neighbor? No! You have been spending your life in idleness. Then, my dear sir, you got married; you assumed responsibilities for the guidance of a young woman, and how have you carried them out? You have not aided her, my dear sir, to find the path of truth, but you have hurled her into the abyss of falsehood and wretchedness. A man insulted you, and you fought with him, and you say that you do not know God, and that you detest your life. There is no wisdom in that, my dear sir!"

After saying these words, the Mason, as if wearied by this long speech, again leaned against the back of the sofa, and closed his eyes. Pierre looked at the stern, impassive, almost deathly face of the old man, and moved his lips without making any noise. He wanted to say, — 'Yes, my life is shameful, idle, dissipated,' but he did not dare to break the silence.

The Freemason coughed, a hoarse, decrepit cough, and summoned his servant.

"How about the horses?" he asked, without looking at Pierre.

"Those that were ordered have been brought," replied the servant. "Do you not wish to rest?"

"No, have them harnessed."

"Can it be that he is going to leave me here alone,

and not tell me all, and not promise me help?" wondered Pierre, getting up, and beginning to pace up and down the room, with bowed head, though he occasionally glanced at the Mason.

"Yes, I had never thought about it before, I lead a contemptible, depraved life, but I do not love it, and I have no desire to continue it," thought Pierre. "And this man knows the truth, and if he had the desire he might enlighten me."

Pierre wished, but he had not the courage, to say this to the Mason. The traveler, gathering up his effects with his skilful, aged hands, began to button up his sheepskin coat. Having accomplished these tasks, he turned to Bezukhoï, and said to him in a polite, indifferent tone: —

"Where are you going now, my dear sir?"

"I?.... I am going to Petersburg," replied Pierre, in a childish, irresolute voice. "I am grateful to you. I agree with what you have said. But pray do not think that I am all bad! I wish with all my soul that I were what you wish that I was — but I have never found any help to become such .... however, I am, above all, to blame for my faults. Help me! teach me, and maybe I might...."

Pierre could not speak further. There was a strange sound in his nose, and he turned away.

The Mason did not speak for some time, evidently lost in thought.

"Help is given only from God," said he. "But that measure of help which it is within the power of our craft to give you, it will be glad to give, my dear sir. When you reach Petersburg, give this to Count Villarski."

He took out a pocket-book, and, on a large sheet of paper, folded twice, he wrote a few words.

"Allow me to give you one piece of advice. When you reach the capital, consecrate your first hours to solitude, to self-examination, and do not again enter into your former paths of life. And now I wish you a happy journey, my dear sir," said he, perceiving that his servant had entered the room, "and all success." ....

The traveler was Osip Alekseyevitch Bazdeyef, as Pierre discovered by the station-master's record book. Bazdeyef was one of the most distinguished Freemasons and Martinists since the time of Novikof. Pierre, after his departure, without lying down to sleep, or asking for horses, long paced up and down the room of the station-house, thinking over his vicious way of living, and, with the enthusiasm of regeneration, imagining to himself the blessed, irreproachable, and beneficent future which now seemed to him so easy. He was, so it seemed to him, wicked only because he had, as it were, forgotten how good it was to be righteous. Not a trace of his former doubts remained in his mind. He had a firm faith in the possibility of a brotherhood of men, united in one common aim of keeping one another in the path of righteousness, and such a brotherhood Masonry now seemed to him to be.

CHAPTER III

On reaching Petersburg, Pierre informed no one of his presence, went nowhere, and spent whole days in reading Thomas à Kempis, which some one — he knew not whom — had sent him. One thing, and only one thing, Pierre understood in reading that book: that was the hitherto unknown delight in believing in the possibility of attaining perfection, and in the possibility of active brotherly love among men, which Osip Alekseyevitch had revealed to him.

Within a week after his return, the young Polish Count Villarski, whom Pierre had known slightly in Petersburg society, came one evening into his room with the same sort of official and solemn air with which Dolokhof's second had approached him; closing the door behind him, and assuring himself that no one except Pierre was in the room, he thus addressed him : —

"I have come to you, count, for the purpose of lay·

ing a proposition before you," said he, not sitting down. "An individual of very high degree in our brotherhood has interested himself in having you admitted out of due course, and has proposed that I should be your sponsor. I consider it as a sacred duty to fulfil this person's desires. Do you wish to join the brotherhood of Freemasons under my sponsorship?"

Pierre was amazed at the cold and severe tone of this man, whom he had seen almost always at balls, with a gallant smile, in the society of the most brilliant ladies.

"Yes," said Pierre, " I do wish it."

Villarski inclined his head.

"Still one further question, count," said he, "which I will beg of you to answer with all frankness, not as a future Mason, but as a man of honor (*un galant homme*): Have you renounced your former convictions? Do you believe in a God?"

Pierre hesitated.

"Yes.... yes, I believe in a God," said he.

"In that case...." began Villarski, but Pierre interrupted him.

"Yes, I believe in God," said he once more.

"In that case, we may start, then," said Villarski. "My carriage is at your service."

Villarski sat in silence all the way. To Pierre's questions as to what he had to do, and how he must answer, Villarski contented himself with replying that brethren more suitable than himself would examine him, and that all that it behooved Pierre to do was to speak the truth.

Entering the courtyard of a large mansion, where the lodge met, and passing up a dark staircase, they came into a small, brightly lighted anteroom, where they removed their shubas without the aid of servants. Through an entry they passed into another room. Here a man in a strange garb made his appearance at the door. Villarski, going forward to meet him, said something to him in French, in an undertone, and went to a small wardrobe, in which Pierre observed trappings such as he had never seen before. Taking from the wardrobe a handkerchief, Villarski bound it around

Pierre's eyes and tied a knot behind in such a way
that his hair was caught in it and hurt him.   Then he
drew him to himself, kissed him, and taking him by the
hand led him he knew not where.   The hair caught in
the knot hurt Pierre; he scowled with the pain, and
smiled shamefacedly.   His burly figure, with bandaged
eyes, with swinging arms, with face both frowning and
smiling, followed Villarski with timid steps.

After leading him half a score of paces, Villarski
paused.

"Whatever happens to you," said he, "you must cour-
ageously endure it all, if you are firmly resolved to enter
our brotherhood."

Pierre nodded assent.

"When you hear a rap on the door you can take off
the handkerchief," added Villarski.   "I wish you good
courage and success."

And pressing Pierre's hand, Villarski went away.

Left alone, Pierre still continued to smile as before.
Twice he shrugged his shoulders, raised his hand to
the handkerchief, as if inclined to remove it, and again
let it fall.   The five minutes which he spent with
bandaged eyes seemed to him like an hour.   His hands
swelled, his legs trembled; he had the sensation of
being tired.   He had the most complex and varied feelings.   What was going to happen to him seemed to
him terrible, and he was still more afraid that he should
show his fear.   He was filled with curiosity to know
what was going to take place, what was going to be
revealed to him; but, above all, it was delightful for
him to think that the moment had come when he had
definitely entered upon the path of regeneration, and of
an active, beneficent life, of which he had dreamed ever
since his meeting with Osip Alekseyevitch.

Loud raps were heard at the door.   Pierre took off
the bandage and looked around him.

It was intensely dark in the room, only in one place
burned a lampada, or shrine lamp, within some white
object.   Pierre went nearer, and saw that the lamp
stood on a table covered with a black cloth, on which

lay a single opened book. The book was a copy of the
Gospels; the white object, in which burned the lamp,
was a human skull, with its eye sockets and teeth.
Reading the first words of the Gospel: "In the beginning was the Word, and the Word was with God."
Pierre went around the table, and saw a large box filled
with something and covered. This was a coffin with
bones in it. He was not at all surprised at what he saw.
In his hope of entering upon a wholly new life, absolutely removed from the old one, he expected all sorts
of extraordinary things, indeed much more extraordinary than what he had already seen. The skull, the
coffin, the Gospel — it seemed to him that all this was
what he had expected; he expected something more.
While trying to stimulate a sense of emotion, he looked
around him: "God, death, love, human fraternity," he
said to himself, connecting with these words confused
but pleasing conceptions.

A door opened, and some one entered.

By the feeble light Pierre could just manage to make
out that it was a short man. Coming from light into
darkness, this man paused a moment, then, with cautious
steps, he approached the table and placed on it his
small hands covered with leather gloves.

The short man wore a white leathern apron covering
his chest and a part of his legs; around his neck was
something like a necklace, and above the necklace arose
a high, white frill, serving as a sort of frame for his
elongated face, lighted from below.

"Why have you come hither?" asked the new man,
approaching Pierre, who had made a slight noise.
"Wherefore do you, who believe not in the truth of
light, and have never seen the light, wherefore have
you come hither? What do you desire of us? Wisdom?
virtue? enlightenment?"

The moment the door opened and the unknown man
entered, Pierre experienced a sense of awe and reverence similar to that which he had felt in his childhood
at confession; he felt that he was face to face with a
human being who, under all the conditions of ordinary

life, was a stranger, but was near to him through the brotherhood of man. Pierre, with his heart beating so that he could hardly breathe, went toward the Rhetor, as the Masons call the brother whose duty it is to prepare the candidate for admission into the confraternity. Pierre, as he came nearer, recognized the Rhetor as an acquaintance of his, named Smolyaninof; it was a disappointment to think that this man was an acquaintance: the newcomer was merely a brother and instructor in virtue. It was some time before Pierre could find a word to say; so that the Rhetor was obliged to repeat his question.

"Yes, I.... I.... I seek regeneration," said Pierre, speaking with difficulty.

"Good," said Smolyaninof, and immediately proceeded: —

"Have you any idea of the means by which our holy fraternity can aid you to the attainment of your desires?" asked the Rhetor, calmly and rapidly.

"I.... hope for.... guidance.... for help.... toward.... regeneration," said Pierre, with a trembling voice, and finding a difficulty in speaking which arose from his emotion as well as from his lack of practice in speaking in Russian on abstract themes.

"What knowledge have you of Freemasonry?"

"I suppose that Freemasonry is fraternity and equality of all men who have virtuous aims," said Pierre, with a feeling of shame overwhelming him at the unfitness of his words at such a solemn moment. "I suppose...."

"Good," said the Rhetor, in haste, evidently perfectly satisfied with this reply. "Have you found in religion means for the attainment of these ends?"

"No, I have considered religion opposed to truth, and I have spurned it," said Pierre, so low that the Rhetor did not hear him and asked him what he said. "I have been an atheist," replied Pierre.

"You seek after truth for the purpose of following her laws through life; consequently, you seek wisdom and virtue, do you?" asked the Rhetor, after a moment's silence.

"Yes, yes," insisted Pierre.

The Rhetor coughed, folded his gloved hands on his chest, and began to discourse : —

"It is now my duty to unfold to you the chief object of our craft," said he. "And if this object coincides with yours, then you will find it an advantage to join our fraternity. The first and principal aim, and at the same time the foundation of our confraternity, on which it stands firm, and which no human violence can shake, is the conservation and handing down to posterity of a certain important mystery, which has been handed down to us from the remotest antiquity, even from the first man, from which mystery perhaps depends the destiny of the human race. But as this mystery has the peculiarity that no one can know it and get advantage from it except through a long and assiduous course of self-purification, therefore not every one can hope speedily to discover it. Consequently, we have a secondary aim and object, which consists in preparing our fellow-members, as far as in us lies, to correct their hearts, to purify and enlighten their reason, by those means which have been handed down to us by tradition from those men who labored for the investigation of those mysteries, and thereby to teach them to be qualified for the reception of one.

"By purifying and rectifying our own members, we endeavor, in the third place, to correct also the whole human race, presenting in our own members an example of honor and virtue, and therefore we endeavor, by all means in our power, to counteract the evil that rules in the world. Think this over, and I will come to you again," said he, and he left the room.

"To counteract the evil that rules in the world," repeated Pierre, and he imagined his future activity in this great field.

He imagined such men as he himself had been a fortnight before, and his thoughts turned to the initiatory discourse that he had just heard. He called to mind the wicked and wretched men whom he should help by word or deed; he imagined the oppressors from whom he rescued their victims.

Of the three objects which the Rhetor enumerated, the last, the improvement of the human race, was the one that most appealed to Pierre. The important mystery of which the Rhetor spoke, although it aroused his curiosity, did not seem to him to be a reality; but the second, self-purification and regeneration, interested him very little, because at that moment he felt that he was already perfectly freed from his former vices, and ready only for what was right.

Within half an hour the Rhetor returned to instruct the candidate in the seven virtues, symbolized by the seven steps of Solomon's temple, which every Mason must make his especial practice. These virtues were as follows:—

1. *Modesty*, the observation of the secrets of the order.
2. *Obedience* to the higher degrees of the fraternity.
3. *Good temper.*
4. *Love for mankind.*
5. *Courage.*
6. *Generosity.*
7. *Love of death.*

"Apply yourself to the seventh," said the Rhetor. "By frequent thoughts of Death, bring yourself to feel that he is no more a terrible enemy, but a friend who frees the soul, wearied by works of beneficence, from the wretchedness of this life, and leads it into the place of rewards and rest."

"Yes, this ought to be so," thought Pierre, when the Rhetor, after delivering himself of this message, again retired, leaving him to solitary reflection. "This ought to be so, but I am still so feeble as to love my life, the meaning of which has only just been, to some small degree, revealed to me."

The other five virtues, however, which Pierre counted off on his fingers, he felt were already in his soul: courage and generosity, good temper and love for mankind, and especially obedience, which last seemed less to him a virtue than a pleasure, so glad was he now to be freed from the exercise of his own will, and to subordinate it to those who knew the indubitable truth. The seventh virtue Pierre had forgotten; he could not remember what it was at all.

For the third time the Rhetor returned, this time more promptly than before, and asked Pierre if he were still firm in his convictions, and were resolved to undergo all that might be required of him.

"I am ready for anything," said Pierre.

"I must still further apprise you," said the Rhetor, "that our order does not instruct by words alone, but by other arguments which have perhaps a more powerful effect on the earnest seeker after wisdom and virtue than merely verbal ones. This chamber, with its ornamentation which you see, must have already made this plain to your heart, if it is sincere, more than any words could have done. You will see, probably, during your further advancement, similar modes of symbolism. Our order takes pattern after ancient societies, which concealed their teachings under the guise of hieroglyphics. A hieroglyphic," explained the Rhetor, "is a name of something symbolizing an abstract idea, and possessing in itself qualities similar to those possessed by the idea symbolized."

Pierre knew very well what a hieroglyphic was, but he did not venture to speak. He silently listened to the Rhetor, under the conviction that some sort of test was immediately to begin.

"If you are resolved, then it is my duty to proceed to the initiation," said the Rhetor, coming closer to Pierre. "As a sign of your generosity, I shall ask you to give me everything of value that you have."

"But I have nothing with me," said Pierre, supposing that he was to be required to make over all that he possessed.

"Well, what you have on you: your watch, money, rings...."

Pierre hastily took out his pocket-book, his watch, and struggled for some time to remove his wedding-ring from his stout finger. When this was accomplished, the Mason said: —

"As a sign of obedience, I will ask you to strip."

Pierre took off his coat, waistcoat, and left boot, at the Rhetor's direction. The Mason opened the shirt over his left breast, and, bending over, lifted his trousers above the knee of his left leg. Pierre hastily began to take off his right boot also, and to tuck up his trousers, so as to save this stranger the trouble, but the Mason assured him that this was unnecessary, and gave him a slipper for his left foot. With a childlike smile of shame, doubt, and derision at his own awkwardness involuntarily crossing his face, Pierre stood up, dropping his arms and spreading his legs, and faced the Rhetor, waiting his next commands.

"And finally, as a sign of sincerity, I will ask you to reveal to me your chief predilection," said he.

"My predilection? But I *used* to have so many of them!" exclaimed Pierre.

"The predilection which more than all others has caused you to waver in the path of virtue," said the Mason.

Pierre paused, trying to think.

"Wine? Gluttony? Slothfulness? Impetuosity? Anger? Women?" He passed his faults in review, mentally considering them, and not knowing which to take in preference.

"Women," said he, in a voice so low that it was scarcely audible. The Mason did not move and did not speak until long after this reply. At last he approached Pierre, took up the handkerchief that was lying on the table, and again blindfolded his eyes.

"For the last time I say to you: 'Examine yourself with all attention! Put a bridle on your feelings, and seek your happiness, not in your passions, but in your heart. The fountain-head of happiness is not without, but within us.'"....

Pierre had already begun to feel in himself this refreshing fountain of happiness which now filled his soul to overflowing with bliss and emotion.

CHAPTER IV

SHORTLY after this, there came into the dark chamber, not the Rhetor, as before, but Pierre's sponsor, Villarski, whom he recognized by his voice. In reply to new questions as to the firmness of his resolve, Pierre said, "Yes, yes, I consent," and with a brilliant, childlike smile, with his broad chest uncovered, awkwardly stepping along with one foot in a boot and the other in a slipper, he marched forward, with Villarski holding a drawn sword across his bare breast.

He was led from the darkened room along several corridors winding back and forth, and at last brought to the door of the lodge-room.

Villarski coughed; he was answered by Masonic raps with mallets; the door opened before them. Some one's deep voice — Pierre's eyes were still blindfolded — asked him who he was, where and when he was born, and other questions. Then he was led somewhere else, the bandage not yet removed, and while he was on the way his attendants related to him allegories about the difficulties that beset his way, about the sacred fraternity, the Eternal Architect of the universe, and the courage with which he ought to endure labors and sufferings. During the time of this circumambulation, Pierre noticed that he was called first the "Seeker," then the "Sufferer," then the "Claimant," while the mallets and swords were struck each time in a different way. At one time, just as they brought him to some object or other, he noticed that there was confusion and perplexity among his attendants. He heard the men surrounding him whispering together, and one of them insisting that he was to be led across a certain carpet.

After this, they took his right hand and laid it on something, while with his left he was directed to hold a pair of compasses to his left breast, and to repeat the words read aloud by one of the number, and which bound him to a faithful observance of the regulations of the order. Then the candles were extinguished; some alcohol was burned, as Pierre apprehended by the odor, and they told him that he could now see "the lesser light."

The bandage was removed from his eyes, and Pierre saw, as in a dream, by the feeble light of the alcohol lamp, a number of men, who, all wearing aprons similar to that which the Rhetor had worn, stood in front of him holding swords pointed towards his chest. Among them stood a man with a white shirt stained with blood. Seeing this, Pierre bent his chest forward against the swords, wishing that they might pierce it. But the swords were withdrawn, and his eyes were immediately rebandaged.

"Thou hast now seen the lesser light," said a voice. Then the candles were lighted again; he was told that he was to see the full light, and once more they removed the bandage, and more than a dozen voices suddenly cried: "*Sic transit gloria mundi.*"

Pierre began to recover himself gradually, and looked around the room in which he was and at the men who were there. Around a long table covered with black sat a dozen men in the trappings worn by the others whom Pierre had seen. Some of them Pierre had known in Petersburg society. At the head of the table was a young man whom Pierre did not know; he had a peculiar badge around his neck. At his right hand sat the Italian *abbate* whom Pierre had met two years before at Anna Pavlovna's. There was still another very important dignitary, and a Swiss, who had once been a tutor at the Kuragins'. All preserved a solemn silence, and listened to the words spoken by the presiding officer, who held a mallet in his hand. Inserted in the wall was a blazing star. At one end of the table was a small cover with various allegorical symbols; on the other was something in the nature of an altar, with a copy of the Gospels and a skull. Around the table were seven large candlesticks, such as they have in churches.

Two of the brethren drew Pierre to the altar, made him stand with his feet at right angles, and bade him lie down, declaring that he must prostrate himself at the Gates of the Temple.

"He ought to receive the trowel first," said one of the brethren, in a whisper.

"Akh! please hold your tongue," said another.

Pierre, with his distracted, near-sighted eyes, looked around him without obeying, and suddenly doubts began to come over him.

"Where am I? What am I doing? Are they not making sport of me? Will not the time come when I shall be ashamed of all this flummery?"

But this doubt lasted only for an instant. He looked around on the grave faces of the spectators, remembered all that he had already been through, and comprehended that he had gone too far now to withdraw.

He was mortified at his doubt, and, while endeavoring to regain his former feeling of emotion, he prostrated himself at the gates of the Temple. And, in reality, the former feeling of emotion came over him even more powerfully than before.

After he had been lying there for some little time, he was bidden to arise, and they put upon him the same kind of white leathern apron which the others wore, put a trowel into his hand, and gave him three pairs of gloves, and then the Grand Master addressed him.

He told him that it behooved him to endeavor never to allow the whiteness of this apron to be sullied, it being the emblem of strength and purity. Of the mysterious trowel, he said that he was to use it for eradicating the faults from his own heart, and courteously laying the foundations of virtue in the hearts of his neighbors. Then, as regarded the first pair of gloves, which were men's, he said that he was not to understand their signification, but must keep them; in regard to the second pair, which were also men's gloves, he said that he was to wear them at the lodge-meetings; and, finally, in regard to the third pair, which were a woman's gloves, he said as follows: —

" Dear brother, these woman's gloves also are destined for you. Give them to the woman whom you will reverence above all others. By this gift you pledge the purity of your heart to her whom you will select as your worthy Masonic affinity."

Then, after a brief pause, he went on :—

" But take care, dear brother, that these gloves are not worn by unworthy hands !"

While the Grand Master was pronouncing these last words, it seemed to Pierre that he was embarrassed. Pierre himself was still more embarrassed, he flushed till the tears came, just as children flush ; he began to look about him uneasily, and an awkward silence ensued.

This silence was broken by one of the brethren, who drew Pierre to the table-cover and began to read to him from a copy-book an explanation of all the symbolical figures worked in it ; the sun, moon, the hammer, the plumb-line, the trowel, the untrimmed and four-square foundation-stone, the pillar, the three windows, and other things.

Then Pierre was assigned his place ; the signals of the lodge were explained to him ; the password was told him, and he was at last permitted to sit down.

The Grand Master began to read the regulations. They were very long, and Pierre, from his joy, excitement, and sense of shame, was not in a condition to understand what they were reading. He heard only the last words of the regulations, and they impressed themselves on his memory.

"In our temples, we recognize no degrees," the Grand Master read, "other than those which separate virtue from wrong-doing. Take care not to make any distinction which may tend to destroy equality. Fly to the aid of a brother, no matter who it may be ; reclaim the wandering ; raise the fallen, and never cherish anger or enmity against a brother. Be gentle and courteous. Kindle in all hearts the fires of virtue. Do acts of kindness to thy neighbor, and never allow thyself to envy the happiness of another. Forgive thy enemy, and avenge not thyself on him, except by doing him good. Having thus fulfilled the highest law, thou wilt discover traces of thy primal and lost greatness."

He finished reading, and getting up, embraced Pierre and kissed him. Pierre, with tears of joy in his eyes, looked around him, not knowing what reply to make to the greetings and congratulations of the acquaintances who surrounded him. He made no distinction between old friends and new; in every one he saw only brethren whom he burned with impatience to join in carrying out the work.

The Grand Master rapped with his mallet. All sat down in their places, and some one read an address on the necessity of humility.

The Grand Master then proposed to carry out the last obligation, and the important dignitary who bore the appellation of "Collector of Alms" began to approach each in turn. Pierre had the inclination to subscribe all the money that he possessed, but he was afraid that this would be construed as an exhibition of pride, and he put down only what each of the others did.

The session was ended, and on his return home it seemed to Pierre as if he had come from some long journey after an absence of ten years, and was entirely changed, with nothing left to him from the former objects and customs of his life.

CHAPTER V

On the day following his reception into the Masonic lodge, Pierre was sitting at home, reading a book and trying to penetrate the meaning of the square formed on one side by God, on the second by the moral world, on the third by the physical, and on the fourth by a mixture. Occasionally, his attention wandered from his book and square, and in his imagination he began to formulate a new plan of life for himself.

The evening before, at the lodge, he had been told that the emperor had heard of his duel, and that it would be for his advantage to leave Petersburg for a time. Pierre proposed to go to his southern estates and look out for the welfare of his peasantry. He was joyfully thinking about this new life, when Prince Vasili unexpectedly came into the room.

"My dear, what have you been doing in Moscow? Why, my dear fellow, what made you quarrel with Lyola? You are in the wrong," said the prince, as he came in. "I have known all about it, and I can tell you honestly that Ellen is as innocent toward you as Christ toward the Jews."

Pierre started to reply, but Prince Vasili cut him short.

"And why did n't you come right to me in all frankness, as to a friend? I know how it was, I understand it," said he. "You behaved as a man who prizes his honor; perhaps, too, you acted too hastily, but we won't discuss that now. Just think of this, though: in what a position you have put her and me in the eyes of society, and especially of the court," he added, lowering his voice. "She is living in Moscow, you here. Remember, my dear," — he made him sit down, — "this is a mere misunderstanding; you yourself will feel so, I am sure. Now join me in writing a letter, and she will come back, — everything will be explained; but if you don't, I will tell you, you may very easily repent of it, my dear."

Prince Vasili gave Pierre a very suggestive look. "I have it from the very best sources that the empress dowager takes a lively interest in all this matter. You know that she is very favorably disposed to Ellen."

Several times Pierre collected himself to speak, but on the one hand Prince Vasili did not let him have a chance; on the other, Pierre himself was afraid to take that tone of determined refusal with which he had definitely made up his mind to answer his father-in-law. Moreover, the words of the Masonic ritual, "Be courteous and genial," occurred to him. He scowled, flushed, got up and sat down again, struggling to perform the hardest task that had ever come to him in his life — to say something unpleasant to a man's face, to say exactly the opposite of what this man expected. He was so accustomed to give in to Prince Vasili's tone of easy-going self-confidence, that even now he felt that he had not the force of mind necessary to oppose him; but he felt that what he was going to say now was to decide the whole destiny of his life: was he to go back to the old path of the past, or to go on over that new one which had been placed before him in so attractive a light by the Masons, and on which he firmly believed that he should find regeneration?

"Well, my dear," said Prince Vasili, in a jocose tone, "tell me 'yes,' now, and I will write her the letter and we will kill the fatted calf."

But Prince Vasili had not time to finish his joke, before Pierre, not looking at Prince Vasili, and with a flash of rage, which made him resemble his father, exclaimed in a whisper: —

"Prince, I did not invite you to come; please go, go!" He sprang up and flung the door open. "Go!" he repeated, not believing in himself and rejoicing in the expression of confusion and terror on Prince Vasili's face.

"What is the matter with you, are you ill?"

"Go!" he cried once more, in a trembling voice. And Prince Vasili was obliged to go, without bringing about any explanation.

In a week's time, Pierre, bidding his new friends, the Masons, farewell, and leaving in their hands large sums for charities, departed for his estates. The brotherhood gave him letters to the Masons of Kief and Odessa, and promised to write and guide him in his new activity.

CHAPTER VI

PIERRE'S affair with Dolokhof was hushed up, and, in spite of the emperor's strictness in regard to dueling, neither the two principals nor their seconds were punished. But the story of the duel, confirmed by Pierre's rupture with his wife, was noised abroad in society. Pierre, who, when he was an illegitimate son, had been looked upon with patronizing condescension, who, when he was the best match in the Russian empire, had been flattered and glorified, had lost much of his importance in the eyes of the world since his marriage; and young ladies and their mothers had nothing more to expect from him, the more from the fact that he could not and would not ingratiate himself into the favor of fashionable society. Now, he alone was blamed for this occurrence; it was said that he was a jealous blockhead, liable to exactly the same fits of ferocious temper as his father.

And when, after Pierre's departure, Ellen returned to Petersburg, she was received by all her acquaintances, not only gladly, but even with a shade of respectful deference, due to her unhappiness. When her husband was mentioned in conversation, Ellen put on a dignified expression, which, without her realizing its significance, she managed by that consummate tact of hers to make peculiarly becoming. This expression signified that she had made up her mind to endure her unhappiness without complaining, and that her husband was a cross sent her from God.

Prince Vasili expressed his feelings more openly. He would shrug his shoulders when the conversation turned on Pierre, and, pointing to his forehead, would say : —

"I have always said he was cracked."

"I said so before you did," insisted Anna Pavlovna; "I said so at the very first, and before anybody else," — she always claimed priority for her predictions, — "that he was a silly young man, ruined by the perverse notions of the day. I said so even when he had just returned from abroad, and when every one was enraptured by him, and you will remember that at one of my receptions he posed as a sort of Marat. How is it going to end? Even then I did not approve of this marriage, and predicted what would come of it."

Anna Pavlovna, just as of yore, was giving receptions on her days at home, and such ones as she alone had the gift of arranging — receptions at which were collected, in the first place, the cream of genuine good society, the very flower of the intellectual essence of Petersburg high life, as Anna Pavlovna herself expressed it. Over and above this discriminating selection of society, Anna Pavlovna's receptions, or "evenings," were still more distinguished by the fact that at each one she managed to present to her company some new and interesting personage, and that nowhere else could one so accurately and assuredly gauge the political thermometer by which the disposition of the conservative court society of Petersburg was regulated.

Toward the end of the year 1806, when the melancholy news of Napoleon's defeat of the Prussian army at Jena and Auerstädt and the surrender of the majority of the Prussian fortresses had been received, when our armies had just crossed over into Prussia, and our second campaign with Napoleon was beginning, Anna Pavlovna gave an "at home." "The cream of genuine good society" consisted of the charming and hapless Ellen, Montemart, the bewitching Prince Ippolit, just arrived from Vienna, two diplomats, the little old aunt, a young man who enjoyed the appellation simply of "a man of great ability," a newly promoted maid of honor, and a few persons of more or less distinction.

The person whom Anna Pavlovna served up this evening, as a choice "first-fruit" for the edification of her guests, was Boris Drubetskoi, who had just arrived on a special mission from the army in Prussia and was now enjoying the position of aide to a very great personage.

The political thermometer that evening offered the following points for the study of society:—

"Whatever all the rulers and commanders of Europe may do by way of indulging Bonaparte, at the expense of causing *me*, and *us* in general, annoyance and humiliation, our opinion in regard to Bonaparte remains unchanged and incapable of change. We shall not cease to express our views on this subject, and we can merely say to the king of Prussia: 'So much the worse for you. It's your own choice, *Georges Dandin*, that's all that we have to say about it.'"

That was what the political thermometer indicated at Anna Pavlovna's.

When Boris, who was to be offered up to the guests, entered the drawing-room, nearly all were already present, and the conversation, under Anna Pavlovna's lead, turned on our diplomatic relations with Austria and on the hope of an alliance.

Boris, in an elegant uniform, fresh and ruddy, and grown to man's estate, came with easy assurance into the drawing-room, and was led up, according to custom, to salute the aunt, and then brought back to the general circle of the guests.

Anna Pavlovna gave him her withered hand to kiss, introduced him to a number of the company with whom he was not acquainted, and of each she would say in a whisper : —

"Prince Ippolit Kuragin, a charming young man; Monsieur Krouq, *chargé d'affaires* from Copenhagen, a profound mind;" or simply, "Monsieur Sitof, a man of great ability," giving each one whom she named a word of flattery.

Boris, since he had been in the service, had, thanks to Anna Mikhaïlovna's efforts and to his own tastes and habit of self-control, succeeded in obtaining a very advantageous position. He had been appointed aide to a man of great eminence; he had been intrusted with a very important errand to Prussia, and had only just returned from there as a special courier. He had thoroughly mastered that unwritten system of subordination which had pleased him so much at Olmütz, according to which the ensign may stand incomparably higher than a general, while, for success in the service, exertions and services and gallantry are unnecessary, but all that is needed is tact in getting on with those who control the patronage of places; and he was often himself surprised at his rapid advances, and by the fact that his friends could not understand it. The consequence of this discovery was that his whole mode of life, and all his relations to former friends and acquaintances, and all his plans for the future, were entirely and absolutely changed. He was not rich, but he would spend his last kopek so as to be better dressed than

others; he preferred to deprive himself of many pleasures sooner than allow himself to ride in a shabby carriage or appear in anything but an immaculate uniform
in the streets of Petersburg. He frequented only the
society of those who were above him and might be of
advantage to him. He liked Petersburg and despised
Moscow. His recollections of his home with the
Rostofs and his boyish love for Natasha were unpleasant to him, and since his first departure for the army
he had not once been to see the Rostofs.

On reaching Anna Pavlovna's drawing-room, an invitation which he considered equivalent to a rise in
the service, he immediately understood what part he had
to play, and he allowed Anna Pavlovna to make the
most of the interest which centered upon him, while he
attentively studied each face and took mental stock of
what possibilities of getting advantage from each might
present themselves. He sat down in the place assigned
to him, next the beautiful Ellen, and began to listen to
the conversation that was going on.

"Vienna regards the basis of the proposed treaty as
so entirely out of the question that it would be impossible to bring it about even by a series of the most brilliant successes, and she questions the means we have
of gaining them. Such is the authentic report from
Vienna," said the Danish *chargé d'affaires*, in French.

"The doubt is flattering," said the young man of the
profound mind, with a shrewd smile.

"One should distinguish between the cabinet of
Vienna and the emperor of Austria," said Montemart.
"The Austrian emperor could never have thought of
such a thing; it could only have been the cabinet that
said it."

"Ah, my dear viscount," interrupted Anna Pavlovna,
"*l'Urope....*" for some reason she called it *l'Urope*, as
a special refinement of French which she might make
use of in speaking to a Frenchman. "Ah, my dear viscount, Europe will never be a trustworthy ally for us."

And then Anna Pavlovna immediately led the conversation around to the bravery and resolution of the

Prussian king, doing this for the sake of giving Boris a chance to take part.

Boris was listening attentively to what was said, awaiting his turn, but, nevertheless, he had been able to look several times at his neighbor, the beautiful Ellen, who, with a smile, had more than once exchanged glances with the handsome young adjutant.

Quite naturally, while speaking of the position of Prussia, Anna Pavlovna begged Boris to tell about his visit to Glogau, and the state in which he found the Prussian army. Boris, without undue haste, speaking in pure and elegant French, related very many interesting particulars about the army, and about the court, but throughout his story he carefully avoided expressing any personal opinion in regard to the facts which he communicated. For some time Boris held the attention of all, and Anna Pavlovna was conscious that all her guests took great satisfaction in the treat that she had set before them.

Ellen, more than any one else, gave her undivided attention to what Boris had to say. She several times asked him in regard to certain details of his journey, and was apparently greatly interested in the position of the Prussian army. As soon as he had finished, she turned to him with her usual smile, and said:—

"You must be sure to come and see me." She spoke in a tone which seemed to imply that circumstances of which he could know nothing made it absolutely imperative.

"Tuesday, between eight o'clock and nine. You will give me great pleasure."

Boris promised to comply with her wishes, and was about to engage her in further conversation, when Anna Pavlovna called him away, under the pretext that her old aunt wanted to speak with him.

"You used to know her husband, did n't you?" asked Anna Pavlovna, closing her eyes, and making a melancholy gesture toward Ellen. "Akh! she is such an unhappy and charming woman. Don't speak to her about him, please be careful about it. It is too hard for her."

CHAPTER VII

WHEN Boris and Anna Pavlovna returned to the general circle, Prince Ippolit had taken the lead in the conversation. Leaning forward in his chair, he had said: "*Le roi de Prusse,*" and when he said it, he laughed. All turned to him. "*Le roi de Prusse?*" asked Ippolit, again laughing, and then with a calm and serious expression throwing himself back into the depths of his easy-chair. Anna Pavlovna waited a little for him, but as Ippolit apparently had firmly shut his mouth not to say anything more, she started the conversation on the godless Bonaparte laying hands on the sword of Frederick the Great at Potsdam.

"'T is the sword of Frederick the Great which...." she began to say, but Ippolit interrupted her with the words: —

"*Le roi de Prusse....*" and again, as before, when all had turned toward him, he begged her pardon and remained silent. Anna Pavlovna frowned; Montemart, Ippolit's friend, turned to him peremptorily: "What do you mean now by your *roi de Prusse?*"

Ippolit laughed, as if he were ashamed of laughing: —

"No, it's nothing at all, I only meant...."

He was trying to get off a joke which he had heard in Vienna, and which he had been anxious the whole evening long to spring on the company. He said: —

"I only meant that we were doing wrong to wage war for *le roi de Prusse.*" [1]

Boris smiled a guarded smile, which might have been taken to signify a sneer or approbation of the joke, according as it was received by the company. All laughed.

"Your pun is very naughty! it's witty, but it's unfair," said Anna Pavlovna, in French, threatening him

[1] An untranslatable joke: *pour le roi de Prusse* means *for mere trifles.* — AUTHOR'S NOTE.

with her finger. "We do not wage war for *le roi de Prusse*, but for good principles. Oh, this naughty Prince Ippolit," said she.

The conversation had not languished the whole evening, though it had turned principally on political matters. Toward the end of the evening it grew particularly lively on the topic of the rewards bestowed by the emperor.

"Now last year N. N. received a snuff-box, with a portrait," said the man "of the profound mind." "Why should not S. S. receive the same reward?"

"I beg your pardon, a snuff-box with the emperor's portrait is a reward, but not a distinction," said one of the diplomats. "A gift, rather."

"There have been precedents. I will mention Schwartzenberg."

"It's impossible," said the other. "I'll make you a wager. The ribbon is a different thing."

When all got up to leave, Ellen, who had spoken very little all the evening, addressed Boris again, and begged him with the most flattering and significant expression to come to see her the following Tuesday.

"It will be a very great favor to me," said she, with a smile, glancing at Anna Pavlovna, and Anna Pavlovna, with that same melancholy expression which always accompanied her words when she spoke of her august protectress, corroborated Ellen's request.

It seemed that from certain words spoken by Boris that evening concerning the Prussian army, Ellen had suddenly conceived a powerful determination to see him. She practically promised him that when he came, on the following Tuesday, she would tell him what it was that made her wish to see him.

But when, on the Tuesday evening, Boris reached Ellen's salon, he received no explanation that made it plain why he was so anxiously desired to come. There were other guests; the countess talked very little with him, and only on his departure, just as he was kissing her hand, she unexpectedly whispered to him, without any smile, — which was strange for her: —

"Come to-morrow evening to dinner. You really must come!"

Thus with his first visit to Petersburg began Boris's intimacy at the house of the Countess Bezukhaya.

CHAPTER VIII

THE war was growing fiercer, and its theater was approaching the Russian frontiers. Everywhere were heard curses against Bonaparte, the enemy of all the human race. In all the villages of the empire, veterans and raw recruits were forming into companies, and from the theater of war came conflicting rumors, usually false, and consequently interpreted in various ways.

The life of the old Prince Bolkonsky, Prince Andreï, and the Princess Mariya had changed in many respects since the year 1805.

In 1806 the old prince was appointed one of the eight commanders-in-chief for the militia, at that time recruiting all over Russia. The old prince, in spite of the weaknesses of age, which had become especially noticeable at the period when he supposed that his son was killed, felt that he had no right to refuse the duty to which he had been called by the sovereign in person, and this new activity into which he entered stimulated and strengthened him. He was constantly engaged in journeying about the three governments intrusted to him; he carried his regulations even to pedantry; he was stern and strict even to cruelty with his subordinates, and he himself looked into the smallest details of his work.

The Princess Mariya had now ceased to recite her lessons in mathematics to her father, and only on mornings when he was at home did she go to his cabinet, accompanied by the wet-nurse and the "little Prince Nikolaï," as his grandfather called him. The baby prince, with his wet-nurse and the old Nyanya Savishna, lived in the apartments which had been occupied by the princess, his mother; and the young

Princess Mariya spent a large portion of the day in the nursery, trying to the best of her ability to take the place of mother to her little nephew. Mlle. Bourienne also apparently felt a passionate love for the child, and the Princess Mariya, often in a spirit of sacrifice, would allow her friend the pleasure of attending the little "angel," as she called her nephew, and playing with him.

Near the altar of the Luisorgorsky church, a chapel had been built to the memory of the little princess, and in the chapel was placed a marble monument brought from Italy, representing an angel with outstretched wings as if about to mount to heaven. The angel's upper lip was lifted a little, as if she were going to smile, and once Prince Andreï and the Princess Mariya, as they came out of the chapel, agreed that the face of the angel reminded them strangely of the face of the departed. But what was still stranger — and this Prince Andreï did not remark to his sister — was that in this expression which the artist had accidentally given to the angel's face, Prince Andreï read those very words of sweet reproach which he had before read on the face of his dead wife: —

"Akh! why have you done this to me?"

Shortly after Prince Andreï's return, the old prince had quarreled with his son and made over to him the large estate of Bogucharovo, situated about forty versts from Luisiya Gorui. Partly on account of the sad recollections associated with Luisiya Gorui, partly because Prince Andreï always felt himself unable to endure his father's idiosyncrasies, and partly also because he felt the need of solitude, he took possession of Bogucharovo, established himself there, and there spent a large part of his time.

Prince Andreï after the battle of Austerlitz had resolutely made up his mind never to go back into the military service again; and, when the war began, and all were obliged to enlist, he, in order to escape active service, accepted a position under his father's command in the recruiting of the militia.

Since the campaign of 1805, the old prince and his son seemed to have exchanged parts; the father, excited by active life, expected all that was good from the campaign; Prince Andreï, on the contrary, not taking any active part in the war, and in the secret depths of his heart regretting it, saw only a dark prospect ahead.

On the tenth of March, 1807, the old prince started on one of his circuits. Prince Andreï, as usual during his father's absences, stayed at Luisiya Gorui. The dear little Nikolushka had not been quite well for several days. The coachman who had driven the old prince to the next town returned and brought documents and letters for Prince Andreï. The valet, carrying the mail, failing to find the prince in his study, went to the Princess Mariya's apartments, but he was not there either. The valet was informed that the prince had gone to the nursery.

"If you please, your illustriousness, Petrusha has come with some documents," said one of the maids employed in the nursery, addressing Prince Andreï, who was sitting in a child's small chair, and with knitted brows and trembling hands was dropping medicine from a bottle into a tumbler half full of water.

"What did you say?" said he, testily; and by an unguarded movement of his trembling hand he poured too many drops into the glass of water. He threw the medicine on the floor and asked for some more water. The maid handed it to him.

In the room stood a child's cradle, two chests, two arm-chairs, a table, a child's table, and the little chair in which Prince Andreï was sitting. The windows were closely shaded, and on the table burned a single candle shaded by a bound volume of music, so that no light might fall on the cradle.

"My dear," said the Princess Mariya, turning to her brother from the cradle by which she was standing, "you had better wait .... until .... "

"Akh! Please be kind enough .... you 're always talking nonsense, and you 're always procrastinating; and see what it has led to now!" said Prince Andreï, in an angry whisper, with the manifest intention of wounding his sister.

"My dear, truly it would be better not to awaken him; he is asleep now," said the princess, in a supplicating voice.

Prince Andreï got up and went over on tiptoes to the cradle with the glass in his hand.

"Had we really better not wake him?" said he, irresolutely.

"Just as you please; truly, I think so. But just as you think best," said the Princess Mariya, evidently embarrassed and a little ashamed that her opinion was about to rule. She called her brother's attention to the maid who was speaking to him in a whisper.

It was the second night that neither of them had got any sleep on account of watching over the baby, who was suffering from a sharp attack of fever. All this time, since they had felt very little confidence in their own domestic physician, and were expecting one to be sent them from the city, they had disagreed about remedies, the one preferring one thing, the other, another. Suffering from sleeplessness and anxiety, they each blamed the other, and indulged in recriminations which amounted to actual quarrels.

"Petrusha, with documents from your papenka," whispered the maid. Prince Andreï went out.

"The devil take them!" he exclaimed, and after hearing the verbal messages from his father, and taking the envelopes and letters, he went back to the nursery.

"How is he now?" asked Prince Andreï.

"Just the same. We must await the mercy of God. Karl Ivanuitch always declares that sleep is better than any medicine," whispered Princess Mariya, with a sigh.

Prince Andreï went to the child and felt of him. He was very hot.

"The mischief take you and your Karl Ivanuitch!"

He took the glass with the medicine which he had dropped into it, and again approached the cradle.

"André, you ought not," exclaimed the Princess Mariya.

But he scowled wrathfully at her, and at the same time with the look of a martyr, and bent over the baby with his glass. "I insist upon it," said he. "Well, then, you give it to him!"

The Princess Mariya shrugged her shoulders, but obediently took the glass, and, calling the nurse to help, tried to give the child the medicine. The baby screamed and strangled. Prince Andreï, scowling, clasped his hands to his head, left the room, and sat down on a divan in the next room.

The letters were still in his hands. He mechanically opened them and began to read them. The old prince, in his large scrawly hand, sometimes employing abbreviations and quaint archaic words, wrote on blue paper as follows:—

"I have just at this moment received very agreeable news — unless it's a canard. Benigsen is said to have gained a complete victory over Buonaparte at Eylau. They are wild with delight at Petersburg, and endless rewards have been distributed in the army. Though he's a German, I congratulate him. I cannot imagine what that nachalnik, Hendrikof, is doing at Korchevo ; so far no reinforcements or provisions have come from him. Go there as quick as you can and tell him that I will take his head off, if everything is not here within a week's time. I have received additional news about the battle of Eylau through a letter from Petinka ; he took part — it's all true. When mischief-makers do not meddle, then even a German can beat Buonaparte. They say he is retreating in great disorder. See that you go to Korchevo without delay, and hurry things along."

Prince Andreï sighed and tore open another envelope. This was a closely written letter from Bilibin, filling two sheets. He folded it up without reading it, and again perused the letter from his father, ending with the words: "Go to Korchevo without delay, and hurry things along."

"No, excuse me, I will not go now, when my baby is still sick," he said to himself, and, stepping to the door, he looked into the nursery. Princess Mariya still stood by the cradle, and was gently rocking the child.

"Yes, what in the name of goodness was that other disagreeable thing that he wrote?" asked Prince Andreï, trying to recall his father's letter. "Oh, yes. Our men have won a victory over Bonaparte, now that I am not there to take part. Yes, yes; he will have a good chance to make sport of me; well, let him if he wants." ....

And he began to read Bilibin's letter, which was in French. He read without understanding half of it, read it simply for the sake of forgetting for the moment what had been painfully and quite too long occupying his thoughts to the exclusion of everything else.

CHAPTER IX

BILIBIN was now acting as a diplomatic chinovnik at the headquarters of the army, and though he wrote in French with French jests and phraseology, still he described the whole campaign with genuine Russian fearlessness, not sparing reproaches or sarcasms. He wrote that the discretion imposed upon him by the necessities of diplomacy annoyed him, and that he was glad to have in Prince Andreï an ingenuous correspondent, to whom he was able to pour out all the spleen which had been accumulating in him at the sight of what was going on in the army. This letter was of somewhat ancient date, having been penned even before the battle of Preussisch-Eylau. Bilibin wrote as follows: —

"Since our great success at Austerlitz, my dear prince, I have been, as you may know, constantly at headquarters. I have conceived a decided taste for war, and so much the better for me. What I have witnessed these past three months is beyond belief!

"I will begin *ab ovo* — at the very beginning. The 'enemy of the human race,' as you are well aware, has been attacking the Prussians. The Prussians are our faithful allies, who have only duped us three times within three years. Consequently, we take up their cause. But it proves that the 'enemy of the human race' pays no attention to our fine speeches, and, in accordance with his rough and untrained nature, flings himself on the Prussians without allowing them to finish their parade, in short meter beats them all hollow — *les rosse à plate coûture* — and makes himself at home in the palace at Potsdam.

" ' I have the most earnest desire,' writes the king of Prussia, to Bonaparte, 'that your majesty should be received and treated in my palace as would be most agreeable to you, and I hasten to take all measures to this end that circumstances permit. I only hope that I have been successful.'

" The Prussian generals make it a point of honor to be gracious toward the French and lay down their arms at the first summons.

" The principal officer of the garrison of Glogau, with ten thousand men, asks the king of Prussia what he shall do if he is called upon to surrender. Fact !

" In short, while hoping to make a great impression solely by our military attitude, lo and behold ! here we are in for a real war and what is worse, for a war on our own frontiers *avec* and *pour le roi de Prusse !*

" Everything is all ready ; we lack only one trifling thing, that is, a general-in-chief. As it has been discovered that the success of Austerlitz might have been more decided, if only the general-in-chief had been older, all the octogenarians have been brought forward, and between Prosorovsky and Kamensky, the preference has been given to the latter. The general comes to us in a kibitka after the style of Suvorof, and is received with acclamations of joy and triumph.

" On the fourth comes the first courier from Petersburg. The mail is brought into the marshal's study, as he likes to do everything personally. I am summoned to help sort the letters and take those addressed to ourselves. The marshal looks on while we work, and waits for the packages addressed to him. We search them over, but there is not one. The marshal becomes impatient and sets to work himself and finds letters from the emperor for Count T., for Prince V., and others. Then lo and behold ! he goes off into one of his blue rages. He shoots fire and flames against everybody ; he seizes the letters, breaks their seals, and reads those which the emperor has written to others.

" 'So that 's the way I am treated ! They have no confidence in me ! Ah, that 's a fine notion, setting others to watch my actions! Away with you.' And he writes his famous order of the day to General Benigsen: —

"'I am wounded, and cannot ride on horseback, and consequently cannot command the army. You have taken your defeated *corps d'armée* into Pultusk; there it is exposed, and lacks firewood and provender, and, as you yourself reported last evening to Count Buxhövden, you must devise measures for retiring beyond our frontier; see that this is done to-day.'

"'Owing to all my riding on horseback,' he writes to the emperor, 'I have become galled by the saddle, which, in addition to my former infirmities, entirely prevents me from riding on horseback and commanding such an extensive army, and therefore I have transferred the command to Count Buxhövden, who is next in seniority to myself, giving him the whole charge, and advising him, in case he cannot obtain bread, to move nearer to the interior of Prussia, since only enough bread is left for one day, and some of the regiments have none at all, — according to the reports of the division commanders, Ostermann and Sedmoretsky, — and the peasants, also, have nothing left. And I myself shall remain in the hospital at Ostrolenko until I am well. In offering, most respectfully, this report, I would add that if this army remain another fortnight in its present bivouac, by spring there will not be a single sound soldier left.

"'Permit an old man to retire to the country, since he is now so feeble that he finds it impossible to fulfil the great and glorious duty for which he was chosen. I shall await your all-gracious permission here in the hospital, so as not to play the *rôle* of a clerk instead of commander at the head of the army. Of men like myself there are thousands in Russia.'

"The marshal is vexed with the emperor, and punishes all of us for it. Is n't that logical?

"Thus ends the first act. In those that follow, the interest and the absurdity increase in proper degree. After the marshal's departure, it is discovered that we are in sight of the enemy, and must fight. Buxhövden is commander-general-in-chief by order of seniority, but General Benigsen is not of this opinion; all the more because it is he and his corps who are in sight of the enemy, and he is anxious to profit by the occasion to fight a battle on his own account, '*aus eigene Hand,*' as the Germans say. He does so. This is the battle of Pultusk, which is reported to be a great victory, but which, in my opinion, was no victory at all. We civilians — *nous autres pékins*

—have, as you are well aware, a very wretched habit of making up our own minds in regard to the gain or loss of a battle. The one who retires after the battle is the loser, so we say, and in this respect we lost the battle of Pultusk.

"In short, we retreat after the battle, but we send a courier to Petersburg to carry the news of the victory, and the general refuses to surrender the chief command to Buxhövden, hoping to receive from Petersburg the title of general-in-chief as a reward for his victory.

"During this interregnum, we begin an excessively interesting and original scheme of manœuvers. Our design consists not, as it should have been, in avoiding or attacking the enemy, but solely of avoiding General Buxhövden, who by right of seniority should be our chief. We pursue this plan with so much energy, that even in crossing an unfordable river we burn our bridges to cut off the enemy, who for the nonce is not Bonaparte but Buxhövden. General Buxhövden just misses being attacked and taken by overwhelming forces of the enemy by reason of one of our pretty manœuvers which saves us from him. Buxhövden pursues us, — we sneak away. As soon as he crosses to our side of the river we cross back again. At last our enemy, Buxhövden, catches up with us, and attacks us. The two generals have a quarrel. Buxhövden even goes so far as to send a challenge, and Benigsen has an attack of epilepsy.

"But at the critical moment the courier who carried the news of our victory at Pultusk returns with our nomination as general-in-chief, and our enemy No. 1 is done for. We can think of No. 2, Bonaparte. But what do you suppose? Just at this moment there rises before us a third enemy, the *pravoslavnoye*, — the orthodox army, — loudly clamoring for bread, for meat, for *sukhari*,[1] for hay, and what not! The stores are empty; the roads impassable. The orthodox troops set themselves to marauding, and in a way of which the last campaign would not give you the slightest notion. Half of the regiments form themselves into freebooters, scouring the country and putting everything to fire and sword. The natives are ruined, root and branch; the hospitals are overflowing with sick, and famine is everywhere. Twice the headquarters have been attacked by troops of marauders, and the general-in-chief has himself been obliged to ask for a battalion to drive them off. In one of these attacks my empty trunk and my dressing-gown was carried off. The emperor has consented to grant all the division

[1] Biscuits, hardtack.

chiefs the right to shoot the marauders, but I very much fear that such a course would oblige one half of the army to shoot the other half."

Prince Andreï at first read with his eyes alone, but gradually, in spite of himself, what he was reading — in spite of the fact that he was well aware of how far Bilibin was to be trusted — began to absorb him more and more. Having read thus far he crumpled up the letter and threw it aside. It was not what he had read in the letter that moved his indignation, but rather the fact that the life there, so remote and foreign to him now, had still the power to stir him. He closed his eyes, rubbed his forehead with his hand, as if to drive away all recollection of what he had been reading — and listened to what was going on in the nursery.

Suddenly it seemed to him that he heard a strange sound there. A great fear came over him; he was afraid that something might have happened to his baby while he was reading the letter. He went to the nursery door on his tiptoes, and opened it.

As he went in, he noticed that the nurse, with a frightened face, was hiding something from him, and the Princess Mariya was no longer by the cradle.

"My dear," he heard behind him, in his sister's frightened voice, as it seemed to him. As often occurs after long wakefulness and keen emotion, a causeless panic came over him; he imagined that the child was dead. All that he heard and saw seemed to confirm his fear.

"It is all over," he said to himself, and a cold sweat stood out on his brow. He went to the cradle in great apprehension, firmly convinced that he should find it empty, that the nurse-girl was hiding his dead baby! He drew the curtains aside, and it was some time before his frightened, wandering eyes could find the child. At last he saw him. The little one, all rosy, lay sprawled out across the cradle, with his head lower than the pillow, and was smacking his lips in his sleep and breathing regularly.

Prince Andreï was delighted to see the child so, when he was already beginning to think that he had lost him. He bent over, and, as his sister had instructed him, felt with his lips whether the baby's fever had gone. The sweet brow was moist; he passed his hand over the little head, and the soft hair was also moist, the baby was in such a perspiration! Not only was the baby not dead, but he was aware now that the crisis had passed, and that he was better. He felt a strong inclination to snatch up this helpless little creature and press him to his heart; but he dared not do so. He stood over him, looking at his head, and at his little arms and feet, which had thrown off the coverings. He heard a rustling behind him, and thought he saw a shadow outlined on the curtain of the cradle. But he did not look around, but gazed into the baby's face, still listening to his regular breathing. The dark shadow was the Princess Mariya, who, with noiseless steps, came to the cradle, lifted the curtain, and dropped it after her. Prince Andreï, without looking around, recognized her, and stretched out his hand to her. She pressed his hand.

"He is in a perspiration," said Prince Andreï.

"I had gone out to tell you."

The baby stirred a little in his sleep, smiled, and rubbed his forehead against the pillow. Prince Andreï looked at his sister. The Princess Mariya's lustrous eyes in the subdued twilight of the curtains gleamed more than usually bright with happy tears. She leaned over to her brother and kissed him, slightly catching her gown in the material of the curtain. Each made the other a warning gesture, and stood quiet for a moment under the faint light of the curtain, as if they wished still to remain in that world in which they were shut off from all the rest of the universe. Prince Andreï was the first to move away from the cradle, getting his head entangled in the muslin of the curtain as he did so.

"Yes, that is all that is left me now," said he, with a sigh.

CHAPTER X

SHORTLY after his reception into the Masonic brother-hood, Pierre, with full written instructions given him for his guidance in managing his estates, reached the gov-ernment of Kief, where the larger number of his serfs were to be found.

When he reached Kief, he summoned all his over-seers, and explained his intentions and desires. He told them that measures would be immediately taken for the unconditional emancipation from servitude of all his serfs; that till this were done the peasants must not be constrained to hard work, that the women and children must not be required to work at all; that assis-tance was to be freely rendered the peasantry; that corporal punishments were not to be employed, but reprimands; and that on each of his estates, hospitals, asylums, and schools were to be established.

Some of the overseers — and in the number were half-educated *ekonoms*, or stewards — listened with dismay, supposing that the young count's speech meant that he was dissatisfied with their management, or had discov-ered how they had been embezzling his funds. Others, after their first panic, found amusement in Pierre's thick, stumbling speech, and the new words which they had never before heard; a third set found simply a certain sense of satisfaction in hearing their barin talk; a fourth, and these were the sharpest, and at their head the chief overseer, perceived from this talk how it be-hooved them to manage with their barin, in order to subserve their own ends.

The chief overseer expressed great sympathy in Pierre's proposed plans; but he remarked that, over and above these reforms, it was indispensable to make a general investigation of his affairs, which were in a sufficiently unfortunate state.

In spite of Count Bezukhoï's enormous wealth at the time when Pierre entered upon his inheritance — and it was said that he had an income of five hundred thousand rubles a year—he felt himself much poorer than when he received an allowance of ten thousand a year from his late father. He had a general dim idea that his expenses were somewhat as follows: interest to the "Society," [1] about eighty thousand rubles, on all his possessions; about thirty thousand stood him for the maintenance of his house in Moscow, and his pod-Moskovnaya, and the support of the three princesses; about fifteen thousand went in pensions; as much more to various charitable institutions; one hundred and fifty thousand were put down for support of the countess; about seventy thousand went in interest on his debts; the building of a church which he had begun two years before cost him about ten thousand a year; the rest, not far from one hundred thousand, was expended, he himself knew not how, and almost every year he found himself obliged to borrow. Moreover, each year his chief overseer had written to him about fires, about bad harvests, about the necessity of building new factories and works. And thus Pierre was at the very first confronted by what he had not the slightest taste or capacity for, the settlement of his affairs.

Pierre each day spent some time with his chief overseer in this business; but he was conscious that his efforts did not advance his interests a single step. He was conscious that his efforts were wasted on this business, that they did not have the slightest influence on his affairs, and were not calculated to help him on with his schemes. On the one hand, his head overseer pictured his affairs in the gloomiest colors, pointing out to Pierre the absolute necessity of paying his debts and undertaking new enterprises with the labor of his peasantry, a thing to which Pierre refused to listen; on the other hand, Pierre insisted on the project of emancipating his serfs, but to this the overseer opposed the imperious necessity of first paying the mortgage held by

---

[1] *Opekunsky Sovyét*, Orphan's Aid Society, the famous bank supported by the State, that loaned money on land and personal property, including serfs.

the Society, and consequently the impossibility of accomplishing the business rapidly.

The overseer did not say that this was absolutely impossible; he proposed, for bringing this about, the selling of certain forests in the government of Kostroma, some river lands, and an estate in the Crimea. But all these operations proposed by the overseer entailed complicated legal proceedings, replevins, permits, licenses, and so forth, so that Pierre quite lost his wits, and merely said, "Yes, yes, do so, then."

Pierre was not possessed of that practical bent for business which would have enabled him to grasp the whole matter immediately, and consequently he disliked it all, and merely pretended to take an interest in it in the overseer's presence. The overseer, on his side, pretended to consider all these efforts advantageous for the proprietor, and troublesome for himself.

In the large city of Kief, the capital of the province, Pierre had some acquaintances; those whom he did not know made haste to pay their respects to him, and gladly welcomed the millionaire, the largest landowner of the whole government. The temptations that assailed Pierre in his principal weakness — as he had confessed at the time of his entrance into the lodge — were also so powerful that he could not resist them. Again, whole days, weeks, months, of his life sped away constantly occupied with parties, dinners, breakfasts, balls, just as it had been in Petersburg, so that he had no time whatever for serious thoughts. Instead of the new life which he had hoped to lead, he still went on with the same old routine, only in different surroundings.

Of the three obligations of Freemasonry, Pierre acknowledged that he was not fulfilling the one that enjoined upon every Mason to be a model of moral living; and of the seven precepts of virtue, two he had not taken to heart, — virtuous living and love for death. He comforted himself with the thought that he was fulfilling one of the other obligations, the reformation of the human race, and that he possessed the other virtues, love of his neighbor, and particularly generosity.

In the spring of the year 1807 Pierre determined to return to Petersburg, making on his way a visit to all of his possessions, so as to assure himself as to what had been done toward carrying out his orders, and personally to learn in what condition lived the peasantry intrusted to him by God, and whom he was striving to benefit.

His head overseer, who considered all of the young count's ideas as perfectly chimerical, — disadvantageous for himself, for him, for the peasants themselves, — had made some concessions. Though he still represented that the emancipation of the serfs was an impossibility, he had made arrangements for the extensive erection, on all the estates, of schools, hospitals, and asylums, against the coming of the barin; everywhere he made arrangements for receptions, not, to be sure, on a sumptuous and magnificent scale which he knew would displease the young count, but rather semi-religious and thanksgiving processions, with sacred images and the traditional *khlyeb-sol*, — or bread and salt, — the Russian symbol of hospitality; such demonstrations, in fact, as he was certain from his knowledge of his barin's character would deeply touch him and delude him.

The southern spring, the comfortable, rapid journey in his Vienna calash, and the lonely roads had made a most pleasant impression on Pierre. These estates, none of which he had ever seen before, were each more picturesque than the other; the peasantry everywhere appeared prosperous and touchingly grateful to him for the benefits which he was heaping upon them. Everywhere they met him with processions and receptions, which, though they embarrassed him, filled his heart with a pleasant sensation.

In one place, the peasants brought him the khlyeb-sol and a holy picture of Peter and Paul, and besought his permission to add, at their own expense, in honor of his name-day and as a sign of their love and gratitude to him for the benefits conferred upon them, a new chantry to the church.

In another place he was met by women with children

at the breast, who thanked him for freeing them from hard work.

On a third estate he was met by a priest carrying a cross and surrounded by children, to whom, through the count's liberality, he was teaching reading and religion.

On all his estates he saw with his own eyes the massive stone foundations of edifices for hospitals, schools, and almshouses, building or almost built, and ready to be opened in a short time.   Everywhere Pierre saw from the accounts of his overseers that enforced labor had been greatly reduced from what it had been, and he listened to the affecting expressions of gratitude from deputations of serfs in their blue kaftans.

But Pierre had no knowledge of the fact that where he had been met with the bread and salt, and where they were building the chantry of Peter and Paul, it was a commercial village where a *yarmarka*, or annual bazaar, was held on Saint Peter's day; that the chantry had been begun long before by some well-to-do muzhiks of the village, the very ones in fact who came to meet him, while nine-tenths of the peasants of this same village lived in the profoundest destitution.

He did not know that in consequence of his order to cease employing nursing women at work on his fields, these very same women were forced to do vastly harder work on their own lots of communal land.   He did not know that the priest who came to meet him with his cross oppressed the muzhiks with his exactions, and that the pupils who accompanied him were placed with him at the cost of tears, and were often ransomed back by their parents for large sums of money.

He did not know that the edifices built, according to his plan, of stone were the work of his own laborers, and greatly increased the forced service of his serfs, which was really diminished only on paper.

He did not know that where the overseers pointed out to him on the books the reduction of the serfs' *obroks*, or money payments, by one-third, the consequence was that an amount corresponding was added to the forced labor of the peasantry.

And so Pierre was in raptures over his tour among his estates, and he fell back fully into that philanthropical frame of mind in which he had left Petersburg, and he wrote enthusiastic letters to his " preceptor-brother," as he called the Grand Master.

" How easy it is, how little strength it requires, to do so much good," said Pierre to himself. " And how little we trouble ourselves about it ! "

He was happy over the gratitude, but felt mortified to be the recipient of it. This gratitude made him think how very much more he might have easily done for these simple-hearted, kindly people.

The chief overseer, a thoroughly obstinate and wily man, perfectly comprehending the intelligent but innocent young count, and playing with him as with a toy, when he saw the effect produced upon him by the receptions that he had himself so skilfully arranged, approached him all the more resolutely with arguments for the impossibility, and, above all, the uselessness, of emancipating the serfs, who were perfectly happy and contented as they were.

Pierre in the depths of his soul agreed with the overseer that it would be hard to imagine people more happy and contented, and that God only knew what would happen to them if they had their freedom ; but still, though against his better judgment, he insisted upon what he felt was only justice.

The overseer promised to do all in his power to carry out the count's desires, clearly comprehending that the count would never be in a position to assure himself whether all his plans for the disposal of his forests and other lands for the sake of redeeming his mortgages to the Society had been carried out, or would ever ask or know how his costly edifices would stand empty and the peasants would continue to contribute their labor and money, just the same as they did on other estates, that is, the utmost that they could give.

CHAPTER XI

On his return from his southern journey, in the happiest frame of mind, Pierre carried out his long-cherished
purpose of going to make a visit to his old friend Bolkonsky, whom he had not seen for two years.

Bogucharovo was situated in the midst of a flat and
uninteresting region, diversified with fields and forests
of birch and evergreens, cleared and uncleared. The
barsky dvor, or proprietor's place, was situated at one
end of the straggling village which extended along on
both sides of the straight highway. In front was a
pond, recently dug and filled with water, though the
grass had not yet had a chance to grow on the banks
around; the house stood in the midst of a young grove,
some of the trees of which were pines and firs.

The *barsky dvor* consisted of a granary and threshing-
floor, the house-servants' quarters, the stable, a bath-
house, and the wings of a great stone mansion, the
semicircular façade of which was building. Around the
house a young garden was planted. The fences were
strong and the paths were new; under a shed stood two
fire-engines and a barrel, painted a vivid green. The
paths were straight, the bridges were well built and had
railings. Everything bore the impress of extreme care
and good management.

The house-serfs who met Pierre, in answer to his
question where the prince lived, pointed to a small building standing at the very edge of the pond. Prince
Andreï's old body-servant, Anton, helped Pierre down
from the calash, told him that the prince was at home,
and led him into a neat little anteroom.

Pierre was struck by the modesty of this diminutive,
though scrupulously clean, little house, after the brilliant conditions of existence in which he had last seen
his friend in Petersburg. He hurriedly went into a small
hall, smelling of pine and not even plastered, and was
about to go farther, but Anton preceded him on his
tiptoes and knocked at the door.

" Now who 's there ? " was the reply, in a harsh, forbidding voice.

" A visitor," replied Anton.

" Ask him to wait ; " and the noise of a chair pushed
back was heard. Pierre went with swift steps to the
door and met Prince Andreï face to face, as he came
out, frowning and looking older than his years.

Pierre threw his arms around him, pushing up his
spectacles, kissed him on the cheeks, and looked at him
closely.

" Well, this is a surprise ; very glad to see you," said
Prince Andreï. Pierre said nothing ; he was gazing at
his friend in amazement, not taking his eyes from him.
He was struck by the change that had taken place in
Prince Andreï. His words were affectionate ; there was
a smile on his lips and face, but his eyes were dim and
lifeless, in spite of his evident desire to make them
seem to have a joyous and lively light. His friend was
not so much disturbed that he had grown thinner and
paler, but this expression of his eyes and the frown on
his brow, the evidence of long-continued concentration
on some one painful topic, amazed and estranged Pierre,
who was not used to see him so.

As usual, on meeting after a long separation, it took
some time to get the conversation into running order ;
they asked and answered various questions briefly in
regard to things which both knew they should have to
talk about afterward at length. At last they began
to settle down a little more on what they had already
touched upon, what had taken place in the past, and
their plans for the future, about Pierre's journey, his
undertakings, the war, and other topics.

That concentration and lifelessness which Pierre had
already remarked in Prince Andreï's eyes was now expressed still more noticeably in the smile with which he
listened to Pierre, especially when he spoke with animation of the past or the future.

It seemed as if Prince Andreï were trying, but without
success, to feel an interest in what he said. Pierre was
beginning to feel that it was in bad taste in Prince

Andreï's presence to speak of his enthusiasms, dreams, hopes of happiness, and of doing good. He was ashamed to tell about his new notions concerning Freemasonry, which had been especially renewed and excited during the latter part of his journey, He restrained himself for fear of seeming naïve; at the same time he had an irresistible desire to tell his friend as soon as possible that now he was an entirely different and much better man than he had been when he had known him in Petersburg.

"I cannot tell you what I have lived through since then. I should not know myself."

"Yes, yes, we have changed much since that time," said Prince Andreï.

"Well, and you," asked Pierre; "what are your plans?"

"Plans!" repeated Prince Andreï, in an ironical tone; "my plans!" he repeated again, as if he were astonished at such a word, "you can see for yourself, I am building; I intend next year to come here for good."....

Pierre said nothing, but still looked attentively at Prince Andreï's aged face.

"No, I wanted to ask," said he, but Prince Andreï interrupted him.

"But what is the use of talking about me?—Tell me, oh, yes, tell me about your journey,—all about what you expect to accomplish on your estates."

Pierre began to tell him what he had been doing for his peasantry, trying to conceal, as far as possible, his own part in the improvements made.

Prince Andreï several times finished Pierre's description for him, as if all that Pierre had done were an old story; and he seemed to listen, not only without interest, but even as if he felt ashamed at what Pierre told him. Pierre began to feel awkward and uncomfortable in his friend's society. He stopped talking.

"Now see here, my dear fellow,—*dusha moya*," said Prince Andreï, who evidently found it just as uncomfortable and irksome in his guest's society, "I am only camping out here, as it were.... came over simply to see now things were going. I am going back to-night to my sister's. If you will go back with me, I'll introduce you to her. Oh, but I think you know her," he added, evidently trying to think of something to amuse a guest with whom he felt that he had nothing in common; "we will start after dinner. But now would you like to look around my premises?"

They went out and returned to the house in time for dinner, talking of the political news, and of their common acquaintances, like men who cared very little for each other. Prince Andreï spoke with animation and interest only in regard to the new farmhouses and other buildings which he was having constructed; but even here, in the midst of their conversation, and while they were on the scaffolding, and he was describing the projected arrangements of the house, he suddenly paused:

"However, there is nothing very interesting about this; let us go to dinner and then start."

At the dinner-table the talk turned on Pierre's marriage.

"I was very much amazed when I heard about it," said Prince Andreï.

Pierre flushed, as he usually did when it was mentioned, and said hurriedly: —

"I will tell you sometime how it all happened. But you know that it is all over and forever."

"Forever?" queried Prince Andreï, "there is no such thing as forever!"

"But you know, don't you, how it all ended? You heard about the duel?"

"And so you had to go through that, also!"

"There is one thing that I thank God for, and that is that I did not kill that man," said Pierre.

"Why so?" asked Prince Andreï; "to kill a mad dog is a very good thing."

"No, but to kill a man is not good — not right."

"Why is it not right?" urged Prince Andreï. "It is not for men to judge what is right and wrong. Men have always been in error, and always will be in error, and in nothing more than in what they consider to be right and wrong."

"Wrong is whatever is harmful to our fellow-men," said Pierre, with a sense of satisfaction that now, for the first time since his arrival, Prince Andreï had really brightened up and begun to talk, and was on the way to disclosing what had made him so different from what he used to be.

"And who has ever told you what is harmful for another man?" asked Bolkonsky.

"Harmful! harmful!" exclaimed Pierre, "we all know what that means for ourselves."

"Yes, we know what is bad for ourselves, but that which is bad for myself may not be bad for another man," said Prince Andreï, growing more and more animated. He added in French: "I know of only two real evils in life — remorse and illness. There is nothing good except the absence of these evils. To live for myself, avoiding only these two evils, is at present all my philosophy."

"But how about love for your neighbor, and self-sacrifice?" protested Pierre; "no, I cannot agree with you. It is a very little thing to live merely so as not to do evil, merely to be free from remorse. I have lived in that way; I have lived for myself, and I have wasted my life. And now only that I am living, I mean trying to live, for others" — Pierre corrected himself out of modesty — " only now do I realize the full happiness of life. No, I cannot agree with you; and you yourself do not mean what you say."

Prince Andreï looked silently at Pierre, and smiled satirically.

"Well, you are going to see my sister, the Princess Mariya. You and she will agree," said he. "Maybe you are right as far as you are concerned," he went on to say, after a short silence, "but every one must work out his own life. You have lived for yourself, and declare that you have almost wasted your life by this course, and you have found happiness only when you began to live for others. But my experience has been exactly the opposite. I have lived for glory — and what is glory? Is it not love for others, the desire to

do something for them, the yearning for their applause?
And in that way I have lived for others, and have not
almost, but wholly, wasted my life. But only since I
have begun to live for myself alone, have I begun to
feel more satisfied."

"But how can you live for yourself alone?" asked
Pierre, growing heated; "there are your son, your sister,
your father!"

"Ah, yes; but they are the same as myself, they are
not 'other people,'" explained Prince Andreï; "but
others, neighbors, *le prochain*, as you and the Princess
Mariya express it, — they are the chief fountain-head of
error and evil. *Le prochain*, your neighbor, is, for
instance, those Kief muzhiks of yours, whom you are
trying to load with benefits."

And he looked at Pierre with a provokingly satirical
expression. It evidently provoked Pierre.

"You are jesting," said Pierre, who was constantly
growing more and more excited; "how can there be
error and evil in what I have desired — the accomplishment has been very trifling and wretched; but I mean
in what I have desired to do in the way of benefiting
them, and have accomplished in some small measure?
What possible evil can there be in poor men, like our
muzhiks, men just like ourselves, who grow up and
perish without any comprehension of God and right,
beyond mere forms and meaningless prayers, being
taught the consoling belief in a future life, in rewards
and compensations and joys to come? Pray what evil
or error is there when men are dying of maladies without succor, and when it is so easy to help them materi-
ally, in my giving them medicine and a hospital, and a
refuge for old age? And is it not a palpable and un-
questionable benefit that when the muzhiks, the nursing
women, have no rest either day or night, and I give them
leisure and recreation?" said Pierre, stammering in his
efforts to talk fast and keep up with his thoughts.
"And I have done this, stupidly enough, feebly enough,
but at all events I have done something toward it, and
you will fail to persuade me either that what I have

done is not good, or that you yourself have any such notion. And above all," proceeded Pierre, " I know and am firmly persuaded that the pleasure of doing good in this way is the only true happiness that life affords."

"Yes, if you propound the question in that way, you make an entirely different one out of it," said Prince Andreï. " I am building a house, I am laying out a garden, and you are erecting hospitals ; and some one else might come along and argue that both were a waste of time. But the decision as to what is right and what is good let us leave to Him who knows all things, and not try to decide it for ourselves. But I see that you want to argue the question." He added, " Give it to us, then."

They had left the table and were sitting on a flight of steps which took the place of a balcony.

"Well, let us have the discussion, then," said Prince Andreï. "You speak of schools," he went on to say, bending one finger, "and of education and so on ; that is, you wish to take such a man as that " — pointing to a muzhik, who, as he passed by them, pulled off his hat — " and lift him from his animal existence and give him moral necessities ; but it seems to me that his only possible happiness is his animal enjoyment, and that you want to deprive him of. I envy him ; you want to make him like me. You say another thing : you propose to free him from work, but in my opinion physical labor is for him as much a necessity, as much a condition of his existence, as intellectual labor is for you or me. You cannot help thinking. I go to bed at three o'clock ; thoughts crowd in upon me and I keep turning and twisting, and it is morning before sleep comes, and the reason is because I am thinking and cannot help thinking, just as he cannot help plowing and mowing ; if he did not he would go to the tavern or make himself ill. Just as I could not endure his terrible physical labor, and should die within a week, so he could not endure my physical idleness ; he would grow stout and die. In the third place, — but what was your third point ?" Prince Andreï began to double down his third finger.

"Oh, yes, hospitals, medicines. Well, he has a stroke and dies, but you would bleed him, and cure him, and he would drag out a crippled existence for ten years more, a burden to every one. It is far easier and simpler for him to die. Others are born, and there are so many of them to take his place! If it were merely that you were sorry for the loss of a good workman, that would be a different thing, — for that's the way I look at it, but you want to cure him out of mere love for him. And that is not necessary so far as he is concerned; and then, besides, what a delusion it is that medicine ever anywhere cured any one! You might rather call it murder!" said he, frowning with disgust and turning from Pierre.

Prince Andreï expressed his thoughts with such clearness and precision that it was evident he had thought on these questions, and he spoke fluently and rapidly, like a man who has not had for a long time a chance to express his thoughts. His eyes kept growing more and more animated, in proportion as his ideas became pessimistic.

"Akh! this is horrible, horrible!" exclaimed Pierre. "What I cannot understand is how you can live, holding such opinions. Such moments of despair have come to me, but that was long, long ago at Moscow and abroad, but at such times I go down into the depths so that I cease to live; everything is disgusting to me.... myself above all! At such times I do not eat, or wash myself..... Well, is that the way with you?"

"Why should n't I wash myself? It is n't cleanly!" retorted Prince Andreï. "On the contrary, I have to struggle to make my life as agreeable as possible. I am alive and I am not to blame for that, and so it behooves me to make the best of it, not interfering with anybody else until death carries me off!"

"But what on earth induces you to live, cherishing such notions? Do you really intend to sit down doing nothing, without undertaking anything?"

"Even thus, life refuses to let me be in peace! I should be glad enough to do nothing, but here on the one hand the nobility of the district have done me the honor of electing me their marshal. I barely got out of it. They could not understand that I had not a single qualification for the office, not a bit of that peculiarly good-natured and commonplace indefatigability which is needed for it. And then there is this house which I had to build, so as to have my own little nook where I could be free and easy. And then, again, there is the militia...."

"Why don't you serve in the army?"

"After Austerlitz!" exclaimed Prince Andreï, gloomily. "No, I thank you humbly, but I have vowed that I would never again serve in the Russian army. I would not, even if Bonaparte were here at Smolensk, threatening Luisiya Gorui; no, not even then would I serve in the Russian army. There, now I have told you," proceeded Prince Andreï, growing calmer. "But there is the militia; my father is commander-in-chief of the third district, and the only way that I could avoid joining the army again was to be with him."

"So you are in the service after all?"

"Yes, I am."

He was silent for a little.

"But why are you?"

"This is why. My father is one of the most remarkable men of his age, but he has grown old, and while he is not exactly cruel, he has too active a nature. He is so used to unlimited power that it makes him terrible, and now he has the power granted him by the emperor as commander-in-chief of the militia. If I had been two hours late, a fortnight ago, he would have hanged a registry clerk at Yukhnovo," said Prince Andreï, with a smile, "and so I serve because no one but me has any influence over him, and I often save him from acts which he would be sorry for afterwards."

"Ah, there now, you see!"

"Yes, but it is not as you understand it," retorted Prince Andreï in French. "It was not that I wasted any sympathy on the rascal of a clerk, who had been stealing boots from the militia. As far as he was concerned, I should have been glad enough if he had been hanged; but I should have felt sorry for my father, which is the same thing as for myself."

Prince Andreï was again growing more and more excited. His eyes sparkled with a feverish light, as he tried to prove to Pierre that his action had nothing whatever of philanthropy in it.

"Well, now, look here, you want to free your serfs," he went on to say; "that is a very good thing, but not for you — for you never flogged any one or sent any one to Siberia — and still less advantageous for your peasants. If they are beaten and flogged and sent to Siberia, I imagine it does them no special harm. The peasant leads in Siberia that same cattle-like existence of his, and his scars heal over and he is just as happy as he was before. Now this might be a good thing for those who are morally perishing, who are preparing for themselves an old age of remorse, who try to stifle this remorse and become cruel and severe, for the reason that they have the power of punishing either justly or unjustly. That's why I pity any one, and in such a case should desire the emancipation of the serfs. Perhaps you have never seen, but I have, — how good men, educated in these traditions of unlimited power, as they grow old and irritable, grow cruel and harsh, and are aware of it and cannot help themselves, and so become ever more and more unhappy."

Prince Andreï said this with so much feeling, that Pierre could not avoid conjecturing that these ideas of Prince Andreï's were suggested by his own father. He said nothing in reply.

"And this is what I lament over: human dignity, peace of mind, and purity, and not men's backs and heads, — which, however much they be flogged and shaved, will still remain nothing but backs and heads still."

"No, no, a thousand times no, I never should agree with you!" cried Pierre.

CHAPTER XII

IN the afternoon, Prince Andreï and Pierre got into the calash and started for Luisiya Gorui. Prince Andreï occasionally glanced at Pierre and broke the silence with remarks, showing that he was now in the very happiest frame of mind.

Pointing to the fields, he told him about his agricultural improvements.

Pierre preserved a moody silence, replied in monosyllables, and seemed to be immersed in his thoughts.

Pierre felt that Prince Andreï was unhappy, that he was deluding himself, that he was ignorant of the true light, and that it was his duty to come to his aid, to enlighten him, and lift him up. But as soon as Pierre tried to think what and how he should speak, he was seized with the consciousness that Prince Andreï, by a single word, by a single argument, might destroy everything in his teaching, and he was afraid to begin; he was afraid of exposing to the possibility of ridicule the beloved Ark of his convictions.

"No, but why do you think so?" suddenly began Pierre, lowering his head, and taking the aspect of a bull about to charge. "Why do you think so? You have no right to think so!"

"To think how?" asked Prince Andreï, in amazement.

"About life, about man's destiny. It cannot be. I used to think exactly the same way, and do you know what saved me?—Freemasonry! No, don't smile! Freemasonry is not a religious, a ceremonial sect, as I once supposed, but it is something much better, it is the one expression of the best, of the eternal, in humanity."

And Pierre began to expound Freemasonry to Prince Andreï as he understood it.

He declared that Freemasonry was the doctrine of Christianity freed from political and religious bonds, the doctrine of equality, fraternity, and love.

"Our sacred brotherhood only has a practical conception of life; everything else is visionary," said Pierre.

" You must comprehend, my friend, that outside of this fraternity everything is full of falsehood and deception, and I agree with you that for an intelligent and good man nothing is left except to live out his life as you do, merely striving not to interfere with any one. But once adopt our fundamental principles, join our confraternity, come with us heart and soul, allow yourself to be guided, and you will immediately perceive, just as I did, that you are a part of a tremendous, invisible chain, the beginning of which is hidden in heaven," said Pierre.

Prince Andreï, silently looking straight ahead, listened to Pierre's discourse. Several times, when, owing to the rumble of the carriage, he failed to catch a word, he asked Pierre to repeat it. Pierre could see, by the unusual gleam in Prince Andreï's eyes and by his silence, that his words were not without effect, that Prince Andreï would not throw ridicule on what he said.

They reached a river which had overflowed its banks, and which had to be crossed by ferry. While they were arranging for the disposition of the calash and horses, the two young men went down on the ferry-boat.

Prince Andreï, leaning his elbows on the railing, looked in silence down along the brimming river, which gleamed under the rays of the setting sun.

"Well, what do you think about it?" asked Pierre. "Why are you so silent?"

"What do I think? I have been listening to what you said; all that is so," said Prince Andreï. "You say 'join our confraternity and we will teach you the purpose of life and the object of man's existence, and the laws that govern the world.' But who are 'we'? Simply men! How do *you* know all that? Why is it that I am the only one that fails to see what you are privileged to see? You see a kingdom of goodness and truth on earth, but I do not see it."

Pierre interrupted him.

" Do you believe in the future life?" he asked.

"In the future life?" repeated Prince Andreï, but Pierre gave him no time to reply, and took for granted that this very repetition of his words was a denial, the more so because he had of old known Prince Andreï's atheistical convictions.

"You say you cannot see the kingdom of goodness and truth on earth. And I did not see it, and it is impossible to see it, if we look on our life here as the end of all things. On the earth, especially on this earth here," — Pierre pointed to a field, — "there is no truth; it is all lies and evil; but in the universe, in the whole universe, is the kingdom of truth, and now we are the children of the earth, but in eternity we are the children of the whole universe. Do I not feel in my own soul that I constitute a part of this mighty harmonious whole? Do I not have the consciousness that in this enormous, innumerable collection of beings in which Godhead is manifest — Supreme Force, if you prefer the term — that I constitute one link, one step between the lower orders of creation and the higher ones? If I see, clearly see, this ladder which rises from the plant to the man, then why should I suppose that it stops at me, and does not lead higher and ever higher? I know that, just as nothing is ever annihilated in the universe, so I can never perish, but shall always exist, and always have existed. I am conscious that besides myself spirits must exist above me, and that truth is in this universe."

"Yes, that is Herder's doctrine," said Prince Andreï. "But that is not enough to convince me, my dear; but life and death are what convince. You are convinced when you see a being who is dear to you, who is bound to you by sacred ties, toward whom you have done wrong, and have hoped to atone for the wrong," — Prince Andreï's voice trembled and he turned his head away, — "and suddenly this being suffers, is tormented, and ceases to be. Why is it? It cannot be that there is no answer, and I believe that there is one. That is what convinces a man, that is what has convinced me," said Prince Andreï.

"Yes, yes," exclaimed Pierre, "and isn't that exactly what I said?"

"No! I only maintain that arguments do not convince one of the necessity of a future life, but this:

when you go through life hand in hand with a companion, and suddenly that companion vanishes, *there, into the nowhere*, and you are left standing by this gulf, and straining your eyes to look into it! And I have looked in!"

"Well, then! You know that there is a *there*, and that there is a *some one*. *There* is the future life. The *some one* is God."

Prince Andreï made no reply. The horses had been long harnessed again into the calash on the other bank, and the ferriage fees paid, and already the sun was half hidden and the evening frost was beginning to skim over the pools by the ferry with crystal stars, and still Pierre and Andreï, to the amazement of the servants, the drivers, and the ferry hands, stood on the ferry-boat talking.

"If there is a God and a future life, then truth must exist, then virtue must exist; and man's highest happiness consists in striving to attain them. We must live, we must love, we must believe," Pierre was saying. "Believe not that we exist for a to-day on this lump of earth, but that we have lived and shall live forever yonder in the Whole" — he pointed to the sky.

Prince Andreï was standing with his elbows resting on the railing of the ferry-boat and listening to Pierre, and, without turning away his eyes, he gazed at the red disk of the sun reflected in the brimming river.

Pierre came to a pause.

It was perfectly still. The boat had long been moored, and only the ripples of the current glided by the bottom of the boat with a faint murmur. It seemed to Prince Andreï that this lapping of the waves corroborated Pierre's words and murmured : —

"It is true; believe it!"

Prince Andreï smiled, and with a radiant, childlike, tender expression looked into Pierre's flushed and enthusiastic face, which, nevertheless, showed that shyness peculiar to him in the presence of a friend of superior attainments.

"Ah, yes! if it were only so," said he. "But let us

be starting," added Prince Andreï, and, as he stepped off the boat, he glanced at the sky, to which Pierre called his attention, and for the first time since Austerlitz he saw those lofty, eternal heavens, which he had looked into as he lay on the battle-field, and something long dormant, something that was the better part of himself, suddenly awoke with new and joyful life in his soul.

This feeling vanished as soon as Prince Andreï fell back again into the ordinary conditions of existence, but he knew that this feeling, though he was unable to develop it, still lived in him. His meeting with Pierre was for Prince Andreï an epoch with which to begin his new life, not indeed to outward sight, which remained unchanged, but in the inner world of his consciousness.

CHAPTER XIII

IT was already quite dark when Prince Andreï and Pierre drove up to the principal entrance of the Luisogorsky mansion. Just as they reached there, Prince Andreï, with a smile, called Pierre's attention to the hubbub at the rear doorsteps. An old woman, bending under the weight of a birch-bark sack, and a short man, in black attire and with long hair, seeing the approach of the calash, started to run in through the back gates. Two women were hurrying after them, and all four, gazing at the carriage, hurried up the back stairs in affright.

"Those are some of Masha's 'Men of God,'" said Prince Andreï. "They took us for my father. And this is the only thing in which she dares think of going against his wishes; his orders are to drive these pilgrims out, but she likes to receive them."

"But who are these pilgrims, — 'Men of God,' as you call them?"

Prince Andreï had no time to reply to him. Servants came out to meet them, and he began to ask where the old prince was and how soon he was expected.

The old prince was still in town, but was expected at any time.

Prince Andreï took Pierre to his own chambers, which were always kept in perfect order for his reception in his father's house and he himself went to the nursery.

"Let us go and find my sister," said Prince Andreï, rejoining Pierre. "I have not seen her yet: she is hidden away somewhere, talking with her 'Men of God.' It will make her very much confused, but you shall see her 'Men of God.' It's queer, on my word!"

"But who are these 'Men of God'?" asked Pierre again.

"You shall see for yourself."

The Princess Mariya was genuinely confused, and her face blushed in patches when they joined her. In her cozy chamber, with the tapers burning in front of the holy pictures, on the divan behind the samovar, by her side sat a young lad with a long nose and long hair, and dressed in a monastic cassock.

In an arm-chair near by sat a wrinkled, lean old woman, with a sweet expression on her childlike face.

"André, why did n't you let me know?" said she, with gentle reproach, standing up in front of her pilgrims like a hen trying to protect her chicks.

"Charmed to see you. I am delighted to see you," said she to Pierre, still in French, as he stooped to kiss her hand. She had known him as a boy, and now his friendship for Andreï, his unhappiness with his wife, and, above all, his good, simple face, quite won her heart. She looked at him from her lovely lucid eyes, and her expression seemed to say, "I like you very much, but please do not make fun of my friends."

After they had exchanged the first greetings, they sat down.

"Ah, and here is the young Ivanushka," said Prince Andreï, with a smile, indicating the pilgrim lad.

"André!" exclaimed the Princess Mariya, in a beseeching tone.

"You must know that he is a woman," said Prince Andreï to Pierre.

"André, *au nom de Dieu!*" exclaimed the Princess Mariya.

It was evident that Prince Andreï's derisive treatment of the pilgrims and the Princess Mariya's inefficacious defense of them were matters of long standing between them.

"But, my dear girl," said Prince Andrei, "you ought, on the contrary, to be very grateful to me for explaining to Pierre your intimacy with this young man."

"*Vraiment?* Are you in earnest?" asked Pierre, with some curiosity and with perfect seriousness, — and for this the princess was especially grateful to him, — looking over his spectacles at Ivanushka's face, who, perceiving that the talk was concerning him, looked at all of them with cunning eyes.

It was entirely unnecessary that the Princess Mariya should have felt mortified on account of her friends. They were not in the least abashed. The old woman, dropping her eyes, though looking at the newcomers sidewise out of the corners of them, turned her cup bottom side up on the saucer, placed next it the half-gnawed lump of sugar, and sat silent and motionless in her chair, waiting to be asked to have another cup. Ivanushka, drinking out of his saucer, gazed at the young men from under his sly, womanlike eyes.

"Where have you been? To Kief?" asked Prince Andreï of the old woman.

"Yes, father," replied the old woman, who was inclined to be loquacious. "On Christmas day I was deemed worthy to partake of the holy sacrament with the saints. But just now I come from Kolyazin, father; a great blessing has been vouchsafed there...."

"Tell me, has Ivanushka been with you?"

"No, I have been all by myself alone, benefactor," said Ivanushka, striving to make his voice bass. "It was only at Yukhnovo that Pelageyushka and I met...."

Pelageyushka interrupted her companion; she was evidently anxious to tell what she had seen.

"In Kolyazin, father, a great blessing has been shown."

"What was that? New relics?" asked Prince Andreï.

"Come, do stop, Andreï," said the Princess Mariya. "Don't you tell him, Pelageyushka!"

"I o.... but why not, mother, why should n't I tell him? I love him. He is good; he is one of the God's elect, he gave me ten rubles once .... he is my benefactor .... I remember it very well. When I was in Kief, Kiri-yusha the Foolish .... he 's truly a man of God, he goes barefoot winter and summer .... said to me, 'What makes you wander round out of your own place,' says he to me; says he, 'Go to Kolyazin, there is a wonder-working ikon; the Holy Mother of God has manifested herself there.' So I said good-by to the saints, and I went there."....

No one interrupted; the old woman alone, in her monot-onous voice, spoke, occasionally stopping to get her breath.

"I went there, my father, and the people there said to me, 'A great blessing has been vouchsafed to us. Holy oil has trickled down from the cheeks of the Holy Mother of God.' "....

"Well, that will do, that will do; you can tell the rest by and by," said the Princess Mariya, blushing.

"Let me ask a question of her," broke in Pierre. "Did you see it with your own eyes?" he asked.

"Indeed, I did, father; I myself was deemed worthy. Such brightness in her face, like light from heaven, and from the Virgin's cheeks it trickled and trickled."....

"But see here, that was a fraud," was Pierre's naïve comment, after listening with all attention to her story.

"Akh! Father, what do you say?" exclaimed Pela-geyushka, in a tone of horror, turning to the Princess Mariya for protection.

"That 's the way they deceive the people," he re-iterated.

"Oh, our Lord Jesus Christ!" exclaimed the old woman, crossing herself. "Okh! don't say such a thing, father. And that 's the way a certain anaral" — she meant to say general — "was an unbeliever; he used to say, 'The priests deceive.' Yes, and he was took blind in consequence. And he dreamed that the *Matushka Petchorskaya*[1] came to him and says: 'Believe in me and I will cure you.' And so he began to beg them: 'Take me, oh take me to her.' And I tell you this as gospel truth — I see it with my own eyes. They took him, stone-blind as he was, straight to her; he fell on his knees, and says to her: 'Heal me, I will give thee,' says he, 'what the Tsar gave me.' And, father, I myself seen the star on her, just as he gave it to her. And so he got back his sight. It's a sin to speak so! God will punish you," said she, admonishingly, to Pierre.

"How did the star look on the holy picture?" asked Pierre.

"And did they promote the Virgin to be a general?" asked Prince Andreï, smiling.

Pelageyushka suddenly turned pale and clasped her hands.

"Oh, father, father! What a sin! And you with a son!" Her face flushed again. "Lord forgive him! Matushka, what does this mean?" she asked, turning to the Princess Mariya.

She arose, and almost weeping, began to pick up her bag. It was evident that it was both terrible and shameful to her to take advantage of benefactions in a house where such things could be said, and yet she regretted that it was now necessary for her to deprive herself of them.

"Now what amusement can you find in this?" asked the Princess Mariya. "Why did you come to my room?"

"No, Pelageyushka, I was only joking," said Pierre. "*Princesse, ma parole*, I didn't mean to hurt her feelings. It was only my way. Don't have such an idea; I was only joking," he repeated, smiling timidly, and anxious to smooth over his offense. "You see, I was only in fun, and he was, too."

The old Pelageyushka paused in doubt, but Pierre's

---

[1] The *matushka*, little mother (that is, the Virgin), of the Petchorsky monastery, or Monastery of the Catacombs, at Kief.

face showed such sincere repentance, and Prince Andreï looked now at her and now at Pierre with such a gentle expression, that she gradually recovered her confidence.

CHAPTER XIV

THE pilgrim woman soon recovered confidence again, and, returning to her favorite theme, gave a long account of Father Amfilokhi, who was such a holy man in his life that his "dear little hands" smelled of incense, and how her friends the monks, during her last pilgrimage to Kief, had given her the keys to the catacombs, and how she, taking only some little buscuits — *sukhariki* — had spent forty-eight hours in them with the saints.

"I pray before one, I worship, and then I go to another. Then I take a nap and go and kiss the other relics, and oh, matushka, such peace, such blessed comfort — never did I want to come up into God's world again!"

Pierre listened to her with an attentive and serious expression. Prince Andreï left the room, and the Princess Mariya, leaving her "God's people" to finish drinking their tea, invited Pierre into the drawing-room.

"You are very kind," said she.

"Akh! truly I did not mean to offend her! I appreciate and prize so dearly such feelings."

The Princess Mariya looked at him without speaking, and a gentle smile played over her lips.

"I have known you a long time, and I feel as if you were my own brother," said she. "How do you find Andreï?" she asked hastily, not giving him time to respond to her affectionate words. "I feel very solicitous about him. In the winter his health was better, but this spring his wound opened again, and the doctor said that he ought to go away and be treated. And I am very apprehensive about his mental condition. His nature is so different from us women, and he cannot ease his grief by a good fit of crying. He carries it in his heart. To-day he is jolly and full of life; but that is caused by your visit. He is rarely so. If you could only persuade him to go abroad. He needs activity, and this quiet, monotonous life is killing him. Other people don't notice it, but I see it."

At ten o'clock the servants rushed to the doorsteps, hearing the harness-bells of the old prince's carriage. Prince Andreï and Pierre also hastened to meet him.

"Who is this?" asked the old prince, as he got out of the carriage and caught sight of Pierre.

"Ah! I am very glad! Kiss me!" he cried, as soon as he learned who the young stranger was. He was in excellent spirits, and treated Pierre in the most friendly way.

Before supper, Prince Andreï, returning to his father's cabinet, found him in a hot discussion with Pierre. Pierre argued that the time was coming when there would be no more war. The old prince in a bantering but not angry tone maintained the opposite.

"Drain all the blood from men's veins and pour in water instead, and then you will have an end of war! Old women's drivel! old women's drivel!" he exclaimed, but still he affectionately tapped Pierre on the shoulder as he went over to the table where Prince Andreï had taken a seat, evidently not caring to enter the discussion, and was glancing over the papers which his father had brought from the city. The old prince went to him and began to talk with him about business.

"Count Rostof, the marshal, has not furnished half his quota, and when I got to town, he actually conceived the notion of asking me to dinner — I gave him an answer that settled him! But just look at this! Well, brother," said Nikolaï Andreyitch, addressing his son, but patting Pierre on the shoulder, "your friend is a fine young man, I like him very much. He warms me up. Many another has clever things to say, but you don't care to hear it. But this one succeeds in warming me up though I am an old man. Well, go on, go on," he added. "Maybe I'll come and sit down to supper with ye. I'd like another discussion. Make yourself agreeable to my little goose, the Princess Mariya," he shouted after Pierre through the door.

During this visit to Luisiya Gorui, Pierre for the first time appreciated the real strength and charm of his friendship with Prince Andreï. This charm was manifested not so much by his relations with Andreï himself, as it was with all his relatives and the inmates of the house. Pierre felt that he was received on the footing of an old friend, both by the stern old prince and the sweet, shy Princess Mariya, neither of whom he had ever really known. Both of them soon grew to be very fond of him. The Princess Mariya, whose heart was won by his genial treatment of her pilgrim friends, looked at him from her big, lucid eyes, and even the little "yearling Prince Nikolaï," as his grandfather called him, smiled at Pierre and liked to go to him. Mikhaïl Ivanuitch and Mlle. Bourienne looked at him and smiled pleasantly while he talked with the old prince.

The old prince came down to supper; this was evidently on Pierre's account. During the two days of his visit at Luisiya Gorui, he treated him in the most flattering way, and often sent for him to come to his own room.

After Pierre had gone, and all the members of the family met, they began to express their opinions of him, as is always the case after the departure of a new acquaintance; but, as is rarely the case, they all agreed in saying pleasant things of him.

CHAPTER XV

ROSTOF, getting back from his furlough, for the first time felt and realized how strong were the ties that bound him to Denisof and all his regiment.

When he went back to his regiment he experienced a sensation analogous to that which came over him on his return to his home on the Pavarskaya. When he saw the first hussar of his regiment, with unbuttoned uni-

form, when he recognized the red-headed Dementyef,
when he caught sight of the roan horses picketed, when
Lavrushka joyfully shouted to his barin: "The count
has come," and the tattered Denisof, who had been having a nap, came running out from his earth-hut and
threw his arms around him, and the officers all came out to
greet him, Rostof felt very much as he did when his
mother and father and sister welcomed him home; tears
of joy filled his throat and choked his utterance.

The regiment was also his home, and as sweet and
dear to him as the home of his childhood.

After reporting to the regimental commander and
being assigned to his old squadron, after taking his turn
as officer of the day and forage purveyor, after getting
into the current of all the small interests of the regiment, and coming to a realizing sense that he was now
deprived of his freedom, and was confined to a narrow
and rigid routine, — Rostof felt the same sense of rest-
fulness, the same moral support, and the same consciousness of being at home, in his proper place, as he had
felt while under the paternal roof-tree.   There was nothing more of that mad confusion of the outside world in
which he found himself out of place and often engaged
in questionable actions; there was no Sonya, with whom
he ought or ought not to come to an explanation; there
was no choice offered him of going somewhere or not
going somewhere; there were no longer those twenty-
four hours which had to be filled with so many varied
occupations; there was an end to that innumerable
throng of people whose presence or absence was a matter of indifference to him; there was an end to those
obscure and indefinable pecuniary relations with his
father; an end to his recollections of those terrible
losses to Dolokhof!

Here in the regiment all was open and simple.   All
the world was divided into two unequal divisions: one
was "our" Pavlograd regiment, and the other — all the
rest.   And he had nothing whatever in common with
this rest.   In the regiment everything was known: who
was lieutenant, who was captain, who was a good fel

low, who was a rascal, and above all, who was his messmate. The sutler sold on credit, the pay was given
quarterly. There was no necessity for thought or decision, provided only that one did nothing that was considered dishonorable in the Pavlograd regiment; but
fulfil your duty, do what is commanded you in clear,
explicit, and unmistakable language, and all will be well.

Coming back again to these explicit conditions of
army life, Rostof felt a sense of comfort and satisfaction analogous to that experienced by a weary man
when he lies down to rest. To Rostof his army life
was all the more agreeable during this campaign from
the fact that after his losses from his gambling with
Dolokhof — an action which he could not forgive, in
spite of the forgiveness of his relatives — he made up
his mind to serve, not as formerly, but in such a way
as to atone for his fault, to be scrupulously faithful, to
prove himself a thoroughly admirable comrade and officer, in other words, a "fine man." This might seem
quite too hard were he "in the world," but was quite
possible in the regiment.

He had also determined, ever since the time of his
gambling escapade, to pay back his debt to his parents
within five years. They sent him ten thousand rubles
a year; now he resolved to take only two, and to apply
the remainder to the extinction of the debt.

Our army, after repeated marches and countermarches, with skirmishes at Pultusk and at Preussisch-
Eylau, was concentrated in the vicinity of Bartenstein,
where they were awaiting the arrival of the emperor
and the beginning of a new campaign.

The Pavlograd regiment, belonging to that division of
the army which had taken part in the movements of the
year 1805, had been recruited to its full quota in Russia,
and had arrived too late for these first actions of the
campaign. It had been neither at Pultusk nor at Preussisch-Eylau, and now, at the beginning of the second
part of the campaign, having united with the acting army,
it was detailed to serve under Platof.

Platof's division was acting independently of the army. Several times the Pavlogradsui had taken part in skirmishes with the enemy, captured prisoners, and once even took Marshal Oudinot's baggage. During the month of April, the Pavlogradsui were stationed for several weeks in the vicinity of an utterly dilapidated and deserted German village without stirring from the spot.

It was thawing and cold; the rivers were beginning to break up; the roads were impassable, owing to the mud; for many days no provision had been brought for horses or men. As it seemed an impossibility for transport trains to arrive, the men scattered about among the pillaged and deserted villages in search of potatoes, but even these were scarce.

Everything had been devoured, and all the inhabitants had fled. Those who were left were worse than poverty-stricken; there was indeed nothing to take from them, and even the usually pitiless soldiery oftentimes let them keep the little that they had, instead of appropriating it for themselves.

The Pavlograd regiment had lost only two men, wounded in engagements, but they had lost almost half their numbers from sickness and starvation. Death was so certain if they went into the hospitals, that the soldiers suffering from fevers and swellings, caused by bad food, preferred to keep in the ranks — dragging themselves by sheer strength of will to the front, rather than take their chances in the hospitals.

As spring opened, they began to find a plant just showing above the ground; it resembled asparagus, and for some reason they called it "Mashka's sweetwort," though it was very bitter. They hunted for it all over the fields and meadows, digging it up with their sabers and devouring it, in spite of the injunction not to eat this poisonous plant. Later a new disease broke out among the soldiers, a swelling of the arms, legs, and face, and the physicians attributed it to the use of this root. But, notwithstanding the prohibition, the men of Denisof's squadron eagerly ate "Mashka's sweetwort," because for a fortnight they had been trying to subsist on the few remaining biscuits — half-pound rations being dealt out to each man, while the last consignment of potatoes had proved to be rotten and sprouted.

The horses also had been subsisting for a fortnight on thatching-straw taken from the roofs, and had become shockingly emaciated, and, even before the winter was over, covered with tufts of uneven hair.

Yet, in spite of this terrible destitution, officers and men lived just the same as usual. Just as always, though with pale and swollen faces, and in ragged uniforms, the hussars attended to their duties, went after forage and other things, groomed their horses, cleaned their arms, tore the thatch from roofs to serve as fodder, and gathered around the kettles for their meals, from which they got up still hungry, while they joked over their wretched fare and hunger. And just as usual during the hours when they were off duty, the soldiers built big fires, stripped and stood around them steaming themselves, smoked their pipes, sorted and baked their rotten, sprouting potatoes, and told stories about the campaigns of Patyomkin and Suvorof, or legends of Alyosha the Cunning, or of Mikolka Popovitch the Journeyman.

The officers also as usual lived in couples, or in threes, in unroofed and half-ruined houses. The older ones looked after the procuring of straw and potatoes and other means of victualing the men. The younger ones were occupied as usual, some with card-playing (money was plentiful if provisions were not), some with innocent games, — *svaïka*, a kind of ring toss, and quoits or skittles. Little was said about the general course of matters, partly because nothing positive was known, partly because there was a general impression that the war was going badly.

Rostof lived just as before with Denisof, and the friendship that united them was closer than ever since their furlough. Denisof never spoke of Rostof's family, but, by the affectionate friendship manifested by the commander for his subordinate officer, Rostof felt assured that the old hussar's unfortunate love for Natasha was an additional factor in the strength of his affection.

Denisof evidently tried to send Rostof as rarely as possible on dangerous expeditions, and to shield him, and, after a skirmish or anything of the sort, displayed intense delight to find him safe and sound.

On one of his expeditions Rostof found an old Pole and his daughter with an infant at the breast, in a deserted, ruined village, where he had gone in search of provisions. They were almost naked and starving, and had no means of getting away. Rostof brought them to his lodgings, installed them in his own rooms, and kept them for several weeks, until the old man got well. One of Rostof's comrades, while talking about women, began to make sport of Rostof, declaring that he was the slyest of them all, and that it was no wonder that he did not care to introduce his comrades to the pretty little Polish woman whom he had rescued.

Rostof took the jest as an insult, and, losing his temper, said such disagreeble things to the officer, that Denisof had great difficulty in preventing a duel. When the officer had gone, and Denisof, who knew nothing about what relationship Rostof bore toward the Polish woman, began to upbraid him for his temper, Rostof said : —

"Well, maybe you are right.... she is like a sister to me, and I cannot describe how offensive that was to me. Because .... well, because ...."

Denisof gave him a rap on the shoulder and began swiftly to march up and down the room, not looking at his friend. This was a habit of his at moments of mental excitement.

"What a deucedly fine bweed all those Wostofs are!" he exclaimed, and Rostof noticed tears in his eyes.

CHAPTER XVI

In the month of April the troops were cheered by the news that the sovereign was coming to the army. Rostof did not have the privilege of taking part in the review made by the emperor at Bartenstein, for it happened that the Pavlogradsui were stationed at the advanced posts, a considerable distance in front of Bartenstein. They were established in bivouacs. Denisof and Rostof lived in an earth-hut excavated for them by their soldiers, and covered with boughs and turf.

This earth-hut was constructed as follows, according to a plan much in vogue at that time: a trench three feet and a half wide, a little less than five deep, and about eight long was dug. At one end steps were constructed, and this formed the entry, the "grand staircase"; the trench itself constituted the abode, in which those who were fortunate, as, for instance, the squadron commander, had a board set on posts on the side opposite the entrance; this served as the table. On each side along the trench the earth was hollowed away to half its depth, making a bed and divan. The roof was so constructed that in the middle it was possible to stand erect under it, and one could sit up on the beds by leaning over toward the table.

Denisof, who lived luxuriously, because the men of his squadron were fond of him, had an extra board in the pediment of the roof, and in this board was a broken but mended pane of glass. When it was very cold, coals from the soldiers' fires were brought on a bent piece of sheet-iron and set on the steps in the "reception-room," as Denisof called this part of the hovel, and this made it so warm that the officers, who used to come in great numbers to visit Denisof and Rostof, could sit there in their shirt-sleeves.

In April Rostof happened to be on duty. One morning, about eight o'clock, returning home after a sleepless night, he ordered some coals to be brought, changed his linen, which had been wet through by the rain, went

through his devotions, drank his tea, got thoroughly
warmed, put his belongings into order in his own corner and on the table, and, with his face flushed by the
wind and the fire, threw himself down on his back, in
his shirt-sleeves, with his arms for a pillow. He was
indulging in pleasant anticipations of the promotion
which was likely to follow his last reconnoitering expedition, and was waiting for the return of Denisof, who had
gone off somewhere. Rostof was anxious to have a talk
with him.

Behind the hut, he heard Denisof's high-pitched
voice; he had evidently returned in a bad humor.
Rostof went to the "window" to look out and see whom
he was berating; he recognized the quartermaster,
Topcheyenko.

"I have given you special orders not to let them eat
that woot, Mashka's what-you-call-it," cried Denisof.
"And here I 've seen it with my own eyes; Lazarchuk
was bwinging some in fwom the field."

"I have given the order, your high nobility, but they
won't listen to it," replied the quartermaster.

Rostof again lay down on his bed, and said to himself
with a feeling of content: "Let him kick up a row and
make as much fuss as he pleases; I 've done my work,
and now I 'll lie down; it 's first-class!"

He heard Lavrushka, Denisof's shrewd and rascally
valet, join his voice to the conversation going on outside
the hut. Lavrushka had something to tell about ox-carts
laden with biscuits which he had seen as he was going
after provisions.

Denisof's sharp voice was again heard behind the hut,
and his command, "Second platoon to saddle!"

"What can be up?" wondered Rostof.

Five minutes later, Denisof came into the hut, climbed
up with his muddy boots on his bed, lighted his pipe in
grim silence, tossed over all his belongings, got out his
whip and saber, and started from the hut. In reply to
Rostof's question, "Whither away?" he gruffly and carelessly replied that he had something to attend to.

"May God and the soveweign be my judges!" he

exclaimed as he went out, and then Rostof heard the hoofs of several horses splashing through the mud. Rostof did not take any pains to inquire where Denisof had gone. Warm and comfortable in his corner, he soon fell asleep, and it was late in the afternoon when he left the hut.

Denisof had not yet returned. The weather had cleared up bright and beautiful. Near a neighboring hut two officers and a yunker were playing *svaïka*, merrily laughing as they drove the *redki*, or mumblepegs, into the loose, muddy ground. Rostof joined them. In the midst of the game the officers saw a train approaching them; fifteen hussars on emaciated horses followed the wagons. The teams, convoyed by the hussars, approached the picketing station, and a throng of hussars gathered round them.

"There, now, Denisof has been mourning all the time," said Rostof, "and here are provisions after all!"

"See there!" cried the officers. "Won't the men be happy!"

A short distance behind the hussars rode Denisof, accompanied by two infantry officers, with whom he was engaged in a heated discussion. Rostof started down to meet him.

"I was ahead of you, captain," declared one of the officers, a lean little man, evidently beside himself with passion.

"See here! I have told you that I would not weturn 'em!" replied Denisof.

"You shall answer for it, captain; this is violence — to rob an escort of their wagons. Our men have not had anything to eat for two days."

"And mine have not had anything to eat for two weeks," replied Denisof.

"This is highway robbery. You'll answer for it, my dear sir," repeated the infantry officer, raising his voice.

"What are you bothewing me for! Hey?" screamed Denisof, suddenly losing his temper. "I am the one who is wesponsible, and not you. What is the object of all your buzzing here? Forward!.... Marsch!" he cried to the officers.

"Very good!" screamed the little officer, not quailing and not budging. "If you insist on pillage, then I...."

"Take yourself off to the devil! Get out of here!" and Denisof rode his horse straight at the officer.

"Very good, very good," reiterated the officer, with an oath, and, turning his horse, he rode off at a gallop, bouncing in his saddle.

"A dog on a fence, a weal dog on a fence," shouted Denisof, as he rode away. This was the most insulting remark that a cavalryman could make to a mounted infantryman. Then as he joined Rostof, he burst into a loud laugh.

"I wescued 'em from the infantwy, I cawied off their 'twansport' by main force," said he. "What! do they think I would let my men pewish of starvation?"

The wagons which had been brought to the hussars were consigned to an infantry regiment, but Denisof, learning through Lavrushka that the "transport" was proceeding alone, had ridden off with his hussars and intercepted it. The soldiers had as many biscuits as they wished, and even enough to share with other squadrons.

The next day the regimental commander summoned Denisof, and, covering his eyes with his spread fingers, he said:—

"This is the way I look at it: I know nothing about it, and I have nothing to do with it; but I advise you to go instanter to headquarters and report this affair to the commissary department, and, if possible, give a receipt for so many provisions received; unless you do, the requisition will be put down to the infantry: the matter will be investigated, and may end badly."

Denisof went straight from the regimental commander's to the headquarters, with a sincere intention of adopting his advice. In the evening he returned to his hut in a condition such as Rostof had never seen his friend before. He could hardly speak or breathe. When Rostof asked him what the matter was, he only broke out in incoherent oaths and threats, in a weak and husky voice.

Alarmed at Denisof's condition, Rostof advised him to undress, drink some cold water, and send for a physician.

"They are going to twy me for wobbewy—okh! Give me a dwink of water; let 'em twy me, I will beat the waskals evewy time, and I 'll tell the empewor. Give me some ice," he added.

The regimental surgeon came in and said that it was absolutely necessary to take some blood from him. He filled a soup-plate with dark blood from Denisof's hairy arm, and then only was he in a condition to tell all that had taken place.

"I get there," said Denisof, telling his story. "'Where is your head man here?' They show me. 'Can't you wait?' 'I have pwessing business; come thirty versts, impossible to wait; let me see him!' Vewy good; out comes the wobber-in-chief, he, too, undertakes to lecture me: 'This is highway wobbewy.' 'A man,' says I, 'is not a wobber, who takes pwovisions to feed his soldiers, but one who fills his own pockets.'—'Will you please keep quiet!' 'Vewy good.' 'Sign a we-ceipt at the commissioner's,' says he, 'and your affair will take its due course.' I go to the commissioner's. I go in. And there at the table, who do you suppose? No! Guess.... Who has been starving us?" screamed Denisof, gesticulating his wounded arm, and pounding the table with his fist so violently that the board almost split and the glasses on it jumped up. "Telyanin!— 'So it 's you, is it, who 's been starving us? Once be-fore you had your snout slapped for you, and got off cheap at that. Ah! what a.... what a....' and I began to give it to him. I enjoyed it, I can tell you," cried Denisof, angrily and yet gleefully showing his white teeth under his black mustache. "I should have killed him, if they had not sepawated us."

"Here, here, what are you shouting so for? Calm

yourself," said Rostof. "You've set your arm bleeding again. Wait, it must be bandaged."

They bandaged Denisof's arm, and got him off to bed. The following day he woke jolly and calm.

But at noon, the adjutant of the regiment, with a grave and regretful face, came into Rostof and Denisof's earth-hut, and with real distress served upon Major Denisof a formal document from the regimental commander, who had been called to account for the proceeding of the day before. The adjutant informed them that the affair was likely to assume a very serious aspect, that a court-martial commission had been convened, and that on account of the severity with which just at that time rapine and lawlessness were treated, he might consider himself fortunate if the affair ended with mere degradation.

Those who felt themselves aggrieved represented the affair as in somewhat this way : that after the pillage of the transport, Major Denisof, without any provocation and apparently drunk, had made his appearance before the "commissary," called him a thief, threatened to thrash him, and when he was dragged away, he had rushed into the office, struck two chinovniks, and sprained the arm of one of them.

Denisof, in reply to a fresh series of questions from Rostof, laughed, and said that he thought some one else had been there in that condition ; but that all this story was rubbish, fiddle-faddle, that he was not afraid of any court-martials, and that if these villains dared to pick a quarrel with him, he would answer them in a way that they would not soon forget.

Denisof spoke with affected indifference about all the affair ; but Rostof knew him too well not to perceive that at heart — though he hid it from the rest — he was afraid of a court-martial, and was really troubled by this affair, which evidently might have sad consequences. Every day, inquiries, summonses, and other documents kept coming to him, and on the first of May he was required to turn over his command to his next in seniority, and appear at the headquarters of the divisions to make his defense in the matter of pillaging the provision train.

On the evening preceding the day of the trial, Platof made a reconnoissance of the enemy, with two regiments of Cossacks and two squadrons of hussars. Denisof, as usual, went out beyond the lines, in order to make an exhibition of his gallantry. A bullet sent from a French musket struck him in the fleshy upper portion of his leg. Most likely Denisof, in ordinary circumstances, would not have left the regiment for such a trifling wound, but now he profited by this occurrence, gave up his command of the division, and went to the hospital.

CHAPTER XVII

In the month of June occurred the battle of Friedland, in which the Pavlogradsui took no part, and this was followed immediately by an armistice.

Rostof grievously missed his friend, and, as he had not had any news of him since he left the regiment, and was doubly uneasy about his trial and the result of his wound, he took advantage of the armistice and went to the hospital to make inquiries about Denisof.

The hospital was established in a small Prussian village, which had twice been sacked by the Russian and French armies. For the very reason that it was summer, when everything in nature was beautiful, this village, with its ruined roof-trees and fences and its filthy streets, its ragged inhabitants, and the invalid and drunken soldiers wandering about, presented an especially gloomy appearance.

The hospital had been established in a stone mansion with many broken panes and window-frames, and situated in a yard with the remains of a ruined fence. A number of pale-looking soldiers, bandaged and swollen, were walking up and down, or sitting in the sun in the yard.

As soon as Rostof entered the house, he was enveloped by the odor of putrefaction and disease. On the doorstep staircase he met the Russian military surgeon, with a cigar in his mouth. The surgeon was followed by a Russian *feldsher* or assistant.

"I can't be everywhere at once," the doctor was saying. "Come this evening to Makar Alekseyevitch's; I'll be there."

The feldsher asked him some question.

"Eh! do as well as you know how! It does n't make any difference, does it?" The doctor caught sight of Rostof mounting the stairs. "What are you doing here, your nobility?" asked the doctor. "What are you doing here? Because a bullet has n't touched you, do you want to be carried off by typhus, batyushka? This is the house of leprosy!"

"What do you mean?" asked Rostof.

"Typhus, batyushka! It's death for whoever comes in here. Makeyef," he pointed to his assistant, "Makeyef and I are the only two left to wriggle! Five of our brother doctors have died already. When a new man comes, it's all up with him in a week," said the doctor, with apparent satisfaction. "The Prussian doctors were invited, but our allies did not like it at all."

Rostof explained his anxiety to find Major Denisof of the hussars.

"I don't know; I don't remember him. You can imagine: I have charge of three hospitals; four hundred sick is too many. It's a very good thing for benevolent Prussian ladies to send us coffee and lint at the rate of two pounds a month; if they did n't, we should be utterly lost." He laughed. "Four hundred, batyushka! and they send me all the new cases. There are four hundred, are n't there? Hey?" he asked of the feldsher. His assistant looked annoyed. It was evident that he was impatient for the too loquacious doctor to make haste and take his departure.

"Major Denisof," repeated Rostof. "He was wounded at Moliten."

"I think he's dead. How is it, Makeyef?" asked the doctor, in an indifferent tone, of the feldsher

The assistant simply repeated the doctor's words.

"Tell me, was he a tall, reddish man?" asked the doctor.

Rostof described Denisof's appearance.

"Yes, there was, there certainly was such a person," exclaimed the doctor, seeming to show a gleam of satisfaction. "But that person, I'm sure, must have died; however, I'll make inquiries; I had the lists; you have them, Makeyef, haven't you?"

"The lists are at Makar Alekseyevitch's," replied the feldsher. "But you might inquire in the officers' ward; there you would find out for yourself," he added, turning to Rostof.

"Ekh! you'd better not go," said the surgeon. "You wouldn't like to be kept here!"

Rostof, however, took leave of the surgeon, and begged the feldsher to show him the way.

"Don't you lay the blame on me," shouted the doctor, up from the bottom of the stairs.

Rostof and the feldsher went along the corridor. The hospital odor was so powerful in this dark corridor that Rostof took hold of his nose, and was obliged to pause to collect his strength before he could go farther.

At the right a door opened and a thin, sallow-looking man, on crutches, barefooted, and in his shirt-sleeves, appeared. As he crossed the lintel, he gazed with gleaming, envious eyes at the approaching men. Glancing through the door, Rostof saw that the sick and wounded were lying in the room over the floor, on straw, and on their cloaks.

"May I go in and look?" he asked.

"What is there to see?" replied the officer.

But for the very reason that the feldsher was evidently reluctant to have him go in, Rostof was determined to investigate the soldiers' ward. The effluvium, which he had already smelt in the corridor, was still stronger here. It had also changed somewhat in character: it was sharper, more penetrating, one could be certain that this was the very place where it originated.

In a long room, brilliantly illuminated by the sun, which poured in through the wide windows, lay the sick and wounded in two rows, with their heads to the walls, leaving a passageway between their feet. The most of them were asleep or unconscious, and paid no attention to the visitors. Those who had their senses, either lifted themselves up, or raised their thin, yellow faces, and all, without exception, gazed at Rostof with one and the same expression of hope that help had come, of reproach and envy at seeing another so strong and well.

Rostof went into the middle of the ward, glanced through the half-open doors into the adjoining rooms, and on both sides saw the same spectacle. He paused and silently looked around him. He had never expected to see such a thing. In front of him, almost across the narrow passageway, lay, on the bare floor, a sick man, apparently a Cossack, as his hair was cropped, leaving a tuft. This Cossack lay on his back, with his huge legs and arms sprawled out. His face was a livid purple. His eyes were rolled up so that only the whites could be seen, and the veins in his bare legs and arms, which were still red, stood out like cords. He was thumping his head on the floor and hoarsely muttering some word which he repeated over and over again. Rostof listened to what he was saying, and at last made out what the word was: this word was "water — water — water!"

Rostof looked around in search of some one to put the man in his place and give him a drink.

"Who looks after the sick here?" he asked of the feldsher. Just at that moment a train-soldier, detailed to act as nurse, came along, and, scraping, made a low bow before Rostof.

"I wish you good-morning, your high nobility," cried the soldier, rolling his eyes on Rostof, and evidently mistaking him for some important official.

"Lift him up; give him water," said Rostof, pointing to the Cossack.

"I will, your high nobility," said the soldier, with

alacrity, rolling his eyes round still more attentively, and craning his neck, but still not stirring from the spot.

"No, there's nothing I can do here," thought Rostof, dropping his eyes; he was about to go on, but felt the consciousness that an entreating glance was fixed upon him from the right, and he turned around to see. Almost in the very corner of the room, an old soldier was sitting on a cloak. He had a thin, stern face, as yellow as a skeleton, and a rough, gray beard; he looked entreatingly at Rostof. A neighbor of the old soldier on one side seemed to be whispering something to him, and pointed to Rostof. Rostof realized that the old man was determined to ask him some favor. He went nearer and perceived that one leg was affected with gangrene, and that the other had been amputated above the knee. Another neighbor of the old man's lay motionless at some little distance from him, with his head thrown back; this was a young soldier, whose snub-nosed face, still covered with freckles, was as white as wax; the eyes rolled up under his lids.

Rostof looked at the snub-nosed soldier, and a cold chill ran down his back.

"But this one, it seems to me, is ...." he began, turning to the feldsher.

"We have already begged and prayed, your nobility," said the old soldier, with his lower jaw trembling. "It was all over this morning. Why! we are men, and not dogs."

"I will see to it immediately, he shall be removed, he shall be removed," hurriedly said the feldsher. "I beg of you, your nobility ...."

"Come on, come on," replied Rostof, also hurriedly, and dropping his eyes and shrinking all together, trying to pass unobserved under the gauntlet of those reproach-ful and envious eyes fixed upon him, he left the room.

CHAPTER XVIII

PASSING along the corridor, the feldsher led Rostof into the officers' ward, which consisted of three rooms, communicating by opened doors. There were beds in these rooms; the sick and wounded officers were lying and sitting on them. Some, in dressing-gowns, were pacing up and down the rooms.

The first person whom Rostof met in the officers' ward was a little slim man, with one arm gone, and wearing a cap and dressing-gown, who was walking up and down the first room with a pipe in his mouth. Rostof, on catching sight of him, racked his brains to remember where he had seen him.

"What a place for God to bring us together again!" exclaimed the little man. "I'm Tushin, Tushin, don't you remember? I brought you back safe at Schöngraben! Well, they've lopped off a little morsel, see here!" said he, smiling, and pointing to the empty sleeve of his khalat. "And you're hunting for Vasili Dmitrievitch Denisof. He's one of our chums!" he said, on learning whom Rostof wanted. "Here, here," and Tushin drew him into the second room, where several men were heard laughing loudly.

"I declare! how can they think of living here, much less of laughing?" wondered Rostof, with the odor of dead bodies which he had found in the soldiers' ward still in his nostrils, and still seeing those envious glances fixed upon him and following him, and the face of that young soldier with the upturned eyes.

Denisof, with his head buried under the bedclothes, was sound asleep on his bed, although it was noon.

"What? Wostof? How are you, how are you?" he cried, in exactly the same voice as when he was with the regiment; but Rostof observed with pain that, hidden under this show of ease and vivacity, there was a shadow of a new and disagreeable asperity in Denisof's expression, and in his words and tones.

His wound, in spite of its insignificance, was still unhealed, though six weeks had passed since the skirmish. His face, also, had the same pallor and look of puffiness that characterized all the inmates of the hospital. But it was not this that so especially struck Rostof : he was amazed by the fact that Denisof did not seem to be glad to see him, and smiled unnaturally. Denisof did not once inquire about the regiment or about the general course of affairs. When Rostof spoke of these things, Denisof did not even listen.

Rostof noticed also that it was distasteful to Denisof to be reminded of the regiment, and in general of that larger and freer existence going on outside of the hospital. It seemed as if he were trying to forget his former life, and the only thing that interested him was his quarrel with the commissary chinovniks.

In reply to Rostof's question how the affair was going, he immediately pulled out from under his pillow a document which he had received from the commission, and the rough draft of his own reply to it. He brightened up as he began to read his document, and he called Rostof's attention to the keen things which he said against his enemies in his reply. Denisof's acquaintances of the hospital, who had crowded around Rostof as a person from the outside world, gradually scattered as soon as Denisof began to read his paper. By their faces, Rostof perceived that all these gentlemen had more than once heard the whole story and were heartily sick of it. Only one, his neighbor of the next bed, a stout Uhlan, still kept his seat on his hammock, frowning gloomily, and smoking his pipe; and the little, armless Tushin continued to listen, though he shook his head disapprovingly. In the midst of the reading, the Uhlan interrupted Denisof.

"Now, it's my opinion," said he, turning to Rostof, "that the only thing to do is simply to petition the sovereign for pardon. They say now there are going to be great rewards, and a mere matter of a pardon .... "

"I petition the soveweign!" exclaimed Denisof, in a voice in which he tried hard to maintain his old-time energy and vehemence, but which sounded helplessly feeble.

"What for? If I had been a highway wobber, I might petition for pardon, but here I am court-martialed because I 'cawy these wobbers thwough clean water,' as the saying is. Let 'em twy me, I'm not afwaid of 'em! I have served my Tsar honowably, and my countwy, and I have not been a thief! and they degwade me, and.... See here! listen to what I wite 'em in stwaightforward language. This is what I wite: If I had been an embezzler....'"

"It's cleverly written, no question about that," said Tushin. "But that is not the point, Vasili Dmitritch." He turned also to Rostof: "He must give in, and this is what Vasili Dmitritch will not hear to doing. Now, there, the auditor himself told you that it was a bad business."

"Let it be bad business, then," exclaimed Denisof.

"And the auditor wrote a petition for you," continued Tushin, "and you had better sign it and give it to him. He"—meaning Rostof—"has influence at headquarters. You won't find a better chance."

"Yes, but have n't I told you that I won't stoop to cwinge," interrupted Denisof, and once more he set out to finish his document.

Rostof did not dare to argue with Denisof, although he felt instinctively that the course indicated by Tushin and the other officers was the one advisable; and although he should have counted himself happy to find a chance to render Denisof a service, he knew Denisof's unbending will and righteous wrath.

When Denisof had finished reading his venomous diatribe, which had consumed more than an hour, Rostof had nothing to say, and in the gloomiest frame of mind he spent the rest of the day in the society of Denisof's companions, who had gathered around him again, talking. He told them all the news, and listened to the tales of the others. Denisof preserved a moody silence all the afternoon.

Late in the afternoon, Rostof got up to go, and asked Denisof if there was nothing that he could do for him.

"Yes, wait," said Denisof, glancing at the officers,

and, pulling some papers out from under his pillow, he went to the window, where stood an inkstand, and began to write.

"You can't split an ax-head with a whip," said he, as he came away from the window, and gave Rostof a large envelope. This was the petition to the emperor, which the auditor had written for him; in it nothing was said whatever about the faults of the commissary department, but he simply craved pardon.

"Hand it in; it's evident...." he did not finish his sentence, and smiled a painfully unnatural smile.

CHAPTER XIX

On his return to the regiment, and having made his report to the commander in regard to Denisof's condition, Rostof set out for Tilsit with the petition to the sovereign.

On the twenty-fifth of June, the French and Russian emperors had met at Tilsit. Boris Drubetskoï begged the distinguished individual to whose staff he was attached for permission to be present at the conference which was to be held at Tilsit.

"I should like to see the great man with my own eyes," said he, speaking of Napoleon, whom he, like every one else, had always hitherto called Buonaparte.

"You mean Buonaparte?" asked the general, with a smile.

Boris looked inquiringly at his general, and immediately perceived that the general was trying to quiz him.

"Prince, I am speaking of the Emperor Napoleon," he replied.

The general, with a smile, tapped him on the shoulder. "You'll get on," said he, and he took him with him.

Boris was one of the few who were there at the Niemen on the day when the emperors met; he saw the rafts with the monograms; he saw Napoleon ride down the bank past the French Guards; he saw the Emperor

Alexander's thoughtful face, as he sat in silence in the inn on the bank of the river, waiting for Napoleon to come; he saw the two emperors get into the boats, and Napoleon, who was the first to reach the raft, go forward with swift steps to meet Alexander, give him his hand, and then disappear with him under the pavilion.

Ever since his entry into the highest circles, Boris had conceived the habit of carefully observing whatever was going on around him and recording it. During the time of the interview at Tilsit, he inquired the names of the personages who came with Napoleon, remarked the uniforms which they had on, and listened with great attention to the words spoken by all the men of importance. At the moment the emperors went into the pavilion, he looked at his watch, and he did not fail to look at it again at the moment Alexander came forth from the pavilion. The interview lasted an hour and fifty-three minutes; this fact he wrote down that very same evening, together with many others which he felt had historical significance.

Thus, the emperor's suite being very small, the fact of being present at Tilsit at the time of the interview was, for a man who prized success in the service, fraught with deep meaning; and Boris, who enjoyed this privilege, felt that his position was henceforth secured. He was not only known by name, but was always seen and taken for granted. Twice he was sent on errands to the emperor himself, so that the emperor came to know his face, and the inner circle not only ceased to shun him as "a new person," as before, but would have been surprised at his absence.

Boris lodged with another aide, the Polish Count Zhilinski. Zhilinski, though a Polyak, had been educated in Paris, was rich, was passionately fond of the French, and almost every day, during the time of the interview at Tilsit, he and Boris used to have the officers of the Guards and members of the imperial French staff to breakfast and dinner with them.

On the evening of the sixth of July, Count Zhilinski, Boris's chum, was giving a dinner to some of his French acquaintances. At this dinner, the guest of honor was one of Napoleon's aides; there were a number of the officers of the Imperial Guard, and a young lad belonging to an old aristocratic French family, who was Napoleon's page.

That same day, Rostof, profiting by the darkness to pass unrecognized, proceeded to Tilsit, in civil dress, and went to the apartment occupied by Zhilinski and Boris.

Rostof, in common with the whole army from which he came, was as yet far from experiencing that change which had taken place at headquarters and in Boris, in regard to Napoleon and the French — to look upon them as friends instead of foes.

As yet, all connected with the army still continued to hold their former derisive feeling of ill-will, scorn, and fear of Bonaparte and the French. Only a short time before, Rostof, in talking with a Cossack officer of Platof's division, had contended that, if Napoleon had been taken prisoner, he would have been treated, not as a sovereign, but as a criminal.

Even more recently, falling in with a French colonel, who had been wounded, Rostof had become heated in trying to prove that there could be no peace between a lawful sovereign and a criminal like Bonaparte.

It struck Rostof strangely, therefore, to see in Boris's rooms French officers, in the very same uniforms which he had been in the habit of viewing in an utterly different light, across from the skirmishers' lines.

The moment he saw a French officer looking out of the door, that feeling of war, of hostility, which he always experienced at sight of the foe, suddenly took possession of him. He paused at the threshold, and asked in Russian if Drubetskoï lived there.

Boris heard the unwonted voice in the entry, and came out to meet him. At the first moment, on recognizing Rostof, a shade of annoyance crossed his face.

"Ah! is it you? Very glad, very glad to see you," said he, nevertheless, and coming towards him with a smile. But Rostof had noticed his first impression.

"It seems I have come at the wrong time," said he. "I should not have come, but I had business," he added coldly.

"No, I was only surprised that you had got away from your regiment. I 'll be with you in a moment," he shouted, in reply to some one calling him from within.

"I see that my visit is untimely," repeated Rostof.

The expression of annoyance had entirely disappeared by this time from Boris's face; apparently having considered and made up his mind what course to pursue, he seized his visitor by both hands, with remarkable ease of manner, and drew him into the adjoining room. Boris's eyes, fixed calmly and confidently on Rostof, were, as it were, shielded by something — as if there were a screen, the blue spectacles of high society — placed in front of them. So it seemed to Rostof.

"Akh! please say no more about being come inopportunely," said Boris. He drew him into the room where the table was set for dinner, introduced him to the guests, calling him by name, and explaining that he was not a civilian, but an officer in the hussars, and an old friend of his. "Count Zhilinski," "*le Comte* N. N.," *le Capitaine* S. S.," said he, naming the guests. Rostof scowled at the Frenchmen, bowed stiffly, and said nothing.

Zhilinski was evidently displeased at the intrusion of this new Russian individual into his circle, and had nothing to say to Rostof. Boris, affecting not to notice the awkwardness produced by the introduction of the newcomer, and still displaying the same easy grace and impenetrable look of his eyes with which he had received Rostof, tried to enliven the conversation.

One of the Frenchmen turned, with characteristic Gallic politeness, to the stubbornly silent Rostof, and remarked that he supposed he had come to Tilsit to see the emperor.

"No, I came on business," replied Rostof, laconically.

Rostof's ill-humor had come on immediately at noticing the annoyance expressed in Boris's face, and as usually happens with people who are out of sorts, he imagined that all were looking at him with unfriendly eyes, and that he was in their way. And, in truth, he was in their way, for he took no part in the conversation that was just beginning.

"And why is he sitting there?" the glances that were fixed on him seemed to say. He got up and went to Boris.

"I know I am a constraint to you," said he, in a whisper. "Come, let me tell you about my business and I will be going."

"No, not in the least," replied Boris. "But if you are tired, let us go into my room, and you can lie down and rest."

"Well, really ...."

They went into Boris's little sleeping-room. Rostof, without sitting down, began in a pettish tone — as if Boris were in some way to blame for the matter — to tell him about Denisof's affair, and asked him if he could and would send in the petition for Denisof, through the general on whose staff he was serving, and see to it that Denisof's letter reached the emperor.

When the two were alone together, Rostof, for the first time, found it awkward to look into Boris's eyes. Boris, sitting with his legs crossed, and pressing the slender fingers of his right hand into his left, listened to Rostof in the same way as a general listens to a report from his subordinate; sometimes he glanced around, and then again looked into Rostof's face with that peculiar veil of impenetrability over his eyes. Rostof felt awkward every time that he did so, and he looked down.

"I have heard of things like that, and I know that the sovereign is very strict in such cases. I think it would be best not to bring it to his majesty's attention. In my opinion, it would be better to give the petition directly to the commander of the corps. .... And, as a general thing, I think ...."

"Then you don't care to do anything. Why not say it right out!"

Rostof almost shouted, not looking at Boris's eyes.

Boris smiled. "On the contrary, I will do all that is in my power. But I thought...."

At this moment, Zhilinski's voice was heard, calling Boris back.

"Well, go, go, go!" said Rostof, and, excusing himself from the supper, and remaining alone in the little chamber, he paced for a long time up and down, and listened to the lively French conversation in the adjoining room.

CHAPTER XX

No day could have been more unfavorable for presenting Denisof's petition to the emperor than that on which Rostof went to Tilsit. He himself could not appear in the presence of the general-in-charge, for the reason that he was in civilian's dress, and had come away without leave of absence; and Boris, even if he had had the best will in the world, could not do this on the day that followed Rostof's arrival at Tilsit.

On that day, the ninth of July, the preliminary articles of peace were signed; the emperors exchanged orders, Alexander received that of the Legion of Honor, and Napoleon that of Saint Andrew of the first degree ; and on that same day a dinner was to be given to the Preobrazhensky battalion by the battalion of the French Guards. The emperors had both agreed to be present at this banquet.

Rostof felt so ill at ease, and so offended with Boris, that when, after the supper was over, Boris came back to talk with him, he pretended to be asleep, and on the next day he left the house early in the morning, taking especial pains not to see him.

Nikolaï, in his civilian's hat and coat, wandered about the city, gazing at the French and their uniforms, studying the streets and residences where the French and Russian emperors were lodged. On the square he saw tables laid out, and men making preparations for the banquet; along the streets he beheld draperies with the Russian and French colors entwined, and the letters A. and N. in monogram. In the windows of the houses there were also flags and monograms.

"Boris is n't willing to help me, and I won't have anything more to do with him, that's a settled thing," said Nikolaï to himself. "It's all over between us; but I won't leave town until I have done the best I could for Denisof, and at least handed his petition to the sovereign. To the sovereign?.... He is there!" said Rostof to himself, involuntarily wandering back to the mansion occupied by Alexander.

In front of the door stood saddle-horses, and the suite were assembling, evidently for the purpose of escorting his majesty on a ride.

"At any moment I may see him," said Rostof to himself. "If I could only put the letter straight into his hands! But would n't they arrest me, on account of being out of uniform? Impossible! He would understand on whose side justice lay. He understands everything, he knows everything! Who could be more just and generous than he? Besides, if they were to arrest me for being here, what harm would it be?" he asked himself, catching sight of an officer going into the house where the emperor lived. "It seems people do go in! Eh! it's all nonsense, I will go and give the petition to the sovereign myself, — so much the worse for Drubetskoï, who drives me to it."

And suddenly, with a resolution which was unexpected even to himself, Rostof grasped the letter in his pocket, and went straight to the residence occupied by his sovereign.

"Now, this time I will not miss my chance, as I did at Austerlitz," he said to himself, expecting every moment to meet the emperor, and feeling the blood rush to his heart at the mere thought. "I will fall at his feet and beseech him. He will lift me, listen to me, and even thank me. 'I am glad of any opportunity of doing good, but to right wrongs is my greatest happiness,'" said Rostof, imagining the words which his sovereign would say to him. And, though he had to run the gauntlet of the inquisitive glances fastened upon him, he went up the front steps of the imperial residence.

From the porch, a broad staircase led straight up-stairs. At the right was a half-open door. Below, at the foot of the staircase, was still another door, leading to the ground floor.

"What do you wish?" asked some one.

"To give a letter, a petition, to his majesty," said Rostof, in a trembling voice.

"A petition? It should go to the general-in-charge; please pass this way," he indicated the door leading to the ground floor. "But he won't receive it."

On hearing this voice, so cold and unconcerned, Rostof was panic-stricken at his audacity; the thought that he might at any moment meet his majesty was so entrancing, and, at the same time, so terrible to him, that he felt like running away, but the kammer-fourrier, who came to meet him, opened the door into the general's office, and Rostof went in.

A short, stout man, thirty years of age, in white trousers, Hessian boots, and a batiste shirt apparently meant for summer only, was standing in this room; a valet was behind him, buttoning a pair of handsome new braces, embroidered in silk, as Rostof could not help noticing. This gentleman was talking with some one in the next room. "Devilishly well made," this man was just saying, but, when he caught sight of Rostof, he stopped and frowned.

"What is it you want? A petition?"

"What is it?" asked the individual in the next room.

"Another petitioner," replied the man in the braces.

"Tell him to come later. He's going out; we've got to go with him."

"Come later, to-morrow, to-morrow. It's too late now."....

Rostof turned round and was about to go, when the man in the braces stopped him. "Who is it from? Who are you?"

"It's from Major Denisof," replied Rostof.

"And who are you? An officer?"

"Yes, a lieutenant, Count Rostof."

"What audacity! Give it to your general. And begone with you, begone." And he began to put on the rest of the uniform handed to him by his valet.

Rostof went down into the entry again, and noticed that on the steps there were still many officers and generals in full parade uniform, and that he would have to pass by them all. Cursing his audacity, his heart sinking within him at the thought that at any moment he might meet the sovereign, and be mortified, and even put under arrest in his presence, appreciating all the impropriety of his conduct, and regretting it, Rostof, with downcast eyes, was hastening away from the house, which was now surrounded by the glittering officers of the suite, when a well-known voice called him by name, and some one's hand was laid on his shoulder.

"Well, batyushka, what are you doing here without a uniform?" demanded a deep bass voice.

This was a general of cavalry, formerly commander of the division in which Rostof served. During that campaign he had won the signal favor of the sovereign.

Rostof was startled, and began to make his excuses, but when he saw the general's good-natured, jocose face, he drew him to one side, and began, in a voice choked by emotion, to lay his whole case before him, and begged the general to take the part of Denisof, who was well-known to him. The general listened to Rostof's story and shook his head gravely. "Pity, pity; he's a brave fellow; give me his letter."

Rostof had only just handed him the petition and finished telling Denisof's whole story, when quick steps and a jingling of spurs were heard on the staircase, and the general, leaving him, hurried to the steps. The gentlemen composing the sovereign's suite were hastening down from the staircase and going to their horses. The equerry, Hayne, the same one who had accompanied the sovereign at the battle of Austerlitz, brought up the emperor's steed, and then on the staircase was heard the slight squeak of steps, which Rostof instantly knew. Forgetting his apprehension of being recognized, Rostof, with many other curious spectators, from among the natives, went close to the doorsteps, and again, though two years had passed, he recognized those adored features, the same face, the same glance, the same gait, the same union of majesty and sweetness. And that feeling of enthusiasm and love for his sovereign rose in Rostof's soul with all its former force.

The emperor wore the Preobrazhensky uniform, white chamois leather breeches, Hessian boots, with the star of an order which Rostof did not know. It was the *Légion d'Honneur*. As he came out on the steps, he held his hat under his arm and was putting on his gloves. He paused, glanced around, and his glance seemed to light up all about him. He said a few words to one of the generals. He also recognized the general who had been formerly commander of Rostof's division, gave him a smile, and beckoned to him.

All the suite moved away from them, and Rostof noticed that this general held a rather long conversation with the sovereign.

The emperor said a few words in reply, and took a step toward his horse. Again the crowd of the suite and the crowd of spectators, with Rostof in their number, followed after the emperor. Standing by his steed, with his arm thrown over the saddle, the sovereign turned to the cavalry general, and spoke in a loud voice, evidently intending that he should be heard by all : —

"I cannot, general, and I cannot because the law is more powerful than I," said the emperor, and he put his foot in the stirrup. The general respectfully inclined his head; the emperor got into the saddle and rode at a gallop down the street. Rostof, forgetting himself in his enthusiasm, joined the crowd and ran after him.

CHAPTER XXI

On the square where the emperor was going, the battalion of the Preobrazhentsui stood facing the street on the right; on the left stood the battalion of the French Guards, in their bearskin caps.

Just as the sovereign rode up toward one flank of the battalion, which presented arms, another throng of mounted men galloped up to the other flank, and Rostof recognized Napoleon at their head. It could have been no one else. He rode at a gallop, wearing his cocked hat, with the ribbon of Saint Andrew across his breast, with his blue coat unbuttoned over his white waistcoat. Riding up to Alexander on his Arabian steed, gray, of extraordinarily good blood, with crimson housings embroidered in gold, he took off his hat, and, at this motion, Rostof, as a trained cavalryman, could not help noticing that Napoleon sat awkwardly and unsteadily on his horse. The battalions shouted "Hurrah!" and "*Vive l'empereur!*" Napoleon said something to Alexander. Then the two emperors dismounted and shook hands. Napoleon's face wore a disagreeably artificial smile. Alexander, with a courteous expression, made some remark to him.

Rostof, notwithstanding the trampling of the horses of the mounted *gendarmes* constantly backing into the throng, followed every motion of the two emperors, not taking his eyes from them. It struck him as most extraordinary that Alexander treated Napoleon as an equal, and that Bonaparte bore himself toward the Russian Tsar also as an equal, as if this proximity to the sovereign were perfectly natural and usual with him.

Alexander and Napoleon, with a long train following them, passed along toward the right wing of the Preobrazhensky battalion, straight toward the throng that had collected there. By some chance, the throng was allowed to press so near the emperors, that Rostof, who found himself in the very front row, felt anxious lest he should be recognized.

"Sire, I crave permission to grant the Legion of Honor to the bravest of your soldiers," said a shrill, precise voice, dwelling on every syllable. These words were spoken by the diminutive Bonaparte, looking straight up into Alexander's eyes. Alexander listened attentively to what he said, and inclined his head with a pleasant smile.

"To the one who conducted himself most gallantly during this last war," added Napoleon, laying equal stress on each syllable, with an unconcern and self-confidence which aroused Rostof's indignation. At the same time, Napoleon glanced round on the ranks of Russian soldiery drawn up before him, and still presenting arms and immovably looking into their sovereign's face.

"Will your majesty permit me to consult with the colonel?" asked Alexander, and he made a few hasty steps toward Prince Kozlovsky, the commander of the battalion. Bonaparte began, meantime, to be drawing his glove from his small, white hand, and when it tore he threw it away. An aide, hastening forward, picked it up.

"To whom shall it be given?" asked the Emperor Alexander, in a low tone, in Russian, of Kozlovsky.

"Whom would you designate, your majesty?"

The sovereign frowned with annoyance, and glancing round, said : —

"Yes, but I must give him an answer."

Kozlovsky, with a resolute look, glanced along the ranks, and his eyes rested on Rostof.

"He couldn't by any possibility choose me?" said Rostof to himself.

"Lazaref," commanded the colonel, knitting his brows, and the first man in the front rank briskly stepped forward. This was Lazaref.

"Where are you going? Stand there!" whispered various voices to Lazaref, who did not know where to go. He stood in trepidation, looking askance at his colonel, and his face twitched, as is generally the case with soldiers summoned to the front. Napoleon bent his head back a little, and stretched his small, plump hand behind him, as if he wished something to be handed him. The faces of his suite, who at that instant surmised what was going to take place, showed some perplexity; there was whispering, some object was handed from one to another, and a page, the very one whom Rostof had seen at Boris's the evening before, sprang forward, and, respectfully bowing over the out-stretched hand, and not causing it to remain a single instant, placed in it an order, on a red ribbon.

Napoleon, not looking at it, closed two fingers, and retained the badge between them. Then he went up to Lazaref, who, with staring eyes, continued to gaze stead-fastly at his sovereign and no one else. Napoleon looked at the Emperor Alexander, signifying by this that what he was doing now he did out of consideration for his ally. The little white hand with the badge touched the button of the soldier Lazaref. Napoleon seemed to realize that all that was necessary to make this soldier forever fortunate, decorated, and distin-guished above every one else in the world was for this white hand of his merely to touch this soldier's breast! Napoleon simply suspended the cross on the soldier's chest, and, dropping his hand, returned to where Alex-ander was standing, as if he knew that the cross must needs stick to the man's breast. And the cross really did stick there!

Officious Russian and French hands instantly seized the cross and fastened it to the man's uniform. Lazaref had gazed moodily at the little man with white hands who had been doing something to him, and he continued to present arms, with his eyes again directed straight at Alexander's face, as if he were asking his sovereign whether it were his duty still to stand there, or whether he should go back, or whether there was anything else for him to do. But as no orders were given him, he stood in exactly the same motionless attitude for some time.

The sovereigns mounted and rode away. The Preo-brazhentsui, breaking ranks, began to mingle with the

French Guardsmen, and took their seats at the tables which had been prepared for them.

Lazaref was assigned to the seat of honor. Russian and French officers pressed around him, congratulated him, and shook hands with him. A throng of officers and the public crowded around, merely to get a sight of the man. The hum of conversation in French and Russian, and bursts of hearty laughter, began to be heard around the table erected in the square.

Two officers, with flushed faces, feeling gay and happy, passed by Rostof. "What a treat, brother! All served on silver!" said one. "Did you see Lazaref?"

"I did!"

"To-morrow, they say, the Preobrazhentsui are going to give them a dinner."

"Is that so? What luck for Lazaref! twelve hundred francs pension for life!"

"How's that for a cap, children!" cried a Preobrazhenets, putting on a Frenchman's shaggy bearskin.

"Marvelously fine; very becoming!"

"Have you heard the countersign?" asked one Guardsman of another. "Day before yesterday, it was '*Napoléon, France, bravoure!*' Yesterday, '*Alexandre, Russie, grandeur*'; one day our sovereign gives the watchword, and the next, Napoleon. To-morrow the sovereign is going to confer the George on the bravest of the Guards. He can't help it. He's got to keep up his end!"

Boris and his friend Zhilinski also came out to witness the banquet to the Preobrazhentsui. As they returned, Boris noticed Rostof standing near the corner of a house.

"Hullo, Rostof! Good-morning; we missed each other," said he, and he could not refrain from asking what had happened to him, so strangely dark and disturbed was Rostof's face.

"Nothing, nothing," replied Rostof.

"Will you join us?"

"Yes, by and by."

Rostof stood for a long time by the house-corner, gazing at the feasters. His mind was filled with painful reflections which he could never bring to a satisfactory conclusion. Strange doubts had risen in his mind. Now he recalled Denisof and the change that had come over him, and his obstinacy, and the whole hospital, with those amputated legs and arms, with all that filth and disease. It came up so vividly in his imagination, at that instant, he had such a lively sense of that fetid odor of putrefaction, and that dead body, that he glanced around to see what might be the cause of it. Then, in contrast, he recalled that self-conceited Bonaparte, with his little white hand: he was emperor now, the loved and valued friend of the Emperor Alexander! For what purpose, then, all those amputated legs and arms, and those men killed? Then he remembered Lazaref rewarded, and Denisof punished and unforgiven. He found himself indulging in such strange thoughts that he was frightened.

The savor of the viands and the pangs of hunger drove him out of this mood; he had to get something to eat before going back. He went into an inn which he had seen that morning. He found so many people there, and so many officers, who, like himself, had come in citizen's dress, that he had difficulty in getting dinner.

Two officers of the same division as his own joined him. The conversation naturally turned on the peace. These officers, Rostof's friends, like the majority of the army, were dissatisfied with the peace which had been concluded after Friedland. They maintained that, if only they had held out a little longer, Napoleon would have laid down his arms, that he had no supplies or ammunition for his troops.

Nikolaï ate in silence, and kept drinking. He alone drank two bottles of wine. The inner conflict which had risen in his soul, instead of finding solution, tormented him more than ever. He was afraid to express his thoughts, and he could not get rid of them. Suddenly, at the remark of one of the officers that it was a humiliation to look at the French, Rostof began to declaim with a heat and violence wholly uncalled for, and therefore very amazing to the officers.

"And how, pray, can you decide what would have been best?" he shouted, his face flushing suddenly crimson. "Why do you judge the sovereign's actions? What right have we to sit in judgment on him? We cannot appreciate or understand the sovereign's actions!"

"But I have n't said a word about the sovereign," replied the officer, who could not explain Rostof's violence on any other ground than that he was drunk.

But Rostof did not heed him.

"We are not diplomatic chinovniks; we are soldiers and nothing else," he went on to say. "We are commanded to die, and we die. And if we are punished, then of course we must be to blame; it is n't for us to criticise. It is sufficient for our sovereign, the emperor, to recognize Bonaparte as emperor, and to conclude peace with him; then, of course, it must be so. For if we once begin to criticise and sit in judgment, then there will be nothing sacred left. We shall be declaring that there is no God, no nothing!" screamed Nikolaï, pounding the table with his fist with quite unnecessary vehemence, as his friends felt; in reality it was demanded by his feelings. "It's our business to fulfil our duty, to fight, and not to think, and that's the end of it," he said in conclusion.

"And drink," said one of the officers, wishing to avoid a quarrel.

"Yes, and drink," replied Nikolaï. "Hey, there! another bottle!" he cried.

END OF VOL. II.